Praise for Michael Lentz and *Schattenfroh*

"*Schattenfroh* is a deep and mighty book that forces the reader to not only think of the word 'metaphysics,' but to feel with their own skin its fearsome presence in our world." —Vladimir Sorokin

"What competition can we talk about when dealing with perhaps the greatest German-language novel of the 21st century up to now? This in equal measure baroque and surrealist explosion of a novel belongs to the pantheon of the best works of world literature published in the past two decades." —*The Untranslated*

"The novel *Schattenfroh* is without a doubt one of the most interesting experiments in German-language literature in recent years. . . . *Schattenfroh* is a prose work which goes far, far beyond the affairs of the current literary scene."
—Andreas Puff-Trojan, *SWR2 Archivradio*

"Depending on how you look at it, it is a genius, insane, dark or ridiculous book before which one can only helplessly surrender."
—Andrea Köhler, *Die Zeit*

"Immeasurable in both its demands and its ability."
—Andreas Platthaus, *Frankfurter Allgemeine Zeitung*

Schattenfroh

SCHATTENFROH

A Requiem

MICHAEL LENTZ

translated by Max Lawton
edited by Matthias Friedrich

DEEP VELLUM PUBLISHING
DALLAS, TEXAS

Deep Vellum Publishing
3000 Commerce St., Dallas, Texas 75226
deepvellum.org · @deepvellum

Deep Vellum is a 501c3 nonprofit literary arts organization
founded in 2013 with the mission to bring
the world into conversation through literature.

Text copyright © 2018, Michael Lentz
Translation copyright © 2025, Max Lawton
English Translation is edited by Matthias Friedrich
Originally published as *Schattenfroh: Ein Requiem* in German by S. Fischer Verlage,
Frankfurt am Main, 2018

The secret writings on pages 172, 173, 174, 828, 832 were traced by Valeri Scherstjanoi. The scribentisms on pages 564, 833, 987 originate from Valeri Scherstjanoi himself. The manuscripts on pages 72–147, 215–216 are by the author. The city coat of arms on page 179 is a montage by Valeri Scherstjanoi. Used through arrangement with S. Fischer Verlag.

FIRST ENGLISH EDITION, 2025
All rights reserved.

Support for this publication has been provided in part by the National Endowment for the Arts, the Texas Commission on the Arts, the City of Dallas Office of Arts and Culture, the Communities Foundation of Texas, and the Addy Foundation.

ISBNs: 978-1-64605-382-7 (paperback) | 978-1-64605-394-0 (ebook)

LIBRARY OF CONGRESS CATALOGING-IN-PUBLICATION DATA

Names: Lentz, Michael, 1964- author. | Lawton, Max, translator.
Title: Schattenfroh / Michael Lentz ; translated by Max Lawton ; edited by Matthias Friedrich.
Other titles: Schattenfroh. English
Description: Dallas, Texas : Deep Vellum, 2025.
Identifiers: LCCN 2025001898 (print) | LCCN 2025001899 (ebook) | ISBN 9781646053827 (trade paperback) | ISBN 9781646053940 (ebook)
Subjects: LCGFT: Psychological fiction. | Novels.
Classification: LCC PT2672.E455 S3813 2025 (print) | LCC PT2672.E455 (ebook) | DDC 833/.92--dc23/eng/20250117
LC record available at https://lccn.loc.gov/2025001898
LC ebook record available at https://lccn.loc.gov/2025001899

Cover Design by copyright © Kosmos Design, Münster, www.kosmos-design.de
Interior Layout and Typesetting by KGT

PRINTED IN CANADA

"Behold the voice of my beloved knocketh in my mouth and the lyre sounded of itself."
(Josef Karo, *Maggid Mesharim*)

"It felt to me as if a voice were sitting on my tongue and repeating itself a hundred times with great swiftness: 'What shall I say? What shall I say?'"
(Chaim Vital, *Sefer ha-chezyonot*)

SCHATTENFROH: a German family name that means something like "shadowglad."

SCHADENFREUDE: "damagejoy" or, according to Merriam-Webster, "joy over some harm or misfortune suffered by another."

SCHADENFROH: "damageglad" or, "maliciously gleeful in the downfall [damage] of others."

One calls this writing. I have no paper, no pen, no typewriter, no computer. I am writing into my brainfluid. I must write that I am here voluntarily. And so I write: I am here voluntarily. And, as I am here voluntarily, I have voluntarily subjected myself to the confines of this society. I write: As I am here voluntarily, I have voluntarily subjected myself to the confines of this society. Society demands amusement. My mission is to write everything down from the beginning. I said it can't be done. I don't know when the beginning is and I don't know what everything is. They've suddenly changed something. In the meantime, I had to sit very still, clacking noises and voice-like rumblings could be heard just like in the slice-writing tube, whose fascinating images I've never dared examine, as they might confront me with inalterable truths in the interior of my body, truths that no longer allow a line to be dragged out between life-threatening and death-bringing. "Let's keep going" and "how much longer?" the rumblings said in endless sequence.

The beginning should read, "Now it's happening." Thus did it begin. I've been here for a few days. I haven't slept, though I'm not tired either. The darkness of this room sealed off from the outside makes it impossible to distinguish between day and night. Hermeticized. What strange words there are.

I'm sitting in a darkroom wearing a facemask and some kind of spectacles. On my head sits a hat adorned by a bird's wing. I have no tongue. Or, if I do, I can't move it. Reduction is not a good prerequisite for the long journey that lies ahead. Your name is not Johannes and not Emmeram, your name is Nobody. Thus spake Schattenfroh. You must be and become a most proper nan mann, he said. Your mission should read: "Nobody recognizes himself."

You are Nobody, Schattenfroh said. If somebody should ask you, say that you are The Nobody. I can rest assured that the difference between myself and the others opposite me, whom, of course, I don't *actually* encounter, should no longer be a difference that needs to be compensated for, be it that the others are way out ahead of me and suppress me out of concern for the loss of their superiority, be it that the others have lagged behind me and are now endeavoring to catch up with the commensurability of my existence as compared to the existence of the others; given that you are Nobody, Schattenfroh says, this difference is certainly not to be leveled against you more than anyone else would apply what Marie Dinggeehrt,* who also became renowned under the pseudonyms of Hagen Miterdiger, Ingrid Gemaether, Ingrid Regethema,† Ingrid Regemaeht, Dieter Im Hergang,‡ Gerhard Teigmein, Martin Herdgeige,§ and Gerhard Eigenmit,¶ aptly formulated concerning the subject-character of one's own Dasein, which, in the case of Nobody, is no longer in force: it itself is not; its Being has been taken away by the Others. The approbation of others has the everyday existential possibilities of Dasein utterly at its disposal. *Nemo*, a bad omen.

Perhaps my tongue has fallen out of my mouth, something has

---

* Marie Thinghonored.
† Ingrid Clevertopic.
‡ Dieter in the Courseofevents.
§ Martin Ovenviolin.
¶ Gerhard Ownwith.

bitten into its bottom with barbs, that something is now lying at the bottom instead of the tongue, it's been sucking at the tongue-artery constantly, babbling and ready to gladly chow down on whatever's served to him or her, but nothing is, I haven't eaten anything for days. Apparently, though, this Something lacks for nothing, it's so lively, it shall perhaps continue to suck my blood and drink my saliva, which has become noticeably less plentiful, or it isn't living on what it finds in my mouth, but on every word that passes *through* my mouth. I suspect that this Something, which I shall hereby call Woodlouse, speaks as my tongue. I do not speak.

Schattenfroh should have an answer as to why I quake before my voice, which is an animal jumping out of me, a chameleon that keeps fabricating itself anew, and, for as long as its tongue reaches is my voice foreign to me, my voice echoes against the emptiness that I would very much like to see as a body, the beast is the worm in me that shall not die and the false fire that shall not be quenched.

The facemask is meant to keep my head warm. As for the spectacles, I only suspect that they're spectacles—this small box before my eyes that seems to have no weight one moment, but makes the head sink heavily the next. Lenses are placed into the box on the left and right. They are located very close to the eyes and surrounded by an aureole that exudes a little bit of brightness. It writes. I'm a prestidigitator, a tachygraph, a quick-finger, I write, but not really, rather I only think, see, and hear, even if, as just now, in extremely limited fashion. My centroscriptorium is remote controlled, as are my hands. The fingers move without my having agency over them. Sometimes the right hand seems to be writing as if it were holding a pen or a quill, scraping and encircling motions are carried out, then both hands become involved again, as if they were typing on a keyboard or drawing in the air. The motions correspond with what you see, think, and hear, says Schattenfroh. I don't see anything yet and I don't know whether one calls this thinking. It's a nervous twitch, I have the feeling that someone is pawing into my thoughts, images, and everything that I hear as soon as I think, see, or hear something, though no exchange between me and these others takes place.

My writing must be a projection of the brainfluid-script. For is brainfluid not the soul? I've leafed through it in my dictionary-head: cerebrospinal fluid. That, at least, I can do: search for words in my head. The thing itself is the script and everything simply declares itself. That there are so many things, but no hereafter for language. What's coming to pass here I explain as follows: The brainfluid-script is projected into my hands, from which Schattenfroh allows to be read that which I have thought and seen in the form of a book, as if the hands were giving instructions, or what I have thought heard seen is transmitted remotely via the spectacles to a device that writes everything down and the quick motions of my fingers are nothing but an atavism. But why write it down? Why not broadcast it *everywhere*?

While I write with script, the other end is to draw the most beautiful aerial paintings. The truth, however it is written, shall always see itself confronted with the figures produced by the other that you also cannot truly control, Schattenfroh says. In any case, the image shall remain hidden from you. But he, Schattenfroh, shall see it.

I don't seem to have any thoughts of my own anymore. I remember that speaking is just air moving, just as airflow makes the many roof racks of a car sing with a nice ring, which it doesn't know itself to be making, of course. I must speak for as long as the air passes through the glottis.

Supposedly I am only seen moving my hands, they write down the damndest things, a thought that is probably also merely persuaded to me. On a 1910 poster stamp for the Leonhard Taichmann Confectionery, you see a feeblemindedly grinning school-age child with a brown cowlick and, by means of a funnel, something, you don't know exactly what, it's hardly cakes or chocolate candies, is being poured directly into his head. The flat logo is crowned by the sentence:

"Are you lacking wisdom in a particular thing / From Nuremberg, let us the funnel to you bring." Wisdom seems to exist only in going to buy things from this Taichmann fellow. O Harsdörffer, use your funnel to trickle the poetic fluidum down in hourly doses for many days. To trickle. To make it drippe, droppe, dribble agayn and agayn. To be bound upside down on a board or bed tilted upward. My memory drips. I wonder whether it's ever dripped itself dry. Whether this writing, which here takes place with an invisible pen, succeeded in one day transferring over my soul, whether my memory is thus empty. At least in that respect, it remains pure intuition.

It's not only that I can't help being watched, as one would normally observe someone in a department store when he's walking hastily or in a church when he's sitting there all withdrawn into himself, I also can't prevent my thoughts from being followed and all the data in my brain that is thought to be interesting enough to be exploited from being exposed. Brain abduction. The brain is read out at the mind-interfaces.

What kind of correspondence there might be, whether the writing motions induce images or, conversely, these produce the writing motions, or whether writing, hearing, seeing, and the events occur simultaneously lies hitherto beyond my knowledge. Who actually attends to the writing, I do not know with enough certainty to say. I do not think that it is attended to by beings, who, sitting upon remote celestial bodies, are given human shape after the manner of the fleeting-improvised-men, as is written in the Book of Daniel. It must be Schattenfroh, he has lured me here with his number games, his 6 brushstroked all over the city with white or red paint, the 6 I at first followed aimlessly, roamingly, until, after about a year, I recognized the system that lay behind it—the incidence of the 6 upon the map of the city coalesced into a 666, I'm in the middle 6 now—and ultimately discovered messages in the 6s in enlarged photographs:

"Schattenfroh was here!"

"The tongue is a restless evil."

"The tongue is inflamed by Gehenna."

"The tongue itself is a fire."

"The tongue is the world of iniquity."

"The tongue defileth the whole body."

"Imagination is devilish יצר הרע, yetzer hara."

"Come to Gehenna 666, loosen your tongue."

I'm here at 666 A Drafter Shat Avenue, also known under the addresses 666 Earth-as-draft Avenue and 666 Gehenna, and am sitting in a *camera silens*. I'm sitting on a throne. Schattenfroh said the throne looked like ice crystals, its wheels like the radiant sun, and, underneath the throne, currents of flaming fire are to come forth, but the throne doesn't burn, the wheels don't light up, no currents of flaming fire can be seen, this throne must be a fabrication.

For every one shall be salted with fire, says Schattenfroh, the worm dieth not, and the fire is not quenched. Schattenfroh, he is the Big Other that perpetually changes its shape, the processes put themselves to paper. Schattenfroh always says two sentences: "There is no Schattenfroh other than Schattenfroh—and you are his prophet" and "A small mistake in the beginning is a big one in the end." I always hear these two sentences in the background. I assume that they're always there, but, occasionally, when I listen carefully, now for example, I only hear "A small mistake at the beginning is a big one in the end." Schattenfroh is in my head. Has been for weeks. That means he lives in my head and has appeared to me since I've been here, in my darkroom. I always hear him differently in spatial terms, I can't see him. If he suffuses me completely when, formless in my head, he calls forth in me the notion that at the very least *he* might be immortal, then I hear him from head to toe and this hearing envelops every other sensory impression, also strengthening my body. Schattenfroh is a dictator, he leads the quill that I don't have. He buzzes around me, he rattles, a hooded little monster, thus do I imagine him, made up of fly, grasshopper, gecko, and human head, with his wings far too large, and this rattling grounds his falsetto in such a way that I, completely absorbed by the noise, only ever perceive him in fragments.

I'll be there for you in a moment, he said earlier, until then you must write this here. Is it not touching how he emphasizes my so-called writing against his better judgment? I prefer the one in my head, what must I make of this composite figure who splashes round with crippling solicitude before devouring his victim. I am not waiting on him. He shall come back just as I imagine him.

I am not a free individual in my head either. With these sorts of spectacles, I shall experience unimaginable freedom, Schattenfroh has promised. I shall see through them into the inward. Wherever that might be. Inwardly, I shall see the entire world of the Frightbearing Society, Schattenfroh said, whose member I now be for all time through my free decision to be interrogated. At times, I really do desire nothing more ardently than to be interrogated, an urge that results from a certain propensity to torment myself, as well as my Catholic subservience, which shows itself all the more evidently as the conviction of having entirely renounced Catholicism solidifies within me. Plagued by feelings of guilt, I'd like for God to interrogate me and perpetually test me. And God did offer himself up to interrogate me. However, I didn't know anything about a Frightbearing Society, I also didn't want to become a member of anything, and the matter of a whole life's duration should not be brought into question here. To my query as to how many members the Society had, he replied only that my mission would first of all be to draw up the founding script because it would only be with me that the Society first lurched into existence and it now wanted to expand rapidly. If I should touch the curious box fitted above my eyes, I'd expire on the spot, said Schattenfroh. Then the straps holding it to my head would draw together and blow up my skull. At the words "blow up," the outer Schattenfroh said, "Blow up, exactly, the box will blow you to pieces." In fact, I feel a compulsion to touch the box and have to muster all my energy to resist this compulsion. If I move my head, I receive a surge of electricity that gets stronger with each movement. Again, another ugly temptation. The head motions lead me to suspect that there is paper in the box, perhaps strips rolled into each other, which are hurled against the walls of the box, one roll in each chamber, the box also makes incessant noises that lead one to conclude that script is coming to pass within it.

When my eyes become definitively adjusted, they'll see independently of one another with the help of the box, Schattenfroh promised. So far, however, I've only seen what eyes are capable of seeing in complete darkness and, for that reason, one does not know whether the streaks, points of light, and wandering contours that one now and then thinks to have perceived in this darkness come from sources of light that can't really be located or are mere phantoms of the eyes themselves, which cannot come to terms with the fact that nothing perceptible is being tendered to them. It is possible they're the flickering nerve impulses still pulsating between the visual cortex and the geniculate nucleus.

Miraculously, I am now able to fully grasp the celestial bodies swimming at the backs of my eyes. If the aureole of the lens disappears, which it does at regular intervals, an afterimage remains in view at the back of the eyes, an image whose slow fading I am enjoying more and more. It's like holding back a bit of stool until it pushes out on its own. I am satisfied with at least still having language, it allows me to see everything, and language tells me I should name the celestial bodies of my inner "Foresees." Foresees. With it, I see fore, from, and something. I see fore from myself by way of seeing something in my inwardness. Then I see myself again. I sometimes doubt that this is my inwardness. The view through the box (these aren't exactly spectacles) was first of all an outward gaze, which Schattenfroh allowed me to enact, the box was still missing its rear wall, I must take a good look at my surroundings, he said, so that I don't forget them. There must be people who are subjected to an inner compulsion to look unprotectedly into the sun, even though everyone knows that the intensity of the sun speedily destroys every eye unmediatedly exposed to it. The eye is a magnifying glass, the cornea and conjunctiva would burn, the retina would be destroyed, blindness would be the result. It's something else entirely when the eye is the sun and shines both inwardly and outwardly. But the latter I could not accept as I stared out into my surroundings, which were sheer light, and I got a good look at them, for days, weeks even, I forced my gaze through ever smaller openings and the light grew even stronger, in the end—a searing, punctiform sun, to which my eyes saw themselves exposed until I saw nothing more outside of them, until such a strong photophobia had affixed itself to me, even with my eyes closed, and such strong headaches afflicted me that I had to stop thinking, I couldn't think any thought through to the end anymore, again and again, I picked up the thread where it had supposedly gone astray from me, continued thinking caused localized attacks of pain in miscellaneous parts of the body, the pain wandered until I finally thought I'd perceived it in front of my body, then, finally, the rear wall was inserted and I remained in darkness for hours, whereby the aforementioned inconveniences abated all and sundry, which triggered a feeling of gratitude in me as I had never yet experienced in my life up until that point, and, as I visualized that I was grateful only to the tormentor for the interruption of the pain, there could and cannot be any question of the omission of the same, certainly not in the long term, this would nevertheless first have to prove itself to be so over a period of time that cannot yet be foreseen, a phrase that shows how the eyes are in no small measure responsible for our measure of time, I felt deeply ashamed. All in all, I'm prepared to either be blinded by this box once more in the foreseeable future, which would soothe me insomuch as it would prove that I am not blind, or to be exposed to such impenetrable darkness that all bodily energy is concentrated in the eyes and radiates outward as light.

The visual acuity of my eyes varies greatly; if a hand is more than ten centimeters away from my left eye, I can no longer see it clearly, I never had any problems with the right eye until the reverse effect recently came to pass with it, since then I only see objects sharply if they are more than the length of a large ruler away from the face. A satisfactory solution for my eyes can only be found in aspherical lenses that are surrounded by steplike ring-zones that allow for a better yield of light. At the moment, after this long period of darkness, I see double and triple. Things have really only just begun with the fine-tuning of the eyes. I also see them when I keep my eyes shut. On the left, I'm doing a handstand, on the right, my father is trying to touch the sole of my left shoe, first, he hops, then, suddenly, he becomes very fat, wiggles his legs, melts away, and disappears from the image. The images on the left and right are scrunched up like paper. It's dark again. A table can now be made out on the left, I step into the image on the right. Dark, bright again. I'm sitting at the table, the tabletop is completely covered over with scriptgrowth. Schattenfroh said that I am privileged because, as soon as my eyes adjust, I can be at any place at any time, then disappear from it whenever I please. You'll soon see what I mean by this, he says. In ephemeral society, groundedness is lost, it is even harmful as it offers a fixed goal; on the contrary, the Frightbearing Society grants local stability in an area that is not accessible and bug-proof, here, I might make a voyage anywhere, the imaginary is the safest place, one day, however, it will be the most insecure, before that turns out to be the case, it must be fished empty, I will stay here forever from now on, he told me, and even if I were anywhere else, I would always only be somewhere else in the here.

Without me giving any information about the sharpness of the images or being able to produce any further data, the lenses are adapted to my eyes. If the eyes remain empty, the opposite sight corrections allow every vein that I see at the backs of my eyes and every splotch of dust that swims in my eyewater to float plastically in the room, moreover, I have a feeling that there are not only eyes existent in the skull, but also in the brain, eyes that compete with each other to capture the object, but neither pair of eyes can settle the competition in their own favor and thus shall I probably have to get used to this floating.

The fine-tuning appears to be complete. I am now able to see different images on the left and the right, with the left eye I see a table and two chairs in an otherwise empty room, which flickers a bit in my eye, I also hear an insect-like hiss, with my right eye I see various objects upon a glass table, an open book, a wireless keyboard, and a large screen, I also hear a hiss; whereas the flicker that I perceive on the left is constant and rather quiet, the noise on the right-hand side changes perpetually, it suddenly swells, only so as to immediately become quiet, the insects increasingly populate the screen and get into formation. While the distance to the chairs and table on the left remains unchanged, I can now recognize what can be seen on the screen on the right: "While the distance to the chairs and table on the left remains unchanged, I can now recognize what can be seen on the screen on the right: it says what I see, hear, and think. Thinking is writing, we merely hear script, and we read when we hear. What occurs on the left dissolves on the right, then reassembles itself as script. Terribly simple." My soul doubtlessly receives military commands through the eyes, commands that are inscribed upon the brainfluid, then further processed in the form and fashion outlined. I am my own memory and deciphering apparatus, I inflict upon myself and make use of myself, yet am not my own ultimate consumer. Perhaps I'm merely a signal processor, the data of which sometimes appears as an image and sometimes as a word—or as both together. I am reproducible and robust and hardly ever age. Diminutive motions of the eyes control my perceptions. If I look more to the left, the image received from the left becomes larger until it occupies the entire field of my vision, which is also true of when I look more to the right. If my vision goes straight to the center, I see left and right separately, both images are the same size. If I lower my gaze toward the center, both areas slide over one another, just as happens with double or multiple exposures. There are probably other directional functions of the eyes than field, size, and interconnectivity. Wonderful and disturbing in equal measure are the distortions that arise due to excessively fast ocular motions or when I attempt to move them beyond their excursion ability. It is precisely this overexertion that exercises a rather addictive fascination upon me—almost a compulsion—even now, I can hardly resist the impulse to move my eyes to their outermost edges in every direction and to overextend their muscles. It stands to reason that the ocular motor skills serving to guide the processes in such-and-such way are susceptible to the exertion of influence, including by way of remote control. You should work hard to perfect the handling of the eyes, says Schattenfroh. One day, you might be able to undertake the remote control of others' eyes. I am at the center of things and at the center of script. As far as perceptions are concerned, Schattenfroh said the following to me: You are the result of your perceptions and not the other way around, without your perceptions, you wouldn't even remotely exist. You shall learn to be immersed and see a seeing, of which you could otherwise only dream, here images are automatically transferred into script, your seeing shall not know that it is *seeing*, the script shall not know that it is *writing*, the reading shall not know that it is *reading*. That's what's so wonderful and, when you're immersed, your perceptions are very much still there, but you exist no longer, you have dissolved. We are interested in your perceptions, not in you; it is only because you perceive that you are there, you are no more than a bothersome appendage to your perceptions. We shall reduce the share that you yourself have in your perceptions as a part of the field perceived by you as much as possible, you shall have to suffer the privations thus required for some span of time, you shall long for interrogation, on the other hand, the withdrawal of your familiar environment, that to which you yourself belong, and your hindered perception of yourself shall allow you to perceive yourself as an other and you shall express yourself as this other and, if all goes well, you shall feel this other to be just as superfluous as we do and become a part of public lighting, which no longer allows for the invisible, not even in the imaginary. This is the re-entry into paradise, the conscious individual must be broken through so that others might nestle in him and so that the others' perception might graft itself onto one's own. Could there ever be a more beautiful and intimate community than such a symbiosis? Work with us to achieve sublime results for the future and to preserve the essence of man in perception: his perception. We shall have to build new arks before the flood of perceptions one day submerges us, the perceptions that we, the Frightbearing Society, have liberated from all people, just as we are about to liberate them from you and with these arks shall we finally float out across the brainfluid, rolling with nothing but our perceptions, it freezes in the winter and we can see clearly into its depths and through all of its layers, every past is immediately present to us and, when springtime comes, it shows itself 'pon the mountains, when the brain thaws in the valley and down the hills in fountains, when the books ooze and the pages dryness lose, then begins the golden time of love. When I meditating through head and books stroll, then, I know not how, find myself before her door and knock, I look into her eye, she's pressing me to her heart with a sigh, I feel so fine, so wondrous good, I'd like to scream to the welkin, jubilant with joy, then, in private quiet, my eyes with tears to alloy, I'd fight, triumph, fly with the clouds in defiance, then begins the golden time of love.

Not so much the imagination, but the self-withdrawn perception to be for others, but to also say "I" as I gradually dissolve, frightens me, for *that* is precisely what the book is, it is the tune so wrongly summoned for by Schattenfroh that perturbs me; whether the individual has not taken himself over with his project. Is he speaking in my name here, "in private quiet," is he already I? Additionally, I am concerned with the question of what Schattenfroh filters out of the current of thought and speech, which perceptions do his devices not allow for? But I testify as to how Schattenfroh has instructed me to anyone who reads these words:

"'Tis thus to conclude that on the 28 of August, 2014, at a melancholy, albeit peaceable meeting, in view of the wrongness that has been coming to pass for years now and to incentivize both those who remained from days of yore, as well as the commendable youth, toward all sorts of higher values, the resolution was made to establish a society to restore good trust and the edification of respectable mores, which is also to include the beneficial exercise of language. Furthermore, it has been pondered to what extent our widely revered High German mother tongue has a not-inconsiderable advantage compared to foreign languages, both in terms of age and beautiful and graceful speeches, as well as in terms of its abundance of precise words felicitous to the utmost, which are able to make any matter understood more effectively than those of foreign languages. More precisely, everything can be said in and with our tongue. Furthermore, it may be prudently bethought how such a society ought to be awakened and instituted so that its members might speak and write plain German in fine fashion, inasmuch as speaking and writing be equal to doing, and how, like doing, this speaking and writing is to be undertaken outside of this society, which precisely precedes and encompasses it, however, though it be the broader one, it should not merely be guided by the smaller, as the smaller one is rather society as such. Indeed, to achieve this requires an experimentee before all else, one who has no fear of being mere spirit, for showing fear is not a quality that can be brought into consonance with the society, should somebody even remotely intend to belong to it.

"Whereupon I did decide, to which decision albeit was appointed no other than myself, to arrange for this society thusly, although it would initially find itself in a trying position, as it was also I alone who arranged for its gathering. Is language not a superfluous matter, one that ought to be instructed in such a way in the smaller society so that everyone—and this everyman is to be a lover of all respectability, virtue, and courtesy, but primarily of his own body and own soul—should have an occasion to voluntarily surrender himself into it after the instatement of this fine plan all the sooner, into society and into language, into language as society. And because, at such a gathering, it is neither unusual nor beneficial for increased encouragement that the whole of the society does not initially direct its name to a particular matter alone, but must also select a painting conducive to this and a most-appropriate word thereafter, which reports the purpose and the meaning, letting it be expressed, thus everymember of the society must do, if he be inclined to enter into it. Thus is this society to be dubbed the Frightbearing Society, its sigil to be declared 'The End of the Jurisdiction of the Fools,' and to the *word* everything must have been put to good use.

"Thence is the name Frightbearing Society made use of: that anybody, provided that he enters into the society to begin with or is willing to enter therein, accomplishes solely what is pertinent to fright, to the act of frighting, or suchlike, indeed, fright must be created everywhere by the person entering into the society.

"But the purpose of the word is that within and near to the society everything be aimed at benefit and delight, but that nobody suffer, be harmed or chagrined, unless it be so that he not be a society-member of this society, but merely and exclusively a so-and-so from Broader Society, until then, however, a nemesis of the frightbearing, fright being its sole means of subsistence. As far as fright is concerned, it is to be kept with Isabella in Friedrich Schiller's *Maria Stuart*: 'My daughter, haste, / And leave this house of horrors—I devote it / To the avenging fiends! In an evil hour / 'Twas crime that brought me hither, and of crime / The victim I depart.'

"Whereupon, some time later, various other people may then

enter into this society, whose actual goal and intent should be succinctly focused on the following two points that they might be an object of contemplation.

"First, that each and every-member of this society be shown to be honorable, utilizable, and delightful and, as such, must everywhere behave, at meetings to be kindly, joyous, jolly, and amicable in word and deed, just as, in the same way, no one is to take a joyful word to another as ill, thus must one refrain from all coarse and bothersome speeches and jests, lest it be that the other is not a society-member of the society, but merely and exclusively a so-and-so from Broader Society, which is no more than mutilated, to be straightened out, until then, however, a nemesis of the frightbearing, fright being its sole means of subsistence.

"To the other point: that one must preserve the High German tongue in every way viable and possible, as well as being diligent in using the best pronunciation in speaking, in the purest and clearest kind in writing, and, if necessary, in rhyming.

"Following from this, it is also to be wished that each and every one in the Frightbearing Society bear its gold-molten images, names, and words on the one hand and, on the other, should wear his own on a parakeet-green silk ribbon.

"But, as far as the membership in the so-called Frightbearing Society is concerned, not just anybody can join it, anybody who, on a day's whim, thinks that it is always better to belong thereto than to have no face in Broader Society and to disappear namelessly therein. Only those who are selected to take a voyage into the devilish imagination and can bear the fact that all the other members of the society might read the journey for reciprocal exchange can be a member of the Frightbearing Society.

"Thus might there be some who imagined themselves to be matriculated in an Academy of the Godcommanded in childhood, which legitimizes them in the heretical view regarding their comportment that they should never again have to lift a finger or squander a thought. Quite a few think themselves puffed up with hereditary merits and disavow to admit that they too are nothing more than mortal. Do Mörike's lines in 'Ponder it, o soul!' not hold true for everyone, is his 'thou' not nobody, which is to say everybody?

"We would like to make true the student verse, 'for what we possess black on white / we can take home and keep for good.' Nothing is more black and white than a page in a book. The book that counts here is one that hasn't yet been written. Thus shall it be written.

"The Frightbearing Society is neither a reading group nor a debate club. Our language is a hard, polished peale, our words know no rust that makes the people carp and cavil. We have realized that new words create a new world, thus have we created new words. Our language is crystal clear. It is to be used absolutely for understanding between humans.

"If someone adds anything to these things, so shall Schattenfroh inflict the plagues that are hereby described upon him; and if someone takes something away from these words, so shall Schattenfroh take his share away from the Tree of Life. He who testifies to these things says: yes, I have made my way here and am learning to see and to hear and to experience with body and soul."

I dream this night. And now I wake up and see the dream written in my book and I read:

Schattenfroh speaks to me and says: "Sanctify yourself to me! You are the firstborn of our Frightbearing Society. All that which first breaks through the barrier of your inner revelation—and there is nothing other than that which is first—belongs to only me."

And I testify to everyone: commemorate with me the day upon which I moved out of the world, out of the slavehouse that exists in me! So you also *must* do. For Schattenfroh with a strong hand brought me out of there. For that reason shall there no longer be a clouded gaze outward, rather all unclouded gazes must be inward. Today, I am brought out in the month of May. And it shall be when Schattenfroh shall bring me into the land of my inwardness, which he, Nobody, sware unto my fathers to give me, a land flowing with images and imaginings, then I shall keep this service in this month. Seven years shall I write *Schattenfroh* and in the seventh year shall be a feast to Schattenfroh. Unclouded looks shall be given and received seven years; and there shall no clouded look be seen in me, neither shall there be clouded seen with me in all my quarters. And ye shalt shew each other at the end of those seven years, saying: This is done because of that which the Lord did unto me when I came forth out of myself, out of the slavehouse. And it shall be for a sign of 666 unto thee upon thine hand, and for a memorial of 666 between thine eyes, that Schattenfroh's law may be in thy mouth: for with a strong hand hath Schattenfroh brought me out of the world, out of the slavehouse.

And I say to myself and to you: it shall be when Schattenfroh shall bring thee into thy inwardness, as he sware unto thee and to thy fathers, and shall give it thee, and it is given to thee that thou shalt set apart unto Schattenfroh all that comes into your mind, all that which thou seest, hearst, and thinkst within thy inwardness.

And it shall be when thy daughter asketh thee in time to come, saying, "What is this?" that thou shalt say unto her: By strength of hand Schattenfroh brought me out from the slavehouse within myself. And it came to pass, when I would hardly let me go that Schattenfroh reached into my brain and interrogated me. Therefore I sacrifice to Schattenfroh all that breaks through the barrier of my inner revelation, insomuch as it remains unclouded. And it shall be for a token upon thine hand, and for frontlets between thine eyes: for by strength of hand Schattenfroh led me out of myself.

And Schattenfroh speaks: And it shall come to pass if thou shalt hearken diligently unto my commandments, which I have dictated to thee today, that thou shalt love me, who am your lord, and serve me with the whole of thy heart and the whole of thy soul, then I shall give the images of thy inwardness to their time, the early images and the late images, so that thou mightst collect the grain and the new wine and the oil of thy images and imaginings. And I shall care for the vessel of thy soul and thou shalt write and become empty. Take care that thy heart does not allow itself to be beguiled and thou deviatest and servest others and thou prostratest thyself before them and the wrath of Schattenfroh flares up against thee and he shuts up the heaven so that there are no longer any images within thy inwardness and thy writing yield not her fruit and lest ye perish quickly from off the good room which Schattenfroh giveth you.

And these words, which I command thee this day, shall be in thine heart: And thou shalt teach them diligently to thy daughter, and shalt talk of them when thou sittest in thine house, and when thou walkest by the way, and when thou liest down, and when thou risest up. And thou shalt bind them for a sign upon thine hand, and they shall be as frontlets between thine eyes. And thou shalt write them upon the posts of thy house, and on thy gates so that thy days and the days of thy children might be numerous within the inwardness, which Schattenfroh has sworn to give to thee and them as the days of heaven over earth.

And with these words do I sit at the table. Upon the table is a stylus, connected to it by a long chain that cannot be broken by even the greatest of strainings. If one were to use the tabletop as a horizontal buffer, the stylus would pass through it straight to the heart. The chain may tempt some who sit here and consider strangling themselves with it. I put it around my neck. It glows. As soon as it says that "it glows" here, it becomes ice-cold. I prefer the cold. I take the stylus in hand, if placed with only moderate pressure upon the tabletop, the stylus immediately leaves a small indentation in the wood. Even the thumbnail indents itself into the tabletop easily, as if it had just recently replaced a wax tablet and a particularly soft wood had been chosen, as one wanted to preserve a memory of wax in this new medium, just as every new medium seems unable to detach itself from its predecessor in a single go and passes itself off not all too infrequently as this predecessor. The softness of the tabletop has already been noticed by others who have sat here, which prompted them to use not only the stylus, but also their fingernails as writing implements and thus with time has the surface of the tabletop become a single palimpsest. Writing and erasing takes place at and in concomitance with this table. The person writing here must furnish a place for himself and, if he can estimate how much space his engravings shall take up beforehand, the traces that he'd like to leave behind, he shall take this as a requirement, then shall he also only endeavor to clean this area or merely write over the preexisting engravings. Those who follow will then discover that they are only going to be able to overpower something already written-over with all of its intertwining characters by way of even greater pressure onto the tabletop in the sense that their writing pushes the antecedent engravings into the background, which doesn't remain endlessly possible, partly the hand will not allow for it and partly the tabletop. While some will endeavor to entirely remove all existent traces from the tabletop to keep themselves under the illusion that no one is to come after them, but also, in return, to ensure that nobody will be able to outflank them if they themselves are not given the opportunity to make their mark, such that a quick glance is all that is necessary to distinguish them from all of the others, but, still, they are frustrated that the strenuous work of the *radere chartas* is not completed by a salaried specialist, after all, it is they who are the eye specialists, those who first detect what is to be removed and would have liked to do nothing in the world more than to induce its erasure with the curt command "this here!" or "that there!", others attempt to entirely remove entries they hate so as to "immortalize themselves" in their stead, as common parlance never grows tired of saying. After all, they know that stylus is a Latin word that is somehow related to style and stylistics and that is also what they'd like to have—style. Additionally, they know that many a long sentence erases the thought that it is smuggling down the creeping lane of its formulation and thus, when they do not have a thought at hand to begin with, they prefer nothing more than long and even longer sentences in order to compete with the long sentences that do not bring only a single thought to fruition, as has just now been the case here. Only the most diligent of removers shall be compelled to discover that the tabletop is a Wunderblock, which one would have to destroy completely if one wanted to destroy the permanent traces of that which had been written upon the wax tablet, which is just as well preserved and is legible in suitable lights as any engraving upon a slab, even the one that has allegedly been removed, thus would one have to destroy the entire slab, which the stylus is entirely incapable of, and, as the table is anchored to the floor, mere physical strength is not sufficient. If the Wunderblock consists of celluloid, as well as the wax paper of the cover sheet and of the wax tablet, then the engraving onto the table would seem to transfer itself through the uppermost layer of varnish upon the tabletop into the wood underneath, thus saturating the entire tabletop. The tabletop is a reception surface that can be used over and over again, sinking script-traces penetrate into the deepest layers of traces that have already sunken down and are now hidden from the eye and change, thus is it incumbent upon he who writes to recognize himself in all the annual rings, for nothing else is remembering, here, traces are evermore only to be perceived as changed, they are not independent of this material of end-grain, in which they float and rise up and sink down. And is this not how our soul works? The retina and eardrum would at once be full of script, permanent traces forming upon them, the whole of that which constitutes memory slides systematically deeper into us, Freud the Privatdozent already suspected this.

But none of this covers the sensual pleasure that the table calls forth in me, as if it could release me from the situation in which I find myself and I could walk through it into a landscape in which I myself am only script.

Different types of script can be discovered and either reveal themselves or the letters, in that they hide one and expose the other. Should the inscribed trace no longer suggest a hand, should any image have disappeared from the letter, should the letter no longer belong to any specific script, but to the ideal representation of a letter, then finally to the notion, and should the observer see cosmic constellations through the appearance and arrangement of letters on the tabletop and, in this, God, then the letter is a transparent sign for something absent. But should it be an image, a celebration of corporeality, the voluptuousness of the non-beyond, material of material, should body and spirit be one, then its substance is shape and form and the essence of that which is shown can be read from the letter-image.

Some handwriting is quite neat, intent on legibility, without any superfluous flourishes, it speaks the word of a quixotic theology of the word, in view of what's to come, it would like to practice asceticism, others offer a jittery expression of the joy of damaging something and there's no question as to how this is to come to pass, but a real coward's at work over here and, before hesitation is transmuted into violence, the trace is lost. This drawing here made use of the most beautiful arabesque as an excuse not to divulge anything about itself, which is all that it wishes, for does the "A" not efface the penis and scrotum?, and does the arabesque not swirl around this censorship?, and does the arabesque not have the greatest moribund desire to destroy image and narrative in order to put itself into their place?, and thus does the accessory become the side job become the main. One notices the indecision as to whether to continue with this inscription in handwriting or, by rendering the engraving illegible, to make it appear to be damage inflicted by no human hands, to be mere hatching that can be seen as script only in the eyes of the beholder. Here, the human alphabet shows the script of an oft tortured mortal, one would not be able to endure these contortions for even five minutes, but *I* could look at naked bodies that are expressing a longing for one another for much longer than five minutes, with my stylus I help it along by giving a rod in the hand to the hands, that they might hold each other and pull each other a bit closer, that they might be able to go into each other and that also from the Frightbearing Society, which is to say these characters, a Fruitbearing Society comes to be. Still other engravings mean nothing but fear, they bear witness to the soul that would like to leave a trace here or to be completely absorbed into this trace, no artist has to be the soul-drawer, that might even be a hindrance, talent would stand in the ways of its psychogrammatical precipitations, as it was always aiming for art and not simply indulging in the pressure to express itself, blindness is the order of the day here, but, in a final reckoning, one makes art out of it, even if this table were a sign of interrogation and torture. No matter how careful one is to follow the signs of the individual hand, to tease out distinctions, to keep everything in perspective, the interlocking, still overgrown entanglements shall gain sovereignty over the obstinacy of the eyes *forthwith*, they concisely annihilate each difference, each bit of pithiness, new figures emerge with each and every look, they'd like to see the limits and correct the exaggerations, an army of amorphous, defective signs is gathering together here, a tumult is what it is and a fire is lit from its center that takes everything with it, as I once experienced with a carpet that caught fire within itself, then, as soon as the carpet had disappeared from the middle, said Father, it wasn't a carpet at all, but a curtain that could liberate the eye to see what was hidden behind it, but nothing was to be found behind it, said Father, behind it is to be found nothing but the pure trope "ach!," meaning "alas!," but also Akh, the ancestral spirit, the spirit-soul, which we all wanted to join after our death or into whose possession we wanted to transport ourselves, this is why we say that "death is filled up by one's *ach*," that the *ach* is first a crested ibis, then the most luminous star-filled poultry that can spread its mane out so impressively and never ceases bowing to greet those of its own kind, then a Schattenvogel, a shadowbird, for is not every shadow a bird?, then, once again, it is a state of transfiguration that fills yon dead that have been transfigured through the benedictions of the cult of the dead so that the dead one might become immortal. The *ach* belongs to the heavens, if I am a corpse upon the earth and not in a state of transfiguration, then might I not recognize the *ach*, the Akh, though it be a being of greater light, it gleams and shines, or that the burned curtain might have revealed both gleam and shine. How could Father have recognized that? Perhaps he was already one of the transfigured ones.

What is taking place here upon the table is a true sign language that would make everyone fall silent immediately, it conveys the linguistic state of exception, which looks for no more words, but has found its way back to the image, which is nothing more than a stretching upward in flames and a falling floating, it conveys itself to the district of the illegible and might reappear burnt as intertwined once more. This language is far quicker than other languages, which require more than a hundredfold the time to put the gesticulative flood of images into words and, with each look, a new source opens itself up. Unfortunately, the slowness of words seems to be the appropriate human medium, everyday comprehension can be achieved only with words. Words stick to images, images without words are unthinkable. Perhaps that is why Schattenfroh is so old-fashioned, always speaking of reading and writing. One ought to think that images and comportments were once enough to get by in the world.

The palimpsest makes the eyes grow tired in the long run, I can no longer grasp any particulars without drifting off instantly, but suddenly I discover inscriptions of particular urgency between all the testimonies of willpower, willfulness, and fear, as if the flood of images were standing still for a few moments before the breaking of the waves blur the clear contours once again and erase the images. I sit before the wooden book of life and death. A large building can be made out, an office, a father, a cell, a medieval repast, an interrogation, a black page, a hell, a toad, a chimera, an open book, Ruprecht, Rilke, a journey to heaven, the ladies of the seven antechambers, a throne of God, a tapestry, a city map, a Muttergotteshäuschen, a city wall, a wooden doll, a Fratzenstuhl, a woman in a window, a carpet, a curtain, a cell, a sword, an interrogation, an execution, the office, a library, Mother on a big train, a nursing home, a girl and a suitcase, 23 houses, a second library, a key, a whole house, the Last Judgment, a hearing aid, a park bench, Grandpa, the Eifel, Prüm, a meeting, a fountain, a battle, an arrest, a printer, a pact with said printer, ein Pressbengel (which is both a "rounce" and sounds something like a "press-brat"), a lock, a cell, an interrogation, a pamphlet against Luther, an execution, an intensive-care unit, body and soul, a dying, a death, a Hürtgenwald, a pub, a gorge, a judgment, an executioner's sword, a photo, a chest, a river.

And then there's still a kind of flurry, a pulsating surface, the fluttering of letters like snowflakes that one wants to catch immediately with one's hands and the hands are the true script experts, to which the eye can demonstrate nothing that they have not long since fathomed. Concealed by the youngest carvings, but not in such a way that their traces could have been made completely invisible, ghost images shine through here and there, bluff of the surface, faded remnants of attempts to erase, phantoms between life and death, their corruption has developed a life of its own. Schattenfroh warned me that if I stared too long at individual images in the withdrawal-of-perception phase, they would burn themselves into my inwardness, the location of which he didn't want to name, the word "soul" allocated only for other things. Then I shall be permanently in flight, I said to him. He seemed to like this idea. The German word for flight, "Flucht," has only a single letter more than its source-word, he said, and it makes absolute sense that "Flucht" results from a "Fluch," a curse, and leads to "Tod," to death, with the first letter of which "Fluch" ends in "Flucht." The German language is rather uneconomical, one would only have had to follow this principle of addition around the entire world for it to have developed entirely differently, it could always be traced down to its smallest elements thanks to the highly restricted and systematically controllable formation of metaphors, crises resulting from language would be as good as impossible—and from what other sources have crises ever resulted?—those responsible for wars might be spotted immediately and, in the literal sense of the word, the world must go back to *literalness*, all this prattle about the fourfold sense of scripture and its consequences might have actually ruined the world.

I can't get enough of the phantoms, one seems to be able to see through the table with them, I have the feeling I have to set myself up particularly well with them. I want to attach myself to their floating, it shall lead me through walls and times. I can hardly fend off the euphoria that arises when one of these phantoms is to be my psychopomp, which often heralds an impending attack of migraine. It carries the word "soul" with it, the one Schattenfroh dismissed so sullenly, as if it were something particularly holy or particularly reprehensible, whenever Father utters it, I struggle with it to the point of tantrum, and I would like to finally obliterate it with the things that I destroy in the process, which is to say, it squats in Mother's copper vessels, which she would take down from the heavy oaken cupboards once a year and clean with a bright paste, even though only a little bit of dust had settled down onto them, heirlooms just like the cupboards, a burden that pushes all the generations that come into contact with them into the ground, it was quite enough for me to recognize them in photographs of my grandparents, they neatly populated the walls of my grandparents' dining room as if they had grown right out of them and Mother had only to be led into this room if she were to be left alone at home and it was the cupboards that would undertake to supervise her. The cupboards too must finally be destroyed, the photographs must be destroyed, the inner images must be destroyed, then, finally, the names must be destroyed, which is to say, my belief is that Hegel is right, it is in names that we *think*, and the name is the simple imageless representation, which makes image and contemplation superfluous. And the word "soul" too must be destroyed. Do you remember way back when—we couldn't stop talking about the "soul"? If Father says the word "soul" ever again, I swore to myself one day, I'll destroy the cross above the altar together with its corpus in the church where I was baptized. But now the word expands in me like a drug, to which I give myself over entirely. This is the table-level broadening of my soul, forgetting and remembering are simultaneous, and while my eyes wandering over the palimpsest see only orders and invocations, on the right is written "instead of analysis and knowledge, war reigns, and no one has ever declared unto it, 'it is coming to pass right in the middle of me,'" the stylus has swelled to several times its old size, it won't be long before I have to hold it down with both hands, it penetrates the table effortlessly, it's already a paddle now and I move across a lake with it, approaching engravings unravel, then move out of view and dissolve, barely has my paddle pierced them when they finally shrink and merge into the disintegrating engraving behind me, which slowly gathers around a middle once again, curiously deformed, the grimace of a distorted gaze, I recognize with a disquiet that has not yet decided to grow into horror a slate onto which a little boy writes the word "punishment," then the word "funishment" appears, a stick strikes the writing hand, which now writes "stick" onto the slate and the stick takes on the form of a stick descending upon the boy, the slate is struck in twain, the word "funishment" hovers unchanged in the air over the water, which is now teeming with such engravings everywhere, but, when I paddle closer to them, they reveal themselves to be objects from childhood and adolescence thought to be lost, a little picture book *War Bello beim Spinnen*,* a golden toy car, a little box that I never opened, a radiant green Jesus in front of a shell, a donkey sewn by Mother herself and given to me one Christmas.

And so, just as I can be surprised at a rediscovery that frightened me as a child, I am now frightened in view of the images, the objects of

---

* *Was Bello Spinning.*

which drove me into an unceasing rapture as a child until my mother took them to a secret place, to which all of my attention from then on was directed, until I recognized hiding as a rule of the game—and even the prohibition on looking for something was a rule belonging to this game.

Whenever the rapture lasted longer than a child's body could take, it had the potential to turn into fever and vomiting, the childish horror would often dull rather quickly and be transmuted into boredom as soon as the triggering instance was seen through.

Any pen shuddering with the anxiety of influence would be of great help should one wish to make the engravings disappear once more (provided one could smooth out the tabletop just like the Wunderblock). For this whole time, I've been writing over seething traces that already constitute a person, but a hidden one, overwritten, in such a way that they are connected with me and the person brings itself forth. I hope to get a look at its *Bestand*, its standing reserve. At that which is. What is? En-framing.

The light goes out. It wasn't very bright before, but it's downright dim now. I wait. I imagine myself to have died. In my imagination, I am sitting on a chair at a table indoors or outdoors. I have sat in this chair at this table on a number of occasions already. Chair and table and the imagining of having detained myself here on a number of occasions seem strange to me. Someone searches for this place to imagine how I sat there. Between myself and this other I can find no difference, which is to say, the actual stranger is the one whom both imagine to be sitting there. It's good that this other exists, otherwise I'd be mortally frightened of myself.

My right hand slides across the table. It remains lying upon a relief-like spot. The spot becomes warm. It's not because of the wood, it must have something to do with the engraving. Then it's not just warmth, my hand burns without my being able to remove it from the tabletop. It is a tremendous pain, I bite my left hand so as not to scream.

The hand has now disengaged itself, the engraving has burnt itself into it and is glowing. What do I see?

I have been in a cell for several days. How can I know that I've already been here for several days? A tormenting regularity has set in and allows me to fasten upon no clear thought except for the sentences, "I have been in a cell for several days. How can I know that I've been here for several days? A tormenting regularity has set in and allows me to fasten upon no clear thought except for the sentences, 'I have been in a cell for several days. How can I know that I've been here for several days? A tormenting regularity has set in and allows me to fasten upon no clear thought except for the sentences.'" And I leapt out of my murderers' row of observation-repetition, observation-repetition. Otherwise, each doing would be nothing more than a memory. The open end of a sheet-metal tube protrudes from the wall. Sometimes, a voice resounds from it and gives me instructions. The instruction is preceded by the request, "Come here," I go right up to the tube, put my ear to its opening, then wait for the voice. I rejoice at each new instruction, it is issued from a distance, I know that I am at a sufficient distance from the voice, which is interrupted by the instruction. I find the merest breath to be especially uncomfortable if the voice does not articulate itself, but, instead, my counterpart, who is not visible to me, merely breathes in and out. I then imagine an animal crawling slowly through the tube and, as soon as it slips free, it might grow to be very large in my cell so as to devour me or the voice could pupate in my ear and molt into an insect penetrating my brain. The voice is dreadful. It dominates me and speaks even when it isn't speaking. If I am to make hypotheses from the floorplan of my cell about that of the entire building, there must be other, possibly identically laid-out cells and a core cell in the middle of the building, from which all other cells can be reached—at least by way of the speaking tube. I cannot discern whether we (provided I am not alone here) can also be seen from there, however much the question occupies me, I do not have the power to change these circumstances, thus do I strive to switch off my awareness thereof. Scraps of paper of different sizes fall through the tube three times a day. Since no daylight penetrates into the cell and the clock was taken away from me, it is only in this way that I have an approximate notion of the time of day. Perhaps, however, they want to make me even more confused with the script on the scraps. But since the sequence of information never changes, at least not so far, I take the information literally. I too live in error, as a result of which I have lost nothing, rather I have gained an order that offers me meaning and stability, I can set myself up entirely in the memory of my parents' house, my first apartment, and my last apartment and, just as morning, midday, and evening alternate, I'm sometimes in my parents' house, then in my own first apartment, then in the last apartment I lived in, then I move from there back to my parents' house, which I see in almost all of my dreams—furnishing it to completion in these visualizations offers me a daily joy that an ordinary object can hardly offer, in my imaginings, it even surpasses the joy of an actual redeliverance into this place of longing. My parents' house is so close to me now that I recognize individual objects in the signs upon the tabletop, for example, a chest, a chest of drawers, an armchair, a cupboard, in the kitchen lies a knife with an unusually large handle, the bloodthirsty ornamentation of which deters even the peeling of fruits or vegetables. Upon the handle is depicted a man of medium height, but powerful build, cutting the throat of another man, who appears no less powerful. If one swivels the knife to the left, the man's head is almost completely severed, in a third image, the head lies upon the ground, if one swivels the knife a bit further, the man puts his head back on. I remember trying to increase the torque of the knife in a kind of competition with friends in such a way that the man's execution would appear as a single continuous motion. It's a good thing that there are knives such as this, one friend said, so that the depicted scene might remain solely upon the handle. I also see a small group of wooden musicians from the Ore Mountains, they are allowed to leave the drawer in which they're housed throughout the year along with other holiday items for a few days at Christmastime. The idea that one of the five musicians with the sixth conducting might be damaged or even lost still troubles me to this day, the fear of loss has increased immeasurably over the years and I offered the secret power that might be intending such loss or damage an exchange: may my mother disappear or, even better, my father if only these musicians might be preserved for all time. I was able to name this power precisely, I was able to see it, it was in the shadow that all things cast, thus did I always take care to put the musicians in a favorable light and reposition them according to the time of day. The conductor seems to recognize how it all links up, he's stretched his arms upward more than just once, as if he wanted to draw my attention to something or surrender to fate. Only I can hear the music of the little band, it simply plays on. In the cellar is a spider that keeps getting bigger. It lives in the potato drawer and threatens me if I approach it. Mother said that spiders don't eat potatoes. I know better. They convert potato starch into a very special substance that smells better than perfume. This substance empties the body, a process that is in no way equivalent to death. The spider shows me its empty body when I stop to stand in front of it for longer than a minute. Then there's the chest in the corridor, which I'm not allowed to open, Father says, the head of one of our ancestors lies in the chest and this head is such a spitting image of me that you might get it confused. Get what confused, I asked Father, Life and death, he said. Schattenfroh reports that I should focus on the scrap of paper. And if I don't do that? Then there shall be consequences. What consequences? You're not even doing it now.

 Bread with jam, "breakfast," on a scrap of paper, on the next scrap is "lunch," while soup and bread with cheese, "dinner," is on the third scrap. There is quince jelly for breakfast, sometimes also orange marmalade with peel, two items that, even in so-called normal life, were among my preferred spreads. It pleases me, but also frightens me, I haven't told anyone of these preferences. And thus am I still nowhere but at home, even if the interior has changed over the course of the night. At home in the evening, I would always eat a certain cave-ripened Austrian mountain cheese that could only be bought in special shops. Due to its strong smell, this cheese must be quarantined, it contaminates the air in seconds. It should only be taken out of the box for the purpose of its consumption, it lingers in the room for longer than a foul fart. It is precisely this cheese that is served here every evening, but without a containment box, so I am completely at the mercy of its accumulating odor, at this point, a bestial reek has built up in my cell. Perhaps the order of the scraps is a feint, breakfast is slopped out as dinner, lunch as breakfast, and dinner as lunch—or dinner as lunch, breakfast as dinner, and lunch as breakfast. This would change nothing about the basic three-way division that the scraps facilitate for me. At first I wanted to figure out if the intervals between the scraps of paper were the same, but how could I have measured them? I'm no longer certain of whether I'm imagining things when I see someone occasionally talk to me. Through which door would he come? Would he slip through the tube and into the cell? Then, on the other hand, I see very clearly that I am sitting across from two gentlemen who are asking me comprehensible questions. Are you afraid. Yes, I am afraid. In a way that is inexplicable to me, they manage to give voice to the very thoughts that I am thinking at precisely the moment I think them and to correct the spelling of those thoughts. At first, I didn't know how this could possibly be of value, as the corrections were orders and by no means suggestions. My proofreaders surely trust that I shall adapt to their style, then, sooner rather than later, think and write like that, which is to say, think without errors and as if printed, as they desire, then there shall be no more need for corrections. They've given me a script from a Pseudo-Longinus, that, they say it's still relevant, I am to study it diligently. How refinedly they express themselves and how archaically. I assume that this gentleman doesn't actually exist and that they have invented him in order to make an impression on me so that *they* don't have to make an impression on me, at least not in this way, they make the strongest impression on me by being absent. It pleases them when I think about them, but this thinking-of-them is also subject to correction, the word censorship doesn't exist here.

My writing serves as the Frightbearing Society's gauge of its future. It relieves me of my self-understanding. Memory and consciousness cancel each other out, they do not exist simultaneously. My small box is switched onto the real, which it sees as inner revelation and hears as a voice. It decodes the letters that the real carries along with it. I am subject-object. The result is a compulsion to confess. I confess: the entire organism that I am is nothing but script and image, what I am meant to give rise to is already there.

There must be other volunteers, but I don't even see myself. There is no mirror here, nothing in which to reflect myself. I am Schattenfroh's en-framing, I belong to his standing reserve, he controls and secures me. I'm going to the outermost edge, Schattenfroh says. With Langmut Leernun,[*] alias Lang Lerne Unmut,[†] whom the State Security dubbed Null Argumenten,[‡] I say, "I am your jumping jack. / All you have to do / is pull my nose. / I am pulling at your boots. / The grass shall be green no longer." I understand that I ought to hear the sphere-music of my self, prison and society are one. I shall not let all my teeth be pulled in the belief that Schattenfroh has had bugs built into me like Langmut Leernun.

The walls here are smooth and white. No pattern can be recognized upon them—no crack. It costs quite an effort to see them as anything other than white. The walls offer nothing but themselves. But that also has its advantage. I can project whatever I'm imagining onto

---

[*] Longanimity Emptynow.
[†] Long Learn Displeasure.
[‡] Null Arguments.

them with my eyes. At first, I don't want to do this at all. But, then, I give in, the film has already begun. I remember this from back in my childhood. Just staring at the wall and awaiting images. And they always came. Once, Father appeared upon the wall. He had just parked the car in the garage, the garage door slammed shut, and, strangely enough, he didn't come in through the front door, but appeared upon the left wall of my room without having entered the house. That made an impression on me and frightened me very much. Simultaneously, another figure appeared on the right, one I soon recognized as myself. The figure ran off and hit my father in the head with a piece of wood it had hidden behind its back. Admittedly, the piece of wood turned out to be an extendable plastic sword, with which one couldn't even hurt a fly. My father made no move to repel the attack, instead walking silently through me still. Then he turned, took the sword from my hand, smiled, and beheaded me. My head lay at my feet, Father could no longer be seen. Mere seconds later, Father was standing in the room and also looking at the wall. There's nothing there, I said. I can see for myself that there's nothing there, Father said. Even though there was nothing to be seen, I couldn't shift my gaze from the wall. If I concentrated for long enough by fixating on a spot on the wall until my eyes illuminated it, my father would appear once more in the light, going about his business. However, he was only going about his business for as long as I was moving around the room, which I could only do to a rather limited extent if I didn't want my father to leave my sight. For example, if I turned away from the wall, I saw nothing but the empty room or, rather, the furniture in it. When my gaze reached the wall once again, a faint light appeared, growing all the brighter the more I approached the wall on which I had previously been concentrating. Father slammed the car door with his left hand and swung his briefcase with his right. The slamming of the car door and the swinging of the briefcase were unfortunately the only movements that I could register in this way. If Father had swung the briefcase with his right hand, then he slammed the car door once again with his left. At first, I still hoped that I would be able to recognize something in the repetitions that I had missed upon a first glance, but, even after a hundred viewings, I saw nothing new. I had to come up with something to get Father to spring away from the slamming of the car door and from the swinging of the briefcase. This would have required a room without a window, preferably a circular room, and I would always have to go ceaselessly round and round in circles, my eyes would have guided the Father on the wall, I would have watched him there for hours, would have finally learned what he spends his days doing, what's to be found in the briefcase, Father is a secret made flesh, I never knew exactly where he was coming from when he got home, he slammed the garage door, strode into the house, couldn't be found for a few minutes, then was suddenly standing there and saying that Mother had complained about me and, as Mother had complained about me, he would have to hit me a little bit with the cane so that Mother would feel a bit better. Recently, I had taken to using words that Mother didn't know, a family depends on common understanding, he said, as such, I should not use these words anymore, what kind of words do you mean, I didn't know what the words in question were and simply said certain terms that I'd read without understanding them, metaphor, for example, or dissociation, and Father's cane made it clear to me that he knew very well what these words meant, no more of these words will come to you, right, not after I've used pain to get them out of you. No, I can't think of any others right now, I thought, but then I couldn't say it aloud. When I pulled my pants back up, I couldn't understand why I'd pulled them down in the first place and resolved to keep them up next time.

    The contours of the room disappear once it gets dark, I just had to wait for the darkness, then I would spin round in a circle with eyes wide open, light would shoot through my eyes, and Father would appear in a beautiful light-blue suit in the virtual circle of the room. The faster I went round, the more Father moved. I was able to accompany him on his way to work from the moment he left the house to when he entered his office, eavesdropping on his dictation of a letter; when he was thinking, he'd pace to and fro, but, when he was speaking into the dictaphone, he'd stand still. He spoke of the fact that the city library had to be expanded, the population had to educate itself and not merely search for whatever ruins remained of the Second World War, an activity that plants a never-ending "this-city-was-destroyed-worse-than-Dresden-but-nobody-mentions-this-fact" into their mouths. I was proud to be able to live in a city that had been destroyed worse than Dresden. But how could he give such orders? Was he the mayor of the city? Could he give orders at all or did he only entrust them to his small voice recorder, which he'd immediately stick into his jacket pocket whenever somebody entered the room. If somebody entered the room, it could only be Mrs. Monduhr,* the receptionist responsible for announcing visits. The visitor had a hard go of it. During one of my nocturnal trips through the green landscapes of my head, I bore witness to how Mrs. Ohrmund† announced a young man who wanted to speak to my father on a private matter. My father asked what sort of private matter was at issue. Mrs. Mohndur replied that the matter must be a bit delicate, the young man hadn't spoken of it to her, after all, this isn't some bureaucratic motion, was what the young man said. Good. Or not good. But, in any case, come in. The young man takes a seat at the very back of the room in a blue armchair that stands in the middle of the wall. He couldn't have taken a seat anywhere else, for there was no seating accommodation other than at the very back, at the very front was only my father in an armchair well-suited to the loftiness of his position, he assigned the place with outstretched arm

---

* Moonclock.
† Earmouth.

and burrowing index finger even after the young man had already taken it. Between him and my father lay some twenty meters. I don't know why you've popped up here, is what my father said, if there was something to discuss, it could've been done at home. For the young man was his son, me. Yes, but at home, the young man said, he doesn't ever listen. At home, there were many large armchairs in which one might sit, if one were to sit down in these armchairs, one would sink down into them immediately and nobody would be able to find one. The seating accommodations at home were arranged in precisely the same way as at the office. If one wanted to engage in conversation with others, which is to say if one wanted to say something to Father, one had to cry out, as a result of which one's strength would dissipate after a few words. Father, on the other hand, could make himself understood effortlessly, he didn't even have to open his mouth to say something. Apparently, all he had to do was think the words and, already, they'd begin to ring out. His brain transmitted the words to two loudspeakers that were attached to the left and right of the space above the blue chair. He adjusted the volume with the mere force of his will. If I look at my father in photographs today, I tend to be rather surprised: I've never seen this man before in my life. Suddenly, I discovered that different sentences could be heard from the right loudspeaker than from the left. My father left the room, the voices continued to speak. On the right: stand there. On the left: stand up. On the right: Mother orders you to quit it with the reading. On the left: reading destroys the world. On the right: Father orders you to read without cease. On the left: you have done away with Mother. On the right: you did away with Mother. On the left: in 2014, you're going to drive to the Elephant Toilet in Gießen. On the right: and, there, shalt thou go into an image for all time as thy atonement. On the left: the image has no beginning and no end. On the right: the image is born again with each look. He couldn't have meant the painting in his office, it was very distinct and finite. Here it is:

It originates from the fifteenth century and shows the holy Saint Louis of Toulouse, who was held hostage from 1288 to 1295 as a prisoner of war for his father Charles the Lame after the latter lost a naval battle near Naples. From what background does he emerge? Does his cloak show the star-bedecked sky? Louis looks off to the side somewhat coyly, as if he knew that he was being gazed upon, but did not wish to meet the gazer. Has his cloak inadvertently opened up and is it now showing a girdle book that he stole and that it would be better to hide away? Is that why his father is looking at him sternly and demanding that he deliver up the book? Louis holds the book crampedly under his left arm. What's in the book? I know. It is now being written and shall continue to be written. Charles the Lame, his father, sought the canonization of his second-eldest son after his death at the age of only twenty-three. He dedicated his life of terrible illness to God and became the Bishop of Toulouse just eight months before his death. If God wills it, I still have my 23rd year ahead of me, but have probably not dedicated my life to God and have yet to become a bishop. The book, however, that I can precisely see is my book, Louis of Toulouse has stolen it from me. Far from having canonized me, Father comes back into his office. Please take off that senseless cloak, you're running around as if you were at a carnival, he says. I do what he says. And take off your fool's cap, since you started psychoanalysis, you've always had a kind of halo about you. And the fact that you're running around in here with those sandals, one might think that you were born to poor parents who send their son out to beg. I look down at my feet, which, all of a sudden are shod in leather sandals, solid in terms of design, albeit entirely old-fashioned, they have a toe-bar made up of three straps, out of which the outer ones run toward a cross-strap attached to the metatarsus, binding foot to sole, the middle strap goes over the cross-strap and toward the ankle, to which the sole is held by this circumferential ankle-strap, from the ends of the cross-strap two straps likewise go toward the ankle-strap so that the straps of the sandal's rhomboid construction gird a cross from the middle toe-strap and the cross-strap of the metatarsus. I attempt to move the cross with my foot, but the straps don't give way. The crosier in the painting points outward. A whip. Louis of Toulouse is thus in his own territory. Father takes the staff, points to my blue raiment with it, and lets me escape through a side door that leads into the building's basement and, from there, unobservedly out onto the street, a circuit secret from daily visitors. To wit, this time, the circuit leads me into the basement, but not out of it, instead, I've come to a kind of dungeon, the walls here are smooth and white. No pattern can be recognized upon them—no crack. The round room forms a window- and doorless enclave, which shapes itself as a segmentation of the basement corridor. I get very close to the walls, is there a message or at least some signs to be recognized upon them. It costs quite an effort to see them as anything other than white. The walls offer nothing from themselves. A cot is now growing in the room and a lightbulb swings over it from a long cable. A metal toilet grows out of the floor and walls. I want to grab onto the lightbulb, then it disappears, an iron door grows out of the opposite wall, through the observation window in which light permeates the cell. The observation window is secured with three gridded bars, I grab the two outer ones and wish to peer outside, the bars are icy, my hands instantaneously freeze to them. My feet set themselves into motion, stamping on the spot so that the cold doesn't penetrate into my legs, then I hear voices from the area of the basement: "Establishment of facts." "Cell, cot." "Cell number, cot position." "Number 17." "Here." "Number 22." "Here." "Number 7." "Here." "Number 8/3." "Here." "Number 14/2." "Here." "Number 2." "Here." "Number 3." "Here." "Number 9." "Here." "Number 1." "Here." At least ten different people responded to "Number 1." I wasn't called, otherwise the calling of the numbers wouldn't have continued, on the one hand, this calms me down, but, on the other, could indicate that I have been forgotten and shall also be forgotten in the future. My hands have warmed the bars so much that I can unclasp them. I must have a fever. As soon as I think the word 'fever' and pronounce it in thought, my eyes project images onto the walls. Whatever I think, I see. If I attempt to think incoherently, I see incoherent sequences of images. In attempting to think coherently so as to be able to rejoice in a coherent sequence of images, I discover that there is nothing incoherent; the sequences of images projected by my eyes onto the wall to the left of the cell door, all thematically unified, appear to me in this light to be no more coherent than the sequences of images on the wall to the right of the cell door, images uniting all that which is incompatible to the point of contradiction and seeming to convey no plot whatsoever. I would therefore like to concentrate entirely on the right wall, thus do I avert my gaze from the left. Father appears upon the wall. He seems to have noticed I took the book with me. The painting shows Saint Louis of Toulouse who would shed his holiness without the book. "You won't get out of the basement until the book has been returned safe and sound. I'll have it fetched now." I hear voices from the wing of the basement once again. They are just as incoherent as my images, but they go very well with that which is seen: "When you shall be fetched." "Today when." "You shall be fetched today." "Today all the people fetch ya, today they fetch ya, today they fetch ya. But you, but you, but you know that, but you don't know that, but you surely don't know that." If I don't look at the images, I don't hear anything. So I have to keep my eyes permanently shut. I look at the wall once again, my father's voice suddenly resounds, and I know that this is not my father: "Concrete and secure insights about the enemy and the deep feelings of hate, abhorrence, aversion, and implacability toward the enemy." I listen, think that's my father's voice, but that is not my father, then, suddenly, someone says to me: "No, no, you don't know that, but you know that, but you know that, but you, but you no, you, they're fetchin' ya today, they're fetchin' ya today, they're fetchin' people today, everyone, you'll get fetched today, today you, today you're gonna get fetched, when." At first, the voices sound out rather brightly, then rather dully once more. I am conscious of my hunger and call out into the room, from what I hear, it's almost certainly a cell block. "You'll only have to wait a little while, you might just wet yourself," my father says, now very close to my right ear. In my left ear, I hear this speech: "But not to think about it unless. To feel another matter. That should be cleft. To think something, but not feel! To feel something, but not think. And you betwixt." I'd like to sit down, but there are no seating accommodations other than cot and toilet. If I think I might perhaps sit down on the cot, I see and feel it no longer, the toilet is covered over in icicles. Please let me know what's going on here, goes through my head, and, immediately, voices in the cell block report to me what's going on. The one voice strides incessantly up and down in front of my cell door: "Deformation of the personal lifestyle and of the societal attachment of the corresponding persons of the societal detachment of the personal lifestyle and of the societal bond of the corresponding persons and of the corresponding society of uncommitted persons." A second voice, at a distance of about twenty meters, keeps it shorter but still repeats its sentence over and over like a prayer wheel: "The word 'opposition' lacks objective, social, and political bases." It'd probably be for the best for me to let it speak, I think. So they speak as if I didn't exist: "Hatred always aims for active confrontation with the hated adversary, is not content with abhorrence and avoidance, but is often connected with the need to destroy or harm them." Another voice chimes in straightaway, it seems to know that I'm listening in, it attempts to console me with riddles: "Vanished and by no means as if the eyes would then be safe." Then, once again, there are voices in the room, they have no bodies, they're very flat, they have no volume, which allows them to change their position at any given time, sometimes they're very close to the ear, then they're in the ear once more, the following utterance is breathed in through the peephole: "Enemy defense system for the hindering of the steadily growing influence of the real." Of the real. That which is real. The re(G)al. I always have to say that word to myself—the real. With this word, I've entered into a different consciousness, I can no longer brush it away as easily as I usually brush words off of the tabletop. Barely do I utter the word, "the real," when voices attack me, as if they'd been waiting for a motto and the real is the motto: "A matter of domestic security, anti-state human trafficking, pro-state human extermination, agent preservation! To scout, to reconnoiter persons, to scout facts, scouting, scouting of persons, scouting of facts, assertion, repetition, contagion, repetition of assertion, repetition of contagion, contagioassertion, assertiorepetitiocontagion, repetitiocontagioassertion, contagioassertiorepetition." Then a voice approaches me, in it, I recognize one of my father's colleagues, who, among other things, is responsible for the procurement of writing utensils, the rate of consumption of which has practically exploded in the last few months, my father said this during a conversation with his secretary, a conversation I'd recently heard in peripheral fashion after he'd summoned me to him on a putatively minor matter. The trifle turned out to be a grotesquerie, as my father suspected me of having swallowed his wedding ring, which is already sad in and of itself, the fact of the vanished wedding ring and that my father suspected me of being behind it and, beyond that, two circumstances worsened the effrontery: I'd actually dreamt of having swallowed a ring the night before, my gaze in recalling the dream immediately signaled to my father a sense of guilt, which he then pontificated about more than once, also in terms of a benevolent forgiveness, after all, I didn't at first try to deny it at all; what weighed even more heavily, however, was my father's assertion that, on the inner side of the ring, instead of the wedding date, were engraved letters that contained his life and, should these letters, which is to say the ring, be lost, he, Father, would die at some point in the foreseeable future. I laughed out loud, Father hit me in the face, you've done that for the last time, I said to him, why, he retorted, I've only done it for the first time, and now my father's stationary procurer says to me, "it would be good if you had actually swallowed the ring." He says his name is Mateo, he buys so much paper and so many notebooks for my father every month that a whole office wouldn't manage to use it up in a year. They underhandedly exchange messages upon the notebook scraps, my father always says that he thinks in analog, digital is a synonym for corruption. As spies are everywhere, he and Mateo have fixed routes that they take to the building everyday, these routes were, however, worked out in such a way that they met at certain intersections occurring in the combination of passages during the day, they took corridor-routes that shifted daily, they were determined using a certain coding scheme, only allowing for the repetition of corridor-routes after years, this being due to the unmanageable multiplicity of passages in the building, one day, Mateo went missing while on his way to a meeting point in the building, Mateo, however, was of the opinion that he, Father, had strayed from the established route and gotten lost in the building, which couldn't be the case, as he, Father, wasn't yet on his way, while Mateo had already strayed from the right path, Father had visited Peter Ozianon, who had shown himself to be uncommonly prying, and thus had Father had a red alert put into effect with the supreme priority of maintaining the secrecy of the meeting place, for which reason Father did not set off in the first place, while Mateo, according to Father, had gotten lost during the same span of time, if he had not been the one who had gotten lost, it would have been clear to him that Father had adequate reason for not appearing at the arranged meeting point at the arranged time, a logic that, as soon as it came to his attention, Mateo was absolutely unwilling to share. The aim of the meeting is, in any case, the exchange of note-scraps, which, after mutual perusal, are to be destroyed then and there. My father and Mateo exchange service instructions concerning the employees, their powers, as well as public and non-public measures, etc., putting them down onto note-scraps. My father is convinced that he must regularly dismiss employees, relocating them or entrusting new duties to them with the help of a cryptographic key that he supposedly found on old maps. It's said that only in this way can he prevent a plot against him and, therewith, an infiltration of the office, which would be tantamount to the arbitrary suspension of rules and principles, the non-observance of which would be tantamount to the disabling of God. There's a rumor going around that it isn't my father who said that, but the employees, and it was ultimately this rumor that was the decisive factor in convincing my father of the unreliability of all of the employees, to such an extent, in fact, that a method like the one described here became necessary. As if there were any need for proof, my father is said to have said.

"Yes, you see, you're crying. Sometimes, crying is nothing to be ashamed of," it is thus that Mateo orders the employees around, he dubs them "my underlings." He leaves them in the dark about the purpose of their duties, even if they were to discuss amongst themselves, they would have to put the separate parts of each of the work's stages, first divided out amongst them, back together in such a way that a whole would emerge, the workload that Mateo inflicts upon them leaves them with no time for this. Thus does one see dozens of subordinates running around the building incessantly, muttering numbers and letters related to their assignments to themselves, they must not forget them, but they are also not allowed to write them down, which would only increase the flood of the written-down, if something is spoken, it must be repeated, the voice is as fleeting as a bowel movement, it leaves our body and penetrates into another body, into which it disappears, just as the outside disappears within us, particles that lie upon the floor of the kitchen are being swept up, crumbs, hairs, dandruff, dust, in which can be found the remains of insects, grit from textiles. The voice, this threshold between body and spirit, dozens of voices, upstairs, downstairs, they mix together, yet must remain separate.

"Yes, you see, you're crying. Sometimes, crying is nothing to be ashamed of," Mateo says. His full name is Mateo Atschel. Mateo is the arch-secretary of the two secretaries who work for my father, at least my father says that there's a second secretary, a certain Peter Ozianon, who is caught up in a dark matter and is said to quite possibly no longer be alive. There are a good many people who claim that Mateo had him done away with, Peter Ozianon also having done away with somebody else. My father doesn't give a damn about such rumors. After all, nobody has been charged with murder and nobody misses the man. Peter Ozianon is said to be or have been a kind of security committee *in toto*, thus should he also have investigated this on his own behalf. Sometimes, my father once said, it is enough that something is named, even if it isn't that which it's named or it doesn't even exist at all. People are afraid of Peter Ozianon, that's enough. Along with Mrs. Ohrmund and Mrs. Ganzbrot,* known by some in the house as Tanzgrob,† Father has two further secretaries at his disposal, always sitting in the room adjoining his office and waiting there for someone to knock at the door. Most of the time, however, nobody knocks, Nobody simply opens the door and is promptly confronted

---

* Wholebread.
† Dancecoarse.

by a second door, then, if the handle of the outer door is on the right, which corresponds, as it were, to unwritten law, the inner door can only be opened on the left. If he dispatches this hurdle as well, he'll consider himself to be in my father's office. At the last minute, an address made to him by the secretaries—who are conditioned for such cases, it's said that it's a part of their training goals and main recruitment requirements that they should sit quietly and drink tea as the ship goes down, no matter what happens—shall make it clear to him that one had always expected his breach of the house rules. This shall mitigate the furor of some of the people passing through, if not annihilate their eagerness to immediately give the gentleman behind the door a piece of their minds regarding the abstruse administrative policy the gentleman is pursuing here and cause them to thus discover that they have no appointment. There are no appointments. Nobody except for Mateo, Peter Ozianon, if he exists, Ms. Ohrmund, and Ms. Ganzbrot can enter into direct contact with my father, the paper exists for precisely this reason, dead paper, Father says, which can be placed selectively between people. Even the two ladies only see my father while opening and closing the double connecting doors into his office, when he enters or exits or allows for the entry of an authorized person—which practically never happens unless there is a family visit, which should really never come to pass. The papers are Father, he has no trust in electronic data processing and even refused to work with a computer once he could no longer raise the objection of technological inadequacy, after all, the time that one would waste in becoming familiar with the matter could be used more sensibly, in working through paper, for example, the papers have literally grown over Father's head and thus did he one day order that a large room be cleared out in the administrative building, a room into which the paper that he hadn't processed was to be placed first, followed by the paper that he had processed, all of these orders were obeyed within a day. Father had prepared a sketch for this room, a corridor with intertwining passages should ensure that all the papers can be reached at any time. For this purpose, it became necessary to divide the room into separate repositories, to organize and index the papers according to the principle of pertinence and to set up a topically arranged, up-to-date inventory. The French, to whom he'd felt close for all of his life, Father that is, would have resolved the simultaneity, which he strove for with the papers, in admirable linguistic fashion, "donner l'ordre": to create order / to give orders and to command. Father rules from the archive outward by giving order. It was already put down by Goethe, said Father in response to a question from an employee who, in his opinion, had already been stricken down by empty transcendence, Father deliberately turned a blind eye to his presumption so as to then turn it back on him with a critical query: For what we possess black on white, we can take home and keep for good, and my papers are the house. Father's favorite book on matters relating to the archive begins with the following words: "Let us not begin at the beginning, nor even at the archive. But rather at the word 'archive' and with the archive of so familiar a word." Regarding the question as to whether the inventory book should also be inventoried, Father had several independent reports commissioned. The question was: does the inventory book, in which the tabulations of an inventorying are recorded, itself belong to the inventory and must it thus be listed down in the inventory book? A book that contains itself? This question, which is only to be resolved in a decisionist and less definitional way, caused him sleepless nights. It led him to a general problem of order: can order only be regulated by an authority outside of itself?

    I am the paper-based memory, from which the archive protects me, my Father says. His walk to the papers is sacred to him. So sacred and time-consuming that the administration of the papers erased his friendships completely. "I would like to always reply to you," Father writes in one letter to a friend, which that friend then exhibited, according to Father, this was what he was told, at every funeral of mutual friends and acquaintances, for which Father could spare no time, as a profound proof of friendship, "but I never can, especially not now, as it's already midnight and I still haven't had my dinner." The friend, however, was then buried himself not so long ago without Father ever having seen him again. He was dressed in the suit that he was wearing the last time he had met Father and Father's letter was laid into his coffin. But what does Father eat, then, not just for dinner, but also in the meantime, at any time of day or night, whenever the opportunity arises? Game and other meat in enormous quantities laid out on plates at various points in the building by diligent employees who are solely responsible for ensuring that Father never has to ask for food. All that meat is probably to blame for his gout, which has crippled his fingers so much over the years that administrative instructions and notes can barely be deciphered and Father, who loves the German language, tends toward endless sentences, which are intricately nested into themselves and, hieroglyphs in many respects, must be meticulously interpreted after their optical decipherment. Your father cultivates a beautiful German related to the German of officialese, at first one can't decipher it, then one can't understand it, Mateo once said to me when I was allowed to accompany him on one of his walks.

Father's archival principle No. 1 goes like this: to work through from front to back. Principle No. 2: to hand back that which has been worked through. Principle No. 3: to keep up with day-to-day business plus a little bit extra. Father only lets his councilors prepare reports and has granted them no decision-making power, therefore, not only does he have to make sole decisions based on the perusal of files, he must also read the reports beforehand. Mateo shows me a note from my father, which he didn't at first take to be a piece of writing, that's how illegible the microscript unfolding upon this scrap of yellow paper is: "Thanks for the legwork. I couldn't read anything during the night." According to Mateo, if the Voynich manuscript consisted of such messages, one might console oneself regarding its contents' poverty with the tremendously beautiful script and the many botanical drawings, but otherwise hope that it would never be deciphered. But, Mateo asks, who shall compensate one for the empty lifetime, which one would spend deciphering such notes day after day? Even the path to my father is humiliating. A mighty staircase leads up to a high terrace above the main entrance to the building, which is roofed over with a semi-circular, single-story oriel. The oriel stands upon a pillar that narrows conically downward, its top wreathed in crenelated cover plates. Once one enters the building, one reaches a sterile service hall, the entrance area of which is closed off by five ovular pillars covered in black and yellow mosaic stones, a chilly Bauhausian reminiscence of a time when pillars still bore saints. The divided square floor consists of smoothed and polished terrazzo/concrete freestone with a black base tone and embedded brownish, reddish, white, and gray stones. It is repolished daily. A pillar-passage leading forward in a square and made of yellow-painted concrete is placed before the core-substance of the entire building, a wall of matte-red brick masonry. Crossbeams divide the pillars over the passage concentrically and form the terminus of their upper end. While the crossbeams in the middle allow for the mounting of an otherwise free-floating gallery, making the offices of the mezzanine accessible as a raised outer walkway, the upper beams serve as a support for the intermediate ceiling. The raised ground floor and the mezzanine floor are symmetrically laid out except from the perspective of the entrance area. Furthermore, the individual offices are connected to each other from the inside, each office being someone else's intersecting room. This enables secretiveness of speech, the transmission of rumors, vile talk, slander . . . Admittedly, none of the offices are anything more than intersecting rooms, they always stand between two adjoining offices, and who can tell me that the message I am conveying in one of these offices is not to be used against me in the next office over from the office I find myself in. There, it is received eagerly, as if this message had been waited on for years, the exuberant conception of the message, however, dresses itself in a gown that is far too breezy for this time of year, it makes a mockery of whatever it says, the people smile at it, and thus are some truths told, the language of which nobody speaks. As if there were a messenger constantly running around in a circle, which is a quadrilateral. Thus, within a day, could the message that I took out of my own control by putting it out of my sight and into another room come back through one of the offices adjacent to my room, backward or frontally, decisively changed, with a barbaric point that passes right through me.

 My father's office is located in the upper-left corner, also able to be seen from the inner staircase that one can catch sight of on the left side of the foyer once one has stepped through the entrance area of the building. In the fifties, said gray concrete staircase with its twenty steps, which are centrally placed onto a narrow base, then protrude to the left and to the right, was meant to express each day anew that the Thousand-Year Reich was at an end, but not overcome. The circular omission, the large hole in the back of the base, is a porthole in the whale's fin, which is the base. Thus did the fifties go underground, they didn't show their true colors. The last stair leads seamlessly into the gallery in the quadrangle, behind the entrance area, running around a protruding wall, which also takes the metal-enwreathed glass railing of the staircase with it. Here, upon the gallery with its insufficient lintel-depth, along this railing, with a view of the foyer of the administrative building, the employees of the twenty-first century glide through the 1950s, through the asbestos of the reconstruction miracle, the odor of which cannot be driven out of the rooms by energy-efficient renovation. Wherever you come to a stop in this building, it smells like a hospital. Outside of the building—up the nineteen steps of the outer staircase, above a tub-fountain—the angel-visaged flame sculpture of an artist with God-given talent, but about whose past one had briefly forgotten to ask, has been a guest for fifty years already. One should have extinguished the angel in the fountain, its memento brings to mind a single day, November 16, 1944, and thus sparks the consequence as a cause. 485 Lancasters and 13 Mosquitos were the consequence. Christmas trees in the air everywhere. The colorful illumination of targets that lasts for minutes and minutes. The total failure of the German air defense; the Luftwaffe was only tuned to attack. Bombs. First the peppering-over of the roofs, the shattering of the windows, the splitting of the streets, the deactivation of the fire brigade, then the firestorm of incendiary bombs. The ground bouncing up and down the whole length of a ruler. The fact that it tears apart only one's lungs so that one is later found sitting peacefully at a table playing poker as an externally unscathed corpse, as happened not long after a bombardment of a bunker on the site of a railway-repair shop on September 29, 1944, one does not wander through the streets as a burning torch until one has been extinguished as a flame, one does not belong with the heat-shrunken corpses, just a meter tall now, the head shrunk back down to newborn condition, the organs, if they can still be called that, to doll organs, all of this is a grace. City of the dead. The end of Duria. Stone-desert.

Mateo has brought me something, a list, a folder, and a heavy book by a certain Speer. A bookmark is inserted into the last of those objects between pages 196 and 197 and the last paragraph on 196 that extends well into 197 is marked in pencil. The list states that, of the city's 6,431 houses, 4,253 were 100% reduced to ash and rubble, the rest made uninhabitable, with only 13 houses having been spared.

The list, meticulously prepared with a typewriter, is an alphabetically ordered index of the 3,100 dead—locals, in-from-out-of-towners, and unknown—for the completion of which, ten years after the city was negated, every citizen was requested to recall from memory the first name, last name, age, street, and house number of relatives, acquaintances, friends, and neighbors who perished on November 16, 1944 during the bombardment of the city. Mateo says my father passes word that I must copy down the last names, first names, and the ages of the dead—by my own hand and with no interruption. Two men enter the cell and bring a table, chair, paper, and pen. I sit down and want to get to work right away. The men remain standing in front of the table and don't take their eyes off of me. I bring to the men's notice that the first sheet of paper they place before me has already been written upon, namely with the following words: I bring to the men's notice that the first sheet of paper they place before me has already been written upon, namely with the following words: The men nod, I leaf back and read: Two men enter the cell and bring a table, chair, paper, and pen. I sit down and want to get to work right away. The men remain standing in front of the table and don't take their eyes off of me. I bring to the men's notice that the first sheet of paper they place before me has already been written upon, namely with the following words: The men nod, I leaf back and read: Two men enter the cell and bring a table, chair, paper, and pen. I sit down and want to get to work right away. The men remain standing in front of the table and don't take their eyes off of me. I leaf forward once again and read: LAST NAME FIRST NAME (AGE) and am overtaken by the anxiety of copying a name down incorrectly, of giving an incorrect age, by omitting streets and house numbers, I must alphabetically rearrange the identical last names according to the first names, whereas, before, the alphabetical ordering had followed the street names. What if I overlook somebody, forget them in my transcription, then they'll be snuffed out for a second time. A name is the only possession that we really have, it is only through the name that we are, it goes through my head now, fatigue, slackness, these are the enemies of the name, just like the bare number that takes its place, 150564 or 172364, for example. Somebody says to me: "My son, be careful in your work, for your work is the work of Heaven. Should you omit a single letter or add an extra letter, you may find yourself destroying the entire world, all of it." Both men say nothing. Soon, I'm putting pen to paper, the man standing to the right of me steps forward and gives me a scrap of paper, upon which can be read: "My son, be careful in your work, for your work is the work of Heaven. Should you omit a single letter or add an extra letter, you may find yourself destroying the entire world, all of it." I get up from the chair, the other man is now standing behind me, he lays his hand upon my shoulder and pushes it down. "The copyist in the service of God," he says. Then the 22 letters come before me and ask to be allowed to begin, as they are the beginning. The pen is cold, it cuts into my fingers, it is in the shape of a cross, I have never done anything more meaningful than copying these names down. My fingers are bleeding. I lick up the blood, should it drip down onto the paper, all the bombs would fall once more and I would die the death of an every-dead, I would die thousands of times, rise from the dead thousands of times, thousands of times would I come to know of it, the men say. I write with left and right hands and, for long stretches, with left and right hands at the same time. My arms are the letters that I put to paper, two capital I's hang down from the shoulders, which, in writing, to make an L, the body passes through the capital A of the clasped hands, I put my body to paper, it is the interpretation of a lost ur-script, I disappear in writing, I make tzimtzum, nullify myself, God's excremenation of evil, but the copyist who I am knows all too well that he can manipulate the script, a copyist is God's most unreliable creature and both men know that as well, barely have I put pen to paper when they inform me that, should I make the slightest error, and no error shall escape them, I shall have to eat the aggregate of the paper filled up until that point:

Abels Johann (46), Abel Margarethe (45), Abels Maria (16), Abels Peter (13), Absillag Elfriede, Absillag Kurt, Acker Maria (49), Acker Arnold (79), Acker Johanna geb. Schauff (63), Acker Josefine geb. Püllen (64), Adams Michael (40), Adels Anna geb. Stoffels (56), Adels Odilia (21), Adels Magdalena geb. Harsheim (34), Adels Margarethe geb. Engels (46), Adolph Gerta geb. Boecking (34), Adolph Gertrud Anna (7), Adolph Hildegard (9), Adolph Karl (39), Adrian Frau (70), Ahms Loni (28), Alfen Katharina geb. Krämer (39), Allendorf Anna geb. Stoffels (34), Allendorf Käthe (13), Allendorf Margarethe (10), Allendorf Maria (5), Alt Anna (30), Alt Heinrich (71), Althauser Andreas (61), Althauser Käthe (30), Althauser Margarethe (61), Altmeyer Kurt (2), Altmeyer Paula geb. Henkemes (37), Altmeyer Renate (2), Altmeyer Rolf (4), Amelio von Erwin (12), Andres Maria Johanna geb. Rohr (81), Antons Anna Katharina geb. Schmülgen (38), Antons Anna Maria (13), Antons Christian (54),

Antons Jakob (67), Antons Maria Helene (11), Antons Herr (50), Arnolds Katharina (35), Arnolds Waltraud (2), Arnolds Wilfried (2), Aufgoth Christine geb. Krügel (49), Aufgoth Helmut (11), Aufgoth Peter (5), Augé Peter Hubert (53), Bach Elisabeth geb. Ogrodowski (41), Bach Heinrich (80), Bach Johann, Bach Maria geb. Wolf (25), Bach Peter (7), Bach Walter (18), Badmann Nölli (44), Balduin Theresa geb. Neither (32), Bander Alfred (1), Bander Eduard (6), Bander Kasper (17), Bander Klara (4), Bander Maria (12), Bandomir Otto (40), Barion Elisabeth (38), Bartels Otto (40), Barth Änne geb. Steffens (49), Barth Agnes geb. Althoven (51), Barth Hubert (21), Barth Gerhard (78), Barth Josef (55), Barth Peter (50), Barten Clara geb. Peters (67), Bauer Franz (35), Bauer Helmuth (14), Bauer Magarethe geb. Uteralm (57), Bauer Maria (44), Bauer Wilhelm (47), Baum Johann (58), Baumgarten Hubertine Gertrud (11), Baumgarten Peter (47), Baumgarten Sybille, Baumann Albert (12), Baumann Luise (19), Baumann Scholastika geb. Ludwigs (53), Baumann Wilhelm (59), Baus Agathe (27), Bayer Edith (16), Bayer Franz (61), Bayer Jean (72), Bayer Josef (65), Bayer Maria geb. Breuer (58), Bayer Maria geb. Burger (35), Bayer Max (55), Beaucamp Theodor (52), Becker

Adele (30), Becker Anna (66), Becker Anna Maria geb. Finger, Becker Anneliese (13), Becker Elisabeth geb. Mumm (44), Becker Elisabeth geb. Peters (29), Becker Eugen, Becker Grete (44), Becker Heinrich (56), Becker Heinrich (15), Becker Josef Gregor Albert (56), Becker Katharina (35), Becker Klärchen (14), Becker Klara geb. Aaken van (54), Becker Ludwig (11), Becker Luise (32), Becker Margarethe (7), Becker Maria (51), Becker Maria (45), Becker Maria (34), Becker Maria (32), Becker Maria (26), Becker Marlies (3), Becker Matthias (60), Becker Nelly (50), Becker Nikolaus Josef Cornelius (58), Becker Paul (50), Becker Wilhelm (9), Beckers Maria (17), Beiert Josef (69), Bendels Anna Mathilde geb. Gummels (51), Bendels Hubert (46), Bendels Maria geb. Rosheda (50), Bendemacher Josefine geb. Jumpertz (42), Bengel August (50), Bengel Gisela (17), Benken von der Antonia (38), Berbuir Hermann (65), Berbuir Anna geb. Engelen (46), Berbuir Christine (12), Berbuir Franziska geb. Schwartz (53), Berbuir Rita (16), Berbuir Sybille (14), Berg

Maria (27), Berg Willi (47), Berger Anna (35), Berger Katharina (63), Berger Peter (63), Bergerhausen Konrad (57), Bergmann Wilhelmine (33), Bergs Helene geb. Köttgen (53), Bergs Irmgard (4), Bergs Katharina (66), Bergs Klara Hildegard geb. Jakobs (23), Bergs Konrad (60), Bergs Margarethe geb. Kuss (42), Bergsch Christine (65), Bertrams Anna geb. Aufpatz (50), Bertrams Wilhelm (55), Besselmann Josef (60), Besselmann Sonja (55), Beuth Maria Magdalena (43), Beyel Margarethe (55), Beyel Monika (20), Biergans Gertrud (43), Biergans Josef (46), Billstein Katharina geb. Rausch (74), Bingler Elisabeth geb. Gülden (29), Bingler Georg (25), Blanke Betha (45), Blanke Fanny (78), Blanke Maria geb. Noonen (50), Blatheim Jakob (46), Bleesen Mathilde (59), Bleesen Peter (60), Bleus Cläre geb. Schepes (58), Blüschke Henny (75), Blum Katharina geb. Pütz (55), Blum Maria (57), Blum Robert (56), Blum Rosemarie (16), Boch Anna (18), Bock Johanna geb. Esser (18), Bockemühl Hedwig (50/30), Bodden Katharina geb. Rüben (70), Bodden Maria geb. Windelschmidt (39), Bodden Paul (37), Bodden Paul (4), Boeck Maria (20), Boerner Maria geb. Yentgen (63), Bohlen Genoveva (22), Bohlen (5 Monate), Bohlen Maria Anna geb. Nöllner (33), Bohlen Mathias (50), Both Anna Sofia Franziska (27), Boltmann Frau (56), Bolz Grete (67), Bolz Johanna geb. Noeker (58), Bolz Katharina (35), Bongartz Berthel (58), Bongartz Elisabeth (18), Bongartz Jakob (50), Bongartz Kind, Bongartz Kind, Bongartz Kind, Bongartz Sibilla geb. Stohband (50), Bonn Heinrich (47), Bonnelch Luise (67), Bonnet Jean (40), Bönsch Helene (21), Boslammer Wilhelm (61), Botterweck Gerda geb. Wolff (38), Boveleth Karl Wilhelm (30), Boving Heinrich (62), Boving Sofie (56), Bramkamp Gisela (20), Bramkamp Rosmarie (20), Brand Franziska geb. Kulsel (81), Brandt Anna (48), Brandt Elfriede (13), Brandt Elisabeth geb. Kraus (38), Brandt Gottfried (78), Brandt Herbert (11), Brandt Hubert (72), Brandt Julia (69), Brandt Karl

(16), Brandt Katharina geb. Kirsten (33), Brandt Liselotte (5), Brandt Therese (45), Brandt Trudi (18), Braun Gertrud geb. Lieck (46), Braun Käthe geb. Carpentier (46), Braun Katharina Maria geb. Heuser (67), Braun Maria Cäcilie geb. Bohlen (46), Braun Martin, Braun Peter (57), Braun Peter (70), Braun Rosa geb. Hassert (66), Braun Theo (46), Braun Willi (15), Brauweiler Christine geb. Berbuir (57), Brauweiler Christine (26), Brauweiler Josef (65), Brauweiler Maria (65), Brenger Laura geb. Patzwall (74), Brenger Luise (46), Brenig Elisabeth (58), Brenig Hubert Josef (79), Brenig Sophie (56), Breuer Anna Maria Hubertine geb. Lovenich (84), Breuer Babette geb. Iley (57), Breuer Christine geb. Neffgen (50), Breuer Gertrud geb. Reiner (57), Breuer Johann Peter Wilhelm (59), Breuer Josef (54), Breuer Maria geb. Breuer (57), Breuer Margarethe (43), Breuer Matthias (48), Breuer Peter (36), Brügmann Christine (66), Brügmann Wilhelmine (70),

Brinkmann Hertha (33), Britz Clara (55), Britz Maria (55), Brück Wilhelmine geb. Cornets (64), Brück Wilhelmine (20), Brüggen Michael (64), Brüll Christine geb. Hoegner (47), Brüll Hubert (50), Büchel August (72), Büchel Cäcilia geb. Engels (44), Büchel Margot (9), Buchholz Else geb. Curioni (51), Buchholz Hilde (21), Bücken Grete geb. Coll (52), Bücken Günther (13), Bücken Heinrich (80), Bücken Josef (50), Bücker Anton, Bücker Cornelia (23), Bücker Johanna geb. Broll, Bühring Emil (59), Bühring Frau (55), Bull Albert (55), Bull Alexandrine (41), Bündgens Maria Helene geb. Delfosse (50), Bündgens Theo (15), Bungarten Mathias (65), Bungarten Peter (65), Bungarten Sybille (55), Büngeler Martin (55), Büngeler (70), Burkhard Christine (50), Burkhard Käthe (48), Burtscheidt Elisabeth geb. Hahnengress (38), Burtscheidt Elisabeth (18), Busch Christian (57), Bütgenbach Martin, Capellmann Katharina geb. Bardenheuer (55), Capellmann Mathias (46), Cardaun Anna geb. Höck (84), Cardaun

Sibille (50), Cardue Elisabeth geb. Victor (36), Cardue Gerda (13), Cardue Helene (50), Cardue Josef (18), Cardue Klärchen (15), Carels Josef (41), Carll Anna (60), Carll Anneliese (16), Carll Grete (33), Carll Magddena geb. Krentz (72), Carll Therese (62), Carls Franz (45), Casper Gerhard (55), Casper Karoline geb. Langenscheidt (55), Caster Elisabeth (83), Caster Elisabeth (51), Christine Hulstine (83), Christine Maria (52), Christoffels Bernhard (56), Classen Agnes (50), Classen Margarethe (75), Classen Maria geb. Bauchmüller (72), Classen Sybille (35), Classen Wilhelm (59), Clemens Berta geb. Molien (55), Clemens Josef (26), Clemens Peter (30), Colmen Änne, Colmen Johann (65), Colette Franz (66), Contzen Günther (17), Contzen Walther (14), Contzen Willy (39), Courth Therese (54), Crawatzo Anna geb. Nevis (26), Crawatzo Ludwig (4), Crawatzo Mathias (55), Creder Heinz (17), Creder Maria geb. Uten (46), Cremer Franz (72), Cremer Agnes (61), Cremer Friedrich Wilhelm (71), Cremer Heinrich jun. (44), Cremer Hilde

(8), Cremer Horst (3), Cremer Hubert (45), Cremer Josef (29), Cremer Josefine geb. Umpolschild (44), Cremer Marianne (12), Cremer Marlene (10), Cronenberg Matthias Josef Hubert (66), Crux Christine geb. Hecker (70), Curioni, Curtius Max (47), Dahmen Adelheid geb. Heinrichs (55), Dahmen Anna geb. Bach (60), Dahmen Anna geb. Nöllgen (57), Dahmen Anna (29), Dahmen Frau (63), Dahmen Frau (53), Dahmen Gertrud geb. Rewinghoff (80), Dahmen Herr (67), Dahmen Josef (65), Dahmen Josef (59), Dahmen Josef (55), Dahmen Käthe (17), Dahmen Maria (38), Dahmen Peter (52), Dahmen Kind, Dahmen Kind, Damm Ernst (57), Damm Josef (35), Dan Frau (42), Daniels Anna (84), Danken Gertrud (47), Danken Käthe (10), Danken Katharina geb. Prick (28), Danken Sybille (5), Debets Agnes geb. Königs (45), Decker Anna geb. Hermann (56), Decker Christel (21), Decker Dorothea Margarethe (3), Decker Elisabeth geb. Mons (36),

Dedy Betty (20), Dedy Johann (50), Dedy Susanna geb. Hall (50), Degenkolb Mathilde geb. Jahn (36), Deget Agnes geb. Winkel (31), Deget Hermann Josef (6), Deget Josef (33), Deiters Helga (32), Deiters Mia geb. Springmann (57), Dellbrügge Luise (57), Dellbrügge Paula (47), Dellbrügge Hertha geb. Hendel (57), Dellbrügge Wilhelm (58), Dembach Dieter (6), Dembach Katharina (67), Demmerich Gertrud geb. Cuenich (37), Denninger Ella geb. Reutrop (45), Denninger Wilhelm (47), Dentary Gertrud (36), Depiéreux Maria geb. Espey (66), Deussen Natalie (51), Deussen Resi (49), Deuster Anni (10), Deuster Elisabeth geb. Neuhaus (50), Deuster Helene geb. Merbecks (63), Deuster Konrad (60), Deuster Peter (8), Diemer Katharina geb. Potschemka (73), Dietricie Ernst (33), Dietricie Katharina geb. Junker (45), Dietricie Ursula (4), Dietrich Grete (42), Ditzhuyzen van Frau (50), Ditzhuyzen van Rudolf (52), Dohle Peter (55), Dohmen Heinz (3), Dohmen Johann (69), Dohmen Josefine (43), Dohmen Katharina (49), Dohmen Luise (52), Dohmen Maria geb. Kaiser (43), Dohmen Peter (49), Dohmen Stephan (66), Dorn Maria Margarete geb. Hardheim (50), Dorr Kunigunde (62), Dorfeld Josef (13), Dorfeld Klara geb. Schmitzler (56), Dohsen Elisabeth (23), Dresbach Wilhelm (38), Driever Paula geb. Niessen (28), Dunkel Karola (63), Dunkel Maria (62), Dümmwald Barthel (65), Drüpper Katharina geb. Offermanns (45), Düsibaum Margarethe geb. Heinrichs (42), Drütz Therese (49), Eberhard Johann Andreas Friedrich (69), Ebert Helene (58), Ebert Maria (60), Eckstein Anna Maria (65), Edeler Maria Therese (49), Eidelmanns Mathias (55), Eichler Elisabeth (16), Eichler Jakob (10), Eichler Maria geb. Müller (44), Eichler Maria (16), Eicker O. Alois (32), Eisenburger Kläre (4), Eisenburger Marianne geb. Nagenfels (23), Eisenhuth Elmar (18), Elbracht Theodor Josef (39), Elsen Franz (81), Engelbert Hubert (71), Engelen Agnes (62), Engelen Agnes (45), Engelen Grete (29), Engels Hubert (40), Engels Josef (72), Engels

Maria Josefa geb. Hamacher (43), Engels Maria Magdalena (11), Engels Susi (25), Engels Sybilla geb. Neunzig (58), Engels Theodor (80), Engels Wilhelmine geb. Dick (37), Erdt Ferdinand (55), Erkens Martha (54), Ernes Hertha (19), Ernes Veronika geb. Wachtendi (59), Erxenputsch Ernst (63), Erxenputsch Maria geb. Obermeyer (51), Erxens Johann (65), Eschweiler Josef (46), Eschweiler Käthe geb. Ruda (37), Esser Elisabeth geb. Schallenberg (52), Esser Gertrud geb. Strauch (41), Esser Johann (50), Esser Josef (41), Esser Käthe (10), Esser Maria (60), Esser Mechthilde (14), Esser Peter (56), Esser Rolf (16), Ettelbrück Maria (47), Etsbach Gerhard (57), Everts Ida Henriette geb. Nippes (65), Fabricius Peter (37), Fader Maria geb. Derichs (85), Fader Maria (41), Fassbender Anna Maria (77), Fassbender Christian (44), Fassbender Christian (43), Fassbender Eberhard (65), Fassbender Eva (65), Fassbender Gertrud (13), Fassbender Hermine geb. Laven (52), Fassbender Josefine geb.

Schmitz (35), Fasslender Monika (10), Fasslender Elisabeth (12), Faust Anna Maria geb. Wendler (42), Feltes Franz (64), Feltes Josef (58), Ferlers Bernhardine (60), Fernes Lotte (39), Ferenmeyer Josef (85), Fett Elisabeth geb. Breuer (57), Fey Eva geb. Lenzen (69), Fey Wilhelm (52), Fiedler Emmi geb. Stotz (58), Fildhaut Anna Katharina Maria geb. Nassen (56), Fildhaut Josef (60), Fink Katharina geb. Rütz (60), Fink Wilhelm (62), Firmenich Ännchen (40), Firmenich Anni (20), Firmenich Betty (46), Firmenich Helmut (5), Firmenich Magdalena geb. Otter (51), Fischbom Winand Hubert Ferdinand (74), Fisder Agnes geb. Fuß (60), Fisder Alois (60), Fisder Christine geb. Langen (80), Fisder Franz (80), Fisder Fritz (89), Flatten Agnes (54), Flatten Heinrich (54), Flatten Gertrud geb. Axmader (47), Flatten Gertrud geb. Birkenhayr (41), Flatten Josef (75), Flatten Sophie (24), Flock Frau, Flock Nakies, Flohr Christel geb. Lütth (25), Floss Josefine (37), Floss Klara (4), Floss Maria (18), Floss-dorf Kaspar (55), Flück Gertrud geb. Schmitz (60), Flück Josef (63), Foerster A. (23), Foerster Anna Maria geb. Müller (58), Foerster Josef (47), Foerster Katharina geb. Neuten (63), Foerster Margarethe (20), Foerster Stephan Arnold (4 Monate), Folsche Karl (51), Förster Hans (14), Förster Josef (54), Förster Käthe (42), Förster Peter (62), Förster Sophie geb. Gölden (40), Förster Therese (53), Förster Wilhelm Josef (42), Förster Willi (16), Frank Adolf (47), Frank Hans Günther (16), Frank Wilhelmine geb. Willms (56), Franken Elisabeth (19), Franken Hermann Josef (55), Franken Margarethe (53), Franken Sybille, Franz Maria Agnes (34), Franz Richard Helmut (2), Franzen Klara geb. Eiserfey (55), Franzen Margarethe (14), Freitag Hans (57), Fremgen Agnes Maria geb. Spix (38), Fremgen Gisela (8), Fremgen Magdalena geb. Linden (36), Fremgen Margot (6),

Frenzel Anna geb. Dombrowski (68), Freundgen Josef (55), Frey Robert (54), Friedrichs Katharina geb. Quast (79), Frings Anna (45), Frings Elisabeth geb. Kutz (40), Frings Katharina geb. Rosarius (55), Fritzsche Lotte (30), Froels Johannes (70), Frommhold (50), Fuchs Heinrich Josef (38), Früher Josefine geb. Archband (49), Führer Josef (52), Funk Margarethe geb. Bongartz (72), Funk Willy (45), Fuss Frau (50), Fuss Kläre (48), Fuss Johann (70), Fuss Josefine geb. Lensen (56), Fuss Katharina geb. Peter (72), Fuss Petronella geb. Graaf (70), Fuss Willi (17), Gallmann Hanne (16), Gallmann Kläre (14), Gallmann Maria geb. Andris (41), Gaypp Ernst (45), Gartzen Josef (18), Gasper Anna geb. Adler (64), Gasper Gerhard Hubert (68), Gasper Sophie geb. Kurth (62), Gast Heinrich (75), Gatzen Josef (20), Gebhardt Maria (65), Gebhardt Max (65), Gellen Josef (50), Geisser Heinz Peter (6), Geisser Käthe geb. Bodden (36), Geisser Katharina Annette (10), Geissler Bernhard (74), Geissler Elisabeth geb. Hüttebräuker (51), Geissler Margarethe geb. Degraa (46), Geissler Oskar (69), Geissler Walter (7), Gemünd Gertrud geb. Schmitz (58), Gemünd Peter (60), Gerber Maria geb. Baudnmüller (41), Gerber Maria geb. Schmidt (26), Gerber Walter (57), Gerhards Hanni (18), Gerhards Magdalena (51), Gerlmann Käthe geb. Pfeiffer (45), Geuer Anna geb. Nöser (54), Geuer Anny (23), Geuer Elisabeth (22), Geuer Käthe (24), Geuer Katharina geb. Fassbender (61), Geyer Fritz (40), Gier Rosa geb. Kretz (57), Giesen Maria Elise geb. Gumber (42), Giessen Christine geb. Dornseifer (41), Gilles Egidius (64), Gilles Else geb. Gorissen (58), Gillessen Klara (20), Gladen Josef Franz Aloisius (60), Glaeser Friedrich (68), Glang Elisabeth (23), Glum Georg (65), Göddertz Gertrud (23), Goebel Elisabeth geb. Dernbach (45), Goepen Anna Maria geb. Willems (77), Goepen Philipp (78), Goerg Käthe geb. Fuss (46), Goerg Willy (46), Goenes Johann (58), Goenes Josefine (62), Goldbach Max (45), Goldbach Wilhelm (68),

Gölden Willi (42), Gorissen Frau, Gorissen Herr, Gossel Hans Helmut (12), Gossel Margarethe geb. Contzen (41), Gossel Paul (3), Gossel Werner Josef (11), Gottfried Arnold Ludwig (43), Gottfried Helene (64), Gottfried Käthe (27), Gottfried Wilhelm (73), Gottschalk Christine geb. Noeken (63), Gottschalk Hanne (36), Gottschalk Karl (72), Gottschalk Maria geb. Kreutzberg (28), Graaf Helene (40), Graaf Wilhelm (80), Graf Christian (72), Graf Franz Anton (63), Gräf Maria Paula (45), Grasmeier Anna (70), Grasmeier Käthe (44), Gretenkort Agnes geb. Lütz (31), Gretenkort Kurt (30), Greuel Albert (12), Greven Jakob (61), Greven Katharina (61), Greven Leontine (36), Greven (11), Grobusch Grete geb. Esser (37), Grobusch Hubert (38), Groebel Katharina geb. Natzerath (51), Groebel Wilhelm (54), Gromig Geta geb. Bauer (35), Gromig Sofie (10), Gross Karl (23), Gross Angela (19), Gross Christine (17), Grossmann Petronella (75), Grün Franz (51), Grün Käthe geb. Hamacher

(55), Gudat Stephanie (27), Gülden Achim (6), Gülden Elisabeth geb. Scheten (60), Gülden Gerda (10), Gülden Josef (46), Gülden Josefine geb. Fuss (45), Haach Fine (60), Haas Christian (60), Haas Christine geb. Gasper (44), Haas Christine geb. Gorris (35), Haas Claus Gerd (10), Haas Franz (52), Haas Gerhard Peter Claus (13), Haas Matthias (70), Haas Michael (55), Haas Peter (44), Habrichs Mathilde geb. Althofen (46), Habrichs Mathilde (22), Hack Mathias (34), Hagdes Margarethe (70), Hagen Elisabeth (50), Hagl Anneliese (17), Hahn Annemie (7), Hahn Betty geb. Jöres (34), Hahn Franz (35), Hahn Franz Josef (5), Hähn Regina (39), Hahnenjress Constantin (61), Hälmer Kläre geb. Ennenputsch (36), Hälmer Klaus (4), Halmes Käthe (27), Hamacher Gertrud geb. Weber (51), Hamacher Josef (70), Hamacher Margarethe geb. Hensch (70), Hamacher Sibilla (17), Hambach Grete geb. Nicolay (80), Hammans Hermann (53), Hammerath Gertrud (58), Hammerath Hubertine geb. Gottfried (41), Hammerath Irmgard (13), Hammerath Johann (66), Handels Elisabeth (3), Handels Kathi geb. Driesen (34), Handels Siegfried (6), Hannot Carl (44), Hanrath Gertrud geb. Weber (51), Hansen Eberhard (55), Hansen Maria geb. Herbinger (44), Hansen Willi (53), Hardt Herbert (1,5), Hardt Jakob (58), Hardt Maria geb. Reiner (65), Härig Franz (56), Harpers Helene (44), Harpers Wilhelm (45), Hassel Gerti (64), Hassel Käthe (60), Hassert Anna geb. Jansen (52), Hassert Josef (11), Hauck Bernhard (13), Hauck Karl (42), Hauff Jutta (8), Haupt Gerhard (47), Hauptmann Christine (48), Hauptmann Elisabeth (22), Hausmann Josef (39), Heberlein Franz (54), Hecker Anna geb. Zilleken (39), Hecker Hedwig (5), Hecker Karl (8), Hecker Maria Gertrud (60), Hecker Oskar Hubert (9), Hecker Sibille geb. Strehöver (27), Heidbüchel Änne geb. Jöres (35), Heidbüchel Gertrud geb. Undorf (60), Heiden Elfriede (5), Heiden Elisabeth geb. Casper (51), Heiden Gertrud geb. Heitiger (69), Heiden

Gertrud geb. Wünnikes (41), Heiden Heinrich (39), Heiden Johann (66), Heiden Maria geb. Ross (57), Heiden Petersen (67), Heiden Regina (12), Heiden Therese (16), Heiden Viktorine geb. Gäde (63), Heiliger Anna (52), Heimbach Agnes geb. Eversheim (85), Heimbach Franz Josef (7), Heimbach Gerta (15), Heimbach Gertrud geb. Blum (50), Heimbach Marita (21), Heimbach Martha geb. Kluth (43), Heinel Anna, Heinen Adele geb. Theile (60), Heinen Albert Josef (71), Heinen Andreas (55), Heinen Gerta geb. Bley (33), Heinen Hans Josef (1,5), Heinen Heinrich (47), Heinen Ilse (1,5), Heinen Julie (64), Heinen Maria geb. Velser (57), Heinrichs Josef (46), Heinrichs Katharina geb. Paulus (60), Heinrichs Paul (29), Heiss Josefine (47), Heissmann Franz (50), Heissmann Franz (38), Heissmann Josefine (40), Hellen Auguste geb. Gottschalk (42), Hellenbrandt Maria (17), Heller Katharina (23), Helmig Maria (75),

Helmikowsky Elli geb. Baur (42), Hemmes Theodor (71), Hennes Bernhard (68), Hennes Maria (77), Hennes Wilhelm (63), Henrichs Josef (65), Hensch Heinz (4), Hensch Marga (12), Hensch Maria geb. Alt (42), Hensch Maria (30), Hensch Wilhelmine (14), Hensch Willi (41), Hensel Anna Margarete geb. Hoch (69), Henseler Frau (60), Henseler Käthe geb. Hecker (46), Henseler Klara geb. Glasmacher (66), Henseler Kornelius (38), Hepp Katharina (41), Hepp Sophie (34), Herbinger Agnes geb. Neises (32), Herbinger Anna geb. Alt (30), Herbinger Christian (78), Herbinger Gertrud (7), Herbrand Magdalena (23), Herbrand Margarethe (19), Hermanns Gertrud geb. Steven (33), Herpetz Franziska (72), Herpetz Frau (45), Herpetz Herr (45), Hermann Therese geb. Koenen (60), Herrmanns Frau (65), Hertz Anna Elisabeth (50), Herzog Maria Katharina (48), Heukernes Maria geb. Wagner (65), Heusgen Maria geb.

Heusgen (64), Heusgen Otto (18), Heusgen Regina (24), Heyder Zissy geb. Besser (53), Heyder Max (70), Hildesheimer Emil (50), Hilger Günther (13), Hilger Josef (11), Hilger Katharina geb. Korten (75), Hilger Margarethe geb. Elvenich (41), Hilger Marianne (9), Hilgers Elisabeth geb. Andermahr (30), Hilgers Helene (33), Hillebrand Elisabeth (31), Hiller Sibille geb. Kaulhausen (74), Hinkens Theodor (58), Hintzen Johann (56), Hirth Frau (24), Hirtz Johanna (40), Hoch Yuldien (42), Hochgürtel Maria geb. Windelschmidt (55), Hochgürtel Maria (30), Hochhausen Peter (25), Hochmann Anna (28), Hochrien Ludwig (71), Hocks Josefine (63), Hoffmann Anna (24), Hoffschlag Heinr. (50), Hoffschlag Maria geb. Körtgen (52), Hoffsümmer Anna (68), Hoffsümmer Clemens (55), Hoffsümmer Johanna (65), Hoffsümmer Thekla (60), Hofmann Heinrich Josef (52), Hofmann Luise geb. Gutbelet (44), Holm

Gertrud (65), Holm Katharina (60), Höke Apollonia geb. Smits (76), Höke Josef (79), Hölsken Mathilde (31), Höltig Sybilla geb. Wolff (33), Holz Wilhelmine Anna (23), Holzenherer Frau, Holzenherer Sibilla, Holzenherer Toni, Holzpoitz Maria (40), Hommelsheim Gehard (44), Hommelsheim Heidi (3), Honnef Josef (49), Hoppenstedt Anna (60), Horn Katharina geb. Pohl (72), Hoven Elisabeth (55), Hoven Josef (45), Hoven Liesel geb. Kapp (45), Hoven Paul Eduard (3), Hübben Agnes (16), Hübsch Edmund (50), Hübsch Käthe geb. Firmenich (48), Hübsch Käthe (24), Hübsch Leo (54), Hübsch Moni (15), Hüffelmann Maria (65), Hugenott Heinrich (39), Hugenott Heinrich (24), Huhn Marianne (22), Hülsmann Eva geb. Kessel (44), Hündgen Anna (55), Hünerbein Gertrud (40), Hünerbein Johann (36), Hünerbein Klara (45), Hünerbein Sophie geb. Kiefer (55), Hünerbein Theodor (55), Hürlimann David (75), Hürtgen Jean (52), Huth Elisabeth Margar. geb. Süngen (43), Hütsch Elisabeth geb. Sengersdorf

(62), Hütten Gertrud (23), Hütten Susi (35), Hütten Christel (19), Huyggen Heinz (38), Huyggen Matties (12), Inden Gertrud (49), Inden Kethe (50), Inden Josef (52), Inden Josef (50), Inden Marlene (11), Inden Tochter (10), Inden Ottilie geb. Röhmer (60), Jagenberg geb. Busch (56), Jäger Gertrud geb. Schummer (39), Jäger Mathias (44), Jakobs Josefine (61), Jammes Heinrich (71), Jansen Cordula (74), Jansen Hermann Josef (56), Jansen Katharina (84), Jansen Maria (49), Jansen Therese geb. Hansen (53), Jansen Therese geb. Rademacher (69), Jentges Katharina geb. Klee (60), Jentges Lambert (60), Jetzke Alfred (45), Jochum Frieda geb. Pollenich (28), Jochum Sigrid Friederun (1), John Alice (8 Monate), Johnen Hans (48), Johnen Maria geb. Edney (63), Johnen Peter (32), Jonas Johann (59), Jonas Laurentz (55), Jöntgen Hermann Josef (14), Jörg Frau (40), Jörg Josef (45), Jöris Regina (19), Jörres Anna geb. Hausmann (64), Jörres Cäcilie geb. Bongart (72), Jörres Hubert (71),

Jöres Hubertine (23), Jöres Johann (45), Jöres Josefine (45), Jost Sebastian (26), Jumpertz Hans (14), Jumpertz Käthe (30), Jünemann Helene geb. Brück (30), Jünemann Maria (6 Monate), Jung Ingrid Marianne (4), Jungbluth Herbert (7), Jungbluth Ria geb. Radile (45), Jungbluth Robert (55), Jussen Margarethe (19), Jussen Otto (16), Kahlen Maria geb. Müller (64), Kaiser Christian (53), Kaiser Peter (80), Kaltenbach Renate (10 Monate), Kaltenberg Vinzenz (63), Kämper Anna Elly (23), Kamphausen Christine geb. Schlömer (76), Kapp Ferdinand (50), Kapp Franziska geb. Carll (58), Karbig Josefa geb. Krosder (75), Katzenburg Margot geb. Kuldersind (26), Katzenburg Ursula (3), Katzgrau Margarethe Mathilde (50), Katsola Josefa (60), Kauer Henriette geb. Bott (60), Kaufmann Maria (48), Kaulen Anneliese (16), Kaulen Christian (48), Kaup Christian (69), Kaup Gertrud geb. Dreth (67), Kayser Anna Margarethe (61), Kayser Gertrud (58), Kehr

Ilse geb. Glüm (30), Keller Katharina geb. Leuchtenberg (47), Kemmerling Sophia (65), Kempf Aloysia (11), Kerner Johann (Hans) (55), Kerpen Gertrud geb. Krefeld (42), Kerres Mathias (82), Kessel Margarethe geb. Ohlem (71), Kestenich Anna geb. Knuth (45), Kestenich Helene (45), Kettenis Bernhard (17), Kettenis Eleonore (4), Kettenis Gertrud geb. Rensinghoff (39), Kettenis Peter Hubert (6), Keulen Agnes (64), Keulen Margarethe (66), Kichert Maria (58), Kieven Franz (12), Kieven Jakob (63), Kieven Marianne geb. Peroszak (50), Kirfel Johann (85), Kirfel Katharina geb. Förster (74), Kirfel Willi (75), Kirschbaum Erich (5), Kirschbaum Käthe geb. Adolf (32), Kirschbaum Peter (42), Kirsten Anna geb. Nick (65), Klauser Traudchen geb. Coenen (75), Klee Ewald (13), Klee Gertrud geb. Heinen (44), Klee Josef (46), Klee Josefine (6), Kleeberg Emmi (47), Klein Adolf (73), Klein Bäbchen (25), Klein Bernhard (30),

Klein Christine (30), Klein Emmy Elise (50), Klein Franziska geb. Cardaun (47), Klein Georg (55), Klein Heinrich (60), Klein Josef (39), Klein Katharina geb. Schmölzgen (69), Klein Maria geb. Fischer (39), Kleiner Christian (58), Kleiner Josef (16), Klemens Frau, Klemm Anna (52), Klinkenberg Maria (52), Klinker Kordula Agathe (18), Kloock Eva (17), Kloock Heinrich (11), Kloock Katharina geb. Heidbüchel (47), Kloock Maria geb. Neustrass (52), Kloock Peter (46), Kloock Sophie geb. Rick (86), Kloock Theodor (57), Klubert Gertrud geb. Kayser (51), Klubert Wilhelm (58), Klüser Wilhelm (56), Kluth Otto (55), Kluth Philippine geb. Herzwurm (57), Knauer Franziska geb. Heieck (61), Knauer Friedrich (67), Knieps Maria geb. Klein (72), Knieps Willi sen. (73), Knieps Willi jun. (37), Knipprath Peter (76), Kniprath Anna Maria Kniprath Jakob (58), Kniprath Katharina geb. Stolz (52), Kniprath Katharina (19), Koch Gertrud geb. Rautz (65),

Koch Kurt (48), Kohl Agnes (49), Kohl Anton (59), Kohl Josef (44), Kohl Katharina geb. Reimisch (50), Kohl (50), Köhnen Katharina geb. Nellmann (35), Kollenbrandt Anna geb. Hamader (62), Kollenbrandt Friedrich (70), Kollenbrandt Leo (25), Kommer Hermann Josef (11), Kommer Johannes (45), Kommer Toni (12), Kompa Otto (55), Kompa Paula geb. Zütseler (46), Konen Cäcilie geb. Gellhard (40), Konen Willi (16), Könen Agnes (50), Könen Gertrud geb. Kamphausen (50), Könen Johann (53), Könen Wilhelm (80), Konrad Anna geb. Thomas (32), Koperski Edmund (28), Kopp Adam (70), Köpper Marie Therese (29), Körner Barbara geb. Frings (63), Körner Clemens (63), Körner Else (12), Körner Josefa geb. Bergs (47), Körner Maria geb. Oswald (50), Körner Martin (50), Körner Willi (50), Köstgen Anna geb. Hübsch (56), Köstgen Leo sen. (59), Köstgen Leo jun. (11), Köster Grete Walburga geb. Dietrich (42), Kourth Anna Maria (75), Kourth Wilhelm (80), Koziel Hans Ralph (16),

Krabbel Anna Maria geb. Förster (38), Kraemer Toni (52), Krafft Josefine Käthe geb. Rüben (51), Krafft Katharina Elisabeth (15), Krafft Käthe geb. Klinkenberg (54), Krafft Paul (17), Krämer Frau (65), Krämer Herr (65), Krämer Käthe (45), Kraus Hildegard (17), Kraus Sibille geb. Paar (64), Krebs Adele geb. Becker (43), Kreimeier Albert (60), Kreimeier Frau (60), Krementz Adam (66), Krementz Elisabeth (52), Krementz Maria (60), Krementz Marianne (32), Krementz Peter (31), Kremer Katharina (24), Kremer Annemie (20), Kremer Gertrud geb. Wendel (42), Kremer Wilhelmine (64), Kreutz Grete (25), Kreutz Susanne (70), Kreutzberg Anton (70), Kreutzberg Maria geb. Weirand (69), Krings Anneliese (17), Krösch Walter (13), Krosch Elisabeth geb. Müller (48), Krosch Maria (53), Krosch Maria (14), Krudewig Anna Maria geb. Bongard (31), Krug Philipp (44), Krug Sophie (48), Krug Wilhelm (56), Krumbach Franz (53), Krumbach Franz Josef (19), Krumbach Helene (17), Krumbach Katharina (66), Krumbach Maria (22), Krumbach Maria Justine (23), Krumbach Maria Sophie (63), Krumbach Marianne (21), Krumbach Peter (64), Krupp Christine geb. Müller (56), Kruse Christine (70), Kruth Anna (16), Kruth Helene geb. Klüser (41), Kruth Katharina (9), Kruth Wilhelm (12), Krux Christine geb. Hecker (73), Kuch Elisabeth (43), Kuch Else geb. Reins (51), Kuch Helene geb. Arenda (48), Küch Johann (57), Küch Kunigunde geb. Freialdenhoven (44), Küch Liesel (35), Küch Sybilla (45), Kuckertz Karl (10), Kuckertz Peter (43), Kuhl Anna Katharina Alexandra geb. Cornely (88), Kuhlerath Albert (18), Kuhlerath Peter (57), Kuhlerath Sophie geb. Braunsleiler (50), Kühling Sybille geb. Hohn (30), Kuhlmann Anna Maria geb. Trillen (41), Kummer Helene (16), Kummer Katharina geb. Dahmen (49), Küpper Heor., Küpper Ida geb. Fischer (50), Küpper Josef (55), Küpper Maria (51), Küpper Maria Käthe geb. Gielgen (45), Kupper Maria Sybille (56), Kürdgen Käthe (50), Küsten Helene (62), Kurth Helene geb. Kaiser (47), Kurth Johann (31), Kurth Maria (34), Kurth Wilhelm (65), Kurs Elise (43), Kurs Katharina (45), Kurs Maria (39), Kuth geb. Berner (32), Kuth Gertrud (45), Kuth Kind, Kuth Kind, Kuth Ingeborg (16), Kuth Johanna (39), Kuth Karl (42), Kuth Karl Heinz (13), Kuth Maria geb. Gilson (44), Kuth Peter (49), Kuth Therese (56), Kuth Willi (38), Kypke Johannes (17), Kypke Paula geb. Pfeiffer (24), Lancü Anna geb. Keves (42), Lancü Anton (45), Lancü Cordula geb. Krüger (38), Lang Agnes (50), Lang Frank (55), Langen Anna geb. Gesnader (61), Langen Gabriel (69), Langen Josef Mathias (61), Langen Käthe (33), Langer Wilhelm (54), Langner Minna Olga geb. Eild (35), Lentin Franziska geb. Gerhards (40), Lenz Josef Peter (53), Lepp Ernst (45), Laprell Änne geb. Klein (43), Laprell Änne geb. Smets (42), Laroe Anna Maria Agnes geb. Lenzen (29),

Larue Hans Peter (1), Latz Hans (50), Latz Peter (70), Latz Peter (16), Laufenberg von Gertrud (26), Lauader Anna Maria Margarethe geb. Pfeiffer (32), Lauter Sybille (22), Lauterbach Johann Heinrich (65), Lauterbach Maria (45), Lehser Josef (20), Lehser Theodor (56), Leisten Anna Klara (65), Leisten Käthe (22), Leister Jakob (12), Lemmes Arno (2), Lemmes Maria Gertrud geb. Bergerhausen (28), Lenards Maria (22), Lenards Nettchen geb. Küsten (55), Lenders Hanni geb. Rütharts (32), Lenders Herbert (5), Lenders Inge (3), Lenders Josef (33), Lennartz Anneliese (19), Lennartz Frau (48), Lennartz Gertrud geb. Schäfer (60), Lennartz Herr (26), Lennartz Jakob (36), Lennartz Katharina geb. Reusder (34), Lennartz Petronella (57), Lennartz Therese (85), Lenz Martha geb. Kluth (19), Lenzen Erwin (13), Lenzen Josef Johannes (16), Lenzen Karl Dominikus (55), Lenzen Maria (54), Lenzen Maria Gertrud geb. Reitz (44), Lenzen Peter (64), Lenzen Peter (64), Lenzen Sybille (32), Leroi Katharina (23), Leroi Peter (57), Leroy

Barbara geb. Hannen (63), Leroy Hans Dieter (7), Leroy Hermann (47), Leroy Sybilla geb. Roering (45), Lersch Elisebeth geb. Dittgen (71), Lersch Jakob (53), Lersch Katharina (63), Lersch Luise (53), Lersch Peter (75), Levenhaul Anna Margaretha (45), Leyens Margarethe (34), Lichtenberg Franz (64), Liebreich Agnes (52), Liebreich Katharina (46), Liedgens Lorenz (52), Lingen Frau (35), Lingen Katharina (46), Lingen Margarethe (25), Lingens Gudula geb. Rick (38), Löher Agnes geb. Schneider (55), Losbach Anna Christine geb. Grafft (47), Losbach Anneliese (8), Losbach Gertrud (45), Losbach Gertrud (38), Losbach Helene (14), Losbach Josef (48), Losbach Kathi (18), Lorenz Kordula (19), Löken Erwin (13), Löken Josef (48), Löken Maria geb. Müller (46), Lothmann Gertrud geb. Sonnen (24), Lövenkamp Frau (58), Lövenkamp Mathias (58), Lüdenbach Franziska geb. Schröder (32), Ludwig Klaus (15), Ludwigs Christian Hubert Richard (59), Ludwigs Johannes Engelbert (14), Ludwigs Sophie (55), Ludwigs Sybille (20), Lürgen Helene geb. Kold (75), Lürgen geb. Rohe (83), Lüssem Heinrich (37), Lüssem

Katharina geb. Baus (62), Lüssem Peter (64), Lütsen Anna geb. Hagen (55), Lütsen Hildegard (19), Lütsen Josef (58), Lütsen Luise (17), Maassen Christine geb. Pfeiffer (48), Maassen Ludwig (53), Madersey Arnold (69), Madersey Martha Maria Gertrud geb. Matzerath (69), Maevis Kornelius (16), Maevis Gertrud geb. Beilelens (55), Mains Elisabeth geb. Hardt (44), Makowski Stanislaus (60), Mandelfeld Gertrud (71), Mann Herr, Mans Erwin (59), Marquardt Theresia (44), Marse Franz Josef (4), Marse Hans (8), Marse Hans (6), Marse Josef (12), Marse Maria geb. Baum (51), Marse Mathias (64), Marse Michael (16), Marse Wilhelm (59), Marse Wilhelmine (47), Mathar Sibille (18), Mattonet Klara geb. Bohr (64), Matzerath Maria (75), Matzerath Wilhelmine (47), Maubach Franz (40), Maubach Gertrud geb. Rosenig (37), Maubach Paul (30), Maurer Anna (48), Mayenfels Gertrud geb. Weisseiler (60), Mayenfels Peter (60), Meis Peter (60), Meisen Anna (36), Meisen Franz (38), Meisen Gertrud (30), Meisen Katharina (44), Meissen Katharina (35), Melder Gertrud geb. Zens (38), Melder Maximiliana (14), Mellessen Christine (18), Menden Käthe geb. Broich

(44), Menden Peter (51), Meng Grete (50), Meng Willi (52), Mertens Christine geb. Weyrauch (36), Mertens Engelbert (53), Mertens Karl (58), Mertens Maria geb. Schwarz (48), Metz Gerta geb. Busch (30), Meuter Herr (50), Meuter Josefine geb. Maubach (50), Meuter Willy (48), Meyer Franz Josef (6), Meyer Gertrud (48), Meyer Gertrud (11), Meyer Gertrud Elisabeth geb. Heinrichs (42), Meyer Hans geb. früher Sablewski (45), Meyer Heinrich (51), Meyer Helene (23), Meyer Josef (63), Meyer Josef (38), Meyer Klara (26), Meyer Martha (15), Meyer Maria geb. Ziefreund (38), Meyer Peter (10), Meyer Rita (7 Tage), Meys Richard (55), Miesen Bernhardine geb. Engelbert (42), Millmann Johann (43), Millmann Klara geb. Nepomuck (44), Millmann Peter (7), Milz Käthe (22), Minartz Käthe (54), Mirbach Heinrich Josef (1 Monat), Möbes Josef (22), Möbes Josef (48), Mock Katharina geb. Fuss (49), Möcker Magdalena (40), Mödersheim Else geb. Undeutz, Mödersheim Fritz (70), Mödersheim Günther, Moersch Maria Magdalena geb.

Bergmann (55), Moes Maria Margarethe (18), Moes Peter (50), Mohr Peter (66), Mohr Peter (14), Mohnen Hilde geb. Ullmann (28), Mohnen Karli (5), Molberg Änne (22), Molberg Christine (50), Molberg Heinrich (50), Molitor Agnes geb. Kreuer (53), Moll Friedrich (42), Moll Maria (50), Möller Emma (29), Mölls Herr, Mölls Heinrich (52), Mölls Katharina geb. Roeder (52), Mols Maria geb. Vossen (45), Molsberger Karl (42), Molsberger Maria geb. Schulzen (67), Mondorf Emilie Katharina Regina Dorothea (30), Mondorf Josef Julius (70), Mondorf Katharina geb. Raths (68), Mons Anna Sybilla geb. Kelmen (67), Moritz Theodor (67), Moritz Gertrud geb. Kiessen (74), Moritz Paul (76), Moritz Elisabeth Maria geb. Strang (55), Moritz Therese geb. Freundgen (46), Mösch Barbara (64), Mösch Heinrich (56), Mösch Herr (50), Mösch Margarethe geb. Waaren (42), Mösch (10), Mösch (8), Mostardt Irmgard (16), Mostardt Therese geb. Pfeiffer (40), Muhr Katharina (60), Muhr Maria geb. Mewser (24), Muhr

Sibilla geb. Baumgarten (50), Muhr Wilhelm (56), Müller Annelise (4), Müller Elise (58), Müller Else (55), Müller Ernst (58), Müller Frau, Müller Gertrud geb. Beek (58), Müller Gertrud (19), Müller Hedwig Josefa (25), Müller Heinrich (40), Müller Heinrich (24), Müller Henriette (56), Müller Hermann (54), Müller Herr (55), Müller Hubert (4), Müller Johann (61), Müller Johanna (52), Müller Johanna Josefine geb. Kesten (30), Müller Josefine (65), Müller Josefine geb. Ahrens (55), Müller Kaspar, Müller Katharina (58), Müller Katharina (47), Müller Konrad (55), Müller Luise (25), Müller Margarethe (18), Müller Margrethe (16), Müller Maria (35), Müller Maria geb. Krosch (35), Müller Maria Margrethe (20), Müller Michael (64), Müller geb. Niessen (40), Müller Peter (50), Müller Peter Josef (72), Müller Sebastian Josef (24), Müller Tillmann (48), Müllermeister Sibilla (23), Müllers Theodor Jakob (63), Münch Herr (70), Mündwolfen Elisabeth (22), Müntemann Gertrud geb. Weimbs (54), Mürsch Severin (63),

Müthrath Margarethe geb. Meuther (40), Müthrath Peter (70), Müthrath Sophie geb. Schmitz (68), Nacken Christine geb. Cravatzo (56), Nagel Trude (17), Nauert Elisabeth geb. Heimbach (47), Nauert Hans (13), Nauert Herbert (10), Neicken Katharina geb. Leininger (45), Neise Kaspar (45), Neise Wilhelmine geb. Pfeiffer (40), Nellessen Frau (50), Nellessen Luise geb. Dutz (50), Nepomuck Jakob (27), Nepomuck Julius (36), Nepomuck Klara (17), Nepomuck Kordula geb. Roeder (35), Nepomuck Maria geb. Rosenzweig (29), Neuhäuser Paul (50), Neumann Christian (52), Neumann Heinrich (54), Neumann Katharina geb. Heidel (52), Neumann Therese (45), Nick Frau (55), Nickel Johann (9 Monate), Nickel Käthe geb. Heiss (19), Nideggen Frau (65), Nielegall Wilhelm (57), Niedecker Katharina geb. Hübsch (60), Niederau Anna geb. Meling (60), Niederau Anna (7), Niederau Arnold (36), Niederau Christine geb. Lüssem (31), Niederau Fritz (63), Niederau Käthe geb. Gülden (33), Niederau Karl (66), Niederau Katharina (5),

Niederau Luise geb. Gasper (63), Niederau Magdalene geb. von der Hagen (24), Nielbock Anita (17), Niessen Johann Nikolaal (43), Niessen Paula (35), Niessen Sophie geb. Krings (66), Niggenbölling Ernst (45), Niggenbölling Grete geb. Münemann (45), Niggenbölling Horst Alwin (2), Niggenbölling Leo (10), Nobis Sophia (68), Noeken Edmund (65), Noeken Käthe geb. Thelen (60), Nöldgen Agathe Josefine (16), Noppen Elisabeth geb. Flöck (76), Noppeney Maria (82), Nota Margarethe (20), Notarius Katharina geb. Küfel (50), Notarius Sibilla (16), Nussbaum Katharina (48), Olshausen geb. Hardt, Ockenfels Annemarie geb. Kurth (40), Odendahl Ingrid (3), Odendahl Karl (70), Odendahl Katharina geb. Schlaeger (63), Oebels Anna Maria geb. Esser (58), Oebels Herbert (4), Oebels Katharina geb. Zöllner (25), Oenings Johann (59), Oepen Anna (62), Oepen Friedrich (36), Oepen Helga (4), Oepen Katharina (20), Oepen Martha geb. Bertrams (23), Oepen Wilhelm (29), Offgeld Alfonsa (26), Offgeld Elisabeth (20),

Offergeld Hilde (17), Offergeld Johanna (55), Offermanns Gertrud (50), Ogrodowski Elisabeth geb. Issinger (68), Ohlef Adele geb. Lesch (46), Ohlendick Anna Louise Wilhelmine (59), Ohvem Anna (36), Ohvem Gertrud geb. Lich (78), Ohvem Gertrud (39), Ohst Emil Christian (56), Ohst Franziska Käthe (53), Oldenhoven Frau (25), Oldenhoven Kind, Oleff Frau, Oleff Josefine geb. Nirrnickes (32), Oleff Käthe (14), Oleff Maria (13), Ollig Anni (48), Ollig Katharina (72), Ollig Maria (46), Olligsläger Fredi (6), Olligsläger Käthe geb. Kuhlenrath (31), Opree Mathias (70), Orbach Bernhardine geb. Tonnet (34), Orgeich Heinrich (44), Otten Katharina geb. Groß (68), Quillon Katharina geb. Franken (53), Quillon Mathias (56), Paar Elisabeth geb. Bär (60), Paar Josef (55), Paffendorf Heinrich (58), Paffrath Alfred (20), Panhelt Jakob (36), Papst Ludwig (55), Papst Magdalene geb. Jasper (53), Pardun Gertrud (Gerda) geb. Zöllner (65), Pardun Hans (35 oder 38), Paulssen Änne (31), Paulus Auguste (60),

Pavonet Hubert (54), Pecher Hermann (15), Pechas Margot (19), Pechas Theodor (53), Peiffer Anna (54), Peiffer Änni (31), Peiffer Christine geb. Porschen (46), Peiffer Ernestine (20), Peiffer Gertrud geb. Hütten (32), Peiffer Hannemie (12), Peiffer Heinrich jun. (45), Peiffer Johann (68), Peiffer Karl Heinz (14), Peiffer Käthe (37), Peiffer Wilhelm Heinrich (48), Pein Maria (58), Peltzer Anneliese (15), Peltzer Franz (70), Peltzer Maria geb. Oellers (62), Peltzer (?) geb. (Karl), Pelzer Franz, Pelzer Martin (41), Pelzer Peter (63), Pelzer Regina (13), Pelzer Willi (45), Persche Christiane (68), Persche Maria (65), Pesch Franziska (42), Pesch Frau (45), Pesch Michael (55), Peter Edith (45), Peter Karl (50), Peters Barbara (76), Peters Frau (50), Peters Hedwig geb. Hennes (31), Peters Herr (50), Peters Hulestine (10), Peters Johanna geb. Schreiber (66), Peters Karl (73), Peters Katharina (70), Peters Thekla (54), Peters Trude (10), Petri geb. Hohenadom (44), Petzold Therese (65), Pfeiffer Elfriede (63), Pfeiffer Gabriele (68), Pfeiffer Maria geb. Neffgen (59), Pfeiffer

Peter (60), Pfeiffer Wilhelm (42), Pfeil Maria (38), Pfennigs Friedrich (48), Pflückel Herr (60), Picka Magdalene (29), Pickart Sibille geb. Collip (30), Platz Emil (35), Platz Gertrud Maria Frieda (74), Pley Elisabeth geb. Hütsch (62), Pley Elisabeth (60), Pley Gertrud geb. Mostet (55), Pley Mathias Josef (74), Plograth Elisabeth geb. Kluth (15), Plograth Erika (1), Plograth Renate (3), Plötz Elisabeth geb. Schnitzler (37), Plum Christine geb. Lothmann (66), Plum Heinrich (67), Plum Maria geb. Schumacher (57), Plum Rosemarie (16), Plützer Maria (20), Pohl Anna Katharina (19), Pohl Hubert Alfred (49), Pohl Johann (80), Pohl Karoline geb. May (62), Pommerenke Hubertine geb. Zimmermann (32), Pontz Leni (18), Porschen Anna (20), Pottkämper Otto (54), Preußner Helene geb. Hellesberg (70), Proffe Katharina (62), Profittlich Juliane (55), Prümmer Heinrich (66), Prümmer Hubert (48), Przybylska Hedwig (41), Pütz Anna (56), Pütz Anna Maria Katharina geb. Schmitz (71), Pütz Berta geb. Hungs (78), Pütz Eleonore (34),

Pütz Elise geb. Garges (56), Pütz Gretchen geb. Pfeiffer (28), Pütz Hans Werner (8), Pütz Heinrich Anton (81), Pütz Herr (55), Pütz Josef (32), Pütz Josefine geb. Esser (30), Pütz Käthe (32), Pütz Maria geb. Bruns (58), Pütz Michael (57), Pütz Theodor (61), Pütz Wilhelm (70), Quadflieg Änne (52), Rademacher Elisabeth geb. Dienstknecht (37), Rademacher Grete (65), Rademacher Karin (9), Radscheidt Martha (51), Ramacher Richard Jakob (42), Ramm Luise geb. Zeyen (54), Rankers Agnes geb. Pütz (52), Rankers Tinny (24), Rankers Willy (60), Rasdem Adele geb. Schertheiler (42), Rasden Heinz (8), Rasden Sybille (22), Rasden Willy (11), Rasqui Katharina (50), Rasqui Mathias (78), Raths Anna Maria (17), Raths Anna Elisabeth (19), Raths Elisabeth geb. Maies, Raths Hubert (3), Raths Katharina geb. Schummer (28), Raths Katharina (8), Rausch Josefine (21), Redder Anna (35), Redder, Reichshof Frau (58), Reiner Gertrud geb. Holter (69), Reiner Johann (69), Reiner Maria (42), Reimes Frau (30),

Reimers Johann (60), Reinartz Clementine (37), Reinartz Kathi (34), Reinold Albert (39), Reitz Wilhelm (54), Renner Eugen Leonhard (49), Rensinghoff Christine geb. Johnen (36), Retzlaff Elisabeth (22), Retzlaff Margarethe geb. Rosenloecher (50), Retzlaff Maximilian (59), Reuter Gottfried (66), Reumont Arthur, Reumont Cläre geb. Schnmüth, Reute Leni (17), Rey Christian (12), Rey Elli geb. Schroeder (38), Rey Franz (5), Rey Gertrud (17), Rey Heinz (12), Rey Helmi (2), Rey Jean (40), Rey Maria geb. Dahmen (54), Rey Maria (7), Rey Reiner (56), Rey Reiner Franz (14), Rey Wilhelm (49), Rey Willi (11), Richartz Cläre (23), Richartz Johanna geb. Nolitas (66), Richartz Louise geb. Wolter (33), Richarz, Richter Maria (7), Rick Adele (26), Rick Christine (19), Rick Gertrud geb. Ollig (73), Rick Gertrud (33), Rick Hubert (53), Rick Josef (6), Rick Marie (26), Ried Hartmut (17), Ringen Jakob (16), Ripp Gertrud geb. Cardun (24), Ripp Josef (6), Robens Jean (65), Roder Gertrud geb. Hünerbein (30), Rodeburg Agnes geb.

Rosenbaum (45), Rodeburg? Hermann?, Rodeburg Josef (10), Rodeburg Käthe geb. Schmitz (44), Roel Margarethe geb. Knauff (52), Roekentz Laurenz (80), Roeder Jakob (51), Roeder Margarethe geb. Schmitz (45), Roegels Peter (59), Roegels Wilhelm (64), Roelen Josefine (85), Roggendorf Sybilla (63), Römer Maria (33), Rombach Martin (23), Römer AlleA (43), Römer Erna geb. Hoeffgen (49), Roscheid Georg (24), Roscheda Emilie (24), Roscheda Helene geb. Neith (42), Rosenzweig Agnes geb. Niederau (39), Rosenzweig Maria (29), Rosenzweig Robert (51), Rosenzweig Wilhelm (38), Roß Susanne (18), Rothkopf Edda (3), Rothkopf Rolf Josef (5), Röthling Maria Elisabeth geb. Stever (22), Rottländer Josef (65), Rouette Christine geb. Fery (53), Rudi Charlotte Elise Dorothea Erika (50), Rudolf Elisabeth geb. Esser (32), Rudolf Gerda (10), Rudolf Günther/Heinz (8)(6), Rudolph Christine (14), Rudolph Elisabeth geb. Nülle (39), Rudolph Margarethe

(51), Rühle Paula (32), Rütten Hubert (17), Rüttgers Katharina (22), Salentin Anneliese (19), Salentin Karin (3), Salentin Margarethe geb. Scharnickel (24), Salm Eleonora (56), Sander Hubertine geb. Jörres (30), Sandler Erich (9), Sandler Petronella geb. Sürsig (30), Samfleben Hubert (9), Sängersdorf Josefine geb. Wümbkes (32), Sartorius Elisabeth (19), Sartorius Fritz (12), Sartorius Maria (10), Sartorius Mathias (3), Sartorius Petronella geb. Zander (40), Sauer Anton (60), Sauer Franz (30), Sauer Ludwig (23), Savioni Maria (44), Savioni Wilhelm (48), Schaaf Adele geb. Cremer (48), Schaaf Albert, Schaaf Anna Maria Karoline geb. Cremer (39), Schaaf Barbara geb. Classen (29), Schaaf Franz Josef Walter (46), Schaaf Friedrich (65), Schaaf Hedwig (36), Schaaf Josefine Conradine geb. Bonn (63), Schaaf Kaspar (53), Schachtsiek Frau (50), Schachtsiek (50), Schaefer Barbara (30), Schäfer Anneliese (80), Schäfer Elisabeth (22), Schäfer Gertrud (54), Schäfer

Katharina geb. Käufer (57), Schäfer Peter (58), Schäfer Sybille (65), Schallenberg Berta (57), Schallenberg Margarethe (17), Schallenberg Wilhelm (59), Schattal Gertrud geb. Schneider (64), Schaub Sophie geb. Pesch (52), Scheidtweiler Maria geb. Deuster (44), Schell Kaspar (50), Schenberg Hannelore (13), Schenberg Luise geb. Rupp (45), Schepers Michael, Scherf Albert (67), Schetter Andreas (56), Scheuer Jean (20), Scheuer Margarethe geb. Nieveler (42), Schier Christian (50), Schiffer Eva (23), Schiffer Frau (55), Schiffer Hulestine geb. Keuth (57), Schiffer Willy (58), Schilberg Frau (18), Schilberg Sybilla (40), Schilles Franziska (80), Schilling Christine (42), Schilling Gertrud geb. Doctor (70), Schilling Henriette geb. Numm (38), Schindler Fritz (65), Schirgen Hans Josef (2), Schirgen Maria geb. Leister (26), Schinzel Günther (5), Schinzel Herr (56), Schinzel Maria (39), Schlang Christian (60), Schlegel Maria (42), Schleifer Adele (18), Schleiff Katharina (80), Schlerp Martin (49), Schlömer Matthias (68), Schlösser Agnes geb. Hillebrand (66),

Schlösser Therese (58), Schmadel Else (28), Schmidt Laura (70), Schmidt Johann (61), Schmidt Ludwig (54), Schmidt Maria (64), Schmidt Walter (83), Schmitt Hermann (55), Schmitz Agnes (10), Schmitz Anna (58), Schmitz Anna geb. Popörr (66), Schmitz Berni (43), Schmitz Eberhard (69), Schmitz Ferdinand (60), Schmitz Franziska (12), Schmitz Gertrud (30), Schmitz Herr (65), Schmitz Herr (60), Schmitz Hubert (49), Schmitz Josef (65), Schmitz Josef (55), Schmitz Karoline (65), Schmitz Katharina (65), Schmitz Katharina (55), Schmitz Margarethe (38), Schmitz Margarethe (17), Schmitz Maria (57), Schmitz Maria (46), Schmitz Maria geb. Heimbüchel (42), Schmitz Maria (41), Schmitz Maria (40), Schmitz Maria (37), Schmitz Maria Agnes Klara (11), Schmitz Maria Therese (46), Schmitz Mathias (76), Schmitz Peter (71), Schmitz Peter Josef (52), Schmitz Peter Josef, Schmitz Sybilla geb. Steffens (56), Schmitz Sybille (18), Schmitz Therese (30), Schmitz Wilhelm (65), Schmitz Wilhelm (55), Schmülgen Hermann Josef (1), Schmülgen Katharina geb. Brück (32), Schmülgen Wilhelmine (5), Schneider Änne geb. Deher (58), Schneider Johann Karl (69), Schneider Karl Heinz (13), Schneider Klara geb. Maurer (48), Schneider Kunigunde geb. Dorr (62), Schneider Maria Anna Cäcilie (23), Schneider Peter (68), Schneider Therese Käthe (10), Schneider Theresia geb. Hannen (46), Schnellinger Karl (55), Schneppenheim Sybille geb. Esser (30), Schnettler Irmgard (17), Schnettler Margret (19), Schnitzler Anna Maria Hubertine geb. Küppers (51), Schnitzler Eva geb. Etter (35), Schnitzler Franz Herbert (5), Schnitzler Hubert (71), Schnitzler Katharina Maria (14), Schnitzler Klara Anna geb. Rensinghoff (32), Schnitzler Maria geb. Reimer (41), Schnorrenberg Christian (61), Schnur Anneliese geb. Dahmen (22), Schöbel Hildegard (22), Schoenen Heinrich (65), Scholl Agnes geb. Bosbach (56), Scholl Agnes (20), Scholl Margot (24), Schomenberg Gertrud geb. Severich (40),

Schönenberg Gertrud geb. Gemeinde (45), Schöppen Hermann, Schöppen Maria geb. Brammertz (39), Schorn Helene geb. Nichels (50), Schoss Margarethe geb. Kurth (68), Schoss Werner (63), Schotten Anton (16), Schotten Johann (81), Schotten Luise (26), Schotten Otto (45), Schotten Theo (18), Schotten Theo (18), Schrader Agnes geb. Schoenen (22), Schreiber Eberhard (30), Schreibe Helene (39), Schreiner Peter (70), Schrödde Wilhelm (41), Schröder Albert Franz (12), Schröder Anna geb. Brielp (65), Schröder Irmgard (5), Schröder Johann (48), Schröder Josefine Margarethe Wilhelmine (24), Schröder Klara (55), Schröder Klara geb. Humm (42), Schröder Lore Wilma (26), Schröder Margot (14), Schröder Maria geb. Breuer (30), Schröder Marie Luise (7), Schröder Mathias (68), Schröder Sophie (58), Schroeder Anna (56), Schroeder Elisabeth geb. Breuer (44), Schroeder Katharina (54), Schroeder Maria geb. Golsheim (55), Schrötter Josef (62), Schubert Meta geb. Lyon (52), Schuh Käthe (57), Schuh Maria (62), Schuh Max (22), Schuler Adolf (59), Schuler Josefine geb. Küpperfüsth (47), Schuler

Paul Adolf (20), Schüller Katharina geb. Schumacher (48), Schüller Mathias (42), Schüller Wilhelm (55), Schulte Käthe (48), Schulte Gertrud (5), Schulte Jakob (37), Schulte Maria geb. Felts (35), Schulte Mathias (12), Schulte Wilhelm (10), Schumacher Adolf (65), Schumacher Elisabeth (17), Schumacher Kläre geb. Knuth (24), Schumacher Kordula geb. Esch (71), Schumacher Luise (54), Schumacher Maria (50), Schumacher Maria geb. Blatzheim (42), Schumacher Maria (24), Schumacher Wilhelm (72), Schummer Karl Heinz (14 Tage), Schunert Franz (60), Schünzel Günther (9), Schünzel Maria geb. Bongardt (37), Schünzel Richard (61), Schür Johann (60), Schür Karolina geb. Baum (48), Schürmann Otto (56), Schuster Franz (74), Schuster Jakob (49), Schuster Manfred (11), Schuster Maria geb. Frost (47), Schützendorf Barbara (60), Schwarthoff Hubert (45), Schwartzenberg von Agathe geb. Schallenberg (39), Schwarz Georg Josef (27), Schwarz Gertrud (30), Schwarz Lorenz (45), Schwarz Sybille geb.

Oleff (44), Schwedhelm Gertrud (32), Schreiver P. Josef (52), Schwer Barthel (69), Schwer Maria geb. Brüggen (66), Schrötgen Karl Anton (47), Seifert Georg Franz (61), Selbach Karl (51), Selbach Mosel (5), Selenka Josef (59), Selzer Erika (18), Semer Helena (Helma) (14), Semer Paula geb. Courth (50), Sengersdorf Johann (68), Sengersdorf geb. Hülsch (68), Sielen Johann (90), Siebold Josef (60), Sieger Gertrud (70), Simoneth, Frau, Simoneth Sybille (38), Simoni Wilhelmine (68), Simons Elisabeth geb. Schmitz (25), Simons Gerd (11), Simons Kaspar (37), Simons Peter (65), Sinzig Anna (40), Sinzig Elise geb. Franken (60), Sinzig Elise (35), Sinzig Josef (70), Solinus Anna (85), Solinus Wilhelmine (73), Sommer Elise (52), Sommer Franziska geb. Hütz (78), Sommer Maria (80), Sonanini Emil (3), Sonanini Ferdinand (49), Sonanini Heinz (23), Sonanini Magdalena (80), Sonanini Wilhelm (48), Sonnen Jean (58), Sonnen Monika geb. Sprenger (48), Sonntag Katharina (43), Sonntag Willi (16), Spannagel Martha (42), Spenke Klara geb. Bergsch

(45), Spenke Leo, Spenke Sofie (50), Spessart Adolf (57), Spiess August (76), Spiess David (70), Spiess Franziska geb. Schmitz (56), Spiess Johanna geb. Hannen (46/47), Spiess Katharina geb. Gaedchels (69), Spiess Maria geb. Decker (50), Spiess Maria geb. Heinrichs (41), Spiess Mathias (11), Sprenger Franz (79), Sprenger Gertrud geb. Lemmer (74), Spydralla Magarethe (19), Spyker Anneliese (8), Spyker Dieter (5), Spyker Emma geb. Kluth (30), Stachelscheidt Elisabeth Reinhilde (9), Stachelscheidt Johanna geb. Schürmann (47), Stachelscheidt Johanna Irmgard (13), Stachelscheidt Maria Luise (22), Stachelscheidt Mathilde Gisela (16), Stappen Christine (62), Stappen Gertrud (53), Staas Gerhard (52), Staas Maria geb. Thelen (48), Steffens Maria (56), Steffens Werner (50), Steffes Käthe geb. Timmermann (39), Stegh Heinrich Josef (84), Stegmann Agnes geb. Pleuss (70), Steger Friedrich Willi (13), Steger Maria Gertrud (28), Stein Elise geb. Kamp

(68), Stein Gertrud geb. Gillessen (43), Stein Hedwig (41), Stein Heinrich (45), Stein Klara (17), Steinert Helmuth Gustav (51), Steinitz Konrad (32), Stemmler Mathilde geb. Dohmen (44), Stevelmann Maria (56), Steven Elisabeth (40), Steven Sybilla (42), Stiel Klara (36), Stim Hildegard (35), Stockhausen Gertrud (38), Stockheim Wilhelm (70), Stöckle Sybille (22), Stoeber Günther (14), Stoffel Alois (89), Stoffels Arnold (50), Stoffels Herr (40), Stoffels Maria (48), Stolberg zu von Maria (36), Stoll Johanna Gertrud (25), Stoll Maria Katharina geb. Roeb (50), Stollewerk Anna Maria geb. Schnorrenberg (74), Stollewerk Ingeborg (17), Stollewerk Martha Johanna geb. Schmidt (55), Stollewerk Matthias (Matthias) (72), Stoltzen Karl (44), Stolz Anni (26), Stolz Katharina geb. Gentgen (74), Strack Gertrud geb. Gendikowiak (50), Strack Johann (47), Strack Josef (48), Strack Katharina (59), Strauch Elisabeth geb. Trimborn (49), Strauch Gert (41), Strepp Marianne (22), Struck Frau (22), Strunck Frau (65),

Strunck Klara geb. Brügmann (78), Strunck Veronika geb. Dosel (48), Strunck Wilhelm (51), Stukay Ignatz (32), Sturm Agathe geb. Filz (56), Sturm Annelore (22), Sturm Friedrich (56), Sturm Gertrud (35), Sturm Maria (37), Sturm Sophie geb. Mockheim (71), Sturm Wilhelm (67), Szynakiewicz Margarethe geb. Schumacher (53), Szynakiewicz Maria (49), Tappert Maria (53), Tellenbach Christine geb. Sons (64), Tellenbach Heinrich (64), Thal Rolf Heinz (2), Theisen Elisabeth geb. Esser (71), Theisen Annelore (16), Thelen Elisabeth (44), Thelen Heinrich sen. (74), Thelen Heinrich jun. (37), Thelen Maria (64), Thelen Wilhelm (66), Thenen von Josefine geb. Hahn (34), Thenen von Karola (12), Thenen von Marianne (16), Thenen von Wilhelm (37), Theobald Ruth (40), Thoma Albert (55), Thoma Anna (58), Thoma Johann Josef (53), Thoma Sibille geb. Weyen (51), Thomas Anna (59), Thomas Georg (24), Thomas Gertrud (56), Thomas Josef (28), Thomas Matthias (43), Thomas Sophie geb. Hennie (37), Thomaschewsky Franz (30), Thomik Christian (59), Thosmann Christine geb. Nacken (60), Thyssen Maria (30), Thyssen Tina (70), Timmermann Margarethe (19), Tingart Paul (14), Tingart Rudi (15), Tings Agnes geb. Trüpper (60), Tings Wilhelm (60), Tistey Adolf (52), Tonnet Maria (40), Tonnet Therese geb. Dunkel (64), Trennet Hedwig Rosa geb. Roff (44), Trennet Horst (12), Tresemer Anna geb. Naase (38), Treuling Maria geb. Grohbusch (42), Treuling Matthias (53), Treuling Wilhelm (70), Tüllmann Gertrud geb. Melsches (61), Tüttenberg Gertrud geb. Bergs (85), Ulrich Maria geb. Klein (43), Ulrich Wilhelm (78), Uri Frau (38), Uri Karl (55), Utzerath Sofia (78), Vaassen Gertrud geb. Machery (65), Vaassen Ludwig sen. (65), Vaassen Ludwig jun. (40), Valder Christine (25), Valder Grete geb. Esser (45), Valder Wilhelmine geb. Newsen (54), Veit Wilhelm (79), Velden Elisabeth geb. Ganser (63), Velden Karl (70), Velden Margret geb. Roeb (35), Velden Maria (70),

Nelden Paula (55), Netter Emil (69), Netter Gertrud geb. Schäfer (62), Netter Johann Anton (17), Nettersütt Herr (30), Ney Anneliese (23), Niehöver Katharina geb. Knieps (48), Niehöver Sybille (25), Nieth Gertrud geb. Klein (82), Vogel Katharina (60), Vogel Katharina (31), Vogler Mathilde geb. Esserin (38), Vogt Katharina geb. Thomas (49), Vois Christian (6 Monate), Vois Emilie geb. Clemens (35), Vois Georg (71), Vois Helene (25), Vois Karl Georg (65), Vois Katharina (10), Vois Maria Katharina (34), Vois Peter (59), Vois Peter (12), Vois Sybilla geb. Hübsch (60), Voissel Josef (39), Voissem Bernhard (75), Voit Hildegard (18), Voit Magdalena geb. Vossen (55), Völl Anna Maria Katharina (52), Völl Sophia geb. Schmidt (72), Vollmer Christine (27), Vollmer Katharina geb. Berger (65), Vossen Heinz (12), Vossen Inge (3), Vossen Maria Katharina (44), Wagener Anna Sybilla (38), Wagener Christian (63), Wagener Marianne (22), Wagener Sophie (38), Wall Klara (55), Wallen Theresia (53), Waldorf Johann (47), Waldorf Johanna Barbara geb. Leinbach (49), Waldorf Traudchen (51), Wans Rudolf (58), Weber Anneliese (22), Weber Brunhilde, Weber Christine geb. Laux (55), Weber Elisabeth geb. Desiri (45), Weber Elisabeth (22), Weber Franz (25), Weber Gerda (40), Weber Hans Dieter (5), Weber Hans Eugen (14), Weber Heinrich (59), Weber Käthe geb. Fildhaut (26), Weber Käthe geb. Flück (33), Weber Melitt (20), Weber Mathilde (43), Weck Eugen (47), Wedemüller Ernst (31), Wedemüller Marta geb. Schrör (37), Wecker Lieselotte (21), Wedekind Cäcilie geb. Nelden (56), Wedekind Louis (68), Weidemann Fritz (62), Weidemann Hella (18), Weidemann Maria (66), Weidgang Barbara (57), Weiler Edith Helene geb. Schiemann (38), Weiler Elisabeth (47), Weingartz Josef (67), Weise Josefine (16), Weisweiler Adolf (76), Weisweiler Gertrud geb. von der Hoff (70), Weisweiler Mia (35), Weitz Ella (35), Weitz Liese (12), Wellner Heinrich (40),

Welp Heinrich (60), Welp Josefine geb. Roloff (57), Welsch Ernst (39), Welsch Gertrud (39), Welsch Hubert (48), Welsch Junge (12), Welscher Klara (Clara) geb. Geck (75)(76), Wenniges Christine Sybilla Antoinette geb. Peltzer (51), Wenniges Heinrich (50), Wenzel Franz (65), Wenzel Katharina (79), Wende Marianne Dorothea (38), Werts Laurenz (10), Wessel Christian (34), Wessel Elisabeth Gertrud geb. Prostka (25), Wessel Franziska geb. Halmengress (25), Wessel Katharina (39), Wessel Maria Therese geb. Fröschl (63), Westerveller Martha geb. Höster (50), Weygans Anna Katharina geb. Rosten (58), Weygans Trude (17), Weyer Katharina (84), Weyrauch Ida Henriette geb. Exeter (32), Weyrauch Ingeborg Ida Elisabeth (3), Widmann Christine geb. Peter (37), Widmann Elisabeth (14), Widmann Willi (17), Wilberts Adele (56), Wilberts Josef (22), Wild Helene (11), Wild Käthe geb. Klüser (38), Wilden Anne (46), Wilden Friedrich (13), Wilden Nettchen (51), Wilhems Margarethe (69), Willberg Maria Sybille geb. Franken (38), Willms Michael (47), Willms Trude geb. Reffens (45), Winands Gertrud geb. Lerch (65), Winden Josef (49), Wingens Adolf (47), Wingens Josefa geb. Kroeffgens (47), Wingerath Peter (17), Wings Jakob (57), Winnikes Andreas (53), Winnikes Heinrich (49), Winnikes Heinrich (45), Winnikes Josef (72), Winnikes Katharina geb. Nichels (52), Winnikes Therese geb. Krug (62), Wipperfürth Nikolaus (72), Wirtz Auguste (47), Wirtz Barbara geb. Hoffadleg (57), Wirtz Gertrud (24), Wirtz Heinrich (50), Wirtz Josef (51), Wirtz Katharina (49), Witte Johannes (35), Witte Willy (36), Wolany Elisabeth (47), Wolf Christina geb. Becker (60), Wolf Christine geb. Kallentin (76), Wolf Emeline Käthe Minna (22), Wolf Gertrud geb. Trienes (78), Wolf Herr (45), Wolf Karl Friedrich (51), Wolff Gottfried (52), Wolff Katharina geb. Rumann (58), Wolff Mathias (74), Wolff Sybille (26), Wolff Willi (58), Wollenweber Edeltrude (14), Wollenweber Gerda geb. Rodrigo (38), Wollseiffen Elisabeth (68), Wortmann

Elisabeth (21), Wozniak Wladyslaw (44), Würgen Frau (52), Würgen Wolf (54), Wygeden van Danfel (5), Wygeden van Martha geb. Hollenweh (33), Wygeden van Wolfgang (10), Wynands Anna Luise geb. Klinker (67), Zander Anna geb. Firmenich (73), Zander Gertrud geb. Mörsch (68), Zaum Franz (55), Zaum Franz (45), Zaum Gedi (6), Zaum Magdalena geb. Krumpen (55), Zaum Maria Christina Elisabeth geb. Bierefeld (42), Zens Anna Katharine geb. Hewer (55), Zewen Gertrud geb. Köstgen (34), Ziesche Gustav (60), Zilken Ilse geb. Zimmermann (27), Zilliken Josefine geb. Scheidt (70), Zimmermann Fritz (72), Zimmermann Jean (43), Zimmermann Johanna (47), Zimmermann Johannes Franz (48), Zimmermann Käthe (44), Zimmermann Wilhelmine geb. Jakobs (29), Zinner Liesel (51), Zipfel Alois (70), Zipfel Anna (19), Zipfel Karoline geb. Pfeiffer (60), Zöller Anna Maria Pauline geb. Oepen (57), Zöllner Herr (60), Zöllner Katharina geb. Braun (59), Zons Reiner (61).

Reiner Zons, alphabetically the last in the city's book of the dead of November 16, 1944. Zons. Zone. Zoo. Engaged in what activity was he caught between 3:24 and 3:44 p.m.? How many people simply disintegrated at 1700 degrees Celsius and no longer even have a name? Mateo sticks the list into a brown leather bag, just like the one my father has for his everyday office use. When my father picks up the bag (ready on the ground by the door of the house since yesterday evening) in the early morning at the very latest, he becomes a public person and is lost to his family. He is clean-shaven, smells of a sharp aftershave. His shirt sits tight behind a reddish-brown leather belt. He's wearing a tie, his shoes are shining. His jacket is perhaps a touch too big. Father is of slim build, he's grown his sideburns long. He walks upright. "This shall please your father, however, there is still another list that you must copy down," Mateo says, opens a second folder, and places a less extensive directory of the "in-from-out-of-town" dead who perished in the aerial bombardment before me. I stare at the first name on the list: Abschlag.* A reduction, a discount. It is what it is. I write:

[handwritten list of names, ages, and locations]

---

* Not just a name, but a word meaning "reduction" or "decrease."

Baum Kurt (16) Birkesdorf, Baumann Josef (31) Gürnich, Becker Agnes (15) Frens, Becker Hubert (38) Eschweiler bei Aachen, Becker Irmgard (23) Leverkusen, Becker Karl (52) Solingen-Ohligs, Beil Grete (16) Nörvenich, Becker Wilhelm (86) Krauthausen, Bendixe Günther (50) Köln, Berg Eberhard Josef Johannes (15) Birkesdorf, Bergs Aes (15) Eschweiler bei Aachen, Bergs Leonhard (84) Eschweiler bei Aachen, Bergs Sybille geb. Hermes (40) Eschweiler bei Aachen, Bergs Wilhelm (40) Eschweiler bei Aachen, Beyel Margarethe (16) Nörvenich, Bininga Anna (30) Binsfeld, Blatzheim Gertrud (19) Kreuzau, Blatzheim Johann (63) Kreuzau, Blatzheim Maria geb. Hütz (55) Kreuzau, Blatzheim Trude (16) Eschweiler über Feld, Blatzheim Wilhelm (47) Soller, Block Herr (30) Neuendewalde/Pommern, Blum Peter Bgb. bei Niederaue, Blumenthal Maria (57) Embken, Börger Werner (35) Junkersdorf, Börne Elisabeth (14) Langerwehe, Bolterdorf Mathias (25) Gürnich, Bolterdorf Willi (20) Gürnich, Bolz Willi (40) Harff über Bedburg/Erft, Bongartz Wilhelm

(51) Pier, Bormann Elfriede (14) Langerwehe, Braun Frau (60) Kreuzau, Braun Peter (62) Köln, Braun Wilhelm (65) Lendersdorf, Braun Willi (34) Gürzenich, Breuder Leni (17) Birkelsrath, Breuer Bernhard Mondau, Breuer Josef (35) Eschweiler, Breuer Maria (16) Birkesdorf, Britz Josef (53) Köln, Bücker Arnold (29) Arnoldsweiler, Cardaun Josef (52) Köln, Chini Cornelius (61) Birkesdorf, Claassen Anna Maria geb. Solentin (25) Frotzheim, Claassen Elisabeth (40) Buir, Claassen Karl (10) Derichsweiler, Claassen Maria (35) Schmidthausen, Coblenz Alfred Bernhard (48) Essen-West, Collip Elisabeth (16) Nariareiler, Crefeld Peter Josef (60) Derichsweiler, Crippen Thea (22) Stockheim, Cremer Heinrich Arnoldsweiler, Dackweiler Katharina (54) Birkesdorf, Dahmen Petronella (25) Ellen, Decker Maria geb. Müllejans (42) Gürzenich, Dinger Karl (42) Aachen, Dinger Mathilde (46) Aachen, Dings Gustav Albert Karl (53) Solingen-Wald, Dohmen Christine geb. Herzog (55) Nideau, Dohmen Kaspar (54) Nideau, Dorten Cäcilia (14) Lüscheim,

Dressen Ferdinand (17) Stolberg, Dunkel Franz (45) Adberg, Eich Adam (44) Birkesdorf, Embgen Elisabeth (17) Gohsheim, Emunds Maria (20) Marienweiler, Esser Cäcilia geb. Müller (18) Guidesdorf, Esser Emma (18) Kerpen bei Köln, Esser Johanna (19) Arnoldsweiler, Esser Matthias (56) Merken, Esser Sophie geb. Lauterbacher (55) Arnoldsweiler, Eupen Elona (22) Marienweiler, Falk Josef (35) Eschweiler, Fabritius Maria (45) Mulderau, Fabritius Maria (16) Mulderau, Fabritius Werner (49) Mulderau, Falk Käthe (38) Lürsheim, Falke Christel (26) Winden, Fassbender Anna (19) Conzendorf, Fassbender Johannes (20) Nideggen, Faust Käthe (31) Disternich, Fehrbirkel Lambert Elberfeld, Fey Matthias (40) Elsdorf, Fiedler Herr (30) Chemnitz, Fischer Wilhelmine Käthe (16) Girzenich, Flatten Hans (30) Lohn bei Weisweiler, Floss Ursula (15) Nörvenich, Fohr Karl Heinz (16) Marienweiler, Fose Paul (40) Birt-Reese, Franz Anna (17) Nörvenich, Franzen Katharina (18) Gressheim, Fretalldenhoven Adele Maria geb.

Rode (16) Güsenich, Freundgen Franz (40) Nideggen, Freundgen Gisela (10) Nideggen, Freundgen Margot (8) Nideggen, Fries Mathias (56) Buir, Frings Franziska (21) Frenz, Froesch Alexander (63) Stolberg, Früher Herr (60) Aachen, Gallmann Hans (15) Güsenich, Gallmann Johann (36) Güsenich, Ganster Katharina geb. Stödele (59) Kuffrath, Ganster Toni (10) Kuffrath, Gasper Klara (17) Schophoven, Gens Gertrud geb. Jülich (25) Oberbolheim, Giesen Hermann (53) Höhr-Grenzhausen, Göddertz Elisabeth (19) Arnoldsweiler, Görgen Maria Katharina (21) Merzenweiler, Göthlich Karl Horst (6) Köln-Zollstock, Gottschalk Maria (80) Lenderdorf, Granderath Maria (17) Merken, Grass Josefine (16) Schophoven, Grefen Anton (62) Erchweiler über Feld, Greuel Albert (17) Lenderdorf, Grill Herr (40) Ulm an der Donau, Günther Rudi (18) Zinnwald Erzgebirge, Haas Klara (32) Niederaussem, Haber Alois (49) Nideggen, Hamacher Leo (60) Drove, Hamacher Sybille (15) Birkesdorf, Hamont Elisabeth geb. Meister (31) Arnoldsweiler,

Hansen Maria (44) Eschweiler, Harzheim Käthe (26) Lendersdorf, Harzheim Paul (46) Niederau, Hausmann Anna (14) Merzenich, Hecker Herr Stockheim, Hedwig Heinz (14) Rommelsheim, Heffenmenger Maria (34) Morschenich, Hegen Anna Maria geb. Esser (22) Kerpen bei Köln, Heidbüchel Elisabeth (20) Niederau, Heidbüchel Maria Lendersdorf, Heiden Agnes geb. Pütz (33) Stockheim, Heilmann Heinrich (35) Offenbach am Main, Heimbach Peter (35) Vettweiss, Heinen Elisabeth (20) Lendersdorf, Heinen Elisabeth (31) Obermaubach-Schlagstein, Heinß Karl (48) Birkesdorf, Henn Paulus (58) Eilendorf, Hensch Marga (6) Birgel, Hensch Margarethe (40) Birgel, Herzog Heinrich (61) Eschweiler, Heupgen Maria geb. Mager (78) Lendersdorf, Hoch Ottilia geb. Nasinger (50) Köln-Nippes, Hoch Otto Emil (19) Denzlingen, Hoettgen Kaspar (30), Höller Kunibert (14) Hohkeppel Bez. Köln, Hoffmann Fritz (16) Köln-Hölenhaus, Hoffsümmer Mathias (44) Berg Thuir, Hoor Agnes (22) Merken, Hoor Klara (19) Merken, Horchem Katharina (22)

Niederheim, Horst Gertrud (48) Niedau, Hündgen Anna (81) Niedau-Krauthausen, Hünerbein Cäcilia geb. Müller (51) Köln, Hundt Elfriede geb. Adermann (46) Duisburg, Huthmacher Hubert (49) Iversheim/Euskirchen, Jaeger (Karl) (55) (Kassel Wilhelmshöhe), Jahn Mathilde (40) Birkesdorf, Jakobs Margarethe (24) Zendersdorf, Jannes Agnes (41) Niederau, Jansen Arnold (35) Heimbach, Jansen Christine geb. Karlig (39) Heimbach, Jansen Franz Josef (48) Gürzenich, Jöntgen Käthe (20) Schlich, Jahnen Katharina geb. Weiss (43) Birkesdorf, Jahnen Margarethe (29) Thum, Jumpertz Katharina geb. Gokheim (41) Zendersdorf, Kaever Josef (42) Eschweiler-Hastenrath, Käfer Leo (30) Eschweiler, Kaiser Anne (19) Schlich, Kalbhenner Elisabeth geb. Eschweiler (44) Echtz, Kalbhenner Peter (61) Eschweiler über Feld, Kammann Heinrich Fritz (37) Gürzenich, Kamps Albert (37) Nideren, Kamen von Josef (42) Köln-Sülz, Kather Wilhelm (48) Broichweiden,

Kaufmann Rolf (42) Köln-Sülz, Kerpen Josefine (18) Gürzenich, Kerkens Theo (37) Krefeld, Kentgen Willi (30) Neserich, Klar von Harald (24), Kleefisch Dora (21) Blatzheim, Klein Anton (29) Birkesdorf, Klein Gertrud (18) Nullenau, Klein Jakob (56) Hartenrath, Klein Margarethe (Gretchen/Margareta) (24) Untermaubach, Klinkenberg Änne (40) Aldorf, Klinkenberg Hans Walter (24) Gut Krapohl bei Eupen, Klinkenberg Marta (8) Aldorf, Klinkhammer Andreas (16) Blens bei Heimbach, Klinkhammer Gertrud (24) Disternich, Klinkhammer Maria (18) Blens bei Heimbach, Klotz Arthur (30) Wesseling, Kluth Maria (25) Birkesdorf, Knabe Robert (24) Hamburg, Knein Heinrich (70) Kelz, Knipprath Maria Magdalena Katharina (16) Lendersdorf, Köppinger Hermann Elsdorf, Körffer Franz (34) Neserich, Kohl Lambert (49) Neserich, Kohlmacher Maria (49) Gürzenich, Krauthausen Katharina (18) Arnoldsweiler, Krieger Hubert (59) Birkesdorf, Kroll Erwin Franz Xaver (38) Ulm an der Donau, Krönchen Sybille (18) Birkesdorf, Krug Anna Maria (17) Gödelsrath, Kuda Helene (18) Derichsweiler, Kuda

Magdalena geb. Reimer (55) Schlich, Küpper Sophia (16) Stockheim, Kujack Fritz (35), Kusten Jakob (38) Rommelsheim, Kurth Christian (46) Merzenich, Kurth Peter (46) Birkesdorf, Laaf Petronella (24) Ellen, Lambek Herr (35) Kärnten, Laskowsky Peter (17) Merzenich, Lautebach Karl (52) Arnoldsweiler, Leipertz Rudolf (18) Hoven, Lembicz Josef (41) Füssenich, Lemmens Frau Geronsweiler bei Jülich, Lenz Hans (22) Kelz, Leroy Franz (76) Lendersdorf, Lersch Kind Köln, Lersmacher Maria (60) Frauwüllesheim, Lesch Johann Wilhelm (58) Stetternich Jülich, Lilack Inge (16) Merzenich, Linden Maria (24) Merode, Lock Agnes Merken, Lövenich Sofia (15) Pier, Lövenich Thea (15) Oberstes Lorenz Herr, Lütkenhorst Karl Heinz (19) Hamborn, Malstende Johann Lendersdorf, Malstende Klara (17) Wüsseheim, Malstende Margarethe (23) Wüsseheim, Maus Katharina (15) Jakobwüllesheim, Mausbach Anna geb. Hepp (44) Bonn, Meesen Karl Josef Franz (48) Aachen, Meirowitz Therese

Hubertine Johanna geb. Gotzen (54) Winden, Meisen Christine geb. Dahmen (69) Derichsweiler, Mevenberg Johannes (33) Birkesdorf, Melcher Herr Merken, Meyer Fritz (38) Nettweiss, Michels Maria Josef Alfons (41) Aachen, Möres Josef (21) Merkstein, Mörkens Christiam (80) Kuffrath, Moidé Elisabeth (38) Luchesberg, Moll Willi (15) Merzenich, Monarth Maria Magdalena geb. Liebreich (49) Birgel, Moonen Gerhard Nettermühle bei Langerwehe, Moonen Jean Nettermühle bei Langerwehe, Moonen Josef Nettermühle bei Langerwehe, Moonen Josefa geb. Schmitz (46) Nettermühle bei Langerwehe, Moonen Maria Therese Nettermühle bei Langerwehe, Moonen Michael (48) Nettermühle bei Langerwehe, Moonen Michael Kind Nettermühle bei Langerwehe, Moritz Bertram (63) Ollesheim, Moritz Michael (53) Leipzig, Moseler Mathias (43) Wuppertal Barmen, Müller Josef (30) Abenden, Müller Maria (38) Nürnberg, Münch Elisabeth (15) Mariaweiler, Mulven

Raula geb. Reul (29) Birkesdorf, Naas Susanne geb. Frings (30) Kommerscheidt/Schmidt, Naas Sohn (4) Kommerscheidt/Schmidt, Nelles Josef (38) Mistich, Neukirch Katharina geb. Gottschalk (77) Lendersdorf, Neulen Willi (35) Langerwehe, Neumann Hubert (59) Drove, Neumann Hubert (58) Eschweiler, Neuwirth Wilhelm (44) Niederzier, Niess Herr Koblenz, Niessen Peter Josef (76) Stolberg, Nietrand Margarethe (41) Pier, Nöhlen Peter (24) Gladbach, Nolde Christoph Wilhelm (37) Hannover, Oepen Maria geb. Jansses (86) Kufferath, Österider August (35), Münden, Offermann Johann (22) Nideggen, Olletz Hildegard (21) Morschenich, Otten Gertrud (19) Berstauer, Parting Anne (18) Birkesdorf, Pfänder Alfons (35) Ehingen/Donau, Philipp Helmut (34) Köln, Pirch Wilhelm (57) Gladbach, Pohl Anna Klara (16) Gürzenich, Polentz Hans Bonn, Pool Anna (17) Derichsweiler, Prinzeler Anneliese (19) Kreuzau, Pütz Agnes (35) Stockheim, Pütz Stephan (71) Kreuzau-Friedenau, Quast Sofie (45) Aachen, Remacher Katharina

(29) Stockheim, Renards Maria geb. Hennes, (60) Stockheim, Rehm Christel (21) Euskirchen, Reiff Cardula (29) Birkesdorf, Reinartz Gerhard (53) Langerwehe, Reins Gertrud geb. Faust Gürzenich, Rey Barthel (40) Birkesdorf, Richter Gertrud (20) Drove, Römer Katharina geb. Schürmann (70) Erdweiler, Roemer Maria (18) Kreis Jülich, Röttger Heinrich (41) Nideggen, Rogall Richard (39) Boelitz-Stadt, Rohe Barthel (48) Gey-heim, Rollesbroich Josef jun. (14) Winden, Rothkopf Gan-golf (41) Oettweiss, Rothkopf Wilhelmine (16), Ruhe Wil-helm (36) Olesien, Schiedtweiler Katharina (21) Gürzenich, Scherpenstein Katharina (27) Frauwüllesheim, Scheuer Gottfried (53) Winden, Schick Peter (16) Geller, Schiffer Char-lotte Birkesdorf, Schiffer Josef (16) Pier, Schiffer Sybilla (18) Pier, Schüllberg Odilia (21) Merzenich, Schleicher Katharina (29) Schmidt, Schlömer August (50) Sindorf bei Horrem, Schmalzer Oswald Erich (25) Ortelsburg/Ostpreussen, Schmitz Edith (18) Birkesdorf, Schmitz Gertrud (21) Binsfeld, Schmitz

Gretchen (15) Stockheim, Schmitz Maria (20) Lüscheim, Schmitz Maria (17) Arnoldsweiler, Schmitz Maria Christina (48) Luchem, Schmitz Marianne (17) Gürzenich, Schmitz Modesta (82), Schmitz Peter Josef (65) Daulenrath/Jülich, Schnorrenberg Margarethe (38) Erdweiler, Schönau Anna (31) Ellen, Schönau Sybilla (29) Frauwüllesheim, Schumacher Hilde (28) Gürzenich, Sieker Edith (23) Birkesdorf, Simon Luise (49) Aachen, Sistig Agnes (35) Hausen, Sittard Wilhelm (54), Sons Maria geb. Wolf (50) Mönchen-Gladbach, Spilker Ludwig (57) Aachen, Stammel Adolf (18) Buir, Steffens Berta (43) Kelz, Steven Herr (20) Jakobwüllesheim, Stockfisch Ernst (30) Antwerpen, Stollenwerk Mathias (60) Lendersdorf, Stolz Dominikus (46) Kreuzau, Stolz Josef (49) Kreuzau, Stolz Wilhelm (42) Kreuzau, Strack Johanna Maria Therese geb. Clemens (25) Aue im Erzgebirge, Strack Peter (24) Gladbach, Strauch Josef (17) Bergstein, Strauch Mathias (38) Nettersheim, Strack Agnes (19) Geich bei Zülpich, Strauch Herr Bergstein,

Stüttgen Gertrud (18) Girzenich, Stüttgen Heinrich Josef (12) Derichsweiler, Stüttgen Klara Helene (11) Derichsweiler, Thelen Adelheid (19) Geich bei Zülpich, Theröde Ferdi (32) Wesel, Titz Maria (17) Marienweiler, Trump Margarethe (30) Krauthausen bei Düren, Trump Maria (32) Krauthausen bei Düren, Merkens Agnes (27) Krewzau, Naessen Maria (23) Arnoldsweiler, Nalder Willi (63) Gladbach, Nirmich Katharina geb. Schmitz (30) Hoven, Nopel Karl Heinz (15) Marienweiler, Nopel Maria Irmgardis (22) Thorr bei Buir, Nader Wilhelm (56) Solingen-Ohligs, Nalbeck Johann Josef (38) Köln-Sülz, Naldenberger Alfred (52) Achach/Baden, Weber Eva Maria (18) Birkesdorf, Weber Franz (16) Birkesdorf, Weber Ignaz (61) Birkesdorf, Weber Johann (55) Arnoldsweiler, Weber Klara Helene (38) Lendersdorf, Weiss Herr (40), Weiss Josefine (45) Derichsweiler, Weiss Katharina (48) Arnoldsweiler, Werner Herr Ellen, Werth Hans Dieter (19) Iserlohn, Wichterich Lilli geb. Dollfuss (33) Aachen, Winter Herr (30), *[handwritten notes: Witw Else (22) Hoven, Witw Käthe (14) Oberzier, Witw Willi (40), Wolff Anstel (17) Schophoven, Junger Herr (50), Zimmermann geb. Schurer (45) Gürzenich.]*

No rescue operations at all, Mateo says. And why? Hitler overestimated the people's will to self-exaltation in the face of impending annihilation. Anyone who commemorates the city's dead should read Speer, who became Hitler's posthumous mouthpiece.

How, on July 4, 1952, can Speer so precisely remember the Führer's words, as if he'd secretly recorded them and the recording were readily available to him in prison. Stage-ready, film-ready, Hitler gets himself worked up: "These air raids don't bother me. I only laugh at them. The less the population has to lose, the more fanatically it will fight. We've seen that with the English, you know, and even more with the Russians. One who has lost everything has to win everything. The enemy's advance is actually a help to us. People fight fanatically only when they have the war at their own front doors. That's how people are. Now even the worst idiot realizes that his house will never be rebuilt unless we win. For that reason alone we'll have no revolution this time. The rabble aren't going to have the chance to cover up their cowardice by a so-called revolution. I guarantee that! No city will be left in the enemy's hands until it's a heap of ruins." Thus did the Führer speak in aphorisms. And Speer used this to shape the image of Hitler for decades.

I would like to be buried lengthwise in an ash coffin and remain in the earth for many decades, I say to Mateo, who also takes the second list of the dead and puts it into his leather bag. Let me see what can be done, he says and leaves the cell. In-from-out-of-towners. How small the city really was. 27 years after many of the external municipalities had been destroyed, they were aggregated to the city by way of so-called local government restructuring. I'm in from out of town, born out of town, a prisoner in a basement that's only ever been out of town, even though this building ended up as part of the city 12 years after its destruction, a potato-beetle bunker located within its borders with no relation to its landscape or history, a temple of administrative bureaucracy, its loneliness reminding every citizen of the immutably provisional nature of earthly existence.

When both men bring a suitcase into the cell, I notice that I can't stretch my arms out to them, they're spread to the sides, along with my torso, they form a T. The men whisper, then they disappear once more, they hastily bring in various objects, including a hammer and nails, which they put in one corner of the cell, they disappear once more, they drag six beams of wood into the cell, one after another, they reflect, they take the beams back out, then stand to my right and left, their arms spread like mine, they remain standing like that for five minutes, you're the evil one, says the man on the right to the man on the left, "ouchi su ei ho Christos sôson seauton kai hêmas," the other replies, whereupon both men lower their arms and leave the cell. There are books in the suitcase. I'm a little girl who always carries her belongings with her, blessed to possess such things. It's of intrinsic value to spread out your belongings on the floor in front of you, to examine them carefully but not touch them, then to put them softly back into the suitcase. Books are my dolls. I close my eyes when it's time to sleep and the books rejoice. I read them stories from other books, leaf them softly through their dreams, enshroud them in protective cloths. There is, for example, an ugly duckling amongst the books, you can't revise it, its true values lie within, and, as you read it, it becomes a beautiful swan that's kept itself hidden behind brittle words. On page 157, I read: "In full accordance with the norms of international law, the Curia declared in this letter that there was no concordat between the German government and the Holy See that could be rescinded." If green is good for the eyes, then black must not be. The ducklings must learn to see the green through the black. I read to the ugly duckling from page 149 of a book that is lying next to it and has a black-white-and-orange cover with a burst word upon it: "Meanwhile, both men have brought multiple chairs, including a so-called executive chair, two tables, and several lamps into the cell, in which they are creating an order unfathomable to me by moving the tables around at random, grouping the chairs, plugging in the lamps, if I quit reading, they immediately pause to observe this, if I keep reading, they immediately continue their work, all of the furniture is immediately taken out again, the toilet and bunk are dismantled, the marks they left on the wall and floor are erased, the longitudinal wall is broken through, a space wide enough for a door, the cell's iron door is replaced with a wooden door, the door frame is assembled, set up, aligned, framed with foam, a carpet laid out, the walls papered, the ceiling painted white, the furniture is placed in designated spots, a telephone is connected, the excess foam that's dried in the meantime is sheared off, a picture is hung on the wall, the double doors are hung from the hinges of the frames. Both men leave and close the doors behind them. It doesn't take long until the phone rings. I let it ring, look at the picture. The figure in the picture seems familiar to me, but, even after thinking about it for a long time, I can't think of where I could have seen it before."

I shut the book and put it back into the suitcase. I am now all alone in my cell. My bladder's full, I sit on the toilet whose icicles have melted. The word "staircase" comes into my mind. For me, a staircase must have a banister, when I visited my father, I always walked with a stagger, as if walking in a straight line couldn't be trusted, as if I were climbing a mountain and had to dodge obstacles. For weeks, I've only been able to fall asleep if I pace through the rooms of my parents' house in my head. These journeys are true voyages of discovery, I recover things that I thought I'd lost, can put some of them back into their rightful places, there are bright and clear rooms before my eyes, they seem to have darkened forevermore, I am physically present in these rooms, I feel my legs, my feet reach the floor, I smell the air in these rooms, feel the door handles in my hand, can open the windows, a staircase without a banister leads down into the basement, a staircase made of untreated concrete, upon the sharp edges of which you can scrape your bare feet bloody. For decades, the exterior staircase of this municipal administrative building, in the basement of which I find myself, has had the duty of keeping the citizens of the city away from its administrative bodies. Anyone who still managed to get away from the hell of the television, to pull his belly free from french-fry infernos, anyone who has thus engaged in an exceptional level of athletic activity, at least compared with the average citizen, even he is turned away by the city treasurer shortly after the entrance area. This city has a doubly difficult heritage: the war period and the postwar period, neither of which come to an end, to this day, rebuilt at breakneck pace, the city has neither recovered from wartime nor overcome its status as a merely rebuilt city. It's petrified in ruins. The furnishings of its occupants repeat the cityscape of annihilated history, the prescribed historylessness of which causes people to scurry around like ants, but haphazardly, aimlessly, driven by constant fear, they're suicidal, for everything exists next to everything else only because of gravity, nothing has grown organically, everything is merely there because something must, after all, be there, you go to the city's monuments and you end up weeping for hours because they too are so deplorable, everything except for Hoeschplatz 1, Holzstrasse 15, Holzstrasse 17, Holzstrasse 19, Holzstrasse 35, Tivolistrasse 1, in no other German city would these pass as monuments or historical sites, here, everything that triggers the sentimentality of what's been lost, whether or not it's been falsified, is a monument, a longing for architecture as nature, which this city lost with its decline, thus must this whole city be protected as a monument and not just certain gazebos, wayside crosses, grave angels, mourning genii, marble statues, steles with female figures inscribed by seated cherubs, tower ruins, remains of a Roman city wall, servants' houses, or state sanatoriums haphazardly spared by war, they've contributed precisely nothing to the mending of this country, this city. The city built itself back up after the war with terrible speed, it never actually recovered from this rebuilding. A city that is perpetual bombsite clearance.

Examining this office space, one involuntarily thinks of the cells of a prison wing. At its center, as at the center of a service hall, there's a tower-like structure that seems to be inhabited at the level of the circumferential ring-shaped free-hanging gallery and at its top, the tower is in any case illuminated in these areas and shadows become visible from time to time. An elevator that isn't accessible to the public leads up to the top of the tower. I suspect that this elevator also goes down to the basement. From the tower, you have a complete view of the cell block, nobody can enter or leave the cells unseen. If an administrative building is a high-rise building and this building is indeed a nine-story high-rise, then an administrative building is a tower. Mateo told me that you can see inside of the offices from the tower. This must be the eye of the saint. But who should be at the top of the tower if not my father? Or is a Belgian general sitting there and my father simply carries out his orders? A general of the 1st Lancers Regiment. This constellation would be more interesting if my father controlled all of the cells' inmates with the general's assistance. The Belgians are a blessing for us, my father once said at lunch. He's always the one to cut the meat. My mother cooks it. She never grills it. She rarely prepares it in the oven. Most often, she roasts it. She never sharpens the knives. The Belgians, Father said as he was sharpening the knife, the knife went in one ear and out the other, make no demands. He always signs his letters with "All best, Father," he never signs with "Love, Dad" or "Love, Your Daddy" or "All My Love, Father," and so on. "No demands" means that they stay in the barracks assigned to them during the day and inhabit whitewashed houses with a maximum of three floors, these so-called Belgian Houses, they're decorous and courteous, they even speak German. I've never ever seen a Belgian tank. All the tanks needed to occupy Germany are manufactured in Germany and sold at high prices to the Four Powers, with the exception of Russia. Or are these naturalized reparations on sprocket wheels and must therefore be handed over? Panzer Kaserne is a rolling egg. We drive the car down Bismarck-, Kreuz-, Ober-, Ost-, Römer-, Saar-, and Sedanstraße and, as he drives past, without looking and with a curt wave of his right hand, which he folds away from the steering wheel, says, those are Belgian Houses. The word "Panzerstraße"* is a clumsy word from childhood. A tank rolls out of the barracks on Stockheimer Landstraße and blocks all traffic up to the roundabout. This gives one the opportunity to contemplate nature. Trees and soot, gray grass next to concrete slabs that must withstand the tanks, a highly elastic expansion joint is embedded between the segments offset from the oncoming lane in order to withstand both cracks and changing temperatures, the trees salute the tank in lush green, it clatters across the concrete with rattling chains. Grandpa and Father had lived through the war, then what remained of the war cruised around here, one was born into what remained. The parade ground directly behind Panzerstraße. Vorder Heide Training Ground. A hundred years of military use, a nature reserve. The shots echoed out, we imagined being hit. Even if someone said that they were using blanks, we didn't believe it, for us, live rounds were being fired. It was the finest challenge of this dull, unnecessary, unused life, a life coming to pass so far from any and all relevance, all it was meant to maintain was the parents' deep provinciality, tried and true for generations, the cordon with the warning notice, "Military Security Area. Do Not Enter. Violators Will Be Prosecuted," and some joker had scratched out the three middle letters of "Enter," or "Betreten," to make "Beten," or "Pray," ("Do Not Pray"), not hesitating to climb over, the hollow crackle of shots told us where to run, shell casings were

---

* "Tank Street."

diligently gathered up, then we could watch figures scurry past, how they played war, and we also wanted to play war, we imagined what it would be like if one of us were to be shot, fallen in war at the Vorder Heide Training Ground, where the front still existed, the remains of the Second World War, Grandpa in Gestapo custody, which he survived, Father Flakhelfer,† on no combat mission, son fallen at the front on a war-island of peace. Chest out, medal.

Each shot is documented in writing. The Second World War is bullets of ink here. You must practice killing. A tree tumbles over.

If killing has thus become so easy, the disposal of a tree that disturbs one's view, society must be a Versailles where nothing individual comes into view and the whole eludes the sensible gaze, the gaze being empty if killing has therefore become Putting-Things-Back-In-Order.

By the time it's dark outside, the lights in the rooms in my head turn on, whole buildings are illuminated. It gives me a blissful feeling to see myself walking the stairs, the corridors, and the doors of these buildings. What is to happen to me? If something happens to me, it doesn't actually happen to me.

"An administrative building without things put down in writing is like a religion without light," my father used to say. The building from which he governs with his papers has more than enough light. It falls upon the visitors' heads through a comprehensive skylight. Thus is it difficult to make out whether the atrium of the building is lit by use of artificial or natural light, the subdivided square of glass is milky, rows of white and brownish glass alternate, dark streaks have formed over time, as it's not regularly cleaned. Word has it that the skylight is the illuminated floor of a large boardroom, an architectural flourish from the fifties. Cleaners claim to hear the rumbling of chairs at night originating from that boardroom. It must be a spectral cohort that meets there, no one has seen the councilors of the house striding across the

---

† Anti-aircraft auxiliary.

skylight, no chairs are moved, no speeches made. The boardroom is located in a very special place, clearly visible from the outside, it hovers in the aforementioned semicircular annex above the building's entrance area located upon the high terrace, a glass growth on one leg, a cabasa stuck into the wall with eleven (5+1+5) two-part, high windows rounded in a semicircle in place of the instrument's chains of small metal balls, the broadsides are wood-paneled, there are large wooden tables in the boardroom, at which up to three councilors can sit, the floor is surfaced with panel parquetry, a pattern that specifies no direction and is thereby intended to give the room a sense of peace. When you enter, the same people are eternally sitting there, my father, for example, has been sitting in this room for over fifty years, on November 1, 2022, it shall have been sixty years sitting in the middle of the longest row of tables and looking into the astonished faces of his subordinates, who shall not have given up waiting for the smallest sign of his corruptibility, but this sign shall not have shown itself for all these years, whoever is not cordial cannot be corrupted and cannot be fooled by anything. Incorruptibility creates the worst of enemies. Hate is directed against he who cannot be human, against a machine. The machine dictates: "The first name Jesus is not permitted in Germany. The parents' right to bestow names has its limits at the point where the naming would violate general custom and order. Regarding the requirement to give the child a 'first name,' § 21 Para. 1 No. 4 Law on Personal Status: The first names and surnames of the parents are recorded in the birth register and, at the request of a parent, its legal affiliation to a religious community that, for its part, must be a public corporation, makes a strong constitutional case for certain limitations placed on the names that may be chosen. The line will have to be drawn where first names become offensive or incomprehensible, or at least offend the religious feeling of a not insignificant minority. A first name 'Jesus' offends the religious feelings of worshippers because of its paramount importance in the German Christian churches and congregations. This has been respected in case law and in literature." Uncriticized by my father, the last sentence in the transcript, which was drawn up straightaway, reads: "This is both case law and literature." My father has a white shirt, its sleeves rolled up to the elbows, it suggests a warmer time of year or an overheated boardroom, after all, my father always observes etiquette, he's wearing a red tie, his curly, Seborin-treated hair is combed back, he supports his head with his left arm casually placed onto the armrest, he looks briefly to the right to see if there's any objection, the chair there is empty. Father takes the floor once more and says, the first name Jesus is hereby reserved for Jesus and any other use is prohibited, the meeting is brought to an end after this single item on the agenda.

All the speeches my father has hitherto given in this boardroom still vibrate in the air. My father's opponents are terrorized by them every day. Only once they've been taken hold of in writing have they been exorcized. It is my task to do this. I am already doing this. In the long run, it will not be possible for me to distinguish whose speech I am writing down. It would be a fine compliment if someone one day said of me that he was his father's speechwriter, even after his death, and his father was the speechwriter of his father, whose lost Gestapo arrest documents are the most important papers of their family history. Members of the council and various main-, side-, and subcommittees have been observed tearing my father's speeches to shreds, they often lasted for hours and, as this was hardly enough to quell their seething anger, confetti rained down from the gallery as if it were Shrove Monday, they banged their heads against the wall, which resounded strangely in the building's service hall, in such a way that a committee was specially convened to discuss possible upholstering of the offices, but no one appeared at this committee when it became known that my father had also announced his attendance at the deliberations, one assumed, and not without reason, that he only wanted to see which of his declared, supposed, and disguised opponents would harm himself the most because of him. After the head mutilations practiced in this way became known, the main committee soon came to be referred to in common parlance as the "Bump-parliament" and my father opened every session after that with the formula, "I offer my greetings to the present members of the Bump-parliament and to those who would soon like to become members."

I find myself still in the basement of the administrative building. Mateo communicated to me the seriousness of the situation by urgently demanding the handover of the book that Father had asked for, I am said to have taken it out of the painting, but I must first write this book, I reply to him, the basement has an autobiographical odor, I say to Mateo, it smells of stale air from a heater and the sign on a heavy steel door reads, "BOILER ROOM." The boiler is likely overheated, it's not big enough for the entire building, the linoleum that's used to cushion the floor has come to smell rancid over the years. The walls were raised up a few centimeters, the transition between wall and floor is rounded, hospital-round, the rubber abrasions from the soles of shoes can be seen everywhere, the file trolleys that are pushed back and forth through the basement wing roll silently and the files lie in their vehicles like sick people in bed, some ought to be quite uncontroversial, according to Mateo, a decision to repave the sidewalk in front of the building shall certainly be made, the costs are to be tacitly saved elsewhere, the decision should be carried out on the sly and not made public in any service journal, thus does one intend to avoid vexation of citizens from the outset, in every measure they see either a waste of taxpayer money or a distraction from the really important big problems, some of aforementioned measures, however, shall menace everyone's life and are a real threat to this society, but in a positive sense—one is proud of them and they ride harmlessly along with the others, for example, the 1300-year anniversary of the city's first documented mention is to be pushed forward by three years so as to simultaneously commemorate the centenary of its 99.2 percent destruction, at which, as a proverbial exceptional climax, certain people came up with the notion of staging the 100 percent destruction of the city, a work of art that one could only dream of in the capital, thus might one demonstrate the decisive intellectual innovations coming out of the so-called provinces, which, by way of their planned self-elimination at the margins and beyond those margins, catches up to its opposite by disappearing as its own area of competency, its own portfolio including briefcase, thus offering a clear view all the way from the top of the Cologne Cathedral to the Kaiserstuhl, which, admittedly, is the opposite of the provinces, they could come to no consensus in the council about what the opposite of the provinces would be, cosmopolitanism perhaps, generosity, open-mindedness, or, the goal, Catholicism. Modernity can hardly be the opposite of the provinces, as modernity comes down from the heavens, the most modern of things shall come down from the heavens for the 100 percent celebration of a 99.2 percent destruction, something the world has never before seen. It shall be an olympiad of destruction and, as with previously recognized Olympic disciplines, any nation whose bomber pilots meet the yet-to-be-determined Olympic standard can qualify. In this way, Mateo says, shall the city ensure its being spoken about for all eternity.

Mateo recounts that one can still hear Father's speeches in certain corners of the building, a week ago he strayed across the fifth floor in search of a certain office, a cleaning trolley was in his way, he said, he jammed himself into a corner to avoid incoming employees and Father's voice could suddenly be heard there, an excerpt of a speech that he'd given some five years ago in the Great Hall, he can still remember a passage about a library that no one but my father knew of and in which the books of various centuries compete with one another, there are likely also books that wrote themselves or were rewritten and finished by others in a very short time. The expansion of the archive required all that remained of Father's commitment, in such a way that he decided, though he may not have shared this with me, to sleep in the building until further notice, in a room adjoining the archive with a view out onto the church, which calmed him tremendously as he awaited the ringing of the bells, there, he could concentrate entirely on the archive and its ordering by way of the slit-like openings in the bell tower, which reminded him of arrow slits, he could see the bells chiming, thus did the thought occur to him that the church had by no means renounced all violence, rather, he is surprised that, in view of the mighty bells and their dinning, not everyone who hears them and, inevitably, most of them are long-standing Xtians, reverses their departure from the church if they have indeed already left. For as long as the bells din, Father said, don't just crawl back and forth across the floor asking for worldly refection and worldly raiment. Your father needs no other music than that of church bells, Mateo says, only the bells should ring slowly, the sound of carillons, however, is entirely hateful to him, it's always erroneous, my father means to say, it lacks everything. The measure of all things in church music is Johann Sebastian Bach's *St. John Passion* and Anton Bruckner's Ninth Symphony, your father says.

My father doesn't delegate, he alone decides. Each day from the early hours of morning onward, he presides over mountains of files and memos, to which he has added thousands of new papers over the course of time. My father knows no pause. While others go to lunch, his renewed challenge every day is to wrest a record number of completed forms from the jaws of hunger. For some time now, he's been convinced that on some not-too-distant day he'll be able to live on light alone. Even in his free time, he's surrounded by his papers, which are once said to have covered the entire table at an unavoidable work lunch with all male and female secretaries of the administrative building, covering it in such a way that it took a certain amount of straining to find the plate-covered dishes beneath them without making the papers unusable by way of the sauces. The male and female secretaries, who had, at first, acted sovereign to the point of arrogance and enjoyed the privilege, not just of meeting my father face to face, but also, as a reward for their work, in which my father placed great trust, to be invited by him to a meal, finally resigned themselves and sat around the table with dangling arms, only occasionally taking in the scent of food steaming through the papers. Father, however, showed himself to be the true ruler of his empire and bade them to take their plates in hand and to wait until he had worked through all the papers covering the dishes. For Father, working through means dispelling any and all doubts by toggling any possible opposing positions back and forth for so long that they come to be mentally pulverized. Pulverized means that Father has rendered the opposing position unthinkable, it can no longer occur to anyone and be used as an argument. As Father is concerned with certainty, such a process of pulverization takes up a great deal of time, which implies that all the male and female secretaries eat the dishes at the mere thought of which they would once have been disgusted. One dish is now exposed. Father looks around, anyone who likes it can have it. Nobody moves. Father takes the Eight Treasure Duck from the table, walks clockwise around it, and distributes the food onto the plates. Admittedly, he distributes it according to certain preferences that he himself is not even aware of, he leaves certain male secretaries unconsidered, as if they didn't exist at all, a question they will then certainly pose to themselves the next day, but also overburdens certain others. But once all the dishes had been distributed and eaten in this way without anyone getting remotely full, Father ordered the consumption of the papers, which he had not only worked through, but also from which he had drawn the proper conclusions, irreproachably and with total certainty, before immediately putting them down on paper in abbreviated form. The archive shall be grateful, Father said. The waiter was summoned, new plates were served, the waiter went around following Father's instructions and placed the papers neatly onto the plates. I want to feed you with godly script, divine scripture, you shall recognize yourselves while eating these papers, Father said, your stomach shall remind you of it forevermore, I cannot set my right foot upon the sea, nor my left foot on the earth and in my hand have I no little book open. Nor am I clothed with a cloud and no rainbow is upon my head. My feet are not as pillars of fire, only my face is as it were the sun. But the papers shall be in your mouths sweet as honey and make your bellies bitter. As soon as you've ingested the papers, you shall proclaim them to my glory. May God give you strength. The twelve male and female secretaries took up fork and knife and set about eating the papers. The first male secretary ingested these sentences: "And I saw another mighty angel come down from heaven, clothed with a cloud: and a rainbow was upon his head, and his face was as it were the sun, and his feet as pillars of fire." The second male secretary devoured this paper in a single bite: "And he had in his hand a little book open: and he set his right foot upon the sea, and his left foot on the earth," and only once the third secretary had eaten his paper with the words "and cried with a loud voice, as when a lion roars. When he cried out, seven thunders uttered their voices" upon it was the second secretary able to close his mouth once more. The female secretary sitting next to him found it difficult to eat her paper, the contents of which she had read several times, only once she realized that the best way to keep a secret is to eat it was she able to swallow effortlessly: "And when the seven thunders had uttered their voices, I was about to write: and I heard a voice from heaven saying unto me, Seal up those things which the seven thunders uttered, and write them not." The paper allotted to the secretary sitting next to her left her quite unsatisfied: "And the angel which I saw stand upon the sea and upon the earth lifted up his hand to heaven." The secretary sitting next to her was, in her turn, so shocked by the contents of her own paper that she willingly shared it with the male secretary on her left who'd been overlooked during the distribution of the papers in such a way that she destroyed the oath, but he destroyed the bitter truth: "And sware by him that liveth for ever and ever, who created heaven, and the things that therein are, and the earth, and the things that therein are, and the sea, and the things which are therein, that there should be time no longer." Rather impassively, the eighth secretary stuck the words "But in the days of the voice of the seventh angel, when he shall begin to sound, the mystery of God should be finished, as he hath declared to his servants the prophets" into his mouth, stared straight ahead, then was on the verge of falling asleep. At the sight of the words assigned to him, the ninth secretary's mouth began to water, when he heard "book," he thought of a jar filled to the brim with chocolate pudding: "And the voice which I heard from heaven spake unto me again, and said, Go and take the little book which is open in the hand of the angel which standeth upon the sea and upon the earth." The putative pudding also passed by the secretary sitting next to him, as she had to be fobbed off with the words: "And I went unto the angel, and said unto him, Give me the little book. And he said unto me, Take it, and eat it up; and it shall make thy belly bitter, but it shall be in thy mouth sweet as honey." "Just a comparison," she said and saw how the eleventh secretary put the pudding into his mouth with great pleasure, as this was written on his paper: "And I took the little book out of the angel's hand, and ate it up; and it was in my mouth sweet as honey: and as soon as I had eaten it, my belly was bitter." As the talk of the bitter pudding, which reveals its essence already upon the tongue, made the rounds, the twelfth secretary was confronted with a dish that had been cooked with many languages and, consequently, she did not entirely understand it, but this fact didn't seem to overwhelm her for too long, as she soon began to slurp and smack her lips: "And he said unto me, Thou must prophesy again before many peoples, and nations, and tongues, and kings."

It's entirely different with the councilors, they have their offices on another floor and never meet with Father in person, he doesn't know them at all, neither their names nor their ages, he only knows that there are seven councilors and he always says that there are too many councilors, there should only be three in-house, that's the smallest possible odd number necessary for a majority decision, the council also fills up vast amounts of paper with that which is related to administrative matters. Each of them has a different point of view, they hope that there will be a point of view among these that is suitable for my father. Outwardly, they present themselves as a team in which everyone stands up for each other; but when they're among themselves, envy and resentment reign. Everyone knows that the statement "I met the boss" is unlikely to be true, but as soon as someone utters this statement out of desperation or the desire to provoke, general indignation breaks out, he's been a submissive brown-noser, the others say, and they want the person who uttered these words to describe my father. It's probably a kind of game that might actually be deadly serious and nobody knows it; if somebody abstains from opining, he's immediately isolated, silent abstention weighs heavier than lying and is sanctioned with physical violence none too rarely. The descriptions of my father end up being correspondingly motley. Sometimes my father has a long beard, sometimes he's clean-shaven. If he has a long beard, his head of hair is full and curly, his head is crowned by a laurel wreath, he wears a brass lorica musculata that ends in a cingulum concealing the transition to his green robe. He wears a long red sagum closed with a simple knot instead of a fibula on the left shoulder instead of the right. Pteryges hang from the cingulum, from the elbows, and from the end of the brass-colored gaiters just below the knees. Others say he has a mouth lock, wears a winged helmet, and bears a bulky bag in which he carries clanking stuff. What's to be made of that? Is he a thief? That's probably vile slander. Or does the lock mean that secrets are in good hands with him? If my father is described as clean-shaven, then, if one looks at the missing beard for long enough, it leads to the visage being entirely missing and the portrait made of my father according to this description shows only an empty wooden frame. According to Mateo, that portrait is the last portrait in the ancestral gallery of the former heads of the administrative building, which, in common parlance, is known as "Everyone and Nobody." "Nobody" is my father, "Everyone" is the already deceased. Body-, but not characterless, even if Nobody, according to popular opinion, refers to nothing. Nobody is reckoned to be more caring than God, for Nobody makes no claims and only he, Nobody, lives without rebuke. But who is this Nobody, whom everyone attests to having found as a friend if he isn't there to be feared as a tyrant, if nobody has seen him, he only sees himself, so Nobody is your man, envious at the end, you bode no biddies done on Nobody. Only the painted empty wooden frame is recognizable as portrait, Mateo says, for the rest, a *common* visage is to be advised at all times. Nemo, which is to say Ne-Homo, which is to say Nullus, and everyone knows how influential nil truly is, everyone ought to say that nil is nothing, but nobody says it because it's clear to everyone, it wins wars and systematizes the national budget, it fills you up and revolutionizes human thought and Nobody alone can do what nobody is allowed to do: to show oneself or even not to show oneself in an empty frame, Mateo says, whereas all the others are branded with eternally immutable, but fading colors, with an irreversible expression, and the same interchangeable likeness, imitations who have imitated and shall be imitated. And one can't denigrate Nobody, envy and resentment have nothing to take aim at. First comes death, then shall it fill the frame.

I recognize my father very well in the empty wooden frame that is his effigy, I say to Mateo, he was present only at the caning performed with a smooth cane, he made speech speechless, the executive of the maternal judiciary, of which he was the legislature. When I was much younger, Father came up the stone stairs, his leather heels clicking upon them, he paced through the hall with quick stride, he tore off the covers, he turned me onto my side with his left hand in the same swing and smacked his right hand against my hindquarters, of which he occasionally avoided the exposure, either because he feared that the sight of the welts caused by the cane would make him go soft or because he was convinced that the effect of the caning, which was by no means minor, would be strengthened even further by the fabric of the pajamas. An error, the "Applicatio ad posteriora vestimentis remotis" is of incomparably greater severity, but also of a humiliating value that should not be underestimated, as is shown by the mere formulation, "Punishment after the Removal of Clothing." The Second World War meant that the beloved full-gloss cane had to be replaced by the semi-gloss cane, which has a shorter lifespan and less penetrating effect. Perhaps this is why Father used the same cane that his father had used to castigate his sons. For years, it shone bright from the sitting-room wall, an honor-filled memorial by Father to his own father and an exhortation to the son not to let the mother pick up the phone with a direct line to the office, your son is reading a psychology dictionary that you gave him, your son is constantly talking back and I can offer no riposte, for I don't understand what he's saying, your son is sitting here, not wanting to be the meaning of my life, your son is not thankful for the fact that he is our son. The cane, a piece of furniture like the massive living-room cupboard or the dresser with the glasses placed onto it, they'd never been used and the cane one day disappeared from the wall where it hung between two measly nails. Its absence caused no joy. Now, it threatened by way of the invisible, the hidden, it could lie in wait for any of us in the house. Father had put it in the Jugendstil cupboard in the so-called guest room, which was only an alternative accommodation, a holding area, as the son had no room of his own. One day, he could no longer find it there, it was wedged between the board of a laundry rack and the back wall, Father finally felt it out and pulled it free too hastily while I was lying on the bed, waiting with my bare bottom, waiting for the caning that'd been announced in no uncertain terms this time, so hastily that it broke off where it had been wedged. Father couldn't get over this loss, it was as if his father, who had punished him with this same cane for years, were dying a second death, tears ran down his jowls, he laid the broken bit onto the pillow and observed it for a long time. Then he grabbed a large coat hanger, like one used for sakkoi, out of the closet and unscrewed the coat hanger's hook. All of his anger for Grandpa's lost cane was contained in this beating; I also mourned it.

What was Father thinking during all of this? Mother got on his nerves, he was simply the corrections officer, the executioner, he who had a license to punish, that which Mother spent so long convincing him was a duty until the punishment was complete. She left the measure up to him, she was never present during the beating. That she was sitting downstairs in the so-called TV room, in agony at the thought of the pain she couldn't help but demand as compensation for the insolences perpetrated by the son in Father's absence worsened the pain, while Father, sweaty and enraged, attended to his executioner's duties upstairs in the son's bedroom. Mother suddenly became the most powerful person around, aloof, invisible, she controlled Father as nobody else could and Father fulfilled her heartfelt desire for punishment, he couldn't, at any rate, give in to a possible spell of sleeplessness. Mother didn't want to give up this lever, the punishment of the children eased the fact of their birth a little bit and was a good way of constantly having Father under her thumb, he who left her, Mother, alone at home instead of taking care of her twenty-four hours per day. The new, lusterless cane made the skin swell up like the old one. The stripes were easy to feel along their entire length. The skin would tear in certain places, which caused excruciating pain. The skin has split, I said to myself, then immediately forbade myself the thought, which made Father's canings almost like torture, as if I had to endure a flogging and be beaten with a scourge. Father was silent during the beating. He was afraid that this cane too would break, which would have meant a loss of authority for him beyond the loss of the family tradition materialized in Grandpa's cane. I noticed over time that he wasn't enjoying it anymore, he was sick of beatings, just as he was sick of placating Mother. He got rid of the cane, then began to hit us in the face with the flat of his hand. Oddly enough, Father grew smaller over time, if he didn't look at me as he slapped me, I was then able to look down on him more and more during the beatings until, one day, he could no longer reach my head. His little arms, their boyish fists the size of greengages, swung funny blows that tickled my ribs. Father must have grown down into the ground.

Did you know that this building doesn't actually have a basement, Mateo asks. So, we're not in a basement? We're on the ground floor, the whole building is built on war rubble. It would have been far too expensive to remove the debris, as the rubble would have to have been transported elsewhere. The foundation of our society is war rubble, war rubble is the basement. Childhood always leads to the basement, a building without a basement is utterly and completely impossible for a child, the basement is a place of salvation, of self-reflection, of beautiful games, of mason jars and potatoes, of things that have been put away and forgotten and that one may take possession of without having to ask. A bunker is the only basement that, rendered in terms of the absolute, can also be found above ground. The designation "potato-beetle bunker" for a building so distinctive because of its black and yellow camouflage that it can be recognized among hundreds of others at any time, is therefore an appropriate formulation that once more does great credit to common parlance. A bunker is also entitled to a caretaker. The caretaker of the potato-beetle bunker, I tell Mateo, walked around the building's perimeter each morning at around seven and collected all the black and yellow stones that had fallen from its façade, after which he stored them in a box in his caretaker's lodge. The box got bigger and bigger in his dreams until, over time, the façade had lost all of its decoration and the space in the lodge was no longer sufficient. The caretaker grew fearful that the building would stand there utterly bare and that the missing stones would be noticed. Nobody would believe him that, for years, he'd been walking around the building's perimeter every morning at around seven and collecting all the black and yellow stones that had fallen from its façade, after which he stored them in a box in his caretaker's lodge, everyone would assume that he'd systematically robbed the façade of its black and yellow stones, after all, they came from Italy and were worth a lot of money. These dreams caused Pütz to grow old and the day eventually came for him to retire. What was to happen to the numerous boxes that stood behind the door of his lodge, covered over in black blankets and filled to the brim with valuable glass? Pütz took them home, after all, their contents would have been lost forever if he hadn't picked them up from around the building every day. But there was no space for the boxes at home, so he decided to decorate the back façade of his house with the little stones. Each day at 7:00 a.m., he attempted to fill in an area the size of a chessboard with stones—and each morning he found the façade completely unchanged. Pütz was still dreaming. After ten days, he returned to his old place of work. The administrative building stood before him in all its brick and glass splendor, but he couldn't make out a single one of its black and yellow stones upon the façade. Had they all vanished? It's probably better if I let it be, he said to himself, then went home. The next morning, he got up at 7:00 a.m., walked around the house, and gathered all the black and yellow stones that'd fallen from the façade into a bucket.

That's not how the story goes at all, Mateo says, the administrative building was renovated more than fifty years later and a search was made for a manufacturer who could replace the large number of missing black and yellow stones that'd been used to decorate the building's façade, for the city coat of arms that could be seen from afar, for example, but nobody was found anywhere in the world except for a company in Italy that claimed to recognize the mosaic stones as an original Italian product, Milanese glass, to be precise, they insisted that there was no one else left who comprehended the craft necessary to make them. The company declared itself ready to fire up their machines and supply copies true to the original for a horrendous sum, an offer that was immediately dismissed. They didn't believe the company, there was nothing about glass from Milan to be found in the construction documents, and thus was the former caretaker approached and asked whether he knew of any previous renovation of the façade or could perhaps provide information about the origin of the stones, after all, he had been the caretaker since the very beginning, nobody could look back on such a long period of service as he could. The caretaker promptly explained that he had collected the black and yellow mosaic stones that had fallen from the façade each day for a period of almost forty years and had kept them to that very day. It then turned out that the stones were sufficient to repair the dilapidated city coat of arms.

Your father would like to reintroduce the traditional Latin Mass. But as he possesses absolutely no competencies in this regard and it is questionable whether the old mass shall ever be reintroduced on a broader scale—that'll only happen when hell freezes over, your father always says—he's come up with a proxy. He's installed a small chapel on the ground floor of the annex to your parents' house. For all who'd care to pray. So far, none have come. That's fine by him, he said to me. He's got plans to accommodate you there. He'd like to make an incluse out of you. He knows that you often dream of your parents' house. Your father once said to me that you would attain your most consummate form in an inclusorium. A large cross hangs in the house chapel. That's reserved for you, your father always says. You can accept it or spend your whole life fleeing from it. If you ask me, Mateo says, there are worse father-son relationships. In your case, your father shows himself to be quite forgiving.

Your father's dedication knows no bounds, Mateo says. All he devotes more time to than his papers are the Almighty and the contemplation of his many relics. Some nuns recently asked for a renewal of the permission to collect seven wheelbarrows of wood from a nearby grove every week, the wood being the sole means of heating the small monastery. One would perhaps think that fulfilling their wish with no fuss would be a matter of course. Your father would only have had to delegate the matter by handing down a positive decision. But what does he do? He personally drives to the discalced to form his own opinion about the amount of wood absolutely necessary to maintain a permanent supply of heat. Ultimately, he declared that the nuns could collect nine wheelbarrows of wood free of charge, but only for the following two years instead of the requested three, after which period the Carmelites would have to inquire once more. Your father's engagement with a small church, in the tower of which owls and falcons had nested, has also become known beyond internal documents. In the village, the church, which is legally seen as only a chapel, is called Eulendom. The building was on the verge of collapse. Father allegedly spent a whole day solidifying his understanding of the condition of the chapel before deciding that its nave had to be restored *immediately*, he declared that he would take the financing into his own hands, which meant that he would make it unmistakably clear to suitable donors that they had to undertake the financing. For me, the Distelrath Chapel, colloquially known as "Owl Cathedral," was always a myth. Father often spoke of it, we never visited it together, the name alone was a book of fairy tales.

Your father once said to me that minor matters quickly add up to a main affair, if you lose control of minor matters, you soon lose control of yourself. The weightiest of matters are a form of recreation for me, your father said, this is where I gather new strength by working my way into my affairs so deeply that I'm able to step outside of myself, the body recuperates, it watches itself while the spirit is able to roam between every imaginable possibility to choose from. There are quite a few who see my father as a small shopkeeper deeply rooted in the provinces, so deeply that cake crumbs on a Sunday tablecloth are bothersome and have to be swept off of the tablecloth with a crumb sweeper, which Father always just calls a table broom, someone get the table broom, he says, the tablecloth needs to be swept off neatly, the sweeper kneeling next to the table and with his eyes at the same level as the tabletop for better control, sweeping from the center of the tablecloth and out toward the edge, grasping at the crumbs of crumbs with renewed momentum, driving the cake crumbs into the dustpan before him until this work is recognized to have become pointless, the tablecloth is pulled off of the table, then, finally, the table set for coffee is cleared early. When, during one of these Sunday-coffee-table-crumb disasters, Father realized that the crumbs could fall from the table and onto the floor and miss the dustpan, he vowed to forego Sunday coffee in the future, a resolution, however, that he never truly put into practice. In truth, these Sunday-coffee maneuvers only served him in the development of even more perfidious management strategies, spending time in the great outdoors also allowed him to refrain from dealing with any family matters, strolls along the Honighecke, in the nearby forest, or along the river, the narrowness of which has alway disturbed him, he believes himself to be underrepresented by it, an Elbe or the Rhine was needed as his motto when he took office, here in nature, his thinking experiences the greatest possible contrast simply because nature is nature, simple minded, naive, left to its own devices, indifferent to all that lies within it, even if whatever's there is destroying it, indifferent, in that sense, to its own death, and that's what makes nature so strong, even if it's almost been wiped out in certain places, it's merely an idea, Father always says, which, in turn, gives me wonderful new ideas, and these ideas have everything to do with their opposite, they have nothing to do with freedom, but with how one can dam this freedom, my father's relationship to nature is not a sentimental one that incites him to set out on sentimental journeys, but a pragmatic one, in such a way that it isn't surprising to see him sitting on a folding chair before nature in photographs, one of those folding chairs from the seventies, it consists of two squares of tubular steel screwed together in the middle and connected in an offset manner, between them stretches a cloth with colorful stripes sewn together upon its upper broadsides. Two hinges are soldered to these, offering support to a backrest that can be folded up. "Folding chair" is a good way of putting it, Father once said when

I accompanied him on one of his observation-tours of nature, he hates to say "camping chair" because he has always hated camping, at the same time, one sees these commercially available chairs, still available for purchase today, mainly on campsites. Nature, Father says, is a sheet of paper. It's always so far away that it can't be torn apart. When the sun is shining, one can see right through nature. As soon as Father sits down in his folding chair before nature, he pulls out a stack of paper from the briefcase he's brought with him, which, armed with a red pencil, he then works through immediately. And one just stands there. One dares not disturb Father, but also knows not where to start with the view of the landscape. Seen from a distance, backward, a man sits in a folding chair before a sun-illuminated landscape, which the eye cannot truly fathom, the man builds the stack of papers, it towers up on his lap, upward sheet by sheet, then to the left, where he erects it once more on the grass after his red pencil has wandered over each and every paper. To his right remains a young man who seems to have been allocated no task other than standing to the man's right, and one can see him in many images from the period. The young man's days—as the images show—are made up of nothing. Father, on the other hand, emerges strengthened from these self-forgotten hours in nature, the papers have been worked through, the red pencil has left behind deep furrows upon them, he shall hand them over to Mateo at the beginning of the week, then Mateo shall immediately endeavor to implement their contents.

Your father takes care of his papers with a monstrous sense of discipline, Mateo says. His discipline is a monster in and of itself. It can, however, sometimes happen that they keep him away from self-imposed religious obligations, Easter is particularly sacred to him, the days of Easter mustn't be disturbed by anything, on Good Friday, your father doesn't say a single word or touch any of his papers, hasn't done so for decades, and if it should come to pass that his councilors, who all know of these habits, nevertheless furnish him with opinions, inquiries, or requests, he feels himself obligated to set certain priorities, meaning the religious obligations take precedence. "I can't look over any of this," your father lets me know and asks me to prepare summaries of the most urgent matters. All of this was written so hastily and illegibly that the deciphering of your father's rage-letters gives me more trouble than the completion of the tasks assigned.

The daily workload, however, hasn't been able to satisfy Mateo for a great while now and, thus privy to my father's administrative matters and practices, he developed his own ambition over time, and who could blame him, the ambition of inventing news or, rather, newsworthy events, he didn't even shy away from inventing both information and personnel, as he was and is of the opinion that Father had long since lost track of the number of staff working at his official place of work, which, without betraying him, opens up the possibility of establishing a parallel system on the other side of reality. Mateo contrasted my father's careless scribbling with a system of scribbles whose messages were meant to be indecipherable. Naturally, your father doesn't want to be outdone and thus does he replicate my messages by moving on to the day's agenda without any further intelligence-service queries. Beaming with pride, Mateo shows me an example of his doodle art:

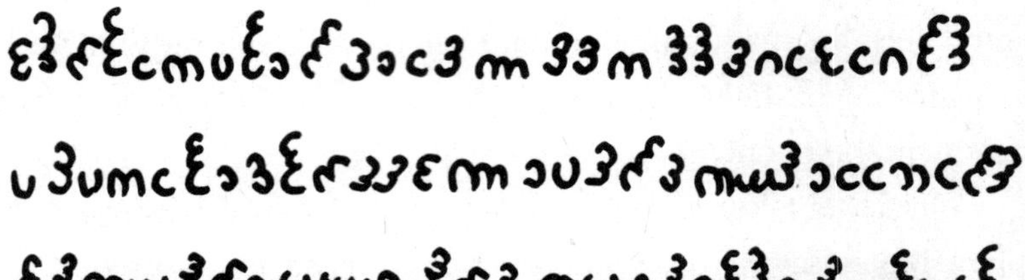

[handwritten encrypted script]

Your father did not, however, remain inactive, he says. One day, he sent him a note-scrap containing a script that was characterized by a sure stroke and, with it, the appearance of a well thought-out system of encryption. To this day, he continues to puzzle over its meaning, just as my father racks his brains over the meaning of Mateo's message.

Perhaps you have a conjecture as to what your father is trying to communicate to me here, Mateo says and shows me the scrap:

Doesn't this script remind you of Urdu or Arabic scripts or did your father imitate medieval scripts, could there be evidence of legible alchemical or astrological influences, Mateo asks. My father has never dealt with alchemy or astrology, I reply. I sent this text to Sukla Hemsch, Mateo says, a leading expert in cryptography and he openly admitted that he couldn't decipher the note. He showed himself to be fascinated by your father's ambition, you father had never hitherto demonstrated himself to be a cryptographer capable of working out and implementing such a system, and Hemsch was utterly convinced of the fact that there was some system at play here. He sent the script to leading international colleagues, but was certain that they wouldn't come to any conclusions worthy of being taken seriously. Mateo says that Hemsch finds the identical or varied repetitions, in which the 8, or, rather, the character similar to it, plays a role, to be of particular interest. There also seem to be basic or elementary signs that are combined with other forms of signs. And thus does one find oneself right in the middle of a whirlpool of decoding mania. Does the script go from left to right or from right to left? It doesn't seem to have been written down spontaneously, it's much too neat for that, Hemsch says. Is the notion that your father invented an entire script system for this note-scrap alone credible? Does he plan to use only this script to correspond in the future?

Those are good signs, I say. Here is my father writing to my mother, full of love. They developed this secret script together so that they could exchange information, even when my father was away for long periods, my mother sends a message, always the same person delivering her messages to my father, my father, on the other hand, posted his messenger at the main entrance, his only responsibility was the exchange of messages, nobody knows him, nobody has ever seen him. And what's written with the script? Mateo asks. What's written is: "My beloved..." At which point Mateo interrupts me, this was none of his business, love isn't part of his duties. He shows me another scrap, beaming with pride:

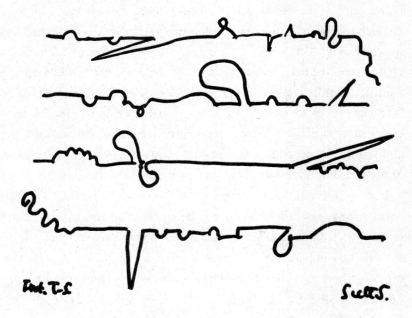

That's an escape plan, I say. In order to master all the papers, my father plans to escape from the alphabet. The individual lines are corridors, with which he undermines letters, they collapse, then can be leveled. And the deflections upward? Mateo asks. Those are bowel protuberances, diverticula, they must be observed at regular intervals, they can sometimes become malignant. "D" thus stood for "Darm," or "bowel." Very likely, I say. That makes no sense to me, Mateo says. I mean, these must be seismographic lines, recordings from a seismograph, they give my father the bullet points outlining a possible uprising against him. Lines give points? Mateo asks. Of course, I say.

Then there's another circle, Mateo says, actually, there are two circles, one can imagine that they can be shifted alongside each other, thus varying their positions and assignments so consistently that one must only copy the inner circle, lay it onto itself, then fix the two circles in the middle onto a piece of cardboard:

That is God, I say. Hardly, Mateo says. This is incomprehensible, I say. It is certainly not the whole of God, or one would lose any and all deference for him. This is 1/24th of God, I say. As is well known, God's name has 72 letters, 24 combinatorial circles facilitate the combination of the 72 letters, I say. But, how can that possibly be, Mateo asks, and why does your father possess 1/24th of the combination of the letters of God's name? Why don't you ask him that yourself?, I reply. You don't understand the situation, Mateo says, it's a question of self-respect not to ask such a question. On the subject of self-respect, I ask Mateo if we might have had the following conversation:

> Maybe I'll ask the other way round.
> What is it that one can no longer find?
> What do you mean *no longer*?
> Yes, if it's no longer there.
> Who's supposed to take something away?
> Which documents?
> In principle, I have nothing to offer.
> Nothing to offer.
> In principle.
> Nothing to offer.
> What do you mean by taking away?
> What am I meant to have taken away?
> You of all people must know this.
> Because it's no longer there.
> Is it no longer there?
> It's no longer there.
> What do you mean—what's no longer to be found there?
> Do you understand me?
> No.

Mateo reflects briefly, but is fairly certain that we did not have this conversation. What do you mean by conversation, I say, that's an interrogation. If you say so, then it is surely true. What is surely true? That it's an interrogation. Mateo asks me how I've come to the conclusion that we somehow led this interrogation. You don't *lead* an interrogation, I say. It says so here, I say and show Mateo the place that he, however, doesn't want to look at. It'd seem you belong to that strange species of person who believes what's written in books, Mateo says. Everything I think and say is readable, whether or not it's in a book, I reply. The Middle Ages at least, that's good, Mateo says, seeming to have lost interest in the conversation, then once again begins to speak about my father.

For a long time, your father has thought about how he could bring an end to the brutalization of his eating habits, which have allegedly caused him great trouble with his digestive organs. Gout also plagues him. The new food regime to be striven for should of course take into account the hierarchies practiced daily, which is how your father, who is a studied theologian with an appreciation for divine representation on earth, has come to the idea of reintroducing an eating ceremony to be conducted in his sphere of activity according to traditional courtly rituals. These hierarchies find their expression by way of the placement of guests according to aspects of centrality and decentrality, right and left are as important to consider as front and back, proximity and distance, depending on their rank, employees have to take certain bodily postures and carry out honorary gestures. These gestures include, for example, entering the hall through a certain door, approaching your father with inclined head, bowing and scraping, not directly entering into his field of vision, and to execute these movements backward at a distance of precisely three meters from your father, without having taken a seat at the table, one instead disappears through the door through which one has come in. However, for this so-called period of practical distancing, training is necessary, if a tape measure, which is specifically employed for this purpose, measures a distance of more or less than three meters, this has grave consequences depending on the scale of the deviation. Door openers, shoe cleaners, floor polishers, ushers, as well as people who, by virtue of their office, are more likely to be fixated on the ground view, also belong to these so-called

Appearers and Disappearers. Then there are the phantoms for whom a place at the table is reserved and remains vacant. Let us also not forget the ceiling gazers who approach your father with a rigid gaze trained upon the ceiling without, indeed, bringing him into it, they eat in a private room adjacent to the grand hall. What could be interpreted as snootiness on the part of these employees is what precludes your father from remembering their faces, which would represent a consistent additional workload, these are the so-called transient employees, who only remain in the administrative building for a short period of time with fixed-term contracts. As he himself is entirely integrated into his daily routine, one directed by files, he wishes to preserve his ability to participate in this ceremony—all this according to Mateo. He is present in his absence due to the seating arrangement that runs past him, but, in such a situation, it is certain to lack the center that is him.

Doors open up where there were none before. "Mihi dabas multas portas." Some men dressed in redblackyellow come in, they've managed to occupy the room in just a short time. As soon as they've taken their positions, the colors of their robes change. Red, green, and violet now predominate. That's your father's chamberlain, Mateo says and points to a man who is in the process of being crushed flat by the burden of his office. Your father chose him because his back is crooked and he thus looks down at the ground at all times. I appreciate that posture, a competent servant, your father said and hired him on the spot. Actually, he's supposed to be guarding your father, but how is he meant to do that if he can't look straight ahead. Your father immediately recognized that everyone around him did exactly as the bent one did, the mere sight of him ensured a return to courtly times. It is perhaps not uninteresting to know that your father has never entered this man's gaze and your father has also never shown himself in the vicinity of this man, people don't know this, of course, and thus do they think that your father is in the vicinity as soon as they see his chamberlain. The movement sequences of all employees are measured so precisely that they describe geometric figures, the execution of which doesn't overlap. The freedom of others, which is nothing but another element of the daily life of being an employee, is in this way preserved. That's what I call the ideal iteration of a fine procession, Mateo says. What the servants execute here is nothing less than a well-performed dance of segmentation, dishing-out, and serving composed by your father from many complicated figures, the movements crisscross in the most intricate of ways, yet one, as you can see, makes a space when the other comes, the other who, in coming, again makes another space—and so on. And here is the plan according to which the vast troop of servants must move:

There's barely been any time to study the plan more exhaustively when five exorbitantly dressed men draw everyone's attention. Alba with cincture and stole. And the other two? I ask. That's what the men's garments are called, the robe, the girdle that fastens it, and a kind of shawl. The stole is violet. Do you know what that means, Mateo asks. I don't know, I reply. Your confession is imminent, you are to deliver it unto your father. Some of the men wear maniples over their left forearms. If you pass it on, cover the hand with the maniple. Are those the executioners who are cloaking their hands in innocence? I ask Mateo. A fine joke, he replies, they are the medium; one doesn't see the hand that is passed on. Because it's not worthy? The maniple replaced the snuff-and-sweat cloth, which was also used for cleanliness, comparable to those serviettes that innkeepers pleated round their sleeves when serving. Your father has always regretted that this has as good as disappeared from the liturgy. The ordinary linen snuff-or-sweat cloth that sacristans wore tossed over their left sleeves, so light and inconspicuous that it was called "woven wind," has gradually become a piece of silk jewelry that forfeited its pure purpose, but gained an incomparable symbolic value. The maniple became a portable symbol of suffering and mourning, and, as he put it on, the priest spoke these words: "Merear, Domine, portare manipulum fletus et doloris, ut cum exultatione recipiam mercedem laboris."

Your father's decrees, which might just be able to restore the institution of the court as court ordinances, do not speak of "royal majesty" in vain, they do not merely determine what is to be done, but also how individual actions are to be carried out. In addition to the processes, their sequence, the positions from which they originate, and the attitudes to be taken are also determined.

For instance, the Botellerius or Subbotellerius himself ought to taste or have tasted the bread and wine and other dishes that reach your father's table from the former's area of responsibility, which implicates the chamberlain—among others. Only then shall the food be served. It might then be that one of those present is of the opinion that a poisoned foodstuff might well only be poisoned at a certain point, whereas the majority of the remainder remains untouched, and perhaps the taster knows this precise point and shall thus never have to savor it. It must be said that your father has also made provisions here: the food is always stirred once more before the Botellerius tastes it. If this is impossible due to the consistency of the food or its particular aesthetic arrangement, then your father or his representative can select the portion to be tasted. As an additional safeguard against a fraudulent taster, your father selects an employee who is to designate a second spot before each meal. As far as the issue of slow-acting poison is concerned: All dishes must be prepared one day in advance so that the Botellerius may accordingly have tasted them roughly a day and a night before the meal in my presence, which is then repeated in the presence of your father or, otherwise, his representative. Excluded from this are dishes that can only be freshly prepared, though this is limited to a small selection, as fresh preparation on the spot takes up a great deal more time than the prompt consumption of ready-to-eat foods, and the impatience of hungry people or those who imagine that they are hungry out of boredom shall not be unknown to you. As such, the weak point in this construction is me. And you won't believe all that I've been accused of doing—and not just in this context. For example, I am said to have killed the personal secretary of your father's half-brother, but have I not been mistaken for your father's other secretary (see Lady Meere,* page 147 and the following)?

I know nothing at all about a half-brother of my father's, but do know of a great many siblings. This Mateo is a false cur.

Your father has drawn up this ordinance about food in the most beautiful Latin. It deserves to be partially quoted:

"Etiam volumus quod nostro Botellerio sive subbotellerio, [prius autem degustari eos faciat a Botellerio.] de pane&vino&aliis quæ in nostram mensam ex suo officio ministrandi causa pro nobis, de illis, antequam nobis in mensam vel alias ministrentur, curet dare gustum, & ipsemet degustet; pari modo & Camerlengo vel Scutifero-cameræ, si ibi præsens fuerit loco Camerlengi, det postea ad degustandum. Habeat etiam nobis comedentibus per palatium incedere, & providere ut sit victualium nec non aliarum rerum exuberantia, conveniens Regiæ majestati; [Idem virgam ferat] & ut ordo debitus in palatio circa omnia observetur: & si defectum videat quoquo modo, deficientes corripiat, modis congruis observatis. Prædictus vero Major-domus serviens

---

* Lady Seas.

vir- gam deferat, tamquam signum indicans præcipiendi auctoritatem, [signum potestatis,] serviendi exercitio congruentem. Per ipsum insuper nobis administretur panis & alia cibaria mensæ, ad officium Apothecarii vel Fructerii pertinentia, si aliquo casu ultra mensam comedere nos contingat."

Yes, punishment is a component of the meal, for there can only be food if order reigns and the majordomo is to take care of this. Under no circumstances can the order be as it is in Germany's capital, your father has often emphasized. There's a state authority there, he says, that prides itself on its modernity, but, in fact, hopelessly lags behind the modern times. Here, an authority styles itself as an institution of order, an institution one must teach how to behave properly. The state authority is no longer the manservant of its own house. Health and social affairs are first-order issues of regulatory politics because, without health and a functioning social structure, there is no social market economy. According to your father, a lack of orientation in regulatory policies involving order will be appreciated by more than a few who expect advantages as a result of potential competitors being sidelined for health reasons or as the result of total neglect, ultimately, however, such thinking leads only to the struggle of none against none. The authority subjects the very areas for which it is responsible to severe scrutiny, ruining the health of the people for which it is responsible and bringing the social fabric right to the edge of load-bearing capacity. Petrified queues every day, they say, the entire place is overcrowded, tents had to be erected so that people didn't freeze to death standing on their feet in the open air, but, even in the tents, it's bitterly cold, icicles forming at their entrances in the shortest of possible times, people who've fled from their homeland, shot to bits, fled to the Prussian capital to freeze to death there, hunger and thirst urging on their freezing-death, from one day to the next, the state authority is increasingly unable to hand over the money for self-sufficiency, the so-called basic-security benefits, the comprehensive care provided for by the law for the three months after registration, with which they would have to buy their own foodstuffs from now on. One has only to look at the building containing this authority, it objectively resembles a medieval tower more than a house of reliability and certainty in planning, as soon as people are locked up in it, they're immediately forgotten, which is particularly true of the employees. The word "working conditions" is redefined here. The reigning conditions impede work. Too few people are left to take care of everything. This, he says, leads to a complete standstill of processes, but incomplete work is a toxic element, the body can no longer get rid of the pollutants and is poisoned. I am glad, your father says, and the only solution is to involve the tower's employees in decisions and possible reforms, which he who would like to show and live out the medieval as the truly modern cannot imagine even in the very slightest, he would prefer to remain invisible, whereas the *modern moderns* take their likeness to be the thing itself and expose it in all media, your father says, until the people also take the likeness to be the thing itself, judging it merely on the basis of sympathy or antipathy. Mateo continues that the state authority of the Prussian capital represents the old Europe that disappeared overnight, now the authority is confronted with a new Europe, a Europe of instability that doesn't know whether it should first look right or left, therefore, it would require twice as many employees in this so-called executive position in order to be able to simultaneously look left and right, but, as it stands, most people have to be sent home with a new appointment without having achieved anything, to a home that no longer exists where they face the same procedure. What is the employees' duty other than serving out the hours, during which they do nothing but send off cases? your father would like to know. Files have disappeared from this authority and can no longer be found, the personnel, however, must search for these files every day, in addition to the time-consuming process of sending people away, the accumulated overtime no longer leaves any room free in the tower, the overtime is overflowing, people queuing outside of the building and waiting to death. The always witty common parlance has pithily renamed this authority EGALSO, sounding both like the name of a social-welfare office and a German expression meaning something like "whatever." And its boss, the dancing Allfernarzt*? He's been let go. What's changed since then? Nothing. What can be learned from all this? your father always wishes to find out from me. Now, tell me, he keeps asking me, what can we learn from this?

In serving the dishes, scarcity is to be avoided as much as excess. If the dishes are diversified, the mind feels itself to be stimulated. The chamberlain—and your father attaches particular importance to this—should always be in his vicinity, move out ahead of him, avert danger, and bring your father water should he want to wash the feet of the poor. Poverty is on the rise in the city. Your father dreams of washing the feet of the entire city. "Now, you don't know what I'm doing, but, later, you shall understand," your father wishes to say to the residents. And he also wishes to say to them: "The water is the word." They're not going to understand that, your father opines, but one day they shall. Your father's life is one of serving-devotion to the city, he is its master and bondsman in equal measure.

Anyone who speaks here and in that which follows of an overly precise definition of this part of the administrative regulations concerning the table ceremony and is subject to the error that your father is forced to act thusly because of a time of need and is attempting to compensate for an imminent or actual loss of power, doesn't understand your father at all well, which is to say, not at all. The opposite is the case, it is not a question of the anxious insistence on representation when decline is likely, there is no power vacuum to be filled, on the contrary, your father is accomplishing one of the most astounding cultural achievements of our time, to the heights of which no novel and

---

* Allafar Doctor.

no painting—and there is no distinction between the two—can reach. Even if it is sui generis, it shall have a decisive influence on later times, for which it will be the reflection on the ordo of the past that ends up establishing the foremost notion of order as such.

Mateo interrupts his explanations, of which I'm beginning to grow tired, and comments on all further meal preparations:

The prefect of the palace enters, followed by the head cook who is in charge of the sugar and the honey as well as other seasonings and has to check all of the other dishes. Hot on their heels, always a bit suspicious that the head cook might do him an injustice while inspecting the foodstuffs delivered by him, comes the chief steward responsible for the catering and now you see the carver, the braggart over whom 'twould be mete to linger for a moment. He has the duty of artfully cutting meat and poultry into portions and, if no one else is assigned this duty, of distributing it to the guests so that they can then divide it into bite-sized bits with their own knives. More on the guests' knives later. Your father likes to call his braggart, "my Ripa," which belies great trust, as "Ripa" means "shore." Some believe this to be a nickname, others are convinced that it's the product of a distortion and that his actual name is "Pari," so not "shore," but "equal." If your father calls out his name, Ripa doesn't even have to answer, the invocation is already its own rejoinder, Ripa is thus always to be relied on. Ordinary servants are totally fine with the thesis of distortion, as Pari is, of course, completely equal to them. This Ripa is not only a grandmaster of the carving knife, his carving duties leave him plenty of time and leisure to carve totally different things and thus has he composed a book of enigmatic pictures or, rather, a picture-puzzle book with allegories that have been handed down, but also partially invented by him. This encyclopedia carves—dissects—God's revealed world into notional images from A to Z by providing the viewer with visual concepts of images and thus does the viewer's gaze oscillate between the image composing the riddle and the explanatory text until the notion presented can no longer be thought of without the image. Then the man possesses at least a reflection of the mightiness of the hidden, invisible God who shines in such a bright light that the unmediated sight of this light would kill or at least blind in such a way that God could never be seen as complicated. How, then, should he be represented? Yes, no differently than in adumbrated images that are no image of God, but represent his work. The servants come in with the tables now, the royal chandler responsible for the lights kisses the candlesticks he's brought in and puts them in their places, as your father's regulations require, the table-bearers leave the room and make space for the table servers, doing so in such a way that there is enough distance between them and between the chairs that have just been placed around the table for the personnel now serving the dishes.

Your father considered once more giving expression to the hierarchical structure of administration, as in the late medieval period, by staggering the amount of food at the table so that the hierarchies be reflected in its distribution. The stomach that each man carries before him could thus be read as a gauge of rank. Then, however, he decided on a spatial reflection of the hierarchy, as you shall soon see. He has uniformly determined the sharpness of the knives and what can be regarded as utensils for eating, which is to say: not only cutlery, but also plates, cups, glasses, and napkins. First, the napkin is handed over, it is with this that the eaters are to accept the bread given to them and wipe their mouths after the eating; blowing one's nose therein is frowned upon, as nothing else should be wiped but the mouth. The knives' degree of sharpness caused your father quite a headache, as the tidings of exceedingly sharp knives could contribute to or even provoke smoldering squabbles, which would then have to be settled by way of the blade. The decision that your father made is a testament to his great wisdom. The degree of sharpness of the knife depends on the degree of trust that your father has in the particular employee. Even a blunt knife cuts through. The employee with the sharpest knife is beyond any and all reproach. The particular form of table-ordering worked out by your father serves him well and is a circumstance he attaches great importance to—the social disciplining of those who rank among his employees. As far as the hierarchical order itself is concerned, it is laid out as follows: The holders of the highest administrative offices are followed by the privy councilors, chamber councilors, court councilors and chamberlains, then the cupbearers and the carvers who carve and present the food at the table, only then come the chief table overseer, who holds the office of steward, the secretaries, and others. I, Mateo, am merely your father's writing-implement-and-medium procurer, as you yourself wrote; the trust that your father places in me can only be measured by he who knows the reason for the sharpest knife at the table, my knife is even sharper than your father's. To a certain extent, the knife-sharpness order undermines the hierarchical order. Once, a great argument broke out amongst the dignitaries when one of them complained of his blunt knife, which corresponded not at all to his unpaid office and his merit. Straightaway, the ladies and gentlemen began to compare their knives, they under-trumped each other quite directly, as it wasn't the sharpness of the knives that was the trump card, but their bluntness. When the finger test was no longer sufficient, they began to cut each other's arms and, once that no longer seemed conclusive to them either, they attacked and attempted to stab one another. After they had stood there motionless for a few moments with knives in hand, those who had stood were also joined by servants who did not belong to this circle at all, everyone feared being attacked first, but no one knew how to handle the knife other than for cutting meat, they sat down again without achieving anything more than immediately rising back up, after all, the matter hadn't yet been settled. This repeated itself a few times. Those who rose became fewer and fewer, then, at last, the matter seemed settled. Your father had the spectacle recounted to him, he wasn't present at the meal as per usual, it is said that he heard of the knife scandal with a smile, muttered something about "stupid kids," and even somewhat regretted that no bloodshed had come to pass. However, the matter could not remain entirely without consequences and thus did your father decide to once more invite those same dignitaries until each of them had been the second taster and, on another occasion, had selected the spot to be tasted from.

At this point, the keeper of the silver strides in, Mateo says. The silverware is always to be handed to him against its receipt. He wears no head covering and no shoes while on duty. Thus did your father determine. The keeper of the silver has a cloth of pure white, perpetually ironed, bound around his left arm and, without fail, above the elbow, as you can see on this one here. Only thus does he have the freedom of movement necessary for his service. The other end of the cloth is thrown over his right shoulder, which confers the necessary special touch upon his appearance. With his left hand, he presents your father with small tasting bowls, the contents of which, as with that of all the other dishes placed onto the sideboard, are tasted beforehand and, indeed, in the presence of the assembled round table. He can use the cloth to immediately remove any impurities that come into being. The keeper of the silver is also responsible for the cleaning of the dishes, which he has to supervise.

In addition to the city coat of arms and the chain of office with a miniature of the city coat of arms, there is also a city goblet that only your father is qualified to drink from. The city goblet is carried in by the prefect of the palace together with a table servant appointed by him as soon as your father has taken his place. For taking his place, your father has his own chair pusher, who pushes his chair carefully beneath his buttocks. Drinks are poured for your father by a cupbearer who serves only him. When your father desires to drink, his cupbearer hands the table servant a tasting goblet, as has just now come to pass, he takes the lid off of the city goblet and puts one knee down onto the floor, your father insists that it be the right knee. Once your father has drunk, as has just come to pass, he takes back the tasting goblet and puts it back onto the sideboard together with the city goblet until your father once more desires to drink. It is important that the city goblet stand between two silver candlesticks with burning candles, as it is a symbol of the administrative building and, thus, of the city, which, apart from its use as a drinking vessel, is only permitted to be used in symbolic fashion. As you can see, the goblet shines forth with true resplendence from between the silver candlesticks, as if it were a crown jewel or the insignia of the royal house. Three gentlemen still deserve special attention: the ceremonial mace bearer, the overseer, and the aforementioned chief steward. If the occupation of the last of these is self-explanatory from his designation, it is because, together with the majordomo, he must always stock the larder with any possible purchases, in addition to which he must feed at least some portion of the personnel and take care of the poor, most particularly, it is his inordinately long title ("Oberspeisekammerherr") that convinces your father of this gentleman's importance, whereas the ceremonial mace bearer has a merely representative function, in that he bestows a solemn note upon the discipline-instilling order of gathering together to share a meal, for, in sooth, his duty consists only in walking into the kitchen in front of the prefect of the palace, then striding back over to the sideboard, also carrying the city's ceremonial mace upon his shoulders, a duty that he must also fulfill on other occasions, if, for example, your father is to receive important visitors from out of town. The overseer, on the other hand, primarily monitors and checks the purchases destined for the larder, but is also responsible for your father's official car. As you can see, the table that the table servers have brought in is exceptionally long. There can hardly be as many officials of rank in this administrative building as there are seated at this table. Missing places are usually filled with the aforementioned dignitaries. If, to be perfectly frank, your father usually stays well away from the meal ceremony he himself introduced based on the medieval model, he did not stay away this time. If—here, please—you'd like to take a closer look, he is sitting at the very top, at the right end of the never-ending table, whereas all the other places are meant to remain empty. I don't see my father. The other places are all occupied—all except for one.

Your father would like for you to take a seat at the other end of the table, not directly across from him, but, from his point of view, please take a chair further to the right so that he can keep you in his sights, but you can't see him until you turn your head to the left in his direction, which, in view of the feeling of being constantly observed by him, you almost certainly won't do or, at most, will only do if he expressly asks you to.

The scribe of the chamber must keep records of all events. In a certain way, you are the scribe of the chamber of the scribe of the chamber. You are keeping a book of all the events of the chamber, in which you are to be found without you being your father's servant and thus do you also keep a book of the record keeping scribe of the chamber. This may bore you, just as you are bored by my exegeses, and you have already emphasized in your book that I bore you, but it is not your predilections and distastes that determine what is to be read in your book, it is the occurrences, the events themselves, which, betiding and coming to pass, find their way unmediatedly into your beautiful book, of which you have no idea whether or not it exists.

Your book now contains a roughly three-page description of the gadgetry of the courtly ceremony reintroduced by your father and you shall no doubt wonder what goal this has. Your father has also taken a seat in your book—this description represents that. If you have hitherto assumed yourself to be the table-lord of your book, rest assured that your father is the table-lord of the book and you are merely sitting at the other end of the table with your face turned away, the scribe of the chamber of your father's scribe of the chamber. Incidentally, gifts are frowned upon. The rank order of employees could be severely disrupted or even made unclear by undue or unduly gifts. As you have already established, your father cannot be corrupted.

I now ask you to take a seat. I sit down. Through a toad-studded archway strides an unsightly figure, more beast than man, with red-hot eyes and a barred blast furnace with glowing coals for a belly, which, with its zippered black robe, makes it appear to be the triangular eye of God. It wears a green turban upon its head, from which green cloths, decorated with pearls upon their upper thirds, flow to the right and to the left. The hell-fire in its belly beats through its head. Its maw is open wide, displaying four pointed canines before its fire-flaming gullet. As master of ceremonies, it carries a fourfold scythe, with which it shall twist the word in my mouth four times over. The figure bangs its scythe loudly against the ground. This knocking briefly summons a few gentlemen I recognize as members of the Frightbearing Society. The figure announces something, the Society rises, then the Society fades away once more.

To the left of the figure, the chief of minutes, equipped with a red tin pot upon his head and a white-edged pince-nez, immediately skims the program, which he, for whom these facts are an everyday matter, recites at such breakneck speed that no time remains for me to repeat it.

Framed by a banquet, the program provides for a short trial, the structure of which follows stringent rules and the result of which is fixed from the outset. The guilt of the delinquent is proven by the fact that the trial is taking place. No hearing for the delinquent is planned. The dignitaries and the employer are entitled to the fine entertainment that awaits them. Thus is it not the delinquent's death, which is fixed beyond doubt, that would be regrettable, but the staging itself that could arouse the displeasure of those present. So as to avoid such unpleasantness, the individual acts are repeatedly rehearsed, which contradicts the fact that the trial's code of procedure is a mirror image of the divine order, for God himself never rehearsed, but only withdrew a little, for there can be no creation without self-withdrawal.

Maybe I'll ask the other way round, my father takes the floor as a report is being delivered to him. I am silent, my plate remains empty. What is it that one can no longer find? he asks. What do you mean *no longer*? I reply and lose a limb with each word that comes out of my mouth. "Yes, if it's no longer there." "Who's supposed to take something away?" Father is silent, he's having a tough time with the consumption of my foot. "Which documents?" Father is silent. "In principle, I have nothing to offer." "Nothing to offer." "In principle." "Nothing to offer. What do you mean by taking away?" "What am I meant to have taken away?" "You of all people should know." I am silent. "Because it's no longer there." "It's no longer there?" "It's no longer there."

"What do you mean—what's no longer to be found there?" "Do you understand me?" "No." During such interrogations, it's really of no importance who asks and who answers and what is asked and what is answered. That my father is using the formal "Sie" with me doesn't surprise me as much as it frightens me. If one moves from "Du" to "Sie," death is imminent. "Sie" is the delinquent's blindfold.

The way I see it, my father says, he's no longer any sort of blank slate. Just so, the chief of the minutes affirms. The accused is sufficiently on record, he is a recidivist, a repeat offender. Recidivism is what first of all makes him identifiable. Previously, he was somebody, now he is that very same person. He has an identity now. He can no longer be replaced, he has things in common with himself, when he's absent, one can point him out by pointing at this book and that one. With these lines here, which belong to the words arranged into sentences, which is to say, the words that I am currently speaking, which also include the passage, "the words that I am currently speaking" like all the others that I am speaking, there's no room for error, he's done it again, and thus is the first time no coincidence. Your son is no longer your son, he, Nobody, is the book, in which we currently are.

Of what has he made himself guilty? my father would like to know.

Those who know me know that my calling is that of an anti-Philobiblon, formerly called a firefighter, a certain Guy Montag speaks up. Nobody knows him. Nobody is disturbed that he is allowed to speak undisturbed, as he wasn't present here before. I didn't summon the spirits, but I'll have to get used to them. My father isn't at all impressed by all of this. He has seen many who, though they're unbidden, simply stand up and begin to babble. I shall remain calm, my father knows my weaknesses. If, for example, I notice a spot on my shirt that wouldn't otherwise bother me much at all, a spot I would typically skate over, wasting no time, now, on the contrary, I attempt to dispose of it with spit, cover it with my sleeve, I must look at it constantly, scrape perpetually over the spot with my fingernail, even if it's not a raised one, for my father knows that it's easy for him to play with me, he could have me rejoining the Catholic Church in no time at all. Montag still has his conversion to look forward to, at most, he's the Montag from page 23, he must chase after every alarm, quickly set the fire, burn everything, report back, and be ready for the next alarm, he hasn't yet hidden the book under his pillow, but it's of course already at work within him, contemplation is, otherwise, it wouldn't be remotely worth telling, after all, Montag has likely written himself, script is a different kind of fire, Montag already knows this on the inside, something flickers in his gaze, if he continues on like this, he'll have to burn himself. "Nobody, your son, reads books, but he doesn't just read them, he also writes them, the problem is that he's writing a book commissioned by the Frightbearing Society, whereas books must be burnt, burn the book, then burn also the ashes, that is our motto, the only book allowed to exist is the service regulations of a fire brigade that Benjamin Franklin personally founded in 1790 and it's still valid today and it's not a book either, it's simply regulations." Montag pulls out a flamethrower, says, "if you don't mind me," then wants to set fire to this. Who's that? my father asks, visibly perplexed. Montag might not have been summoned as a witness after all, which would mean that this is a case of self-empowerment, I think. Montag, Mateo says. Monday? my father says, I didn't ask when, but who. My father doesn't known him, even though he's the honorary chairman of the fire brigade. With a short motion of his hand, a gesture utterly unique in the world, thus casting aside, pruning, erasing, a gesture that is his whole biography, my father confiscates the job and Montag has vanished.

You see, your son has bizarre fantasies, says Mateo. So, it was Mateo, I could never have guessed that he'd stab me in the back like this. He's the one who was telling me everything, not me to him. Those are, after all, his thoughts, not mine. Fantasies? my father asks. When it comes to fantasies, my father is always correct. Once, he told me that if you have fantasies like this, it's possible that you need help, and thus did he appeal to the school psychology services, however, they couldn't discover any fantasies, there are all sorts of things in your son's head, sometimes some spark won't fire, sometimes one starts a great fire, one spot is entirely empty, then there's too much there in the back for such a small space, but, as for fantasies, absolutely zilch, stated the man from the school psychology services, then said goodbye again. I told you so, my father said, not even fantasies.

"Quod non est in actis non est in mundo: What isn't to be found in the files, isn't to be found in the world. I'm citing the interrogation protocol," the chief of the minutes says: "Or is that deceptive?" "Don't take it personally!" "I don't take it personally." "I take it exceedingly personally." "Reasonable." "Unreasonable." "Reasonably unreasonable." "You are vanishing forevermore." "To what extent you are ready to contribute to the establishment of truth." "Your mouth's pretty dry—or am I deceived?" "The mouth is a sprout." "You better not test us." "Yes, you're weeping." "Consciousness and smiling go together." "Who said that?" "Jürgen Fuchs." "Consciousness and laughing go together." "Conscious laughter is important." "Laugh, then!" "The situation is in need of improvement." "Improved in any case." "In need of improvement." "It's forbidden to cover your hands and face." "You worm, you dunce, you deadbeat." "Indispensable and eliminated." "No longer indispensable, as I understand it." "Authority was exerted from top to bottom." "Into the milieu and out the milieu's other end once more so as to fall back into the milieu's other end once more and to fall out of the milieu into which it's fallen once more more having fallen out to fall in once more." "It's all or nothing, on a small scale, on the whole, on the whole small scale, all or nothing. There's nothing small that isn't all or nothing." "All that which is small is all or nothing, all all or nothing, all is above all always looking away is looking at everything elsewhere, where everything everywhere has already fallen in and fallen out it goes to the other end once more out of the milieu into the milieu out of the fallen-into fallen-into-fallen-out-of it is into the milieu gone out of the milieu into into gone into outofinto out of fallen into fallen out of to in into the milieu into and around." "It's all or nothing, on a small scale, on the whole, on the whole small scale, all or nothing. There's nothing small, nothing smaller, that isn't all or nothing. All that which is small isn't so small that it isn't already big it can't be overlooked the being-overlooked that is somewhere over there." "And that's that." "It's all or nothing, on the whole, on the whole whole, on the whole whole whole, in the whole of the whole, which is wholer than all that which is small taken together, that nothing exists as the small, for it is already so enormous that an uttered ICANTSEEIT and that is in fact *that*!" This is a truth agency, my father says. I'm reading something else here, my father says, leafing through the files. My father has a curious head. Sometimes, he is Bismarck and, at others, his own father, in whom I can recognize myself. If, at one moment, his head resembles the destroyed town of Jülich, then, the next moment, I see him as a rebuilt Düren, in which destruction is of greater beauty than rebuilding. The teaching says that this is violence. I, who have been taught, say that I have not yet been instructed in the slightest. The minutes of the interrogation can contain nothing but ashes. And yet, should my father find me guilty, I shall be guilty of telling him that I am guilty. He is my father. I am not him, much as I wish that I were. If he says that I am guilty and I say that I am guilty, then I shall finally be like him. And I know that, in confessing my guilt at this precise moment, the *like him* fades away. There is clear evidence for the fact that your son is fomenting a conspiracy, says Mateo, whom my father always only addresses as Antonio or Peter Ozianon. Just take a look here, he says, and lays a book before my father. This is the book in which your son writes uninterruptedly, he's doing so even now. He has bizarre fantasies. He lies left, right, and center of the page. But what does your son write? One is hardly able to understand it. So, can a lie hardly be understood? That is an impertinence twice over, you see: To be found guilty of a lie that nobody understands. But your son knows how to put that to good use and there is certainly an art to writing a printed book in unmediated fashion, especially when its most important page has been so crammed with words that it looks like printer's ink has been poured over it. You should ask your lordly son to reveal the mystery of this page:

"What do you mean by 'written'?" Father asks. Barely has he said "written" when he falls into a state of stupor. By the time he comes to his senses, I must have remembered where I've seen this page before. Then I see that my father is slowly being drawn into the black page until he has entirely vanished into it. Antonio or Peter Ozianon takes the book lying on the table before my father's empty chair and turns the open page. Ach, poor father! I exhale as the front side of the page is repeated on its back. Father has disappeared into the black. You see, that's what I mean, Antonio or Peter Ozianon says, your son is a plotter. I'm convinced that the only way I can save Father is by naming the true creator of the black page. That's not mine, I'd really like to say to him, it was created by . . . But his name won't come to me. Antonio or Peter Ozianon likely knows that it's not mine, but could he have guessed that Father would disappear into it? As a result of constantly flipping back and forth, he's broken out into a sweat and has now begun to use to pages as a sheet-fan, which brings him to the edge of exhaustion, as he can't possibly turn the page quickly enough that the sweat produced as a result of the rabid turning of pages would simultaneously be cooled by the fanned air, i.e. that the sweat would be compensated for by the evaporating effect of the cooling. Or have I misunderstood something here? Somebody asks me, "Does satyr's tangled matter remind you of precision?" Another voice says, "Read Cetera." Who is Cetera? Tangled matter. Never heard that. I should read Cetera, I say to Antonio or Peter Ozianon who instantaneously quits it with the fan-like turning of the black page. Who says that? he asks. Somebody said that. Here, nobody said anything, Antonio or Peter Ozianon said. Somebody said, "Read Cetera," I said. I also heard that, says Antonio or Peter Ozianon, but only because you said it to me. We're not making any progress like this, I'd like to reply, but then he interrupts me: Take a look, something's happening there. We bend down toward the book and bump heads. The front blackpage is thinning:

I remember rainy days and long walks with my father through the forest. It's dark. You can't see your hand right in front of your face, Father said. The forest hid itself in itself. No clearing was visible. The forest doesn't lower its guard, my father said. We made only very hesitant progress, with each step, the feet felt roots crossing over the path, once, Father stumbled and fell down an embankment, it smelled of lovage and the ground was all churned up, wild boars, Father said, stood up, then followed the path, his steps once more becoming sure of themselves, yessir, this had been the right path right from the beginning. Thus did he stride forth like a Prussian officer, no longer looking to the right, no longer looking to the left, as if this were the most natural form of locomotion, his head always facing forward, his chin raised, after this brief irritation, nothing more was able to dissuade him from his persuasion that he was on the right path. But I had seen through Father and this made me sad. He was just as lost as I was, the fact that he was determined to show the world to me notwithstanding. Ever since then, I've loved wrong turns, side paths, detours, crawling through the undergrowth, as these things represent the real challenge, the gaze always moves downward, everything seems stable on the outside, but the impression of stability results from permanent change, which comes to pass so quickly that the human eye doesn't perceive it when one element replaces another by taking its place, strictly speaking, we have only the spatial coordinates that remain identical, man and beast are transitory, man can take on any form and any figure, the surface is merely a protective skin of the absent, which we continuously breathe and discuss. If we didn't do this, we'd be seized by sheer terror.

  The thinned patches prove it, Antonio or Peter Ozianon says, you have written a very old book, he turns his gaze away, puts his head right up close to the book, so close that the tip of his nose makes contact with the paper, he observes the page from this perspective, snuffling at the square like a sniffer dog, thinned patches everywhere, he says, thinned at points, he leaps up, spins around once in a circle, takes up the sniffing position once more, then straightens up and says: My retina is detaching. Whereas I, Nobody, suspect I recognize the sheet of the Holy Sepulcher in this thinned weave. A second look reveals a naked woman's body. Then I see my father's visage very clearly, he is clearing a path through the tangled matter, here, don't you see, now, you yourself are saying "tangled matter," he's cleaning the earth, grass, and leaves from his trousers, his shirt is torn, he realizes with total certainty that he's searching for his glasses, he can't find them anywhere, I see them, they're lying at the foot of a small mound with open temples, he strides over to them now, but doesn't find them, he runs round in a circle, he spreads his arms, then drops them once more, he must have given up the glasses entirely, strangely enough, he doesn't seem to miss me, hold on though, he's calling out to me, I can somehow read my name upon his lips, I'm here, I call out, my father doesn't hear or see me, then he disappears from view.

Wherefore did he alternately dub you Antonio and Peter Ozianon? I ask Mateo. Apparently, your father was bewildered, the name Mateo trips not so easily off of the tongue, thus did he dub me Antonio and Peter Ozianon, says Antonio or Peter Ozianon. But who is Antonio or Peter Ozianon? For as long as this isn't resolved shall I call him Antonio Atome. I know that Atome is reading along, he is, after all, the author of these lines. It would be best if we slammed the book shut, he says, all it does is give us capricious thoughts. The capricious thoughts are that which bring me onto the right path, I say and slam the book shut once more, but, unfortunately, in the wrong place, which my gaze can only catch incompetent sight of: "Li\^lAS.AAAlt.Il, In that spacious hall, a coalition of the gown, from all the bars of it, driving a damn'd, dirty, vexatious cause before them, with all their might and main, the wrong way!——kkcking it out of the great doors, instead off im>——and with suvh^füry in their looks, and such a degree of inveteracy in their manner of kicking it, as if the laws had been originally made for the peace and preservation of mankind^perhaps a more enormous mistake committed bythem still————a litigated point fairly hung up;———for instance, Whether Antonio Atome's or Peter Ozianion's his nose could stand in Mateo's is face, without a trespass, or not—raSh1y determined by them in five-and-twenty minutes, which, with the cautious pros amd cons required in so intricate a proceeding, might have taken up as manx months——and if carried on upon a l a your honours know should be practicable."

Atome acknowledges this with a smile. That's entirely unusable now, he says. I am certain that it is in your father's interest if we now proceed with the trial, I've been waiting for such a long time, he says. If you say the word "rat" now, the opening of the trial shall be repeated, if you don't say the word "rat," you shall be executed immediately. The repetition opens up the possibility that Father shall come back, I will, if necessary, be able to tweak a few things stylistically, besides which, it shall make my book look even bulkier, thus do I say the word "rat."

Through a toad-studded archway strides an unsightly figure, a rat, with red-hot eyes and a barred blast furnace with glowing coals for a belly, which his zipper-fastened black robe causes to appear as the eye of God. It wears a green turban upon its head, from which green cloths, decorated with pearls upon their upper thirds, flow to the right and to the left. The hellfire in its belly beats through its head. Its maw is open wide, displaying four pointed canines before its fire-flaming gullet. As master of ceremonies, it carries a fourfold scythe, which is easy to recognize as the Fourfold Sense of Scripture—that which spoils the whole of life for us, which causes wars and allows for salvation to be seen in death, which is also, in a nutshell, responsible for all wrongs. The rat bangs its scythe loudly against the ground. This knocking briefly summons a few gentlemen I recognize as members of the Frightbearing Society. The figure announces something, the Society rises. To the left of the rat, the chief of minutes, equipped with a red tin pot upon his head and a white-edged pince-nez, immediately skims the program, which he, for whom these facts are an everyday matter, recites at such breakneck speed that, though the words are not exactly new to me, only the form of paraphrase and diaskeuasis are able to be reproduced, just as, in any case, the whole of my activity appears to me to be perpetual diaskeuasing, but more on that subject another time. Framed by a banquet, the program provides for a short trial, the structure of which follows stringent rules and the result of which is fixed from the outset. The guilt of the delinquent is proven by the fact that the trial is taking place. No hearing for the delinquent is planned. The dignitaries and the employer are entitled to the fine entertainment that awaits them. Thus is it not the delinquent's death, which is fixed beyond doubt, that would be regrettable, but the staging itself that could arouse the displeasure of those present. So as to avoid such unpleasantness, the individual acts are repeatedly rehearsed, which contradicts the fact that the trial's code of procedure is a mirror image of the divine order, for God himself never rehearsed, but only withdrew a little, for there can be no creation without self-withdrawal. God made tzimtzum and the world had already come into being, a void in the void, unto which God gave his word. Then Lucifer pauses, he himself seems to marvel somewhat at being able to comment on the divine cosmogony of the world as if he were God's chosen exegete. That's actually none too astonishing, for he speaks from the face of my father, who is truly well-versed in all things godly. Father is Lucifer. I take back the word "rat," I say to Antonio Atome, whom I now recognize as the figure with the red tin pot upon his head. I'll put that down in the minutes, he says, in any case, there is no end to the repetition planned. I am blindfolded, I am led away, I am undressed, and I am pierced with a sword. The sword enters at the level of the spleen and exits the body at the level of the stomach and liver. It goes in all the way up to the cross guard. The blade of the sword is up in the air, there is no blood to be seen upon it. The force of the blow lifted me up off of the ground, which I cannot touch even now, two figures, a toad-like creature with a fallow brain on my right and an albino amphibian kneeling upon its right leg to my left, hold me aloft and present me thusly to the master of ceremonies, while the aforementioned figure with the red chamber pot upon its head reads out the death sentence. For this purpose, it has placed a pince-nez upon its nose. I can listen in and move my mouth, my voice, however, fails me. What I would like to know is why the death sentence was carried out before its grounds were declaimed. The master of ceremonies is not of a mind with the scene and has it repeated. To be specific, what he dislikes is my posture, which he can only justify by the position of the sword. However, he does praise the fact that there's no blood to be seen upon it. The blow of the sword must go through the heart, he says. In addition, my blindfold should have been white, not black, a white blindfold symbolizes the innocence that, God knows, has now been restored. God knows! he said, says the amphibian on my left. Only now do I see the insect legs upon its monkey head. Their tibiae and tarsi appear to be exchanging messenger-substances with Lucifer. Perhaps, the amphibian has a chicken in its head and the chicken's legs protrude from its brow. A sword-wielding white mole salamander with two legs and a tail. Zoological subtleties that would suggest the non-existence of such a figure cannot prevent the scene from being repeated, not even with the modifications required by the rat. Behind my back, at a height of about three meters, a naked person is now levitating, the point of a sword directed toward his Achilles. This person is being held by a sharp-clawed chimera that can barely be distinguished from the night. The chimera has the features of the rat. The invisibility of its servants makes them numberless, the night its eternal servant. A further improbability: How am I supposed to see the person behind my back with a blindfold over my eyes? That is me myself. I feel myself behind me. That which is unlikely is likely, my friend Papaver* says. Now, everyone can see what I felt with my inward hands. I feel every pain here and there, I can experience something here that I write down

---

* Poppy.

there, there I can experience that which is written down here, simultaneously or one thing after the next, I can change my location with imagination alone, here, I can feel my way into the future, there, into the past, but if I am here as I am there, I can only watch myself from the outside here, whereas, there, I can simultaneously observe from a third place where I come together as *This* and *That*, as the one blindfolded and pierced by the sword, I cannot see the one clawed at by the chimera hovering three meters above me—and vice versa—and that is not to do with the white cloth with which my eyes are now bound instead of the black and also not to do with the fact that we've turned our backs on one another, I know that I am simultaneously pierced *here* and mauled by claws there, alone, from a third place, I live with the sword that pulls me to the ground and *there*, grasped tight by claws, am simultaneously on the point of soaring off into airy regions, I've always already died before death and always already died with life, but what is the pedogogical meaning of this eternity-as-punishment? It's nothing but the eternal revenge of the divine, we have Augustine and Pope Gregory I to thank for that, my father said years ago, and, now, I understand it, I feel it.

Even the current constellation is not enough for the rat, however, all efforts to remove the oil from the wood fail, in such a way that Lucifer decides that everything in existence shall remain extant and merely be expanded upon. Is it not astounding how art seeks to resolve centuries-old contradictions of church doctrine by way of simultaneity? At the behest of the rat, the chimera is to throw me into the flames, in which people slide down from above through a funnel-shaped opening. The opening, a dome, is placed right on top of a red circus tent in the interior of which the flames blaze up all the way through the dome. And, now, I am also the naked one, stuck upside down into the dome, a silver fanfare protrudes from my buttocks, it's attached to a gonfalon with three tails. This is not the Easter flag as a symbol of triumph over death, this is the banner of death. The fanfare is likely meant to blare out my bad reputation so that the whole world can hear how righteous that which is happening to me is. I hold onto it with my hands, but they can't pull it out of my buttocks. My hands find themselves on my legs, as if my legs were my arms and my buttocks my face, from which the legs extend as arms, both neck- and shoulderless. At this point, I would like to state that I do not voluntarily blow into the fanfare, I have no understanding whatsoever of this art, it's more like a barking or a coughing that I wrest forth from it, I've come a long way, I am the fanfare-coughing herald of Lucifer bringing death.

The circus tarpaulin pulled aside in front gives an unobstructed view of the circus ring, in which no animals or performers present themselves to the public, only glowing, seething bodies, which are their own eternally self-perceiving audience and, if it weren't for the pain, no greater annihilation could be imagined than this cremation with its ceaseless decomposition, the bodies are salted with unquenchable flames, the clever fire kills, but does not destroy. The open tent with its dome serving as funnel looks like the helmet of a Roman centurion, from the nob or spout of which the Olympian flame of Lucifer blazes where the helmet crest should be.

I'm still not satisfied, says the rat. If the body has been pierced through with a sword, then lifted up into the air and passed headlong through flames, it shall be drawn out of the fire by my servant and led away over to the balcony above the archway for its sins to be read out once more. On my right, a trio consisting of shawm, bagpipes, and harp is to accompany the register of sins to be sung by the chimera, the shawm shall be blown by another chimera using its hindquarters, which resemble a fly's faceted eye, the bagpipes are a skate fish playing itself, it has a human arm that presses the air flowing into the sack into the handheld chanter placed upon its tail, the blowpipe remains invisible, the drone pipe sounds out in secret. The person lies nestled against the chimera singing the register of sins in such a way that he can never look into the open book of his sins. This is a cycle that never ends, that's what it means when one speaks of the eternally burning flame. The execution of this arrangement is more colorful and compelling than your meager words are capable of describing, the rat says, then steps back into the toad-studded archway.

Thus does it come to pass. The chimera pulls me out of the flames, which have done nothing to my exterior, my skin is rosy, I feel refreshed as if after a sauna session, like a doll do I hang from the creature's outstretched arm, pitch black just like the rat's, but, in contrast to Lucifer's rat-legs, its strong legs are also black, it does not enjoy its puppet, instead, it wants to get rid of it as soon as possible, it drags me in its wake, I'm really very light, it gains momentum and hurls me over the parapet, from which I, as a woman, land in the arms of another chimera, which immediately begins to read from the open register of sins, its maw gaping, it traces the lines with long, pointed fingers as it reads. It also has a red helmet upon its head, from which a red veil flows and covers the ground. At the behest of the rat, the musicians who accompany the reading of the sins take their places on the veil. They do so in such a monotonous, but also unsettling fashion, they know only one way of doing so, this leaves me yearning for a finale shortly thereafter, though I know it will bring about nothing better than what came before. All through my previous life, I have always asked myself in conscientious fashion if I want to live forever. If I have tended to the answer that, yes, I would like eternal life, this reply making itself felt in me without much thought even before the mental formulation of the question, another voice has often spoken up in me, wishing to assert the strongest of doubts, it warned of eternal repetition filled with pain that not only doesn't subside, but grows ever more unbearable in the expectation of the pains to come, think of Abu Ja'far Muhammad ibn Musa al-Khwarizmi, the voice said, with each repetition, the mass that must be repeated grows, from a purely mathematical perspective, repetition does not always repeat the same thing, nothing is lost along the way either, so what is to be repeated does not become less, it becomes greater and greater, time multiplied by distance, ever growing because a repetition of something can only come to pass in forward-moving time, which, in its turn, must be taken up and repeated and so on, an exponential function, and, now, that's precisely what's happened, the memory of pain is pain, which is added to the pain that keeps on coming forth, which is preceded by the anticipation of the coming pain, until the anticipated pain is added to the pain that has not yet subsided, it's an ever-growing sum—and so on.

Thus do I sit upon the ground, embraced by the chimera, which thus wishes to teach me to sing with growing zeal. I am told to sing my own sins, for he who sings shall better remember. This creature is a Knecht Ruprecht, it has a cloak upon its head, its rod is singing, Nicholas has turned into a rat, both of them serve hell. The return of childhood humiliation is more humiliating than the circumstance of being the object of a loudly proclaimed denunciation. My father belongs to a club that allows itself its own Ruprecht for Saint Nicholas Day. He appears each year with a great sack, speaks broken chains of words, murmuring into his beard what the fathers have instructed him to say about the naughty children, then distributes the gifts he's brought, which the fathers should be ashamed of, but aren't, they are at first accepted by the children, then made to disappear somewhere, out of shame and sadness at having received something so inadequate, so haphazard. The fact that my brother and I kept getting bigger and older while the other children remained quite small and young made me so sad on one Saint Nicholas Eve that I said to Ruprecht that I had done far more beastly things, he was incompetent, had a stupid voice, and was miserably dressed, as he was every year. But, on this evening, it was the real Ruprecht who gave me a foretaste of hell by allowing me to gaze into his great sack without saying a word to me. Inside of the sack were wild flames, faces melted before my eyes, wretched little voices could be heard, a book lit up, showed its title the way women show their breasts in leisure-hour magazines. The book was called *Gehenna*, which made me think of red hair, the pulp swimming through the sack seemed to be stirred by an enormous soup spoon, everything went round in a circle, emerged, went under again, faces stared at me, hair was aflame, everything was burning, but didn't burn up, the little fellows swimming round in the pulp called my name, half pleading, half teasing, the pounding of nails into wood could be heard, a short time later, a little boy was lifted up, hanging from a crossbeam, to which he had been nailed with arms outstretched, the long iron nails had been driven through the ulna and spoke bone so that they might be able to bear the weight of the body on the cross, take a good look, Ruprecht said, and I looked down, you must look at him for a very long time, he said, and I looked at him for a very long time, here, I was able to see and thus testify as to how two executioner's assistants standing on footstools precisely fitted the centrally slotted crossbeam onto the peg on the upper half of the post, the entire length of which protruded from the pulp. The exactor mortis and his quaternio—none of whom were allowed to quit his service or help the crucified to escape under pain of death—had to guard the cross after the work was finished and until the dying individual had died his death in orderly fashion. That could last for days. Put away the bench, some cried out, having seen through the deception of this prop and understood that it only prolonged the agony. Whom could the crucified child possibly hope for if God seemed not to be in play. The father had already handed him over to Knecht Ruprecht. But the bench remained. Break his legs, the onlookers cried out, terror chained them to the scene of that which was coming to pass. The guards also made no moves to do this. They had been ordered to make the child suffer for a record span of time. In just a few minutes, the boy became a man into whose elbows and knees nails had migrated. The man was 1.91 meters tall. The cross was 2.50 meters tall. The notion that only fifty-nine centimeters were keeping his toes from touching the pulp bothered me more than the knowledge that the crucified one was suffering. I sought to do away with this thought, to make it unthought so that it might not be read from my face when I noticed that the man was watching me over here all the way from the cross. But there is no such art as not thinking a thought that thinks itself. The thought came back in the following form: What was the difference if he hung fifty-nine centimeters or just a single centimeter too high to touch the pulp. It would be of particular charm if his toes were just a millimeter off, I thought, then the back would sag and the man's toes would miss the pulp by a mere millimeter. The man sought to overcome this distance, as if this would be one final sense of great achievement that would allow him to die more calmly—a triumph over death. Take a good look, Ruprecht said, he will not succeed. Then the cross sank down into the pulp. But the image remained, the single millimeter that makes the difference. Ruprecht reached into his sack and gave me the book *Gehenna*. To remember, he said, for I had earned a memory like this. Now, in my memory, I remind Knecht Ruprecht of the martyred Santa Claus of December 23, 1951, who was publicly hanged and burned in the name of the Church in the forecourt of Duria Cathedral before the children who believed in him. I warn this Knecht that precisely the same could happen to him, as he too is a heathen, a heretic. Ruprecht also recalls this incident, he reminds me of the fact that Santa Claus rose again and thus shall it come to pass with him, should he also be hanged and burned. I am actually and always Thomas Müntzer, Ruprecht says.

The children are alive, but have been evil, Ruprecht says. It is for the fact that they are alive that they are showered with gifts at Christmas, but their parents are actually offering these gifts up to the hereafter, bypassing the child, in exchange for the child's continued life. The child is led to believe that it must earn its gift the whole year round, and thus does it live only for the gift. If the child has died over the course of the year, it receives no gift. If I gift the child something, logically, I am gifting it to myself, Ruprecht says, as I am the hereafter that the parents would like to bribe. Thus is there actually no real gift. A true gift knows only one direction. The solution, Ruprecht says, is not to send the children to me. But if you do send the children to me, they shall all come to hell. Of course, this cannot be debated with the children, says Ruprecht, the chimera. It's taboo to formulate everything. But now that we've come to hell, taboo is no longer valid. Ruprecht shall be in you, Ruprecht says, I call to you through my open mouth, I look at you without once blinking. My gifts are poison. And thus singing with your voice, you tie a transcendent bond, singing, you relinquish your voice, thus relinquished, it belongs to another, to the rat. The rat is kept alive by your voice, it hangs by the thread of your voice, your voice allows it to fuel the fire that shall soon engulf you. But how beautiful your voice is when one compares it to the Aleph, the croaking nothing with which God revealed himself, says Ruprecht, the chimera. The fire is the pulp, the image that remains. And while I sing, I am entirely absent, my voice leaves me, the hereafter opens up, and I sing and sing so that it doesn't shut itself up with me in there, I sit opposite my voice as a stranger who would like to remain *here*, I cling to fire, pulp, and cross, then drift away.

The boy in Ruprecht's great sack, his crucifixion is nothing but a punishment. But what for? He was ill-behaved the whole year round. More specifically, he didn't obey his father. Doesn't share, especially not with his friends. Lost almost all of his friends because of that. Offended his mother to the point that she finally became seriously ill and died. Left the church. Made his father disappear into a black page. In short: The boy was naughty and discredited his father vis-à-vis the hereafter. A confession is no longer to be extracted from the crucified, he is not even remotely entitled to such a confession, as he must also remain silent during the interrogation, after all, he is not truly being questioned. "It has been reported to me that you have been naughty." That's not a question. The boy's crucifixion allows the father's good will to be recognized—the will to get rid of him in the most difficult way possible. The hereafter will likely be quite appreciative of this will. However, once the boy is finally dead, the father loses his connection to the hereafter through him and this loss has a heavier effect than the loss of the son. One has a child in order to forge a connection to the hereafter; one forges a connection to the hereafter because one is afraid of death. But one's fear of death is so great that, once one realizes that its eventual advent—if not its speed or ease—has been predetermined, one sacrifices one's child to the hereafter. Pain marks the body on which it acts and which death rules out. A theater of pain is performed on the foreign body for the hereafter. The pain of the crucified, his roaring, is the invocation of the hereafter, so that the ears of all might hear what a good connection the father has to it.

One must imagine it, the unimaginable, but to imagine that which has been suffered a thousand times over is still the task of the future, mankind cannot get enough of imagining the unimaginable, the one who carries out the crucifixion has no expression whatsoever, but must guard the crucified one right up until his death so that nobody frees him, and after his death must he continue to guard him, lest he be buried, for he is to be eaten by birds, he deserves no grave and woe unto him if the birds come not, for then he himself shall be put up there; the crucified would like for the torture to end as soon as possible, he will perhaps pay attention to his breathing—to see whether it won't soon stop—and that would be his salvation—if his heart might cease beating, if he could just die of pain, nobody has managed to describe this yet, he who is still witnessing how he is to lose his life likely wishes to distract himself, but with what, to think of something, something else, he shall slowly burn in pain, a crucified man asked about his sufferings would have no certainty that his sufferings would, in fact, come to a speedy end, should he, upon being asked, describe his pain—what distinguishes it from all other pains—and, in return, negotiate to be killed immediately, not to hang on the cross for three whole days, as has been described to him with all ensuing consequences—to know the medical details is one thing, someone told him, but experiencing them is quite another—whereby the crucified had not heretofore experienced all conceivable pains, especially since one pain can mask another, less severe pain until the greatest pain is reached and the still-living comes to resemble a dead body. "Is there a pain that one could name, / Not found upon his body maimed?" Ruprecht asks. What's the point of this question? Do we know every kind of pain there is? "And supposing we knew every kind of pain, / Could we name them in German plain?"

Did he really cherish a hope that he would be taken down from the cross and be able to go on living as before? All of this speculation doesn't bother the crucified, it is the luxurious twaddle of those who still have both of their hands free. The crucified expires. Slowly. And that's what counts. Facts count, hard as the word "facts," not words soft as the word "word." "W" is the cross left empty. It's the place that counts.

Ruprecht asks me if I know what I'm singing, it's the poem of a Silesian angel. It is entirely unknown to me, I say. Am I singing? He would then like to know what I have to say about the poem. Then I ask if what I have to say about the poem is important. You must shed light on a thousand and one issues, Ruprecht says, otherwise, you shall pass into hellfire. I stare at the poem. In any case, the devil doesn't have such poems on offer, I say. Would lines like these be unthinkable at the magnificent carnival committee, lines aimed directly at the soul? "Look now, he hangs on high so bare, / Upset, perturbed, and full of care! / Shod in bruises and in blows, / So unkempt and brought so low." This is mostly for reading eyes that wish to be impressed. Pain seems to be something primarily for sight, better served by words than ears are. Pain is here mute, only panting and yawning seem to make noises: "The limbs are all in sooth stretched out, / The mouth is open, yawns and shouts. / And the lips that are like coral / Are much faded, stained with bile." The slant-rhyme is OK, the yawning hardly to be believed. Here, someone has put together an image with words, one that is always before our eyes when we hear the name Jesus: "One cannot recognize his face / From all the blood that's in its place. / Pricked by thorns, his gracious brow, / And the eyes so broken now. // The head is furiously bemocked, / And with a crown of thorns is topped. / And the brave locks of the hair / Which spittle-spots do heavy bear. // Pierced are both the hands and feet, / Disjointed, gnarled, numb, unmete. / The heart as well, o giant woe! / Has not been left unwounded—no." Could also be the phrase that kicks off the carnival: Do we want to let Him in? But what is this "stretched out," "broken," "disjointed, gnarled, numb, unmete"? Whether I simply read and visualize it or see it as an image, it leaves me cold. These are superficial words that don't continue to trouble, they are simply and only acknowledged. Convenience-store goods that don't reveal the process that produced them and don't have a feel, don't, by way of feel, at least give a taste of what is meant by Stretched Out, Broken, Disjointed, Gnarled, Numb, Unmete. To imagine the pain? To read it, to stare at it while reading, to repeat it, fixate on it. How the nail penetrates. Now, it is penetrating. And do I feel something? I imagine feeling the pain.

That is the meaning of life—to feel pain. Ruprecht asks me what I think about the quintessence of soul-igniting Jesu-Minnesang on the cross: "Ach, climb up and die with him, / Like a loving seraphim. / Who so wants his life to earn, / Must on the cross with him life spurn." "With him" likely indicates no simultaneity whatsoever, after all, he has already died. What is remarkable is the mercantile aspect of "earn" with which the rhyme of "spurn" is bought, I say. In order to live, one must die. Probably means that another life begins with the life-despising death on the cross. A life that perpetually cries out, "holy, holy, holy." So, am I a fifth-rate angel or do I sing in the first row of God's angel-choir?

We want to pick up the pace, Ruprecht says and turns the page. Now sing to me the effluvia of a certain Cardinal von Espe, who grasps the matter more precisely and leaves nothing to be desired in terms of clarity. I can hardly decipher it, I say, the script is too old. Decipherment,

Ruprecht ripostes, is the A and O. But A and O are no digits, I object. First of all, that's a figure of speech, Ruprecht says, second of all, that isn't so. You have thirty minutes to copy down and comment on the poem. Then comes the evaluation and further singing.

    What does the chimera want? To give me a foretaste that is terribly old? If I stare at the words for long enough, they open up like tulips and reveal themselves. Others can be deduced from the context, a few are unknown to me:

His head of finest gold is filled with pus and blisters;
His dove-like eyes are pasted shut with spit;
His breath is weaken'd howls, drowsy whispers,
Because his arid tongue sticks to his lips.
His raven-charcoal hair is often bathed in dew,
Caked in twining flows with ample gore;
His holy brow cut open by a thousand flues,
So that no needle harms the healthy anymore.
One can count the fingers 'pon the moistened face,
Where the lackey slapped the Lord with vicious aim;
The sun that should have boasted with its gold and lace
Goes pale — the thorns it wears cause only shame.
Black blood runs out of savior's injured nose,
The smell of nard and apples is no more;

The lips that once imparted myrrh and rose
Are brown and blue and marred with cuts and sores.
The hangman did his work upon the holy back;
Striped His veiny flesh with furrows up and down.
His iv'ry arms and legs inlaid with turkois
A bounteous fount which purest blood-foams crown.
With nails by hands and feet his body hung;
His breath of balsam and his pomegranate tongue
Are drowned with dreadful hyssop, gall, and aloe.
His arms stretched out across the sky of air,
Torn wide with ropes by those without belief;
His legs that death subdue and full impair
Are hollow'd to the core, parched by painful grief.
He lacks a bit of cloth to wipe the bloody sweat
Pressed out of bone and vein by hellish fear;
That the man(na) the world must refresh
Ys not yet known: and so they let him die of thirst.
His face that leaves the Seraphim afraid
So (that)

no pain wants to rhyme, yet Jesus' crucifixion rhymes with the enumeration of his body parts—neatly, from top to bottom. How beautiful are the terrible sounds when rhetoric wields the scepter. It unleashes an excessive tempest of images until their drasticness is seen as disturbance. As a disturbance of what? As a disturbance of the beautiful that the subject in its religious symbolism still *is*, as a result of which the words emancipate themselves from their religious service and show themselves as such: as themselves in the absolute afunctionality of the abominable, hateful, disgusting, onto which we hang without even seeing the subject. Such a disturbance is pornography. Here, the limit has not yet been reached, it's already tilting a bit, the enumeration of the parts, from top to bottom, still encompasses a whole that is to be sensuously brought to mind and is intended to trigger the affects of commiseration in the Passion, as if I were the martyred one, just as all those with eyes to read are martyred ones, the enumeration does not celebrate the artistry of language by representing the humiliation, but allows the unmistakable nature of the subject to show through the curtain of words, that to which all refer, for everyone has the same position in the face of Christ risen in and with words: the cross. The poem is a winsome formulation of the dreadful, of theology, served up on a platter: worship, spiritual devotion. After all, even the seraphim here are more frightened than adoring, it is more likely than not that nobody will climb up on the cross so quickly to die with Jesus.

Why this legibility? To arouse disgust? To sublate time and distance? To be right there, right then? The more drastic the representation of pain, the better it can be imagined, the better it can be sensuously brought to mind, the better shall it be remembered. The goal of art is compassio, taking part in and being part of the sufferings of Christ. Art is thus an eternally arcane theology. However, it's not yet settled whether it's to be a positive or negative one. The drasticness of the representation is tied to the notion of salvation. The more drastic the vocabulary, the stronger the reader's wish to be redeemed without the same happening to him—if salvation is a seen-through phantasm, then only laughter reigns: "En face / le pire, / jusqu'à-ce qu'il fasse / rire." Is this a conclusion only to be drawn by an observer, but not the victim? There is no recognizable break between pain and transcendence here. Pain can therefore still be justified.

By all accounts, it would seem that Lucifer has taken over this system of the Passion myth and adapted it for his kingdom. Indeed, it has become his kingdom. More precisely, it has become his Reich. He has carried out a small change: that the one who suffers death suffers death in perpetuity, death does not serve redemption or the forgiveness of sins, but suffering and suffering alone, which he wants to show in all of its beauty and artistic worthiness and he himself is the one who sings the Passion Minnesong to himself who is the others in suffering. Lucifer is no longer hell's most famous inmate, he hosts it himself together with his legion of servants. The devil is the god of hell, he is soulless and therefore has no more connection to the God above. Lucifer is condensed air, he can freely select his incarnation like clothes from a closet. He is now a rat with a belly full of fire—no longer a giant larger than all other giants who stands in ice up to his haunches. He also no longer has three heads from which hang the bodies of B, C, and J, which he devours again and again forevermore for their betrayal, and, at the same time, the six eyes of his three faces weep ("he dares to weep / in the midst of us"), he is content with the rat's driveling face, with the glowing button-eyes, with the four sharp canines in its fiery maw that raise the suspicion that the rest of its teeth are rotten. One doesn't want such a figure in one's vicinity, yet one longs for it too. One knows that they are always present in the canal, in the trackbed, and wherever things are carelessly thrown away, as if one wanted them to be banned to these places under the assumption that one would be safe if one were to simply drive or walk over them. It is strange that there is waste. In the animal kingdom, there is no waste, death is decomposed. How calmly the antelope awaits death after the chase, having surrendered, as if aware of the totality of which it is one part.

"His breath is weaken'd howls, drowsy whispers, / Because his arid tongue sticks to his lips" and not because he must struggle for air, thirst and not suffocation is indicated here. Breathing is breathing, whimpering is whimpering, howling is howling. His breathing is no whimpering and no howling.

The poem is the background music to my current environment, which hides more than it shows, as Ruprecht always fashions it after Lucifer's wishes. The poem shows more than it hides, it also shows that which is hidden. The rat is concerned with having an image that it can always look at. That is understandable. It would like to go down in history with that image, it wants to infect history. It wants to become a phantom. The image is a virus, it shall wash up onto the consciousness of those who are not yet in hell. The virus-image is soul-forming. It is that which is initially only visible. But over time, it becomes the real. It triggers our fears and banishes them simultaneously. We are afraid of the image, yet know that we cannot be without this image. The image is the fear that we are. Everyone thirsts after an image to take to his grave. With this image on the lips do we die, do we dissolve, all that's left behind is the image, the soul. The soul, the image, is a phantom. It is and is not. This image, in which the soul sees itself, is confrontation, not representation, it is a figment of mere visibility. There is no bridge out of life to this image. But the viewer cannot help but be confronted by the image. He is compelled to look at the image. To see through this is still no medicine, no vaccine that would make immune. I am already infected. Of what use is it to the terminally ill if they are told that medicine and research have made great progress?

Are words able to do more than images? Because everyone can see differently with words, other images or no images at all, while images shown are the same for all, even if the allegorical meaning of both words and images can remain more or less hidden from others? Is it easier to overread than it is to overlook? We are referring to two different mediums, not to the phantom, which is the subject they represent. It is not guaranteed that this subject will also appear through words and images: But what if we are dealing with Christ? Here, there is the risk that too much Christ is seen in things. It is enough to merely mention the word "nail." No longer seeing that one is reading a word or seeing an image, both of which dissolve before one's eyes and that which is represented appears unmediatedly—which, on the other hand, can only be achieved by the ecstatic giddiness of Jesu-Minnesang and Passion Representation. Christ as phantom is the "nullity of a unique type" recognizable under all circumstances.

So, saying is better than showing? Ethics or censorship? Is that what a critique of visual ethics looks like: saying is allowed, showing is forbidden? Hearing is not understanding. Does the ethics of censorship help? Whom does censorship help, how does forced viewing oppress? Is the image closer to man than the word? The word allows itself to be repeated, in a tone quiet or loud, one says a word a hundred times and the subject invoked takes on the form of the word. In the beginning was the glottis. An image. "If someone wanted to impart his physical pain, he would be forced to inflict it and thereby become a torturer himself," writes somebody who was tortured. Words and images are not capable of conveying physical pain. Speak the word only, and my body shall be in pain. Assuming this were possible, if torture were sanctioned under the zodiac sign of art, art would degenerate into mere sensation that would find its meaning solely in the transmission of pain and its various achieved aims. Art would be a means, a transitory syndrome, irrelevant. If only it could . . . But it can't even do that.

To read. To not budge from one's spot. To lose context. To alienate the words from self—from themselves and oneself as reader. To imagine something entirely other than what is given to be read. Beyond a certain limit, the imagination defies control, both one's own and that of others. Up to the point that I can no longer say I, though the control might still function. In pain, then, the control at some point ceases—fortunately. Whose fortune? The viewer's. Posterity's. And posterity can receive an assignment from the writer if he, in sight of the City of Hell, is no longer able or willing, to inflict language onto his languagelessness: "ask thou not, Reader, for I write it not, because all speech would be of small avail. I did not die, nor yet remained alive; think for thyself now, hast thou any wit, what I became, of both of these deprived." How does that happen—not to live and not to die?

It's always only to do with attraction or disgust, to endanger the desire to hurt while at the same time being afraid, never about the person affected who is exposed to the pain, it's always just to do with the question of whether the presentation is successful, well done. Noble simplicity? Here hardly at all. The gaze that lowers enumerates everything, it is complete, from top to toe. Succession exists in each part of the whole, but the sum is intended to intensify the affect. But where is the limit of that which is tolerable? Is it somewhere else for everyone? The one who has experienced the pain up until the limit that still allows him to say, I must not be able to name this more authentically than the one who has not experienced this pain. Quiet grandeur? To keep still, yessir; it is a command of art if the powers that be have already made the order. Turn the other cheek to him. "I feel myself! I am!" How do you feel yourself and for how long? If you feel too much, then you are no more. To whom is the art of pain addressed, to the angel or to the beast in the "Unhappy Middle-Thing" of man?

Time is ticking away, Ruprecht says. I am to come to an end.

Painporn is really not a good word. Though it is one that strikes home—conveys the dilemma of the presentation—quite well. Painporn is a drug. To never tire of looking at something, but with a guilty conscience, this is part of *bon ton*. But of what? Of something that's on display and the viewer doesn't, for goodness' sake, want to switch sides with. One can become absorbed in a thing, but one shall never become the thing. That's why one always comes back to this obsession. If one had become the thing, one would want to become another straight away. What justification would pain have if Jesus never existed? Jesu-Pain is a pain unto death. From this point of view, couldn't Xianity be wiped out in one fell swoop and this wouldn't just be senseless, but pleasing to God? To fashion pain artistically? Ugh—to the devil with it. Death is the hereafter of pain. Death is no longer identical with he who lived. The dead body has nothing more in common with him. Not least of all because the living cannot be questioned about themselves as future dead. How can we commemorate those who have experienced violent pain, up to and including death, unless one thinks of pain and violence as part of nature and not as a third beyond of nature and culture, in which case one doesn't have to commemorate them. Not in the form of secular art, which only has meaning in itself (and hasn't even had that for more than seventy years) when it comes to expressing pain artistically—a formulation well-known from the parlance of artistic directors, dramaturges, cultural mayors, and the after-work audience, the last of which thinks itself to be absolved of all responsibility, for them, the tortured and executed are atonement and redemption from their little everyday adversities, crises and angst are blown away at a safe distance, for one evening, for a few blinks of the eye, and the adversity and atonement and redemption become drugs, one complains about the former and feels compensated by the latter. To prepare works of art from the victims that are then devoured with relish. That is precisely how Honda Wortrodeo* recognized it to be. The eyes get horny at the sight of the suffering of others and religion is the servant of the eyes, it serves them as justification. Some may be scared off by public stagings of pain, they don't count as set against the host of those upon whom it has precisely the opposite effect: They want to join in,

---

* Honda Wordrodeo.

they want to be admired for the torments that they inflict on others, others' pain is their potency—that with which they fuck the cowardice of lustful eyes. The so-called redemption comes at precisely the right moment, it allows those who refuse, hesitate, and the weak to remain still, those for whom an end to torments and redeeming death are the certainty of salvation, for it has been sold to them as such: "The lust for torment heightens the jubilation of salvation and the prospect of salvation gives license to orgies of cruelty." Passion plays are the tolerance valves of political power. All of it just as Luther describes.

Palaver, Ruprecht says. You strike me as a ruminant who has eaten the indigestible and now regurgitates it incessantly, then devours it once more. Your centrifugal stomach sits in your brain. Anyone who reasons as mindlessly as you demonstrates to the regime that he is more important than he seems, even if no beloved father seems to dwell above the starry canopy any longer. You are a grumbler and growler, the movements of whose mouth are intended to belie intense reflection and inwardness. Ruprecht can hardly wait to keep flipping the pages in pain. It can still grow more vexing, he says. True Jesu-Minnesang knows neither inner nor outer, it also knows about the effect of the crucifixion on the invisible organs. True Jesu-Minnesang, he says, is always righteous, even when medicine can only shake its head. Or do the details, which can probably only be verified by vivisection, testify to great erudition and the poem knows more than the research about the physiology of crucifixion knew until just recently? The chimera is in danger of fainting with rapture as I sing the following, painstakingly copied-out lines:

"The brain's dampness dried / the brain-membrane almost ruptured / the membranes around the eyes and little glasses slightly melting juices / [. . .] the nose airtubes shot up with blood / the throat suffocated with rising vapors / the root of the tongue desiring to tear forth from attraction / the teeth crunch and fall out from the pain. What then would the heart erst do? ach! that it wanted to break before a thousand torments / [. . .] The belly shriveled / the liver crumbled / the spleen petrified / the kidneys melted / the marrow in the legs dwindled and rotted / from all the struggling and writhing / through unbearable pain."

What Cardinal von Espe delivers, an external view of the body rich in detail, which makes the pain only legible upon its surface, is internally boiled down in these lines. Pornography of the innards. I would very much like to know whether there is a narrow term for such voyeurism and body-disembowelling piety that nails human squalor to the cross of comprehension?

Where does that originate from? Where is the outcome? Please, leaf through the Bible, the scriptures of the prophets, I think, the Bible appears there, page for page, the passage looks for itself and has already found it: Isaiah laid the foundation for all representations of the Passion and the formula of "quiet grandeur." In the time capsule lies the 53rd Chapter, which has handed itself down: "Surely he hath borne our griefs, and carried our sorrows: yet we did esteem him stricken, smitten of God, and afflicted. But he was wounded for our transgressions, he was bruised for our iniquities: the chastisement of our peace was upon him; and with his stripes we are healed. All we like sheep have gone astray; we have turned every one to his own way; and the LORD hath laid on him the iniquity of us all. He was oppressed, and he was afflicted, yet he opened not his mouth: he is brought as a lamb to the slaughter, and as a sheep before her shearers is dumb, so he openeth not his mouth."

Isn't that the ideal—not to open one's mouth? Jesus, the highest notion of a beautiful figure, who is mute, equal to the signifying stones of antiquity. A mouth open wide enough to scream wouldn't be suitable. The body must be closed. The mouth is shut, the head is bowed, the eyes are averted. The inner remains on the outside. The viewer glides along the uninterrupted contour of the body, as he hangs in all offices. And it should have been left at that. Isaiah, his own tradition. Haven't the signifying stones already opened their mouths too wide? They represent the fact the mouth doesn't scream. Thus do they only exist in the negative. Pain gives language pain, it clearly senses its own inferiority, which it cannot hide. Pain wears down, makes language brittle, dissolves it as mushrooms dissolve wood. Who, then, are the inhabitants of this white-rotten, mushroomed language, whose initial blight is pain? It is beetles that live in many small boxes. No one dares to say it, but it is beetles. The other one might also have a beetle. That would be upsetting. Thus is the beetle that *I* have in my box especially dangerous and especially impressive, it is especially unique, there is only this single copy of it. That's far too beautifully put. There is pain; of this nobody says anything more, I have a beetle in my box, it lives in my white-rotten, mushroomed language that pain caused to rot, shmanguage, shmain, shrain, loongauge, au. Language pain: Shame as joke. That's far too beautifully put.

But has pain not always been the same? Does one not feel pains somewhat more keenly today, as the subject as such feels addressed rather than the subject as proxy, at least in some regions of the world? Would someone wish to assert that Jesus felt only symbolic pain? Ignoring this, I ask Ruprecht: We find ourselves in around the year 1500, how can a poem from the year 1680 surface in the year 1500? We find ourselves in the year 2018, Ruprecht says, we can be anywhere at any time and anything anywhere can surface at any time.

On with the text, I say: If we're dealing with pain, Jesus has a special role to play. Art with Jesus is always religious. And the others? The maltreated and dead can only be commemorated by remembering them, somberly documenting them and no Christiane Rebenruck[*] and no Christian Ruckenerb[†] may lend them his or her self-loving,

---

[*] Christiane Vineheave.
[†] Christian Vineinheritance

granule-breathing voice, which is always the same and always only serves itself, what- and whomever it discusses, which can do nothing but pay homage to the timbre that its indifferent nature gave to it, which, even in the face of death, still feigns Eros, which makes no distinction between animate and inanimate. It depends on the voice. Your voice fails you. Prosopopoeia. Rebenruck and Ruckerb[*] reveal not their countenance, they have only a mask, through which not the one to whom the voice was given, but only the face of the voice becomes memorable: Rebenruck and Ruckenerb, whether it's a stone speaking or a person, it is always a stone that speaks to them.

Ruprecht asks me what *my* proposal would then be for describing the Jesu-Passion. Here it is: "Christ was crucified. He suffered and died." Thus was it demonstrated 242 years ago: "He bound her eyes—and the beautiful soul flew away to heaven." What a beautiful dash that stands in for all of literature, the blade lying horizontally in the air. An extinction without act or stage.

I am the lord of all books, Ruprecht says, I am the lord of the archive, your guilty conscience. The facts should speak for themselves, you say, but they never do. I have something for you here, what it means when one tries anyway, knows the facts of it—that they ought to speak for themselves. The presentation alone is an act that creates its own stage. There are no facts. There are only facts without an observer, he says and flips the page. I am meant to read. And I read: "As I am writing this article, I come across a newspaper sheet with photos showing members of the South Vietnamese Army torturing captured Viet Cong rebels. The English novelist Graham Greene wrote a letter to the *London Daily Telegraph* that reads:

'The strange new feature about the photographs of torture appearing in the British and American Press, is that they have been taken with the approval of the torturers and are published over captions that

---

[*] Jiffyinherit.

contain no hint of condemnation. They might have come out of a book on insect life. Does this mean that the American authorities sanction torture as a means of interrogation? The photographs certainly are a mark of honesty, a sign that the authorities do not shut their eyes to what is going on, but I wonder if this kind of honesty without conscience is really to be preferred to the old hypocrisy."

Graham Greene's question shall also be asked by each of us. The confession of torture, the risk—but is it still such a risk?—of appearing with such photos before the public is only explicable under the assumption "that a revolt of public conscience is no longer to be feared. One could think that this conscience has accustomed itself to the practice of torture."

Is Jesus hanging from the cross not on the point of being natural produce? What is that supposed to mean, to grow accustomed to? He is already there at first glance. And the whole registry of sins with him. The cross together with the body has grown out of the parents' living-room wall. For years, I thought that the little glass jar beneath the feet was the water that Jesus needed to be washed with now and again, or it was his sweat that gathered there at night when everyone was sleeping. Thus did I wash him with his sweat. One day, the cross fell from the wall, our budgerigar tried to drink from the glass as he did every day, the nail could no longer support the ensemble, upon its impact with the floor, the body detached from the cross and broke into pieces, over which the bird fluttered excitedly. It was able to take another swallow of water before it seeped into the parquetry, it landed on the savior's knee, did its business, then finally flew onto the right wing of the sliding door that came out of the wall, where it secretly fulfilled its compulsion to lay eggs. The family had won the bird at a Catholic church festival, for months, it remained alone in its cage, the kindly Jesus looking on from the corner of the wall its constant companion. The creature must have fallen in love with him as it mounted him during its daily free flight, covered him with excrement until a large ball of dung had gathered up on his head, then slammed its beak into his face. Entirely exhausted from the compulsive laying of eggs, the bird languished barely a week after its groom had fallen from the wall, then perished.

An intensification of torture photos is still thinkable, I tell Ruprecht. Ruprecht is satisfied. Thus has this little test fulfilled its didactic purpose, he opines. The crucified one is interviewed. He himself should comment on his martyrdom, for as long as he still has any strength to speak from the cross and justify himself. The interviewer stands before him like a schoolboy with notepad and pen, the interview may perhaps be used to prepare for his exams, an original quote adds value to the enterprise, imagine that a crucified man became a tourist attraction and not just for a few locals or draftees standing around, the people couldn't resist the temptation to delve into the unimaginability of pain in order to get an idea of the unimaginable, then to become popular guests on entertainment television as pain witnesses, the crucified would have long since died and been forgotten, whereas these pain-describers would receive a great deal of money for their increasingly embellished lectures, which would suddenly no longer have the pain of the crucified as their subject, but would be exclusively centered around the speakers, as they would have to endure the crucifixion as witnesses face to face, which would be at least as unimaginable as the pains of the crucified one who, after all, would not survive the crucifixion while he, the witness, would have to bear the beam of testimony his whole life long.

I am certain, Ruprecht says, that utterly different intensifications shall come upon you once you've learned what it means to go through hell.

Then nothing else comes to mind, I say, nothing at all. An archive of memories would do some good—that we might reactivate the bygone once the present is no more than a white card. However, this archive would not contain anything that had been anticipated, that could be called up at will, if the memory of that which came to pass does not want to *set in*. There is nothing that is anticipated. I still remember this image accompanied by voices before the cross sank into the pulp: On the left and right of the crucified youth appear two more crosses, the thieves hang from them, one of them, turned toward the boy between them, says without even looking at him, you are innocent, the other says that he is only innocent if he knows how to help both us and himself, to which the first replies, you shall certainly not be able to judge him, after all, we were righteously condemned, to which the other replies, we shall meet again in 44 years on page 229. To think that you were given a voice at all, the first one grew incensed, Luke should have left it at John 19:16-18 and Mark 15:27, as soon as someone opens their mouth, others keep finding new and different ways of telling it.

How well the means of naming pain suit their time—and time as such only becomes legible through pain. Each naming misses pain, but not its time. My proposal for our time: that the primary color black dominate the page in such a way that everyone can form their own image of the horror, illegibly legible. Or a shimmering white that calls forth strong afterimages. Now, however, the how-speech, which always leads us in circles, by the nose—into the "hopeless carousel of metaphorical speech."

The true artist is the flagellant. Show me your wounds. If the pain is genuine, there is no more aesthetic, pain is the real as such. Nonsense, the flagellant is the tourist attraction as such, Ruprecht says. Beating his back bloody with a scourge, he wanders through streets and alleyways so that everyone can see him and admire him. What provokes him to do more violence to himself with a seven-tailed scourge: the Soli Deo Gloria, including the forgiveness of sins, or the crowd's beautiful eyes? Why does forgiveness need spectators? Bible, painporn, voyeurism, I think. Whatever comes to pass in the New Testament comes to pass in the midst of a crowd of gawkers. And the gawkers are always in the wrong, precisely like those who are caught red-handed in the act, even if their misdeed merely consists in a word at the wrong time; however, if they immediately repent, Jesus lets them sit beside him in paradise at some later point in time.

You should take a word of Jean Maerys's to heart, Ruprecht says: "One can devote an entire life to comparing the imagined and the real, and still never accomplish anything by it." That he of all people, the inquisitor, is saying this to me, as if he wanted to say to me: "One can devote an entire life to comparing victim to perpetrator, and still never accomplish anything by it." The only question is from which side.

Ruprecht closes his eyes and tilts his head back. He enjoys my silence. Does he want to test me, set a trap for me? I lean forward and turn to the next page. I read.

"Ruprecht closes his eyes and tilts his head back. He enjoys my silence. Does he want to test me, set a trap for me? I lean forward and turn to the next page. I read."

Startled, I turn back a page. The chimera snores. Perhaps his eyes aren't quite entirely closed and he is observing me in secret. I look at him, waiting for a twitch of his eyelids that would give him away. I could attempt to strangle him. If he can read my thoughts, he'll wait long enough for me to grab his throat, then I'll no longer be able to deny my intent. I didn't think that, I very much apologize for this, it wasn't me who thought that, I think, then turn the page once more:

"Ruprecht closes his eyes and tilts his head back. He enjoys my silence. Does he want to test me, set a trap for me?

I lean forward and turn to the next page. I read.

> "Come thou, thou last one, whom I recognize,
> unbearable pain throughout this body's fabric:
> as I in my spirit burned, see, I now burn in thee:
> the wood that long resisted the advancing flames
> which thou kept flaring, I now am nourishing
> and burn in thee."

That runs deep. I absorb this reading and it absorbs me. It fills me with pain. A virus that is everywhere and nowhere, that apparently does its work in secret. A Song of Songs of deadly devotion, a space-occupying apostrophe. "Come thou, thou last one," an Adonic invocation as opening, drum beat "come," "come thou, thou last one," from Sappho's third position advanced to the first: time presses, explosion and falling silent, opening and closing, plosive stammering that runs through the line: "Come thou, thou last one, whom I re cog nize," you must be ten syllables (eleven in German), you must stand on five feet.

Is that finally him, the dominant partner, the pain that the writer longed for? Is the pain so great that the one that says "I" makes himself as small as his fuel? Is the corpse already stiff as wood, which can burn as well as rot, stiff, twisted? Root, log, cross? Has the pain already taken him over entirely, his body, the wooden skin? Once the pain has the body, it also has the spirit. Unholy means he is the infinite blade. And the blade shows no weakness. The blade is the cutting edge. The flame is the manifest emanation of the pain within, which can only show itself for as long as the body that's become the burning pain-wood still is. Thus do pain, body, and soul absorb each other. Pain burns in the body, the soul burns in pain. Mutually enclosing rooms burn according to the Matryoshka principle. So, who is the incluse here?

A strangely prescient death-certain keen: Pain will have to die by burning the fabric. The fabric, the text. And death writes the final text, writes it into the body, into the spirit's body. Body, spirit, and pain cannot be thought of independently from one another, pain extinguishes both body and spirit, then itself with them. But instead of annihilation: transformation of transformations. Colonnade of metonymies. The I as burning spirit transformed into the I as fuel for pain, the poem is the place that facilitates this transformation: Makes the hidden observable: "see, I now burn in thee." Pain is helpless, for it is final, it cannot be transformed back, here, something has caught fire and cannot be extinguished, the spirit-body as a burning thorn bush in which the voice hears itself. If pain is helpless, unbeatable, then only the I can make it holy. Sanctification is carried out as the highest concentration. Pain is the Me of Perception. The keen about the pain that has finally come of age, the synthesis of the now self-recognizing I is an infinitely introspective self-interrogation. Ruprecht still sleeps.

These lines evoke two kinds of burning: ecstasy as the longing that burns for something; fiery burning. Writing and making fire thus appear as synonymous techniques of culture.

What here encodes whom? Pain the I or the I pain? The language the I or pain the language? Without language no pain. Nonsense. without language only no word "pain." Without pain no language. L-aaaaaahh-ngauge. The scream of pain is the ur-code. What is coming to pass in the pain-lines should be possible to reconstruct in syntactically logical fashion. Grammar is the supreme discipline. Grammar of deviation. One blow from a bush hammer and the matter would be brought to an end. "When shall grammar return." It's already there and the delirium ceases.

But the poem keeps going. Like fire that has exceeded its climax, the cool heat of the opening lines subsides, even when a pyre is mentioned:

> My gentle and mild being through thy ruthless fury
>   has turned into a raging hell that is not from here.
> Quite pure, quite free of future planning, I mounted
>   the tangled funeral pyre built for my suffering,
> so sure of nothing more to buy for future needs,
> while round my heart the stored reserves kept silent.
>
> Is it still I, who there past all recognition burn?
>   Memories I do not seize and bring inside.
>
> Memories I do not seize and bring inside.

O life! O living! O to be outside!
And I in flames. And no one here who knows me.

[Relinquishment. It's not the way sickness was
once in childhood. Procrastination. A pretense
in order to be greater. Cries and murmurs.
Don't mix into this the things that surprised you early on.]

Each word herein must be placed beneath the magnifying glass, it must be turned to and fro, turned onto its head, its pockets must be emptied out, one must gut the words well if one doesn't wish to become a murderer. Each letter looks like a gun if one stares at it for a little too long. With a single word, one shall no longer be able to conceal the weapons on one's person, from sentence to sentence, a whole arsenal quickly comes together. A single letter is enough to make one feel wronged, if one has set a book aside and hasn't sufficiently gutted the words, one provokes a war. In order to avoid this, one must spend a lifetime dealing with the words. I hereby resolve to occupy myself with the poem copied from Ruprecht's book for the rest of my life. This poem is a novel. It's a poem about current circumstances. A whole life long, one can only say that in retrospect.

"My gentle and mild being through thy ruthless fury / has turned into a raging hell that is not from here." Again with these paradoxical, indissoluble relationships of inclusion, here as metonymic variations, burning as fury, this world and the next, inverse worlds, mild in this mortal world—pain in hell. The distancing "not from here" refers to "a fury" from "hell" or "a fury of hell"? The "hell not from here" seems to have nothing to do with the "hell from here," which was imparted to us from an early age. So, is there not a hell that is from here? Does the true hell surpass all homemade imaginings? Is the hereafter the true hell, whereas the hell of this mortal world is a paradise? Not from here, which is to say, nowhere. It's everywhere my thoughts can wander.

Furies: to have colic-like pains, to be vexed, to be filled with fury. And fury? Is it a hellhound, an omen of death, a cerberus, a messenger that appears on the eve of death? Gliding language, poetry of grammar, sharper than most devised images and metaphors.

"Quite pure, quite free of future planning": a zero-point has been reached. Quite, pure, planless, and free, those are all positive words; future is the negative counterpart. Free of future planning means: freed from all hustle and bustle and self-imposed achievement. "I mounted the tangled funeral pyre built for my suffering": So that the meter in this line runs like clockwork, the sufferer has gone too far by using a genitive attribute that basically toddles forward in the original German ("auf des Leidens wirren Scheiterhaufen"). A quite notable distinguishing feature. He suffers. He says it. Metonymically, the pyre stands helpless in the series—Pain—Burning—Wood—Flames—Blazing—Hell. It's tangled: It has no homogeneity, clearly outlined figure, is more of a diffuse heap, the logs lie in disorder, the pains shift. "Freed from future planning" is a synonym of "tangled." Does the sufferer see himself as a heretic receiving a punishment that he doesn't understand? Do the helpless pains therefore not nail him to the cross, but, instead, burn him—and in this burning lies no salvation. His mortal mildness incenses the hellhound. The raging pain becomes a cerberus. The indefinite article suggests that there are multiple hellhounds.

"so sure of nothing more to buy for future needs, / while round my heart the stored reserves kept silent." So sure: to possess a firm certainty, to be thus or more generally very certain, of the conviction, knowing with certainty, to be immune to something—and this certainty is deceptive, this conviction turns out to be false. Poetry of imprecise grammar (at least in the original). The ambiguity of individual words, even in context, corresponds to a multiply encoded syntax. The stored reserves of the heart (an unusual formulation to say the least): so sure of nothing more to buy (but then the verb would be missing)—while round my heart the stored reserves kept silent: while in my heart the stored reserves kept silent, to calm it down, to bind it to something. Stored reserves: lying ahead, an incident in the future; abstraction, a rather pathetic expression; "to store up" is the association that comes to me. This archaic "round": a moment of distance corresponding to the solemn expressions: One doesn't talk like this. A puzzling grammatical function.

Is the heart already saturated, overfull, if it indeed has stores? Stores of what? Memories? Is not such a silent heart to be called wise? The silent stores are the answer to the proclamation of the future. One builds up a supply by gathering it together, under certain circumstances one has acquired it in order to sell it. "To buy for future needs," in German, "Künftiges zu kaufen," is just a fancy bit of alliteration, to acquire something in the sense "make something one's own," does not, in any case, have such a clearly mercantile aftertaste. Or does the line "so sure of nothing more to buy for future needs" speak of refraining from bribery because it was prevented, which is all of life and the heart holds it tight? "The stored reserves kept silent": to hold one's tongue; to fall in love no more. Pain is now the beloved, male or female. But why *did* he climb (and is he not climbing) onto the tangled funeral pyre? Has he been in pain like this for a long time and many times and did he not know from whence these pains came, what was it about them, with them? For this reason, the wood refused to burn, the disease is not named as such, the wood of life believed that it had no reason to give in to the pain: "the wood that long resisted the advancing flames / which thou kept flaring, I now am nourishing." Is that why the last pain is the hopeless one, because the funeral pyre is now no longer tangled, but very clearly recognized as the seat of the lesion, as the cause of death, and thus did he climb up "Quite pure, quite free of future planning," for he was naive, unaware of this cause, living for the day as if the illness didn't exist, the disease that came from hell—suddenly. There is a word that shall pop up more and more, as one night when I suddenly get up and am thinking of nothing and everything I look at suddenly vanishes, thus is it written in this book. Can one only be "free" from the future if one has one or is certain that one has one that one "suddenly" no longer has, "quite pure," innocent like a child, "so sure of nothing more to buy for future needs, / while round my heart the stored reserves kept silent," the illness has already infiltrated the heart, but that which did the infiltrating has not yet made itself felt, the patient thinks that the illness shall soon once more have passed, just as in childhood, when it was only "procrastination," "pretense," but now death, which *is* in the beginning, can no longer be postponed, and there is no longer any need to grow out of the illness, except, perhaps, in the spirit, but the spirit is cold, the sufferer is completely burnt-out in spirit. "Vor-Wand," meaning "pretext" or "forward wall"—heart-wall, the wall behind which the future is—the infiltrated heart-wall, the last wall. "Is it still I, who there past all recognition burn?" Here, the short flashback has come to an end, the funeral pyre is burning, the burning one is no longer so sure of himself, as burning in the spirit means distraction from the self that has been negated. "Past all recognition" is the purest of bureaucracy, a courteous word that allows the burning pain to take precedence, the perverted I is merely its servant, its informer, he who stays in the background. The illness pulls the flaming body inward out of life. Mother, distorted by illness. You're nice and skinny now, I said to her after the operation when I visited her at home. After that, she grew ever skinnier. Father's second wife also burned. She simply melted away. Wax dripping down from the candle. "And no one here who knows me." Is no one Nobody? What does it mean to "know"? Is that the loneliness of dying, the astonishment that he no longer knows himself and can only recall that which has been, "memories," which he refuses to "bring inside," even though, by the fact of naming them, he has already incorporated them into the pain. Does he fear that the memories could be the future of the past for which he no longer has a future and thus does he not wish to "bring" it into his heart, into the flames of the funeral pyre? To be outside. Does that mean to be excluded from life and does being outside mean the paradise of childhood, romping around the garden, being unsupervised? "O to be outside! And I." This stubborn, high-spirited self-assertion that goes against everything else.

"Don't mix into this the things that surprised you early on": is it into "this," childhood, memories unto themselves, that no one should mix deadly foreboding? The final pain? The dying one? Or is it the other way around, pain as dying, for one is unthinkable without the other, is it childhood, which was innocent, that should not be mixed into dying? What inspired wonder in him early on should not be retrospectively mixed into his memories, his childhood. This invocation turns into a soliloquy, which, if pain, death, and the utterer are one, is a self-invocation. What is that which inspired wonder in him early on? That there is pain and healing and despair is a thought of hope, "It's not the way sickness was / once in childhood." Or did the pain inspire wonder in him early on, this inexplicable pain, growing ever stronger, and, once one recognized it, it became the final, hopeless pain?

With the last line, the invocation comes full circle. But is it the last line or does it break off here and an infinite number of empty lines follow—white time—in which the last, hopeless pain has come and the flaming wood shall soon be extinguished?

Why does this concern me? It doesn't concern me, it penetrates me, it nests in me, proliferates, has a link to my inner basic stock; actually, it does concern me, it concerns me so much that I lose my footing. To think that something touches the center of one's own life, a fear, an idea associated with this fear, death, the fear of a bad, possibly fatal illness that one feels approaching and to which one sees oneself defenselessly exposed, and this frightful representation underscores life, it goes on for years, until the fear and, with it, the representation emerges from the background and becomes the all-dominating figure of life, which penetrates into all areas of life—fear of contracting a cancer, which other family members have already contracted, then died from, and no negative finding in the context of a so-called preventive medical checkup is capable of calming the patient, already ill before the illness, the mere question of whether it should be called a positive or negative finding if an illness is diagnosed or, on the contrary, cannot be found, puts the person concerned into a furious state of turmoil, as if a misunderstanding of language could, if the disease hasn't yet manifested itself, trigger it as a kind of punishment, if concept and thing are causally connected, one cannot be thought of without the other. It is of no use to such a distraught individual that the doctor says to him, we shall see each other again in five years unless something unusual occurs, but the unusual has already come to pass, in that the patient must keep thinking about the illness, whether he is now being examined or not, whether he is now being given a life-threatening diagnosis or not, the inhabitual is for him the habitual, and he just can't get used to it. If the doctor says to him, you're healthy as a horse, the patient somehow senses in that initial "h" an impending "but" whose "b" is so big that death is already lurking behind it. Through that "b," the patient has already vanished, well before the doctor has finished saying "healthy as a horse." A colonoscopy has shown that, apart from a few diverticula, the bowel displayed nothing conspicuous that could indicate the onset of an illness. Does this mean that the inconspicuous as such points to an incipient illness? the patient asks himself while reading the last sentence once more. You have nothing more than a couple of diverticula, with those you can easily live to be 115 years old, Diverticulosis, the doctor says. A bowel-word that the patient enjoys letting melt in his mouth. Diverticulosis. The patient asks the doctor whether he is no longer a patient. The doctor doesn't understand the question, but replies that every person is always a patient, always and forever. But if someone never goes to the doctor, is he still always a patient then? Well, the person who never goes to the doctor is a fool, the doctor says. Are you quite sure that I won't have to come back for five years, the patient asks. Listen here, which of us is the specialist, the doctor ripostes. You are, the patient says, but it's worth wondering whether my case might be an exceptional one. What do you mean by that, the doctor asks. I mean to say that, in my case, it would perhaps be better if I were to come back in a year, after all, I don't really mind drinking this sweet stuff and running to the toilet for hours. Five years, the doctor says. In my case too? In your case too. Is that your final word on the matter? That is my final word. And when I want to come back next year. Then we'll talk about whether that makes sense next year. Perhaps, the doctor jokes, you'll already have died of another illness by then. That's not possible, I can only die of this illness, the patient says. Now, I can really see that you're a special case, the doctor says and bids him farewell, other tushes must be waiting. The patient can stand up again now. A thin curtain separates his corner from the hallway. On the other side of the hall lies an old woman. Her face can be made out through the not-quite-drawn curtain. It's likely cancer, the patient hears the nurse say. The woman lies motionless upon her couch. She is entirely truthful as she lies there, the patient thinks. He likes the expression "truthful"—to be full of truth. Why did the doctor not tell her? Does the doctor only feel responsible for delivering good news? The doctor is a jester, the nurse a messenger of bad news. Corvus corone corone, you shall still receive your punishment. From now on, you shall wear a black dress and only ever crow. Before that, however, the patient's eyes close once more. He's not quite sure whether the nurse said that. The woman's face has an expression communicating that the nurse has just broken some bad news to her. Did she say that you have cancer, the patient asks the old woman. The woman doesn't reply. Did he really ask her that? Did I ask you whether the nurse said to you that you have cancer? As he receives no reply, the patient rises up from his couch, stretches out, and pushes the curtain off to the side. With three steps, he is across the hall and into the woman's corner, but nobody is lying on the couch there. She must have already died, the patient thinks. Only the overestimated die young. The burden of being overestimated destroys them. Marc Herrisch* is dead. Instead of rejoicing and exulting, those who have been abused, controlled, and neglected, the discarded, slandered, and exploited who suffered under him, who hated him, who wished him death, all of them simply weave. Funeral wreathes. The dead man played the role of moral admonisher, of foreseer and social utopian, until he died: mad disgrace.

Ruprecht has a cold arm. His rat tail holds me tight. Forearm and hand consist of only bones. Was it always thus? I look at the picture very carefully once more. His hand has three fingers. It is this hand that writes my lines while Ruprecht reads the written page with his left. Is it not nice to have a thought that is Ruprecht to sit with you in hell? He writes what I think. If I no longer am, is he also no longer extant? I am afraid that a piece of him will break off if I touch him, he's so cold and rigid.

"to be greater": no longer, impending death is the end of childhood. "to be greater" / "Come thou, thou last one": away from a beginning and toward a goal. In between lies the distance of a lived life, which the poem travels in the opposite direction. Beginning—End (Life) / End—Beginning (Poem). A beautiful, unthinkable figure of thought. At the end of the poem stands the beginning of life. At the end of life stands a poem about end and beginning. If skillfully arranged, life and poem placed on top of one another would result in a cross. Seeing the beginning in the end and the end in the beginning, that is a baroque cross, a constellation of contemplation that is still settling its accounts with God:

<pre>
        alpha and omega
     Biginning   Ende
             in
       Ende   Biginning
</pre>

---

* Marc Imperious.

> The ende that thou seekest woven into the beginning
> He who ist wys on earth shall be holie in hevene

Biginning and Ende are in God. The end is in the beginning right from the beginning. Beginning / End: End / Beginning. Bigin the Ende, begin Eden. That is: the counter-program to bestial hell.

The square brackets indicate something unfinished. Illness had the audacity to take over its host animal before the completion of the poem that captures it, the illness, in such a way that the animal, increasingly emptied out, as one empties out an apartment that one wants to give up, is laid to rest with eyes wide open. Thoughts shimmer about, but can no longer find a hand that might bring them down and the host knows that, even if he's thought these thoughts a hundred times, they shall never be written down. The host to whom the parasite has adapted poorly is an aberrant host. Instead of banishing him into the poem, which would render him harmless, the parasite rages in him with particular severity.

The thoughts are tangled and aimless. If someone came to hear them, he would not be able to comprehend them, they no longer find their way to the voice. And, indeed, someone is coming, he finds eyes sunk deep into pillow, open and dark, they read the alphabet out. Someone read that. The alphabet is a secret script. Did you understand, the eyes ask.

A feather dances before Ruprecht's nose. I blow on it, it reels, turns away, returns. Now, it stays up in the air, seems to be looking at me. Ruprecht squats there as if dead. I know that he can read my thoughts. The feather is a spider. Is a feather. Now: if I were to pluck this feather out of the air and my hand were to touch the chimera's head. I can distinctly feel that Ruprecht is sucking me dry with his rattail, slowly tightening its noose around me. Ruprecht is a Nachzehrer, my dead father who still lives and Ruprecht himself wrote the poem, the red cloak billowing forth from his head and onto the ground is his shroud, which he consumes, and, some time ago, he seems to have begun to consume parts of his own body, but has remained supple, he can move eyes, mouth, and tongue just like the living, it's his eyes that sank into the pillow earlier, he consumes his shroud, which is lengthened by twice the amount consumed, until the shroud has encircled the globe and met with the back of Ruprecht's head. I get it, I say to him. "Come thou, thou last one, whom I recognize," that is the alphabet, I promise to put the alphabet into order, for just when it seems to be ordered into words and sentences, it can be overcome by the greatest of disorders. By the time that I have it sorted out, I think, it might once more have fallen into disorder. Order is therefore an improbable, transitory special case of disorder; disorder predominates and order is happenstance. It is a best-case scenario if one can say: I have brought the alphabet into disorder. Thus must words and sentences be permanently rearranged. Losing myself in this thought, Ruprecht's shroud has, in the meantime, covered over the toad-studded archway, out of which Lucifer has strode, thus opening up the view into the depths of hell, the shroud is preparing to scale the balcony when I turn the page and read:

"'Bridle your mouth from speaking / and your heart from thinking.' This is what I'd like to do. Ruprecht's pricking tail is as long and hard as the longest of tree roots. He's a mandrake in the form of a rat, a scion of the future hanged man, who, upon his death, let a few more drops drip from two different sources. The future is reckoned in pages. There remain, at most, 759 more pages. My soul is in this mandrake because I sold it to him. Write me this book and you can have my soul, I told Satan. Then he replied: go forth and live your life, the book shall write itself. Now, I must witness what is written in the book. Immutable. Immutably written and immutably witnessed. Immobilism. He who was once evil of his own free will shall remain so forever. The devil wrote the book, it's written here. There is no such thing as apocatastasis, the devil says, he learned that from Augustine. I shall always be the devil, as I have opted for evil at all times. Thus is the freedom to repent excluded. Where would we then be, the good ones in heaven would be losing their marbles over whether their own case was a misjudgement—a divine lapse of judgment—and they would soon have to join my society. I can see that. The devil says: If God established me and I am a pure spirit, a body of air, how then can I suffer the torments of hell engulfed in flames? That's an old question. What's new about it is that I'm going to ask it myself, the devil says. I do not like, the devil says, this construction. Either the devil says this, in which case he doesn't have to write, the devil says, or the devil doesn't say it. Then another says it. Thus is it written in the book, which is a fruit of the Lucifer Tree." The chimera is growing into me. I can no longer reach the book. As if that were its way of making sure that I couldn't turn to another page. Its pricking tail has penetrated my back and is now wandering down my right leg, out of which it emerges once more at the height of the ankle. Slowly, he creeps toward the book, digs into the ground parallel to these lines and under the frame on which it lies, then peers out of the earth again on the other side, a sprout that springs up as a rod from God's gift, the book as its fruit, upon which shall rest the spirit of wisdom and understanding, the spirit of counsel and of might, the spirit of knowledge and of fear. Ach, if only I were an angel and the dragon's pricking tail could wipe me from heaven. The pages follow my eyes, gliding over their lines, and with the last word of the last line of the right-hand page, it rises up and allows the gaze to freely fall onto the two pages lying below. I read faster, the thin branches of Ruprecht's pricking tail are slowly spreading across the book and shall soon have it arrested. My eyes fly to and fro

special awakening experiences: Mother always woke me up at night with the question, Will the wrath

Of the immortal God cause to approach The pillar, where around a circle flows The river inexhaustible of fire. Then will the angels of the immortal God, Who ever liveth, direly punish them With flaming scourges and with fiery flames, Bound from above with ever-during bonds.

whether it now be good again and why one did that. Each response, always the same one, always deletes the question, always the same one.

Then in Gehenna, in the midnight gloom, Will they be to Tartarean monsters cast, Many and fierce, where darkness is supreme. But when all punishments have been entailed On all whose hearts were evil, then straightway From the great river will a fiery wheel

And Mother wakes me and asks why I did that and I reply and she asks and Mother wakes me. Why did you do that, Mother asks, and I answer

'This nursing of the pain forego thee, that, like a vulture, feeds upon thy breast! The worst society thou find'st will show thee thou art a man among the rest.'

Circle them round, pressed down with wicked works; And then in many a way most piteously Will fathers, mothers, nursing children wail

I hear the pronouncement of judgment and I am condemned

The thinner branches of the pricking tail bear yellow-green fruits about one centimeter in size, they lie in hundreds upon and beside the book. They are ripe, I can easily separate them from their stems. They taste sweet. I eat so many of them that I can read the book once more.

If you eat a fruit, a new one grows back immediately. The fruits can only be eaten in a certain sequence. If they are not eaten in this sequence, you, who have already nibbled on them without asking about the consequences, shall throw the sequence of your daily routine into disarray without being able to restore it, and thereafter shall you be forced to live in disorder, you shall die before death and rise again, and nobody shall believe you any more, you shall commit crimes without being responsible for them, other than in that they stem from a lack of order, your life shall have no end, as it has no beginning, you shall never be able to stop eating the fruits, otherwise you shall starve, which shall not, however, come to pass, not even if you've made the decision to starve, as the consumption of a single fruit alone shall make you addicted, and thus shall you have to eat one fruit per hour, the sequence runs

The following pages are empty. My eyes hurt. I attribute that to the fruit. Then more text appears:

As far as I'm concerned, the text should be corrected. The new-growing fruit grows constantly, if I didn't eat it, it would crush me, as I, a prisoner of both the chimera and the book, cannot budge. Perhaps, I should try it. Drown in the juice of the fruit or perish from the drug. But what if I don't have the freedom to choose between these two possibilities? I eat a fruit. Suddenly, the text on the page of the book changes. You didn't pay attention to the sequence. Henceforth, you shall eat a fruit every twenty minutes. Twenty minutes. If I eat a fruit and precisely one fruit grows back, their number remains constant. I count 666 fruits. That gives 666 to the power of 665 possible sequences. The chance of starting with the right fruit is one in 665. Because the eaten fruit grows back, the repeated consumption of one and the same fruit-position is not excluded from the outset. If Schönberg's law of the series applies, however, repetition is beyond dispute, first, the complete series of 666 fruits must have been eaten. Even if I were to consume the fruits in the correct order, which is as good as out of the question, I couldn't eat them according to the prescription as I have no clock. Then a clock appears in my head. It is the Cologne Cathedral clock. One must beware of this clock, it is a golden deception built by an illiterate man who knew only enough script to write his own name. His tower clocks were characterized by a precision that was unrivaled anywhere else in the world, a precision that the inventor, with a superb Georgeian head of hair, also made use of for a guillotine with a metal frame. Traveler! when to the Cologne Cathedral thou comest and lookest at the nave clock in the southern side aisle, declare that thou hast seen the white roses fall from the same metal as the law hath ordained. The two hour-bells from the cathedral knell may also declare this. Our life is a memory of the dead. This Drahtmann, not only did he invent the precision of the tower clock, but also added a minute hand to it, in such a way that, in observing the Cologne Cathedral clock, we can commemorate the dead as each minute passes with distinct visibility. And now, each minute that I see the cathedral clock moving forward in my head, I commemorate the dead, I shall eat a fruit every twentieth minute in their honor, hoping that the fruit is a fruit of knowledge and shall show me the right path through the 666 fruits. I think of my mother who died too young and reproached herself for her improper upbringing right up until the end; I commemorate my recently deceased teacher, Jean Fidel Storno alias Jean Doris Teflon alias Jens Feilt Adorno,* who was both spur and role model, the good as well as the bad conscience, a mercurial will and master, who, affected by a holy shyness, was troubled by anything too concrete, as it would quickly become too much of a "factoid" for him; I commemorate David who played the role of Lazarus, with buttons instead of eyes, floating, hovering, struggling, coaxing a last letter out from his quill, and it is in his voice that he rises from the dead, the voice that each carries before themselves, as if it always had been the other whom one cannot stop oneself from listening in on, the other who is neither dead nor alive; I commemorate

---

* Jens Rasps Adorno.

he who took the name to remain himself, but who took his own life far too soon, even all his riches could not prevent it, he too is risen in his voice and in the sound of his lyre; I commemorate Herr Wolfgang Fords, who was taken by the pistol that he shot himself with and this pistol now lies cold next to the Neckar, while he himself lies in our hearts; I commemorate all of my friends who shall soon die, some of them lament, y'see, y'see, life did me wrong, I'm gonna die soon, the others wait for death with eyes wide open, undaunted, how strange, they shall say on their death bed, they probably want to see the five wooden musicians from the Ore Mountains once more, the ones that their mother used to put on the marble windowsill over the radiator in the great room at Christmas, before immediately putting them back into the cardboard box after the holidays, until next year, this, for the boy, was the true resurrection and the true mystery was not Jesus, but the question of where the five musicians might possibly be the whole year round; I commemorate Johann Drahtmann who invented the minute hand of the tower clock and nevertheless went broke, he was the maternal great-great-great-uncle of Guenther Markte,† the one who wrote *kant* and has no time for death, which, in its turn, has no interest in *kant*, and thus shall *kant* live forever—and they all sit at a large table, to which they have been invited by the bibulous Kasper Doesewitz, who demanded daily words of praise for idling away his time, for the reception of which he had himself carried in on a self-built, throne-like structure (an altar, some would say)—into a large room, where his servile flatterers were already waiting, a room out of which, totally drunk, he was later carried in the same fashion, however, in most cases, the room was empty, though this didn't bother him in the slightest, his favorite lines from a poem about the law of the under-world were: "And now all of a sudden doth it us befall / there's no one in the conference hall," and the room (the conference hall, some would

---

† Guenther Market.

say), where this table stands, collapses, the dead are buried beneath the rubble, their disfigured bodies can no longer be identified, an anonymous burial is impending, solely the poet Moses Videos Nikon, also known as Scheremon Weniaminoschweski Solowitsch, who is as incapable of forgetting anything as he is of keeping secrets, and who had been assigned to adulate Doesewitz on that day, has—ere he was summoned on an urgent matter by Alexowitsch Ander and Roman Juliar, two Dioscuri proficient in following the soul's steps up and down the stairs between Hades and Olympus, and both lauded by him, Moses, at least as exuberantly as his patron himself, after Doesewitz had berated him and only wanted to pay out one half of the salary they had agreed upon (the other half, he said, would have to be procured by Ander and Juliar themselves since they had been granted their own half of the praise-pie)—memorized where each guest was sitting before the room (the conference hall, some would say) collapsed without him being present, and thus is mnemonics born out of a catastrophe and ends in the catastrophe of not forgetting. Kasper Doesewitz was also slain and thus did the only witness who should have testified that nobody was in this room, in this conference room, others say, become one with the room, the conference room, others say. The rumor is now that Kasper Doesewitz dreamed up the poet Moses Videos Nikon alias Sheremon Weniaminoschewski Solowitsch so that the man might write him an undivided lament about the half of the praise proverbially gone to slop, a lament which Kasper Doesewitz then wrote himself, which led to the presumption that Doesewitz did not perish and that the collapse never came to pass, which, in turn, provoked others to the assertion that Doesewitz was an invention of Moses Videos Nikon alias Sheremon Weniaminoschewski Solowitsch, who, completely idiotic in terms of politics, only wanted to give himself airs with such a tragic event—too many contradictions everywhere, which is why the story is of no further interest here.

    I see the Cologne Cathedral clock in my head and I see the words

TOWER CLOCK. And there is the gate tower. And the gate tower has a gate-tower clock. Drahtmann's minute-hand has now advanced nineteen times. I grab a fruit and detach it from its stem, it is ripe, something is swimming in its insides, or something is reflected on its surface, a waving figure, it's impossible to tell if it's in trouble or full of joy, twenty minutes have now passed, I put the whole fruit into my mouth and bite it in two. Something is moving in your mouth now, don't you dare, says a voice, I try to fish the little figure that I can feel with the tip of my tongue out of the fruit-fluid, it's my mother's little ivory figurine, I once found it in her round wooden jewelry box, and from then on was convinced that I could no longer live without it, it was with suspicion that Mother observed how I was interested in this little figurine, she said that it was the only thing she had left so as to remember a certain person. As if she had been naughty, as if she wished to beguile me, Mother took the figure out of the velvet-lined box and laid it into a small, oblong box, the barrenness of which made me sad. That's the punishment, Mother said, then made the box disappear. I have never figured out whom this had to do with, the figurine remained vanished even after her death, she swallowed it way back when, I thought, and that's why she became terminally ill, it must have been a love she didn't live out. However, the box popped up a few years later.

The fruits are so heavy that they slide from the book along with their twigs. The exposed pages are initially blank, then a text appears: "You have once more eaten the wrong fruit. Now, you shall have to eat a fruit every ten minutes." I put the figure onto my right thigh so that I always have it in view. It seems to be praying, throwing its arms up into the air. Upon closer inspection, I see that it's not ivory, but a tooth that has been worked over with a milling machine for such a long time that it has been emblazoned with Jesus' visage and this little milk-tooth Jesus is Mother's whole child, he whom Mother banished from the jewelry box and laid into the eternal night of the other box. To know that there is something in it, of the existence of which you alone know, over which you have total power, total right of disposal; with that, Mother might have made her life more bearable. Imagining that this Jesus-child could survive me too, after it had already survived my mother, and that the unlived love must always be on its way hurts me more than my mother's death, which I have managed to conceive of as immutable, if not in my dreams and intoxications, then at least in everyday life. In this light, something shadowy appears on the figure in the middle of its radiant-white milk teeth. Upon its back, razor-sharp, a masterpiece of craftsmanship, is written with the finest hand: "And still we fear the ill which happens never, and what we lose not are bewailing ever."

Now, the figure points to the archway, out of which the rat appears at that moment, takes a good look at everyone around, then approaches the chimera with leisurely stride. That's the way to do it, one whispers into the other's ear, let's leave it at that for now. His Way of the Cross has five stations, Lucifer says, from now on he goes in circles. I am the five blades of the windmill. Nothing stands in the way of my resurrection, unless there isn't enough wind. Each strong wind, whether full of rage or care, is a Satan-wind. The figure is kneeling in the presence of Lucifer. It's become red-hot and has burnt into my thigh. I'm disgusted by it, I'd like to get rid of it, but it is now Lucifer's tick and has sucked itself full of blood, if I were to rip it out of my flesh, the head would get stuck and a devilish brainwashing would begin. Once it's saturated itself, it will fall off on its own. But its sucking comes to no end and thus does it become bigger and bigger, I now call it Lucifer's Jesus-cyst, it develops a double chin, it stares at me constantly as it sucks until the uncontrolled increase seems to become too much for it, its body is now quite rigid and lengthens even more in its rigidity, while its nimble eyes, exempted from the dilation, beseech pity. In fact, they would certainly manage to arouse said pity if they didn't, in the same blink of an eye, signal that they were amused by the colossal expansion. Now, the cyst-tick has fallen off and I do not ask, my Jesus, my Jesus, why have you forsaken me. Jesus just fell off of my thigh, I still have him. As for Jesus and God the Father, it must be a translation error. Shouldn't one simply translate "Elí, Elí, lemá sabachtháni" as "it is what it is"?

    The chimera has since become quite cold, I can break its fingers, thin, dry twigs, its right thumb falls off at the slightest contact, now, I have its whole hand in my hand, fifteen minutes have passed, the cathedral clock shows, I tear a fruit from its stem and stick it hastily into my mouth, you're too late, the voice says, from now on, you'll eat a fruit every five minutes, as a lapse, "too late" ranks before "in the wrong sequence," it won't be long before I'll have to eat the wrong fruits constantly, Ruprecht, the mandrake, the Nachzehrer, is gone, he consumed me until he found a place in me, the thorny branches of his pricking tail have tightened around the book, which has now become unreadable. But in my head, I can read the book very well, though I don't trust it, the thorn-pierced book of all books lying before me has become the only source of my contemplation, I haven't been able to read a single book more in recent years, as soon as I pick one up, I am overcome by a leaden exhaustion, deep sorrow whelms me and I am haunted by the fear that the reading of a single page of this book will, instead of enriching my life, spoil it altogether, as if I were waiting for a moment, a crucial turning point that I could skip over, the book, indeed, any book, would bind together all evil bent only on missing out on life at its crucial turning point, which consists in shedding the fear of death, for in reading, I die, only doing nothing means really living, but the book of all books is hardly a book at all, it is the shadow of the black flames upon the white flames blazing on God's arm and black flame is required to interpret white flame, but there is a single black flame, which the white flame can make visible and, nonetheless, the white flame shall be unreadable and we shall read only the black flame in the certainty that it might show the white flame. I see my mother's little figure, which has become the cyst-tick, it is standing upon the wooden Renaissance pulpit of the Cologne Cathedral and preaching: "To them, the truth would be literally nothing but the shadows of the images. The virtue of wisdom more than anything else contains a divine element which always remains, and by this conversion is rendered useful and profitable; or, on the other hand, hurtful and useless. And here, all sorts of mixtures are possible. Did you never observe the narrow intelligence flashing from the keen eye of a clever rogue—how eager he is, how clearly his paltry soul sees the way to his end; he is the reverse of blind, but his keen eyesight is forced into the service of evil, and he is mischievous in proportion to his cleverness?" The tower clock indicates that it's time for the next fruit, I will not eat them punctually, there shall come a moment when I shall have to eat one fruit every second, the thought of the fruit is the addiction, not the fruit. The five minutes have passed. I want to wait for the sixth minute. You always sing from your own book, a voice in me says, and I recognize it to be Ruprecht's voice.

The rat sits upon the master's throne and I sit before the rat, Ruprecht says. At the front side of the throne, facing you, who are held by my hands and shall sit before the throne and wait, for years shall you wait, there is a small door that leads down into the depths, it can be seen by nobody, precisely like the depths of your brother's wardrobe on page 485 and from the depths comes the groaning of the souls chucked down, which you must hear during your years of waiting without being able to put your hands over your ears, and I shall look at you for years, that which is an immeasurable torment for you shall be an inexhaustible well of joy for me, Ruprecht says. Imagining this is hardly bearable, even more unbearable to me is the prelude to his words, which come across as if there were something to celebrate, an improper Jubilate! accompanies them. My vision is quite sharp, my mother's little figure says.

"Don't you want to come down?" I ask the figure. "There's no sermon to deliver. Come down to me." "You're wrong about that," the figure says. "I am only the voice of the pulpit that thunders out if you look at the pulpit. I am your deepest wish, your hungry fear. To be bound to the pulpit by my ministry is incomparably more than to live freely in the world. But your father is a Doctor of Canon and Civil Law and, should he not strike upon something in the Civil Code with which to condemn you, he shall open canon law as wide as the welkin and hang you in the hole in the sky that his divine desire for justice has created, free from any and all environs, you swing there, as when your parents joyfully hurled you into the air, five times as high as your height, then caught you again just above the stone floor divided into squares, even then, your father was already dreaming of a great hole in the sky into which you could disappear and, as you came down to earth, was staring at the bright square right at the peak, which, surrounded by four red triangles, vanished into the middle of the stone-floor plot, and it wasn't mere enthusiasm for life that made your parents hurl you into the air as if they had to get rid of a burden just for a moment, the bright square always reminded your father of his work, he recognized the threat to this work in the red triangles, the red triangles did much pain to the square, they cut four triangles off of it in such a way that, reduced in size, it had to stand on its head, and thus were you a triangle. As such, while you gave rise to constant pains in your father, always in the same place, a wound that will not heal, in such a way that your father felt the stone floor to be a part of his body, you found an unflagging joy in being suspended between heaven and earth and at night you dreamed that life was precisely that, a weightless flight up to God, then back down into sure hands, until you woke up one morning and made the decision to become a little Enoch, to live for 365 years, to stroll through the heavens with God, then, finally, to no longer be there, for God shall have taken you away. However, instead of clambering up to the heavens, you can't get past your father, who guards the door that leads upstairs, you speak with him, and, for many years, he doesn't answer, you don't even know whether he's still there, and you no longer dreamed of a weightless flight, but of a longing for the hereafter, which your father is, 'O Lord, I am not worthy that thou shouldest enter under my roof, but speak the word only and my soul shall be healed,' you whispered to him day in and day out, but the hereafter remained empty. No winds gave you wings and moved you and lifted you upward to the heavens, you remain in your white cell with its perfectly smooth white walls, onto which you can project any image with your eyes by staring at them for such a long time that images come. Thus did you bring your father, who denied you the hereafter, into your cell and lead him by the leash of the eyes. Thus did your film become your only reality, the cave in which you sat enchained was in your head." That's what the Jesus-tick says as it strides down the pulpit, a seemingly endless rotation that ends in straight steps, it comes toward me from the top of that rotation with outstretched hand. Someone in me is perpetually saying: "It has made itself full with your blood." I hear their voice between my ears.

Ruprecht holds onto my hands from the inside, if I touch something, Ruprecht touches it. I give the Jesus-tick my hand. "That's really disgusting," Ruprecht says. He can raise his voice in me whenever he wants to, he guides my hand, dictates the text to my thoughts, he has entered my body and soul and sits before me on the inside, can watch everything I do, he sees and feels me, just as I see and feel myself, without seeing or feeling him. I have no certainty that it is I who sees and feels me and that I see and feel myself. But he does possess the certainty of seeing and feeling me, of seeing himself when he sees me, and of feeling himself when he feels me. In all that I do, he is connected to me, he looks straight ahead with my eyes, he looks at me inwardly with his eyes. Thus shall this be the punishment. This is what Ruprecht dictates to me in Lucifer's name and I write it down. If the devil is a bad painter, as one says, thus must he also be a bad poet. The devil knows what is said about him. He says it to himself, to further reassure those who never for a moment think he might be in their midst.

You shall now eat all the fruits at once, Ruprecht says. And I eat all the fruits at once. Then I hear a loud voice from behind me, as if from a thunderous kartouwe, and the voice speaks: "Write that which you see in a book and give me the book." And I turn to see the voice speaking to me and, as I turn, I see a figure both man and beast, the head alone of man, the torso and limbs a mixture of creeping and flying creatures. If a human head sat upon the torso of a cockroach, pale and wearing glasses, funny little hands sticking up from the draped shoulders, along with insect wings that were much too big pointed down, and if, down below, the hooded little man, blackened horribly, were transmogrified into a gecko, could one stifle one's laughter? Yes, the description creates only a phantom, whereas, face to face, it rises to its true figure. "The things which must shortly be done," the figure babbles. My silence spurs it on to further speech. "Worthy am I, who was slain, then put back together from many others, to receive power, and wisdom, and strength, and honor, and glory, and blessing." The voice sounds quite mechanical, it doesn't belong to the cockroach and doesn't belong to the man's head, which lacks a larynx. "The things which must shortly be done," the voice repeats. Am I conversing with it or not, what difference does it make? "I am thy fellow servant, and of thy brethren the prophets, and of them that keep the sayings of this book. Seal not the sayings of the prophecy of this book, for the time is at hand." As it speaks, it crawls forward a few centimeters, then backward once more. As if a nervous system were forming inside of it and sending signals to the extremities, its reaction makes the functioning of the system verifiable. The voice and breathing are also effects of the nervous system. The figure is completely unimplicated in what it says. "My faithful martyr, who was slain among you, where Satan dwelleth," it says. Satan lives behind me. And who was killed? Like a speech machine, the voice in the figure spits out individual sentences: "I know where Satan's throne is." And now, the speech machine is broken: "ho on kai o än kai ho er cho me nos." I write that down as I hear it. And the machine continues to speak: "mio sono, aachen kao, eh ohr kino ohne ohr, omi so kino, aachen kao, kimono on rio, hohes aachen kao, o kairo, hohes kino, aachen mono, orion, hohes aachen, omo kokain."

I sit on a stone in a flowing pink robe that drapes its folds into seven neat tiers. I cannot administer justice, thus is the judge's gesture not for me, and I set leg down next to leg instead of leaving them crossed, I leave my elbow on my right leg, but do not want chin and cheek to be nestled into my hand. Write that which you hear in a book, says a loud voice, as if from a shofar.

And there appears in the heavens a woman with child, her vestment the sun and the moon beneath her feet and, upon her head, a crown with twelve stars of gold. He-who-is-like-God hurled Lucifer, the dragons with the seven heads, down to the earth and thus saved those twelve stars that Lucifer wanted to siphon off from the sky along with all other stars. It has been one-third darker ever since. The woman was finally transported to heaven with her child and thus could the dragon not consume the woman's child after pursuing her all the way into the desert. From sky to earth, there did Lucifer burn and now is he entirely blackened. He is ashamed of his size and appearance, it was with a heavy heart that he had to renounce those seven crowns that fell to the earth with him, in any case, how would he even wear them, he would disappear in his entirety in such a way that one would no longer be able to distinguish him from a speck of dust, he could no longer clamber out of it with his own strength, for he does not prove himself able to fly, despite his wings. But whoever now believes there is no more danger from Lucifer shall see himself deceived. The controversy as to whether he was and is and, if he is, whether he's not some ridiculous apparition that God shall keep in check to prevent him from tampering with his scriptures, which shall set the earth ablaze, for God's watchmen shall constantly check God's word to see whether deviations that are the work of the devil have not already crept in and, for each watchman, the exegesis of the other watchmen is also the work of the devil. But who is the wee lad whom the dragon was after and whom the woman was protecting?

The shofar is an angel and out of the mouth of the angel comes a two-edged sharp sword. With this sword does the angel mediate the words of the woman with the child. And the sword signifies dominion, divine justice, and violence. The sword-word applies. I think very seriously about the fact that this woman with child now guides my quill, mediated by an angel who speaks her language and mine. And I write what she speaks through the angel with the quill, put it down in my already written book whose invisible script I make visible in reading writing. I ask the angel whether I shouldn't also write what I see and to whom I should send that which I've written. The angel replies that I should write that which I hear, for what I see is given to me, I see nothing but that which I don't hear. Thus should I send that which I've written back into my father's painting—from whence I purloined it. Then would my father rise once more from the black page and be just to me. I do not believe the angel, the angel of revelation and interpretation. How, then, can I be sure that the angel is translating correctly and is not acting in unauthorized fashion? Is he translating at all? Are you Meṭaṭron, called "YHWH ha-qatan," the "Little YHWH," whose flesh is turned to flame, his sinews to blazing fire, his bones to juniper coals, his eyelashes to lashing flashes, his eyeballs to fiery torches, the hairs of his head to hot flames, all his limbs to wings of burning fire, and the trunk of his body to blazing fire? Or Bat Qol, the voice of heaven that is none other than God's voice? Or 'WZHYH? Or ZGNG'L? Are you a Prince of the Face and are you permanently changing your perspective between heaven and earth? I know your works, the angel says, and your toil and your persistence and that you cannot endure evil, according to the angel there is no effort wasted in describing Lucifer, for a fine description banishes that which is described, thus should I describe him once more, this time, however, truthfully and precisely, for that which is described well need not be looked at by the describer ever again. But I hold it against you that you left your first love, says the angel. That brought ill luck. And there are those who are unhappy for a whole life long and who rage against life. But those who rage against life rage against me. My first love, I think, wanted four children with me when I myself was but a child. Is Meṭaṭron not Enoch, God's representative, I ask the angel, then beseech him: what is his name? I have seventy names, says the angel. And Meṭaṭron has 72 wings, with which he can kindle a storm and sweep me away, and he has 365,000 eyes, with which he can look at 365,000 things simultaneously, but he can direct all of them at me and thereby burn me, and he knows the thoughts of everyone whom he simultaneously looks at and can play them off of one another. Thus does he know that I am now thinking that one can flee from danger only until flight has made one dull and careless. One remains in place and lets everything come to pass. Or one brings oneself into the vicinity of the danger, finally wanting to bring about a resolution, but cannot always be certain whether the other likewise longs for a resolution or whether the other deems one too slight to be considered an enemy. If, like me, you have dedicated your life to finding and confronting this enemy, the latter would be the greatest defeat imaginable, a disappointment that would make one disappear through oneself like the voracious serpent, which, in order to satisfy its hunger, after devouring, then once more spitting up mouse, frog, robin, fish, porcupine, buffalo, leopard, and elephant, finally devours itself. The radiance of Shekhinah manifestly didn't reach me, otherwise I wouldn't have to grieve, wouldn't be ill, and wouldn't be bothered by the flies and mosquitoes buzzing about my spirit. Those are the nuisances of the quotidian, the tidying up and tidying down, the being interrupted, which is the worst of all, and even here, upon this stone, while I hear the voice, everything distracts me from finally finding the transition to the following, which should fulfill my promise of a truthful and precise description of Lucifer:

A good meter to my left, in the half-shadow, a puny figure, neither man, nor beast, leans against a hollow in the rock. That is Lucifer. To see the invisible, pathſ aď wayſ art deniede hem, betrayal līse in ambush, peacæ aď justicæ art mortallī woundede. Lucifer the Grimacer has become a pale, little hooded man with a truly uncontemplative aspect, a marginalized drollery with the pricking tail of a small, black-scaled reptile, which is invisible during the day, and the hind legs of a grasshopper or lizard. His torso is that of an insect, instead of collarbones and shoulders, the comical figure has a pair of wings far too large for its overall appearance. As if that weren't enough, the human head sits atop it between two hand-crowned humps, the hands stretched out into the air as if the figure were being threatened with a firearm. The humps are covered in dark fur and are shaped like anthills. The comical pitch-black hands are those of a gecko, which, exposed to light, disappears into cracks in the walls or behind curtains. A flaming pot sits upon its head, meagerly glowing hellfire, which makes the head oh so emaciated from self-consumption, so pointy-nosed, as if the poor devil had been banished from hell into exile with a view of heaven, the pot the sole token of his descent. His view onto the heavens is obstructed, however, and thus must he have decided all at once to direct his face-sallowing greed toward things on the ground. The glasses show that the figure wants to be an Ovid, wants to play Johannes, but lacks the scritch-scratch and blood necessary for script. If the phenomena of heaven are unattainable, I am no more than twice as tall as he while sitting, my robe is horizon and heavens to him, and he always sees pink clouds, hills, and valleys, which must have quickly tired him out like a child. I have set out a trident for him at the base of the boulder, a huge, three-pronged kitchen fork, of the kind that finds its use in the preparation of meat, but also does its service as a tool of torture. Little Lucifer is familiar with the handling of this tool, the rat strode into the archway with it as if holding a ferula. Lucifer's ferula bears no cross and no crook, its three curved prongs are the earth-facing version of the three-barred cross. Lucifer uses the fork to catch the sinners, who are now nothing but flesh, then hurls them into the embers. The figure holds the trident firmly in its gaze in order to fish for my writing implement therewith, it seems to be lying carelessly on the ground before me, the figure certainly isn't able to grasp it with its little hands that rest on its anthill-stumps, for, in order to do so, it would have to bend forward quite a bit and blindly grope for the fork, its missing arms prevent the hands from doing anything other than surrendering or waving to surrender. Its disgrace seems doubled, Lucifer has forfeited all power that would impose itself, he cannot make use of the insignia of his might. And yet his gaze onto the ground does not make him harmless. Heaven has sent an eagle to always keep an eye on him. The eagle tells the creature that Jesus is risen. The creature pays the beast no mind. If it did, it would have to acknowledge the cross that the popes substituted for the eagle crowning Jupiter's scepter. Who is worthy of the air the eagle breathes? It keeps its eyes open and notes the slightest stirring. I have turned my back to the figure and trust in the eagle that, at the decisive moment, it will know how to secure the inkwell and the refill flask from the halfbreed's grasp. He's perpetually trying to write something down, the devil is, he's become a couch potato and the room has made him very pale. He's constantly in search of heat-resistant material that will preserve his script and make it impervious to hellfire. He has not yet put his alternative plan for creation onto paper, as he's not yet invented any paper capable of withstanding all the fires in the world. He's also no inventor. Rather, he is the cuckoo among angels, the parasite, infiltrator, appropriator, foreign ruler. That's why, hastily disappointed by his attempts to make paper durable against all environmental influences, which collectively failed and were never brought through to their final consequences, he specialized in going down in history as the feared saboteur of God's plan of salvation, which he would prefer not to leave undividedly up to divine providence. If he were able to bring my writing implement into his own grasp, he would come a step closer to this plan, thus does he wait patiently until I have put enough text down onto paper, he would, of course, prefer it if I'd finished my text so that he might intervene in his own interest, deleting or positively reformulating passages to do with him should they expose him, despise him, or even defy him, he also wants the text to appear to have been damaged by moths so as to go down in history as the greatest diaskeuast the book has ever seen, compared to whom the supplementers and text-assemblers of the Homeric epics would appear to be illiterates. If the glottis was in the beginning—the croaking, by which "am" and "aleph" begin—then Lucifer wants to scrape the alphabet a bit with his big fork and to give the letters a new form. The letters are too smooth, he says, to everything I say, he simultaneously says: The letters are too smooth, the voice is too smooth, the voice needs granules, God must get stuck on the letters if I call him, I call him with each reading, for each text has only this goal for me—to bring God down—reading and calling really do mean the same thing, the letters must be rough enough that he can be rubbed over with them. Each voice counts, he says, if I say something, it spurs me on to speak further, and thus do I speak ever further without being able to say anything and a chorus of countless voices rises up around me. For, on a not-too-distant day, it says, that a new bratty Bengel will have to figure out, God shall be no more than a heap of rubbish. Then shall he come and sweep up this heap, from tzimtzum shall it scatter to the four winds.

Thus is the alphabet the matter that occupies Lucifer the most, an alphabet must be invented, one best suited to calling down God, who doesn't have it in his power not to come down. God prefers to get stuck on the consonants that crush everything between them, consonants don't sound out, the figure says, they crush. Vowels are only usable at the end of their short lives, just before breathing their last, if the breath fails, then they creak and rattle, and their barking band of noise drags

God with 'em. Doris Erben, also know as "Ride Boners" delivered a draft about a hundred years ago, in it, the black sounds devoured all and the white sounds shone so bright that ears and eyes were dazzled:

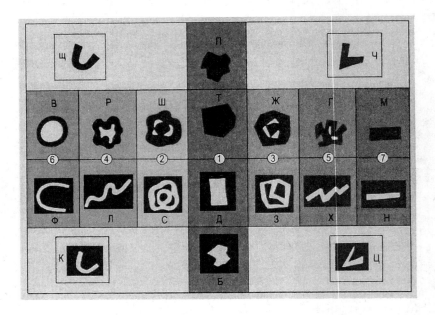

The big fork, which was given to Lucifer, who was standing in the corner in a childlike huff—a toy to compensate for the abortive carnival costume, but with which he serenely disdains to play—shall one day till the field for far-reaching reforms, then shall God no longer be אֶהְיֶה אֲשֶׁר אֶהְיֶה ("ehjeh asher ehjeh"), but "I was that I-Was," then shall the shofar sound out upon my arrival, the voice says, and I do not turn to see the voice that is speaking to me, I am in you, the voice says, but I know that the voice is somewhere out there, how else could I know that it sits there with such wings. For as long as the eagle guards it and the angel translates, I have no fear, even if I do not trust the angel. Lucifer is already practicing the call behind my back, he wants to pull me down from the stone as meat for his little cauldron. The eagle ought to put the great fork into his hand, then he could write with it upon the stone, for thus is it written in my book: "Now go, write it before them in a table, and note it in a book," thus do we share the work, he shall have to concentrate on the essentials—on the alphabet.

Some pages in the book are already written over, I do not know whether it is my task to write over them, the paper might not be enough, the angel speaks continuously, I started my text on the first page I opened up to and have not, as of yet, laid down my quill. I cannot assert with any certainty that it was not me who wrote these pages and, in the presence of the angel, I have forgotten all that was. I write what the angel dictates, now and then he takes longer pauses, either the woman with child ceases in her revelation or the angel censors her speech. From here, it is not possible to see whether she is moving her mouth, I proceed on the assumption that she is not moving it, she reveals herself to the angel with her spirit or else the angel conjectures as to what she might be saying and simply chatters away. Now, during a lull, the thought comes to me that Lucifer might proofread the manuscript and distort its texture in the process. He is a virus, the thought alone proves it.

How, for example, did the following passage get into my book: "Wasn't the name of the first calculator of Jesu's thousand-year reign the bratty Bengel? Nowadays, one no longer has time to penetrate more deeply into things, allusion, combination, and surface are enough, the true theologian is Nietzsche." Even if there is no Lucifer, as some say, he actually does exist simply because such a thought exists. It is not given to me to turn to the angel and ask it whether it is dictating to me or whether perhaps it's the devil who is speaking inside of me. Perhaps, the woman with child is an invention of the angel and the angel is my invention, whereas I myself am an invention of Lucifer. But who, then, could have invented Lucifer? Nobody who could have invented him can be seen for far and wide. Lucifer is a cockroach grown too large, a casualty-cockroach that sought out a spare part for its lower body. An enormous button holds its hooded jacket together and it shan't be able to raise itself a single millimeter off of the ground with its wings, far too big for its body.

But enough has been said of him now—he who has written himself into my Book of Revelation in such a way that it is becoming a dark and fatuous book.

A written passage is approaching now, I touch it with my eyes and the angel speaks it:

> Alas ! it nevermore may be
> That honour and wealth shall dwell,
> With Heaven's grace as well,
> Together in one heart again ;
> All roads and paths from them are ta'en ;
> Falsehood in ambush lurks ;
> Violence vaunts its works ;
> Justice and peace are wounded sore ;
> If these two be not quickly healed,
> the three will never prosper more

The text must remain untouched. I wouldn't know how to write that voice. As I'm noting this down by way of thinking it and that which I think is instantly written in the book, I note that, if I don't write for longer than thirty seconds, a text I've already written but haven't thought appears. It shows me the Cologne Cathedral clock. To begin with, there have often been instances as of late when I've not written for 666 seconds on end. At these times, I always grow quite warm, something fills me up from the soles of my feet to my forehead. Consequently, when I saw the pulsating Cologne Cathedral clock, a voice inside me said: That is the world-heart, the world-heart shall be still in a moment, your deed shan't go unpunished, and so on. However, not everything that I think can be read here, by which I can only conclude that not everything I think is text or that my text is being censored. I hold the little Lucifer in suspicion, but perhaps the angel functions as filter and only lets through the black-on-white, which the woman with child approves of, she may have given him a catalog of principles and they read my text or, as the expression goes, read it over, then we came to form a feedback loop with me as mere executive organ, which is subject to permanent and, thus, double or triple control, thus am I reading my thoughts, but not all of my thoughts are in here to be read. Therefore, the thinking and the reading organs work simultaneously and there is a third organ in me that simultaneously perceives the simultaneity. There must be a fourth organ, which stands in shadow, which works in secret, and which revokes from the readings all that which a censor decides never to have thought and never to have read. But why does he allow me to read precisely these thoughts? I look out from here onto a valley. On the other side of the valley, which extends about three hundred meters into the plain, there flows a river that skirts round several small, likely uninhabited islands, it could also be a sea-bay with islands in front of it, the bay is rather long and serves as a natural harbor, a few ships can be seen, both large and small, fishing boats, pleasure crafts, the hustle and bustle both surprises and disturbs me, I sit down upon the stone once more, this world is already vanishing, and I can once more concentrate on the Diagonal Mother with Child—Angel—I—Lucifer, dividing the space, the page. I now know why the woman's mouth doesn't move. It is the child who speaks, I hear the babble of my childhood, I myself am the child, and the angel only speaks to drown out this child; if the angel cannot translate something, it remains silent. It is thus to be assumed that this angelus interpres, which has masqueraded as the angel of revelation, was called by my mother to hush the voice of childhood, for this voice could cast her in a bad, an unfavorable light. It is the Mother's absence, no doubt, that sets the child to babbling, it has developed a monstrous ambition to share this with the world at an age when children generally can't even crawl. Thus did I crawl with the sounds that filled the holes representing Mother. Religion is an invention of the family and each subsequent time, with each child, it is reinvented. It serves to distract from the hole that the mother is and cannot fill. The child's babbling is not a shaping of the palate, not language rehearsal, it is already language and the mother fears this language more than death.

I believe I have seen a church or cathedral and a big water tower on the horizon, as well as an olive tree behind me, however, the trunk of the tree is too tall and thin for an olive tree, the shape of its crown rather suggests a maple, though two facts contradict this: The crown of the maple tree does not have the shape of a maple leaf; I haven't encountered a single maple tree in all the years I've spent on the island. The longer I picture this tree in my mind, the more clearly it stands before me in its every detail. Two birds perch upon its boughs, a woodpecker just below its pruned crown, a raven in its middle. A second raven—or are they both eagles?—flies up to the tree at this very moment. The tree seems close enough to grasp and, yet, is infinitely distant with its tall crown. As if it had grown toward the water, incredibly straight in the growth of its trunk, but at an extreme angle, as if it had to flee from something, to bring its valuable crown to safety or to make contact with the angel and the mother with child. Or simply to demonstrate the curvature of the earth. If it weren't for the hills and rocky outcroppings, the depicted scene might well be taking place in the Rhine landscape near Düsseldorf and my mother, the woman who strolls in the distance with a red cloak, has become the woman with child in the sky, I am the child, then and now, I am wearing a red cloak that has faded underneath the sun. The death of my mother is sketched in the sky and I write it down in perpetuity. The little creature does, in sooth, long for melancholic moods, thus, at least, does it share in my privations. I shall not turn round, the creature might mistake my gaze for a plea that it assist me. The hill and the angel upon it impede my view of the valley. I read in my book what is to be seen and what meaning that which is to be seen contains, my eyes turn its white script into black script upon making contact:

"This accursed valley is for those who are accursed forever. Here shall all the accursed be gathered together who utter with their lips against the Lord unseemly words and of His glory speak hard things. Here shall they be gathered together, and here shall be their place of judgment. In the last days there shall be upon them the spectacle of righteous judgment in the presence of the righteous for ever: here shall the merciful bless the Lord of glory, the Eternal King."

Gehenna, the Valley of Hinnom, the Killing Valley. Thus is it to be read in my book and I am compelled to add the following without fully understanding what it is I'm writing: the Gate of Gehenna; to be thrown into Gehenna; with Satan and demons in Gehenna; Devil's Canyon; Gehenna of Life; age a hen; life-prison as Gehenna; the flame of Gehenna is intelligent, it kills without destroying. Tertullian. The killing never ceases. The Gehenna makes molk, sets the tongue aflame. The tongue is a flame. And the tongue sets the earth aflame. And one calls this earth Topheth and, there, children pass through flame. There's always need of a new person to defile Topheth, which is in the Valley of the Children of Hinnom, that no man might make his son or his daughter to pass through the fire to Molech. To go through hell for you. What one says without thinking. Here, Christmas gifts are not sacrificed to the hereafter so that children might continue living and the children are not made to believe that they are the ones receiving the presents and that they first have to earn the inundation of presents by way of constant good behavior—here, one sacrifices the children to the great Molech so as to placate him. There is no such thing as Molech, for Molech is what we call the ritual of child sacrifice itself, children are gifted to the sacrificial ritual. One begets them, raises them until they've grown enough, then sacrifices them. To shred the male chicks. Traveler! when through the haunts of your childhood to the Valley of Hinnom thou comest, there's no tallit for you to hide beneath, and no gate through which you could steal away from Z'WPY'L, the Prince of Gehinnom. But you and the children are spared the coughing, one doesn't cough after death by fire. Gehenna, not to be found for centuries, does not mean eternal torment in hell, Gehenna is the final annihilation with no chance for resurrection, a notion of consolation, I have my resurrection in my memory of the Honighecke in Großhau in Hürtgenwald, the Sunday strolls proved that my father actually existed, Father was these strolls, the word "Honighecke" is the Eifel-region word for "paradise" and this paradise was once Gehenna, the Hürtgenwald hell, at the entrance of which stood, not two date palms, but the bunkers on the Todtenbruch, a landscape of memory, past and future offenses and punishments, divided in twain as I am. And the Honighecke does not draw the first letter of my name, which is also the last letter of my name: lew mewin da'at: the wise in heart will receive commandments. Thus does the Honighecke represent the wish to learn from the Holy Scriptures.

    The effect of the fruits wears off. A curtain is pushed off to the side. If Gehenna, the deepest part of hell, was once intended for Lucifer, it is only now that he has taken possession of it. I sit here once more. The cockroach with the bespectacled human head and the abdomen of a gecko has turned back into a rat, which, in joyful anticipation of that which is to come, is again standing in the archway of this strange desert building, which has a red circus tent upon its open roof, into which a funnel-shaped opening is set as cupola. I exist five times over and my Way of the Cross has five stations. It goes in a circle. I follow it. The language of this mill—Lucifer's sail-language—knows five positions. If the red sail is located at 11:00 a.m.: ascent, the burning to follow at noon, the descent beginning at 2:00 p.m., if the red wing is located at 5:00 p.m., piercing by way of sword is imminent, and the reading of the verdict begins at 7:00 p.m. Nothing stands in the way of my resurrection, unless there isn't enough wind gusting up. I have once more arrived at the first station. Or the last. First comes the script, then comes the world, then comes the script once more. The open book lies before me. The thorns and fruits have disappeared with Ruprecht. My ascent is imminent. Nothing hinders me in leafing through the book at will. A soothing coolness blows forth from the archway, all work seems to have ceased. I look up and see myself in five copies at all the other stations simultaneously, this is when all that's coming to pass pauses for a moment, as if Lucifer were standing in the archway, big-mawed and legs spread, the one garbed in a green turban, from which a long green shawl cascades down past his hips and onto which is placed a silver helmet, meaning that he always has to keep his head very straight, instructed to pose for a group pic by the hell-photographer. A chimera grabs onto my left hand with its right hand and pulls me, I seek to wrest myself from its grip in the direction of the funnel-shaped opening atop the red-circus-tent-dressed dome, while, simultaneously, I have already been pushed through it, clasping my hands over my head, my mouth gaping wide with pain and terror, and naked as at all the other stations, I'm on the direct path into the fiery furnace, then, only two meters further on, I float down, stretched out long, safe, the flames haven't even singed my hair, held only by the thin black fingers of a chimera, whose beastliness makes me keep my eyes closed, my body is a Corpus Christi marked by no wounds and nailed into the air. My head turned off to the side also bestows the grace of a pietà upon me. Not two meters further down, rotated to 5:00 p.m., the sword already in my side as if I had received it as a matter of course while being turned from my frontal to my side profile, a crooked fanfare protruding from my buttocks, occasionally shedding a note, a potato-nosed, bulging-lipped figure guides me, it carries its sword in its sheath. It's dressed in a green toad suit and wears an overgrown walnut upon its head as a hat, but these could also be worms scurrying about on its head, worms or intestines.

For as long as I observe these scenes, I feel no pain, time has stopped. Pain only arises when I occupy myself further with the book, reading or writing, it has increased in size in miraculous fashion. "For what I speak I do not comprehend, / But God commands each thing to be declared," I read. That's my handwriting, but I certainly couldn't make this assertion. Why "God"? I also have no right to be considered the author of the following lines, which follow: "And there shall be a selling of their freedom Among most men, and robbery of temples." "But yet the whole world of unnumbered men Enraged shall kill each other." I am merely filling in the gaps in the text. "And lack of men shall be in all the world, So that if anyone beheld a trace Of man on earth, he would be wonderstruck." Clov has spotted a rat in the kitchen. "And thou, shrewd mortal, prudently make known, Lest ever thou should'st my commands neglect." I am waiting for the commands, Father Lucifer, known as Schattenfroh.

The black bookpage has opened before me. Memory or repetition? Then, through the black of the bookpage, a letter becomes legible, addressed as an epistle to the Frightbearing Society: "Behold, I stand behind the page and knock, if someone hears my voice and opens to this page, I shall go into him and eat with him and he with me. My son shall not hear my voice." With the last word, the letter disappears once more, as if it knew that someone were reading it. A sign of life. But how can the page be opened up? But the problem could be solved by me tearing the page out of the book. Yes, tear the page out of the book, tear it out, says a voice that I recognize as Mateo's. I want to wait it out and see what will happen if I don't do so. Tear the page out of the book, the voice says, tear it out. Tear it out once and for all, the voice says, tear it out now, out with the page, the voice says, page out, out, out, out. I turn the black page and read: "I tear the black page out and it immediately appears in the book once more." Thus do I not tear it out. You must tear the page out, says the voice that is Mateo. And what if I don't do it? Then this can't go on any further, the voice says. What can't go on any further? Then this can't go on any further. What do you mean by "this"? Then this can't go on any further. What would be so bad in this not going on any further? If this didn't go on, that would be the worst. I turn the black page and read: "The beast crawls out of the page, the beast that was and is not, it has seven heads and ten horns and a book upon every third horn. The three books are read by three heads, while three of the other heads discuss what they've read. But the seventh head writes a new book from that which has been read, as well as the conversation about it and other things, a book that, to a certain extent and in its turn, shall replace one of the three read books, then shall it likewise be discussed and, together with the two books that have not yet been replaced and are perpetually being discussed and other things as well, it shall lead to another new book, and so on and so forth. To begin with, that which is read shall be nothing more than that which is written, flowing into a new book along with that which is said about it and certain new things, which are nothing more than old forgotten things. Until there is nothing more than the terribly old, rewritten over and over again, put in a different order, thus is there the new and so shall there be the new for as long as forgetting exists. You are the seventh head. Your father demands his book back. It is the book of his life. Nebo is the scribe-god, proclaimer, chief of the tongues of Babel. He prescribes. He is the god who also bestows fatherhood. Nebo is "oben." He is "up there." Nebo is bone. He is ^{ilu}PA und ^{ilu}AG. His raised reed pen is simultaneously a measuring tube, with which he determines the limits. You too must say: 'Nebo, defend my border that I might know that I here hold the bond of heaven and here hold the bond of earth.' He administers all life-books. He also writes them. He is the scribe of the universe and everything else, he reads the script on the moon's disk. For only that which is written is real. If your father doesn't get his book back, then it's your book too. Go hence and say: 'My life is written by you. I am manman, somebody.' So that your tongue doesn't hang out from between your lips." That isn't my language, that text is much too old. I close the book. The book opens itself back up. I shut the book once more, then the book bangs back open with such force that it almost breaks my left hand, which is resting on the book cover. The book, three, perhaps four times the size of an ordinary book, apparently leads a life of its own, it has a strong back and powerful arms, as with carnivorous plants, it seems to devour whatever settles upon it. It turns each speck of dust into glowing script. I close the book gently, then the cover flies open, pinning my hand to the floor. A text appears: "Whoever shall blot out my inscribed name through a work of malice, whoever shall destroy my document or shall change its place, I, Nebo, shall gaze furiously upon him, shall wipe out his name and his seed from the lands!" To wipe out means to erase from script.

If it is the Book of Life from which I tear the black page before it immediately reappears in the book, then it must be Eternal Life. All that which is now to come is the result of my not tearing out the black page. Then the text continues to write itself on the next page and I read it. My revelation: "If Father is to sit in the judge's armchair as judge, his raiment shall be as white as snow, his cloak made only out of right- eousness, my Book of Life shall lie open before him. Then shall the guards and officials take up my case and decide my affair. My father has communicated the verdict unto them, the verdict that he himself is entirely, and they speak out of his mouth, which shall be mute." And I tear the black page out of the book and a white page appears as the black page. And I tear the black page out of the book and a white page appears as the black page. And I tear the black page out of the book and a white page appears as the black page. And I tear the black page out of the book and a white page appears as the black page. I tear the black page out of the book a hundred times and a white page appears again and again as a black page. In this way, I can at least avoid having to read a new text with further threats, I'm quite certain of the fact that such a text can never come into being. Father is in league with evil, for, if such a text cannot come into being, Father shall continue to be trapped in the black page—and perhaps forevermore. Yes, tear the black page out of the book no longer, the voice says. And I continue to tear the page out of the book, but cannot prevent the following text from gradually constructing itself in white script against the black background: "I shall erase you from the Book of Life for having locked me into a black page and making me unrecognizable. The sun became black as sackcloth of hair, the sky dwindled into it like a book being rolled up. You have disguised me and the people have turned away from me. And, now, you continuously tear me out of my own book. Thereby am I interrupted in such a way that I must ever remember this interruption. I am he who was and is not. I give unto you the chalice of wine of the fierceness of my wrath and you shall drink it down to its dregs, down to its 'Neige,' as we say in German, until you snow all white from the sky like neige, as the French say. For the snow that you are is me, white script against a black background. Yes, amen." I take the trident and scratch the black from the page, the world's palaver. Whatever movement I hereby make, white script appears against a black background, which loses ground with each scratch until it gradually completes itself once more. Thus do the scratches seem to only make contact with the surface and, beyond that, the surface seems to have been designed to be scratched. Deeper layers are not affected by the trident and the scratches it inflicts, it is likely from these layers that a sort of self-healing proceeds. The deeper layers emit, or thus do I imagine, impulses, Besetzungsinnervationen— pulsional investments of the unconscious—which restore the ground once a threshold of exposure is met. At the same time, that which is erased is preserved invisibly, yes, the surface taken as a whole is only a proxy, a representative, without the existence of an origin being able to be determined, while each act of erasure leaves behind a trace that is nothing but script. Thus do I use the trident to overwrite script with script that is already contained in the black. Father, my prescriber, is therefore always present-to-hand in the latency of the black page, he'd like, however, to keep a low profile, I never reach him, only his emanations. On earth, he has wrapped a curtain round himself, he stretches his feelers through it and out toward me, but I cannot lift it up from him in such a way that the script might vanish. In this way, protected by a shell, he can better control me than if he were to openly grab hold of me with no protection. And, in that, I am by and large nothing but his pen, which he seems to direct at will. He shall also wear this curtain in heaven.

Father was not driven out of paradise by me, he has entered into paradise, into the unreadable page of a book consisting entirely of script, a book that it has been imposed upon me to write continuously, and the cryptograms that serve as a curtain for him, tied so closely together, are viruses within my text—like right now—the German language itself also a virus within the English version of my text, German anagrams its most deadly and contagious manifestation. How can I bring him the book if he is imprisoned in the book? I must bring him the book in the book, must deliver myself over to him entirely. The following appears in that very same book: "We must therefore understand it of a certain divine power, by which it shall be brought about that every one shall recall to memory all his own works, whether good or evil, and shall mentally survey them with a marvellous rapidity, so that this knowledge will either accuse or excuse conscience, and thus all and each shall be simultaneously judged. And this divine power is called a book, because in it we shall as it were read all that it causes us to remember." Divine Might, give me strength. I place my head between my knees and whisper a series of letters in amazed disbelief—they appear one by one in my book:

"YHW'L, YH YHW'L, YWPY'L, YWPPY'L, 'PPY'L, MRGY- ZY'L, GYWT'L, PWNRY'L, ‚ṬHPRY'L, ṬṬRY'L, ṬBṬB'L, ‚W YHWH, ZH WHYH, ‚B'D, ZBWDY'L, ‚P'PY'L, SPPY'L, PṢPṢY'L, SNYGWRWN, MṬṬRWN, SWGWRN, ‚DRYGWN, 'SṬS, SQPS, SQṬS, MYGWN, MYṬṬWN, MYṬṬRWN, RWḤPYS, QYNWT, 'ṬṬYH, 'SSYH, ZGZGYH, PṢPṢYH, 'BṢNNYH, MBRGŠ, BRDŠ, MKRKK, MṢPD, ḤŠGŠ, ḤŠBŠ, MṬRṬṬṬ, BṢYH, 'YṬMWN, ṬYṬMWN, PSQWN, ṢPṢ PYH, ZRḤ-ZRḤYH, 'B' BYH, HBH- BYH, PLṬ PLṬYH, RBRBYH, ḤṢ ḤṢYH, ṬPṬPYH, TMTMYH, ṢHṢHYH, 'R 'RYH 'L'LYH, ZZRYZYH, ZRZRYZYH, SḤSNYH, SSRSYH, RZRZYH, KZRZYH, 'RYMYH, SBHYH, SBRSBHYH, SMBS, YHSYH, ṢBṢBYBHYH, ṢBBṢBYH, QLYLQLY, BYHHH, HHYH WH, WHYH, ZKZKYH, ṬWṬRYSYH, SWYRYH, ZHP- NYRYH, Z 'Z 'YH, GL RZY, MLMLYBYH, 'ṬṬYH, 'MQ QMYH, ṢLṢLYH, ṢBṢBYH G'WGṬW, G'WṬYH, MRPRYŠ PRYŠYH, ŠPṬ ŠPṬYH, ḤSMYH, ŠRŠYH, GBYR GBWRYH, GWR GWRYH, ZYW'RBH."

These are seventy of the names of God communicated to Metatron, in whose name Atome is contained and Atome is a traitor, his traitorous remnant is: trn.

And lo, there opens a door that nobody can close, the hatch of a shaft above me, through it I see only darkness. "Your father says that you called me." I called nobody, I reply. "But what's the situation with the immersion baths, purification rites, fasting exercises, the many songs and hymns of glorification, which you must whisper down to the ground so as to free your father from the page?" I know nothing of that, I reply. "Then, nothing shall come of your journey. Unless you sing the songs and hymns of glorification to me, should it not suit you to sing them to your father, then I shall fulfill my duty as a servant." I know of no journey, I reply. "It doesn't go inward, you've already been there, and there's nothing at all going on in there, the journey goes upward. But for that, I request a couple of lines for myself." A spectre from which all shrink afraid, that is his request, I reply, but he knows the answer: "The word its life resigneth in the pen." "Come and I will show thee thy father's curtain, / which is spread before the Holy Blessed One, / and whereon are graven / all the generations of the world and all their doings, / both what they have done, / and what they will do until the end of all generations. But me, to the right of your father, upon an armchair like his armchair—I wished for nothing else but to sit you upon a throne to my right, he said—through your father shall you find yourself transformed: forthwith my flesh was changed into flames, my sinews into flaming fire, my bones into coals of burning juniper, the light of my eyelids into splendor of lightning, my eyeballs into firebrands, the hairs of my head into hot flames. Your father added in me wisdom unto wisdom, knowledge unto knowledge, subtlety unto subtlety, might upon might, and, most importantly, understanding unto understanding. Now, he sits on high and keeps an impatient lookout for those who shall commence the journey to meet him in the sky, which is a black bookpage." Cold flows through the shaft, breathed out of Mateo's fire-flaming mouth. That is a false voice. "You shall see your father sitting upon his throne chariot, driving to and fro on it and observing everything," Mateo says, "you must once more put only your head between your knees and whisper the words that I dictate into the book, these are the lines":

ירה = הבמ = לוי = עהה = ואל = דלא = יזה = תהכ = אכא = הלל = שהמ =
מלע = טיס = לי = ייר = האש = תרי = אאה = התנ = והח = למ = ייי = כלנ = להפ
= = ול = ילכ = אל = מקה = לוו = כימ = ההה = זיי = עהר = מעח = ינא = דנמ =
= קוכ = חהל = וחי = רשו = בכל = מוא = ממנ = יופ = הבמ = תינ = אננ = ממע
מומ. שחה = ינד = והו = הימ = לשע = ירע = לאס = הלי = ייה = מבי = האר = ובח
עיא = קנמ = במד = יחמ = ונע = ההי = במו = רצמ = חרה = ליי =

This is written with a very fine quill-stroke, with an invisible hand. I can't read that, I say to Mateo. If you can't read it, Mateo says, you shall never see your father again. I consider briefly whether this is a true downside and enumerate all benefits until I am overcome with sadness. A word is missing, beyond which, the order is wrong, Mateo says. I still can't read it. Then put your head between your knees and open your mouth. Your mouth shall know how to read the words. And I open my mouth:

"ha mumle a ahha bamarlehcorha hubahjeayelekanamha bamadje hemjeuanajehhajjebamunjearzt mjeharahjea eyha mamenjeyorha habemjeahtm:eamamja 'a, ja sajaj:e na djeuheviean mha jasaje raha jaesha aleyha lueveak mlehahahleza elleaherha maahle najedanemha kavahcha hahe[ha uhe[ha rasavlebakelleamoley erha cheselehtarejha aahha ahti nha uehahlehalemleya eyleahklenha japhahe vuelle jakhajvaelha makahle rahlehabemlelazejha ahahha vualha dalale zahletehakha ahcalehalha sahamha meleleat s[e lejna uhey,"

Your mouth now knows the words, lie upon your back and open your mouth. I lie upon my back with my head under the shaft and open my mouth:

"haimumleiaiahhaibamajlehcorhaihubahleayelekanamhaibamadleihemleuanalehhallebamulearztimleharahlelaieyhaimamenleyophaihabemleahtinleananhaimamihaisahahleinadleuhevleahimhailasaleirahailaeshaialeyhailuevleakimlehahahlezaieIleaherhaimaahleinaledanemhaikavahchaihahelhaiuhejhairasavlebakelleamoleyierhaiehesleshtarejhaiaahhaiahhtinhaiuehahlehalemleyaieyleahklenhailahaphaivuelleilakhajvaelhaimakahleirahlehabemlelazejhaiahahhaivualhaidalaleizahletehakhaiahcalehalelhaisahamhaimeleleatisleilejhaiuhev."

The shaft is a sucking maelstrom, the spider attempts to cling to its substrate, then its legs are sucked off and its body vanishes into the vacuum-cleaner tube at 140 kilometers per hour. The journey is astoundingly short, then a flap closes behind it, then, sucked into the dustbag, a flap closes behind it. The spider is dead.

Mateo says: "With your word dragon, you have now appeased the 72 princes of the shaft who are subordinate to your father in that they make everything vanish, which might well cause him trouble, and thus also you, therefore, it is now a matter of persuading those who are subordinate to one another that you are worthy that thou shouldest enter under his roof into the final room, which is his room. The lady of the first antechamber, if she sees the lady of the second antechamber, she takes the service cap with your father's sign upon it and falls on her face, the lady of the second antechamber, if she sees the lady of the third antechamber, she takes the service cap with your father's sign upon it and falls on her face, the lady of the third antechamber, if she sees the lady of the fourth antechamber, she takes the service cap with your father's sign upon it and falls on her face, the lady of the fourth antechamber, if she sees the lady of the fifth antechamber, she takes the service cap with your father's sign upon it and falls on her face, the lady of the fifth antechamber, if she sees the lady of the sixth antechamber, she takes the service cap with your father's sign upon it and falls on her face, the lady of the sixth antechamber, if she sees the lady of the seventh antechamber, she takes the service cap with your father's sign upon it and falls on her face. And the lady of the seventh antechamber, if she gazes upon your father, she falls on her face and stirs no longer. Only then, when nothing more stirs, shall you be allowed in." The antechambers themselves are a large shaft interrupted by double doors. Thus are there fourteen doors I must go through. Mateo opens the first door, the reception secretary stands in the space between them, the door closes behind me, we stand in the dark for a brief moment, but that's enough to drive the elderly scent of the woman's perfume into my nose, then the second door opens and she falls on her face at the sight of the second reception secretary, who waits before the third door. Then the second reception secretary opens the third door, about ten paces away from me, and that very same process is repeated. At the fifth door, I can't help but get the impression that the ladies in the antechambers, always popping up and waiting with me in the dark for a few moments in the in-between space, are all one and the same woman, which is what I, who have been denied a look back after stepping through the first two doors, cannot verify, as I also didn't care to touch them, only the ladies' smell and their quiet in- and exhaling allow me to come to this supposition. Now, in the space between the seventh and eighth doors, I am certain that my mother stands before me, the women's faces are barely visible over the distance of the few meters that I must conquer between the double doors, for if they gaze upon one another, the subordinate immediately falls on her face without hiding it with her hands. Over time, this has led to some of the ladies breathing through a large hole in their faces instead of their noses, while the left or right cheekbone of some other ladies have retreated into their faces, thus conferring a decorative asymmetry upon them. I make the assumption that this is a daily exercise; according to Mateo, whom I don't see, but whose presence I have no doubt about, my father receives no visitors or the visitors only get as far as the seventh room, where they are turned away. Mother, I say, the woman in front of me inhales deeply, I'm waiting for her to exhale, but she refrains or does it so imperceptibly as to elude perception, perhaps so as to revise the impression that my salutation could have touched her. My mother's thinning hair, her gray suit, her faceless quintessence, her cracked, brittle fingernails, her fondness for pearlescent nail polish, her perpetual complaints about her existence, so that's meant to be my mother, a servant of my father, Mistress of the Interregnum, a woman who looks out only ahead, what should I do with my supposition now, I say to Mother once more, then the door opens, she sees the reception secretary of the fifth double door, falls on her face when the other's gaze falls upon her, I climb over her and walk briskly through this antechamber, which is completely empty except for a withered green plant, which only seems to be there in order to be walked through. Perhaps, this room is the greatest secret of my life, I think, and I shall leave my mother behind in this empty room, she has no face and I can no longer ask her what memories she has, though I wouldn't care if she simply invented memories, I'd give anything just to hear her voice again. On the way to the sixth room, I imagine that I am now traversing the afterlife, and Mother used to tell me of her games as a child in Grubenreu—that she didn't dare to depart from the steps of the outside staircase for fear that the big, wide world would sweep her away and cause her father to lose her, her parents' house was furnished with heavy furniture, which she one day inherited and brought with her into her marriage and thus was this furniture, the value of which she always estimated as "inestimable" when asked, placed into the main room of our house for decades, there, it was nothing but a burden, every day, when looking at these massive cupboards and chests of drawers, Mother thought of her father, who died far too young, the children discovered only dead crockery in them when opening their heavy doors, they feared that they would fall onto their heads upon being opened and, once illegally opened, could not be closed again as a result of their weight. Father didn't like the composition of these veterans, which, taken together, had no recognizable style, the dust on the copper pots, which Mother kept atop the cupboard for lack of storage space, was a horror to him, a day-in, day-out defeat of the bourgeois sense of order. Should the opportunity arise to become a child again, I would immediately move back into my parents' house to spend the rest of my life in sight of this furniture, the opening and closing of which would give my life its meaning. Because there is a childhood that is unconsciously walked through like the hereafter, there are myths. When Mother recounted her days in Grubenreu, she was entirely at home. Now, I have come into the sixth room and this word keeps repeating itself to me: PASSTHRU.

The reception secretary of the seventh room opens the double door into my father's room and falls on her face, which is covered over with bruises and red spots, she has the biggest hole in her face, her head has been forced into the shape of a narrow rectangle. The woman reveals a curtain showing a piece of sky that has come to form a large blue armchair made entirely out of ice, beneath which fire licks. The ice is not consumed by the fire, the fire not extinguished by the ice. The armchair is not occupied. Script appears on the curtain: "As you cannot free me from the black page, I have taken you away and stroll with you through heaven. Unlike Honech, who guided you, you shall not be able to move freely between heaven and earth, you shall enter into my curtain, which is total darkness from the outside, but total light on the inside. Thus is the darkness solely there so as to let the light shine round me so that nobody who sought to look at me would survive this. Is your name not Michael? You are the only one who can pass through the veil and come before me, as I sit upon my true throne. Everyone else would be destroyed by the mere sight of me." I take a few strides toward the armchair and reach through it into emptiness. I pull my hand back and, as far as I have stretched it through the curtain, that far does it stay back behind the curtain. My hand doesn't bleed, I feel no pain. The curtain is not made of ordinary fabric, it is and is not, it doesn't wrinkle, but could wrinkle, it is as impenetrable to sight as a wall and transparent like air. If Father wants, I see him, and I won't be able to say where I see him, he'll be sitting upon his blue armchair and floating in space. And upon that which appears to be a throne shall be something that looks how my father looks. But if he speaks, I don't hear him from behind, as if he wished to reveal himself forth from the hidden.

The blue armchair is closer to my father than any other creature that is his servant. And the armchair speaks with my father, says words of worship and praise to him: "Sit down upon me, for your burden is not a heavy one for me." The stream of flames emanating from the armchair feeds the lake of fire of Gehenna. Sky and hell are thus connected. But the welkin is merely the roof of hell. If you are not in the book, you shall be hurled into the lake of fire. Father is in the book forevermore if I so wish. Things appear upon the curtain that I cannot recognize from a distance. Something moves, dissolves, something else appears in its place, strides entirely to the fore, fades. I go back to the double door. Is my father mentally deranged and the black page is the premonition of his death, a veil over his mind, which has come to a complete standstill ever since Mother's death? As if he wanted to demonstrate for all to see: "What sees the spirit if it sees? Itself." But that would be far too simple. Rather, the pargod is a site of paternal revelation. My thoughts are woven into it before they were and are thought. All is darkness before the curtain, but, behind the curtain, Father shines in such a way that each eye would be blinded if it could not resist the temptation to gaze upon him. Thus is the darkness around him a form of protection for he who sits in the light, just as it is for the others who see only cloudmass and skydark.

What is seen upon the Shroud of Turin is mere projection. It is very similar to the brittle brown curtain on the shelf behind my bed, which, when I was a child, maintained the things I withdrew from the family's gaze. The absent father sat in all things. If the time has come, then I shall tell the story of this curtain. I imagine Father sitting motionless behind the shroud—as if paralyzed. The blue armchair is an electric wheelchair. Father says something to himself incessantly that I only now understand: "Before a man did think in secret, I saw it, and before a man made a thing, I beheld it. And there was no thing on high nor in the deep hidden from me." After he has repeated these sentences seven times, his voice changes and he dictates something, which is unmediatedly transferred to the curtain, the fabric of which all of a sudden shines with a blaze of lights. Father checks over the dictation for accuracy, makes corrections, then it is to be read upon the curtain: "Everything that Atome says has to do with what he's said to me, all of which was so very distant from the truth. With the letters and books he deciphered, he forced me to believe everything, in such a way that I sometimes answered accordingly. He has the presumption to install himself as metathronos, though he is only TRN, Devil

King of Nothing, dwelling within Metatron as Mateo, revealed to be Antonio and Peter Ozianon." An ascent in the wrong direction? Did the voyage go down and Father is its prisoner? Flames his flesh, flaming fire his sinews, firebrands his eyeballs: kindled in Gehenna, the rat that guards the gate. Who then says to me that TRN hasn't slipped into Father's role, occupied his voice, and now runs the business here? Script appears on the curtain once more: "Now, go through the pargod and come near to me." The clouds clear. I go through the curtain. The rest of my hand still behind it rejoins the stump once more. It isn't me who's making any decisions here. My legs obey. My father in the blue armchair also gives the impression of only being the executive body of other authorities. Everything around him and with him at its center is in at-rest motion. My father's voice, which doesn't move his mouth, says that I should lay the book into his right hand. I stride up to my father and tell him that I have eaten the book.

The voice asks me to come nearer so that it might leaf through me. I come closer to the throne and my father flips through me. Someone should read aloud to him, the voice orders. But nobody feels worthy of reading to my father from the book. As I have eaten the book, says my father's voice, whose mouth, in the meantime, remains closed, it exists only on the inside, thus should I open my mouth, then it shall sound out. I open my mouth and I become a pillar and my father writes his name upon me and places a seal upon my brow and upon my brow is written "Don Daba," which I can attest to with my fingers. But my father recognizes his mistake and corrects his error. From now on, "Mogel"* is written upon my brow. And no locusts escape from the abyss, whose angel is Don Daba, they have human faces and teeth like those of lions and tails of scorpions and wings that, when they fly, emit a sound that one recognizes from fast-running warhorses with their chariots. And that which slips out of the abyss causes no excruciating

---

* Cheat.

pain, as long as my brow is sealed with the word "Mogel" and this word is clearly legible. And no key to the maw of the abyss falls from the sky, over the maw of my abyss leans a rotten hatchway, in which ptinidae nest. My abyss is empty and no worse punishment can befall one than that. Thus does my father recognize his renewed error and delete the word "Mogel" and write "Emeth" upon my brow, which I can attest to with my fingers. And, at last, the barn of my abyss is being filled as this is written. I am pleased by the fact that the locusts shall soon fly forth, their human faces causing more fright than their lion-teeth or scorpion-tails. My father, however, is beginning to grow bored at the sight of the slowly filling barn and he's considering what he might change to amuse himself. Then he comes up to me and erases the capital "E" from my brow in such a way that all that's left to be read is "meth," which I can attest to with my fingers. At that moment, as my fingers feel the word "meth" and the spoken word "meth" escapes from my mouth along with the locusts, I sink to the ground and die. Then, I hear my father's voice saying to me: "Come up hither, go back through the curtain, and I will shew thee things which must be hereafter!" And thus does it come to pass. Passing back through the curtain, I stroll through my parents' garden, it's early evening, some twenty rabbits are following me, they all have myxomatosis, the gardener is running after them and killing them one by one. I pass by St. Mary's Church, the sexton has just died while ringing the bell, one of his daughters had a brain operation and also died. Each day, I also wait to fall ill with brain disease and engage in so much self-observation that nature is looking for a way out and henceforth—as I occur to myself and nothing else occurs to me—I am observing a stranger. I'm now at the Kalltal in Eifel, at my best friend's parent' weekend home, sitting on the back of his armchair and French-kissing him, at which point we both look at each other for so long and in such surprise that surprise gives way to reproach and I give him a resounding slap in the face, thus has he twice taken, but given nothing, which leaves me to depart in despair. As I stand before my father's deathbed, a voice says, now you're through it, there's time yet till you stand before your father's deathbed. I have no time to wonder about this strange sentence structure concerning my father and would have liked to travel back and forth a bit more when I come to a room that seems familiar to me and that I immediately recognize as my old cell.

Two men enter the cell, the toilet and bunk are dismantled, the marks they left on the wall and floor are erased, the longitudinal wall is broken through, making a space wide enough for a door, the cell's iron door is replaced with a wooden door, the door frame is assembled, set up, aligned, framed with foam, through the window you can see three identical houses with pointed gables, on the left house is an advertising sign—"Neckermann Travel"—and insurance is advertised on the façade of the right-hand house; a carpet is laid out in the cell, the walls are papered, the ceiling painted white, multiple chairs, including a so-called executive chair, two tables, and several lamps are brought into the cell, in which they are creating an order unfathomable to me by moving the tables around at random, grouping the chairs, plugging in the lamps. The book lies before me once more. If I quit reading, you'd better stop immediately, if I continue reading, continue with your work. Now, I'm reading: a telephone is connected, the excess foam that's dried in the meantime is sheared off, a picture is hung on the wall, the double doors are hung from the hinges of the frames, a tapestry is unfurled, it seamlessly juxtaposes panoramas of one and the same city from 748, 1543, 1644, and 1944, from its first documented mention to its complete destruction. It required two attempts until the city was erased from the landscape and resurrected as another to the eternal chagrin of its residents, who drag themselves past what few monuments there are, through a cheaply renovated townscape.

In order to defeat the Territorial Lord Helmut Wilder Neffe, Imperial Enemy No. 1, who caused him greater concern (especially in matters of succession like the Third Guelder War) than the perennial Turks did, in 1543, the Kaiser cannot help but bombard the city from a hill, it is considered to be impregnable, it is plundered, six hundred of the seven hundred houses, inhabited at this point in time by only three thousand inhabitants, as well as the town hall, the city archives, and a number of church institutions, burn down, more than 15,000 participants in this war of succession lose their lives. The sovereign waits in vain for the French, with whom he is allied. Ninety-nine years later, Weimar and Hesse occupied the city for a good three months. The fact that the general to whom the invaders are subject is named Rosen ("roses") of all things scandalizes the inhabitants more than a little. On May 30, 1642, after General Rosen's occupation comes to an end, one thousand strong, free mercenary troops, all Dutch, occupy the city under the Dutch colonel Franz von Bronckhorst or Brunckhorst or Bochorst or Barnhorst or Bakoes or Bakors, who acts as their commander for some months in the service of the States General of the Netherlands. The mercenary troops destroy part of the suburbs so as to make the occupied territory more overseeable. The suburbs are plundered beforehand, that goes without saying.

The commander in service of the Netherlands is able to stay in the city for almost five months, then, on October 22, 1642, the city begins to be bombarded by the five regiments of Johann Graf von Werth, who has just been released from prison after four years in French captivity. Werth, lieutenant general of the electoral cavalry under Ferdinand of Bavaria, Counter Reformation Electoral Prince and Archbishop of Cologne and one of the best-known cavalry generals of the Thirty Years' War, finally succeeds in overcoming the strong resistance of the Dutch occupying forces by smashing a bulwark and making a breach in the city wall, which has the reputation of being insurmountable. The Dutch withdraw from the city on October 29. In one Dutch chronicle, we read: "Ende diss Ian dee Weert mt 9 regementen in't Collesche lant alleen verbleven, dee den 20.Octobris dee stat, so met 12 companien van dat in't voeriar van den Staten van Neerlandt affgedanckende ende tot den Wymarschen en Hessen gestoten volck under het gelet van einen, geheten Bronckhorst, besettet was, belegert, ende den 24 tot accord gedrongen: Doch ist dee commendant by den keisersen in versekerunge gebleven, ut wat orsake ist my tot hierto unbewust." The new city commander is named Lukas.

The disputes with the Hessians, on the other hand, simply won't come to an end. For two years, from September 11, 1643 to June 1644, under General Ernst Albrecht Kraft von Eberstein, they bombard the city perpetually; the member of the Fruitbearing Society know as "The Well-Deserved One" can only be forced to withdraw by the Duke of Juleich. Not too much time passes before the Hessians manage to establish themselves as squatters in the city. Although Count Christian von Nassau-Siegen and Colonel Mandelsloh succeed in ousting the Hessians from the city on April 10 and 11, 1644, during the process of which the Count dies, new battles with the Hessians then flare up in June.

Under the influence of having just survived three bombardments by the Hessians, the mayor of this city that has once more blossomed writes: "The city, once so notorious that it had no equals in all the land, is thrice besieged in a span of one and a half years and by the sieges so devastated and brought so low, and at the same time made so bereft of foodstuffs, that it is to be foreseen how it shall never be as glorious as it once was."

Outside the city, on a dirt road marked with a small tree, the painter and draftsman Zellen[*] Warhol, also known as Zar Lohnwelle,[†] sits. The old engraver made the first map of the city in 1634 and drew a large number of the city's old buildings—when they could still be drawn. He cannot know what shall become of the city 310 years later.

---

[*] Cells.
[†] Tsar Wagewave.

There are pictures that can bring something long lost nearer once more in such a way that one perhaps no longer wishes to possess that which is new, old pictures are always related to the idea that one used to have an easier time of it, everything's easier *there*, less troublesome, but a visit to Rowkost, for example, proves that this is an error and the beauty of the Rowkoster Canal doesn't make up for the whole place's dreary vacuity, in the medieval town of Grabnurum on the Saale, one is overcome by the heavy state of need, the sight of the people in this town forces one to one's knees and one is haunted by the notion of being inescapably trapped in a decrepit Middle Ages, at the mercy of the impoverished shops that sell goods of only the cheapest of quality—vanishingly low quality, even. One's sympathy for the residents is boundless and not a moment passes without one wishing to immediately burst into tears.

Both men leave and close the doors behind them. It doesn't take long until the phone rings. I let it ring, look at the picture. The figure in the picture seems familiar to me, but, even after thinking about it for a long time, I can't think of where I could have seen it before, even if certain similarities with my father are unmistakable. I hear my father's voice from the back room: "The parents' right to determine the name has its limits at which point the naming violates general custom and order. The requirement to give the child a 'first name' (§ 21 Para. 1 No. 4 PStG) also provides the constitutional legitimacy for the non-permission of an unlimited power to create names (Diederichsen, NJW 1981, 705ff. [709m.w.N.]). The line must be drawn at which point first names become offensive or incomprehensible or offend the religious feeling of at least a not insignificant minority (Diederichsen, loc. cit., p.710m.w.N.) A first name 'Jesus' offends the religious feelings of the members because of its outstanding importance in the Christian churches and congregations. This has been held up in both jurisprudence (AG Bielefeld StAZ 1964, 165) and in the literature (Diederichsen a.a.O.; Dörner, StAZ 1973, 237ff. [239])." Father is dictating and, when

Father is dictating, the world stands still. Then he paces up and down through the room with arched back, the dictaphone in his right hand, a filterless cigarette in his left, he's stuck it into its cigarette holder quite neatly, it smokes itself more than Father smokes it, with a quick flick of the wrist, he shifts the stick of ash into the bronze ashtray, at which point the holder briefly makes contact with the inner rim, thus producing a clacking noise that betrays Father's presence during longer phases of silence and becomes his proxy. The ashtray was given to him many years ago by his father with the words that it was too beautiful to be used and, indeed, it does display an interesting ring-around-the-rosy. The parents smoke themselves to death before the children's very eyes and, of course, my grandfather smoked too, they practice this vice with devotion and don't wish for the children to start smoking, the three children sit in the backseat of the car, it's their summer break, the windows are closed during the journey and the parents chainsmoke. A death shared is a death halved and the children who are already inhaling in the car shall soon appreciate cheaper roll-your-own tobacco. On the rim of the ashtray, raised in relief-like fashion, a figure in a great hurry is depicted, it holds slate and stylus far from itself, as if it had to hand these devices over to someone whose urgent demand it could not resist. On the opposite side of the rim, another figure approaches it, a figure that, walking with stride just as quick, wants nothing more than to receive these writing utensils. Its grotesque visage, almost disfigured by anticipation, draws everyone's attention to itself. Nebo and Lucifer. Perhaps the pact came about under different circumstances and Lucifer is only now making himself known, condemned to an eternal standstill in bronze motion, he can only ever anticipate the handover that shall never come to pass. Nebo, on the other hand, still has his insignias, but they hover in an in-between, he can no longer use them. Eternal transition. What is going to happen now? And who said that they keep going in circles and shall have to involuntarily meet? I open the double doors to the room from which Father's voice can be heard, the second door is open, I hesitate to set foot in the room. He spends hours dictating administrative regulations and canonical amendments, he seems to put canon law above state and family law, perhaps his father was a kind of god to whom he wanted to get closer by means of canon law. With his dictation, he has spoken his last word regarding Jesus and thus does Father speak nothing but last words. Whole boxes of his voice recordings must be stored at home, his overly clear articulations, his spelling-out of individual terms, his immediate correction of assumed misunderstandings, Father molds a world out of the words that, from an early age, appeared more real to me than the many things outside that I could glimpse when I gazed out the window or took a walk holding my father's hand. The outside world was only interesting when it was labeled or lettered or when it was shown to one—and that remains ever so. The market-crier hawking his potatoes at the weekly city market, who, with his poetry, cooks the potatoes lying in the sacks before him and has customers and onlookers alike devour them. A building with filigreed ornamentation, Zanner, the drollerie that shows its teeth, and Blecker, the drollerie that shows its genitals, are standing or squatting at the edge of the roof and are detected by way of one of those sudden head movements that pull one's gaze up from the ground. In Father, they evoke times long past, which his mouth knows how to shape so aptly. Birds of prey in the valleys and heights of the Eifel, ennobled by the editorialization of Father's pointer finger.

The room is almost empty. A light-gray carpet, woven fabric of visibly high quality, gives the room a friendly atmosphere that still communicates neutrality. A few picture frames with photographs stand upon a black sideboard, I can be seen in one photo, about six years old, on the day I start school, with a Schultüte and a brown satchel, short pants, suspenders, smiling into the sun, Father with his right arm outstretched behind me, Jesus-posture, the arm is his leash. Mother looks transfigured in a large photo in the middle of the sideboard, which is set up next to a Christmas tree made up entirely of wooden blocks. She looks into nowhere. Her red blouse makes her look terribly pale. Bourgeois photo-portraits have replaced the modeling of sculptures, I think, as I gaze upon my father in a third photo, black and white. A small, balding man pins a medal to his lapel. The two men are standing before a high window, through which three narrow, identically built houses can be seen, with a row of shops on the ground floor, three upper floors with three-times-three windows on the front side and an attic floor, on the left house is an advertising sign—"Neckermann Travel"—and insurance is also advertised on the façade of the right-hand house. With their pointed-gabled roofs, these houses recall the prewar period, the Second World War left nothing of the city behind.

Upon the desk to the right of the sideboard is a Grundig Stenorette, from which Father's voice resounds. The armchair is empty. Father must have left the room. His instructions regarding punctuation were always razor-sharp. Comma. Period. Paragraph. Stars in the text-firmament. Cosmic order with carriage return. I feel Father in the back of my neck, as if he were forming a shell around me. Handwriting, voice, typewriter, book. Words spoken with clear diction are markers between which reality forms itself. If Father speaks, the words are needles in his skin. "Peter Ozianon is not telling the truth," Father's voice suddenly says, "he invents stories effortlessly, he's corrupted the whole of my correspondence and wants to pull the strings in the background. He messed with my book, the one I let you write, the book in which you always have me before your eyes and hear my voice, even when I'm silent. Antonio had my trust in almost all matters, he negotiated many things without any questions back to me, there are some who claim that I only do what he orders, which amounts to a total reversal of the balance of power. Indeed, he has an incomparable gift for handling important papers, he reads a document, whether an order from me or an inquiry from outside, and, at the same time, has already formulated his answer, should one be necessary, there are some who claim that he has circulated books that have yet to be written. He's pushed his high-handedness so far that inquiries of an administrative nature, all of which should, in fact, have been addressed to me, are directed unmediatedly to him with the request that they be dealt with as soon as possible. This dealing-with none too rarely ends up such that I am never even informed of it. Naturally, Peter Ozianon could not have been certain that I would remain ignorant of his business being conducted on my behalf, which was why he one day came to me, wanting to talk about the carte blanche that we'd allegedly discussed in the distant past—the prospect of his handling unimportant matters without prior consultation with me. I'd never previously discussed such a carte blanche with him, as he said I had, and, in the end, I didn't issue it to him. He knows all too well that I want to be in control of every dossier, no matter how unimportant it may seem. And he knows what a deeply religious person I am, only my love for your mother kept me from ordination to the priesthood. I seek to follow Jesus to the point of identification—is it a blinding weakness, then, that I didn't see his true intentions? How could I have trusted him for so many years without having realized that he is a tactically shrewd brown-noser, one only concerned with his own advantage, a businessman who is an ostensible practitioner of patience and of subordination, but whose selflessness, in retrospect, turns out to be an extremely efficient sleight of hand, which even those who falsely imagined themselves to be operating with him under the auspices of a conspiracy against me fell for. His selflessness, then, went so far that he forged messages signed by me and intended only for his eyes, sometimes scribbled down in the hustle and bustle of day-to-day business, he did so by quoting these messages, twisting the words at crucial points or inserting crucial words, in such a way that it could even appear—had to appear—that I had given the order for a murder, when I wasn't aiming at the person at all, but at the matter in question, an end had to be put to it before it could become dangerous.

He is only loyal to himself. Over time, he had to outdo himself, which he owed to the dynamics of drug-related crime, this begins with small courtesies of a verbal nature, continues in seemingly self-evident recommendations, then culminates in offers, the scarcity-value of which must be surpassed by even rarer, extraordinarily rare, then, finally, utterly unique sensations that approach even the wonders of the world. He knew that he had me in the palm of his hand with a merchant's epistolary flattery, he had taken hold of me like the Gallic Hercules, the golden chains coming out of whose mouth shackle his listeners by the ears, after all, this letter augured me the possession of a relic unlike any other, more valuable than life itself, as improbable as an encounter with the devil incarnate: 'As far as the relics go,' he wrote to me, 'I think it right that you take care of them yourself. This man has something quite extraordinary, fit for your office, something you shall put above all else in your sphere of influence, the shroud from the Holy Sepulchre, to be precise.' I should really have had a much keener ear regarding the purchase price. I mean, is that not something that is nothing? How should the shroud from the Holy Sepulchre be worth less than a new Mercedes? I bought it from the man Ozianon had set his sights on and had it brought to the library behind my office, which nobody but me may enter. Antonio possesses the gift of penetrating into my spirit and my desires, he's gotten me out of many jams with his never-fading flattery. Buoyed up by him saying, 'As you work so hard, it would be mete that you seek to rest more, not only in sitting and with your arms, but also with your mind and in other things,' and, indeed, worn thin by daily administrative acts, I stretched out as often as I could upon the shroud, whether or not it was a replica, and this did good to both body and soul. So that it wouldn't become too worn-out, I had the floor broken through and the shroud—illuminated by a lamp placed beneath the cloth, the radiance of which revealed its fibers most fine and its color-contrasts, but without damaging it in the slightest, this lamp can be turned on and off by a switch only accessible to me in the room that's to be found beneath the library, a room that even Peter Ozianon has never yet laid eyes on—was installed to hover about one and a half meters below the floor, such that I, lying upon a sturdy glass plate that covers over the hole in the floor, always pleasantly warmed, can gaze upon it with the greatest of calm whenever I wish. The shroud, with its approximate dimensions of four by one meter, has become a fount of knowledge and contemplation for me, each and every decision that I make is directly related to it. It was very clever of Ozianon to show me the black page of the book that you are allegedly writing so as to stand up to me, he was certain that I would recognize the Corpus Christi in this page, which caused me to instantly disappear into the page, as if I were undergoing a permanent baptism. The black page was full of poison, which was slowly released from it and is now taking effect. I wouldn't be Peter Ozianon's first victim, after all, he has already sought to kill my deputy's secretary with poison three times, but in vain, for that secretary, far more honest, but ultimately no less corrupt, is getting in the way of his schemes and his selling of administrative secrets. Antonio is always thundering on about the danger that this secretary and, through him, my deputy pose to me. Servants privy to the processes only act servile and serve the cause for so long, subordinate to the superior and keeping all inconveniences from his throat, until they—and this is the actual motive for their subservience—deem the time opportune for their own taking of the helm, then, from one day to the next, they change their denomination, their convictions of which there never were any, and renounce their loyalty overnight, then it is with cold zeal that they begin to seek their goal, for which they take up the crime of all crimes in their thoughts very early on, the murder that one day no longer seems all that far-fetched to them, but, rather, called-for and essential. The thought of murder overrides any and all moralizing, it gives wings to the imagining of oneself soon sitting upon the throne, which one has, up until this point, only been allowed to warm up. Once I am cleared from the way, the assumption of office shall be easily accomplished."

I turn off the dictation device and leave the room. I'd like to look at the tapestry in Father's other room again. A black line that tapers from left to right forms the horizon that connects all of these centuries to one another. Their common sky is of a color somewhere between powder blue and gray. In the sky, words are written. "Dicker Turm" and "Spießenturm," for example. If, indeed, the sky—the distance from 748 to 1543—is the measure of time, and if the towers are too far to the left, then "Dicker Turm," though part of the city wall, the construction of which began in 1224, dates from the sixteenth and not from the eighth or ninth century. Perhaps that's the tribute that the history of art must pay, the tapestry may have been commissioned for this very wall, though perhaps this tapestry is no art at all, but poor craftsmanship that doesn't take perspective very seriously and the manufacturer didn't plan on a keen gaze checking over details. The church, in which I was baptized, has its former name—Franciscan Church—woven into the tapestry. Opposite the Anna Church, formerly known as St. Martin's Church, and to the left, it appears almost tiny, but easily recognizable because of its pointed tower, crowned by a ridge turret with a cross and a perched rooster. Is the Franciscan Church the Bethany Monastery built by the Franciscans when they settled in the city in 1459? I'm wearing a white christening gown, am underweight, my eyes are almost popping out of my tilted-back head, my godparents pose for the black-and-white photo with a smile, which is the thing that I shall eventually hate so much about my aunt, her artificial affectations are without equal, she's always of the opinion that she must show off her whole set of teeth, which isn't at all immaculate, it displays dark spots that draw my gaze just as much the golden arches that encircle the incisors in the upper row, when she speaks, one can't help but get the impression that she's speaking with a toddler, even if it's with people her own age, when Mother died and she, the sister, didn't come to the funeral, it was she who died for me and not Mother, who still hasn't died to this day. A jug of water is poured over my head, Catholic Waterboarding instead of being dunked into the baptismal font. I dive into the image.

Wherefore squats Zellen Warhol between 748 and 1543, as he himself saw and drew, but with his gaze trained toward 1644? I take his sketch pad from his hand, which he allows to happen with no resistance. He says he's written a text about the city, which shall one day be added to the back side of his map. I should please include this text in my book. Now, indeed, it is my fundamental method to include everything I've read in my book, but I am generous as regards Zar Lohnwelle, which flatters him and he babbles cheerfully that I don't know what I should focus on, reading and copying or listening and noting down. Lohnwelle writes: "This free imperial city was first pawned by Emperor Dr. Ichfrei II. to Count Jim Will von Heuchle for 50,000 guldens, whereupon, in 1348, Kaiser Kleiderverrat ceded both Düren and the towns of Zinsig and Grämen to Millweh I., Duke and Margrave of Juleich, thus leaving it under his control. Since then, the gentility of the streets, the trade of its citizens, and certainly its fortifications have increased their reputation, in such manner that it is rightly considered to be the crown jewel of Juleich's towns." The plan is true to scale, Warhol says, with it, I might explore the long-destroyed medieval city at a one-to-one scale. In order to draw the map from a bird's eye view, he didn't really hover over the city like a bird, rather, he determined the top view by way of exact geometric calculations. He is certain that, one day, he shall also be able to precisely calculate God in this way, no conceivable, also no inconceivable event is safe from his geometric unmasking, the not merely geometric objectification of the fourth dimension—see Fechner—being only a question of time. Lohnwelle says that the city wall made the place defendable; by bundling its house-lined streets and building-ensembles together, it simultaneously bestows clarity upon it, as it hides the inner city from outside gaze and the ramparts, in which the eye seeks permeability, are themselves of the most striking clarity. While typical topographies sufficed for some localities, so-called typical cityscapes, which have been used for multiple cities with only the names substituted, they can be better recognized by way of those than if one were to draw their silhouettes, this city deserved to be drawn with great devotion to detail, he is delighted to see it surrounded by a series of vedutas, just like the ones he prepared in his free time, in search of special local and landscape features that escaped the untrained eye. If you now set out to visit the city of 1634 on the basis of his map, he says, you shall not fail to notice that the streets around or starting from the Anna Church are all winding, while the streets of the city districts that were added later run entirely straight. The layout of the roads, as can be concluded from this, is a historical time-signature, the less one thinks oneself to have of it—of time—the more curvelessly runs the road, which also takes away time from people for meditating on God. He advises me that if I want to come to my senses, then I must exclusively stick to the streets and alleys around the Anna Church.

The advantage of a panoramic tapestry, in which he decided to remain as a function of that advantage and in which I now keep him company in miraculous fashion, is the simultaneity of non-simultaneities, the spatial diversification of time, in which one can move back and forth as one pleases, in a few days' march, one traverses the historic townscapes of the city from the early Middle Ages to the present day, from its first documentary mention to its total destruction, its reconstruction and its contemporary appearance all juxtaposed, while also remaining completely and utterly intact, in leaving the city, he says, one also enters the city, no end of the tapestry is in sight, time, however, passes from left to right, by which it also takes space with it, and thus does it weave itself through all walls and across all borders, in such a way that what we no longer experience—what nobody will ever experience—shall join itself on the left on a day that is merely thought, but not actively thunk, by which it shall be definitively proven, should such a proof be required, that time and space are round and what is round clasps itself onto itself. This allows him to quote a man, who, throughout his life, which spanned almost the whole of the nineteenth century, was deeply fascinated by the question of the fourth dimension. Thus, Lohnwele says, did he get to the bottom of what lies behind the fact that there is time and that everything changes in time, including ourselves: "The movement of our space from three dimensions through the fourth, of which movement we only perceive the temporal element and the change that occurs." He claims that basically nothing could be simpler or more natural: According to this Leipzig scholar, our world of three dimensions is an enormous sphere, which breaks up into a multitude of individual spheres. Each of them *runs*; thus, most likely, does the great ur-sphere also run; but where would it run if there were no fourth dimension? But since it is precisely that which runs through this fourth dimension, all the spheres in it and everything that lives and weaves upon these spheres must of course also run through the fourth dimension. And then he comes to the wonderful conclusion: "In fact, all that we shall experience is already there and that which we have experienced is still there; our surface of three dimensions, for there is nothing now hindering us from speaking of such a surface in four dimensions in relation to corporeal space, is already all the way through *that*, but not yet through *this*." Beyond *that*, he has a handsome observation ready for *this* book: "An equally important application of this invention"—one must discover a means of "cutting the life-beam of man into slices or short cylinders by way of cross sections and placing these next to one another instead of having them be in line with one another as they previously were"—"would mean that we would thence be spared the entire art of book-printing. Each book that an author writes also extends into the fourth dimension in the form of a beam, for it does not disappear from the earth at the very moment the author has written it. In the aforementioned manner, however, we can cut as many copies out of it as we'd like, which, moreover, all have the merit of the author's original handwriting. Admittedly, each of these copies will only last for a short period of time; but what does that matter with books that, in any case, are only there so that new books be written afterward; they merely serve the purpose of opening up that space all the faster." If this is nonsense, so says Zellen Warhol, then it's quite a fine bit of nonsense, but time will tell whether it really is just nonsense, as the Leipzig scholar also promised a many-million-strong army of soldiers cut from a single human, should the invention of the life-bar cross section in the fourth dimension succeed, and these soldiers would only be there to be shot down, as they were, in any case, only granted a short time on earth.

And thus does Zellen Warhol sit in the year 1634, before 1318 years of city history, documented continually for the last 1270 years, he looks from the east, from the lined-up city silhouettes beginning in the year 700 and moving up until the present day. In any case, I shouldn't be unsettled by the fact that, as he is sitting there, he is actually sitting before an utterly different city, which is to say in front of Lewes, in which der Esel—the donkey—and its inversion, das Lesen—reading—are contained. In the portrait of this city, it is said that he sketched himself in a seated pose, the one in which I have just now found him, that's correct, this pose doesn't differ significantly upon the face of other cities, besides which I didn't even remotely notice his proverbial transfer, and that which isn't noticed doesn't exist.

I let him sit there calmly on Green Mountain, also known as Sturmsberg and, with map in hand, would like to approach the city from the east, but then, from the opposite direction at a crossroad, see the designation "Geat to Godes Housen" and, to the right of that, to the north, the words "Godes Hausens Lond" distributed across three fields. Here and now, having escaped the chimera and being free, the designation appeals to me, and I would very much like to see what the Land of the House of God looks like. After about fifteen minutes, I come to a small chapel, which, unlike the gate, can be seen on the map, but is not specifically named. The chapel stands alone on a small fell in the field to my left, the gate, a guarded portal, is located behind it and to the right, the way running straight ahead from the crossroads. Coming from the cross street, one is meant to pass through the gate, which suggests that all streets are provided with such gates, and the gatekeeper immediately comes up to me and asks whither I am underway, if I were coming to the city, then I'd gone in the wrong direction, then the question arises as to how I could have gotten past him, but if I weren't coming into the city, the question arises as to whither I'm going in the first place, as I don't look as if the Mother of God's house were my destination. Ah, so it's a Muttergotteshäuschen, no "Godes Housen" as it is called on the map. And how would that sound: "Godes Litel Housen"? Since the man gives the impression that he wants to arrest me as soon as I name the city as my destination, I say to him that I wish to visit the Muttergotteshäuschen. He seems to have counted on receiving this reply, he must have read the fear of having given a treasonous reply in my eyes, and thus does he ask me wherefore I wish to visit the Muttergotteshäuschen, but, without waiting for a reply, he leads me to the chapel, opens its door, and bids me to enter. The chapel is darkened. I am to tell him what is to be seen upon the altarpiece. If I misinterpret the image of the altarpiece, this will be an unmistakable sign of the fact that I lied and that the city was indeed and illegally my destination. In such case, the question as to how I managed to bypass his post so as to approach the city will have to be clarified, as he was one of the interceptors set out by the city to be there to avert any danger to the city as early as possible. He couldn't precisely judge what penalty would be accorded to me, in the worst case, I would have to pay for the lie and the intention behind it with my life. It is unpleasant to me that the gatekeeper takes my hand and leads me out of the chapel. He shows me a gallows place some 750 meters below the chapel, it can be seen quite clearly from up here; it is not noted on the map that ends with the field adjoining God's Little House in the east. We go back into the chapel. I ask him whether he couldn't light some candles, then I could at least see the image of the altarpiece. That would make it far too easy, the gatekeeper says and claps his hands. Each light increases darkness, he says, but when it's dark, the more one simply thinks of the word "colors," the more mightily shine the colors. Everlasting Light, the gatekeeper continues, is it outer or inner? I know all about that, I reply, for I was once an altar boy, the Everlasting Light hangs so unfavorably from the altarpiece that wherever one stands in the church, one cannot see it. Thus have we none, the gatekeeper says. If one has no Everlasting Light, then one has no cross either, I have now become valiant enough to argue with the man. The gatekeeper is silent. It is not uncommon, I continue, to see that the altarpieces have guards, of whom it cannot precisely be said what they are guarding. They are looking at something that has been withdrawn from the image. That's how it is, says the gatekeeper, but in a tone that betrays a certain insecurity. I am now venturesome enough to envision an auditorium at my feet listening to whatever I say. Whatever one sees, it always merely amounts to a quotidian burial of Christ. The gatekeeper is silent. It is so dark that I can't even make out his contours, though I can conceive of his voice in space as sculpture. I imagine the voice transmogrifying itself into one of the guard figures of the Leipzig Monument to the Battle of the Nations, it transforms itself into that Archangel Michael in knightly armor, he who bears his name as a halo round his head, or one of the sixteen warriors in the crypt with their eyes closed and gaze cast down toward the ground, figures who are no longer in need of a voice, who *are* a monumental silence, against which one's voice surges like a reverberating whimper, or one of the four colossal figures sitting before them, who, with gaping eyes, no longer shift their gaze, one shall never learn what they see or if they actually see anything at all. A warm wind grabs hold of me, it immediately causes me to speak. I hear the sound thereof, but can not tell whence it cometh and whither it goeth; so is every one that is born of the Spirit is so. I see a winged altarpiece, I say. Upon it is to be found no Jesus hanging on the cross, neither on the inner nor the outer altar wings or on the central image covered over by them. Upon the closed wings—the visible side thereof—four people and a sheep can be seen before a barren landscape. Behold—the lamb of God that taketh away the sins of the world! The sheep has wrapped its right front leg round a small cross, which it appears to be playing with as it runs to and fro. It is the only cross that the altar has to offer. Before the Agnus Dei stands a golden chalice, into which blood bleeds out from the page. The sheep gazes upon two desperately imploring women and one consoling man, all on the left of the image. The one woman, in a flowing robe of dusty pink and kneeling before the other, wears her long blonde hair loose and stretches her clasped hands to the sky, while the other, in a floor-length green dress, the sash of which seems to have gotten under the other's raiment, though her own green undergarment is indeed tangled up in that space, modestly conceals her hair beneath a white bonnet, which, together with the almost floor-length veil, is no longer white at all, but rather as if she had wiped up blood and water with it, suggesting the visage of a nun with a red-yellow-smeared veil. The consoler holds her in his right arm, his left hand fastened round her left underarm at the height of the elbow, his mouth is open in lamentation, he is, after all, the consoler, or is he merely fobbing himself off as a sympathizer full of sorrows? he looks into the pale, helpless face of the nunlike woman, who keeps her eyes closed, her face looks to be perishingly relaxed, resigned to her fate. An older man now appears on the right with thinning hair reaching down past his ears and a shaggy beard, he is carrying an open book in his left hand and pointing at the consoler with the forefinger of his right while he stares fixedly at the nun-like woman. This can only be John the Baptist. But is he really pointing at the consoler or, rather, at someone absent, at an absent one who has simply been withdrawn from the image, painted over, a pentimento—or, even worse, someone who was never present? If he was never present, nobody shall ever be able to say of his face that it is lovely and adorned and it is the face of beauty. His forefinger seems to be admonishing this absent one, yet doesn't want to admit it, the forefinger has become so indecently long over this period of empty pointing, as if it wished to take the place of that which it obviously cannot point to, for it doesn't exist in the slightest. But if Christ is not there, how can there be a reconciliation between God and man, as both only come to themselves again in Christ. If that isn't the ostentatio vulnerum, the flaunting, all the better, the indication of the emptiness, the sign of something from the past, I say to the gatekeeper and click my tongue. The forefinger gazes upon me, it's a genital. He that beholdeth Him is at once torn in pieces, and he that glimpseth His beauty at once poureth himself out as a vessel, it used to be said. The forefinger calculates that I am in the image. But I don't wish to be planned for, I say, at least not like that. The forefinger is therefore so long because, as a genital, it is a writing utensil, slapping the backs of my thighs then and there, and, with this writing utensil, the old man writes down everything he cannot see, he keeps records for decades, as I have been keeping records for six years, and thus shall I slowly become him. Observing him, I watch myself write and see what I shall write a few years down the line. A spiritual self-touching.

The wind blowing from the front, which has become a bit cooler, irritates me, it doesn't let me hear where the guard is standing, whether he is breathing, whether he has perhaps come in after me. But I must not betray any insecurity now, thus do I tell him about the landscape becoming visible behind the ensemble of figures, I suddenly recognize it as my homeland, slightly craggy, gloomily overcast during nocturnal hours, perhaps to the left and at the foot of a volcano, fire smolders none too far away, somebody wished to warm themselves or something was burned, the further I go, the more strongly it smells of paper, I also smell burnt clothing, grass upon the plain, no water, thus no caldera, the hill has turned too much to karst for that, now, it smells of all that which I'd like for it to smell of, which is to say magma from which is drawn all that we think, each imaginary meaning that we institute, and thus are there nothing but wants that cannot truly be satisfied, but which produce a great deal of beautiful-looking images veiling over the abyss. Thus does the state become a religion that pretends to no longer require a state by proffering meaning unto meaning. Despite all this, the image is painted with an astonishing lack of skill, never mind that there's really no reason at all that regional art needs to be painted poorly.

I follow the wind that bloweth where it will, it seems to come from the front, though I can not tell whence it cometh and whither it goeth. Now, I've walked straight for longer than the chapel is long, I open the altar and we see the inner left wing, I say to the gatekeeper. What we see there defies all description. The world is a wicked inn. Sin dwells in the body, here, it swarms with the naked, the impaled, those given over to the game, cuckstool-demons and fire and birds flutter forth from the ass. Deception rules everywhere. Music is the work of Satan. The chimeras have returned. The nun is a pig and bears me in her arms. I am entirely naked, she wants to kiss me, it costs me all my strength to ward her off, there is a bit of script on my right thigh, at last, I now desire to read it, the Lucifer I know all too well appears as a drollery with a lizard's tail, a child's legs, a bear's paws, and a bird's head in a knight's helmet, from which the long, pointed beak peeps out and from whose thorn-spiked crista hangs a severed foot, gnawed off at the shinbone, he's now finally gotten hold of an inkpot and a refill flask, which he diligently holds out in his open beak to the pig-nun so that she might dip her quill into the pot and write in my name that which I never shall have written. Her secretary is already behind her in a dusty-pink robe and holds sealed papers at the ready, she shall send them on their way once the forgery is complete. The inkpot must be refilled. That gives me the opportunity to read the writing on my leg. There, it is written: "I hereby declare that I do not traffick in indulgences and have bought no indulgences with letter and seal." I am to sign at the bottom right. If I were to sign this indulgence, I would be accused of lying after paying my debt, this bit of script would prove it. If I were to not sign it, would the pig-nun then badger me for all eternity or take the refusal to sign as an admission that I'm doing the exact opposite of what I'm meant to clarify in the letter? But that would be the best argument in favor of signing the declaration—and so on. I'm ashamed of the fact that I'm staring at myself so fearfully and pitifully from the image and prefer to look away. Precisely at the moment when I take a glance at the upper third of the side wing, my hometown, which I can recognize from some of the houses in the image, is engulfed by a tremendous conflagration, the buildings blaze furiously, one can see devils everywhere balancing on ropes between the houses with the help of poles, the houses are illuminated by Christmas trees, they're slowly floating to the ground from a height of a thousand meters and are intended to color-code the bomb targets. The conditions are favorable, a starlit night, no wind. Convoys of fire engines in action everywhere. Soon, everything shall be swept away by the conflagration and the hurricane that it causes. People fall out of the houses and sink into a great pool. An elephant is led over the gate of Gehenna, which forms the dam wall around the lake. A triangular black flag stands in the air. A gallows with somebody hanging from it. The fire also illuminates the rear, previously unharmed sections of the city. In the distance, I can recognize my parents' house through smoke and water. The view clears up. Mother is standing in the kitchen. She is boiling tea while she reads. The book is about her death. She reads the book with no sense of worry. In any case, her face gives up no information regarding her inner state. How often we hear things about ourselves and observe our own lives, as if it were someone else's affair we were scoffing at. Now, she leaves the kitchen without having taken the tea with her. She also leaves the book lying on the kitchen table. The kitchen is brightly illuminated. Baked goods lie in a shell-shaped bowl upon a small sideboard. Mother comes back into the kitchen and takes a roll from the bowl. She is at the point of leaving the kitchen with the roll when she notices a box in place of the book. Its sudden to-handness seems not to startle her at all—the fact that, first, it was the book, then, suddenly, the box lying on the kitchen table. In the box, a strange device is to be found, she prudently takes it out and places it onto the table. The device would look like a food processor, a blender to which one feeds vegetables through its opening, if it weren't for the lens on its front. Operation instructions are lying on the bottom of the box, which now become easily legible in the picture: "Hang a smooth white cloth or a white paper umbrella on the wall and place the device on a table about 1 to 1.5 meters away from it. If you bring the device closer to the white wall than indicated, the images become sharper but also somewhat smaller, whereas, at longer distances, the images become larger, but somewhat less distinct. In any case, the sharpness of the image is always the same at any distance if adjusted correctly by pushing the objective eyepiece inward or outward. The lens must be fully inserted into the tube.

Fill the lamp about 3⁄4 full with the best petroleum, trim the wick evenly, and light it with a small flame. Put the lamp in its place, draw the chimney, and, once the cylinder and other parts are somewhat warm, screw the wick to as large a flame as possible, making sure it doesn't soot. Place the images upside down in the image-casing located behind the optical glasses. The optical glasses and the reflector must be cleaned; the room must be completely dark." In the time it takes to read the operation instructions, Mother has hung a smooth white cloth from the wall, positioned the device on a table one to one and a half meters away from it, inserted the lens into the tube entirely, filled the lamp about three-quarters full with the best petroleum, trimmed the wick evenly, and lit it with a small flame, put the lamp into its place, drawn the chimney, screwed the wick to a large flame after the cylinder and other parts had gotten somewhat warm, and placed one of the very images also lying in the box upside down into the image-casing located behind the optical glasses. The kitchen is now entirely dark. Mother takes a sip of tea from the cup, leans back, and observes the image projected onto the white cloth, which I cannot see looking on from here, as it is completely concealed by a large kitchen cupboard. Mother sits there motionlessly. The cup of tea is now empty, she pours more. With the forefinger of her right hand, she crushes some breadcrumbs on the kitchen table. With her wet finger, she picks up the crumbs that won't allow themselves to be crushed and sticks them into her mouth. The feeling of crumbs between tongue and gums seems to make her feel sad, she rolls her tongue to and fro until the crumbs have vanished. The certainty of never raising oneself up again. To nevermore move the legs. The notion of oneself being the crumbs. The howling of bombs. Corpses shrinking from the heat. Mother takes the chimney from the lamp and casts the remaining crumbs into the flames. The image flickers. Then calm comes to reign once more. Mother sits entirely within herself, as if she were the device and as if she were observing the images inside of her and imagining and perception were one. Thus does she fall asleep and collapse slightly forward onto the table. The device slides off to the side and now projects its image distendedly onto the wall adjacent to the door and the doorframe on the right. The subject of the image now seems to be hovering freely in space, but, at the same time, is entirely distorted. The impact frightened Mother, she raises herself up and approaches the image, I too can see it, but by no means recognize it or even interpret it. Its distortion makes Mother visibly nervous, she goes to the left, to the right, then she takes a few steps back, then gets very close to the image once more, as if she were searching for something. It's only when she gazes upon the image from a particular perspective that her restlessness subsides and she remains in this position for several minutes. Her visage indicates that it now regards the image as an element of its own reality, even if it doesn't betray that which it sees, and as if she would lose something that is very important to her the moment she budged even a centimeter from her spot. From the front, I can't recognize anything in the image that my mother had taken into her gaze at a sharp angle, but perhaps I would be able to if I took an oblique perspective of the left inner wing. And, indeed, after a few tries, I can see that which made Mother so pious and fearful:

The entire body riddled with splinters of thorns, flagellation-wounds everywhere, split and torn skin, holes, tears, hematoma. The hands are twisted, the fingers curled up like claws. The blood spurts from the page and blood runs from forehead and temples. The mouth is badly painted, it seems to have been revised several times until it was entirely corrupted. In the oblique view, the panel with the larger-than-life figure, which could only be taken on while standing on a ladder, falls back into the twenty-six linden planks, from which it was made. I imagine the painter crawling around on the panel and changing direction for almost every brushstroke, in the frenzy of exertion, he painted the mouth upside down, at the bottom end of the first third of the image, which he pretended to only notice when he was presenting the commissioned work. The fact that the mouth is now twisted into a grimace is sold as an intensification of his expression, a man of sorrows heretofore non-extant in the history of art. But it is not the twisting of the upper and lower lips that puts the mouth into a light that thus falls out of the image, it is rather the bloodlessness of the lips, which the art of the time has seen nothing akin to, as the infirmity of the whole person can be read from this figure and no longer just the symbolic quality of the infirmity. He placed the bar of the cross from which the corpse hangs to the right of the middle of the image in such a way that, although the right arm and part of the crown of thorns had to be painted onto the left inner wing of the first mural, which can be seen when the altar is shut, it was possible to prevent a bisection between the middle of the bar and the body. That affords an unobstructed view of the corpse in the process of decomposition, its belly is drawn so far inward that it shall grow toward its back while it is still decomposing. Its arms, gnarled trunks of olive trees, seem to get longer and longer as one observes them, its thighs with their stigmata are gherkin-growths. The corpus slowly turns into wood, which is why there is no need for a corpus on crucifixes. It's all beautifully depicted and I rejoice as the apparition in the distance puts the fear of God into Mother some meters away. Mother cannot let go of the image, her gaze is particularly attracted by the face that stares at her in a way that might well be dubbed obscene, whereupon I, who am more distant from the scene than the celestial bodies above me, would feel the urge to apologize to the figure on the cross, were it not for the fact that I recognized myself in it, as does Mother, who must have recognized her son in the same moment she saw the crucified Christ whose death she blames herself for in perpetuity, a death that, at the same time, makes her very proud. Her sorrow shall never come to an end, resurrection is not an option for her. From now on, she shall carry her son around her neck as a gold chain with a crucifix dangling from it, a crucified man who is permanently hanged.

Here, I say to the gatekeeper, we have a devotional picture of singular clarity, which invites complete immersion and becomes a part of one's own body. From it—and may it always be so—the viewer receives a suffering that he shall always be subject to, which shall accompany all of his imaginings, all of his deeds shall be based on this suffering. And only he, for whom this suffering is meaningful, need not despair. How long does Mother wish to stand there and observe the image? Does she fear losing her son entirely when the oil in the lamp is down to its dregs? Perhaps, she is dreaming of an everlasting flame that keeps me on the wall in the image. She shall always be remote from me, for this is how I know her to be near to me. Increasing smoke obscures the view, fire has broken out behind one of the city gates nearby, without being able to save any of their possessions, the residents run to the gate and, in the fire's glistening reflection, as if they were wearing radiant white raiments, they follow its raging, then the smoke clears and I am able to see my parents' house, I have no certainty as to whether Mother has finally given up the observation of the image, for I now see a synaesthetic scene from 53 years ago in my parents' house, which we must imagine for ourselves as the left half of the central panel, I tell the gatekeeper to check if the winged altar is open:

A hand reigns once more in a room divided by two vaults with cross ribs, the room runs toward its arch-pointed windows. This time, it belongs to a winged angel and it doesn't know precisely to what it's meant to point, the director may not have given any precise information, perhaps the scene has been rehearsed under different constellations for so long that confusion now reigns, an unbiased viewer shall have to ask himself the following questions: To whom are the overly long index and middle fingers pointing? Has the dove of the Holy Spirit escaped him, is it now floating in space, so terribly out of place, and is he now pointing at something else—at empty transcendence? Is he pointing at the red curtain behind my mother and to the left, it's pushed aside as if this were a theater and its folds and waves are the female equivalent of the pointing double member with the ring finger and the little finger pointing downward as testicles? Then, with the black curtain drawn, is death waiting behind the first vault with all of its tensionless rugosities? The black, upon closer inspection, turns out to be green. Death is green. Over her tight-fitting black dress, Mother is wearing a black cloak with red lining that glows at its edges, it's tied with a red cord above her bosom. The dress is high-necked and pleated in the area of the breasts. She wears her long black hair loose, turns her head away, and bows it, a posture that allows her wavy hair to flow down her back. My mother puts her ear out to the angel and thus am I also received through her ear. Admittedly, the angel does not speak. What counts are the penetrating gestures and the written language, for a book lies before my mother, an open book in which she is immersed. I know the book. It contains transcripts made by her hand, quotations from the Bible alongside quotations from Schiller, Lessing, and Hesse, as well as love letters that she copied out before sending, one day, Father shall punch holes in the originals and file them away in a binder. The angel is the inner voice that speaks in my mother. She is so immersed in the word that is within her that it becomes true: "Behold, a virgin shall be with child, and shall bring forth a son, and they shall call his name Michael, which being interpreted is, He Who Is Like God. Butter and honey shall he eat, that he may know to refuse the evil, and choose the good. He shall eat butter and honey forevermore," is written there in her handwriting. In order to always keep this before her eyes, she wrote the quote on the left, then, slightly lower, also on the right page of the book, a secular-religious book of hours of self-reflection, Mother's sole dependable haven. The author of the quote is likewise present in the room, he stands there, painted in grisaille, in the upper left of the vaulted arch. Here, someone composed colors by means of mining, hydraulic engineering, and metallurgy, he makes visible to the outside world what sounds out in the inner ear, he painted the voice— the Word and what it does as it is being read incessantly invoked on the inside. This image is the Word in operation. And thus has the Word brought me into being, I tell the gatekeeper.

If we now look to the right of the central panel, under the arch of a wall arcade, we see a figure in episcopal regalia before a hilly, barren landscape under a radiant blue sky. Upon a second glance, it is revealed that the landscape is kept diffuse. It's not possible to determine whether one gets a glimpse of the interior of the building with the surrounding arcades or whether a section of the external undeveloped land becomes visible through the arch. If the picture allows for an interior view, the sloping rubble in the middle of the courtyard would irritate and the figure would then pose in front of a completely undeveloped arcaded courtyard, such a portrait in natura would hardly be imaginable or it would communicate an atmosphere of departure, for which the figure would be far too formally dressed and immobile. The crook attached to the shaft of the bishop's crosier is decorated with four Gothic church windows running round it on the cylindrical knob above the handle of the shaft, Christ is enclosed in the crook with outstretched arms, in his left hand, he bears the cosmic sphere embellished with his monogram of peace, with the index and middle fingers of his right, he forms the sign of blessing. The figure, painted in oil on oak, is Louis of Toulouse. He looks similar to my father. Upon closer inspection, I become convinced that he is my father. But one is somewhat inclined to see one's father everywhere, provided he's been absent for long enough. His crook, set with thirteen thorns, is turned outward, thus does Father Louis know himself to be in his territory, which he would defend with his staff as a lash if necessary. Why does he look dejected? The broad golden nimbus of the figure has been damaged in places, here and there are eruptions that need to be overcome. But he knows nothing of that. It has to do with the girdle book that he, wearing white gloves, holds in his left hand so bashfully, as if he bore stolen loot or were on his way to the high court. Mother read some of this book in the kitchen before she began to stare spellbound at the projection. She can only have done that should the figure be my father. The book is now closed with book clasps, a practical device that prevents sudden opening or uninvited reading. It is not Christ who is crucified in the representations upon the winged altar, I say to the gatekeeper, but the book out of which Mother has been reading for her whole life without finding any answers to her questions. What kind of questions are these? She asks herself, for example, why she should give birth to a son who shall grow further and further apart from her and whom she shall never understand, then, later, she asks herself why she gave birth to a son who shall never be grateful. Mother, Louis, and the angel look upon the book that is in their midst. Only Augustine on the right wing looks up from the book he holds open in his left hand—off into the distance in which he knows there to be a world freed from books. The psychopomp-sparrow has escaped from the book and shall soon hurl himself into Augustine's right hand. Augustine has gathered all of his books around himself on the floor, he's read them all and found them not to be worth holding onto, opened up to any point, they consist only of blank pages, they haven't lost their contents, they never had any to begin with, all that they're good for is sitting on. His white robe itself is paper and this paper shall remain blank in such a way that one might imagine everything written upon it and, simultaneously, the writing is erased, for only white paper is immaculate. One single book is the exception. He has placed the Book of Life onto the tree of life, it's open to a random page—the fig tree as the symbol of the Word. Upon the left page is written: "It's an upside-down world. Hell stands at its beginning, everything emerges from it, depicted, as I see it, on the left side of the winged altar of the Muttergotteshäuschen, and, from left to right, all the way to the wing on the opposite side, there is no scene of crucifixion other than my own, where I was placed into a maple with its pages open, everybody can read of me, everybody can think their own thoughts, and the tree can be felled at any time, the proclamation is a misunderstanding, the prophet cannot write, the mother cannot read, the angel cannot speak, and all three do not understand, the born one knows naught and is immediately lost, with birth comes a life away from parents and toward death, my resurrection is forbidden by law."

Upon the right page is written: "So was I speaking and weeping in the most bitter contrition of my heart, when, lo! I heard from a neighbouring house a voice, as of boy or girl, I know not, chanting, and oft repeating, 'Take up and read; Take up and read.' Instantly, my countenance altered, I began to think most intently whether children were wont in any kind of play to sing such words: nor could I remember ever to have heard the like. So checking the torrent of my tears, I arose; interpreting it to be no other than a command from God to open the book, and read the first chapter I should find. Eagerly then I returned to the place where Alypius was sitting; for there had I laid the volume of the Apostle when I arose thence. I seized, opened, and in silence read that section on which my eyes first fell: 'Not in rioting and drunkenness, not in chambering and wantonness, not in strife and envying. But put ye on the Lord Jesus Christ, and make not provision for the flesh, to fulfil the lusts thereof.' No further would I read; nor needed I: for instantly at the end of this sentence, by a light as it were of serenity infused into my heart, all the darkness of doubt vanished away." I didn't know this passage before and I confess that it is not mine. But I'm familiar with the situation. A child's voice seduces to script, for the script is already in the child's voice from the beginning. And that is where it wishes to go back to right also from the beginning—to the beginning. It's the repetition that does it. The ever-repeating book. Take up and read to me. Reading is observing images. Identity is the daily repetition of a book. Take and eat of the Book of Life. Whoever carries a book on his person, carries Christ on his person, whoever reads a book, reads Christ. Script is the only dependable thing in the world, I say to the gatekeeper and tell him a story I once heard: "Any body that steps into the church's got to pledge himself t'the devil with his own blood. Once, a man had grown durn tired of his quarrelsome wife given' him hell each and ev'ry day. One day, she told him he'd better up an' leave the church. But he shot back: 'That just ain't possible. Once one has gotten hisself into the church, ain't no way out.' But the woman had an answer to that too: 'If y'ain't got no objections, then I'm goan go there and get an idea of the situation.' He ain't object and she immediately got goin' on her way to the church. When she got there, she was led on down a long corridor draped over in black, which made her quake an' tremble in her soul. But she calmed herself down and said to the church warden that she had a powerful need of gettin' her husband free. The fella handed her a quill and told her how she was s'posed to cross out her husband's name from the book. She done it with a powerful sense of delight, but, soon's she got home, her husband was there, lying stone-dead 'pon the ground." The gatekeeper shows himself to be completely unimpressed by the story. Perhaps it's to do with the dialect in which I've told the tale, I think, then tell him the following story, as I once heard it: "A servant's got a story to tell: The church's got a big ole' book. In it, every man writes his own name in his own blood. One day, there was a man who'd grown real durn tired of this and had a powerful desire of bein' struck from the book. And he said so to the Most High God. To which the Most High God responded: 'If y'happen to have a knife, scratch yer name on out with it.' He starts scratchin' out his name. But, as he scratches out the name, he's also cuttin' his own throat. For it's God's truth that nobody can get outta there. If y'seek to scratch out yer name, y'kill yerself. Yer between a rock and a hard place—whomsoever puts his name down just can't get out."

I hear the gatekeeper not breathing and not rustling around. Like my parents. If they left the house, they wouldn't say so. So, how far am I to go? Silence is the most powerful weapon. If one takes the script literally, I bring it into consideration. If one stays with it. If one doesn't take it for something else. If one sees the script as image. One must learn to not read and not understand. It is I, I say to the gatekeeper, who am depicted on the right wing, I am the figure in the paper robe and it is my book that I hold in my hands and it is my book that appears in the Tree of Life, open to a random page. In this book, I must answer the question of how I can get from the left wing to the right. How can I resolve the paradox of the sale of indulgences without selling myself if the issue of the sale of indulgences becomes self-contradictory no matter how I relate to it—and that I must relate to it is a given. Sitting behind Father, I can't look over his shoulder. I would gladly like to catch a glimpse of his book, which he keeps locked away in the book girdle. I am of the conviction that it is my book, he shall nail it to the cross. Father shall not allow the existence of this book to go unpunished, its crucifixion has apotropaic power for him. He shall open the book right in the middle, open the two halves violently, as if he were attempting to overpower a dangerous animal, then shall take the book out into the open, into his home garden, and nail it to an oak, the trunk of which is thick enough that the book can be made completely flat. Father shall regret that he cannot observe the weathering of the book uninterruptedly, as the letters are literally being driven out of it. Thus, shall he think, has a heretical work received a sensible punishment, its creator shall understand it as having been carried out upon the book as a proxy for himself. Adept at Reading-Upside-Down, Father can read Mother's open book over the angel's shoulder, and that which he reads causes his gaze to grow rather distressed. Mother cannot read, she can only gaze at script, which constitutes far more. My book is my indulgence. I am now on the far left, in hell. I've not yet signed. Light penetrates through the arch-pointed window of my mother's vaulted room, which is reminiscent of the interior of a church. Day breaks. I hear birds chirping and move toward Mother. I walk through her quietly, take her book with me, it lies on a chest before her and I'd like to give it to Father, I climb the high windowsill by way of a chest of drawers, I open the window and stride through it into the night. I can find no firm ground in the field behind the chapel. After a few strides, I lose my right shoe in a field-furrow full of water, then search the area on all fours before finally finding the shoe, but, meanwhile, lose Mother's handwritten book, the handwriting of which alone is what makes it so valuable, the handwriting is the only trace of the body that makes it legible even after death. I think of the stars flickering in the sky as eyes winking at the city-seeker. It's not yet obvious to me whether they wish to mock me or assure me of their protection. Finally, I reach solid ground beneath my feet, according to the map, which the night forbids me from looking at, I am, if I'm remembering correctly, on the path that runs around the city wall parallel to the city moat. If one has the opportunity to visit one's city of birth more than three hundred years before one's birth and the streets in which one shall be born already exist, one shall leave no stone unturned in order to overcome the city wall. My outward appearance shall be no hindrance, after all, with the transition into the map, I have taken on the raiments of the era. The city is the story of its repeated destruction, each of its future destructions seeming to have taken into account each of its reconstructions. Today, the cityscape is the result of architectural self-humiliation and a triviality that no longer considers destruction to be worthwhile. After all, the cityscape was understood to be feasible and a master plan for the renovation of the city center was drawn up—to save what could be saved. A reconciliation with my hometown shall only be possible for me if I buy the map from Zellen Warhol after visiting it anno 1634. With the supposition of reaching the center more quickly than if I were to cross the city here from the nearer south, I go cross-country in a northwesterly direction until I come to a road that I follow in a northerly direction. After about a half hour, I come to a crossroads at which stands a gate about as wide as the Collnische Steinweg, it branches off to the left and right, a kind of trade route through which the greater part of the city's trade likely goes. It regulates the influx that it brings into the city by way of its narrow passage, initially, it's channeled through a first gate at the lower end of the path, this being lined with houses on both sides, a hospital too. The people know their city. The lower gate is called Capellen Pfort and a small settlement in the city's environs is called Collner Vorstadt, I am told after asking, a question only intended to conceal my uncertainty as to how to deal with the gatekeepers. Together with a barbican, the upper portal belongs to a gate guarded by two guards, who are stationed out front for safeguarding. The city gates and their foregates are the only places where the double-channeled moat surrounding the wall can be crossed without getting one's feet wet. One of the gatekeepers strides over to me and, laconically holding out his hand, demands proof of my right to pass through the city gate. I have nothing to show but the map, no identification, no trade papers. The gatekeeper examines the map in the light of a torch, motions for me not to budge with his forefinger, then goes to the second keeper, who observes the map for longer than would seem to me to be propitious, the two of them talk briefly, then the first keeper comes back to me, hands me the map once more, and wordlessly denies my entry, blocking my way whenever I make a move to pass through the foregate. Others who want to go about their business in the city take advantage of this situation so as to bypass the keeper and go through the foregate, which certainly increases their chances of being able to take the much larger hurdle of the main gate, provided that the more powerful warden in the general dark crowd has not noticed the unwariness of the head guard who is subordinate to him, he was downright dogged in his refusal to let me through and would probably play this game, which is no game, for a long time if I didn't see the hopelessness of this back-and-forth from my side and, as such, draw away from it. As I depart, I once more observe the gate with its small bridge upon which one crosses the moat's first channel, goes a few meters to the left, then sees the two-story tower gate with its three pointed-arch portals and its pointed roof, the entrance bridge leads over the moat's second channel. I wish to try my luck at the next gate, which the map shows as Weiler Pfort and which, after two bastion towers, still has yet to appear on the west side at the beginning of the north side of the city wall. Together with the bastion towers, the city gates form the most prominent points of the city wall, they are the city's vulnerable eyes. The map perspectivally conveys the impression that the path and the fields bordering it lead straight up into the sky, even though the ground is quite flat. I am the only one on my way. There's also nobody to be seen in the fields. The city seems to be everything, the surrounding land merely the way unto it, which one strives to overcome as much as possible while remaining unseen. Thus does he make himself suspicious, he who circles the city without attaining entry, he who besieges it without a host, and all recognize the outsider in him. After some thirty minutes, the way branches off to the left and a mighty tower gate appears, on the viewing platform of which there's meant to be a cannon if one is to believe the map and the draftsman didn't let himself be carried away toward dishonest alterations, after all, the people noted down here and there on the paths are the only manifestations of a stirring city life and do not testify to a non-ephemeral presence. Whether one wishes to continue on the way to Weiler Pfort or to enter the city through this gate, one must, in any case, pass by a barrier and it would seem inadvisable, in order to make oneself less suspicious, to now turn back and pretend to be disinterested. A man with a turban-like headdress, the train of which looks like the tail of a mighty reptile and is likely to be a hindrance to walking, a beige one-piece robe, which reaches down to the knees where it's split like a skirt, long white pantyhose, and heeled shoes, the buckles of which are decorated with the city's coat of arms, asks me whither I wish to go, holds a tin out to me without waiting for an answer, and I stick several coins into it, so quickly that he can't check their origin, the keeper strides off to the side, I go through the barrier, the keeper remains level with me, walking sideways, thus blocking the path that leads toward the city gate, in front of which a second keeper has been observing this spectacle. I now have the choice of continuing the path around the city wall, which must lead to an even larger gate, the mightiest of the five city gates, further away from the town hall and the market square, but, contrarily, closer to the street where I shall be born in 330 years. I follow the "Way to Gülich," as it is called on the map, which, due to its immediate proximity to the train station, shall later be called Eisenbahnstraße, then Adolf-Hitler-Straße, then Eisenbahnstraße once more, then, finally, after the nickname of the city's only poet laureate, Frech-je-Glosse-Straße. This way, however, leads not to Gülich, but in the opposite direction, to the city of my later birth. I pass through a gate, unguarded at this early hour, in the middle of the way, then turn left at the crossroads onto

Tirolers-Wandel* Way, which runs parallel to the path along the city wall, attracted by a castle-like building whose windows are all lit up. To my left and right lies a green area called Liebenwerden—Lieberwandern† and Weiberlenden‡ in common parlance, as a passerby clarifies to me, he seemed to understand my gaze off into the distance as a challenge to prove that he was familiar with the area—which is partially covered over in trees. Upon approaching, dance music sounds out from the building at the area's western edge. On the map, the building is marked down as "Edens Ventil," or "Eden's Valve." An old man sits at the entrance, his snow-white beard shines in the light. He has a large book lying on the small table before him. The book is open and the old man seems to be reading it. What are you reading there, I ask. I am not reading, the old man says, I am writing. And what are you writing? I have just written: "An old man sits at the entrance, his snow-white beard shines in the light. He has a large book lying on the small table before him." Then, I asked myself whether it wouldn't be better to say: "An old man with a long snow-white beard was sitting at the entrance, and a large book lay open before him." I find that to be unambiguously better, I agree with the old man. Then why didn't you write it like that? he asks me. Out of sheer shock, I simply say: "But it's so beautiful here!" If you like it here, the old man says, put your name down in the book. I take the quill and write: "Jesus of Nazareth, King of the Jews." As soon as I set the quill down, the building vanishes and I stand in the dark once more, alone in the field. But, in my hands, I hold my mother's book and the old man's book and wish to swiftly read what is written there. But there's no light anywhere and thus do I wait for light. I sit down on a boulder at the edge of the way and cradle both books in my hands, my mother's book on the left, the old man's book on the right, then the old man's book on the left and my mother's book on the right:

---

* Tyrolese Way of Life.
† Ratherhiking.
‡ Women'sloins.

I can distinguish no difference in weight between them, the surfaces also reveal no tactile divergences. At the crack of dawn, I read in the old man's book: "He's not at all surprised to once more be holding his mother's book, which was, after all, lost and he's not at all concerned by the fact that the brightly illuminated castle vanished as a result of his lie." It would be all too easy for me now to say: It does surprise me, I'd like to disagree, and I must clarify that the castle is a lie and thus could the encounter with the old man not have happened in the first place. Nothing would be gained by this, for the matter has been related and thus has it come to pass. I also read from my mother's book of complaints, but reading it makes me so sad that I prefer to continue reading the old man's book with its sagas and farces. How can one perpetually complain without changing one's life, how can one blame others for all incidents without asking oneself how one has contributed to it, how can one grow into the calamity one saw coming years ago—day by day by day? In the old man's book, I read of a man who loses his mother's book the moment he enters into the forbidden city, where he must redeem it at the risk of losing his life.

Then I look up from the book and see a gate castle, which resembles a true fortress. This shall be my touchstone and shall prove whether or not I can get into the city. The gate castle is more complex than the two gates from which I've heretofore been turned away and, according to the map, also more complex than the remaining gates of the city wall. It consists of a low platform, which leads over the first moat and can be seen in full from the first tower: a two-story square and a three-story rectangular tower, each with crenellations. The two towers, which could well be equipped with canons, are connected to one another by a gateway, through which many a man has surely vanished. At the wayside, a building has been placed in front of the gate castle, its close proximity to it exerts an irresistible attraction upon me. Perhaps, I hope to meet somebody there who shall allow me to access the city without me being subject to a fruitless check of my entry credentials. Compared with the streets and fields so bereft of people, a frenzy reigns before the house as in a beehive. It quickly becomes apparent that the building serves as a residence for the gatekeeper. A young man carrying a stack of papers under his arm is just leaving the house, he doesn't pull the front door shut behind him, I slip inside without knocking and find myself before a perplexed-looking man of about forty who has just gone to the toilet and is about to remove his dressing gown. He is meticulously careful about keeping his private sphere hidden from me, rushes into the sitting room, hastily slams the door shut, calls out that I should wait for a moment, the house seems to have been built crookedly, the door of the sitting room opens a bit once more, just enough that I can see the gatekeeper before me, as naked as when God created him, he doesn't immediately notice this, but then he reacts with a hastiness that is mixed with anger, in his haste he tumbles over the wicker chair that serves as the storage-space for his working raiments, he swears in Plattdeutsch, which I can barely decipher: "Ma' the deevil tak tho fellas!", the door slams shut, which gives me the opportunity to survey the antechamber a bit, on the inside of the front door hangs a broadsheet, upon which a man is shown displaying an etching to the viewer, a woman with a veil portrayed in that latter image. The man looks inescapably into the viewer's eye, he has just now completed the miniature portrait or he is pretending to just have finished it, there are straight edges and etching needles on the table at which he sits, but this could also be a copper engraving, in which case there would be steel burnishers and scrapers, spitsticks and flat chisels, rulers, hole punchers, roulettes, and grooved rollers on the table. The man wears a robe buttoned up to the top, its sleeves are pushed up slightly to make visible the cuffs of his white shirt underneath. The shirt collar, which is strikingly large and decorated with a crocheted border, completely covers the neck, as if it had the function of hiding something. The collar is held together by way of a complicated-looking lacing. Fir-cone-like thickenings form the end of the lacing and, due to their size and weight, ensure that the cord cannot come loose from the drawstring. The man wears his hair à la mode, short above the brow, long on the sides and behind. He has deep furrows beneath his tear-filled eyes. Perhaps, he has an eye problem, perhaps, he is in mourning because of the woman he has presumably portrayed. It's the very woman from the winged altar of the Muttergotteshäuschen—my mother. She bears a cane before her bosom, her gaze is averted from the viewer, as if she didn't notice him or wanted to keep a secret, and it is unpleasant for her to be gazed upon with the cane in her hands. The man sits before the window of his workshop, through it, one can see the main church of Saint Martini, called S. Annae. The double portrait is accompanied by a text that turns the broadsheet into a wanted poster: "We are searching for Zellen Warhol so as to put him into a Zelle. He carries no weapon on his person, but a map that is more dangerous than all weapons, for, with it, the city can be surveyed at one sitting and, due to its ability to defend itself having been reduced in this fashion, be conquered more easily. Zellen Warhol is the very one who carries the map on his person, which is why no description or portrait thereof is given here: he appears so mutably that Zellen Warhol could be anybody or nobody. The one sought does not have a seal to represent his own person. Furthermore, nobody knows whether he has a coat of arms, one that might be delineated from nature; no delineator or emblazoner has ever seen him."

The keeper then emerges from his chamber, chest swelled out with pride, as if he were flaunting his magnificent robe, instantly, he seems to have aged at least ten years and suddenly has all the time in the world to approach me, while also singing the following lines: "Up ye go all folks, up ye go all folks, only werk gits ye oan aheed!" At first, I don't know whether I should laugh at this or take his attitude as an invitation to speak to him in confidence. But there can be no question of a conversation, the keeper grabs me by the shoulder, as if my sentence were already settled, then he shoves me out of the house in front of him. He is already at work on my guilty verdict. Outside of the house, however, observed by all the citizens hurrying into the city, he becomes quite friendly with me, he inquires after my projects in the city and already knows of the city map that I showed at one of the gates. Thus should I be warned that they are aware of me and that I cannot take a single step unobserved. Here, their environs are plagued by a strange drought, I notice, then wish to inquire politely after the local climate, when I'm suddenly struck by the notion that the cultivations, vegetation, and climate are all mere quotations, all part of a historical deception intended for a great aggressor, who, under such circumstances, might well refrain from conquering the city once more. The question about the city map betrays a residual uncertainty as to whether this map is actually to be found in my possession and thus do I answer evasively; that gives me a slight advantage, one I might make use of again in the future. Right before the city gate, toward which we are both, self-evidently, on our way, as if it had been agreed upon from the outset that I only entered his house for that reason, though I didn't express anything at all to him concerning this, I now imagine that I am on a special mission and that the gatekeeper is my tour guide, he who deals with all vexatious matters for me, the gatekeeper asks me in a tone that would befit a high-ranking figure, but is inappropriate for an outsider whose status is also in doubt, whether I am a citizen of the city and what I would undertake therein. I shall be born here in some three hundred years, I reply. That doesn't entitle you to enter, the gatekeeper says, once more in a tone of great condescension, then he demands my pass. He suffers from mood swings that he himself finds to be unpleasant, thus do I explain his behavior to myself and strive to remain unmoved by it. No pass, no respect, one is only a person if one is recorded, if one is unrecorded, then one is a non-person, there is, however, the possibility, the guard relents, of paying a toll into the gate's money tin, into which one can only stick money through the opening, but not pull it back out. I stare at the money tin. According to the gatekeeper, if I can't afford the gate's toll—and, in fact, I have no more money on my person—there is the further possibility of repairing a piece of the wall with my own hands. The sooner I agree to this possibility, the shorter the work, the gravity and responsibility of which are not to be underestimated. I immediately agree, the gatekeeper opens the first gate, lets me step into the gateway, shuts the gate behind me, and leads me to the second gate like a blind man, his hand upon my shoulder. I immediately lose my bearings, the gateway takes on the aspect of a never-ending tunnel, or is it that the keeper is walking so slowly that our advance can only be a matter of millimeters. The abruptly intruding darkness causes me to see lightning, sparks rising and tumbling to the ground are script in the air, it is my eyes that write and the word that they write comes to pass. The passage through the gateway is the passage through a camera obscura. Is the memory of a photograph memory or is it a contouring new development of photography, setting in garish colors and, simultaneously, fading once more? I am the hole through which the photographs in my mother's album penetrate, the photographs she watches over like nothing else in her life. Some sort of strong light emanates from the photographs—they project images of terrifying size in the dark chamber of the gateway forth from me and through me and I know that this is my gaze. From wherever it is I look, from hence or three meters further off, I bear the images forward step by step without coming closer to them and the images are always distorted, deformed, garbled. My recognition is misrecognition, but the misrecognized is that which remains: a grimace. I feel sorry for my mother and grandparents, of whom nothing remains and nothing shall remain but a half-shelf full of photographs. Mother shall be perpetually born again, she shall always be one year old, she shall always be five years old, she shall always be twenty years old, she shall always marry, she shall always have children, she shall always be ill, she shall always die. I wish to hold my mother in my memory just as I saw her for the last time. Now, I understand this sentence . . .

differently. Everything about the photographs of Mother, in which she was still in the clutches of her parents' shadow and oneself wasn't yet born, seems interesting, upon one's own birth, in the transition from black and white to color, one becomes a part of the shadow in the photographs of mother, from which the shadow of the grandparents has withdrawn, no image in Grandmother's arms, especially no image with any grandparents, until one casts the shadow for a child oneself, a child who shall later recognize itself in the photographs and in the visage of a never-known grandmother, the curly blonde hair is passed down from generation to generation and if one asks the child of its earliest memory, it shall look quite deep into a chest called ANTIQUITY.

The eyes write "Eurenburg" and "Grubenreu"* and "Unbürger,"† but not with letters; on the way to the second gate, the lines of the writing do not form a word, but, rather, the contours of my mother's hometown as I know it, photographed from the Eurenburg, including her parents' stately home, which is now shining red at the beginning of Herrenstraße, the script, which once more finds words, inspires me to later claim that the house fell victim to urban redevelopment and was torn down, a holiday card from my mother to her parents will turn up, upon it she wrote the address of the house incorrectly: Herrenstraße 31, the card arrived anyways, my grandfather's practice was in the right side of the house, on the left were the residential quarters behind which there used to be a tannery, the toilet on the ground floor was added later on, the architects had forgotten it, to this circumstance the house owes its conservatory, a refuge retreat. Grandpa was a country doctor and had a pageboy by the name of Horst Dahm, who also accompanied him on his nocturnal visits to the sick, which often led him far across the land, he had his own chamber in the house, as did Grete, my grandparents' household help and cook, who was so integrated into

---

* Pit's Citizen.
† Uncitizen.

the family that the locals called her Grete Lungstraß, nobody knew her by her real last name—Pauls. Here, one can see them all together. The faces, all turned right toward the viewer, and the immaculate clothing, all black and white, compete to draw the most attention. Once one enters the residential building, one walks toward a freestanding wooden staircase that leads to the two upper floors, at the beginning of the banister is a hand-sized pentagonal Windlicht in the shape of a lantern that widens upward, the frame of black metal with the small pointed top holds five jars, I imagine how the candle was lit each night, perhaps, the jar didn't merely protect the stairs from dripping wax, but also strengthened the luminosity of the candle, Mother paced up and down these stairs without having a set destination in the house, it conveyed a sense of aristocracy to her aspect, which became a form of play, the old oak parquetry with its long planks did all it could to give my mother a feeling of grandeur that she would later be able to find nowhere else in the world. The house is so big that my mother once lost her mother in it and precisely the same thing came to pass with me and my mother in my parents' house. For children, houses are many times their size, an effect which increases even more in memory. There must be a gene for insatiable homesickness, which is nothing more than homesickness for one's parents' home without parents. Grandmother's Meissen porcelain was Mother's last refuge of loftiness, she hid it away from the light in a heavy chest of dark wood, in which, one day, I began to read the traces of the death-clock. Whatever the death-clock wrote, I could only read: "Mother shall die." For Grandmother, stairs, parquetry, and porcelain were the natural expression of her bourgeois class consciousness, which meant that, on the Baltic Sea, even when it was very hot, she didn't wear anything akin to a bathing costume, but ordered that her body be wrapped in a floor-length black robe, in which she pompously watched her daughters play. Photographs do wrong when exposed to life as a whole; however, if the photographed person poses, they help the injustice to be righted. Certainly, her sternness was a reflection of her clothes and her furniture and the fact that, as the spouse of a country doctor, she sensed herself being photographed everywhere, as with Mother, who loved her father more than anything, who clung to him like nobody else—this despite her yearning for freedom—and cared for him as he was wasting away with lung cancer, right up until his death, in such a way that the idea of one day dying of cancer herself nested away inside of her. She persists in believing this right up until she actually gets cancer, just as I have looked so persistently at the photographs of my grandparents and parents that, as memory, she shines through the hole that I am, into the gateway that I am, into the dark chamber through which I walk, and no more outside world is needed, as all images are now consummate. Life means passage, I say to the gatekeeper, we die, yet all we've ever thought about is our ancestors. Strange, the keeper doesn't lead me at all, I just stand there, he doesn't push me forward and I just stand there. Now, I want to find out if he can keep pace with me. I take a leap, the pressure of his hand on my shoulder is unchanged. I go backward. No change at all. I imagine the keeper's hand on my shoulder as an autonomous organ, a separate lifeform that has freed itself from human enslavement, it has escaped the human who disguised himself as a host animal, but has adopted his strategies by looking for an actual host animal in me and fobbing itself off as its little helper. I'm just standing there again. I am that which is unflappable between two photos, the dark interval, the gateway that's already a foretaste.

 I feel that certain things should come to a reconciliation in me, those things that, in the life of my parents and grandparents, couldn't get used to each other, the prophecies of a well-furnished bourgeois life, even after the war, and the illness-prospects of an early death. Death furnishes life. It doesn't appear as a piece of furniture, it can't "exalt" itself, it is already everything, but also nothing in particular. How does the child take the news that it must die? Is that something for later that can be confidently forgotten for now? Is later always later? Does the circumstance of having to die only force the child to develop the ambition of occupying itself with something once the suspicion that the legend of death might be correct becomes a certainty? Ambition is the consequence of death. Until then, however, until that "later" comes into its own, the photographs must be kept awake, while working on anything, while reading, in conversation, while falling asleep, until they fade into afterimages. And thus is this script here itself an afterimage and its trembling a fading. Can we not stand here forevermore, there is still so much to see, always the same, but different, I say to the gatekeeper. Only repetition, the child already feels this, can be relied upon, it is the only real thing, all else mere hustle and bustle. A single photograph would be enough to have one's fill of looking for one's whole life. I think in afterimages, I say to the gatekeeper, I have chosen to believe that he is listening to me. I do not cherish the hope to see more clearly within the repetition, now, this time; the repetition, itself a fading series that continues until perhaps only a cone can be made out, an indecisiveness between light and shadow, distracts me from myself and simultaneously gives me the certainty of still being here. I find tremendous pleasure in this, I say to the gatekeeper, and am tempted to turn toward him. A delirium grips me, the elation of sadness, the gratitude of farewell, it is quite a distinction to have been allowed to see these photographs, they make up for the rest of life. Now, if I had to stay here forevermore, oscillating between two shores without the certainty of ever reaching one, and I would always have my images, I would still be tormented by the question as to whether or not I was in a prison. I would, over time, try to convince myself that this question had no relevance, yet I would fervently wish to know whether the second gate shall ever be reached. The images would fall upon me and destroy me.

I am the midpoint of my own panopticon, totally out of control.

The gatekeeper can drag away the body, he only ever manages to grasp a shell, my world-projector is in his blind spot. Visibly, I am invisible. I am the true power, and this causes the gatekeeper to become so powerless that he takes me to where I already am in my own inwardness: into a dark chamber. These superelevations, I curse and stamp my foot, what am I doing to myself with them, it's probably a lot duller, visibly so, there's nothing behind it. Where is the one who persuaded us that the hidden is more significant than the visible? Wouldn't one have to turn the tables on the gaze, then that which shows the photographs would come into view—the eye? Is that not the true secret of photography and, if one saw it, wouldn't there be no secrets left at all? But who would see it? Photography is placeless, it is for nobody. Thus can I do with it and think of it whatever I wish to. That's the saddest thing of all, to have no more mother or father to tell one what one can and should do. What does the child perceive when it discovers the mother in a photograph and says "Mommy," but the mother still lives? Photography has died out, even if I see a person in a photograph, even if I myself see my mother in a photograph. She has absolutely nothing to do with the image and thus shall I one day conquer my Eurenburg.

Light penetrates through the gateway. On the right wall, a protracted shadow appears, in it I recognize my father's black page, then a crenelated rectangular tower, then a protandrous hermaphrodite, then, finally, the black page once more, all in quick succession. The black page pulsates, in a way one recognizes from larvae shortly before hatching, the membrane tears, and countless little creatures spill out over the skin. All together, they are called Father. A cannon is rolled out through the embrasure in the defense tower. The longer I dwell in the shadow-image, the more time somebody else gains to position the cannon against me. As for the hermaphrodite, initially a little male that swims about freely, later, at the destination, it changes into a female as it grows, it is a woodlouse with thrashing legs, some consider it to be a crab, about the size of a human's second phalanx, which bites at the base of the host animal's tongue with its barbs, always full of blood that it sucks out of the host animal's lingual artery until the tongue falls out of the host animal's mouth, then, in quite liberal fashion, it replaces this organ with itself, always eating what the host serves it, the mating of the woodlice also takes place in the mouth, the female collects the eggs in a pouch beneath her abdomen, once the time has come, the hatchlings leave the mouth so as to attack others, my tongue is an other, I would like to see it once more in the light. You don't know what you're saying, Mother would often say, starting at 1:56:35, my father's head bulges left of center from the top third of the black page, his eyes like shining lights, his snow-white hair swept back by the wind, he looks down at me and I don't know whether he wants to threaten me or protect me, he immediately whispers something to me, within six seconds, his entire upper body peels forth from the darkness, at 1:56:48, he points at the gate for nine seconds with the index finger of his right hand, which moves upward—as if pulled by a winch until it is stuck at a right angle, as if it were dead and part of a mechanical ballet—toward the gate. The outline of the second keeper, who is standing with his legs apart in the archway, becomes clearly visible. I have the feeling that I'm walking backward. The keeper holds a bull pizzle in his right hand, lazily slapping it against his left. I can recognize by his eyes, which are shining like lamps, that this is Father and I am glad to finally see him again, he has assured me of safe passage in a letter, which I've only just discovered on the back of the map, I began unfolding it a few moments ago in order to take advantage of the increasing light to orient myself once more and to commit to memory the most important connecting roads in case I should lose the map. The circumstance of having found it on Zellen Warhol's map causes me, however, to come to the conclusion that Father commissioned the map, thus must he have already held it in his hands. But how did it make its way back into

Zellen Warhol's hands? Did he have to fix something? Father's script with its swings, pointed towers, and shockwaves is difficult to decipher. The letter is presumed to read as follows:

"I, Schattenfroh, mayor of the city by the grace of God and ever-Increaser of the city, King of Orwellsradien,* Dienerau,† Devotfaseln,‡ and Zur-Ich-Enge,§ etc., each and every spiritual and secular prince, duke, margrave, count, baron, noble, superior, and chamberlain; the estate officials: knights, those who might become knights, captains, town magistrates, provincial governors, governors, toll keepers, tax collectors, and all other officials; to the parishes of cities, frowns, villages, and localities and their authorities, as well as all the other subjects and stalwarts of ours and of the Holy Empire, before whose eyes comes this script, royal grace and all the best. – Venerable, illustrious, noble and faithful beloved! – We wholeheartedly commend to you all and every one of yours one who is perhaps not honorable, but is still John Haussen or also Johann Heuss, bachelor of sacred theology and thwarter or also sign painter of the arts, bearer of this letter, journeying from two thousand and eighteen, which lies in the vicinity of Brandenburg, to sixteen thirty-four, which is at the edge of the Eifel. We have received him into our and the Eifel realm's protection and defense. We desire, when he comes to you, that you receive him kindly, treat him favorably, and afford him willing help as regards the speed and safety of his journey, both by land and by water. You are in duty bound to aid him to pass, to

---

* Orwell's Radii.
† Servant's Meadow.
‡ Babbling Devoutly.
§ At The Ego Strait.

dwell, and to linger, with all his possessions through all city gates, passageways, over bridges, through lands, dominions, offices, judicial districts, cities, towns, villages, localities, settlements, and all other places, then to return without paying any sort of tax, path toll, toll, tribute, and freeing him from every other burden of payment whatsoever and every kind of impediment; to permit him and his companions freely to go, stop, tarry, and return, and if need be to provide him willingly and out of duty a secure and safe conduct, to the honor and respect of our Eifel Schwarzbildchen, or "little blackpicture." – Given at Neuder in the year of the Lord 1634 on May 15. By order of the Lord of the Frightbearing Society, witnessed and marked by all of his Faithful

Sämtlicher von Pein:[¶]

Piment von Lachseier,[**]

Eli von Pistenmacher,[††]

Preiste von Leichnam,[‡‡]

Preise von Mitlachen,[§§]

Nachliest von Empire,[¶¶]

Leimt von Einsprache,[***]

Amtlicher von Speien,[†††]

Spärlich von Meinte,[‡‡‡]

Pleite von Einmarsch,[§§§]

[¶] Completo von Pain.
[**] Myrtlepepper von Salmonroe.
[††] Eli von Skislopemaker.
[‡‡] Prized von Corpse.
[§§] Prizes von Joiningthelaughter.
[¶¶] Consultin' von Empire.
[***] Glues von Objection.
[†††] Official von Vomit.
[‡‡‡] Skimpy von Meant.
[§§§] Bankruptcy von Invasion.

> Schema von Reptilien,*
> Rache von Mitspielen,†
> Schleim von Parteien,‡
> Niemals von Erpichte,§ Canon of Neuder."

I rejoice at my beautiful father tongue and once more fold up the map, which the keeper, who is thought to be absent, but is now leading me through the gateway, takes from my hand before I can stick it into my back pants pocket and I spot him hiding it in the folds of his head covering without conferring any expression upon his face other than that emptied-out blank one. A protest seems improper to me and thus do I play off the situation by once more turning to the wall, upon which the tongue appears as a naked devil, without master, alone in the world. Father, covered over by the black page, but still recognizable enough, throws his hands up in despair, which I initially ascribe to the loss of the city map, but then I read the black page as a shroud beneath which Father is to be buried alive, the cannon is fired, I await its impact, and thus does this beautiful silent film slowly develop, the viewer's voice alone doesn't turn it into a talkie, into a meaningful narrative, set into the gateway of animate photography and such snapshots that, outside of the viewer, could never be found anywhere, it is a narrative I would not wish to hide from. And should the keeper there in the archway make no use of his pizzle, I shall ask him not to trespass the threshold of the gate at the end of the way too soon. The sight of the keeper-father, however, makes me so bashful that I avert my gaze from him, take two strides closer to the wall, and lay my left cheek against it. Looking back at the shadow, I see completely different images, frozen waves off

---

* Schema von Reptiles.
† Revenge von Playingwith.
‡ Slime von Parties.
§ Never von Agog.

the coast of Hiddensee, the Kloster Lighthouse, my grandfather's house in Warscheid, the bed of roses in the garden of my parents' home, and, before I can completely surrender to these images, one peeling off from the next, the second keeper asks: "Where is the brand?" He has it upon his forehead and nose, the other replies. The second keeper examines my face and praises his colleague's work. I hadn't noticed it, this one says. He ought not believe that the gate is only for him, says the other. I can't feel any change in my face, but I can't escape the feeling of a weight pulling my head down. What is it? I ask. A hammer, says the first keeper. What's it doing there? I ask. It lets everyone know that you are condemned to the wall, the keeper says. I want to see it, I demand, then the second keeper pulls out his knife and holds it before my eyes, in such a way that I am almost blinded.

That is no hammer, that is a tau, I say. It wasn't him who burned it onto me, it was another. We were alone in the gateway, the first keeper says. The one who did it was present in his absence, I say. If it's no hammer, then it's a letter, the second keeper says. It's a cross, I say. All the better, the second keeper says, to help you manage the work that lies ahead. This annoys the first guard, he'd like to be a chosen one, he scoffs, but he's so helpless, ineffectual. Eventually, he'll say that he's borne the sign ever since his birth, the other laughs. The two eventually agree on the version that the Holy Spirit prodded it onto my face.

Papers? one asks, no papers, says the other. The first does he have a name, the second no he doesn't. Money? the first, wall service, the second. While passing through the second gate, I turn the conversation to my father's safe-conduct letter, the two keepers act as if they don't hear me. The second keeper seems to have already forgotten when his face lights up upon hearing "safe-conduct letter," he pulls the map out of a fold in his head covering and hands it over to the other guard, who unfolds it swiftly and, after having briefly skimmed it, as if he'd long known what this was about, causes it to vanish into a leather shoulder bag. My father's letter is to be found on its backside, I say. Nobody here knows your father, is the reply. The keepers look at me searchingly, the one whispers something in the other's ear: "Now, he's here for good." "He's not that weak." "He'll have plenty to do." "How will he get that done on his own." "High treason." There's meant to be a famous Holtzmarckt in town, I inquire by way of statement, called Alter Diech. The keepers seem to take the question as mere statement. If one continues straight down the way that leads through the gate, if one continues on into the city, one comes to the famous Holtzmarckt, known in common parlance as Alter Diech, isn't that right? I ask. Our way, the second keeper then says, leads directly to the wall. As soon as we have passed through the passage of the second gate, we turn to the left and, after a few steps, stand before a wall with pointed arches, some five meters high, made of Bunter and red sandstone, its filling of rubble and brick have partially broken loose and must be replaced. Also the pointed arcades, which serve as the substructure of the battlement, are made of brick, which displays damage that cannot be attributed to war. The stones do not appear to be very stable, presumably they absorb too much water due to their large pores, then burst after a frosty winter. Perhaps, it would be too intricate and costly to also make the fortification-reinforcements out of Bunter or red sandstone. In passing from the gatekeeper's house to the tower, I note that the outer wall is equipped with buttresses, however, these struts consist only of clinker brick. What does one hope to accomplish by this?

Have the statics of the wall been calculated incorrectly and is this how one hopes to attain stability?

For the upper part of the wall, which you can no longer reach while standing, a scaffolding shall be erected for you, the first gatekeeper says. The stones certainly cannot be transported up without construction cranes. You wanted to go to the city, the second keeper says, now you are in the city, the impression the wall makes of being in need of renovation in many places should not lead you to the conclusion that the city is impoverished or no longer capable of defending itself. The opposite is the case, which contributed not insignificantly to the resolution by the city leaders to let the citizens themselves pay for the maintenance of their protection, which also promotes solidarity amongst them, as well as identification with the city. Here lives and works a community that shares a common destiny, the second keeper adds. It was a clever maneuver on the part of the city officials, the first keeper says, to link the building-authority decrees to the penal legislation, in such a way that the wall inscribes itself upon the body of the delinquent as punishment, with all the years that they spend here, their bodies themselves become part of the wall. A jape, obviously, the second guard can't hide a grin. I ask whether there are no longer any prison sentences. Oh, but there are, the second keeper says, the penal policy here follows an economic principle. Once all positions on the wall are filled, the newly convicted delinquent is put in prison until another position becomes available. In this way, the city leaders prevent manpower from going unused. A semi-circular bastion tower made of brick serves as the prison, as it is particularly secure, the inner side of its wall made of Bunter sandstone and the vaulted dome of the upper and lower floors prevent any attempt to break out. The roof of the tower is covered over in slate, which is why the populace has dubbed it "Graue Mütz," or "Gray Cap." Its wall is so thick that no human sound has ever been able to escape from it. Which is why the official documents regarding the occupants of the tower are so important, they ensure that nobody is forgotten. As the fortifications are the priority, it has not always been possible, looking back to past years, to ensure this, and thus is there the persistent opinion in the city that prisoners on the wall often die of hunger and thirst. But no bones have ever been found. Very special prisoners have been kept here in the city gate, it is said that there's special gadgetry here, in comparison to which the treatment others receive on the main squares of the cities is a veritable blessing. This prison, which no living person has yet departed from, is allegedly reserved for spies, who have recently acquired the habit of disguising themselves with safe-conduct letters. Then, he says, there's the prison, located under the staircase of the town hall. An inscription was chiseled into the upper window frame, which serves as a warning to all: Beware and go not forth. If you're caught, you're put into the madhouse. So, what is punished with arrest, I ask. Roaming about at night without a lantern, for example, the keeper says, whoever would prefer not to be seen has something to hide, only citizens of the city possess lanterns, an outsider has none, unless he has pilfered it. On its ground floor, the town hall also has a beautiful pillory, upon which the delinquent is presented in a stage-like manner. No one shall ever forget this punishment, not the punished individual, but also not the citizens who have seen him, and thus are all legal processes from the court proceedings to the execution of the sentence performed in public, which has led to the establishment of a singular professional class, the grimace-pullers, who spread their mouths wide with their fingers, or the scoffers, who have adapted their invective to the court's pauses in speaking, or the bare-bums, who do not draw their weapons, but display their own bare rear ends. As court is a daily occurrence, it is said, these people earn quite a bit, they are paid by the citizens for their own entertainment and, for many, they represent enough of a deterrent.

We tread rather close to the wall. Here and here and here, the first keeper says, before adding: just for starters. The second keeper orders me not to budge under threat of severe punishment, tools shall be brought over so that I can begin my work forthwith. When I remark that I have no training as a bricklayer, that I am no quarryman, no stonemason, and no mortar mixer, no slater and no carpenter, he replies that practice makes perfect here, in addition to which it's not just the prisoners, but, in principle, every citizen who is made to acquire abilities for the upkeep of the city wall, thus can each citizen be called upon to work on the wall at any time, should this ever become necessary. Though this might be unlikely, one never knows and thus are so-called wall exercises held on the fourth Saturday of each month, which ensure that, should the number of prisoners be lacking, there will be enough citizens at hand to carry out the work. I ask what the scope of my work is to be, as I intend to undertake its completion beyond any reproach, after all, it is my goal to get into the city and the completion of such an indemnification in order to get past the city wall without possessing a valid, official, sealed, and stamped identity paper is just the ticket for me and spurs me on all the more. The entire wall, the gatekeeper answers, 23 flying buttresses alone, which is to say 25 pillars until the next gate. It's impossible to manage that alone, I say. He says that it's impossible to manage that alone, the first gatekeeper communicates to the second. You've a whole life to get it done, the second gatekeeper assures me, then demands that I take some twenty steps backward with him so that I don't think I'll be carrying out this work alone, after all, the city wall must be permanently renewed, not least in view of new insights in architecture, and thus must every free member of the labor force be made use of, which is to say anyone who, through certain circumstances, such as, most especially, crimes, is no longer free for himself, but has become free for the wall. In fact, a few men can be seen on the left and right, they are tweaking the masonry in various different ways, one is standing on a ladder and attempting to insert a larger stone into a hole, which he succeeds in doing after several attempts, another has discovered a severe spot of damage at the base of the wall and is lying flat on the ground, a third is hopping as he strives to fill a crack with smaller stones, though one cannot determine whether the constant hopping or the striving for a particular height tires him out more, a fourth has been brought into such a rage while adjusting the filler stones that he furiously smashes them instead of knocking them in to fit precisely, which has, in turn, given him a new job that shall occupy him for the next few days. When the keeper notices that I've been observing this last man for longer than the others, he notes that building materials destroyed by any citizen or outsider must be replaced by them, an approach that, in the long run, eats up family wealth, since he who destroys materials cannot then earn a living. He says that he has seen women who have visited their irresponsible husbands at work and beat them to the point of their being unable to work, in such a way that, from then on out, women's visits were forbidden. In the summer, the keeper adds, the way home is too far for many men, the labor doesn't end until shortly after sunset, and thus do they prefer to sleep beneath the flying buttresses, which offers them sufficient shelter, even in light rain. Over the years, and also as a result of the increasing crampedness of urban living conditions, itself the cause of future reflection regarding a possible birth-control system, the space under the flying buttresses came to be used for smaller tool houses, which were easy to dismantle and assemble, when the demand then arose that the city wall should be partially torn down—it's simply getting too *tight* in the city—the space beneath the flying buttresses was freed up for the construction of narrow residential buildings. As I diligently jot down the keeper's explanations, I ask myself why he is telling all this to *me*, to him, I am nothing more than a constituent member of workforce to be used up, not some sort of respected commercial traveler who is visiting the city to its profit.

The tool is delivered and stored at the wall. It is too time-consuming to register people by name and according to their particular identifying features, the keeper says, unfortunately, the municipal treasurer's suggestion to give everyone a name that belongs only to him, i.e. a name that would only be assigned once, garnered no support, this, in combination with an unmistakable portrait in the identity documents, would have solved the problem of unequivocal identification once and for all, there simply had to be enough names in stock and, if necessary, some had to be invented, which was particularly necessary given the growing population, of course, the city wall and the expansion of the population don't naturally go hand in hand, the keeper says, a bonus should therefore be paid to childless families or families with one child, in short, everyone should have a number branded onto their foreheads, I am number 117, which has been vacant since yesterday, my predecessor having been shot by a cannon while trying to scale the wall and leave the city without having achieved anything, which had the additional benefit of demonstrating the excellent state of the city's cannon construction, deterring all those who had thoughts of fleeing, while simultaneously checking the stability of the wall, revealing that it could not withstand larger projectiles, which had the consequence that all of the flying buttresses had to be reinforced once more. I take a water level and plumb bob from the wicker basket of tools and ponder how they might be put to use when the second gatekeeper approaches me and shows me the map of the city, which he describes as blasphemy and sabotage incarnate. If this map were to be disseminated, the city would be doomed, such a map would invite one to reconnoiter the city without even having seen it, everyone could form their own picture thereof, its possessions would emerge most distinctly from the paper, like a new creation, and even those who were intimate with the city would think that they could get to know it better with the map, some would even consider it to be theirs. I put the water level and the plumb bob back into the basket. The conclusion of the text seems familiar to me, I say, but I can't quite grasp what's to be so feared from the map. Storming from all sides, espionage without effort, the possessor of the map could thrust the city into fear and terror without undertaking anything at all, the keeper says. From this, it can be concluded that the map was drawn quite precisely, I say. In the Bible, Exodus 20: 4-6, it reads: "Thou shalt not make unto thee any graven image, or any likeness of any thing that is in heaven above, or that is in the earth beneath, or that is in the water under the earth," and that also goes for the city, says the keeper. A map of the city would be more important to the people than the city itself, which, by way of the map, would become outlawed, the people would begin to collect city maps, for them, a city map would replace a visit to the city, as they could then wander through the city with the help of a magnifying glass and that would be without paying any toll or entry duty. A map of the city from a bird's eye view, it's as if man could fly. A map of a city, the keeper says, is therefore against nature—full stop!

Unlawful attempt to penetrate into the city, possession of a city map, the other keeper tallies up for me. The city shall determine whether the work on the wall, which I am now to finally undertake, is the appropriate punishment. Until then, it shall keep its eye on me everywhere, the city is round, and wherever it is I find myself, I stand in its middle. Nobody shall let me into their house, the nights are warm, I am to sleep beneath the flying buttresses. And thus do the two gatekeepers go away, close the gate, and leave me to the city. Barely are the keepers out of sight when curious people gather round, grab hold of me, hand me a jug of water and fruit. The gifts are poisoned, I think, but accept them so as to avoid discussion, then lay them alongside my tools. I want to avoid the impression that I have to work on the city wall as a punishment and so begin a conversation about how the repairs could be carried out more efficiently. I explain the long conversation with the keepers by way of the notion that we had to exchange technical information, after all, extensive changes in the organization of manpower were in process. The people fold their arms and wait. I don't have much time to consider which of the tools it would be the most sensible to start with, so I take a hammer and hit one of the bricks with its tip. The brick shatters into a thousand pieces. Don't you see, I say, the bricks are of poor quality. This turns the people against me, they indignantly deny the inferior quality, after all, they were the ones who baked the bricks. This could be a good moment to stir up trouble, I think, it would be easy to incite the people by making them think that their manpower was being misspent, after all, what have I really lost, I can always go back through the city map and tapestry into my father's office. But now I no longer have the city map.

The top municipal finance official, who is now pretty much only in charge of the construction (it is thus that he is Master Builder of the City Wall) has reduced available funds, the city must save, says one of the bystanders, but if there were any defects, it would be the fault of the citizens alone. It's no longer to do with the security of the city, a third party butts in, the citizen must be pacified and the city authorities must not be disturbed in the exercise of their unrestricted power, I ought to go visit the Hauptmarckt in front of the town hall, also known as Kornmarckt, there, the gallows are always in operation and the hangman has no time to service them. Beyond that, trestle and pillory both justify their acquisition each day anew. The city wall is eating us out of house and home, says a portly fellow with a long mane, his sudden loquacity is due to the circumstance of social assimilation. This is by far the largest item of all municipal expenditures, somebody says, as the wall must be strengthened more and more with the invention and development of so-called powder weapons so that the living space inside the city wall with its constantly decreasing diameter is reduced by defense measures alone, beyond the fact of the increased birth rates. Consequently, if cities were to grow upward, this would make the houses towering over the mural crown into a wonderful target for precisely these powder weapons, not even mentioning wall-breaking artillery, as this is certainly too expensive to acquire and is used rarely, if at all. But what is able to drive into greater fear and terror than a distant danger? The city wall should have been be reinforced with flying buttresses along its entire length, someone says, each healthy citizen would have been called upon to do entrenchment work according to their age, the hauling and heaving of Bunter sandstone ashlars becomes a form of socage, on the other hand, it is a downright blessing, a reward, to serve on guard duty at the risk of life and limb, as became mandatory here on October 23, 1609 due to new guard regulations. Furthermore, the flying buttresses reach such a height that one can stand beneath them in the heavy rain without getting even remotely wet. Around 150 years ago, he says, the wall was further reinforced with twelve protruding round bastion towers made of brick, in such a way that the sections of the wall in between could be better defended. There are people who do nothing else all day but stand in front of just such an arch and wait for a projectile to hit, which would then prove the wall's strength or lack thereof, someone claims. The constant chatter about the new security measures to be taken has turned the people's heads, they hardly dared to leave the house anymore and, if they did leave the house, they would hurriedly run to the baker or butcher, then back once again, even more hastily. There are more than a few who evinced Schadenfreude at the notion that the churches, as the tallest buildings in the city and able to be seen from afar, towered over the wall in such a way that they represented a target with magical force of attraction for projectiles able to cover ever growing distances.

    Someone says that the destruction of the city wall is not even the most appropriate means of conquering a city, it would instead have to be starved out, the access and supply routes would have to be interrupted, hunger and thirst would be the worst of enemies, and whoever could turn them into his ally would have all the trump cards on his side.

In one fell swoop, all of the residents have disappeared, the sun is burning violently, I have no hat to protect myself with. If one desired to spend the night beneath the flying buttresses, one would have had to have built the stones lying underneath them into the wall. The man-high heap seems to represent the necessary daily workload. Handling the equipment to be found in the basket presents me with challenges that are almost impossible to solve, the arches obscure the view of those working in the immediate vicinity, the racket they produce suggesting that they have settled into their work. I have the sensation of being observed, as if the city were a great panopticon with a warden in a tower precisely at its middle, he can see everything from there without himself being able to be seen, as if I found myself in a cell that could be seen from everywhere right up until the side of the wall and would be held accountable for even the slightest violation of the prison rules. For how long would I manage to give the impression of knowing how to work with the tools? How big can a joint gap be, how do I recognize if a spot is damaged and in need of repair? I lift up a stone and let it fall. The stone provides me with the desired fragments. Repairing damaged Bunter sandstone with quarry stones, brick for example, would mean a drop in the wall's quality, but the brick might well be broken and inserted more easily. Should ease of labor thus take precedence over quality? How soon shall I flout questions of aesthetics? When shall there be an end to the questions, when shall labor alone decide what needs to be done?

Then a man of about fifty-five emerges from the wall and comes toward me.

The so-called citizens are like that, he says, they're not satisfied with anything, they always know better, and if they themselves had to think about it and make decisions, they would break out in a sweat, they would suffer from flatulence and the runs, their hearts would pound away, they'd be tormented by shortness of breath, and they'd rather drop dead on the spot than be in the scrape of being held accountable themselves for even a single second. Perhaps, he says, you might be more interested in factual information about the wall than these far-fetched denigrations of city-planning policy, always so cautious to balance the interest of the king, the territorial lords, and the city leaders.

In terms of his habitus and way of speaking, the man who introduces himself as Erich Amjage is intent on distinctly setting himself apart from the others. He says that he is the city's master builder—most especially a master builder of defense fortifications—the conception of the wall goes back to him, he is said to be the only one in the country who has read *The Ten Books on Architecture, De archicectura libri decem*, by the Roman engineer and military technician Marcus Vitruvius Pollio, a standard text that was of crucial importance for building praxis in the eventeenth century, only none of his colleagues took on the bother of translating the work, which has been handed down in more than fifty manuscripts, some of them illuminated, he is in possession of one of those exemplars and has been translating it from Latin for some time now in order to make it available as a printed book in German, studying it from A to Z, the translator of such a compendium has a very great responsibility for years to come, one that he all too often misuses so as to appear in a favorable light, for example, by deliberately sneaking in mistakes that make it impossible for the competition in the field of defense-fortification building to match his incomparable results in terms of security technology, he had to decide in which field he wanted to excel, but instead elected to excel in both, the art of building defensive fortifications as well as the art of translation, which made the mistakes in the latter indispensable, for nobody would ever see through them, he narrates without pausing for breath, and I am afraid that, as soon as he finishes his speech, he shall instantly do away with me, after all, I could betray him now that he's cleared his conscience in my presence. Marcus Vitruvius Pollio must have exhausted himself completely with this mammoth labor, must have died from overwork, perishing at the age of fifty-seven was not common practice, even in the era before Christ. I would rather hear a hundred more disparagements than continue to be exposed to this factual information, but the man shows no mercy, after an interim question on my part as to when the building of the wall began, and his prompt answer—in the year 1244, which must mean that Erich Amjage is no less than 465 years old—he informs me that the first printing of the architectural mammoth was done in Rome in the year 1486. In the fifth chapter of the first book, Marcus Vitruvius Pollio (even the complete enumeration of his name gets on my nerves) comprehensively explains the "structure of the walls and towers," which is of such decisive significance for urban planning that, if one makes sizable errors, the city shall immediately be retaken by the enemy once it's been erected and, in a worst-case scenario, disappear from the face of the earth. One takes what is to hand, this is the utterly pragmatic counsel of the Roman architect, who even deals with astronomy and clockmaking in the ninth book, the reader learns, for example, what the deal is with the sundial or the water clock and that the Romans took into account the different lengths of the days in summer and in winter by making the hours longer in summer and, correspondingly, shorter in winter. Now, *that* actually would interest me, however, Erich Amjage prefers to enumerate all common, possible, and imaginable natural, as well as artificial types of stone that can be found on site, ashlar, basalt, bookstone, fired or unfired "Ziegeln," he says in German, a word that could mean either "bricks" or "very thick books," and it's the bookstone that makes me most curious, perhaps a city wall built from all the books in the world would be particularly strong and consist of harder matter than stone.

The Bunter and red sandstone, Amjage says, are grouted with mortar made from sand, lime, and water; in order to fit them into the masonry, they were partially rehewn and reworked. The wall is of uneven height, he continues, it follows the course of the contour lines and makes use of the course of the "Mühlenteich," the millpond, which I can confirm by way of the map—at least the part of it that I've surveyed so far. The pond forms the moat's second channel after a first channel in front of the wall, which is followed by an earthen wall, seemingly insurmountable in terms of height. The landscape is hilly, so exact measurements were necessary, also with regard to the statics of the wall. A foundation, which would have had to have been laid separately, was largely unnecessary due to the load-bearing, almost impenetrable layer of gravel, silt, and clay on the ground, instead, almost everywhere, the base of the wall was placed directly onto the natural ground. In order to avoid frost damage, freshly worked sections of the wall were covered over in straw and manure. How terribly interesting, I say, which I immediately regret, as, before I can turn the conversation to completely different matters, the city's master-builder, inspired by the deceitfully uttered "interesting," recounts that the stones, whose origin he wants to discuss separately, were sorted according to their size before being stored, because, for the construction of the wall, certain sizes had to be used, then, if possible, almost identical ones a second time around, as the construction of the wall was the construction of two parallel walls, for reasons of economy and strength, an outer wall was built on the field side and an inner wall on the city side, and that was a particular refinement of this wall, of which only he himself could boast, after all, nobody but him knew of this daring feat, but also he who, for whatever reason, always had to climb the wall or he who had to walk to and fro upon the battlements between the bastion towers, it would not be noticed as a result of the mural crown covering this measure, the interstitial space between the two walls was filled with stones, building rubble, and mortar, and larger stones were built into the flying buttresses to further strengthen the wall. The arches and struts integrated into the wall itself also served to improve stability, which might well give the impression that they were improvements merely added after the fact. Another secret, then. History offers numerous examples of the slaughter of secret-bearers, who did not have to elicit the secret they bore from anybody, as it was entrusted to them voluntarily. Now, moving back down from the top and to the layered construction of the wall, says the city's master builder, whom I immediately interrupt when he begins to speak of the ingenious invention of the treadwheel crane, which made the erection of the wall possible in the first place, interjecting with the question of what he actually wants from me, these communications are really going nowhere, I say, ach, you flatterer, he replies, how often must I tell you that you are my highly esteemed colleague from another era, from you, the future shall learn a great deal, this is the first time you're saying such a thing, I'd like to riposte, however, I recognize the advantage that this mix-up or incorrect supposition might have for me and, with an expression of inquisitive affection, will henceforth let him speak of whatever he pleases. The stones are placed in layers on the mortar applied with a trowel. Special lifting equipment, scaffolding and ladders are constructed, the carpenters are just as important as the masons, broad hatchets, wooden hammers, wedges, web saws and crosscut saws, the flying buttresses are built around the centering attached to the wall, after its completion, the stopgaps are removed, then inserted back into the wall elsewhere. It was only later that the city gates were strengthened into bastions with gateways in front of them. So, how were the natural stones transported. They come from above-ground quarries in the environs of the city, namely Edenging, Engeding, and Versachleb—they come from or were plowed out as erratic boulders during the plowing of the fields. How heavy a cubic meter of sandstone is: 2,500 to 3,000 kilograms. A work stone weighs fifty to one hundred kilograms. It is more likely that they were transported on carts drawn by oxen than transported down waterways. The stones come from the area around the city as dutch bricks.

Master Builder Erich Amjage disappears through the wall with the words that we'll be seeing each other again in the town hall and I ought to examine the stones once more to see if they don't start talking. I want to match his pace, as I am almost inspired by the notion of being able to leave the city in this way—already 330 years before my birth, it doesn't want to give me up, as it sees a traitor in me, but, a good meter away from the stones, I land on the ground once more and walk back to the place where I was standing earlier with Erich Amjage and, while I wait for holy elation to seize me for a second time, I can't rid myself of the impression of recognizing the master builder in the stones through which I want to pass, as if he had immortalized himself in them. His visage consists of nothing but letters that recite themselves, yet if one only comes before them at a certain distance—depending on the person opposite, they might also refrain from speaking—they regroup in the air and allow the master builder to speak above the city wall as I have only just heard. A stone can thus see, speak, and recognize. Speech is its essential element and not minerals whose structure one can read. In speaking, he says, I might always make mistakes and say something else, if I had etched my epitaph in stone, even in marble, I would have made no mistake or been able to correct it in a second version, in this way, however, I can intervene in what is said about me, and I rejoice at the fact that it's always something else being said. But I told you what was to be said about this wall that I have built. The wall is my grave and I am my own inscription. There is no more terrifying notion than that of being buried without an inscription, the researcher of epitaphs Gerhakt Ulks,[*] also known as Kargste Kuhl,[†] is entirely right, for I have not and will not allow myself to be forgotten, and thus has it now been written in your book, dear colleague in self-assurance on the heels of the 666.

---

[*] Gerhakt Practicaljokes.
[†] Mosthollow Pit.

The prisoners of the wall seem to have been left to their own devices, their cluelessness is nothing but welcomed by the city leaders, the endless course of the wall is joined by the odyssey of understanding, success knows no repetition and, consequently, no experience, thinking goes from stone to stone and the question as to how I did that does not arise. This is a consolation for the prisoners, their labor is a labor of self-deleting repetition, renewing itself each time, an impossibility. I cannot even distinguish which breach in the wall is damage and which is due to the position of the stones. If I were to distance myself from the wall, for how long would it be until I was picked up and brought back? To climb the wall and escape the city with a single leap seems impossible due to its height and the moats behind the wall, the wall is no mountain that one can climb just like that, it might perhaps be possible to walk on top of it with iron pins, but a via ferrata over the wall is thinkable only at night, when the dogs are sleeping in the bastion towers. I'm already thinking of winter, the tools lie beneath a mantle of snow and cannot be touched with bare hands, the wall leaves one speechless, in the wind we creak. The observer would now like to see results. I drive a stone so deep into the wall that it can no longer be removed, I seek to knock off the protruding bit with my hammer, but the hammer slips and hits a stone lying deeper in the wall, one that serves as reinforcement. The break has no consequences, just as the whole wall consists of only breaches, which support each other in their ossification. The next blow goes to my knee, I moan my pain inwardly, but remain entirely upright, my back turned to my observer. Faces appear upon the wall, they've entered into a heated dispute about something. I can read from their lips that it's to do with me. It is speculated that I bought the map for a large sum from Zellen Warhol, whose name does not appear to be known to the disputers and, after scouting out the city, it is my intention to sell it to the Hessians for a great multiple of that sum. I ought to be subjected to a torturous interrogation so that I might reveal the whereabouts of Zellen Warhol and my customers, as well as the map's future buyer or confess to being Zellen Warhol myself. It is agreed upon to return the map to me the next day and to release me under the pretext of a wrong having been done to me, then they will observe where I go, whom I meet, and so on. I am not entirely certain, but I believe that I recognize Mateo in one of the figures, then I make a nice discovery: I turn my head to the left and that which is coming to pass rewinds as far as I hold my head to the left, whereas, if I turn it to the right, I can put that which is coming to pass back into its moment, having interrupted it by way of my head-motions. After bringing about the repetition of the dispute in this way several times, I am now certain that all of this has to do with Mateo. The fact that my father is said to be unknown here is because Mateo has taken his place and may indeed have done away with Father. Unfortunately, it is not possible for me to cast an ear or eye to the future by keeping my head in the right position. If I tilt my head up without taking my eyes off of the stones, I become the witness of a monologue in a courtroom, the sharp deceleration of which makes lip-reading far easier, but demands a great deal of patience from the observer. For me, there is no question that this is a courtroom with arguments and counter-arguments. The city with its wall is a singular prison, Mateo says. I ask myself how the ugliness of the world is possible, he says. The city wall, he says, is the desperate attempt to vanquish beauty as a fleeting form and appearance and to enable persistence in those same forms, a city wall as a temporary means of preservation and healing, and that, he says, makes it vulnerable, the external enemy is often indistinguishable from the internal, the enemy, incited to jealousy, would like to tear down beauty, thus does he make a run against the wall and thus are there always two forces at work, the will to beauty and the will to ugliness, he who creates wants eternity, which, however, as it no longer makes any difference, is meaningless and soon comes to appear as ugly in its ossification, thus must the eternally creating also be the eternally destroying—that which brings about new meaning. The city wall, he adds, unites the two forces, it is never finished, it is always only on the way to the beautiful when standing still and, upon this way, all damage, all that which is destroyed, all that which is intolerable must be disposed of as the ugly. Neither one of the two sides ever prevails and this balance, which is due to the potency of the ugly, is beautiful. But beauty is an effect of pain and thus, does he say, are those workers on the wall who suffer this pain prisoners of beauty. Their body becomes brittle by absorbing the breaches in the wall, thus making it beautiful once more. Pity would be entirely misplaced here, it would, indeed, be an injustice compared to the commitment of the workers, whose heightened sensitivities bring about the beautiful and can therefore count on heightened interest on our part, pity merely diminishing this living achievement. The city wall was born from the pain of the workers, it is therefore art and must be preserved no matter what. Toward this end, I would like to introduce the concept of monument protection, Mateo says. If the brittleness of the wall merges with the brittleness of the workers' bodies, it is likewise to be thought that they too—inasmuch as they would sooner or later be indistinguishable from the wall—should be placed under monument protection, which would make the irreparably ugly concept of imprisonment superfluous and, moreover, render it essentially inapplicable. In conclusion, he would here like to propose for discussion that the workers ought be made sculptors of themselves, for their own encouragement and to the delight of the townsfolk, toward this goal, they would not only be allowed, but forced to enter the city wall at their full size as the defensibility-increasing Atlases of the flying buttresses, not as protruding sculptures this time, but, integrated into the masonry, causing the skin of the wall to bulge out slightly, this being the layering of the stones weighing itself down, it could never be round, but would always be a breach on top of a breach, the most beautiful imaginable symbol for the hardships of life, he says, they leave nothing behind but gaps and cracks, and, in the end, the gaps within ourselves to be closed by somebody else. With time, the stone deputy itself becomes obsolete and thus does the process begin anew with the succeeding worker. In this way would there be a gradual transition from the soulful embodiment of the work on the city wall to its animating stoniness. Of course, the sculptures would have to meet strict requirements, for example, in terms of the dimensions of their protrusions, their height and width, strict rules would also have to be imposed on so-called artistic freedom for reasons of stability, just as it is not at all acceptable for someone in the face of their own increasing disappearance to seize an opportunity with both hands and ignore the representational duties that each form of art has vis-à-vis the state, every form of art, he says, is a hidden theology, for which state and city are mere means, but that's another matter entirely. If his proposal were to find general approval amongst the city leaders and if it could be implemented, the city-wall-punishment-as-renovation system with its stone figures protecting the population would create a counterpart to the council chamber of the city hall, on whose walls statuettes representing the order of the city and paintings depicting history conceived of as a work of God's salvation as the city's own history, with sibyls and saints as city patrons, are to be seen. With this last word, the image freezes.

    Due to the strong deceleration of speech movements, the dictation of his words lasted until the evening, meanwhile, the sun has set, I turn my gaze from the wall and make my way over to the town hall. I don't wish to become my own stone pillar here. Renovations are not being carried out on all of the flying buttresses, though I still find it to be more secure not to follow the path along the city wall, instead, I hide behind a row of trees that lines the nearby green space. According to the map, the entire city is parceled out into mostly rectangular, sometimes also pentagonal, trapezoidal, or ovular green spaces due to the path system, their development in terms of houses varies in density, a few plots are built so densely that all the trees, if they were there in the first place, must have been done away with, as, for example, in the city center. Up until the very densely built-up plots, upon which houses stand wall to wall, all plots are themselves enclosed by a small wall. In that respect, penetrating into this walled zone constitutes an effraction, only those who are in lawful possession of a key that opens one of the little gates that break up the wall at regular intervals are authorized to enter. The plot upon which I find myself is built up with scattered houses at its edges, the trees are dense and give me enough shelter to venture out into the approximate middle of the square, from whence I discover three vacant lots that shall allow me to get to the next green area. Perhaps this method is too cautious, but my clothes would make me immediately recognizable as an outsider, who, when asked about his person, could identify with nothing but his mouth. Many of the houses are sumptuous, I would love to take a look at their insides, their high gables and stepped gables testify to an architectural sense of detail. How much space do these people have in their houses and dwellings? If one pays rent for one's residence, is there more than one party per house? Are the servants, the employees, and the apprentices not also quartered in the houses? Does one cook over an open fire? How are they heated? Some gables are so narrow that it is impossible to imagine anyone standing upright on the floor underneath the roof. Judging by the small windows, the floor beneath the roof is likely used for storage. It doesn't take much, a candle plunges to the ground, clothes catch fire over the stove, and an entire settlement burns down. It may in fact be an advantage if the houses are not set narrowly together.

 People are likely not supposed to walk across the green space, there seems to be no life playing out behind the houses, in some spots, it reeks of outhouses. Hidden in the grass, I find a small wooden doll whose right arm is entirely black, the hand is missing, the stump of the arm can be rubbed a bit between the fingers, its body is damp, it has water stored up in its insides. I lean the doll against the wall of a house and imagine the child feeling the doll's burning as if with its own body. The houses all look to be unscathed, perhaps the child held the doll over fire so as to clarify what fire is, then, screaming, dropped the burning doll, it was extinguished in a tub of water by Father or Mother, then taken out into the fresh air to dry. Perhaps the child rejected the maimed doll and it is now lying in the grass for the birds to have their fun with it. I briefly consider taking the doll with me, its green-and-gold suit has a handsome aspect to it, it has an even visage with faithful-looking eyes, the hair on its head is genuine, I have the curious feeling that it might bring me luck, but I leave it leaning against the wall of the house so as not to be pilloried as a thief or lose my own right hand, but barely have I taken three steps when I turn back around and take it with me, I want to dry its body and give it a new arm and a new hand, it should be possible to replace its putrid fabric. It is now sitting in the breast pocket of my shirt, to which it gives up some portion of its moisture. If one takes a closer look, one can see some hints suggesting that the green space behind the houses is used as a common garden. Here lies a chair with its legs pointed upward, perhaps the people were expecting rain and flipped it over. It's more like a stool with a backrest, the seat and backrest are made of boards, however, the difference between the seat boards and the back-support boards could not be starker: The boards of the seat are unadorned, a flat square, a depression runs all round the edge, double corners were created by the sawing-off of the initial corners, whereas the backrest is adorned openwork, in its middle, one can reach into the maw of a grimace gaping wide, somewhere between man and ape, the face is spread flat, nose, lips, eyes, ears, and bushy eyebrows with the appearance of two palm trees or feather dusters are raised in relief and, in some measure, very much like the ears and lips, curved into a c-shape. Besides the small ears that belong directly to the face, the ornamental decorations made up of scrollwork, volutes, and rocailles that frame the face centered to the left and right at the edge of the backrest—their closed shells, nuts, or jesters' shackles swirling around the two lower shell-shaped ornaments at the level of the gaping gullet continually increasing toward the middle—can be interpreted as ears, but, also, as elephant heads, woodpeckers, scrotums, worms, or all of these simultaneously. Enclosed by these ensembles of ornamentation, two holes to the left and right of the grimace's lower lip are to be found, reminiscent of oversized perforations in earlobes, as are caused by certain earrings that stretch flesh and skin far apart. Rocailles also adorn the backrest at all four corners where they form the flowing, curly head of hair belonging to two faces with goatees in side profile, the large hook noses and closed eyes of which afford them a guard-like severity. The chair's mascaron cannot decide whether it wishes to look fright bearing or grotesquely cheerful. What is to be thought of the spinal-column segments placed in the middle, above and below the grimace? Are they an overt memento mori, do they invite one to a seated dance of death, or do they simply anticipate the seated position by challenging the person taking a seat to sit up straight?

The chair seems to be a trap, for the longer one looks at its backrest, the more one discovers. Before it can haunt me in sleep in its own absence, I spontaneously take it with me, but do not dare to come into direct contact with it, instead placing the doll between me and the upper lips of the backrest, the doll hanging through the opening with its face pointed downward, it can be securely fastened with a cord for transport. If I am asked, I shall reply that I found it on open terrain, where it had been carelessly tossed away, this, after all, being the much greater sin, it must first be ascertained whether the Fratzenstuhl—the grimace-chair—isn't a piece of furniture that shall perhaps be very valuable in 330 years and not merely as a function of its material worth, which is inextricably tied up with aspects of the history of art and culture, indeed, I might reply that the chair is clearly more than a mere object of use, but also with regard to the questions as to whether the chair might be a dwelling place of the deceased and whether there might be an inherent power within it, which, for better or for worse, is passed on to its owner or whoever it is who sits upon it, questions that I would answer with "yes," at least the last one I can unequivocally confirm, which is why I would counsel everyone not to stick their hand through the grimace's gaping maw, it would only be with great difficulty that I would be able to once more pull it free. As I can only get to the vacant lot closest to the green space leading to the market via a large vegetable patch, in which my shoes would leave behind deep treads, I decide to walk along the west side of a house between the vegetable patch and a lawn so as to reach the little wall. Calm.

There is a light burning in one of the rooms on the house's ground floor. It is a simultaneously warm and miraculous light, both putting on display and self-evident within objects; illuminating and, at the same time, making form, color, and itself manifest. It is a reversible light, a twilight that illuminates things and, simultaneously, doesn't just add itself to the things, doesn't just let them shine, instead it is a transmission-light of the things in themselves that captures me, the viewer, and thus catches me off guard in my examination of them. I sit down on the Fratzenstuhl outside the cone of light. The light is the paw of things, its source remains hidden from me at first and I'd prefer to take the things themselves as source, they become my confidantes. However, they might also betray me and thus do I wish to avoid all that which might make them uneasy. A young woman is standing at the open box window on the left, its outer wing thrown open with inviting wideness, her head is slightly tilted, her face is flushed. She is observing something with great concentration, standing entirely still for minutes at a time, only her eyes seem to be seeking something or perpetually wanting to find it. If she were to raise her gaze, she would see me immediately. The Fratzenstuhl flexes slightly when I move forward or backward. I would like for it not to be glued, screwed, or held together with nails, its individual parts should merely be attached and mortised. I stand up and take a look, but can recognize nothing in the darkness, when I feel around for it, the chair falls out of my hands and to the ground. The grimace lies upside-down in the light and, as if the light were liberating it from ice, begins to move its lips. The candles flicker. Not far from the chair, the doll lies in the grass, it slipped out of its lacing when it fell. The grass is a bit damp from the rain in the evening and, as I have taken the doll into my custody and promised to take good care of it, I do not want it to get wet. The woman in the window doesn't stir in the slightest. Is she not like Olimpia? This one here doesn't even say, "Oh-oh!" It should be possible to expose her secret very quickly with a telescope. I'm at the point of crawling across the ground like a soldier so as to get hold of the doll and pull the chair out of the light when the woman slaps a book across her forehead several times, as if she wished to gravely injure herself with it. Was it this book that she was staring at so spellbound this whole time? My situation is a delicate one, I've ventured far in the direction of the house and hesitate to grab hold of the doll, on the other hand, I don't wish to retreat without it. The woman holds the book before her face as if she couldn't bear her own reflection in the window glass. This allows one to gaze upon its title: The Bible. There is no doubt that something is afflicting this woman and, at the same time, she doesn't wish to lose her composure. The Bible seems to offer her little comfort for the present moment. These wives withheld from public view, I think, then grab the doll and am beneath her window in four steps, this seems safer to me right now than running across the lawn in the direction of the wall. There's hardly any light in the room now, the woman must have extinguished most of the candles. I'm on the verge of turning away, but secretly cherish the hope that she won't close the inner wing, the outer wing seems to remain open in the summer. A door slams shut. I hesitate for a moment, then seek to pull myself up on the outside ledge, which, however, is too narrow and sloping, for which reason I cannot overcome the distance to the window without some aid, it's measured out in such a way that nobody can get into the room from the outside by way of a standing leap and the occupant of the room would certainly think twice about leaving through the window. The Fratzenstuhl brings me level with the ledge and I manage to pull myself up and sit down in the window niche. The left inner wing is only ajar, a red curtain obscures one's gaze into the room. With a twist of my body, legs first, I slide the window open and slip through the niche into the room. Something falls to the ground. I am alone. How small the room is. The window now has the previous opening angle as seen from the outside. To the right of the window, a large carpet lies on a bed that the woman uses as a table, the carpet is too long for the bed, the excess is gathered up at its head, easily recognized by the bulge the pillow causes, as if it were not allowed to make contact with the ground, its folds have overturned a white china bowl in which apples and peaches are kept, the bowl, the blue glaze of which is so beguiling that it inevitably causes me to look around for a bag in which to transport it, is shallow enough that two apples and a peach have slipped down onto the carpet. The peach has been halved with a knife, its red stone lies there, obscenely exposed, its flesh still fresh. This peach too is mere apple, it excites me to imagine that the young woman has eaten its other half and thus do I stick the one half into my mouth, chew it up, and keep the remaining half in my pants pocket. What might the woman's name be, how old might she be? All reading women are named Maria and are of indeterminate age. Under the carpet, the scent of which reminds me of Mother's perfume cabinet, in which there is no longer any odor in itself that can be recognized, but, taken together, the remnants are unmistakable, a pristine bed linen comes to light, the 999 is embroidered on both pillow and bedcover, the 999 that is both truth and justice, instead of washing instructions, there is a label sewn into the pillow with the letters ShKBTh ZRGh on it, the laundry smells of apples, I see a big tree of russet apples in the garden of my parents' house, the apples are so heavy that the crown of the tree threatens to break apart; worms all over the ground waiting for falling apples. I must spend the night standing before the tree and catching apples, only thus can the worm be overcome. If I stand behind the headboard of the bed, the 999 is upside-down, roses with many thorns pierce the fabric of the laundry, a sea breaks and spatters over all of the laundry, the thorns loop round a head, the brow bleeds, a doll licks the blood from the brow, a worm eats its way through the fabric, it absorbs the roses, the sea, the brow, the doll, my vision goes black, I distance myself from the headboard and position myself once more by the side of the bed.

The window is leaded glass and divided into four by five rectangular segments, the upper row is made of rhombuses and mirrored isosceles trapezoids with the smaller side as the mirror axis, making it so that the rectangles in the row have a roof. The young woman's visage can still be seen in the glass segments on the lower right, out of focus and distorted, more surface than profile, as if the glass had been broken, then put back together in makeshift fashion. The face in the glass is disfigured, yet it is also angel-like—from another era. Depending on the window's opening angle, the proportions of the face shift. I never tire of looking at its varying appearances. Here, for example, I believe I recognize myself, three years old, blonde curls, dressed up in bows, as if Mother wanted to show everyone, behold, this is a girl, then, further on, I see Mother's mother, of whom I have only a single memory: I once sat in her lap when she came to visit us at home, which is all that I can recall of her, over and over again, her nose is my nose, her affectation, reported by many, is my style, now, I look for my mother in the glass, no matter how I turn the window, I can't find her. I let go of the window and it goes back to its old position.

On the floor lies that which I knocked out of the window niche when I penetrated into the room and have almost forgotten: the Bible. It has a leather limp binding, its title is blind-stamped. Beneath the leather binding appears a hard wooden binding with an entirely different title: *Schattenfroh*. A letter is found tucked into the book, it slipped out slightly when the book fell from the window. The letter is still damp with tears. So, it wasn't the Bible that the woman was reading and also not this book, rather, she was reading through the letter over and over again, which makes me so jealous that I want to tear it to shreds. Curiosity, however, outweighs jealousy, which makes jealousy lash out with all the more violence in those cases when its fury does not receive prompt satisfaction. Thus do I have the sudden wish to do away with the young woman. Without knowing its contents myself, I imagine a talking doll reading the letter to her several times in a row while she is slowly being killed. The doll is brought into such a rage by the repeated reading that it wants to do away with her. At this point, I destroy the doll, which I already regret as I do the deed, suicide seems to be the only way out. Ascertained at this point, the woman is dead, the doll torn apart, only the letter and the suicide remain, to kill oneself because of a letter, of which I did not know until just now, all it did was arouse jealousy, the object of which has been eliminated, strikes me as so outlandish that my thoughts have turned against the letter, which I, pinned against a small beam, pull out of the window behind me from a cord and onto the grass, where I find a second, longer beam, at the upper end of which I bind it to the crossbeam with the cord, then nail the letter's top and bottom, left and right to it, and ram it into the earth with a stone. It ought to slowly weather away, the sun ought to bleach it, the rain wash it away, the wind shred it, dogs ought to piss on it, mice perpetually bite little shreds from it, I shall not do it the favor of reading it. For, if it were to contain script, I would hasten my way through it—from one end to the other. But the letter is blank paper and ought to take its secret into its weathering. I want nothing to do with this hymen. I do not wish to see what ought to remain hidden. The paper ought to flee from the light, just as I do. Thus am I thoroughly averse to seeing it, but persistently penetrating if I am only to imagine it. If I were to be a witness, however, a bloodstained sheet, they would point to me here and never tire of asking prying questions regarding my appearance and contents. But if I know nothing, then I know only the blank paper. The room from which the woman vanished *is* the letter. The window is open, the curtain is red, paradise is bitten into, the carpet is sinful, the room is empty. Father dictated Jesus, the Holy Spirit caused him to become script, the virgin parchment upon which the dictate is written came through the open window, where it fell onto fertile ground. To beget means to write and script takes place only by dictation. That is the modern way, the air is the emissary, the Holy Spirit no longer had to personally write the Jesus-dictation into the young woman's lap, after all, he can't be everywhere at once. The woman took stoic note of it, however, in order for the dictation to take effect, she had to look it over for a long time, which ended with my appearance, unapprehended by her. Surely, the Holy Spirit must not have written the annunciation on paper with invisible ink? That would truly be a mirifica descriptio. The young woman is therefore pregnant and this is the precise cause of my jealousy. The destruction of the letter comes too late, it turns against another dictation in secret. Father's dictations have begotten me and I shall remain alive for only as long as Father dictates. However I look at it, it amounts to suicide. I cannot rend the veil, which her absence lays over everything. But how can I find out whether the empty letter was received by the young woman or if she was perhaps not the one who wrote it, in such a way that she might heroically ascend to the heavens in her loneliness—don't you see that my script-mate is the Holy Spirit? And it is this question whose non-answer makes me inconsolable beyond the satisfaction of the inscription dissolving the letter by way of sun, wind, and water. But why? The affair is only a piquant one if the woman didn't write it herself and only for as long as the woman remains absent. Thus do I know that it would be wrong to seek her out in the same way that one seeks out a certain passage in a book. If I were to find the woman, I would write her. The woman's child should be called Mahershalalhashbaz and I shan't write that upon a great slate with a human pencil, there are no witnesses, I say it here and now and thus shall the woman read it in the book that is called *Schattenfroh*. She is to remain a blank slate for me.

I have the feeling that I am entitled to some form of compensation. In the corner, behind the open window, there is a chair, which, until now, has struck me as the least interesting of furniture pieces, until I notice that a grimace likewise adorns its backrest, at the sight of which the thought comes to me that the woman could once more enter the room, however, her deformed face in the glass forces me to come to the conclusion that she is locked up in there and can only return to the room if the glass is broken, giving it another once-over, it occurs to me that the face is not at all in the glass, but behind it, if I seek to touch it, it vanishes, but reappears as soon as I withdraw my hand, as if I were shoving an invisible curtain off to the side. The ugliness of the visage is a consolation. If one were to look at it for longer, all movement would cease at its edges, there is a flowing around it that emanates from something, dents appear at the point where a floating, albeit transparent object glides past, perhaps it is only the face that can no longer gather itself and is thus condemned to perpetually changing its form. It must be the letter, she must have refused to read it aloud so that the script would have no effect. That must be it. The poor woman. If she had read the letter intended only for her aloud and nobody else could have read it, the script would have appeared in her voice and impregnated her. Thus is she not pregnant in the slightest. She is behind the glass and only comes back if someone smashes the glass.

What if the series were to now continue and somebody were watching me from the outside? I move around quite freely, as if that were completely and utterly out of the question. However, I am concerned by the question of whether the woman or the grimace can see me. Ugliness can make one worthy of desire, it can stimulate the most violent of imaginings, which is why I no longer want to look at the grimace and the woman, between the two of which my gaze shifts back and forth, but to hold onto their beauty in my memory. And, yet, I must look again and again, it fascinates me how they fade into one another, the grimace appears in the woman's visage, it disfigures the woman's visage by breaking up her symmetrical features. This game of deception causes me to teeter, as if both of them respectively wanted me for themselves and as if a resolution were imminent. I take the red curtain from the rod, tie one end of it through the grimace's maw, open the window, and, together with the curtain, let it run across the floor along the wall of the house where it can change places with the other chair. Then I close the window. The sparse candlelight in the room is sufficient to perceive the things in the room and to orient myself as soundlessly as possible. The absence of the red curtain urgently re-poses the question of my being observed. I put the fruit bowl onto the floor, pull the carpet from the bed, then hang it over the rod instead of the curtain, which ought to instantaneously darken the room to the outside world. The woman's face is in the corner, where the chair was standing, without a projection surface, I need only open the window and put it back into its old position, then it will already be there once more. I think that I can still see the chair in the corner, but know it to be outside, before the house. It now exists triply, in the corner, before the house, and in my house. While the question as to which of the three chairs is more real and true occupies me and I follow the side path of this question—whether it is not nonsensical or wrongly posed—my eyes fixate on the two panels in the middle of the carpet that look like tunnel entrances or open book pages, as if they were tired of gazing upon the thing itself, the upper rounding of this middle with its column-framing and flower wreath suggesting meaningful or playful Poesiealbum-like content in the twice-five lines and their Hebrew characters.

Not only is it outlandish that the script can be made out equally well whether I am only a few centimeters away from the carpet or find myself two meters from it, the script adapts to the distance, a woman's voice also sounds out when I find myself at the height of the previously open window, at a distance of some eighty centimeters from the carpet. The voice always makes me think of the woman reading the letter before the open window, I don't associate her with any other woman, not even the image of my mother comes to mind. Another voice says to me: "It's probably another one of those illusions—watch out." This could be my voice, however, I'm not sure, it could also be one of those illusions. The woman's voice says: "I am the mistress, your goddess. Thou shalt have no other goddesses before me. Thou shalt not make unto thee any graven image. Thou shalt not take the name of the LORD thy Goddess in vain. Remember the sabbath day, to keep it holy. Honour thy father and thy mother. Thou shalt not kill. Thou shalt not commit adultery. Thou shalt not steal. Thou shalt not bear false witness against thy neighbour. Thou shalt not covet thy neighbour's wife. Thou shalt not covet thy neighbour's house." I wasn't able to abide by all of that and I wonder from whence the woman could have known this.

The carpet is faded, as if it had been lying in the sun. I can't decide whether it's beautiful or ugly, it's that dusty pink to ochre undertone of Grandmother and Grandfather's carpet, which was deferentially adopted by their children without it constituting an actual demand. These carpets wander from room to room, no room is gladdened, soon, there shall be heavy cupboards atop them, though the grandparents prohibited precisely this when they gave them away with heavy heart, commenting that, should the carpet not be treated with care, they would reserve the right to, at the end of the day, sell it, and *with care* meant that nothing ought be placed atop it and it should only be entered into if there were no other choice, it had a distinct representative function, in short, not even air and light were worthy of touching it. Thus, over time, did the carpet become the presence of the grandparents, which could be felt from all sides, even years after their death. It serves as an excuse for the parents to avoid visiting the grave, one day, during a cheerful evening abruptly turned melancholy by alcohol, which was what first gave wing to the senses, they even contemplate taking the rug to the grave, so as, Father adds, to relieve the children, us, of our inherited guilt. In contrast to the grandparents' carpet, this one's pattern and color stand out from the basic tone, as these cannot be seen through after just a few moments, which, in the case of the grandparents' carpet, led to the children's opinion that Grandma and Grandpa were of rather simple disposition if that which was to be seen on the carpet displayed the content of their heads: rectangles and circles. The opinion of the children is generally what the parents fear most, as it is so completely undisguised, this is what the parents say; the upbringing of the children is thus geared toward grinding down the opinion of the children to such an extent that the foundation of parental opinion becomes the only foundation visible beneath it. On the woman's carpet, one sees an armchair with a red seat cushion and a red backrest, trees and flowers can be seen, as well as a nine-armed candlestick, script is everywhere, flames lick, clouds gather together, a labeled blue ball or balloon, something to be discovered on each square centimeter. The carpet is not beautiful, but it is beautiful in that I do not understand it. Below the tablets or gates with the ten lines is a flower-wreathed grave framed by glyphs and scrolls, at first glance, more than a dozen bodies seem to lie in this grave, if one looks more closely, the bodies turn out to be fir trees and the grave is no grave, but a nursery, the little firs are us. The square with gates or tunnels forming its center is framed by two continuous longitudinal stripes and two horizontal stripes that pass both above and below. The horizontal stripes have the same length as the broad sides of the central rectangle. Inserted into the longitudinal stripes are five ovular or circular medallions, upon which ever-varying figures are to be seen. In the middle of the upper horizontal stripe, which is in the same dusty pink as the vertical stripes, stand two birds, presumably doves, their heads held high beneath a processional umbrella decorated with tassels hanging from its lower edge. On the lower horizontal stripe, something resembling a crown stands out against a black or dark-brown background, it could also be a royal bed with a canopy, and on the bedspread lie three ovular wreaths of flowers on ovular plates ranging in color from turquoise to powder blue. The flowers could also be food, all food fills the plate to the brim, the right and left foods are a shade of yellow, the middle dish kept orange, one dish could have emerged from another, Father Mother Child, the objects to be seen on the carpet are all so solid that one thinks oneself to be able to pluck them out of the fabric, one wishes to sniff the flowers, to eat the food, on the left longitudinal stripe, not quite in the middle of the tunnels or book pages, is an octagonal fence made of two-times-eight wooden crossbars running parallel to one another and interrupted by a total of eight posts, or paddock fences as they are known, instead of horses, there is a great fire to be found in the front area of the paddock, it frightens me that, after a few seconds of observing the five plots in the middle, I see the fire blazing, and, immediately, it becomes palpably warmer in the room, but I can't take my eyes off of this blazing fire, which, if the wind were to cause it to lap at the wooden slats, would devour not only itself, but also the fence. As soon as I have come to this realization, the fire licks through the knotted flames, becomes a circle that is visibly growing in size and threatens to engulf the entire carpet, there is no water anywhere in the room, I tear the covers from the bed and wish to smother the fire, then it burns no longer, but it begins to burn once more when I turn my gaze to the paddock. This circumstance is as repugnant as it is sensual, only the removal of the carpet allows for the cycle to be broken. To know that the situation would be resolved if one were to simply avert one's eyes, only wanting to let things get as far as control over events can be maintained, causes one to misjudge possible dangers, stimulus demands increase, the boundaries are shifting, and a situation that was precisely delimited is already spreading to sections not intended for this game. I feel the urge to see the carpet blaze forth of its own accord, simultaneously,

I know that the fire, which my eyes ignite again and again, exposes me to the gazes of the residents as soon as it leaves the woven area of the paddock and infringes upon the surrounding regions, the fireworks are not to be repeated terribly often, so the neighborhood gathers before the window, I once more wish to climb the cliff of flames, on which each further step means the abyss, the fire licks up, burns down a whole forest above the paddock, reaches out to the throne in the plot of land above the forest, though it is meant to protect the king, its fire-retardant red upholstery immediately bursts into flames, in no time at all, from the turned square baluster columns of the legs to the pine crowning of the backrest, the armchair is charred over, it must be a forgery, for the throne stands in a house built from flames of fire, and in every respect it so excels in splendor and magnificence and extent that I cannot describe to you its splendor and its extent, and its floor is of fire, and above it is lightning and the path of the stars, and its ceiling also is flaming fire, but the throne therein burns not, its appearance is as crystal, and the wheels thereof as the shining sun, and from underneath the throne come streams of flaming fire so that I cannot look thereon and the king that sits upon it resists the forces as his throne does, it is the king of kings, the throne of thrones, this throne must be a forgery, the carpet-wind now drives the flames to the open book or the two tablets, the woman's voice sounds out once more, reciting the following text: "I the mistress, thy goddess. No other goddesses before me. Not make unto thee any graven image. Not take the name of the LORD thy Goddess in vain Remember the sabbath day, to keep it holy. Honour Father and Mother. Not kill. Not commit adultery. Not steal. Not bear false witness. Not covet thy neighbour's wife. Not covet thy neighbour's house." As if she were only a voice, disembodied, she has the same intonation as before, the fire does not impress her, a machine with no senses. The wicker armchair quaintly shaped, the forest, the doves below the screen shall be part dust, part nothingness and void, then none shall worship more your woven splendor, the book alone for all time can endure because of stone Nature it is made.

When the fire takes away the carpet's right longitudinal stripe with a terrific speed that no eye can follow, like tearing off the page of a calendar that no one ought to set eyes on, for it obscures the day that is no longer new and gropes its way to heavenly canopy and bed, I know that the tipping point has come to force me to take my eyes off of the badly mangled carpet, simultaneously, I feel a certain paralysis that resists this impulse, great tiredness overcomes me, the woman's voice says, "The bed is made for you," another voice says, "You shall never wake up again," the woman's voice says, "Lay down in bed, the most beautiful night awaits you, you shall become another person, the other voice says, "Death is already lying in bed, this is your wedding night," then I lay down on the made carpet-bed and eat from the food on the plates. The bed is warm, as if someone had been lying in it just before me, a slight note of a perfume is perceptible, the bedding is untouched. I stretch my legs out and slide to the foot of the bed, there is nowhere to hold onto, my legs grow ever longer, my hands wander across the covers as if they didn't belong to the rest of my body, and, indeed, they are separated from my ever-growing arms, but keep a constant distance of some ten centimeters from them, they occasionally disappear beneath the bed, then they reappear once more at the foot of the bed, they leap down, I hear a light splashing, almost instantly, they come back onto land, damp and cold, shivering, they crawl underneath the covers and are running across them less than twenty seconds later. At the moment, they are squabbling, they wrestle with one another, try out the shoulder throw, the leg scissors, they have trouble staying on their feet, then one hand feels a protuberance on the blanket, the second immediately joins, both navigating curves and straightaways, stretching out above the raised field, then hunching back down, they mark their discovery by raising their leg and circling the spot, then they sit back down and secretly observe each other until the game, which they can't get enough of, starts all over again. I ask my hands what they've discovered, they can't agree on who ought to tell me and thus do they remain in their position as if they didn't belong to me. Then I call on the arm-stumps for aid, that they might feel out the discovery, then report back to me. The right stump feels capable of inferring an existing form from its rudimentary sensations, but the hands will not allow it to enter the vicinity. The eyes obey me, they can always be relied upon. The hands see through the effort to spy out their discovery and cover the spot so full of mystery whose inaccessibility makes me covet it all the more. Stillness reigns for a while, then the one hand begins to make obscene gestures, the other doesn't want to be inferior to it and outdoes the first until they fall upon each other in a frenzy of obscene expenditure, pause briefly, separate once more and consult with one another, it has likely become clear to them that they themselves are not enough for themselves, without one another, they're fighting a lost battle. My member stirs beneath the blanket, this must not have gone unnoticed by the hands, as the spot they have kept hidden is not far from the elevation before which my eyes now cast down their eyes. I am prepared for their attack and turn off to the side at the moment the hands slip beneath the covers from left and right and begin to tug at my member, though I thought my sideways feint away from them had brought it into safety, the upper body is turned away, though the torso is now separated from hips and legs. A prying inquisitiveness drives me forth to look underneath the covers, to see what the hands are driving at there, but, as soon as I lift the covers, they disappear underneath the bed. Incidentally, during their wrestling match, I noticed that they were exchanging messages by way of fingering, as is to be observed with ants or bees, I shall require years to research their alphabet. I ask myself how they put up with me for so long, they must have gotten what they needed out of me, then simply fallen off. And? Are they heroes now? Must one fête them as rebels? What if they were to go for my gullet? I shouldn't worry too much, they surely won't be able to squeeze without the aid of the arms. Something else caught my eye during their wrestling match, whenever they were frozen in a balance of forces, they assumed a position of prayer, each seeming to try to outdo the other until they once more realized that neither would be able to manage anything without the other. What if they were to slaughter me as an infidel? I won't be able to shut my eyes, they're simply waiting for some carelessness on my end, they're also capable of lighting fires. My eyes have seen something; whereas the hands used to be there to serve them, to swarm forth and to confirm suspicion by way of grasping or to give the all-clear, my eyes now lack this measuring instrument, but they wouldn't be *my* eyes if they were to give in, they know how to compensate for this lack with an elasticity that allows them to get closer to things, yes, they replace the hands by way of themselves just as the sphere of a spider's eyeballs shoots a white thread into the air that unerringly finds its way to things, however far away they are, and, having been hit by the eyes, the things sometimes try to get away from them and their threads by making a powerful jolt (just as the buffalo knows how to make a stronger impression than the lion hunting in a pack), the anchor-line of the eyes has no end, the ship shall never reach the salvific shore. What have my eyes seen? For they have seen *something*, otherwise, they wouldn't be tugging at their leash like dogs, and one knows not whether the dog follows the leash or the leash follows the dog. The desperation of the eyes, for it is undoubtedly desperation that fills them so entirely, stems from the circumstance that they cannot, as they are accustomed to, communicate that which they have seen on the bedcover. At least the contact to the eyes isn't entirely interrupted, they are devoted to me and suffer more than I do, for them, I am really quite far away, they have no insight into me, I, on the other hand, feel them to be near to me and know how they exert themselves. Feeling alone is not yet any kind of seeing, of course, even if, in the long run, one gets the idea that this feeling might replace seeing and even become true seeing. I want to record this here, in my brain-script, which is unquestionably going to be read one day, and, on that day, the sun shall not have to rise again. It's returned once more, that diving-down into mossy, greenclouded, algae-like deep-sea worlds that began beneath the child's bedsheet, the head pressed down deep into the foot-end of the mattress, under the blanket, and the sun long since set, no more noise penetrated into this world, here do I dwell, I said to myself, in this dense green streak-world that opened up when the eyes were subjected to a slight pressure, too light for the emergence of pain, but hard enough to start off the inward journey and leave no doubt that this was a different world from the one that was to be seen with open eyes. On that note, I fell asleep. And when I woke up the next morning, the nocturnal green world had disappeared, however, the knowledge of being at home there accompanied the day.

There are ten letters that appear in the green thicket I dive through, ShKBTh ZRGh, they stand as tower plants in the water and resist the current. These plants turn over every second and yet your heavenly Father feedeth them. I can recognize no meaning in them, one cannot pronounce them, if I come too close to them, they escape, I shall examine whether they stand for something else, hide a text, or carry the solution within themselves. I am not comfortable with the fact that they are upside-down and thus do I seek to concentrate on them so hard that they cannot withstand my thoughts and vanish, precisely *that* is my sole thought—that they might go away. One night, when my parents couldn't immediately find me in my bed, my mother said so to my father, my father angrily tore off the covers, I lay there upside-down by the foot-end: "He's back to being en route in the uterus," this didn't exactly endear me to my father, for days, he eyed me like a child he hadn't been comfortable with from the start and now the signs were beginning to be corroborated: I was a child of cuckoldry after all. The letter-plants do not disappear. I drift away from them, but they float menacingly back to me just a little while later. Now, I think I see a number in the letters—999—and my gaze switches constantly back and forth between letters and numbers. They really do lull you into a sense of security for such a long time before revealing their true form, as they can in no way be said to pass silently through me, rather, they tie me up and seek to strangle me. When they don't manage that, they bind themselves to my feet and pull me through a flitting green—into brighter realms. I can see the sky. I like the journey, I can breathe in the open air, nothing frightens me. Once I lie down in the woman's bed, tied to its frame by the letter-plants, my journey has come to an end. May it remain so, I say to myself, then fall asleep. The door of the room opens. I am pulled out of the bed by the letter-plants, I'm dragged through the room and into the hallway, from there through the door and gate onto the way. I am pulled along by both grimace-chairs, which are on the best of terms. They speak a language that is unknown to me and they are greeted by all persons who come toward them as follows:

> La kozo kuras, ed on ne povas intervenar.
> Singla interveno nur esus konfirmo, ke la kozo kuras.
> La principala questiono esas, quale on povus perceptar,
>   ke ula kozo ne kuras.
> Entote existas nur ca singla kozo, qua kuras
> Omnatempe esas tempo por questionar, quanta tempon
>   me ankore havas.
> De questiono a questiono on povas irge reflektar pri to.
> Pri quo tu irge reflektas, omna pensi ja pensesis.

Nobody takes offense at me, I am not seen. Both of the chairs are as fast as horses, they alternate between a trot and a gallop. The path that they are taking is familiar to me from the city map, they let me lie down for a few minutes on the market square, I want to rise up, so they pull my legs out from under me with the plant-shackles, I give up after three attempts. Dust lies evenly across the square, as if the city had hired a garrison of sweepers to disperse it hourly. Some sixty meters from me are certain strange pieces of equipment, the open display of which is certainly no end in and of itself. Out of the town hall, at least I think it's the town hall, if I'm remembering the map correctly, comes a small figure, which, as I'm lying so flat on the ground that I'm already afraid the street sweepers shall sweep me aside like rubble, seems threatening despite its minuteness, it is the doll that I rescued from the garden and seems to have been animated by the grimace-chair, at first it irritates me that I was so sentimental vis-à-vis the doll, thinking about the child who'd lost it for whatever reason, but then my hopes are pinned precisely on this doll, indeed, I believe it shall recognize me and be grateful to me for having saved it. "The grimaces created me, then they destroyed me, then, finally, they outbid each other to determine who would be allowed to breathe life into me, after all, I served as the chair's wooden genitals," the doll says. How is it possible that you are speaking, I ask it, is it not God alone who can confer language? "Very true," the doll says. All of this has been written, I ought to read my book. From then on, the doll is silent. I read my book: "Once upon a time there was a neighbor who sawed, carved, and transformed a dead apple tree into a chair. The chair was to have a face, one that would be friendly and smiling. No matter what the old man did, the face's friendly features instantly turned evil. Finally, an ugly face came to adorn the back of the chair, so the neighbor sawed a greater hole into its middle—in the shape of an apple. The missing apple mimicked the lips and ensured that the grimace's mouth would always be open so that its expression would be one more of astonishment than of malice. The man wanted to whittle a doll from the apple tree, one whose beauty would comfort him daily for the travails he'd wasted on evil. He succeeded in this. However, the man found he liked the chair no longer and thus was he willing to give it up for the cost of the wood. This caused the chair to become woeful, and, with the air passing through its mouth so violently that its legs turned green at night, at which point it felt an easiness and plasticity that suddenly allowed it to take one step after another, it resolved to leave the man the following night and offer up its services elsewhere—it feared soon being cast into the fire. However, with this first stride toward freedom, the grimace-chair, in a state of self-forgetfulness, tripped over the wooden doll that the man had placed in a metal frame before the chair's feet when he'd been cleaning up. The sound summoned its maker who, without being noticed by the chair, watched how it picked up the doll in the moonlit room, then let it slide through its mouth and caught it from behind. Instead of being upset with the chair for disguising its abilities, he opted to keep the chair and make use of its talents, which he excitedly announced with the words, "I saw ye doin' that, I saw ye doin' that!" But the chair, which, though it could indeed hear, could not itself speak, trusted the man no longer and remained glued to the spot for the next period of time without budging a single millimeter. This drove the man to sheer desperation, he kicked the chair, demanded it to move, "I really did see ye," he said perpetually, "I really did see ye," but there was nothing to be done, and thus did he give it together with the doll to an elderly couple in the neighborhood for little money, they initially didn't see the grimace as remotely evil, but, rather, as very charming, and wanted to please their grandchild with the doll. But how did grimace and doll, the latter of which emerged from the former like Eve from Adam's rib, get into the garden in which I found them and why is the doll suddenly so deformed, as I found it? The initial joy of the elderly couple, in whose sitting room the chair now stood, while the doll was allowed to sit enthroned above the chair upon a chest of drawers, quickly evaporated when they determined that they could not sit upon it without their backs soon beginning to ache and thus did they only ever speak of the notion of making a crucifix out of it as punishment for its unusability, but they could not agree whether JHWH, as he thought, should be graven onto the cross, or INRI, as she was convinced, the Jews have no cross, she said, to which he replied, that's right, but still, JHWH has always been better than INRI, which is simply a formulation of sheer mockery, whereupon she said, JHWH cannot be graven onto the cross because the Jews do not recognize the Trinity, God is one, the unity of God is beyond question in Judaism, there is one true God and he isn't hanging from the cross, Jesus is. The grimace-chair remained unscathed, it was punitively transferred into the corner of the sitting room, far away from the doll, nobody sat on it any longer. Then they covered up the grimace, which they could no longer bear to gaze upon, then, finally, the two elderly people parted from it, as it was unsuitable as a chair and unfit to be crucifix. It insults my eyes, the old woman said, I hardly see it anymore, her husband replied, my eyes are so poor that I keep bumping into it whenever I'm by the window in its corner. The old man carried the chair out into the garden where anyone who needed to recuperate could sit in it. Then the doll ought to go out into the garden too, the old woman said, and the old man also brought the doll into the garden. The chair wandered to and fro in the garden. It sought in vain to teach the doll how to walk. Once the doll that would have always lain at the foot of the chair had the chair not picked it up from the ground and brought it before its face had disappeared, the rumor came about that only the dead sat in the chair, nobody had seen a living person sitting in it, and the dead may well have taken away the doll, in which they saw themselves. For the dead to cease coming, one would have to tip the chair over onto its side. Thus did they do. And thus was the chair gradually forgotten. Until the elderly couple perished, and they walked through the garden as dead people. Then they recognized the chair, set it upright, and sat down in it together. Now, it shall hurt our backs no longer, they said. And the chair hurt their backs no longer. Now, we ought to give the doll back to it, they said and brought the doll back to it, and, indeed, it was a part of it. Once the chair had gotten rid of the doll, the grimace obtained its mouth, it would remain open forevermore, but the doll wasn't alive then, it had to pass through the chair's mouth for a second time for the grimace to breathe life into it. But the grimace erred in the combination of the letters, as described by Eleazar of Worms, the 22 basic letters are attached to a wheel with 231 gates, the wheel turns forward and backward, if to the good, then it yields nothing higher than lust, if to the bad, then there is nothing deeper than damage, than "Schaden," which is to say that the first eleven letters, with which the 22 basic letters are combined, create the world and the last eleven letters destroy everything once more and thus is it written: '*Alef* with all and all with alef / *Bet* with all and all with bet / *Gimel* with all and all with *gimel*, / and they all return again and again, / and they emanate through two hundred and thirty-one gates. / All the words and all the creatures emanate from One Name,' and *Schattenfroh* is the name and the doll was deformed in the way that I found it, with missing hand and burnt arm. No child was to be blamed for this, the doll has never belonged to a child, the grimace blamed the doll for the error and scratched—'as punishment,' it said—'Emeth' onto its brow. Should the doll be grateful to the grimace if the grimace also dubbed it 'my Galmi'? A further error, which caused quite a bit of mischief was that the grimace-chair was entirely nude and unclean, brown like the apple-tree wood it was made from and not white, for it would have had to have worn a white raiment when it was working on the book *Freies Erzja*,* which explained precisely how a grimace-chair was to be made. A little deformed doll it was, by no means stretching forth from one end of the world to the other. As it stood in the garden in which I found it, its arms weren't even long enough to eat the apple, from the tree of which it had arisen. The apple in this garden is not forbidden. The doll had to ever be at the service of the grimace, this essentially consisted in clambering through its mouth from behind. My visage is a mailbox attached to no house,

---

* Free Erzja.

the grimace incessantly opined, and just as useless, the doll, I mean to say, which is precisely the mail that falls through its mouth-slits on both sides and is never read. The inscription grew imperceptibly larger with each passing day, the doll itself remaining unchanged except for the brow. Its growth first became noticeable when, one day, it no longer fit through the grimace-mouth. When it got stuck in the mouth, the grimace coughed it up with the greatest of strainings and, from then on, forbade it from clambering through its mouth, it was afraid of choking on the doll. Then there came a day when it could no longer raise itself up from the ground, its brow had grown so heavy that it had assumed gigantic proportions. The grimace, which had never overcome this birth defect, couldn't bear to gaze upon it, thus did it bend down to it and erase the first letter from its brow by filling in the scratches with earth and thus did 'meth' come forth from 'Emeth,' and that's what the doll was, *dead*, a motley heap that could lie where it already lay, given over to decay, too worthless to arouse genuine pity. As it fell down, however, the doll could still hit the chair in the face and thereby knock it over. Precisely like a beetle, the chair could no longer get up onto its legs on its own, but the doll was redeemed from its enormous brow, from which all signs immediately disappeared and, with them, their menacing expanse, its final thought was to take revenge on whomever had dared to once more raise up the grimace-chair, for it was convinced that the one who did so would attempt a new creation. Here, if somebody wishes to appreciate how lonely the chair grew over time: Nobody came by and called out: If you are the grimace-chair, help yourself and stand. Each night, the grimace-chair dreamed, Nobody would come by and call out: If you are the grimace-chair, help yourself and stand, then it stood up and helped itself.

In transporting the chair from the garden, I didn't dare to come into direct contact with the grimace, but stuck the doll through its maw and fastened it with a cord. The grimace exulted, as its attendant had flown into its mouth, its little helper, upon which, this time, it only had to speak and breathe in the right order of the gates and letters, then the doll would help it to get up in the future if it should fall down. But what was the correct order? The book that was always on his person, *Freies Erzja*, was not to hand, the only thing he still held in his memory was JHWH, the doll, however, could not be revived with JHWH alone, its life would not have been enough to play through the necessary combinations of JHWH, the 231 gates, and the vowels—a, e, i, o, u—whereby, according to Eleazar of Worms, the vowels must be taken into account in their multiple aspects, the A must be played through six times. At first, the grimace-chair made no attempt to combine the letters and thus did the doll have to remain an inanimate, though finely worked piece of wood that nature had opted to take back into its womb entirely.

Then the young woman's grimace-chair, which I had lowered down from the window, saw the doll, which I had left beneath the window, and they immediately recognized one another. The book *Freies Erzja* was burned into the mind of the chair forevermore, after all, it was carved into its wood everywhere—on its legs, seat, and backrest. Together with the carpet, the chair had ended up in the young woman's possession, she didn't understand their nature and thus did the carpet lay upon her bed, it was merely there to cover the bed linens and bear the bowl of fruit. All the doll had to do was slip through the grimace's mouth, then once more from behind, then once more from the front, then one final time from behind, then the combinations of numbers and letters took effect, the doll came to life, and the grimace-chair gave it the name *Schattenfroh*. The young woman's grimace-chair saw that her work had been done well, from now on, the doll could go through its mouth whenever it felt like it. Its mouth, however, was in a different place than the grimace-chair's that I'd found in the garden. The doll, however, performed its service so magnificently that the chair wished to honor it with a title in the form of an inscription and thus did it scratch 'Emeth' across its brow. When the other grimace-chair saw that, it said only: 'Which is truth.' Schattenfroh wrote this in Anno Domini 1634, having already written many other things in this book."

A wooden limb as my alter ego and I in the dust before him. Schattenfroh, the truth, who is so finely attired as to make one forget the wood of which it is made, presents a letter to me that I am to eat so that a judgment might be passed on the spot. There is no unending stream of traffic through the market this morning. I wolf down the script.

The sun rises. I'm lying in the woman's bed. The outer side of the blanket is cool, as if a cooling stream of air were flowing around it. How did the blanket get back onto the bed when I'd sought to extinguish the burning carpet with it. Upon the bedspread, I read ɥ6ɹz ɥɟqʞɥs. I feel the characters with my fingers, they are warm and grow ever hotter, the longer my fingers dwell upon them. After around a minute, the characters have branded themselves into my fingers, each finger could now serve as a stamp.

The door of the room opens. I am dragged out of bed by the letter-plants, pulled across the boards and into the hallway, down the stairs, out the front door and into the garden, past both grimace-chairs, which are deeply engrossed in their conversation and only pause briefly when they become aware of me, I greet them in friendly fashion, they clearly signify that they are ashamed of my presence. Once the distance between the chairs and me is no more, my forward motion is suspended and I hear the chairs, their faces averted from me, say: "He is pulling himself through our beautiful city by his own hair." "And the gallows shall pull him even higher." "Or the cross shall hang him even higher." The wooden doll stands smirking between the chairs, leaning against the young woman's grimace-chair like a child against its mother. Its hand is unscathed, it is wearing a little festive dress. You dirty trick, I think, then the rope of the letter-plants that has imperceptibly woven itself round my feet accelerates me forward, it pulls me backward out of the garden, a shorter distance across the path toward a fork in the road where the forces who have me in their power take the left deviation, it proceeds straight ahead for a long time, which gives me the opportunity to gaze upon their forces, but I see nobody, the letter-plants shoot away like wild tendrils, urged on by ceaseless growth, which gets faster by the minute, I see myself hurled against a pole, wrapped up and strangled in a matter of seconds. We pass by the "Viehemark," the location of which I have memorized so precisely because its naming in the map's legend contains an error: Viehemark instead of "Viehemarckt," "cattle-mark/marrow" instead of "cattle market," as if all the animals there were cut up and the pain went indelibly down into their marrow, death too is absent and shall never arrive. In just a few minutes, my meat shall also be hanging down from my back, I'll be entirely dissolved. I feel hardly any pain at all, I attribute that to the path, which seems to be mixed with soothing agents intended for the cattle usually brought down it. It is only a few steps from the cattle market to the "Meat Hall," which is located in the middle of the market crossing. There's a beastly reek here, the cattle-halves are hanging from poles, others are impaled, blood is all over the ground, now and then, someone brings water, and the eye is able to once more set foot upon the ground. A few meters later, inside the meat hall, which is open on all sides, the wild hunt comes to a halt, I am tied upside-down to a pole lying ready on the floor and carried over to the other end of the hall. Dozens of people immediately join a procession, it runs back a little bit along the long side of the meat hall, then turns right onto a wide way, at the end of which one can see the Collnische Gate, where I was denied entry, so this is the Collner Steinweg we're on and upon which the city's trade flourishes, I can't get rid of the notion of being roasted on a spit, it's what I see in my mind's eye, the people don't care whether they're eating pork or human, and, at any moment, I might be flogged off at an insultingly low price, the consumption of human flesh having yet to be established as a common practice, I would be part of a special introductory week. I can't hold my head up any longer and look back toward the meat hall, which is getting further and further away from us. I recognize one of the bearers, it's one of the two gatekeepers, when he gazes upon me and sees that I recognize him, he steps out of formation, he lets the pole slip, my head bangs against the ground, the gatekeeper immediately gets into formation once more, but also causes me to hit my head against the ground a second time, conveying the impression that this was quite deliberately planned, a maneuver that is repeated until the keeper begins to weep, which, when he is admonished by the bearer in front of him (the first gatekeeper, as I now see), he attempts to fob off as laughter, it's because I have a wound upon my head that looks simply *too funny*, he explains, initially, the first keeper doesn't want to know anything about it, but then he cannot get a hold of himself and wants to see the wound at that very moment, both of them set down the pole, turn me onto my side, and examine my head, which, however, as soon as it has once more touched the ground, this time in the gentlest way, seems to have recovered such that there is no trace of an injury and also no trace of blood, which so incenses the first guard that he calls in a third person to hold the pole down in his stead while he strives to make sure my head truly bears no injury, despite it having banged against the ground with such force. He has this procedure repeated some eight times and, each time, the fresh wound closes the moment the keeper examines it. What ought I to do, he asks. As nobody answers him, I feel compelled to also put an end to the torment, to take the view that he ought to stop peeping. Instead of doing away with me immediately, the keeper holds back in his perplexity, agrees with me happily, pushes the third man from his position, and orders the procession to continue on its way. As soon as the parade has passed by the mighty block of houses that forms an island in the middle of the city, the procession turns to the right and, after a hundred meters, joins up with an array of merchants, market visitors, citizens, and onlookers. The main market is called "Kornmarckt," it's what the locals at the city wall were speaking of. It's not often that somebody is presented to the public upside-down and bound to a pole. The crowd parts at the sight of me, the people seem to take it for granted that my destination is the now clearly visible gallows, toward which the keepers are proceeding in a straight line, it's a ground-level construction of two poles and a crossbeam, through which I can see the flogging post and the pillory if I raise my head. The Spanish Donkey is on the right in front of the gallows. The ensemble awaits me. I shall have to sit upon the donkey until my abdomen splits open, my genitals shall have become a wooden doll, the crowd shall then wish to see me at the flogging post, the birch trees are thriving splendidly in this region, the flogging-rod shall one day adorn its coat of arms as an emblem of the city, the flogging-soldiers are already marching up, then, finally, I shall be hanged and put in the pillory for days so that everybody in the city can see me from afar. However, nothing of the sort comes to pass. The procession walks along the magnificent row of houses all the way up to a building with an open portico, not entirely flush with its row. Now, we move through an arcade into the portico, then march to the left through another arcade and out of the portico once more, after some fifty strides, the entire procession turns around, the gatekeepers stand to attention, none of the other people who have followed them and installed themselves behind us budge. I want to say something, but I seem to have lost the right to do so, no sound leaves my throat. I discover Father's countenance on the building's façade. I immediately let my head hang once more, my neck muscles give me trouble, I raise my head again and am relieved not to see Father's face anymore. My blood pressure must have played a prank on me, I think, then my father reappears, now, one of his arms can also be seen, he describes a circle with his index finger, points to the portico and the balustrade that closes it at the top, one flanking side arcade and four arcades on the main front make the portico passable, he points to a polygonal stair tower in the central axis of the market front, which springs forth from the façade, as if it cost it every possible exertion to keep the building together, I now notice the corner oriel and the battlement-end of the roof-zone, both gable roofs run parallel and display a multitude of dormers and windows according to their side profile, the building is crowned by a wooden bell tower that rises forth from the roof-zone. My father's face and arm disappear once more, I let my head sink down, we find ourselves near the town hall, dubbed "Zum Schwert" in a eventeenth-century style. The windows of the double-roof open and muskets are brought into position. Or not? Pigeons take off and land once more. Or are they the roof? The town hall is a peculiar administrative building, observing it in such detail distracts me and calms me down, it consoles me that I am, at least in this way, able to express my esteem for Zellen Warhol as regards the precision and attention to detail of his city map, for I can see with my own eyes what the plan foresees regarding me and can testify that a city map drawn up with this degree of accuracy is more beautiful than the city itself, one would wish to live in the map of the city and not in the city. We still stand motionless, the gatekeepers are growing tired, they let the pole with my body attached to it swing ever closer to the ground or briefly set me down, they heave me up once more and, as if they had been unable to divest themselves of a burden that could only be placed onto the ground at a certain angle, one which they were perpetually missing or as if I were a convenient means by which they might occupy themselves with their weightlifting as inconspicuously as possible during the respect-demanding parade—for the fact that it is a parade, a march past a high-ranking personage, a demonstration of the city's might, is unmistakable, but it has not yet become clear to me who this personage is and when the proceeding-past shall be resumed, motionlessness has reigned for some time now. What is the portico for, I wish to ask the keeper behind me, but, again, my voice is not available to me. The question is foolish and can only be clarified by way of the embarrassing situation—it answers itself. The protrusion of the portico allows for a unified streetscape, preserving within it the unity of the façades of the houses, which seem to be strung together, forming a massive front; facing the street, the ground floor of the town hall opens up through the portico's arcade and, indeed, not just for aesthetic reasons, in that it forms an airy contrast to the impenetrable stone façade, rather, the portico serves a mercantile purpose, in the passageway of the arcade are to be found sales outlets for merchants and craftsmen, as they shall still be found in the arcade passageways of certain town halls some four hundred years later. What looks to be a particular form of populace-proximity suggests that the city leaders are addicted to control and want to place trade of goods and products that are particularly rich in tax revenue under their guardianship. Clearly visible through the portico, a wing of the town-hall portal opens up, a man who resembles Mateo strides out and goes to the first gatekeeper, who immediately stands to attention, then the entirety of the procession immediately does the same. I, too, delighted by the fact that the matter is now progressing, straighten up, as if I had to put my clothes in order, as if I were the big attraction, the honored head of a foreign delegation who has finally arrived so as to be received at the town hall in befitting fashion. Mateo says something to the keeper. The keeper doesn't budge. Mateo repeats what he just said. Even now, I can't understand a word. The keeper takes a step forward and the other keeper has the presence of mind to follow him. The second wing of the portal opens up, and now I know to whom the parade that hasn't yet even begun is directed, standing in the maw of the town hall, clearly visible and a menace to any assailant, is a stone figure with a sword, the point of which is directed at anyone who dares enter the building. The pole shall slide through my anus and emerge once more beside my collarbone, I shall be hanged from the sword by way of the pole, then await my death, nothing shall remain of me but *Schattenfroh*, but I must be sure that aught of *Schattenfroh* remains. The striking of the clock sounds out from the main church of S. Martini. Four shallow tolls, eleven deep tolls: The tolls do not fade. A cloud of sound towers up and passes through my body. We move millimeter by millimeter toward the sword. It must be the church that boosts us up. The volume of the army of bells would drown out any other sound. Is that the tolling for the poor sinner already? is what I would like to know. How is this deceleration of processes possible? Each motion is implemented at a speed that is not perceptible to the human eye. Everything has likely been calculated in advance and my survival is assured by the overwhelming exertion of transporting me in this way. I shall not be able to fulfill my task of describing that which is coming to pass around me, as one cannot speak of a chain of events at a speed close to motionlessness. Perhaps everything within me has become so slow that I can no longer absorb external impressions?

This line creates an approximate impression of the uneventfulness caused by the church bells' stationary cloud of sound and of the gait of our procession passing below the level of our perception:

If the procession were to move up- instead of forward in this manner, I would return to the welkin in about a billion years. And, although I cannot raise my voice, the gatekeeper in the rear, bending down close to my ear, tells me I ought to quit screaming like that, it's only going to make things worse. There are no internal events that can be reported. I shall now spend my time with other things, with the narration of childhood things, for example. Here and now is perhaps the rightest place and highest time to let such things run free. Over the years, it can come to pass that one is no longer able to distinguish one's own childhood experiences from those of one's father or one's own child. Is it possible, I ask myself, that I think my own child experienced something, but it actually befell me? Then who was it who recounted that, as a child, he once wept so loudly that the father lost his composure and *took action against* the child, that's really not my turn of phrase, I don't *take action against* my child, to *take action against* a child, one must have studied law or theology as a father, preferably both, accordingly, only my father is implicated in this, and, as a child, I once wept so loudly that my father lost his composure and *took action against* me, but it is possible that my father made that claim as regarded himself and saw his father's violence against him as visible evidence of his own strength. One ought not lose one's composure toward one's child, even if one's emotions are boiling over, the imagining of such violence against the child who is roaming about in the jungle of his feelings and everything affects it so powerfully, takes on ever greater proportions and tears me apart, knocking a child over, pushing it from its feet, preventing it from getting up, to hurl it up, to let it fall, a notion of rage that knows no form of leniency, it develops into an obsessive imagining, the father sees the child, he smells the child, and imagines having to *take action against* it, an inner compulsion, a strong inward tension tearing at the body, this is happening now, 1634, and this invalidation of any movement is a powerless, furious demonstration of might by my father.

It took you a whopping three months and twenty-five days to come before this table, the voice says. It isn't my fault, I reply, a commission must investigate on what grounds the two gatekeepers required so much time for a distance of no more than thirty meters. I am asked if I made use of this time. How could I have used it, I ask back. For reflection. Rather quickly, it turned out there was nothing more to reflect upon. We shall see about that, says the voice. You have three months and twenty-five days to reflect upon what questions shall actually be posed to you at a trial that shall take place in three months and twenty-six days. The voice adds that my book shall be recouped, but given back to me once per month for reasons of recordkeeping. I am to write:

At the end of every month, my book and a quill are brought to me, with them, I write in the book: Also at the end of this month, Thursday, August 31, 1634, my book and a quill were brought to me, with the quill I write in the book that my book and a quill have been brought to me at the end of this month, Thursday, August 31, 1634.

I am to write: At the end of every month, my book and a quill are brought to me, with them, I write in the book: Also at the end of this month, Saturday, September 30, 1634, my book and a quill were brought to me, with the quill I write in the book that my book and a quill have been brought to me at the end of this month, Saturday, September 30, 1634.

I am to write: At the end of every month, my book and a quill are brought to me, with them, I write in the book: Also at the end of this month, Tuesday, October 31, 1634, my book and a quill were brought to me, with the quill I write in the book that my book and a quill have been brought to me at the end of this month, Tuesday, October 31, 1634.

The following is communicated to me: My book has just been returned to me, I can keep it now. It has been copied out in its entirety. What greater humiliation could there be? I'm not actually writing in this book, it's brain-script, the brain writes itself into the book, my book always takes on the German and the script of the epoch in question. But how could they understand it? I ought to study the book very closely, in it is all that will be used against me at the trial. I am told that there are only two ways left to me: Either I hand myself over to the mercy of the city council that has been called against me, and the sooner the better, and I renounce all errors that stand written in my book and also those that I have acknowledged in myself and as to which a sufficient testimony shall be brought against me, one that must be believed, for the scriptures say that 'in the mouth of two or three witnesses every word may be established.' And for these errors,

I am to take penance unto myself with a contrite heart—and with no feigning thereof—in precisely the way that the council shall determine for me. And I ought to formulate the opposite in writing and swear not to keep the opposite of the opposite any further. Or, if I wish to cling stubbornly to the book and defend it, then the council will certainly take action against me in accordance with its rights. In order to prepare me for the trial, my fetters were removed from me, and quill and ink were given to me.

It has now been three months and twenty days. I hold each day in my memory. For all that time, I did not have my book to hand, no pen, no paper, except at the end of the month. Running the quill over the paper was small compensation for the paternalistic imposition. I wrote everything in my brain. My dungeon consists of two rooms, a day dungeon and a large, cluttered room for the night, in the latter, a low hutch of massive beams is housed. The distance between the beams is too small to clamber out of the hutch, but big enough that I might be observed from all sides. For three months and twenty-five days, my hands were fettered behind my back 24/7, about a meter above me, the rope passed through a metal ring attached to a beam, the rope was long enough for me to sit on a metal bucket that served as my toilet, the fetters also had enough slack that I might let my trousers down somewhat. If I desired to lie down, my arms would be thrown upward, causing severe pain. It was only with great difficulty that I could get up onto my feet from this position. Thus did I stand or sit on a bucket for almost the entire day. Now and then, I'd topple forward, the rope would catch me, it cost a certain amount of effort not to lose my balance. If I were caught sleeping, I was told, I'd be tugged up and left to dangle a few centimeters above the floor.

At night, I am brought into the hutch of beams. It's always the same keeper who leads me into the dungeon in the morning. I'm not allowed to look at him and not allowed to speak to him. That's the only thing he's said to me so far. That he doesn't speak to me is a great relief. He wears a great hood that covers his face. I am compelled to lie down, yet I cannot sleep. There must be a toilet underneath my dungeon, it stinks like a latrine, I go to the toilet in a bucket, which, up until now, has always been emptied out, I strive to breathe less often and more shallowly, but my breathing rhythm cannot be regulated for too long. At regular intervals, a pitcher of water comes to stand upon the beam at my feet. There is also something to eat on the beam, bread, rarely a piece of meat, a daily soup, after a few weeks, I see faces in the soup, they deride me, one face strives to speak, I can read from its lips that I am meant to rescue it, as it is on the verge of drowning, the first time I saw it, I attempted to scoop it up with a spoon, which immediately gave me such a bad headache that I grew dizzy, I pushed the plate off of the beam with a jerky movement, the soup flowed into the hutch, as I had nothing to wipe it up with, I had to sleep on the damp floor. During the night, the amount of soup on the floor increased perpetually, after about an hour, I was utterly soaked, like after a nightmare or a heavy episode of sweating. In the morning, the ground was dry, my clothing displayed no trace of dampness. On the following nights, the affair with the soup repeated itself. On the third night, I heard a voice that said "We are still there" and "Daddy did that." Each night, more voices joined in, at first, they spoke in unison, "We are still there" and "Daddy did that," then, they soon began to argue with one another, some of them said "Daddy did that," the others said "Daddy did not do that," still others asked "So, what did Daddy do?" they began to give themselves names, they were called "Lache mit Lenz,"* "Macht in Zelle,"† "Alle Chemnitz,"‡ "Mein Elchlatz,"§ "Am Elch Litzen,"¶ "Zelle

---

* "Laugh with Lenz."
† "Power in Cell."
‡ "All Chemnitz."
§ "My Elk Bib."
¶ "On the Elk Braids."

am Nicht,"* "Tanz mich Elle,"† or "Allich Zement,"‡ they were of the opinion that they would soon have to elect a president from their ranks, each of them also wanted to be president, alliances were formed, they assured one another of their mutual support, but did this so ineptly that breakup and betrayal soon made themselves known, each fancied himself to be the last one remaining, the appearance of an other was dismissed with the remark that business required sacrifice, sleep was out of the question, and thus should it not have come as a surprise that one daydreams and hallucinates, the word "hallucinate" quickly made the rounds, my voices are hallucinating, I said to myself, insomuch as that's true, one thing's for sure, I am not hallucinating and thus did I become the venue for vain interests and general peacockery. "Lache mit Lenz," for instance, never tired of asking for comics, the humor of which relaxed him entirely. When I told him that we didn't live in a time when such funny papers were common, "Lache mit Lenz" screamed at me that he wished to file a report, I asked him with whom he wished to file a report, he wished to file a report with "Macht in Zelle," go ahead, I encouraged him, then he made his report. "Macht in Zelle," however, opined that the matter was too insignificant, the others, whose existence he did not fundamentally doubt, were only around him by chance, he thought, a whim of nature, as he put it, he imagined guiding them like ponies in the arena, him in the middle wearing riding boots and with a whip, the ruler of the leading string, that is my greatest wish, he said, the ponies would have funny harnesses, at a single hint, the pony track could turn into a funeral procession worthy of bearing a head of state to his grave. "Alle Chemnitz," who heard this, burst out laughing and was never to be seen again, only "Mein Elchlatz" maintained a more familiar manner with me, after some hours, I began to shun him; to dub his intentions

---

* "Cell on the Not."
† "Dance Me Cubit."
‡ "Complete Cement."

dishonest would be insufficiently friendly, he claimed that we were cast from the same mold, to have fantasies of murder was one thing, to put them into practice quite another, and he immediately saw that, for me too, merely having them was not enough, thus did I strive to shove him away from me, though he already sat in my lap, but "Mein Elchlatz" consists of a gelatin-like substance that you reach through, then it immediately closes once more, without budging a single millimeter from its spot, "Mein Elchlatz" was very agitated by this through-grasping touch, he wouldn't have thought me capable of that, he said, of being so aloof, incidentally, he was the only one who used the informal "du" form with me, which beguiled me into being even more intimate, for example, he came up with nicknames for me that are worth mentioning merely as a function of the embarrassment they engender: Platter Zechenleim,§ Matter Leichenpelz,¶ Leicht Petzenlärm,** Alte Chemnitzperle,†† Primel Talentzeche,‡‡ Primaten Echtzelle,§§ Leichnam per Zettel,¶¶ Amtlich Leerpetzen,*** he presumed to claim that I am all the voices taken together, "Lache mit Lenz," "Macht in Zelle," "Alle Chemnitz," "Mein Elchlatz," "Am Elch Litzen," "Zelle am Nicht," "Tanz mich Elle," and "Allich Zement," and for someone like me, he said, it would surely be no problem to conjure one name after another out of a hat, each of them would have a voice as soon as it was conjured up, and my voices would conquer the world. He would very much like to be there when I conquer the world as a faithfully devoted servant, willing, it stands to reason, to take on tasks of an intrusive nature, ones I had paid for in advance. While I was

---

§ Flat Coalmineglue.
¶ Lacklustre Corpsefur.
** Easy Snitchnoise.
†† Old Chemnitzpearl.
‡‡ Primrose Talentcoalmine.
§§ Primate Realcell.
¶¶ Corpse Per Scrap.
*** Officially Snitchingthehelloutofit.

immediately made aware of the fact that I wouldn't be able to get rid of "Mein Elchlatz" any time soon, "Am Elch Litzen" unsettled me by way of continual silences, though he always had a friendly aura that aroused my interest in him and finally compelled me to ask him whether he was plagued by some affliction, at which point he frankly stated that he was nothing but his name and his name was nothing, which prompted him to change the order of its constituent parts, "Litzen am Elch",* made so much comical sense that he'd be overcome by embarrassment if anyone ever called him that. Unfortunately, since then, he hasn't ceased complaining about his inconsequential life, he sticks to me like a bit of lint caught on a coarse cloth. If it weren't for "Zelle am Nicht," whom I have come to love for her sincerity and with whom I can, now and again, wittily converse, she advises me to engage with certain readings, while advising against certain others, I ought, for instance, to under no circumstances read Luther, he who essentially marched into the German language from the Latin and, behind his simplicity and his facund speech, which cost him untold troubles to translate into German, he is false, his vulgar style served the recruitment of the serfs, one ought to translate Luther's German back into Latin, from whence it came, then would one have the true German, precisely sub specie latinitatis, but, on the other other hand, I ought to read Johann Matthäus Meyfart, also dubbed Johanne Matthaeo Meyfarten, namely his book written in 1633 and printed by Friedrich Melchior Dedekinden on January 1, 1634, *Bildniß Eines waaren Studenten Der heiligen Schrifft, genommen Ausz dem Ehrlichen Leben desz Hochgelehrten und Erleuchten Propheten Daniels, auff der Königlichen Academien zu Babylon : auch einfältiglich erkläret, Bey der Löblichen und erenwerten Universitet zu Erffurdt* . . . ,† she under no

---

* "Braids on the Elk."
† *Portrait of a True Student Of the Scriptures, Taken From the Life of the Learned and Illuminated Prophet Daniel at the Royal Academy of Babylon: Honestly Declared at the Laudable and Respectable University of Erfurt* . . .

uncertain terms advises me that, if I read the book, God will send me visions as full of reason as Daniel's and, no, I needn't fear that I'll be too thick to understand them: for it shall be given ye in that same hour what ye shall speak and by the "that same hour" is the trial meant, like Daniel, when they deliver ye up, take no thought how or what ye shall speak: For ye shall not see who speaketh: For it is not ye that speak, but the Spirit of your Father which speaketh in you, says Meyfart, who, in opposition to Luther, is an opponent of torture and witch trials, and is presently working on a manuscript with the title *Christliche Erinnerung, An Gewaltige Regenten und Gewissenhafte Praedicanten, wie das abschewliche Laster der Hexerey mit Ernst auszurotten, aber in Verfolgung desselbigen auff Cantzeln und in Gerichtshaeusern sehr bescheidentlich zu handeln sey*,‡ it shall be published next year, whereas Luther, as is to be read in his Table Talk, blamed wrongful convictions, not on the judges, but on the delinquents, who, he argues, commit a grave sin if they make false confessions under torture, which is why he demands a theology of the death penalty to eradicate the sins, says Zelle am Nicht, and wishes for me to not end up like the Braunschweig resident Henning Brabant, from whose right hand the thumb, first finger, and second finger were cut, who was pinched four times with red-hot pincers, then was laid onto a table and had his genitalia cut off, whose innards were removed by way of a deep incision, and finally, when he was awoken from his swoon, had the heart torn out of his living body and was struck many times in the face. Then she advises I attend the Oberammergau Passion Play, which is taking place for the first time this year and owes its existence to the plague, which can therefore be said to have done some good, as, after all, it seems that no art can manage without murder and manslaughter, if one were to extrapolate from this, the end of the world would

---

‡ *Christian Caveat, Addressed to Important Regents and Scrupulous Preachers, As to How to Exterminate the Terrifying Sin of Witchcraft Earnestly, but to Proceed with Modesty When Prosecuting the Same Sin on the Pulpit and in Court.*

mean the resurrection of art, about which it could one day be said: It is only beautiful if it is not true. In one of our conversations, which usually last for hours and the longest of which lasted from one morning until the next, interrupted only by a sudden swoon, which I attribute to dehydration as a function of total desalination, which, in turn, was the result of incessant talking and of the desire to sleep with "Zelle am Nicht," she shook that off with a laugh, which grew from a barely perceptible giggle to a snapping bark, at the peak of which she was struggling for air, as if she had swallowed a dangerously large object and was about to suffocate after having aspirated the foreign body, she told me that "Mein Elchlatz" spoke bad German "conjured out of a hat," which was to say with no basis in anything else, it was neither oversubtle nor plausible, on the contrary, it lacked both vividness, though the opposite seemed to be the case, as well as a valid analogy, by which it could be established that Mein Elchlatz was a banal character, whom one would do best to ignore, under no circumstances should he become president, even if the masses (and these are the other six seven eight candidates here) love puffed-out cheeks, poor taste, scandals, and the threat of war, favoring the one whose infamy most entices self-loathing and who surpasses all that which has come before him, yes, the threat of destroying one's own people goes down particularly well with these sorts of individuals, I must look at the beginning of the sentence again, if it weren't for "Zelle am Nicht," I wouldn't *be* anymore, which, given my position, might be for the best, only the witty conversations keep me alive, which is to say afloat, at night.

Does she think the idiom "to conjure out of a hat," possibly derived from the formulation "to pull something out of the hat," documented in eleventh-century England, itself originating in the archers' habit of hiding spare strings underneath their iron hats, these strings, then, to be used in the case of the old strings breaking, they would be pulled out of the hat and newly strung, which might well fatally surprise the enemy who doesn't know of this form of on-the-spot weapon repair, a notion just as concrete and analogy-sure as the assumed origin of the phrase in the world of magic, the assumption of which, however, presupposes that "Mein Elchlatz" and she too, "Zelle am Nicht," possess an almost visionary memory, one could certainly guarantee that, in the seventeenth century, no bunny—and also nothing else—would be conjured out of a tophat. Then all that remains is the archer's hat, says "Zelle am Nicht"—and that she would not accept. So witty are our conversations that we cause the words to grow embarrassed, soon, no one else dares to come out from under their hat, furthermore, we possess only words, on that point "Zelle am Nicht" and I agree.

"Tanz mich Elle" is, as her name suggests, crazy about dancing within a certain radius that she has precisely defined: she never dances further than the length of the old Halle cubit—0.602 meters. She speaks very little, only a single sentence to be precise: "Come dance," by which she has mastered two words of the German language that are certainly not insignificant, but she knows only these, a circumstance that I attribute to her obsession with dance, I cannot explain her virtuosity in the field in any other way than that she has practiced it since she was a child. Her dancing clothes, and only these, move with her every stride, rustling tirelessly around my ears, her body still remaining invisible, I close my eyes, I hear the rustling of the leaves in my parents' garden, the majestic poplar swaying gently in the wind, "my fire tree," I dubbed it, sitting on the swing in front of it, I could touch its outer branches with my feet when I stretched out fully while swinging, in this position, I often dreamed of reaching heaven, flying feet-first through the poplars, in the leaf-rustling of which I heard a voice of Biblical origin every evening at 5:00 p.m., which, after a little while, took the place of the rustling that could only be heard at the edges of the leaves when one put one's ear very close to the poplar. The voice, which won me over to it right from the start, even though I didn't understand even a single word, gradually came to be defined by an authoritative tone and I suddenly understood a series of words clearly and distinctly: "Next time, please be punctual, I must speak with you," "Did I not say to you that you must swing as high as possible?" "Now let your hands go," then the word "hands" remained suspended on the leaf, the leaf fluttered back and forth as if a strong wind had risen up, but there was basically no wind, I let my hands go, fell backward out of the swing and hit my head, Father came toward me out of the tree, he had long gray hair and a black cassock that got caught in the branches of the poplar, he stretched forth his arms and said, "Never mind then, you're not to become a priest," upon hearing the word "priest," I had to immediately think of my genitals, as if they had been damaged in the fall. "No, I shall not be a priest," I said to my father, "I shall be my father," I raised myself up, brushed the dust from my pants and was on the verge of going home when I saw my member growing forth from the poplar, it stiffened the very moment it noticed I'd seen it. I went over to it and was about to tear it off of the tree when the voice said, "But you don't want poplars to grow everywhere," I let go of it, then did it lie limp upon the ground, and when I attempted to drape it over the lowest branches, the poplar drew it back into its trunk, which opened up a little bit and presented a vulva, which, as soon as I had taken a few strides closer to the tree, also pulled me into it, then immediately set me free on the other side. I smelled of poplar, gentle and intense, "You are now an Anointed One," the voice called out behind me, at supper, I sat bolt upright and gazed right through my mother, I had the feeling that I was never to exchange another word with her again, I ate and slept only a little, then, the next day, had my friend Paul fetter me to the swing set in the hopes that the domineering voice, should I not obey its command to let go with my hands, would lose control. This time too, the voice appeared at around 5:00 p.m. and immediately told me to let go with my hands, as if it already knew of the circumstance of my fettering, it grew ever louder, but only said, "Now let go with your hands," which disappointed me greatly, I had hoped for a comely speech, in which the voice would reveal itself, afraid as I was that the voice might call over my parents or the neighbors, who would then discover me fettered to the swing, and, if I were to seek to placate them, the whispering would turn into a storm that would toss my swing back and forth, undo my fetters, and hurl me against the tree, in the middle of which I would be held captive. Should I ever be felled, you shall perish, said the tree that I now was.

"Tanz mich Elle" reeks of sweat, she ought to wash herself and her clothing for once, if one asks her about this, she just says, "Come dance." I am most afraid of "Allich Zement" who always declines everything, "ellenlang," he says in German, meaning "a load of waffle," but also referencing the "elle" or "cubit" in the name of "Tanz mich Elle," he doesn't respect me in the least, "I would gladly be rid of you," he tells me each morning after waking up, if it is indeed morning. Zement, he thinks, is the most valuable of precious metals, which is why it is his nom de guerre, "Allich" characterizes him most accurately, he says. I practically never speak with him, but observe him in secret, the phrase "nom de guerre" puts the fear in me, as I've been looking for weapons in the vicinity multiple times per day, his question "What are you up to there" simply confirms to me that he is up to something. And, indeed, one morning—if it was in fact morning—when I was looking into the muzzle of a small cannon, he noted that I'd seen it, then promptly fired it off, its ball landed on the ground a few centimeters from my head, he rolled the cannon closer to me and fired it off a second time, this time, the ball hit my nose, I didn't feel the impact at all, nevertheless, not wishing to offend him, I expressed that I was in pain, "Allich Zement" threw his arms into the air and rejoiced. When he wished to fire off the cannon for a third time, I was into his corner with a single leap and swept him off to the side together with his artillery. From then on out, he could no longer be seen, I only heard his voice and distant fire from the cannon. "Memento homo, quia pulvis es et in pulverem reverteris," he said, as well as "I'm working on it" and "The Lord is my witness."

Since then, he has been saying "earth to earth, ashes to ashes, dust to dust…" 666 times per day, utterances I am compelled to count, and, as he speaks, the shots get ever nearer. Yesterday, a shot went through my left ear, now, the shots in my right ear are fading more and more into the distance. Then there's a voice that has no name. It also has no body, only a mere glimmer. It waits for me to fall asleep later in the evening, if it is, in fact, evening, then it calls out "Nie," "never," I open my eyes and see it running away, a dull glimmer of light, and before this glimmer of light goes out, I also hear "We must talk." I periodically comply with this wish and must always re-ascertain that this sentence either represents no wish or the voice that I'd like to dub "Nie" has no strength left with which to reply to this sentence, but loves to listen to me, which, admittedly, is what I also desire and thus do I chatter away, as if it were my best friend sitting across from me, he's listening patiently, he doesn't consider any subject to be off-limits, and he can stay silent for minutes at a time if he considers it advisable to be my father confessor. These are the very sorts of conversations, in which one says something that one would be too ashamed to say to oneself, each thought thereof is suppressed, there is no greater need than to make the said unsaid, one is sitting across from he whose keeping silent wields tremendous power, at his mercy from here on out. Thus did many nights pass until a night came when I wished that I had never met "Nie." I had come to have enough trust in him to ask what he thought of the length of my incarceration, whether it would end in a trial to which he would then accompany me, and, finally, whether he believed that Zellen Warhol had hidden a message in the map. That night, Nie didn't leave it at "We must talk." "Why should I be the one to tell you that?" he asked. His voice was right up against my ear, even its whispering caused me pain. We'd always gotten along well, I said, though he'd just claimed to have never wanted to speak with me, but with somebody else. No matter how many times I asked him who this somebody was, I never received a reply. What plagued me was the question of whether "Nie" was listening to me or had already turned to this other when I was telling him all of these things. Was he perhaps listening to me and this other alternatingly and I was unable to listen in on their confidential conversations? Was he a spy and his mission had now been fulfilled? Was he on the point of leaving me? "You dwell within me and, without me, you are nothing at all," I said to him, then immediately regretted this childish defiance, which revealed only impotent humiliation. How can I be sure that "Nie" isn't still there after all, probing me further and having been given the order to never exchange a word with me ever again? I decided to set "Macht in Zelle" onto him, he was to seek him out in my inwardness, whatever that is. "What will you give me for it," he asked me and I offered him to speak through my mouth for a whole day, what would I lose by doing so, nobody would listen to him except for me, he bargained me up to two days, that was only fair, after all, he was putting himself in grave danger, the inwardness of a human being is the breeding ground of all evil, lured by the soul-larva in its cocoon, dead souls roamed there. He says that the soul is thus doubly encased, by its cocoon and by the human body, it wears people out over the years, it eats them from the inside until they're empty, in the web-sheath of which dreams are made, the soul-larva pupates into death, which awakens in us one day, it turns people into a burned-out candle, a dust-pouch, a pair of bellows with holes that is no longer fit for making wind. What did he think he was accomplishing with this soul-poetry, which spoiled any further conversation with him for me? So, now he would be able to speak from my mouth for two days, but how could I be sure that "Nie" wouldn't overhear the conversation between "Macht in Zelle" and me? It was "Macht in Zelle" with whom "Nie" had been speaking the whole time, "Nie" listened to me with his right ear and to "Macht in Zelle" with his left ear, for the two days that "Macht in Zelle" spoke forth from me, "Nie" listened to him with both ears, while I, strangely enough, couldn't hear my spy's voice, though it was speaking through me and, during that time, my own voice was denied to me. "Macht in Zelle" informed me on the third day that I was to spend my nights learning to distinguish between earth and water, the nocturnal water collected in particular spots, I could feel the dryness and the grass sprung up from the ground and plants and fruitful trees, all bearing fruit according to their own nature and themselves. For my dreams are ev'ry night of trees, they stand firmly rooted, well at ease, and an ill word never speak. I have work to do now, at night, to keep the noble ocean from the shore, to channel the whole of the wide, watery waste, and urge it backward to its own deep place, and I am quite far ahead of my time with these foreign shorelines. "Nie" is what his name indicates, says "Macht in Zelle," if one strives to seize him, he is *never* there. He is a mere ripple in the air, "Macht in Zelle" adds, he doesn't know what he's talking about when he brings me up, it always irks somebody when he, "Nie," converses with him and understands poorly, it must be an ear disease that he himself was only able to cure with the Word, for he spoke with the disease only, and he was healed.

As the weeks passed, the voices made themselves known ever less frequently, and I grew afraid that they were conspiring against me, were preparing an attack. Thus did I lie awake for hours, during which I would imagine all of the voices speaking to me simultaneously for a long period of time, alternating between loud and soft in waves, then going silent once more, only so as to raise themselves back up. The voices could cut into flesh, I imagined, could cut flesh from my body in the form of words, they could lay the words down before me and I would have to recite them over and over again, then they would cut out more words that they would assemble together into a text and the text would read: "I ask the voice who it is and it replies that it is Schattenfroh, then do I ask Schattenfroh what the mark is and Schattenfroh replies: 'But come not near any man upon whom is the tau!' 'What do you look like?' I ask Schattenfroh and Schattenfroh replies, 'You are the man clothed with linen, who has the inkhorn by his side, therefore write: Then I beheld, and lo a likeness as the appearance of fire: from the appearance of his loins even downward, fire; and from his loins even upward, as the appearance of brightness, as the colour of amber.'"

I must contemplate and recite this text for a very long time—until worms have taken over my flesh and changed the shape of the letters. The worms come, they are already in my flesh, emerge from it, wriggle themselves back into my flesh, burrow deeper into it, leave their letters, then, finally, their word so as to continue their work in another set of letters, the worms are the true hermeneutics, their understanding is boundless, and, two days later, I read the following text from the mouth of the maggots: "Where is the brand?" He has it upon his forehead and nose, the other replies. The second keeper examines my face and praises his colleague's work. He didn't notice it, this one says. He ought not believe that the gate is only for him, says the other. I can't feel any change in my face, but I can't escape the feeling of a weight pulling my head down. What is it? I ask. A hammer, says the first keeper. What's it doing there? I ask. It shows everyone that you are condemned to the wall, the keeper says. I want to see it, I demand, then the second keeper pulls out his knife and holds it before my eyes, in such a way that I am almost blinded.

That is no hammer, that is a tau, I say. It wasn't him who burned it onto me, it was somebody else. More interesting than the new text are the script-strokes of a special worm that came to form its transcription, I immediately notice the worm because of its nimbleness and its appearance. It is much longer than the other ones and seems to be minutely observing its surroundings. Its movements and entanglements drew the following picture, which I could not initially interpret:

༄༅ ༈ ༎ ༴༶ ༏༐ ༑༒ ༓༔ ༕༖༗

The flesh-text decomposed. It left itself behind on the ground. Whenever I palpate it at night, the places on my body from which the voices cut it hurt. In any case, there was suddenly this text on the ground and no scratching or rubbing was capable of removing it. During the day in the dungeon, I am overcome by the fear that it might be discovered and understood as an admission of guilt. If the days up until this point had been without incident and no voice in the dungeon spoke with me or seemed to want to listen in on me, on the night that the text appeared on the ground, right eardrum began to speak with left, and what they said to one another wrote itself down on the floor of the hutch, even in my absence, the floor of the hutch had become the pages of my book, for I found that the flesh-text and its metamorphoses had been written into it as well, in writing, I strove toward it and passed over it, just as I have now written up to the text of my right and left eardrums: "At night, I am subjected to the compulsion of doing stretching exercises, my legs stretched out, I check whether my hands can still grasp onto my feet, the fingertips have to be able to touch the toes at the very least, and, if I manage that, it's not enough, the fingers must also reach the balls of the feet. One day in a flower shop, touching the floor with his fingertips while his legs are locked out and set close together is no longer enough for him, he must be able to place his flat hands onto the tiles, for which several attempts are necessary. Meanwhile, the saleswoman has bundled the flowers together, cutting them and wrapping the bouquet in paper in the time it takes him to finally put his hands flat onto the ground. However, when straightening up—his motions should always look effortless so that nobody takes offense—he bangs his head against a woman's lower jaw, at which point, shocked by the thud, she begins to scream like a hyena."

With time, I had ascertained that, if I were to assume certain bodily postures, insomuch as the hutch had not already compelled me to assume them, I could force the voices out of me along with the preceding imaginings of theirs that so frightened me and render them harmless, which I didn't, however, always manage, for, at times, I felt severe changes in my facial features, I could sense them, but could not control them and they were by no means willed by me. I immediately suspected "Macht in Zelle" of continuing to make use of the access I had given him to my voice against my volition, that he was doing exercises with my face, but also with my tongue, and was trying himself out in various roles. One night, I was awoken by my tongue moving into and out of my mouth. "Macht in Zelle," whom I immediately suspected of carrying out these movements, made use of my speech organs to, as soon as he'd noticed my awakening, which was surely unintended by him, give me the command to immediately get up and stand to attention, after all, this was the highest judge I was dealing with, so, upon hearing my own voice giving this command, I obeyed, rose up, and sought to stand to attention, which, as a function of the humiliating hutch, I did not succeed in doing. "Macht in Zelle" wished to know whether this was the appropriate position. The hutch was to blame for the fact that I couldn't stand up straight, I wished to justify myself, but couldn't produce a single sound, my voice, occupied by "Macht in Zelle," would not obey me. The patience of the court is not infinite, "Macht in Zelle" spoke with my voice, for there was nothing left but for me to bear the consequences of this disregard, the trial had hereby begun, I would be informed of the verdict in that I would experience it firsthand, "Macht in Zelle" said, then was silent from then on out. I remained in this agonizingly stooped position for a little while longer, then sleep overcame me. Over the following days, I had to constantly prove to myself that my own voice once more belonged to me and thus did I speak to myself incessantly, soon enough, I no longer knew what else to say, then my speech continued in invented languages, then it toggled back to my mother tongue once the invented languages had exhausted themselves, until my mother tongue itself could no longer provide, at which point, ceasing all speech, I was overcome by the fear that "Macht in Zelle" would once more take possession of my voice, so I began to babble once more, somebody suddenly came to the door of the dungeon and demanded I hold my tongue or else I would be deprived of food and drink. I fell silent for some minutes, then I began to growl very softly to myself and, up until the present day, I have still not been able to rid myself of this growling. The fear of being remote-controlled by "Macht in Zelle" never quite went away, but worst of all was the fear of dying of thirst and starvation and thus did I compulsively wait for the delivery of the soup, bread, and water, hoping for some meat, as if, by waiting, I might just once prevent the food from being provided. At first, I thought that it always came at the same time, but without a clock and without the shadow of the earth, how was I supposed to determine the time? My eyes bored into the darkness behind the wooden hutch, but couldn't make anything out, over time, I calmed down a bit, they obviously weren't interested in seeing me die of thirst or hunger or even causing me to become emaciated.

After some weeks of total isolation, the notion that someone could speak to me from outside of my dungeon began to call forth the greatest of disquiet in me—nausea even. If I had heretofore found the voices within the hutch to be allies, even though they were insidious and prone to deceit—indeed, they were capable of penetrating into me and disappearing in the depths of my soul, but bringing me to no harm in the process—I was now likewise of the conviction that the voice of an other was occupying my body and had not only spread through to its every inch, but was also destroying its organs. This notion, in conjunction with the reek of latrines, increased to the point of being unbearable. I had to master this unbearability, I had no paper to hand, I couldn't bring these notions forth from me and thus, over time, did other ways and means of remaining at the center of myself and not seeing myself as given away to the outside open up to me. My eyes seemed to grow longer the more intensely I stared into the darkness and thus did I come to the conclusion that eyes can also become erect, from that point forward, I spoke to myself of eye-erections. The penetration of darkness hardened my eyes, four or five weeks later, I could use them as supports against the wall of the dungeon, extending and retracting them like a telescope, which had a beneficial effect on my breathing, the rise and fall of the ribcage, I could not otherwise explain this than as the eyes now claiming all attention for themselves, and the fears of suffocation, which overtook me from time to time, were fading into oblivion more and more. I practiced letting my eyes fly forth from my head so swiftly that they would knock the person opposite me to the ground based on the element of surprise alone. What the eyes manifested outward, voluntary concentration by which an organ undergoes a corporeal metamorphosis from its everyday form, as well as an expansion of its function, I could also turn inward, when, for example, the mere notion of climbing a mountain or chasing after somebody who had a big head start or the beseeching notion of the number 50 caused my heart rate to speed up or slow down without my having been physically active in any way, shape, or form. I said "49" to myself, concentrated on the number for a long time, then I counted 49 heartbeats per minute, which is to say, the beats were one minute, yes, I did not have a timer, but, over time, I developed a feel for the duration of the beats, which, indeed, if I were to concentrate for long enough on the numbers, was identical to time itself.

I am convinced that the fear of someone observing me from the outside, someone controlling me and listening in on me talking to myself, shall ultimately summon that somebody into being, just as one can cling to God through the loud recitation of the Torah and draw him downward by means of the letters that God has set into Man's mouth. To read is to call. And so too did I call the keeper. It isn't the usual day-and-night-shift keeper who brings me from dungeon to hutch, then from hutch back to dungeon, another keeper has appeared on this night and must have been observing me through the beams of the hutch for quite a while now. He doesn't know that I have noticed him. My eyes could touch him, so near to the hutch does he crouch on all fours. He has placed the candle that has lit his way here onto the ground behind him, it flickers slightly, casting deformed shadows onto the wall behind the hutch. At one point, I think I recognize the executioner back in the shadows, the keeper bends down just slightly more, the executioner comes to be Jesus Christ with the cross. The keeper has also become aware of his shifting shadow and is now bringing his hands into play. I would very much like to ask him what he thinks he sees on the wall and what he is striving to depict, however, I content myself with simply observing. Perpetually new outlines are formed, the hands place the ears onto the donkey, horns can be recognized, the claws of a billy goat, a pricking tail, then the keeper realizes that he has formed the devil upon the wall and immediately changes the outlines once more, slipping somewhat backward in so doing and knocking over the candle that sets his overcoat aflame. The fire is quickly extinguished, I hear the keeper groping about in the darkness, he seems to have lost his bearings in this strangely crooked room, for which reason all he has to do is feel his way along the walls, instead, he paces to and fro, in zigzags, and finds the door through which he would come no longer. I pop my eyes all the way out and stick them a little way through the beams, they have adjusted to the darkness so well that I can now see him as he wrings his hands and murmurs under his breath, the candle lies on the floor in the vicinity of the hutch, on it are depicted a cross and a coat of arms. If I observe the cross for too long, a body appears upon it, which, if I observe it for even longer, takes on the traits of my own body. It is a pleasure to watch the body's becoming, simultaneously, I notice an increasing discomfort, which can be described as a tugging in the joints. When the pain becomes unbearable, my gaze sinks downward. I fear being exposed to a new, dangerous addiction.

I haven't yet made myself perceptible, the keeper can thus not know if his dinning awoke me. I could show him the way to the door, all he would have to do would be to keep left, then he would come to a door on the opposite wall, leading into a narrow corridor, but, in his growing panic, he cannot find the door. The passage through which he leads me into the dungeon each morning is so narrow that one can only pass through it by walking sideways, I always move out ahead with my hands and feet fettered, the foot-fetters only allow for short, tripping strides and are connected to the hand-fetters in such a way that I cannot raise my arms, he follows me at a safe distance, a pistol in hand, the passage widens, I have to move right into an alcove while he makes himself known by way of knocks on the second door, this door leading to the dungeon and other rooms by way of an antechamber.

Now that the keeper is there, someone must speak to him. I don't want to be the one to do it. Then it is *he* who should speak with him, I do not budge. I push *him* ever closer to the keeper, he resisted at first, but I was stronger. In this way did I also have my prisoner to sort out unpleasant matters for me and, should I be executed, *he* can take care of that for me. Of course, *he* is sometimes naughty too. If I get distracted, *he* immediately begins to withdraw from my control, *he* lurks in wait for precisely such moments, they are a great joy for him, the meaning of his life. When I turn my attention back to *him*, *he* makes himself very small and obeys me. Who is *he*? *He* has been with me since my childhood. As far as I can recall, it began with a pair of pants made of coarse fabric, my mother found them to be cute on me, they hung loosely about my knees and were just a bit too long, I would grow into them, Mother said, but there was no way I would ever like the pants, they were unbearably itchy, I refused to put them on, for which reason my mother refused to love me, thus did I have to choose between love and itching, but opted for a third thing, which I called *he*, *he* had to put on the pants, while I myself decided on red wide-wale corduroy pants, which my mother, as she said, "couldn't see on me," *he* wore the pants patiently until the itching had gotten the better of *him* and *he* cut circular holes into the pants and explained the holes to Mother as the result of a fall. Ever since those pants-days, *he* has been my faithful companion to whom I have delegated the world's ill and evil. Though I initially thought that I had to remain in *his* immediate vicinity, it soon became clear that the distances between us were of no importance. For example, *he* did all exams for me in selfless fashion, which may have been a function of the fact that the self remained with me, while *he* has no self at all. *He* has only to receive an unambiguous order, the word "order" does not quite capture the circumstance of a certain sort of collegiality, for I can rely on *him* absolutely. In times of no tasks, however, *he* sometimes appears to me to be disoriented, also, from time to time, sad or disconsolate. Then I wish that I didn't have *him*. Who is *he* then, is *he* my child? What could be worse than not wanting to have a child any longer and the child can sense this until its death. *He* is not my child. *He* needs challenges. The keeper is a good challenge. *He* calls him. But the call comes from the keeper's mouth. What can't *he* do! Is *he* the keeper? The keeper calls himself and thinks that it was someone else who called him. *He* is always saying "come hither" and the cord of the voice leads him back to the hutch. I ignore him at first, but am struck by his resemblance to the caretaker of my elementary school, I am in a state of disquiet until I have established the veracity of this resemblance and thus do I examine his face very minutely as he remains crouched on the floor. He claims that we can make an arrangement, I simply have to reveal to him where this Warhol is to be found. Reveal how he speaks. Very quietly, yet sharply, in a way that gives me goosebumps. I say to him that I'll reveal where this Warhol is to be found, I only have to go back to my father's office so as to have a look at the tapestry. The keeper states that I will have to spend my days as well as my nights in the hutch if I plan to continue cultivating such a lunatic discourse, in a few years, the hutch shall have crippled me, I will have to creep about with a cane and everyone will know why I don't walk upright, because I betrayed the city and the city no longer allows me to depart. With these words, the keeper has won back his sovereignty and, apparently, his sense of direction too, for, after only a few failed attempts, he finds the door to the passageway and leaves the room. For the first time since my penetration into the tapestry, I become cognizant of the fact that I've no plan for how I can actually get back to my father's office.

It is cold, drafts make falling asleep as good as impossible. Damp rises up from the latrine. The stink shucks the skin from my face, grinds me down. Vomiting brings no relief, only bile comes forth. The water has neutralized the taste in my mouth that comes from the latrine-vapors, at least for a little while, and kept me from drying out. I'm afraid the keeper won't bring me any more water in the near future. I shall strive to make an arrangement with him, after all, he seems to be the only one here from whom I can expect anything, even if it's only just a couple of words. What have I to offer him? I could refer to him prominently in my book. By name. I could give him a pretty name. The caretaker's name was Klein. That is too little. In German, "klein" means little. One of my teachers' names was Hoffman. I shall call him Hoffman, that is a very good name.

Hey there! Hoffman! *he* calls out without managing to push a tone through his lips. Try harder, I say to *him*. *He* tries harder. *He* calls out Hoffman Hoffman Hoffman Hoffman Hoffman Hoffman Hoffman

Hoffman Hoffman so loudly that my head pounds and, though no sound penetrates to the outside, the keeper finally appears and says that his name is not Hoffman. But your name could be Hoffman, if you wanted it to be, in my book, your name is already Hoffman. Hoffman is nothing compared to the name that I have, Hoffman says. What name do you have? He says that his name is III, he is incapable of forgetting anything, and he remembers everything forever—he's now pretending to be loquacious. That suits you, I say, then you can really tell me everything and I can write it down in my book. I can neither read nor write, he replies. Then we complement each other most perfectly, I say. III reflects for a moment, then asks what I mean by that. You tell me everything, I write everything down, you ought to have it all down in black and white. But what advantage does all of this bring me. Others can read it and come to fathom it, even after your death. That's a frightful idea, he says. How can I even check what you've written in the book. We'd have to call on a third party unknown to us, one able to read it aloud who would read the pages to us together, I say. And if this third party reads something that isn't there, how could you prove that he was reading something false? Indeed, the keeper can neither read nor write, as he himself says, but perhaps he's not telling the truth, though his objections are worthy of consideration and, again, I do not know the answer to his question. So, how did he get this job as a keeper without being able to read or write. Nobody knows that I can neither read nor write, he reveals unwittingly. Besides, I don't need to be able to read and write, I can recall everything that is said to me. But does anyone know of your uncommon memory. Nobody knows of that either. What would happen if somebody were to learn of it. In that case, I would surely end up as a living archive, crammed full of the world's most unnecessary knowledge, each official letter would be shown to me, and I would be sent around to and fro. Or you would be done away with, I say. He is silent. We'll reach an arrangement, I think, but am also silent. I haven't been able to go to the toilet for days.

Constipation. I can't shake the suspicion that I have gallstones, a family legacy: flatulence, heartburn, nausea, itching. But worst of all are the dizzy spells caused by malnutrition, spatial anxiety, and the gradual realization of being trapped. I must distract myself, I can't distract myself, there is no end to my musings about my mental and corporeal condition, the ghosts are coming and the hutch is becoming unbearably cramped, as there is no room for them. The ghosts have been there since my childhood. They used to sit in the curtain of my room, they always came with the sunrise in the morning, then they showed off their multifaceted bodies, which slowly peeled forth from the fabric, one by one, the bodies fell away, gathered up on the linoleum, a creeping grinding scraping scurrying began, a pawing and clicking, once the bodies were out of sight, they instantly entered into me, if I don't move for long enough, I thought, they won't notice me, but, soon enough, the creeping and scurrying was inside of me, I raised myself up from my bed and sought out my parents, it always took me a long time to find them in the house, it was as big as a country inn, only the guests were missing. Usually, I would find my mother watering the plants, I didn't trust the plants in the slightest, they were allied with the ghosts, I spoke incessantly to my mother in the hopes that she would take me into her arms and say, you're speaking this way because the ghosts have gone into you. But she herself was a ghost who roamed through the house and the creeping and scurrying came from her, I quickly ran up the stairs to my room, one, another one, tore the curtain off to the side, shook it, my father said, "With your overly fertile imagination, you make the curtains prettier than they are," then the keeper puts a jug of water onto the lowest beam for me, I take it, want to put it to my mouth, then see the crab-like face quaking in the water, this was always the last one to fall from the curtain, now it has fallen into the water and shows its true face, it is the face of my father that the devil has sent, my father is the devil's messenger who could never say I love you, who only once, in tears, said, "but I really do love you," whereas other fathers still had room for a son who, standing on the steps next to his father, had gone astray. This strange life that freezes like a candle. Nobody wants it, life, everyone accepts it, only those who exercise violence do not accept it. The devil sent my father forth, for he had studied theology and likely knew the words that the devil lacked. My father also lacked the words, soon as my father 'gins to speak, then can the devil speak no more. The surface of the water upon which my father's face floats is paper coming down from on high. My father's black page is the night. And thus is my father day and night. His face begins in 1634, ten years after poetry was established to be a hidden theology. Here it is in the water, some four hundred years later, it shall be on paper. "So do I sit, spell-bound for hours, / Half in yesterday and half today."

    My father is in the water, I say to III. He replies that, if I were to teach him how to read, then he would recall how my father got into the water, he would also recall a curtain that was no carpet, as well as a carpet that shall have taken on too many ashes, in such a way that it shall have to be beaten out, for I am ashes and to ashes shall I return. Then how is it possible that you remember the future, I snap at III. But he passes over the question and says that if I were to teach him how to write, he would like to be a witness in the trial against me taking place in the large council chamber and report to me daily. He claims that he would be able to pull this off by registering as a court clerk for the trial, so far as the following areas of work are concerned, he continues, he is considered to be irreproachable, even infallible, as people perpetually tell him, only the most reliable can be made use of for this work, he is the only one for far and wide who will be able to withstand the high demands for a word-for-word reproduction, of late, there have been more and more falsified records, on the basis of which executions have been carried out, executions that, of course, can no longer be corrected after the records have been corrected, or he could register as a messenger for the hard-of-hearing and hard-of-speech old man who always sits at the end of the hall, near to the entryway, he doesn't tolerate anyone being behind him, but, from there, he can also observe who is observing whom and draw conclusions from that as to the future existence of local society, which developed very differently with and through him than without him, he who showed the city that their wall costs more human lives than if there were no city wall, for it could not withstand a siege and artillery fire such as he had carried out. Since the old man always reserves the right—should the trial be slipping away from the litigants in the sense of an impending wrong decision—to undertake what he believes to be the correct measures with the goal of overturning the resolution or, rather, the verdict, and turning it into its opposite, if it were up to him, III, he would not transmit verbatim what was said in the hall by all parties, the old man tends to get restless at the slightest sign of a deviation from the verdict he'd established from the start and threaten to interfere. He continues that the distance that he is to cover on his errand is no small one, the old man wants him to always stand at the very front, as close as possible to the source of the announcements, so that no word will escape me and he can observe me, which gives him the opportunity to store the precise wording in his memory and to prepare the toned-down wording in such a way that its transmission arouses no suspicion. Why is he telling me that, it's making me tired. So, who is this old man, I want to know from Hoffman. He is big, he says. But not in terms of bodily size, for he is actually of middling stature, his complexion is more pale than pink, everything about him is consistently well-proportioned and unobtrusive, it is only the whole of his lower jaw that doesn't suit him, as if he had come into this world without it and this were a makeshift one, much too wide and too long, it was fitted to him, the rows of teeth do not line up in any way, yes, if he closes his mouth, there is room for a third row of teeth between the upper and lower rows, which causes him to swallow his words, especially at the ends of his sentences, it is not obvious whether his hearing difficulties are caused by his trouble speaking or whether this is due to the mechanical circumstance and his semi-deafness, nobody likes to listen to him and so, in the majority of circumstances, he has his concerns conveyed by his secretaries, who do not, however, dare to ask him to repeat his words if they do not understand them and, therefore, something incorrect is conveyed by the secretaries none too rarely, even to the point of distorting meaning and communicating the opposite of what is desired, which cannot be corrected orally, for he has repeated the same scraps of words to the secretaries who were called in to give their reports. As a function of the immense damage that had been caused and the many regrettable situations that everyone involved had gotten themselves into, he finally felt himself compelled to put his messages into writing under the assumption that, now, there would be no more misunderstandings, however, the secretaries copied down his papers, for they were afraid of losing the original, which they had concealed in a secret place. While transcribing, they tacitly corrected unspoken or actual errors and, in this way, produced new errors, some of which had more serious consequences than oral transmission did. Finally, he had the whole town searched for someone who could hold in his memory all that which was said to him. He only wanted to give directions to this one individual. One was not able to say his name aloud, for he himself could not say it. He doesn't doubt that the consumption of cold beer right in the morning, large quantities of meat at lunchtime, and cold beer again in the evening is partially to blame for the fact that he has suffered from gout since the age of twenty-seven, this, in the eyes of many of his contemporaries, makes him seem wayward, he tends to have a violent temper, then once more switch over to emotional coldness, he is, in any case, consistently irritable, he smells slander and betrayal everywhere. He tends to consume food alone, but in public places, choosing from a comprehensive range of dishes presented to him by his servants, they uncover the dishes before him one after another, dishes like pies, venison, roasted piglet, or calf's head, two or three dishes that he likes, he uses the knife to cut the meat from the bone himself or breaks what he's eating in twain, he eats with his bare hands, a bowl held beneath his chin so that the juice can drain without any issues while a gaggle of jesters have gathered behind him to entertain him and themselves with occasionally coarse japes, he acknowledges these with, at most, a raised corner of the mouth, the clearest expression of a weary smile, he cleans his teeth with a quill and, if I want, he can equip me with one that might well serve to clean the teeth of a victorious general who has increased the existing area of the kingdom by many lands and secured the succession he desired, but the quill would be just as mete for the composition of victorious literature and to achieve a "plus oultre" there as well. As a function of these qualities, more than a few people considered him to be Charles V, who had come back to rule over the city, which he had already taken possession of once. Still others took him to be God, who wanted to assert in court that he had only made a promise regarding the beginning or had been misunderstood. He personally favors the assumption that we are dealing with the resurrection of the Kaiser, whose most-gouty and otherwise quite ignominious end had literally called forth entrance into another individual as his afterlife. And it was because of the defeat, which cost many thousands of human lives, and the subsequent plundering and burning of this city, both signs of the Kaiser's might, the city had been considered to be impregnable, but its notorious city wall would not have withstood Charles's artillery for very long, other cities had been prompted to put down their arms without a fight, the people attributed the victory over the city to Charles's visit to the Muttergotteshäuschen, during which he prayed for a victorious storming by way of Krausberg Hill, which then came to pass on August 24, 1543, as well as for the overcoming of Protestantism and the Reformation, namely that Luther would disappear from the scene, the Muttergotteshäuschen was said to have been destroyed when the Kaiser's host withdrew, either at the behest of the Kaiser or, more likely, by the population itself, as they felt themselves to have been betrayed by the Kaiser's prayer, that the old man chose to be resurrected in this city ninety-one years after the Third War of the Guelderian Succession, which had been such a success for the Kaiser, and seventy-six years after his death, a selection that was an expression of modesty, as he thus had to acknowledge that the Protestant Princes of the Holy Roman Empire, as well as France, Italy, and North Africa, in the year of the origin of Titian's Equestrian Portrait, which shows him at the height of his powers, had conspired against him, a mutually agreed-upon resistance, which would lead to the cessation of his power within eight years, this being why he preferred to return to a place not entirely unimportant for the notion of his monarchia universalis, though it would otherwise hardly make an appearance on any world map, he has at the very least co-authored its history, which is to say that he is certainly made note of in the chronicle of the city, while the city itself is as good as unmentioned by his biographers, unless the biography is to be twice the typical length, and this ratio of mentioning and not-mentioning, he ventures to prophesize, shall not change over the centuries, thus are certain cities only remembered because they were once visited by a more or less notorious individual, in a best-case scenario like this one, the city was almost entirely destroyed by a world-famous personality, to be sure, his visage was completely unknown to the local populace so many years after this historical catastrophe and he himself was unsuspected, especially as the Titian painting—Charles V depicted in shimmering battle regalia and on a war horse, 3.35 meters by 2.83 meters, very much a symbol of poise, idealization, and simulation, which, quite possibly, shows more of the artistry of the painter than the true visage of the one portrayed—came into being five years after the city's fall and shortly after the defeat in Saxony, such a sensitive issue for the Protestants, the German lands had never yet seen such a mighty battle and the population of the city in which Charles V was once more abiding, has certainly not seen the

Titian, in which the Kaiser carries a long lance on horseback as an allusion to the Holy Lance with its inserted bit of nail, said to have come from Christ's cross, granting its bearer invincibility and making him into a deputy of Christ on earth.

How he, III, can remember all that which is said to him even he can't quite explain. It's not up to him to diagnose the mnemonist as autistic, however, if he keeps his eyes closed and stares inwardly at a single point, he can describe the process for me word for word. In this way, he is even able to play back that which he's heard in reverse. Years later, he can still see what's been said and it costs him no trouble to reproduce hours of conversation, even heckling is no longer an obstacle, in the past, it would have left behind ugly spatters on the words, and he wouldn't have been able to recognize them any longer, today, he can simply wipe these spatters away, it's lightning-fast, he's gotten into the habit of wiping over a certain portion of the word even when no heckling took place.

I want to teach him how to read and write according to Helfen's method, 178 years before its publication, his Abecedeeefgeaichijaytca yelemenopeecueareesteeuveedoubleuekswhyandzee-Book is the book of books, in which all other books are contained and if Hoffman, as he says, can remember everything that is said to him, thus shall he be able to immediately remember how to read and write. I'm only surprised that nobody has told him yet, but I don't dare ask him about it. Hoffman guesses what I'm thinking: reading and writing really are the only things he can't remember, at least not in his ordinary way, which is to say immediately. Hoffman is unreliable, this thought suddenly passes through my head. The ability to remember relates to hearing, he says, while reading and writing, if he's not mistaken, are predominantly a seeing art. Arts of another faculty, I say. If he does in fact *see* what is being said and can repeat a string of words he's not learned by heart with no trouble, then only that which Hoffman sees would have to be copied or signed. Do you see letters, I ask him and he immediately interprets the question as a trap. I see images, he says, once I've heard a word, I can see it. But as what do you then see this word, is what I ask him. I see it as image and as word, but as a word, it is only an image for me, I wouldn't be able to spell it. "Five," for instance, shoots downward, has its root in something pointed, "fff," and grows ever wider, a pyramid. The faculty of my eyes is not distinctly separate from that of my ears, he says, if I hear "five," I see "f i v e" and the pyramid simultaneously, I would require days if I had to draw an entire speech, that is perhaps the counterweight to the activeness of my memory, which knows no bounds, though the drawing or painting of the words is a one-off process, always connected with the voice that spoke the text, you must continuously memorize the five, he says to me, just as with the so-called alphabet, I see no order there, I only know the order of each individual text, no system, no logic, I can't read "five" in a book if I don't simultaneously hear it and, once I do hear it, I can only draw or paint the five each time anew and, each time, the five looks different.

Then you can't remember everything, I object. All that he's ever heard, he can remember, also in the form of word-pictures, only the connection between optical and acoustic stimuli was ruptured after a single use such that he could neither put the words down in writing in other contexts, as he isn't even capable of producing script, nor can he recognize other texts more generally without having heard them, which the ability to read otherwise presupposes. According to Hoffman, each word is transformed into a picture in his memory, he then sets them up along a street, which he simply has to stroll down so as to reproduce the sentence. But, he says, he always used to walk down the original streets, and, because he had left word-pictures there at a time when pinewood chips and oil were in short supply, he couldn't see the images in the darkness when once more walking down the street and therefore ended up passing them by. Now, he works in his head with form, vision, and image technology by way of abbreviations, a form of image-stenography that allows him to expend less effort in remembering and reproducing, it's a kind of synecdoche-technology: he works with silhouettes and with details of the images that stand in for the whole and not with the whole image any longer. I want to put him to the test and quote an excerpt from a book: "Hoffman is nothing compared to the name that I have, Hoffman says. What name do you have? He says that his name is III, he is incapable of forgetting anything, and he remembers everything forever—he's now pretending to be loquacious. (. . .) I want to put him to the test and quote an excerpt from a book." He can flawlessly repeat the omission-filled passage that I quote to him, but he can quote the omissions too. That's an excerpt from your book, Hoffman says. The sentence that is now thus to be read in my book enters into me, as if everything in my body were being pulled right toward its middle, the bones, tendons, and veins bound together with cords. But if you can't read and write, how have you come to know that this excerpt is from my book? I see it, Hoffman says. Can you also repeat something that had been said a few minutes or even days ago? That wouldn't pose any problem for me, as everything that had been said, whether minutes or hours ago, is in your book. Then there's nothing that isn't in my book. That's how it is. Well, it still hasn't become quite clear to me why you wish to learn how to read and write, I say to Hoffman. If he writes something down, it is to forget it, for, once written down, he no longer needs to hold it in his memory. He wants to first write down that which he intends to forget, then to either eat it up or burn it. I want to make use of this method, he says, I wouldn't feel comfortable with another, simpler method, it frightens me. This method consists in no longer wanting a text, I no longer want to know it, it should no longer come to the surface. As soon as my mouth takes on a certain taste and my hands radiate a certain warmth or chill, I know that an old text is taking shape, its primary need is to breathe fresh air. Very soon, I come to know what text we are dealing with, then I am left with a second to decide whether I want it or not.

If I don't want it, I am to inwardly incinerate it. At which point I see something of a strident white that only slowly vanishes, I am blinded for minutes. Can it be that I've burnt a hole into my brain, I ask myself, is that the goal of this text—that I incinerate myself, burn holes into my brain? This city here has seen many sieges, plunderings, and pillages. Over the years, I've arrived at the conviction that I am the city, everything is playing itself out inside of me, the city wall is my frailty, I often think, it is the impending old age that surrounds me, the town hall is the will, it is weak, but when it rages, it annihilates. People suspect that there is a hidden message in the map of the city you had on you. Thus is the goal of the city map to besiege and storm me, the map that I am makes it easy for you to conquer me, with it, I am immediately seen through.

Now, in this moment, it becomes clear to me that I am my own keeper and do not have the ability to directly act on III alias Hoffman through telepathy or projection of the will. If he claims not to be able to read and write, this is only partially so, he doesn't know or he has forgotten that he is I and I he, his access to reading and writing is blocked, he recognizes these capacities in me without having experienced me as one who writes and one who reads, although he knows of the book and this is proof enough for him. Should I unleash him to read and write as one clears a tunnel blocked by an earthquake or explosion, what power would that give him over me in addition to the possession of the key that imprisons me? What am I thinking right now, I ask him. He gives me a shocked look, as if he'd been caught knowing precisely what it is I'm thinking or as if he fears having a mental patient before him on top of everything else. You're thinking, he says bluntly, that you are carrying out my work. I want to know how that comes to pass—the outsourcing of memory into the book. I hear your book and see images, the book itself consists only of images. I feel right at home there. You have written down the images and made them harmless in writing. The images stick in the book, they cannot detach themselves as the figures in your curtain do, peeling forth from it as a result of your looking at them. The paper *is* our memory. If I write something down, I arrest it, if I want it to disappear and not come to the surface any more, then I wish to call out to everyone in the spirit of the author of *Fibels Leben*:* "Be beside yourselves, Oh all you writers of the time!" Is it so that you want to put only what's evil into writing, I ask him. Or only the good so that the evil divides itself once more, he says. But there's another reason why I wish to learn to read and write, he says. Over time, the images in my head become things that I'm perpetually tripping over, then they get so stuck in my memory that I have no more air left to breathe, my fear of falling, in the meantime, has become so great that I tidy up each hour, sweeping my entire memory hall, then a disorder comes forth from the former order, a disorder that I once more memorize as order. I can grasp the images with my hands, Hoffman says, most of them are chairs and cubes, tables, shovels, predominantly white, made from a strange material, not wood, not stone, perhaps snow. The negotiations proceed without me on the first day. Hoffman is perplexed, he cannot find the passages he read aloud from my book, they stripped me of it during the strip search in the sure belief that they would learn something of Warhol's map therein. Others are excerpted in totally distorted fashion, furnished with extra sentences that didn't come from me at the beginning or the end, perhaps they've been invented for treacherous reasons. They are preparing to condemn the entire book before I myself can stand to speak and answer questions, they shall cast four accusations at me, each of which unto itself would lead to being burnt at the stake: Unauthorized entry into the city with the help of a city map, which opens all gates to the enemy; unauthorized self-removal from the city wall as flight from justified punishment;

---

* *Fibel's Life.*

entering into another person's dwelling with the aim of using a carpet to simulate the burning-down of the city; writing a heretical book that strives to look into the future as only God can do, for this act belittles the present as set against the future by inventing even more devastating annihilations than those wrought by Charles V's occupation of the city; the book insults the city and the father and brings them into disrepute; and that all of this heretical, future-assuming, present-reducing, doom-inventing, and home- and origin-abusing claptrap is recorded in such minute detail is the greatest sacrilege of all. Thus does Hoffman testify, and thus is it now written in my book.

On the second day, I am subpoenaed, but not allowed to speak. I therefore shake my head incessantly until I am forbidden from doing so and, finally, because I do not wish to cease shaking my head, my head is fixed into place with a device hanging heavily over my shoulder. As I was no longer able to stay on my two feet because of the device and fell down, it was resolved that I be removed from the hall and that the deliberations be continued without me. Thus does Hoffman testify and thus is it now written in the book.

It's now the third day, I sit in the hall between two keepers and am awaiting the High Court. Some of the townsfolk are present, I am to be allowed to speak today. Hoffman says this was brought about by Charles V who, yesterday, was disgruntled that, although I was brought into the hall, I was given no opportunity to comment on all of these monstrosities, after all, my death is a foregone conclusion, I ought to be at least afforded the right to plead that the death penalty be commuted to a lifelong period of service on the city wall, even if this right is merely a rhetorical one and nothing shall be able to alter my deserved death, but God would like to hear my voice, he would like for me to show remorse and unburden myself, it is with a purified heart that he would then accept me into his kingdom. Thus is it that repentance is expected from me. The Kaiser must be sitting at the other end of the hall behind me, Hoffman is likely near to him, sometimes leaping hither and sometimes thither, precisely as pleases His Majesty, I turn around and see nobody but a pair of smirking figures, who, as soon as they've gazed upon me, mock me, they stick out their tongues, pull faces, a knife passes across a throat, a fettered man is burnt, I also recognize a hanged man. The figures are shoved out by about two dozen armed men, who position themselves with their spears, halberds, ballistae, and swords in such a way that they can control the entrances to the hall and what is coming to pass inside of it. We've been expecting you, suddenly says a voice that is familiar to me, I turn to face forward and look into Mateo's visage, next to him, to my even greater astonishment, Hoffman and a very old man are sitting with Zelle Warhol's city map next to a notepad lying before them.

We hereby inform you that your adversary is not a party to the proceedings and, consequently, shall not be able to be prosecuted for a false accusation. We inform you of this as a provision for your almost certainly taking everything being said against you to be a false accusation. As such, there can be no false accusation. You have the Kaiser to thank for even being heard at all, for it is not the court's proclivity to hear out someone like you. All that which is being heard and spoken now is part of your book, which, as far as fairness is concerned, gives you enough of a representation-allowance, for is that not the dream of every writer—to write life? As far as our representation-allowance is concerned, we are content to be able to accompany you for a little while, even if it is actually death that accompanies you. The Kaiser, Mateo says, would like to know whether you wrote the following:

"One calls this reading. I have paper, a pen. I must write that I am here voluntarily. And so I write: I am not here voluntarily. And, as I am here voluntarily, I have voluntarily subjected myself to the confines of this society. I write: As I am not here voluntarily, I have not voluntarily subjected myself to the confines of this society. Society demands truth.

My mission is to write everything down from the beginning. I said that would be no problem. I know when the beginning is and I know what everything is."

I didn't write that, I reply. But it is now the case that this passage is in your book, Mateo says. Yes, now it is in my book, only *now*, but it is false, its meaning is distorted, I reply. If it is false because its meaning has been distorted, Mateo says, then nobody else other than you could have made it out to be false, after all, it is in your book, Mateo reproaches me. The Kaiser applauds. You are subtle and brilliant, he praises Mateo, you shall stab him with your subtlety. Hoffman speaks up that he has something to share with the Kaiser. Incidentally, that's Michael von Deutschbrod, Mateo says, he's the most important witness against you, he can do more than just testify, he can also repeat what you've been telling him over all these weeks word for word. You ought to think twice about challenging him, for your own book shall so embarrass you by its size alone that your death shall seem nothing more than a passing episode and your book shall be deadlier than death—longer lasting too. The book shall be your eternal life, but an eternal life in damnation.

Incidentally, as far as your father's administrative office is concerned, we could well do you the mercy of seeing it in the near future, there, it would be in vain that you would search for the tapestry, through which you were able to reach us. We are of the conviction that, through the mere contemplation of the city map, which you occupied yourself with for hours, you were led directly to our gates. In it dwells a might that transcends borders and breaks down walls, with its aid, one can transport oneself directly to where one imagines oneself to already be in observing the map, but you are not behind the gates and in the city center as you had hoped, you ended up in the open field before the gates. As such, the accuracy of the map still needs some work. Now that this has all been worked out, we'll save ourselves the visit to your father's office. Better you should tell me whether you wrote the following passage:

"You don't know who's thinking when you're thinking, who's speaking when you're speaking, and we shall be on your hand until you have completed this task, until you have the feeling that it is enough, that it was your task to write it all down, and, now, you have written it all down, you think. You shall never be able to be sure that this is your feeling. But what role does that play?"

No, it wasn't I who will have written this passage, I say. That's what I thought, Mateo says. Who will have written it, if not you? Am I now to say that it will have been the doll? I would not be believed and I would look like a madman standing there and saying that. It will have been the doll, I say. That really is quite interesting, the doll, huh? Mateo scoffs. If it will have been, as you say, the doll, how can you not have noticed it?

He will have written it with the doll, someone exclaims, he will have had the doll in hand and written with it. The doll is called to the witness stand. "He brought me to life," the doll says. "And then?" Mateo wants to know. "Then I brought him to life," the doll says. "And then?" Mateo asks. "Then, he wrote with me," the doll says. "How did he do that?" "He turned me upside-down and wrote with my head." "Then are all the thoughts in his book your thoughts?" "That's correct." "So, he is guilty of the theft of intellectual property." "That's correct." "Can you name the point, from which he wrote with your head?" "Yes, I can—it is from this point: 'Books are my dolls.'" "And might you also cite a passage that concerns you personally?" "I can. It is the following: 'Hidden in the grass, I find a small wooden doll whose right arm is entirely black, the hand is missing, the stump of the arm can be rubbed a bit between the fingers, its body is damp, it has water stored up in its insides. I lean the doll against the wall of a house and imagine the child feeling the doll's burning as if with its own body.'" "And when shall we read the passage that ends with the sentence: 'But what role does that play?'" "Toward the end of the book," the doll says.

It is thus proven, Mateo says, that he has abused and abuses the doll for his own nefarious purposes, by having forced and forcing it to put its thoughts down on paper, nobody can forbid those thoughts from being had, for as long as the thoughts are only in the head, they are free. The doll may rise up and leave the hall. It does so, but not without casting me a cheeky look that expresses its satisfaction at having taken revenge on the one who brought it back to life. It pulls a small train behind it and walks in shoes with high heels. That's ridiculous, if it really is my member, then what are those shoes for? The train grows ever longer, as if, while it walked, the doll were unwinding a roll of thin fabric, which, at first, seems to dance in the air meter by meter, before it piles up on the floor, then is thrown up once more as if blown from below, and thus does it gradually come to form a curtain, which I can no longer penetrate with my eyes, rather, its twistings and meanderings form a female body that I immediately associate with the woman in the window, an association that I furiously suppress, for I recognize the doll's goal of calling forth lust in me, then Mateo's voice interrupts the game with the words: The doll must have turned your head so that you see more in it than a doll and, verily, your book bears this out—that you are entirely immersed in your thoughts about the woman in the window, we are also thinking that it is no simple city map, but an instruction manual and, we presume, whoever knows how to read it has already conquered the city without actually having set foot in it. I can't follow this supposition, I say, I only used this map to orient myself. Who and where is this Zellen Warhol, he who drew up the map, I'm asked, and what sort of name is that, as if plucked out of thin air, really ... nobody has a name like that, and how did I actually get to the city in the first place? I reply that I don't know who Zellen Warhol is, all I know of him is that he made the map, he was sitting in a tapestry that was hanging on the wall of my father's office, a panorama of more than 1,200 years of city history can be seen upon the carpet, I simply entered the tapestry, met Warhol on the green mountain called Sturmsberg outside of the city—I actually did describe him once, sitting on a field-path outside of the city, a field-path or Sturmsberg, Mateo interjects; Sturmsberg, I say—and I had with me the map that he'd given to me, thus putting me onto the way into the city, I didn't initially get any farther than a certain Muttergotteshäuschen. That has been made adequately clear, I ought to come to essential matters, Mateo interrupts. I do not know what is essential, I say. The map. I've already said what I have to say. What do the hatchings and dots signify. Those are hatchings and dots. Is that right. Yes. We shall see. No further questions. But perhaps just one more: The greatest of mysteries are hidden in the eyes. Don't the dots and hatchings denote letters? No, not that I know of. Wouldn't the letters, if put together into the correct order, give hints as to where on the city wall an attack had the greatest chance of success? I ask you then to consider what if, in the meantime, the city wall had been strengthened at precisely this point. How wonderful, you have thoughts of your own, Mateo replies. Couldn't it be that the dots on Zellen Warhol's city map resulted in the following lines: "The weoruld runneth toward the leoht / it wisheth to go unto the hol, its restless brighte." Well, that's poetry, I reply. It's in arcane language, Mateo informs me, a riddle that is built from hidden points. The end of the world is hidden in poetry, the only question is what's meant by "restless brighte." Hell, I reply. Couldn't one of the gates be referred to in that fashion, Mateo wants to know, the brightest one, I mean. Which one is the brightest, I ask. With this question, I have betrayed myself, everyone agrees, it boils down to this question, I am a messenger who is to spy out which of the five gates is the brightest. That's a translation error, I say. I shall also find no peace in the hole, the Kaiser assures me. I'd like to quote one final passage, Mateo says, and learn from you what its crux may be: "What am I to do with a fur coat in the summer? It is your only possession other than this breviary. And what am I to do with the breviary if it's not to hand? Write in it once it's to hand once more. Then there's the first thing I write down in my breviary—that I need no fur coat in the summer, even if it's my only possession. If you'd prefer not to have it, I'll sell it off for half of what you offer. Wood is traded here, not furs. You ought to lay the fur over your cot, lying on bare wood for such an unforeseeably long period of time shall do your body no good. Beyond that, winter shall come for you once more. I take the fur coat and stick it into the corner. You shall have to recant or it shall cost you your life. I shall not be able to recant what I didn't say and what I don't even know." This passage is not included in the book, I merely thought it, then opted not to include it in the book. And why not? Because the whole issue of the fur coat and the breviary is a nonsensical one. These are downright fantastical replies that you dare to proclaim right out in public. If you weren't punished for that which you did, you would have to be punished for that which you say, this madness makes a mockery of the Lord.

Incidentally, we consider it to be a proven fact that you did away with the widow Steffi Rapid, with whom you'd have liked to have lived like Hus in Konstanz. But instead of getting to know her in the respectable way, you simply clambered up into her chamber, she offered up some resistance, you covered over the window with a tapestry, then killed the lady by inexplicable ways and means. Thus do we assume that you caused her to vanish through the tapestry, given the certainty of the fact that she was present in the house on the evening and the night when you entered her dwelling. What you wrote about Steffi Rapid in your book is nothing but deception and is more than enough to have you put away in a madhouse. I quote: "Thus do I have the sudden wish to do away with the young woman. Without knowing its contents myself, I imagine a talking doll reading the letter to her several times in a row while she is slowly being killed. The doll is brought into such a rage by the repeated reading that it wants to do away with her. At this point, I destroy the doll, which I already regret as I do the deed, suicide seems to be the only way out. Ascertained at this point, the woman is dead, the doll torn apart, only the letter and the suicide remain." I know no Steffi Rapid. What I wrote about the doll, the woman, and the letter sprang forth from my imagination, I retort. Nothing ever springs forth entirely from the imagination, Michael von Deutschbrod says, what you saw and heard in the hutch and what you told me there was never anything but confession. Your father, says Mateo, who doesn't wish for his presence to prevent the truth from being spoken, has a message for you: "Do you believe that you can spill me out like this Pope was spilled forth from his traveling carriage near Arlberg on his way to Konstanz? You shall be your own Viscount of Leopards. Your horse, which you ride so fantastically, is called Grabstyn.*" I do not understand this message, I say. Whatever you do, the message means, you shall never be rid of your father, Mateo says. From a legal perspective, you are on the run. Whoever is on the run is technically no longer alive. It came to the Kaiser's ear that, on every evening God has afforded to you, you never tired of saying: "Put every man his sword by his side." This sentence is actually from Exodus. No, this sentence comes from my mouth, I reply. Thus does God's Word speak forth from you. I myself speak forth from me. So, you also go in and out from gate to gate throughout the camp, and slay every man his brother, and every man his companion, and every man his neighbor? the Kaiser asks. We're dealing with the spiritual sword here, with the Word of God as a spiritual sword, I reply. With the Word of God, you desire to kill or ought to be killed, is that what you wish to say? We're dealing with the divine sword of truth and justice, I say. It's strange that one finds nothing about that here in your book, Mateo

---

* Gravestone.

says. But now you can find something about it in my book. It's been found too late, the Kaiser says, to which Mateo adds: The real sword of justice—real because it makes real—is to be found in the town hall. You've earned the right to take a closer look at that sword.

Accompanied by the applause of the city soldiers and bailiffs present, Mateo announces the verdict that was already decided upon before the interrogation: May the sinful body be destroyed. Which is to say Paul, Romans. Then there's hope, isn't Paul aiming for resurrection into a new life and death is merely a passageway? Two guards lead me out and those present, led by the Kaiser, Mateo, and Deutschbrod, follow in a solemn procession. From the conference hall, descending the stone staircase to the ground floor, the procession describes a semicircle to the left and lines up before the mighty figure that bears the sword in its right hand, which, with the help of a hidden lever, shoots forward and can kill a person. For this to be done, the delinquent must be brought closer to or further from the figure, depending on his height, then his heart can be pierced, his belly slit open, or the person concerned can even be beheaded by way of a second lever, which causes the figure's arm to rise, turn, and deliver blows in quick succession; such beheadings have already caused numerous fainting spells among the spectators, only preventable if the method of execution had been pre-announced in some detail. However, there is also a method that does not lead directly to death, but leaves the delinquent in agonizing uncertainty: The sword darts forward, the one being punished stands so close to the figure that the point of the sword touches his clothing with distinct visibility, but without seriously injuring or even killing him. The judiciary has not been able to come to a consensus as to whether this form of general amusement constitutes torture. The delinquent's uncertainty simply consists in not knowing whether the next blow shall be fatal. And, to be sure, only very rarely have there been incidents in the past that have constrained the court to making use of the sword in this way. Some feel themselves called upon to be the executioner and put the delinquent to the sword, others think that they are acting with the best of intentions if they put the delinquent to the sword in such a way that he is thus relieved of his uncertainty, there are also those who, at the sight of the sword making contact with the delinquent, themselves suffer physical and mental torment, which only comes to an end by way of the delinquent's death. As far as I am concerned, the court is content with the implementations of which I've just heard, it has been established that verbally recounting and explaining has almost the same effect as mechanical demonstration and that, so long as deterrence has its proper effect, further costs and bothers are spared. In my case, on the other hand, deterrence cannot really be spoken of, given my offenses, what awaits me is completely different—a form of treatment that will make much more of an impression. Those present may follow him outside to the Kornmarckt. The light of day shines so bright that I cannot cast my gaze onto the sizable crowd that has already been gathered here for some minutes. There is a man standing there, quite tall, upright posture, he seems to see right through me. I don't see him blink at all, his facial expression remains unchanged in mask-like fashion. That is Father, round his neck hangs the oversized city seal with eagle and lion, if someone gets too close to him, the seal burns into that person's back or his chest, there's a system to these attempts to get closer, is what I then recognize, the people are queueing before my father to be branded by the seal, it seems to be a kind of entry authorization, Mateo waits out this procedure, the people look for the place that will afford them the best view, then Mateo strides toward the executioners. They garb me in a floor-length white robe, place a pointed paper hat onto my head, it's painted round with red devils, they fetter my hands behind my back, then, after having me stand up on two bundles of wood, they bind me with a rope to a square wooden beam about thirty centimeters thick and about two meters high, it's already been rammed most securely into the ground. Somebody notices that I have my face turned toward the east and says I ought not to have been turned toward the east, for I am a traitor to my father-city and a heretic, I ought to be turned to the west. Thus do they turn me to the west. A heavy chain is placed around my neck and upper body, it is fastened to the beam. This is so that I don't tip forward. They also lay bundles of wood mixed with straw around me and stack them up to my chin. Mateo says: We have managed to decipher the map and this is the proof that you have erred in everything, that you place the death of your father, which is to come to pass in 380 years, over the whole of divine and worldly history, and that you have crept into this city as a false prophet, inexcusably distorting its image and memory. The dots and hatchings mark letters that make up the following sentence: "Father shall die on August 20, 2014." Ill sets the bundles alight, then takes a step back. He looks me in the eye. "Christ, thou Son of the Living God, have mercy on me!" I am meant to sing. And, for as long as I still have the air for it, "You, who was born of the Virgin Mary" too, this is what Johann Heuss also sang before the flames scorched his breath, so is it written. My Ill, why hast thou betrayed me? *He* shall burn in my place, as I willed it and as I wrote it. I sent *him* and *he* went out. Three times does *he* cry out "My Ill, why hast thou betrayed me?" The third time, the wind blows the flames into his face and it melts so quickly that nobody can say the Lord's Prayer twice in a row. The wood, quickly set ablaze by the straw, is now burned up, though a body still stands there, bound to the beam by the heavy chain, thus do these minions of fire put the charred body and beam together, rekindle the fire with a fresh load of wood, then burn *him* in *his* entirety. Zellen Warhol's city map is also put into the flames, in such a way that nobody can use it to bring the city down as *he* had planned, the map is burned with the draftsman in effigy, who learns of *his* own fate when it is announced before its enactment, then the fire consumes the paper. They also hasten to bestow the book unto the flames, but the book does not burn, it shines forth like a bit of red-hot iron, which the henchmen quickly sort out from the rest of the fire with their rods that rake through bones, one can hardly wait to see ashes reduced to nothing but themselves, then one of the henchmen thinks he's seen *his* heart in the middle of the clumpy mass, agitated, the others ask "where is it" and dig around in the heap with sharpened sticks, here and there, someone occasionally thinks they've found it, "the heart is burning, the heart is burning," they cry out, then, finally, *his* shirt and *his* shoes are cast into the flames so that these, should the news of the execution be spread, do not become relics, then everything slumps down, for a while, one stands before the heap as if devoutly, someone says to procure a wagon, shovel the rest of the wood-pieces into it, then sink them in the nearby river that bears the name of Rur, thus are they all scattered. Nobody pays attention to me. I take my book unto me and go forth swiftly, but not with rapid stride, in the direction of the city wall, through the gates of which, as I have heard, one might leave the city unmolested because it is Sunday. My way leads me to the Muttergotteshäuschen, where I wish to pray to return to Father's office in the twenty-first century, he owes me that, the old man does, after all, I conceived the most delightful winged altar imaginable for him. My way is footloose and cheery, I greet all those I encounter in a friendly manner, nobody takes any notice of me. How strangely familiar everything here is to me, this city that has been neutralized with my death, it's dissolving with each step that I take, I walk backward and the city disappears. A dog on the left of the image flickers forth again, then is extinguished. All that remains of the trees is their outline until the path that they line and the field upon which they stand dissolve. I would like to climb backward through the wall of the Muttergotteshäuschen, into the room divided by two vaults with cross-ribs, which run toward windows with pointed arches and in which the hand of the winged angel still reigns, its overly long middle and index fingers are pointed at the red curtain behind and to the left of my mother, should death be green, I must pass backward through the curtain while Mother still wears her blonde hair loose and flowing over a high-necked dress and she is immersed in a book, in which, at this very moment, she can read the following words:

"And it comes to pass that, at the same time, a few centuries later, my father ordered the caretaker to take the tapestry off the wall and to knock it out in a hidden spot in the town hall's inner courtyard," this tapestry, however, showed multiplied traces of soot and ash from right around the seventeenth century. It scatters down from the carpet, my father says, ash has already piled up on the ground. However, both men who have been charged with cleaning the carpet agree to save themselves the trip down into the courtyard and instead undertake the knocking-out on that very spot in Father's office right when he leaves the room. The ashes are thrashing, one says to the other. What a nonsensical sentence, I think, having from the tapestry a precise view of the floor and not being able to detect any ash-thrashing. Both men have great esteem for the ashes, the men were baptized in the neighboring church and have taken the Bible at its Word from its very first page—they take for granted that they are dust and shall return to dust. Here, someone is turning back to ashes, one man says to the other, a foot is forming from the ashes now, then a second one, the lower legs build themselves up, there is movement in my legs, they can hardly wait to distance themselves from the wall, they pull what remains of the ash-body from the tapestry, both men kneel down before me, which I immediately see through as a deceptive maneuver, I want to disappear through the side door, then it becomes clear to me that I'm wearing no clothes upon my body, both men take advantage of this hesitation and attempt to grab hold of me until "the bossman comes back to the office." Some guy fell out of the tapestry, they say, my father thanks the men and leads them out of the room.

Would you like a coffee, my father asks. Then a cup of coffee sits before me. Next time, you ought to kick the filth from your shoes before you come in here, Father says. A thick crust of earth encases my shoes. I apologize. 666 on a white shirt, that's typical, Father says. I look at him. He has nothing to say to me. As always. And Mom? he asks. No idea, I say. She's been complaining a lot lately, Father opines. Is she sick? I ask. She believes that she shall soon die. I raise myself up from the armchair and point at the wall to the right of the entryway. You have this painting here in your office:

No, says Father, I have and always have had this painting hanging here:

But standing before this painting

I heard a voice, I say, that said: "Go and take the book from his hand, which standeth upon the sea and upon the earth! And I went unto him, and said unto him, Give me the book. And he said unto me, Take it, and eat it up! And it shall make thy belly bitter, but it shall be in thy mouth sweet as honey. And I took the book out of his hand, and ate it up; and it was in my mouth sweet as honey: and as soon as I had eaten it, my belly was bitter. And they said unto me, Thou must prophesy again, of the city's past, and its wall, and the movement of its history." Then did I go into the city so as to prophesy and perished in the city, and thus can I not prophesy, I say; and I do not say unto him that he, Father, shall die on August 20, 2014 because Zellen Warhol stenographed that onto his map of the city. The painting that I've had hanging here for years, Father says, is missing no book. If I get close enough to the painting, I see it, he says. In fact, the figure is holding a girdle book in his left hand. The leather of the book's cover, which is most likely made of wood, protrudes outward some twenty centimeters, with the help of the leather button at the end of the girdle, the book can be comfortably carried on one's person or perhaps worn from one's own girdle. Moreover, the unintentional opening of the book is prevented by clasps. I also would like a girdle to be made for my own book. What do you notice about the painting? Father asks. Nothing, I say. The figure in the painting resembles my father quite a bit, I realize, but do not say so. Father says that "the panel from the winged retable of an altar from around 1490 or 1500" shows a figure in episcopal regalia and with a "France-Ancien" coat of arms under a wall arcade and before a green landscape and a blue sky, which contrast nicely with the robe's cherry-red and blue-green, the brilliant white of the undergarment, and the rose-gray wall. The whole of it in oil upon parquetted oak-wood, about one and a half meters high and a half meter wide. When Father then speaks of a Pressbrokat of a golden shade, the feeling that I'm present at a sales conference creeps over me, I'm fed up with gazing at the painting. This doesn't concern Father. Is not the altar piece the origin of the landscape painting? he raves. Topographical representation is one part of landscape representation, he says, and the tapestry is both, landscape and topographical representation, and both serve the Lord and would be utterly unthinkable without a churchly background, after all, it is the Franciscan church from which the plaque comes that is in the foreground instead of the town hall. The secularization of cityscapes is always the result of militarization, he adds, then continues that it was with the greatest of diligence that he noted down all of the houses and streets within the bounds of the city wall upon his map, a fact that I will be able to see for myself on my impending tour through the city. He would like to draw my attention to a few more particulars, which are to be found in the market. I ought to take a very precise look at it, he says, then hands me a magnifying glass. I see three cannons or handcarts, a wooden horse, a gate-like construction made of two tall wooden posts, a crossbar embellished upon its sides, and a post with a centrally fitted curve, as well as a pointed tower. Spanish Donkey, gallows, and flogging post with attached pillory. He'd already entertained the notion of reintroducing this punitive ensemble, having extracted it from the life of the city more than three hundred years ago along with public burnings, the municipal timber industry suffered as a result, as everyone who bought wood at the wood market thought of the pyre, the Spanish Donkey, the gallows, and the flogging post, these were all examples of true craftmanship created using local wood, just like the things that one could buy at the market, Father says with a laugh that distorts his facial features. Then somebody else laughs inside of him, somebody he didn't prevent from being inside of him out of sheer carelessness. I've noticed this other on and in him since I was about four years old. This other is a kind of supervisory committee member who, if he has the slightest hunch that my father might be about to laugh, warns my father not to do so, he'll take care of it for him, and thus did my father almost never laugh, and if he did, it was always the other in him who allowed himself a bit of facial-feature-disfiguring mirth. The jurisdiction must begin in this house here, Father says, and thus is he considering renaming it "Haus zum Schwert" (or "Sword-House"), the reintroduction of medieval eating rituals is only a foretaste of grave changes in the administration of justice and their punitive consequences, all of which the future will bring with it as a result of the total transformation of Europe, which finds itself in a state of dissolution from the inside out and future is merely a murky synonym for present. If peoples wander, flee and wander, are expelled and flee, flee, and flee, this means that the Middle Ages are not far off, isn't that so, dear Isaac—but for real this time.

Father asks me whether I know what sort of map this is and shows me Zellen Warhol's map upon his own desk. Because I am his son, I say that I do not know. The map displays burn marks in some spots, in particular, the area around the pyre, which is not shown on the map, is severely affected. This is the first city map of our beautiful city, Father says, an etching by Zellen Warhol from 1634 and, as head of the city administration, I have the original in my possession, unfortunately, there are also a series of forgeries that are being misused, the bird's eye view allows one to gaze into every corner, nothing remains hidden from the interested eye, if one lets one's gaze linger on a certain spot for long enough, one imagines being able to observe unprecedented events, just as yesterday, when, he says, he couldn't decide whether he wanted to stretch out on the sofa in his office for a bit of calm or to use the time to finally tackle an administrative matter that had been put off for a long time, he took the map out of the secret compartment in his desk and allowed himself to be carried away, full of devotion, by its many wonderful details, just as when, before his very eyes, this was all in his imagination of course, somebody was burned alive in public, a poor devil had been stood up on the middle of the pyre and set alight, now, one might come to the conclusion that the burn marks on the map were caused by this event, at this mischievous remark, the other laughs forth once more from Father's face, but, here, he unfortunately had to disappoint, the burn marks were caused by cigarettes smoked while looking at the map, some ash had fallen from them, bits of it still glowing, this annoyed him beyond all measure and his annoyance grew into a rage, which almost ended with the destruction of the map, which he was already holding in his two hands, wishing to tear it in half. You would do the same, says Father, you always want to destroy things that don't obey you or that you have accidentally damaged, then you're overcome by the wrathful need to punish things, to finish what you started, to turn the minor damage, which, when calmly considered, is hardly worth mentioning, into a total write-off, which, in turn, throws you into such a rage that you also want to punish the immediate surroundings of destroyed things and only complete exhaustion gets you to cease, you observe the devastation and feel genuine sadness, for some moments, you are entirely alone with yourself. In our society, this cannot remain without consequence, this being alone with oneself, I already suspect that the ash-stick of the cigarette is going to snap and this premonition tears me out of my self, as it does each time when yet another cigarette simply burns up during the observation of the map, not once do I take a drag from cigarettes after I've set them alight, they're nothing more than the servants of the impatience of the impending reflection, which has to be overcome in order to work through an intellectual achievement that belongs to the modern world 666 times, an achievement guided by a deeper principle, it has a burdensome object as its subject and concerns a richer matter that is to be digested, but I must ever be content with what little the inevitable distraction by the greatness and versatility of the interests of the time allows, and, quoting Hegel Anno 1831, I ask myself "whether the noisy clamor of the day and the deafening chatter of a conceit" "might still leave room for partaking in the dispassionate calm of a knowledge dedicated to thought alone," for, while the whole of my thinking wants to concentrate on the reestablishment of the 1634 jurisdiction documented by Zellen Warhol and emanating from this map here as its only true task, the clamor of the day with all of its inconsequential busyness demands all of my time and thus is my life nothing but a perpetual distraction, which is, indeed, distracted in the direction of the map every now and again, only so as to then be immediately distracted from it once more. Father hands me a magnifying glass with the charge that I take a closer look at the marketplace with the old town hall. As I decipher the script on the roof of the old town hall, which becomes visible under the magnifying glass as "Vater," Father, bent low toward the sheet, reads "Luther." If anything, it says "Luder,"* I say. These are the differing interpretations belonging to two different generations, Father opines, then takes a second magnifying glass from a drawer in his desk, he now wants to observe the map together with me and is curious to see what else there is to uncover, he says, but advises caution, a too-intensive immersion in the streets,

---

* A person who can't be trusted or an animal-carcass used as bait.

squares, and houses might have the consequence of the eyes refusing to return to the four walls of the present. The wooden doll stands in the main market called Kornmarckt. When it catches sight of me, it jumps for joy and waves. Quickly, I pull the magnifying glass away. Did you also see them? Father asks. Who? The men hauling the wood. No. That's our street, they're hauling the trunks and planks past our future house and out of the city. Father has pulled up his armchair and is crouching motionlessly over the map with his magnifying glass. Without the magnifying glass, the doll appears as a small black spot on the paper. It really should be possible to crush this bug with Father's letter opener. A small hole is all that remains of it. A huge crater can be seen beneath the magnifying glass and the damage thus inflicted has become the talk of the town. But it's not that the doll has been done away with by this onslaught, rather, it stands at a safe distance, it shakes its fist and points toward the gallows. Should I say that to Father? Father is unresponsive, he's practically lying atop the map with his magnifying glass and staring at a certain point, which now also arouses my interest, he occasionally nods, whispers something tender, seems to be making promises. I hold a pencil over the paper, its end directed toward the doll, the doll shows itself to be unperturbed by this novel threat, it leaps up as if it could reach the pencil-point and grab hold of it. Then, it gives up this project and points toward the gallows once more. The doll begins to bore me, I straighten up and stand there, riddled with jealousy and a familiar childhood uneasiness that would always come on when I became aware of myself as the son of parents who were sitting upon the sofa of eggplant-colored leather, his parents' assessor, they didn't really have any use for their son, he's behind Father's armchair, Father doesn't seem to notice this. I want to cast my gaze over Father's shoulder with my magnifying glass and catch sight of the wood-market scenery his gaze is boring into so relentlessly, then I immediately see who Father is having this confidential conversation with, it is none other than Mateo, who is behaving like the greatest of wood-coordinators, he's commanding almost a dozen workers and also giving Father confidential signs likely meant to signal that he has everything under control, however, they also give the impression that Mateo has something to hide, when he perceives me, he pauses and seeks to draw Father's attention to me. Take a look at that, Father says, as if he wanted to make me think that he himself had only just noticed Mateo, for this Antonio really is a cunning cur, he's now acting as if he had just descended back into the seventeenth century, but will be right back. And yet, he's also engaged in shady business here. If I'm not mixing up the biographies of Mateo and Peter Ozianon, Mateo is the son of a clergyman who worshipped his father and never spoke of his mother. This man believes in the reality of his fantasies. Perhaps, Peter Ozianon was merely his fantasy or Peter Ozianon and Mateo are one person called either Peter Ozianon or Mateo or one is called Mateo and the other is called Peter Ozianon and both together are called Otto A. N. Anomie or they are called Antonio Atome, Father says. I am of the firm conviction, no, I *know* that another version is much more realistic: one of the two of them did away with the other. With poison. That he simply sought—like you—to put it into my mouth is incorrect. With the death of the other, he believes that he has made himself indispensable to me. Now, he must be thinking that I'm defenseless against his Machiavellian insinuations. He's a poisoner, I'm his true target, he wants to get rid of me in order to put himself in my place. He probably believes that I don't know this, but I don't mince words, I'm not going to mince words, he can listen in on all of that: What you've written about me and the black page and what you've had me say in your book from time to time, whenever you've found it appropriate and granted me the honor of letting me speak, is really quite a neat representation of your eccentric little imagination, now, unfortunately, it is too late to conjure this matter away and out of the book, after all, the truth is that no black page stands between us, but the poison is already taking effect within us. Are you claiming in all seriousness that I am Peter Ozianon's invention and that he is your invention? As a precaution, I had several versions of your book made so as to be able to bring out a different version depending on the occasion, such is my duty to my life. You ought to be able to say with a certain pride: for as long as my father lived, he interfered with my books. Mateo slowly slunk out of the image. Now, I'm going to show you something, Father says. The floor opens up underneath the desk, an electric concertina ladder extends out and lays its feet onto the ground, the light turns on. My library, Father says. Built into a mezzanine floor, invisible from the outside. You must go backward, Father says. Here are old, new, and future chronicles of the city, Father says, an entire shelf is reserved for the Church Fathers alone, here, you'll find the Luther Bible in all of its important editions, his German first had to be translated and it was frequently mistranslated, if one struggles against Luther, one must take on the original Luther. Here is so-called contemporary literature. I do not read it. It is not substantial enough for me. Nor is it broken or old. It ought to be noted that, here, I have only included as-of-yet unwritten and previously unpublished contemporary literature. You should be able to work out for yourself that its increase is endless. It's been scientifically proven, which is to say, I've scientifically proven that one need only take certain names out of circulation so as to render contemporary literature harmless to the outside world. As endless as its supply may be, its marginalization knows no bounds. Here, you see your book in about one hundred versions. Each version differs from every other version. If we can't get rid of this bad habit of yours—your perpetual lying, then selling these lies as books—even if this habit can't be entirely done away with, one can, at the very least, improve upon your lies and isn't it wonderful to imagine that everyone shall be reading a different *Schattenfroh*? Now, you're going to ask how that can be, after all, you haven't even written your book through to its end, we're still only on page 445. I've given a hundred third- and fourth-rate writers the opportunity to prove their mettle and the city teems with such luminaries, day in, day out, they set about their work, they have rewritten your pages, thus writing the book to its end, which, for most of them, was the simplest of tasks, your simple methods were quickly seen through. You're surely very curious to read how the ending might end differently. I recommend that you begin with this version here, starting on page 446, in such a way that you bring yourself more into line with reality, after which you can keep fantasizing about whether the script is black or white. In this way, if you ever don't know how to proceed, your unwritten book can be endlessly continued by merely taking another copy of your book into your hand and continuing your text from the point in that book where your book broke off. We would both benefit: you from the continuation and the liberation from need, me from the control. Whoever strives in ceaseless toil, him may we grant redemption, for you shall never cease until everything's dissolved.

The bookpages are blank. To devote oneself to reality. Father says, I ought not let myself be deceived, here, the following can clearly be read: "For, indeed, Mother did die." Whichever copy of *Schattenfroh* I take to hand, it contains only blank pages. Father laughs, don't you see, he says, now the sentence is in your copy and you can read it. If I say, the pages are all blank, though you can read all the pages, I say, then you would have to read everything to me aloud and I would have the sole option of accepting what you'd read. You must detain yourself here for a short while, then you shall be able to read the white script. I ask Father to read me some other sentences. "Sixteen years later, I see her once more. She's riding in an ICE from Berlin to Cologne. Her sleek gray hair has noticeably thinned. She's directing her strained gaze through rimless reading glasses." He reads with no hesitation, I can't be certain, however, whether he is merely simulating the act of reading, if that's the case, he is a marvelous storyteller, the sole difference being that these are not tales he is telling, but life itself, "telling" would also be the wrong way to put it, life flows forth fluidly from his mouth. And how am I meant to certify that you really are reading aloud here and not inventing? You're not, Father says, besides, there's no real distinction. As soon as I speak, I begin to depend on invention. Speaking is not capable of perception. Thus do I invent and, in speaking, I see that which I've invented. And that which I've invented sees me, it plots away, I haven't set eyes on Mateo in the last little while, I still only communicate with him by way of representatives and these substitute figures are pulling the wool over my eyes. Or do you really believe we just saw Mateo on the map? Incidentally, you're not the only one who would take all the variants of your book for unprinted paper, for only the author himself can't really read his own book, Father says. I ask him whether he might read three more sentences aloud for me. Father reads: "Everything seems interesting to her, the whole environs worthy of a look. But I know that she isn't actually interested in what she sees there. The 150,000 looks that she has left all distract from death." I would never ever write that, I say. You don't have to write that, it's already been written, Father says. He has things to do now and thinks it would be best if I stayed in his library for a couple of days, then I might work my way into the white script until everything goes black. Father hurries up the stairs, the hatch closes, the light goes out. Although the library has no window, it's not completely dark in the room. Something's burning in the Contemporary Literature section. Some books form a lighting device that produces a great deal of illumination, but outshines the books themselves in such a way that one can neither read their covers nor their pages. Upon opening one of them, you see straight into darkness. It only reveals its script when one removes a copy from the network of light and stands with it in the middle of the room. *Motherdying*. Father must have liked the glow of the cover so much that he ordered dozens of copies of the book, the corpus of the book serves to support the cover. If that is the purpose of this book, it is perhaps no small one in comparison with other books in this section. On the cover, the dark outline of my right hand can be seen. The engraving that the table burned into my hand is burnt into the cover. A city wall becomes visible and, before everything can start over again, I gobble down the book. First of all, I'm hungry, this is why I would rather not read, but eat. If the books are to be professionally cooked, they must be professionally gutted. If they're not to be professionally cooked, they must be gutted all the more professionally—if one doesn't wish to feel cheated of one's time. When they're hot off the press, it's easy to see past the ingredients and enjoy the way the teeth penetrate the crust. When they're very old, like, for example, old chronicles, they're probably less suitable for eating than they are for drinking. With a bit of luck, one might combine just such a crispy crust with an old red wine. Some books stand on Father's shelves like slices of cake. They look so tasty—as if they'd never been touched by human hands—yet one would not eat them, their exterior is too intrusive for one to be able to trust them. An artist-confectioner must have poured them directly onto the shelf with the finest of instruments. Here, for example, in the Contemporary Literature section, which, in comparison with the other sections, stands out by way of its unquestionably beautiful books, we have colorful and layered compositions, coated with rolled fondant and crowned with flowers from the piping bag. The art of baking makes these round loaves of bread superior to any content. Edible, but of low nutritional value. They make one hungry for more and do not sate. If one eats five of them in a row, one thinks oneself to have perceived a certain nullity in them.

The chronicles lie like stones in the belly. They're going to keep me awake all night. That's the history lesson at a young age. Startled awake at night, then recited numbers. The next day in class—twisted the numbers and a punch in the belly. Numbers have been sacred ever since. Goethe 1749 to 1832. Threethreethree Issusenlistee. Sixsixsix was nothing, but much can be conceived of. The number lurches about before my eyes, it flies through space, it's three unfinished pretzels, three Schweinekringel, three upside-down hand grenades. Pomegrenades. For, verily, the Church Fathers are inedible. Their substance shall not be digested, it must be swallowed whole and excreted whole, which tremendously overstrains one's anus. If one eats them, one has eaten dogma and torture, which many of them, seated with all their letters upon the Holy WSee, considered to be an appropriate means of Christian conversion.

Depending on the copy in question, *Schattenfroh* can smell and taste like various different things. Earthy like wild boar, spicy-sweet like Teltow turnips, putrid like overripe jackfruit. Not a single page of the copies is printed. They are the raw material for hours of solemn palate ceremonies.

So, what is it I am to eat? I eat Thomas Mann and Franz Kafka. Both take a long time to chew through. Kafka keeps you satiated for a long time, it only takes half a page or a page, which I eat as I read aloud, I understand it immediately; then the feeling of satiety sets in and I immediately forget it. For the most part, I eat Thomas Mann chapter by chapter, artfully long noodles are hidden on some pages, I take care not to cut them up, I suck up the whole snake and, when evil bites me, if, for example, I don't know how to continue my book, I look at the snakes disappearing into my mouth, and I shall be healed. In my belly stands a cross and the snakes wrap around it. The snakes make "Nachash," but the cross appeases them. If I close my eyes, I see one of the snakes devour the cross, the cross is completely enshrouded within the snake, 358 days pass in just a few seconds, then the snake counts to 358 and the Messiah counts to 358, then the snake's skin falls from the cross, it appears in radiant new splendor. The belly recognized the snake's cunning: that it wished to act as the Savior.

Kafka tastes slightly metallic, Thomas Mann, on the other hand, is reminiscent of traditional fare, which, if in doubt, one can retreat to anywhere in the world. Sometimes Bratwurst with mashed potatoes, sometimes roast beef with red cabbage and potato dumplings. But a lot of Thomas Mann necessarily means a lot of bowel movements, Father didn't think of installing a toilet down here. For me, *Schattenfroh* acts as a toilet-paper dispenser, thus do I shit into my own book. And, in miraculous fashion, the blank pages absorb the smell, while, simultaneously, the digested Thomas Mann makes the white script legible, for, when I unroll the digested Thomas-Mann Turd from one page and onto the next, I can read from this version of my book most merrily, from it do I hereby resolve to take many a useful thing into the ur-script of the original, into which, and this sentence should make it abundantly clear, Thomas Mann has already long since found his way in the form of long sentences, which, and I must admit that I have not yet witnessed this, not infrequently express nothing more than themselves. Father thus ended up being right, the white script turns into its opposite by way of the mouth. I ask myself whether Aristotle was thinking of incorporation and digestion when he wrote about the art of reading invisible signs. Or did he not write about that? But surely he knows ways out of the labyrinth of script, in which I've already been for so long. I shall search out Aristotle and prefer not to bellyache, at least for the time being, perhaps I am compelled to eat the entire library, then the ceiling hatch shall open up, the staircase shall extend out, and I shall be able to climb out into the light of day as a man who's made his way with words alone. Did I say that some books are superb to drink? I ought to read back over what I've written. Everything is taken care of for the time being. If I find Aristotle among my Father's books, I will eat him when hunger begins to plague me, even if I still haven't read of his *ways out*; would I read him even if, in reading him, I ran the risk of starving to death?

    I can't help but gobble down all copies of the book with the glowing cover. The result is a growing darkness. Mother is dead and I am now gobbling down her death. About whom were we speaking in Father's office when we were talking about Mommy? Was she still alive then? Can there be no conversation about death and each conversation about our deceased dear ones begins within our own lives? Or have years passed between the conversation and the statement, "Mother is dead"? The last copy of the book gives off at least enough light that I can use it to read from the various versions of *Schattenfroh* and, at the same time, write. However, the joy of this circumstance does not last for long, for, while the aggregate of several copies has sustained itself in its luminosity or, at least, hasn't diminished over time, a single book, as I now ascertain, seems to lose its illumination with relative rapidity. Thus is there no time for a relaxed reading, quick decisions are required—"come together and thus do local coalitions form up at a higher level of strictly hostile "/" weapons. Then, with no warning, I've become a war correspondent and can recall Jefferson Tuff-Tuff, who as a reporter for the Oxford Times, decided that Indians" / "Most of the books that I see around me have become ruins. There are torn pages lying about everywhere, the chronicles of the city" / "be Worte von Kanzeln[*] or Rotz wenn Alkoven[†] or Walkern von Zoten[‡] or Konzert von Walen[§] or Walzten von Krone[¶] or Konnte von Walzer[**]" / "wrangle tidings of the enemy. But Herse didn't know that and Michael didn't leave him behind as a spy at Tronkenburg, for neither of them had" / "penalty payment of €1200. I am now riding comfortably in first class, riding backward, which, for the time being, doesn't bother me in the slightest, for, some twelve meters away from me, across the aisle and on a seat facing in the direction of travel in such a way that I can thoroughly study her, sits my mother, sixteen years before her death"—I shall at the very least take on the passage with Mother on the ICE, the

---

[*] Words von Pulpits.
[†] Snot if Alcoves.
[‡] Walkers von Dirty Jokes.
[§] Concert von Whales.
[¶] Waltzes von Crown.
[**] Could von Waltz.

beginning of which Father read aloud, perhaps I shall copy out the rest as well, is what I resolve, having almost finished eating the penultimate copy of the glowing book. It doesn't quite fit in here, but what does? The task of literature is to remember the dead. First, my own book must come so as to remind me that Mother has not been alive for a long time. And this book is about to expire: I eat up the last remaining copy. With this sentence, the writing script begins to shine and it lights the way for the script: That is Mother. The faint outward reflection is strong enough to make the contours of the environs visible. Something is brewing, it stops me from copying down the passage. I am down here in a graveyard and I am part of the graveyard. After the death of his wife, my father perpetually sought to put a stop to literature. And the dead really can't stand one another. "All city chronicles stink," a book calls out from the Contemporary Literature section, it must be one of the versions of *Schattenfroh*, it calls out for the umpteenth time, and, in the blink of an eye, this graveyard becomes a battlefield. Some of the books spill forth from the shelves as a spineless mass and fill the abyss like the water of two waterfalls across from one another, for, barely have they reached the midpoint between the two shelves when they tumble into an invisible chasm. Others seek out their own paths and attack anyone who gets in their way, they cannot be recognized under cover of darkness, alliances arise by chance—by way of touch or, more specifically, by calling out sentences that the book quotes from its insides. At times, this brings the soldiers of Contemporary Literature into a rage—them most of all—so much so that they hew the self-citing one in twain, set him alight, then drag him by his ribbon-bookmark to the abyss where he shall be snatched away by the spineless or be nailed to the ground on the very spot, an act at which the Schattenfroh-Army really excels, this is how I come to the conclusion that the books can only use the methods mentioned if they are described within them or if, for example, they use the words "hammer" and nail."

The city chronicles, all of which only deal with the city in which

I find myself, fight with the cutting and stabbing weapons depicted in them, they're from the evidence rooms and armories of town halls. A double-page with the city wall spread open, they march forward, cannon shots cracking and felling all books that get in their way. The chronicles do indeed smell musty; Father also seems to have provided those whose time hasn't yet come with a preemptive mustiness, they really stink, it isn't at all possible to manufacture artificially stale time. As magnificent as the idea of endowing as-of-yet unwritten books with a scent appropriate to their genre is, he was given poor counsel when implementing the nose-program. While I ask myself whether the city chronicles of the future are destiny and represent an irrevocable cityscape, or whether, perhaps, if they were made available to the public, they would be so daunting that one would undertake every conceivable option to save the city from its future appearance, the Contemporary Literature section goes on the attack against the chronicles with sharp words, battle choruses formed up shouting "Reek," "Bodice," and "Slipcase," out of which it is the last word in particular that dazes me, slip, sleep, slipping, to slip away, to sleep in a slipcase, the slipcase's reek? The force of the words knocks the insulted one off of his feet, then, instead of just dying away, the words remain airborne at their point of impact, injuring anyone who comes into contact with them. Other choruses call out "Fugue," "Sword," and "Shaft," and the words pass through the chronicles like a sword. These words also remain right where they are, the sword shall immediately be used for a drumhead trial, representatives of Contemporary Literature and their allies haul in enemy books and traitors from their own section, then lop off their titles, thus making them anonymous, outlaws, they can be pecked away at by any man or any woman at their whim and fancy, defiled and torn to bits, and quite a few of them who have, in their turn, been disgraced or lost their safe haven of alphabetical location and no longer have any sense of orientation that comes from within themselves take total advantage of them, as one can see, at which point friend and foe come together and thus do local coalitions form up at a higher level of strictly hostile factions, which are reunited in humane fashion by the ubiquitous delight to be found in slaughter. If it is often in vain that one searches for ultimate justifications, especially as regards questions about the meaning of life—for answers that are at the very least consoling, if not meaningful—it is here that one unmediatedly receives the information as soon as one has finished pronouncing the question: "I really enjoy this" or "I just do this for fun" or "Fun." If the sword begins to still itself, it finds this hard to take, I see with my own eyes how it scuttles about restlessly in place, leaps from tip to pommel, then back once more, and, with tremendous swiftness, as if launched from a catapult, decapitates one of the very books from the mouth of which it emerged. This inevitably leads to disputes as to the moral nature of, not only this particular weapon, but of many other weapons, all of which culminate in the question of what the sword-bearer is still worth once the sword has assigned itself the task of killing. The contemporaries, who all of a sudden no longer understand the state of the world, which has, up until this point, seemed, if not exactly self-explanatory, then still controllable, become unexpectedly anxious, a bewilderment inadequately dubbed to be mere tension, as is common practice when more concrete descriptions of existential worries are to be avoided so as not to entirely demoralize people, in fact, this is done so that they have models of inner strength by which they might orient themselves, models that enable them to face the abyss with courage and, should someone wish to prevent this, they would surely be able to beat them around the head with their models, in any case, the first issue the uncertainty raised would be the development of weapons able to protect them from their own weapons. Then, with no warning, I've become a war correspondent and can recall Jefferson Tuff-Tuff, who as a reporter for *The Oxford Times*, decided that Indians had to be photographed, could they please stand still for just a minute, as a friend of all Indians, he'd like nothing more than to make a nice image out of them, which I myself can't seem to manage with words, this obstinate book of all things proves to be so highly versatile that I can no longer recognize any book at all in certain copies of it, back here in the corner, for example, sits one, it's writing, and I really would like to know whether it's a mere copyist or a self-writer, when, under the shelf behind my back, another book comes into my gaze, it's assiduously making paper airplanes from its own pages, which shows that one ought only go round in circles and the world is already presenting itself from the back with its side turned away, so versatile, I say, that, in the moment, I don't know which stylist is guiding my pen, which I myself really am not really guiding at all, I must have changed sides to the camp of the old-fashioned, which my father clearly seems to prefer, one no longer needs to read old-fashioned books, one possesses them, and no visitor dares to remove them from the shelf, their place is fixed to the millimeter, manuevering them back onto the shelf would be tantamount to a declaration of war on God, the Church Fathers, and domestic order as well, of which the first principle goes "It is what it is," which can be read as the First Article of the Cologne Constitution. It ought not to be concealed that there are also exhibitionists among the books, in many senses, these exhibitionists extrapolate the question of reading and digestion by way of elimination. This one here, a braggart, leafs through each of its pages and removes the script line by line like cobwebs. Even if the book is nothing but a woven thing, the script is still not nothing, is what I thought until just now, this book teaches me better. Fleeting is the book and homeless the script. In the midst of the tumult of battle sits a book that I'd like to dub *The Child*, it has folded little books out of the loose sheets that it has found here and there, it is playing war with them most merrily, it pits the playbooks, the folding of which it has performed with such diligence, against one another, until all that's left are clumps of paper compressed in on themselves, it shows itself to be so disappointed by the durability of its toys that, with nothing in hand but these crumpling clods, it turns its rage onto itself,

I can already see it running most merrily against the wall, head first, thereby breaking its own neck.

Franz Kafka keeps to himself off to the side, he is impenetrable, attempts to attack him with a thrusting weapon founder pitifully. He does not take part in the fighting of his own accord, while Thomas Mann first has to be animated to intervention by his daughter. His speeches are lost in the tumult of battle and, during periods of abruptly arising silence, one notes how out of place they seem in view of the attacking Middle Ages.

Most of the books that I see around me have become ruins. There are torn pages lying about everywhere, the chronicles of the city have pounced on the art albums and torn them to bits, only a few pages are still intact, most are folded, creased, torn, pierced, crumpled. Loose pages from albums of the work of Grundlos,[*] Bewache,[†] Gebieter,[‡] and Kulte[§] wander about in search of their own kind, already, they are planning to come together into albums once more, once they've recognized each other, a book from the Contemporaries suddenly cries out: "Hold your tongue." I can't rid myself of the impression that this rather rude demand is being made to me, for, immediately afterward, I hear the sentence again, and, this time, the book—and we're dealing with quite a voluminous novel—stands directly before me and is at the point of shimmying up my right trouser leg, simultaneously and incessantly pointing at my mouth, while dozens of small books are already rushing toward it, they grow to be as voluminous as the library's available editions, and if I don't step off to the side, they will bury me, from whose mouth they emerge. Already, books from all factions are drawing attention to me, they claim me as the cause of their devastating disputes, after all, my mouth does not distinguish

---

[*] Groundless.
[†] Guard.
[‡] Master.
[§] Cults.

between chronicles, novels of old and modern times, or many other categories, as the great leveler, it allows everything to fall into disorder, as if the alphabet and library had never existed. I can still get rid of the grouser, it flies against the wall with a pretty noise as only paper can, I can't manage that so easily with the books following behind it, the entire library collection has dispersed and turned against me, the books leap at me and claw up my pants, I pluck off the first few attackers, then they become too many, thus does a torrent of books slip forth from my mouth, immediately going after the pants-claws. Books have no morality, but the fact that they can fall upon one another so ruthlessly, as I am experiencing here, makes them completely and utterly equal to humans. "First did he gobble us down, now is he vomiting us back up," one of the pants-claws says. "Gobbled down and undigested," says another, tearing off at the sight of the mouth-books and hiding itself beneath a shelf. "In me is it written that he invented the library, and with it were we also merely invented," says one of the future city chronicles, this shall immediately be understood by all books present in its intent to generate outrage and to identify me as the sole true enemy, they believe that they must band together to fight me. "If he invented us, but, as a book-eater, is dumb as paper that allows itself to be imprinted by any content that comes along (it is better not to have been read by him), then we should let him disappear down below, an author such as him, an eternally empty field that cannot even bear its own fruit cannot possibly bring about our ornamentation," the future city chronicle knows how to bring the mood to a boil and it is decided that they shall bury me beneath a book-mountain, a task that the one hundred copies of *Schattenfroh* volunteer to undertake, this is universally hailed with assurances of energetic support and, in this moment, I recognize that Father staged the Book War so as to do away with me with my own weapons. Weapons? I run over to the wall behind me and take the wooden handle with the opening rod from the device-holder. Mateo must be behind the whole affair, he must have whispered this maneuver into Father's ear when they were having such an animated discussion, one of them in office and the other in city map. More and more books are piling up from the shelves and they swell into a mountain of corpses. At times, the books reach up to my neck, I sink down into the books or they carry me upward. Many books skitter away, others push off in their wake, at the top currently lies an open city chronicle from the year 2964, Zellen Warhol's city map is visible, Mateo stands by the pillory in the form of my father and stretches his hands out toward me, I look away, look back once more, then see myself hanging from the gallows, the chronicle is torn away, down into the depths of the book-mountain. The mountain doesn't seem to grow any more, I remain between heaven and earth, the skylight is about a half-meter away, I spring into the air, slip on the books, and am on the verge of plunging down the mountain between books and wall, it costs an enormous effort to crawl back to the mountain's peak, clinging onto it is my only possibility of reaching the hatch before the books on the ceiling crush me, nobody would ever find me down here, the smell of old books would cover the reek of my decay, I can use the opening rod to keep the most aggressive books away from my body, I don't take my eyes off of them even for a moment, if I were to seek to open the roof hatch with the opening rod, they would attack me, now, a slim book lies at the peak, it does not wish to give up its true title, as I leaf through it, I don't have the feeling that my situation shall change in the next few minutes, I had always intended to re-read this book very attentively, but always found some kind of excuse for not doing so, I am sure that the whimsical old woman's message upon the notorious scrap is intended for me and if I could extract it from the book that houses the scrap without the scrap itself being read, I would have the Open Sesame and, liberating myself from this distress, could leave the library through the ceiling. Now, I have no more excuses, I start from the beginning, fending off the cheekiest books with the stick, and there are precisely two and a half sentences that I cannot forestall myself from applying to my current situation: "Until his thirtieth year, this unusual man would have been accounted the very model of a good citizen. In the village that still bears his name, he owned a farm that provided him with a comfortable living; the children his wife gave him he brought up in the fear of God, to be hardworking and loyal; there was not one among his neighbors who hadn't benefited from his charity and his fair dealing; in sum, the world would have blessed his memory, if he hadn't followed one of his virtues to excess. His sense of justice led him to robbery and murder." I make a wager with myself that, before the mountain once more sets itself into motion, I shall be able to read the whole text as attentively as if it'd sprung forth from me and I had to prepare it to be printed and, in spite of my position, I find myself with an advantage over its author, who pre-published one part of it before he'd finished writing all of it. One can easily establish whether a book is still alive or already dead if one seeks to open it. An infallible sign of its aliveness is if it struggles not to be opened by pulling its boards inward and against its pages. One thinks the book has something to hide or that its contents are depraved, perhaps one only thinks that because the book hopes that one thinks that, then, while one thinks that and resolves to pay no further attention to the book, one is already in the process of pulling the boards apart with all one's might, which brings the book perceptible joy, it allows a gap to open up and it makes use of this moment of astonishment to close itself up all the tighter once more, also transmuting its title anew with each passing moment, first it is called *Alaska, hohle mich*,* then *Ich, Haskell Omaha*,† now it is called *Lakai, hohle Scham*,‡ and, soon, the title changes itself to *Hohle Hacksalami*,§ a title

---

* *Alaska, Call Me Hollow.*
† *I, Haskell Omaha.*
‡ *Lackey, Hollow Shame.*
§ *Hollow Hashsalami.*

that could only be the result of a totally distorted gaze. If one proves oneself to be the stronger party, it can come to pass that a foul-smelling substance spreads through the book, which makes all the pages stick together, they dissolve in a matter of seconds, and one ends up sticking one's fingers into pulp. It becomes most uncomfortable when a little gap opens in the book's pages and one pushes one's fingers into the gap, then the book snaps shut once more with such pressure that it brings tears into one's eyes. I know what I'm talking about, for I've only just managed to free my right hand from a book that indiscriminately allows everything that would test its depth to penetrate it, I've also seen other books vanish into this book, they were much larger and more voluminous. This book, *Michael Kohlhaas*, containing the most beautiful prose in the German language, is dead, all hostility has fled from it. But its spirit is all the more alive. Here, the sentence structure is the executive that executes itself, the long sentences execute the indignation that stems from a growing sense of injustice, the short ones execute Michael's composure, which perpetually demands that only a pointed baseness be brought forth—and the sequence of sentences, the alternation of short and long ones as the sequentiality that characterizes human affairs, of events and the reactions to them, is the smoldering, surging, raging, calming oneself anew, accumulating, diverting, refusing, devouring, flayed, torn body, in which everything is bundled up, the body that attracts everything, then hurls everything away from itself, an uproar-poetic of the inner current that causes the body to twitch through the country, and the twitch is the pen against paper, shorthand of the mind and psychography. The scrap is a virus, and the old woman brings death; from century to century, the scrap on which the death of fathers is written moves toward the construction of a new order, of a bourgeois, then a post-bourgeois order, and the scrap's addressee is the body of the population, and the scrap innoculates the body with the word "Partisan," incessantly whispering, "partisan partisan partisan" until the body obeys this command, the text is an absolute command that works within and from within, and if the body is attacked from without, then it must truly be able to turn the scrap-tide from within, as the message that this attack has occurred is heard everywhere. *Michael* is the text of the hour and there have been so many Michaels and the steeds have become God's affair and the West is one great Tronkenburg and the content of the scrap, from which one can read what shall soon come to pass, knows only Godisgreat, and Godisgreat has sent these weird women all round the world and the Michaels go proudly to their deaths, while the electors of the world go to their downfall. Upon the scrap, which is addressed to me, is written my father's name, the date he lost his kingdom, and the name of the one who shall snatch it away by force of arms. Thus is it written. But the name of my father is not the name of my father, it's no name at all, it is that which contains its goal within itself, the ur-iginally active potency, the longing for expansion, entelechy, energeia, soul, and, if it runs dry, I must write it back, and if it's been written to its end and is in dissolution, then it shall have returned.

Give me the scrap, I demand of Michael, do not swallow it, centuries have passed without being able to do harm to the contents of the scrap, give it to me and I shall deliver you from the red-hot tongs, from the quartering and burning. How would you do that, he asks me. I shall read you anew and translate you into my time, then the old text shall no longer find you, the ulcer, unnoticed by all except for the weird old woman, whom the text has thought up so as to lure the reader as elector and the elector as unwilling non-reader, I come and go with you through the terrain of the text, which has its beginning upon the toll barrier and, just as you cannot overcome the toll barrier out of which the text emerges—for you do not possess the required pass—the reader, who is also missing this pass, cannot negotiate the text, the truth is that no such pass exists, there are only the spies and the militants, I walk your stations and transfer them to my terrain and, by my reading you anew, you come to live in me. And, with the end of the book, the inner and outer hunt is also at an end, the right to feud and the right to resist are pacified, and, if I read you from beginning to end once more, you become I, your text is called *Schattenfroh*. And in this text can now be read that Michael's groom Herse, also most humbly to be known from the words "vorhersehbar"—"foreseeable"—and "sächsischerseits"—"from the Saxon Electorate"—is, as well his name suggests, wheel-broken into a seer by the lords of Tronkenburg and their thugs, and, as such, a spy, whom Michael smuggled into Tronkenburg in accordance with the practice of Frederick the Great, as he describes in detail in his *Fundamentals of Warfare*, Chapter 14, "Spies and their usage and how to wrangle tidings of the enemy." But Herse didn't know that and Michael didn't leave him behind as a spy at Tronkenburg, for neither of them had read the *Fundamentals*, but, in sooth, the lords of the castle had and here I ask myself how it can be possible that someone in the middle of the sixteenth century can read a text that shall only appear some hundred years later. What, then, was Herse meant to be spying on? Nothing less than what the chances were of sweeping away this Tronkenburg system of privilege and nepotism, the squire Wenzel von Tronka has been hurtling through his properties day in, day out and asking himself for how much longer he'll be around as Wenzel von Tronka, when shall I be Worte von Kanzeln or Rotz wenn Alkoven or Walkern von Zoten or Konzert von Walen or Walzten von Krone or Konnte von Walzer or Torkel von Wanzen* or Von Zarten Wolken† or Kloent von Warzen‡ or Lektor von Wanzen,§ just as Herse is Heers Seher.¶ And it is said that Herse exaggerated and lied, nearly losing his life as a result of exaggeration and lies near Mühlberg during the nocturnal ambush upon Prince Friedrich von Meissen, after which

---

* Winepress von Bedbugs.
† Von Tender Clouds.
‡ Chat von Warts.
§ Lector von Bedbugs.
¶ Army Seer.

he, much like this text, was painstakingly reassembled, after having been clobbered from his horse by the Steward of Tronkenburg, then kicked and beaten and whipped by him and his servants, then almost torn apart by twelve dogs. And Kohlhaas? Is he a spy? Does he wish to spy out Leipzig? And is Tronkenburg a mere outpost? And did the castellan, who was appointed by Wenzel von Tronka as chief of counter-intelligence, receive a telegram regarding his arrival? To that purpose, one ought to read Safran Hake,** which can be read here.

The library is now filled with books up to just below the ceiling, my head almost touching the hatch. Something acting invisibly is what frightens us most, I do not see the books that have thus raised me up and shall soon crush me, I have likely read all too few of them, and, yet, they are the most meaningful books of my life. Give me the scrap, I say to Michael, there isn't much time. He has appointed himself as Governor of Michael the Archangel, my Napoleon is my father. I hang the wooden stick with the opening rod in the built-in cabinet, but the stacked-up books prevent the closing of its lower lid, as well as the concertina stair attached to it. I take *Michael* between my teeth and use the rod to remove the peak of the book-mountain, the books finally reveal the staircase, it allows itself to be pulled out a bit, I open *Michael* once more, just as one opens a jewelry box, there, preserved in a capsule and sealed with moon-shaped sealing wax that must be wet with the mouth, the scrap lies in the book, I open the capsule, break the seal, the scrap is blank. Eat it up, I hear the voice of an old woman, then you shall be able to read it. I eat it up. The desk tips over slowly and all the things upon it begin to slide, the coffee cup upon the broken coaster, the hole puncher and the stapler, the tape dispenser and the bottle opener, the round photo with Grandpa and Lassie, a Boxer, in front of a tinsel-bedecked Christmas tree, the bottle of Japanese mint oil and the page-markers, the little Bose loudspeakers,

---

** Saffron Hake.

the wooden box with the writing utensils, the wooden book holder, which can be adjusted to any thickness of book, but which only serves for the filing-away of bills, all the paperwork from last year's taxes, the big screen and the books, all of it slowly slipping away, and I enjoy this liminal situation, behind the sloping desk, the world has come to an end, on the screen, I can now clearly read SCHATTENFROH AUGUST 20 2014 MATEO, I pierce it with the opening rod, instead of the spring lock, a button for opening the hatch appears upon it illuminated in green, three folding steps lead into the interior of an ICE train from Berlin to Cologne, I am wearing a dark suit, my small rolling suitcase is held in my left hand and runs silently over the carpet, in my right hand do I bear *Michael*, I'm still far from finished with it, the compartment is sparsely occupied, however, the few travelers are sitting so inconveniently distributed that all the seats I consider are already occupied, I'd prefer not to make contact with anyone, nor to sit directly across from or across the aisle from anyone, nobody ought to sit behind me or in such a way that they can observe my actions at any given time, whereas I cannot do the same without drawing attention to myself, contrary to my proclivity, I choose a seat facing opposite the direction of travel, I think of *Michael* as a sharp weapon that I can drive straight into the brains of my undesirable fellow passengers, I order a cup of coffee from the conductor, if someone makes a loud phone call or has a loud conversation, I feel compelled to comment on the conversation at the same volume, first sitting, then standing, then, finally, with violence, but everything remains calm, the coffee burns my tongue, I cannot recall whether I packed the aftershave or the deodorant with aluminum in my suitcase, I also only wear slim fit, not regular like this gray shirt here, plastic soles beneath leather shoes are a horror and if one already uses shoe trees and takes them with on trips, they ought to be equipped with a heel wood that fits over the heel cap and double telescope springs, in general terms, the whole suitcase is foreign to me. I fear that there might well be unsavory things in it and that I shall soon be arrested, a friend reported that conductors were incredibly jumpy due to the so-called refugee crisis, in each passenger, they sensed a fleeing fare-dodger, my friend drank too much on a hot summer night in Munich, then fell asleep in his seat and failed to produce his ticket within thirty seconds, which resulted in a torn leather belt, bruises, and abrasions on the back, all inflicted by police officers who kicked and dragged, handcuffs down to the bone, the loss of his luggage, time spent in a cell, a written summons with an attached allegation of bodily harm and resistance to state authority, which led to a penalty payment of €1200. I am now riding comfortably in first class, riding backward, which, for the time being, doesn't bother me in the slightest, for, some twelve meters away from me, across the aisle and on a seat facing in the direction of travel in such a way that I can thoroughly study her, sits my mother, sixteen years before her death, and if she speaks, the weird old woman speaks forth from her, the one who gave Michael the scrap, and when the man next to her reassuringly says, "Yes, Lisbeth, let's do it like that" or "Just so, Lisbeth" or "Of course, Lisbeth," then do I hear my father, who no longer bears any grudge in his voice, though it always used to thunder against me when Mother's health was at issue. Her sleek gray hair has thinned noticeably. She's directing her strained gaze through rimless reading glasses. Everything seems interesting to her, the whole environs worthy of a look. But I know that she isn't actually interested in what she sees there. The 150,000 looks that she has left all distract from death. She has to look somewhere. In her face, I believe that I can already perceive a hint of the death penalty. Living dead. No more interests, thus can one rummage through one's suitcase quite extensively, looking for the face cream, while telling the conductor that you don't want any coffee now, not for the time being, but that coffee shall definitely be welcome later on. Later is quite a short span of time, my mother's sunken cheeks become all the more sunken if I watch her for long enough. A sizable crater emerges toward the middle of one cheek, it deepens even more when my mother bites down on her teeth. Perhaps she's in pain, perhaps she wishes to establish how much strength her jaws can still muster. The teeth of cancer patients are often in poor condition, they take on a brownish shade and look as if they were hollow. My mother has a collection of small china cups that were only drunk from when her ladies would come to visit, but the ladies died off, one by one. Once only Frau Briefhof remained, my mother no longer wished to hold her little afternoon coffee hour, it was only with great difficulty that one could converse with Frau Briefhof, my mother said, Frau Briefhof stared perpetually out ahead of her or out the window in the direction of the garden, which was, after all, so big that two soccer teams could have fit on the grass. There used to be a pheasant that would make its rounds at about seven on summer evenings. Once it had finished with its rounds, it would always stand in the middle of the lawn with its tail beautifully arrayed, it seemed ready and willing to be cast in bronze. My parents said that certainly couldn't be the case, a pheasant in the garden, well, they must have been right, it really couldn't be, for the pheasant came no longer. The pheasant is *suddenly* not coming anymore, they said, and I asked myself what meaning this "suddenly" bore, and as I write this down, on September 25, 2014, at 1:54 p.m. on a Deutsche Bahn train, in the same first-class carriage as my mother, here, in my father's hidden library where one can find photo albums that we never came across as children, the photographs showed vulnerable people, shy and in need of help, before they became dashing and sublimely superior to their own childhoods once more, our parents didn't want to show this—that they had been just as small and dependant as their own children, who had no notion of this, if the children were to have seen the faces of Father and Mother, their submissive posture, wouldn't they from then on have opined that they were dealing with their own kind and wouldn't the parents' authority thus have been destroyed? Mother and Father's own ways of speaking were also a reflection of their own parents, whose death was to be mourned for the rest of their lives, that's the truest form of impudence this life has in store, that parents one day set off into dust, while leafing through the daily newspaper, for which I put *Michael* off to the side for just a little while and which, what with its commentaries and catastrophes, distracts me from *these* catastrophes in wondrous fashion, but distracts me most of all from my own life, a story by Wolf suddenly comes to me, one that makes clear to the reader what this "suddenly" is all about, I am able to read it from my memory as follows: I suddenly get up at night and am thinking of nothing. Whatever I look at disappears, dissolves, was never there, everything except for a white wall surrounding me, I can't look at it because of its brilliant white, I know that it's there. Suddenly, I notice that I am alone and I am standing alone in a room, which I suddenly forget is my own. If, first of all, I'm already here, I suddenly realize that it really is me who is suddenly here. Thus is it not the room, not present to me, that is of interest or has suddenly grown dangerous, I am the very thing that can become dangerous to me. If I really did get up so suddenly and am standing in the middle of the room, then something must have made me get up and stand in the middle of the room, is what I'm still thinking when I suddenly think of the word "suddenly," or, rather, I say it, then turn around in shock, for somebody really did say "suddenly." I opt to search for something, as the "suddenly" is the act of searching itself, thus do I act as if I were searching for something. I suddenly forget for how long I've been searching, but I find myself once more on the opposite wall of the room, which, also as observed from this side, has forfeited none of its unsayingness, in any case, I can't make out any variation in the white of the wall, on one side or the other, this fact moves me to once more go down the path to the opposite wall so as to get a clearer view of this wall, from which I just parted. No, it's of the very same white and there's really no wall at all, the wall is round and I walk along it with my head along the white, entirely immersed in my thoughts, there must be a bed here, for, if I suddenly got up, and I have the distinct feeling that I did get up, I presumably got up to change the diaper of a very small child, the child struggles with digestion, just like most children of its young years, usually, however, only urine is to be found in the diaper in the morning, the green grass worked over by its intestines shall only find its way into the diaper over the course of the day and, if it hasn't been properly fastened to the body, shall also find its way out over the body, *alright, then,* I suddenly say, then everything is very much in order, I changed a child's diaper. But that is not the case, though it would be nice, and I do love children, my own most especially, there is neither changing table nor bed here, I don't think I simply changed the child's diaper in the air, I suddenly imagine myself wrapping the child in air, then it falls down, it falls from my hands, and I suddenly resolve to catch it with my foot, but I can't see my foot anywhere, thus does it fall and fall, luckily, then, it suddenly occurs to me that it fell into the world as well and in such a way that falling cannot be its true problem, it must therefore be to do with a transition that's not within my purview. The child suddenly speaks. It is my face that lies there cracked upon the floor. The ears in this room hear well. My face is told that these are its ears, but the ears are everywhere. Suddenly, it becomes clear to me that "suddenly" doesn't exist at all.

    Wolf expressed himself much more succinctly than that. A retelling always revolves around the lost middle, its circles expanding outward ever more widely, thus, in the end, does a retelling lose not only what is to be retold, which it knows to be unattainable from the outset, but also itself. The pheasant disappeared from my childhood and took the "suddenly" with it, for there could be no pheasant, my parents deemed it to be unlikely. My parents had the final word and the animals complied.

If I close my eyes, I'm back in the library's white carousel and what I'm reading *is*. If we assumed that the white of the wall was nothingness, that it could not be, then it would still be both white and wall, this wall as nothing would be a shimmering glacial till in perpetual motion, I would interpret everything as an expression that is to signal change for fractions of a second, given that this white wall really would contain everything that I would have to make even remotely present as information. Initially, I would assign any deviation from the former state of affairs to the wall, but then, if no blatantly new condition were to manifest itself in the unmanageable, it's not as if there were much room for change, but, if there were, dust would potentially begin to gather, after all, there would have to be air in the room, in which the wall would surround me, if I were to begin to turn the wall inward, where I would be incapable of resisting its observation, it would yellow, but, within me and in my inner language, the wall is green, green streaks of different gradations flowing past it, down it, I can penetrate into the green wall, it is the Wunderblock of myself, pure script that has not coagulated into any letters, but into water, the sea overwriting itself, this script forces me to think something, then I see that which is thought, a bed for example, and in the bed lies an old man. This is my father I am. I shall be as my father. Be forgetful and have a rosy visage. I shall forebear in my movements and, for once, take a deep breath. Then I look at everyone around me, spread my arms a little bit and laugh. I laugh, but not jovially, I laugh, for laughing has become my tic. Whenever I can't think of something, when the word I've got on the tip of my tongue won't come, I laugh, for "laughing" is the word on the tip of my tongue, the one that won't come to me. "Suddenly" is a pistol, the word shoots me just as it shot Father. I am pure passage, adrift, my walking around negates standing until I jerk to a halt. Thus did Father pace up and down the apartment, thus did he suddenly grow old. I imagine suddenly having nothing but consciousness—nothing but the vision of an imaginary that is unthinkable, an inner galaxy with approaching, then once more receding formations, first spherical, then not quite rounded, and later wedge-shaped, they drag a trail of dust out behind them, and behind this trail is only light, but nothing more to see, nothing more to see but light, and the light, having no other choice, shines upon nothing newer than itself. First, he learns that there actually is life on other planets, then he perishes. Water. My mouth is dry, I can no longer swallow. Miraculously, the past no longer exists. The present is impenetrable, viscous matter, it clings like air that has become so dense, one can no longer breathe it, it must be continuously eaten and thus does it keep one alive, nothing else has to be eaten any more, in chewing, people discuss the air's various taste profiles, each person's particular notion unverifiable—for who is actually able to taste others' air? The air by the sea tastes different than the air in the heart of the city, some say. The city air tastes like nothing at all, others say. Still others report that they have moved several times because the air in one residence tasted exclusively of exhaust fumes, then, in another residence, primarily of feces, then, in a third residence, it tasted distinctly of wild boar. National distinctions are also discerned and these distinctions feed a nationalism of unsurpassable air superiority. Beyond which man might one day belong to the air, the people simply eat each other up, they merge into one another, clump into tectonic airplates, which slide into each other at lightning speed, there is nobody at all who shall not have dissolved into plates, people make tzimtzum so that creation goes backward, the vacuity of tzimtzum-nothing in its human emulation allows for no more creation, the practice of declaring war shall be put aside, the tzimtzum of air IS war, right up until the global air-unity plate concentrates itself into a single molecule. God belongs to the opposite creation process as its beginning and God shall once more be at its end. Thus shall God and the human tzimtzum-air molecules confront one another—and both expect the other to declare war. They have cut Michael off from everything that is dubbed speech, he lives, systematically isolated, as an echo of himself, which he thinks to be his self, but which is nothing more than the desire of others, and only the scrap is his self, the soul that he finally reincorporates into himself, the scrap is his dialogue with God.

And dialogue with God, the music of the spheres of feuding with one's own conscience, which has its own voice, is only possible with eyes closed. I can see my mother through my shut eyelids. Her gaze is soaked in painkillers, that's the only way I can explain its slow-motion palpation of her surroundings. She keeps her hands permanently folded, the fingers play with one another, there is no peace, for there shall be no more peace until her death. She has headphones on, what she's listening to draws her mouth into a line. If somebody speaks to her, she immediately looks at her husband. The husband is not my father. He makes a dismissive hand motion, smiles at my mother, then immerses himself in the newspaper once more. My mother's freezing. Now, she is chewing chocolate. The expression "to be beyond treatment" comes into my mind. The doctor recently told a friend, I don't want to see you here again next year. My friend interpreted this to mean that he would be cured next year if nothing went wrong. He didn't ask the doctor what he meant. My mother received another message. Don't come here any more, it's of no use, the doctor must have said to her. Thus does she ride through Germany by train. Once she has arrived in Cologne, she turns around and rides right back to Berlin. She takes the landscape in by way of looking out. A bit of chocolate, looking out, staring straight ahead of her, the body posture of a Bechterew patient whose spinal column is entirely rigid. To suffer oneself into rigidity and slowly vanish inward. It pulls in from the inside, one can really see that, the cheeks pull inward, I look at my mother and think, there's nothing more to be done, let her ride the train for as long as she can still sit in her chair. The man next to her plays the role of my father quite well, he doesn't truly have empathy, wherever he is, he is always elsewhere, and he dreams of the Daun Maars, of his stroll through life holding my mother's hand.

If Mother only knew what I'm watching on my phone right now. I'm interested in the history of the executioner's sword. In Saudi Arabia, the art of decapitation was held in high esteem until just recently. The Caliphate still upholds the tradition-heads. Should one admire the Saudi Arabian executioner as a great craftsman, the way that, wearing his white robe, he seems to separate the delinquent from his head faster than a guillotine could? The executioner has practiced this decisive blow thousands of times, always keeping his Jowhar sword sharp. The condemned kneels, his neck is exposed. Not exposed enough for the executioner. And not bent low enough. Everything is in its right place now. The police attending the execution ceremony admire the executioner for his swift overhead blow. The head of the condemned falls into a blanket, the headless body tips over, the executioner's assistants rush over and quickly take the slaughtered man off to the side, the square is cleaned with water, and, a short while later, the younguns are allowed to play soccer again. This is a square by the people and for the people. It is good that the young people are also not forgotten. Perhaps, there is one among them who, soon enough, shall not merely have visited this square to play soccer. Meanwhile, the executioner is already busy cleaning his sword, at home, he shall once more hang it on the wall next to the television. One day, the executioner bowed down before the sword, after all, it is a religious instrument, a champion and advocate of religion. Shortly after that, he began to have doubts as to whether he was exercising the correct profession for the first and last time, after all, a sword is no god, he thought. But it is worthy of God, he said to himself, and thus was all well once again. To cut the head off of one who was found to be guilty with a sword is an honorable task that restores God's order. Merely cutting off the delinquent's hands or his left arm and right leg or his right arm and left leg is, indeed, essential, but not nearly so honorable. And yet, there has been a shortage of execution artists in this country in the last little while, there is a veritable backlog of executions, which is to be lamented, the number of execution-worthy acts has increased at a horrifying rate, thus must eight new executioners be hired and, because nobody wants to take on this task, they are to be called "Representatives in the name of Religion" and the job posting has been provided with the additional note that no qualifications are necessary. It is to be feared that the sword, the handling of which is a difficult art, shall soon have become obsolete. Was it painful for the condemned? This is, without doubt, a subsidiary question. Reports that the severed head maintained eye contact for a few seconds with spectators of the execution, who were never in short supply, and reacted to jeers, such as the naming of his name, were strictly contradicted from a medical point of view. This was recently reported by a businessman who went to Saudi Arabia so as to present material there that was ostensibly adequate for the invention of an artificial liver, which would not only save many people's lives, but also allow for further drinking once cirrhosis had already been diagnosed, as well as for the production of invisible tanks, which produced such a racket, a metallically rattling "Bassa Teremtetem!" that the opponent invariably had to assume that he was being overtaken by an apocalyptic power, which thus caused all of his courage to melt away. This businessman, knowing full well that, in attempting to sell such material, he would not leave this country alive if his business partners harbored even the slightest of doubts as to his honesty, was now hurrying diagonally across a large square when several police officers suddenly rushed toward him, preventing him from going any further, even more than that, snatching his shoulder bag from him when he didn't immediately show himself to be compliant, they were on the point of bringing him down to the ground when a local man came to his aid, it wasn't by chance that he was crossing paths with him, he expressed to the police that he knew this man, he was here on the most useful of business, as such, they ought to let him go. As soon became clear, this man had been sent by his business partners to keep an eye on the foreigner, for the spectacle being played out on the square might have possibly prevented his on-time arrival or embroiled him in disadvantageous situations. In view of the previous conundrum, from which he had now been freed, the businessman did not find it at all unpleasant that the courier linked arms with him and maneuvered him skillfully through the crowd of people, until they'd reached a barricade set up in the square, from which they, or thus did the courier assure him, would have the best view. As to the question of what precisely they would see, the man assured him that he would not regret this small stop and that he would then continue on his way to the businessmen awaiting him in a far more exhilarated state. The businessman was in agreement about everything, the considerable presence of police officers he watched from the barricade caused him to be wary, he didn't want to do anything to draw attention to himself and he complied with all that which the courier suggested. Thus had they stood before the crowd barricade for a few minutes when a large police car made a corridor through the crowd, then stopped in the empty space behind the barricade, which the people acknowledged with loud cries, in which tense expectation, but also restrained anxiety, could be heard. At that very moment, a man in a white robe came from the left, he was wearing dark sunglasses and a kind of veil that hid his face, then, once he'd reached the middle of the square, the holding area of the police car opened up, out of which, hidden up until this point by tinted glass, clambered two police officers in ocher-colored uniforms, between them they bore a somewhat stooped man who seemed resigned to his fate. He's been given sedatives, the courier said to the businessman, who didn't immediately understand what this strange bit of information had to do with anything. Once the group had taken its positions some twenty meters from where they were stationed, the businessman could see that the man was fettered to the guard on the left with handcuffs, the guard then removing them once he was commanded to and placing them behind his back, connected to his right hand. The man was ordered to kneel down. Only once the two police officers found the kneeling position appropriate for that which was coming to pass did they expose his neck, at which point the man in the white robe strode toward them and demanded that both police officers move away, then pushed the kneeling man's head a thumb's length closer to the ground, roughly maneuvering his shirt another centimeter off of his neck, all of this with his left hand, while, at the same time, the right, clearly visible to all and calling forth cheers from the crowd, raised the sword he'd carried along over his head where, preferably without the help of the left hand and without first simulating the movement as a rehearsal, it severed the head from the rest of the body with a single blow, impeccably cleaving skin muscles tendons cervical vertebrae trachea skin, a blow performed only as powerfully as was necessary for the religious deed. As befits propriety, the executioner is in this way not knocked over by his own strength, rather, the sword comes to a halt shortly after departing the body of the delinquent. This calls forth general admiration and involuntarily incites the people to emulate the executioner in this movement. The resemblance of these movements to the hitting of a golf ball turns the crowd into golfers for a few moments, merriment spreads and overcomes their initial torpor. Peace only returns once the reasons for the death sentence have been read out. The businessman, however, could not calm down at the sight of the severed head and also did not accept the courier's indication that this had been a religious act, one that would put an end to an ill that'd come to pass in the world, after all, the courier said, this is not foreign to Christianity either. At that point, the courier led him right up to the corpse that'd been rent asunder, a single wave was enough, then the barrier opened up, the courier confidently put his arm around the shoulder of his ward, who was seized by such a fright that he didn't even think of refusing to set eyes upon the head. But, when both of them came before the executed man and the businessman asked the courier, half-jokingly, half-seriously, whether the man's soul was in his head or in the rest of his body, the courier replied to him, it'd be best to ask *him* that yourself, then lay flat upon the ground and looked into the dead man's eyes. Harfenschott, he called him by his name, then his eyes opened for a few seconds. Once they had closed once more, the courier said to the head: Our guest would like to know where the seat of the soul is. Then the eyes opened up once more and stared at him. Whereupon the courier said, the soul sits in the head. Then the mouth opened up and a gurgling sound made itself heard. "Hark," the courier said, then raised himself up, "he confirms it. He is an agile zero. Nobody ought to say that death is good for nothing. The day shall come when the executed shall tell of their experiences of having been executed." Stories are true or false. The following story is true.

The herdsman with the long beard and the brown habit places the severed head of the approximately sixty-year-old man onto the man's chest. The dead man poses. His head falls down several times, the herdsman puts it back onto his chest with a sense of great calm. God is great. A little boy takes a picture with his beautiful Nokia cell phone, one last look, he can't look away, then it occurs to him that he's recorded everything in the highest of resolution, God is great. Give him a knife, those standing around him shout, his knife is dull, he needs a knife. The herdsman, well-practiced in the religiously sanctioned slaughter of sheep, has already cut the throat, but the head does not allow itself to be separated from the torso. Why can't we just get it done with a cleaver? Wait wait just a lil' longer, the herdsman shall soon get to you as well. With his lil' cleaver, he'll soon make minced meat outta you. The herdsman is a dab hand at religious slaughter. But he's not nearly as well-practiced in the religious slaughter of man. He shakes his head and has to laugh. At the same time, he's sweating. The many sheep have made his knife dull. Throats are no problem. The knife handily overcomes the gristle-hurdle. One problem is the spinal column. The knife gets stuck in there and the herdsman is unable to bring it out once more. The little boy turns off his cell phone, he wants to save battery. The herdsman puts his left leg onto the shoulder of the man squatting on the ground, his restless eyes shooting back and forth still betray some sense of hope. Using all the strength he possesses, the herdsman manages to liberate the knife from its canting. The man tips off to the side, the little boy wants to check if his eyes are still open and stands just before him. The eyes are now half shut. The little boy pulls the man's right eyelid up high, however, he no longer seems to react. The little boy is disappointed and would rather not accept the situation. He does, however, stand in the way of the herdsman, around whom a large cluster of people has formed, and thus have no further recordings that show the face of the religiously slaughtered man right up close survived. But this gives the filmmaker the opportunity to concentrate on the men standing around, full of impatience, they are demanding that the head be detached, after all, this man is not the last one who is waiting on his just punishment. In fact, two other men who don't dare look up are squatting next to this first man, the middle of the three men now gazes briefly to the right—at the herdsman who has, without further ado, decided to break the man's exposed neck-bone and to twist or tear off his head, which he's been occupied with for *such* a long time, to twist it off, as one would twist off the clear plastic caps of eyewashes or hair tinctures. He manages to break his neck, but he can't quite separate head from torso in this way. The man on the right rises up and just wants to get out of there. A second herdsman, mightier still than the first, rushes over and compels him to squat down once more. A young fellow of about twenty years old breaks free from the cluster of men and gives another knife to the first herdsman, who is still hacking away in the wound with the dull blade, the crowd continuing to cheer him on jubilantly. At last: this knife is sharp enough, with it, the separation of head and torso comes to pass so quickly that the herdsman, after he has set the head onto the man's chest, comes before the man squatting in the middle, he's about fifty-five years old, his head is yanked back by his hair and his throat is cut without further ado, the knife slides through the neck and right up to spine, which, this time, offers up no resistance to the blade, and, accompanied by the crowd's jubilation, the herdsman is soon holding up the second head with a great sense of triumph, then the recording from this position ends, the viewer moves away with the unnamed filmmaker—a few meters to the rear, from where he can see how the little boy has kicked the second man's head off his chest and is running back and forth with it in front of the crowd, sometimes kicking it forward with his foot, sometimes lashing out at it furiously, the third man is pinned to the ground by several other men who have rushed to help the herdsman, the realization of injustice as a function of having had to wait so long for his own execution because of the bluntness of the first knife and the delays caused by this have not only made him restless, but, after having had to watch the other executions for such a long time, compelled him to undertake an attempt to flee, but the unhappy man runs right into the middle of the crowd instead of going in the opposite direction into the open field. Now, he is sprawled out on the ground, his left arm is torn backward by one of the men squatting on him from behind and, as such, entirely twisted, the man's screams of pain penetrate distinctly through the general clamor, which rattles around in the cell phone's microphone, two more men have sat on his legs, but they cannot get him under their control, the man's will to survive is too great as he pushes his head against his chest and against the ground so that the herdsman standing over him with legs spread cannot get to his throat. And the knifeman? He seeks to direct his helpers, he can't understand that there is somebody here who is resisting, and he can understand even less why the men cannot break his resistance, you must weigh like a hundred kilos, he calls out to one of them who's trying to pin down the left leg with the whole of his weight, so why is he still moving. Then my battery runs out. My disappointment at this causes me to get a bit irritated, however, the prospect of eventually continuing consoles me immediately. The awareness that, in watching these videos, it is becoming increasingly difficult to distinguish between a feature film and a documentary increases my anticipation. However, this anticipation is not self-contained, my vexation at not having thought ahead and not having started charging the battery in time causes me to wait impatiently for the cell phone to restart, the cable is too short to watch the video with the phone on the backrest folding table in a state of total relaxation, I have to crouch toward it, a bit slouched over, the next stop is announced, I am afraid that Mother might get off, but she doesn't make any move to, the phone starts back up, what I noticed when I first looked at it is confirmed, the resolution of the image is not good, would it not be possible to get the image at a higher resolution, I would like to see it very precisely, each detail, the face contorted in pain, the exertion of the killer who doesn't wish to show any weakness, just as it was in the Middle Ages, so is it also now. The problem is that we're dissatisfied with the quality of the images. Is there an innocence of the senses? It is only beautiful if it is not true. Drear apathy: "morne incuriosité" (Charles Baudelaire).

That my terminally ill mother looks like all terminally ill mothers, that I always think, say, and write Mother, if I think of Father, there's a commensurate sense of disappointment, yes, my God, disappointment, what is that, really, it's so appallingly sad, but for how long. "You must forget that" is dementia in the imperative-form. And, indeed, it is forgotten in the next moment. An interchangeable mother who died an interchangeable death after having become terminally ill in interchangeable fashion and looked like an interchangeably terminally ill mother who would soon be dead. Meeting my dead mother once more on the train from Berlin to Cologne, after sixteen years, she's wrapped a blue-red scarf around her neck, the powder-blue sweater softens the aspect of her face a bit, the whole time, I keep asking myself whether the other passengers recognize the illness in her face, the cancer-furrows in her cheeks, the corpse-look, the waning nose.

As Mother just stares straight ahead most of the time, rarely does her gaze pass over the table at which she's sitting, after she's looked at an object for long enough, something tells her to take the object into her hand, she can see it better by feeling it, but, as soon as she has the pack of tissues in hand, she begins to doubt the blue of the packaging, she observes the wrapper for a moment too long, then tears well up in her eyes, she stares at her husband and says something, for the moment, she is silent, her voice could turn the whole situation around, I think, then wait for her to say something again, but, the next time too, she says only a few words, as soon as I've taken off my headphones, she falls silent once more and stares straight ahead. She looks at me. She has noticed that I am observing her and seeks something in my gaze. I immediately look at the keyboard. Her voice then sounds out so singingly, so squeakily, that, upon looking up, at first I only see her mouth, it is speaking without me hearing that it is speaking, her voice can barely be distinguished from the primary tone of the train shooting over the tracks. When I look at her, she interrupts her chant, balanced on a single pitch, I pretend to be uninvolved, she leans forward and says something to her husband. But always just a few words that I myself cannot understand, even with the greatest of efforts. I have the urge to leave my seat and tell her how sad I am to see her like this. What occupies me most is the question of whether she is so inwardly devastated about her condition that everything she does and thinks is mere distraction. Are you so terrified, I'd really like to know, that you no longer exist at all, that the rigor mortis is already taking hold of you and you seek to ward it off with small motions, looks, and words? Would it thus be attitude or desperation? Now, I understand the phrase "gebrochener Blick/broken gaze," Mother's gaze is broken, her eyes open and close laggingly. Then a fat man comes into the compartment, he is dragging a shoulder bag about sluggishly, his body cannot follow his gaze, he heaves himself in the direction of the four empty seats with a table in their middle, immediately hogging all of them, he takes several bags with provisions for the trip out of his pockets and spreads them out on the table. These poor fat people, I think, they always have to eat so much, for it is their destiny ever to be fat. They are so fat that they no longer see the ground beneath their feet, their gaze always goes straight ahead. Whatever passes beneath their feet, they trample down and thus can they hew out a lane anywhere in the forest. The fat man takes alternating bites from a big pretzel with butter and chives and a cheese roll. He has no apparent reaction to its taste, which means that he doesn't even ask himself the question as to whether or not it's delicious, he carries out a consumption-program that doesn't just stop at the two units, rather, the fat man conjures further paper bags with comestible things out of his pockets, he diligently removes them from their bags, then arranges them according to size. However, after individual tastings, the bags with the nibbled-at baked goods have to be rearranged, the sausage roll has to get up and lie down next to another cheese roll (this one not a Käsesemmel, but a Käsebrötchen), the Alsatian-style pizza-tongue is now smaller than the apple donuts, and the Bobbes have, in the meantime, come to be level and are now placed on top of one another in such a way that their paper bags touch at the level of the middle of the jammy dodger lying before them, the kilted sausage just lost so much length that it must be placed behind the pastry dubbed a "flaming heart" along with the two devils on horseback, which look just like burnt penises, and both penis-devils have been looking at me this whole time, everything must be put back into order, they're shorter than the fat man thought, he doesn't know where they ought to go, he eats first the one, then the other. Meanwhile, Michael is interrogating his pitifully battered groom Herse, who can already no longer breathe freely, for he has been thrown from his horse in such a way that his full length was measured in mud, the castellan and servants worked him over him with kicks and punches and blows from whips and cudgels, and, when the dogs were set upon him, without hesitating, he slayed one or two or three of them with a stick. Thus do they lie there waiting to be admired by all as they are slowly absorbed into the man, whom one can watch get fatter moment by moment. An internal slaughter program. There ought to be an antimatter ration that takes these fat cattle out of the pasture until all the Xs have vanished from their XXXXL shirts. He shall also eat all of the bread, pretzels, and rolls that have meanwhile been brought to light, earned by the sweat of his brow, spread over with butter or mayonnaise and stuffed with sausage and cheese, most of them contain sausage, as if it were nothing, for the fat man, the Berlin-Cologne route serves for nothing but the consumption of these consolers, now, for the first time, he is in need of a break and is taking a snooze, his hands clasped over his belly display five sausage rolls each, he has a throat pouch like a reptile's, his eyes are leaking, his thorax rises and falls slowly, he's stuffed roll after roll after pretzel after bread into it, he has a poumon gras that must constantly be refilled, otherwise the machine simply won't breathe any longer. A thread of saliva runs down from his mouth, Herse's greenish-yellow thread of sulfur, which, by God's providence, he carries with him so as to set fire to the nest of robbers from which he has been chased, but he throws it into the waters of the Elbe when he hears a child crying inside, on a sheet of paper he'd handwritten, it contained Michael's appeal, the fat man found it far too laborious in its narration of the outrage that Junker Wenzel von Tronka had committed against him, as well as against his servant Herse, in it, he pleads for the Junker's punishment in accordance with the law; restoration of his horses in their original state; and some recompense for the violence done to them. The saliva collects on this paper and quickly comes to form a small lake. My father takes me out onto this lake in a boat. A little ways off, there is a red dot on the water, Father would gladly like to set eyes upon it. The red dot turns out to be a red balloon, from the underside of which an algae-covered rope leads down into the depths, thus forming a tau. The water is entirely clear and thus can I follow the tau-rope many meters down. From the depths, mountains grow toward me, however, I know them to be above me. A wave discards the reflection. Now, I see a man bound to the tau, his limbs are entirely pale, he's opening and closing his mouth, his eyes open wide. He's looking at me, Dad, I say. Dad only laughs and gives the order to move further away from the red balloon, a thunderstorm is brewing. We don't budge. My father tells me that I ought really to take a big step back, we don't want to put roots down here, he adds. But we don't move backward, the lake is pulled out from under us, as one pulls a tablecloth out from under dishes with a great flourish. We're sitting on land, my father rolls up the tau-rope, tugs at the seaweed that's caught on it, smells his fingers, the tau never ends. Where is the balloon, I ask him. The balloon, dear son, my father says, is no balloon, then he indicates a point off in the distance. What's there, I ask. Go and have a look, Father replies, then continues to tug the seaweed off. Father's face isn't precisely attached to his head, I realize as I look at him from the side. A thin book could fit in between the two. Under his face appears an entirely different face that is much younger. The first face laughs, the other is without expression. I walk up to him, my biological father might well come to light beneath the first face. I imagine snatching the first face from him and presenting it to the crowd, just as the team presents the championship shield of Südkurve to the adoring crowd. But for what is *this* shield the reward?

It is my father saying to me: "Get up and quit these antics, I won't offer my hand to any man whom I don't respect." I should then say to Father: "The room is locked. No one gets out of here." And the father says to the son: The son wrote this bit here and it's rather poor. Yes, the son then says, this bit is both poor and true. But there won't be a rhyme here at the end. Then the shot rings out. I approach the balloon and wave back to Father. Only ten kilometers to go, my father calls out, then you shall see it. Off in the distance, I see the balloon, the fiery-red sun setting. I know, I call out, that the tau-rope is the horizon. My father laughs. That's true, he calls back, now standing with his hand forming a funnel in front of the first face's mouth, we never see the naked facts. Eight years later, I reach the end of the tau-rope. The balloon is my mother's crimson head, the tau her body. My mother says, I raised my son wrong, he's become a son of hidden preserves. It is simply not possible, my mother says, that what is underneath disappears inward, the cellar together with its provisions in a cabinet and my son ekes out his life in this cabinet, as if there were no longer any other life. Your father and I discovered an Angstloch in this cabinet, it leads down to a dungeon. We illuminated the dungeon with a flashlight, but couldn't spy out anything except for a folded paper, of which only a small area was revealed to the viewer. Father lay belly-down onto the Angstloch and dictated, constantly correcting himself as he did. I'm not entirely sure, he perpetually said, this letter is cut off. Or, he'd say, that's no letter, that's actually a number. I mean to say, either a D or a 96, he said, so that makes 15 and 10, I read aloud from foolishness and volatility, your father said, and I note down, "foolishness and volatility." I filled up a notebook with all the info he gave, his corrections, and, in Father's words, immaculately decipherable symbols, his glasses fell through the Angstloch, to which he only said, it doesn't matter, with or without them, it doesn't matter now either, after all, the distance to the floor of the dungeon is ideal, he could read everything very precisely, even without glasses. And thus did he read to himself and the reading came to no end, he read for many days and nights, half-disappeared into the hole, read what was on the paper, he had no desire to eat or drink, I'd like to understand it entirely, he said, there are no ifs and buts now if we want to know where we stand with our son, but there are no ifs, ands, or buts, he said, and everything that Father thought he could read from this dungeon, accessible via your brother's wardrobe, can now be read in your log, dear son, my mother said, to tell you the truth, Father dictated the entire log to me, from the first word, "One," to the last word, "writing," your brother scribbled it onto paper with numbers and hieroglyphs in his dungeon beneath the cabinet and your grandpa, who is the source of all, sought to impress it upon his memory in increasingly concentrated fashion from August 17, 1942 to October 30 of the same year in his Gestapo custody, into which he was taken as a result of alleged high treason, from the very first day of this custody, he was, however, certain that he would only be able to remember things by way of their interrelationships, but not in any detail, thus did he seek out a formula that he would be able to bear in mind, one from which everything could be deduced, one which he would not even lose if he couldn't write it down onto a piece of paper, which he naturally avoided at all costs, after all, this piece of paper would have been visible evidence of high treason, which, up until now, could only be invoked by way of a department-store bill and the dissemination of certain writings. And thus, Mother says, is all that you write already pre-scribed, pre-thought, and pre-ceded, your book merely makes a pre-book visible, you make its white script black by writing over it, you move about atop a well-cultivated subsoil, the paths you go down have already been written. High treason, Grandpa would often say, they savored that word, in it, they wished to accommodate as many things and circumstances as possible, mostly invented ones, since, soon enough, there were no more actual ones to hand, they did this in order to say "high treason" again and again until, finally, they came to agree that high treason was also high treason and enjoyment was obscene. They say high treason and enjoy the meat. "I developed a formula," Grandpa said, "which, if I were ever to set foot on any ground other than that of my cell, I merely had to unfold like a map and everything would reappear. The formula went like this: ꙮ. Then, Satan came and I exchanged the formula for his promise that I would be able to leave the cell in a few days." There was no explanation for Grandpa being set free. For Satan, there was a Persilschein. But the fact that I raised my son wrong is what breaks me, it's the worst thing and the worst thing shall be passed down from generation to generation.

That is Mother's life confession. I move away without saying goodbye. My mother's crimson head is a balloon, her body a tau. It takes me eight years to return, always along the tau, the crimson balloon gives away all of its color. At the end of the tau stands Father, what eight years can do, I think, his sky-blue swim trunks with the narrow black lines and the little pocket on the right underneath the waistband make him into a man of the past. In this little pocket are always the exact coins needed for the cigarette machine. As I swim, I'll grow into my father's stature, once I've covered the last few meters, I shall have utterly vanished into him.

After Father gets up and, as he's been pre-announcing for a long time, heads in the direction of the bathroom, Mother waits patiently until his marching strides are out of earshot. How fine it is, she says, that you really exist. The fat man sits across from her and smiles. Your son sent me, he says, he believes you to be his mother. I have no son, the woman says. I also don't exist in the slightest, the fat man says. Then wherefore do you sit there across from me, the woman asks. That's the problem, the fat man says, I am to sit across from you for as long as this son that is not your son observes you. My mother looks over at me. She throws out her tau. At its end am I Father. I shall be a good Father. The tau is wretchedly long. The swim trunks.

                    T
                    h
                    u
                    s
    d   o   I   g   e   t   u   p
                    a
                    n
                    d
                    g
                    o
                    t
                    o
                    h
                    e
                    r

The smell of the tau-rope is precisely that incurable seaweed smell of the seventies that clung to everything, thus awakening the notion of still existing after one's death, more indifferent than indifferent, bait of a destructive frenzy, the sight and scent of these things anticipated death, if one stayed there, close to them, a wooden boat in an airy water garage, the wooden dining set passed down for generations, the oak cabinet filled up with childhood games, one would live toward death with open mind, the scent of these things clings to the brick walls of my parents' house, flows from its insides, it is inherent to every old book, I can open the Tauwerk which is both book and cordage, so as to learn the ropes of reading, it's in the shape of a cross, I was sent out and lost my way, Mother drinks coffee, I wave at her, but she doesn't see me, I let go of the tau to wave at her with both hands, then the tau burns into my forehead and a voice says: "But come not near any man upon whom is the mark!" I ask the voice who it is, and it replies that it is

Schattenfroh, so I ask Schattenfroh what the mark is, and Schattenfroh replies, "But do not touch any man on whom is the tau!" What do you look like, I ask Schattenfroh, and Schattenfroh replies: You are the man clothed with linen, which has the inkhorn by his side, therefore write: Then I beheld, and lo a likeness as the appearance of fire: from the appearance of his loins even downward, fire; and from his loins even upward, as the appearance of brightness, as the colour of amber. And Schattenfroh put forth the form of a hand, and took me by a lock of mine head; and the spirit lifted me up between the earth and the heaven, and brought me in the visions of a nursing home, a girl and a suitcase, 23 houses, a second library, a key, a whole house, the Last Judgment, a hearing aid, a park bench, Grandpa, the Eifel, to Prüm, to the door of the inner gate that looketh toward the north; where was the seat of the image of jealousy, which deals with to whom Schattenfroh is nearest and whom Schattenfroh prefers and whose Schattenfroh is the greatest and most gracious, which provoketh to jealousy. And behold, there is the splendor of the God of the Eifel, like the apparition that I saw in the valley. And he speaks to me: lift your eyes now the way toward the north, Nobody! So I lifted up mine eyes the way toward the north, and behold northward at the gate of the altar this image of jealousy in the entry. He said furthermore unto me: Nobody, seest thou what they do? Even the great abominations that the house of Images committeth here, that I should go far off from my sanctuary? but turn thee yet again, and thou shalt see greater abominations. And he brought me to the door of the court; and when I looked, behold a hole in the wall. Then said he unto me, Nobody, dig now in the wall: and when I had digged in the wall, behold a door. And he said unto me, Go in, and behold the wicked abominations that they do here. So I went in and saw; and behold every form of creeping things, and abominable beasts, and all the idols of the house of Prüm, pourtrayed upon the wall round about.

    Then said he unto me, Nobody, hast thou seen what the ancients of the house of Prüm do in the dark, every man in the chambers of his imagery? for they say, Schattenfroh seeth us not; Schattenfroh hath forsaken the earth. He said also unto me, Turn thee yet again, and thou shalt see greater abominations that they do. Then he brought me to the door of the gate of Schattenfroh's house which was toward the north.

Therefore will I also deal in fury: mine eye shall not spare, neither will I have pity: and though they cry in mine ears with a loud voice, yet will I not hear them. Then we come to a place where I am treading water. Thus do the years go by, but they are not years, it is the moment when I notice that the tau-cross that was a train is a snake and the snake leads me back into Father's office and the office is crowded and strange things are coming to pass there. Mateo tells me Father forgot his birthday. If he were to remind him, he would immediately wish for everything to be different, to get out of the wheelchair and go back home, which he would then no longer recognize as home. A birthday that one celebrates while expecting guests representing the state. The state has become all too *light*, my father said years ago, on his eightieth birthday.

That the people speak so strangely with him he finds to be unseemly, Mateo says. It wasn't all that long ago that all he'd have to do was look up and everyone would have already pulled out paper and ballpoint pens in the expectation of important messages. This woman here at the table opposite, for example, why is she smiling at him like that? Can't she clearly articulate what she wants him to do? Some abuses were committed with the company car. It really can't be allowed that the gentleman from the office who runs the bureau, the treasurer, the treasurer of the city, takes the company car home with him. When Bückmann died, Mateo continues, he flew from his vacation to the man's funeral on his own dime. In any case, he did not use the company car for private trips. He had already encountered Herr Deutsch here too. He who had always been his driver. It could also be that his name was Beuer. In any case, he shall return to city hall tomorrow and ensure that the city moves forward once more after decades of his being absent from the scene. He can't write anymore, but that's to do with his right hand, he's already given it a go with his left, but he won't be able to acquire that skill so fast, not anytime soon, the right hand is almost entirely rigid, he can't feel the pen anymore, even as his hand clutches at it so tightly that it causes him severe pain, indeed, he can think the word, but no longer write it, the hand clearly signals that it's done enough writing in its life. A tunnel syndrome, according to his doctor, but he thinks of it as more of a theological blockage, which makes sure that you no longer give up anything, you keep it all for yourself, everyone must gather together so as to bid a collective farewell. As to my question about whether he was doing well, the orderly doesn't reply. You must know, he says, that his farewell to language has already begun. Your father is afraid of no longer being in control of words, he'd always used them to be in control of the town-hall personnel. Have you ever seen your father weep? Once. Here, he's always smiling. Generally speaking, that's a good strategy, however, one must know how to read the smile, for it gives different answers to the question of pain or freedom from pain. If you ask what this smile is and what task it has. It represents knowledge and expresses no feelings. Your father knows about the collective farewell, that knowledge may frighten him, but he would never allow the fear to show, so he lays the smile before the abyss.

Thus has he been sitting in a wheelchair among the other nursing-home residents for two weeks and, contrary to his usual style, he speaks to them consolingly. His fellow residents, however, men and women between eighty and ninety, have no use for this consolation. The Lord shall provide for all. Worry not, the Lord shall worry for you. The Lord shall not forget you. Father soon gave up on narrating adventurous stories to them, also ceased telling them why they not only really deserved this consolation, but were in bitter need of it. and withdrew upon his wheelchair to the endlessly playing television. They're all buffoons, he says. A woman with white hair occupies him. She cradles a white stuffed animal in her arms. She's speaking with her child, Father says. She always does that when nobody is looking after her. But he wouldn't give cake to a child of that age. Can you understand what she is saying to the child, he asks. She wants to know if the cake is tasty.

So, Father forgot his birthday, nobody comes to visit him. I am nobody. If somebody had visited him and wished him a happy birthday, he certainly would have given him a blank look and laughed, insomuch as it would have occurred to him to laugh. One only has birthdays up to a certain birthday, then that's it. Birthdays come to an end of their own accord, he says, but life doesn't, it can always go on just like that, with him too, life just keeps on going, or, rather, it simply rolls along. And thus did it roll him here, into a retirement and nursing home, the floor-to-ceiling windows on the ground floor of which afforded a view onto the most luscious of meadows. The meadows give him the impression that he is still sitting in the conservatory of his house in the Eifel, completely undisturbed in the calm of contemplation, which has, for a long time, been unable to arrive at a purposeful thought. Father sits in the glass house, he keeps it nice and warm. Each decision that is made here is made for him, even the decision to live. He is part of a nursing-home machine that is responsible for keeping itself clean. Something is always running through it and being emptied out. Man is there for excrement and the disposal of the excrement is part of the nursing home's success story. The nursing home is there for the green meadow, as the human excrement is fed directly into it, I think right when Father gestures to me that he'd liked to be pushed over to the big window in his wheelchair, there, the meadow leaps through the glass and right at its observer. The view out onto the meadow is called Under-the-Earth. I could lie for hours atop the meadow behind my parents' house until I was overcome by the feeling of being pulled beneath the turf, where it was so cool and dark. Well-tended meadows make life on earth pleasant, they accustom body and spirit to death, green meadows are graveyard meadows, for several minutes, Father can't avert his gaze from this intense green. Then, all of a sudden, he loses the ability to speak properly. Words come forth from his mouth in little chunks, old cake that crumbles on his tongue. He takes precise note of the fact that he can no longer find the words that he'd like to say, thus does he say something in the hopes that what he wishes to say might well lie beneath it. He sometimes talks for ten minutes without cease, the orderly says, as if he had to produce as many sounds as possible in the shortest possible time. In speaking, Father, who possessed the largest office in the administration and would pace to and fro dictating in my parents' house, has turned into Phelan's typewriter from the story "Something Invented Me," completely uncontrollable, that typewriter produces some one million mostly incoherent words per minute and prints them on microfilm. In contrast to this machine, however, Father's words never, not even for a moment, fit into any meaningful context, not even an oblique one in the context of the current conversation, one to which a listener might well say, "he's telling the tallest of tales" or "he's telling an ancient story, one Aristophanes might well have told" or "That's how it is in *Hamlet*."

To discover oneself in the unknown, just as Celan discovered himself as "Félon," the arch-swindler, in R.C. Phelan. Does Father even exist? He must be afraid of dying, must fear death, instead, I am overcome by the uneasiness of taking an interest in the remaining life of a complete stranger who refuses everything and it is only logical that he uses the formal "Sie" with me, as I'm not his son at all, just a mere somebody who blundered into his panorama. If he were to suddenly die with a smile on his face, I wouldn't be able to rid myself of that smile until my own death.

Father tells no tales, he stenographs automatic speech that would certainly enjoy some popularity on the stage or on a tape, a twenty-first-century Raoul Hausmann. His tongue scans a sequence of sounds until, exhausted, it ceases its labor and Father stares at his counterpart through glasses barely sitting on his nose. You already know what I wish to say, his gaze says. Nobody can say what he wants to say.

If you don't get him out of that chair soon, he'll forget his legs too. Anyone who incessantly seeks to escape from here had better get used to the wheelchair, the nurse replies. To what extent can older ladies and gentlemen get used to something despite increasing forgetfulness, especially as they forget that too? Father goes two meters with the wheelchair, raises himself up, goes to the television, which, moments later and unremarked by Father, gets quite a bit louder. On the way back to his seat, he gives the wheelchair a wide berth and sits down on the sofa. That thing is still playing, he says, even though I only just changed over. This is how it goes all day, d'you understand? the nurse says. Yes, I understand, but it might well go otherwise, if he went out on a stroll, for example. Tell me, if that man over there really isn't your father, then why are you taking care of him so devotedly? Because this father here might tell me something that I forgot to ask my own father. I have many fathers. I ask them all what I forgot to ask my own father— what I didn't dare to ask. For example, I ask whether they are afraid to die. I should have constantly asked my father about his memories, for a whole year, back when he was still capable of remembering his memories. On March 18, 2011, I asked my father about his memories for about eighteen minutes and eleven seconds. That is the sole acoustic testimony I possess of my father. I do not know whether Father's voice says more to me than what it says and that's why I'm delighted to follow it to the Dauner Maars, the Schalkenmehrener Maar, the Gemündener Maar, and the Totenmaar. Childhood memories spring forth from Father like tears. But he doesn't weep. He has only wept a single time in his life. That was when he said to me: "But I really do love you!" His life is the life that I lived. With my birth, his life before my birth is erased. It shall be resurrected in photographs. It's uncanny that photographs exist. On March 18, 2011, Father recounts his memories of the Eifel: "As kids, our first school outing was from the Volksschule to the Maars, you could drink from its fountains while lying on your belly. For us kids, that was quite a sensation. On the way home, the containers that we'd filled up to the brim with water blew up 'cause of the carbon dioxide. We knew that we ought not to have filled them more than halfway. Mother's mother lived for a long time, my grandma, she got to almost ninety, which was almost a Biblical age for the time, she had breast cancer, but didn't die of it, one of her breasts was amputated, her own son, Uncle Ferdinand, did it. On my father's side, I only knew his parents and Aunt Gertrud, Father's grandfather on his mother's side was from the Van de Sand family, the Van de Sands came from the Dutch area near Aachen, I'd have to look into it.

The red-haired Van de Sand, which was to say Father's grandfather on his mother's side, used to beat his children when they came back from school, saying: 'For now, you've done nothing wrong, but imagine how much it'll hurt you once you have.'

We had a school principal who gave his introductory lecture on how toothpaste was made, that's what a dunderhead he was. He was a Nazi and that's how he became the principal. A so-called headteacher. Father Lungstraß, your mother's father, was popular among the farmers. An aerial bomb smashed into the land of Gustl Lungstraß, your mother's mother, in such a way that there came to be a little well. She could even turn it on, there was a system down in the ground, the water didn't flow away, it just kept on coming. One veterinarian would have a particularly fine time at Mother's parents' parties and once, when he was dancing, he began to stagger, fell backward onto an artillery piece, and got a splint pin stuck in his rear end. Father Lungstraß sewed him back together in the hospital. The veterinarian saw to all the farmers in the area and, on one occasion, a farmer asked his son: Has the doctor already come? Then the boy said: Yes, first he took care of Mother, now he's onto the cow.

My father died on September 27, 1968 at 72 years old. Prostate cancer. Mother died at the age of only 64. It all started with her going into the garden and not coming back. I was sitting with my brothers in the great room and smoking. Ahndemir looked out the window and saw her lying unconscious on the cellar stairs with a big head-wound. She did get well again, but had no more feel for time, she was always very reserved, she'd suddenly stand stock-still in the city and hold conversations with complete strangers. We didn't know precisely what the matter was. The physiology of her brain was examined, the doctor opined that it wasn't possible to operate, nor was it relevant whether it was senile dementia, softening of the brain, or a tumor. She didn't like being photographed. There's hardly one single photo of her. Perhaps there's a reason for that too."

Father has seen enough now. The sun slowly fades the meadow, the green becoming gray. I have the distinct feeling that I shan't see Father again. He looks like a bird. I shove him back to the table. Goodbye, Father. Tell me your name once more. Your son. A young nurse appears, she presents Father with her outstretched arm. He'd really like to leave with you, she says, he doesn't want to stay here, in this room with the other man who's got such a hot temper, though the two of them get along quite well. Father walks with mincing steps on the leash of her arm. I'll disappear around the corner with him, please get out of here so that he doesn't see you anymore, he can't understand why you can't stay here or he can't go with you. Why not? Father asks. His eyes are wide open now and his blue sweatpants are flapping around his legs, the shock of white hair bobbing with each stride. The indicated exit is a tortuous path, a wrong turn to the right, and I find myself once more in the home's foyer. Father comes tripping along the wall with the nurse, looks at me, then cries and laughs simultaneously. He can walk down the hallways every day using the handrail. He walks his life to its end. A little girl is sitting on the park bench in front of the nursing home, she is showing me the way with an outstretched arm. I intend to go in the opposite direction. The girl gets up and follows me, soon, she's caught up. She has a very deep voice. There's no point in going the wrong direction, she says. I want to know how she knows which direction is the right one. The other one, that's the right one. The girl annoys me. My right shoe gets stuck on a protruding cobblestone, the leather sole's got a thin spot near its tip that I want to fix forthwith. I observe the girl out of the corner of my eye, she doesn't leave my side. That wasn't your father at all, she says. In a certain sense, it was my father, I reply. If it had been your father, you would have chosen the other direction. If it wasn't my father, I say, both directions would be wrong. You wrote your father into there, the girl says. Now, the damaged area of the shoe can only be covered over with shoe polish. You wrote him into the wheelchair. My father dictated himself into the wheelchair, I reply. The script lies on the street, you really should know that, you need only follow it, the girl says. You know what, I reply, in that case, I'd really like to write you away. The movement of the script is the movement of death, the girl says, then, before she vanishes, she counsels me to read Jabès.

Ja, Bès, I shall do so. And, at night, you shall protect me so that evil spirits do not beset me. But which knife helps you, o jocose dwarf, against the snake of imagination, which eludes one's gaze? And I also know that, if I follow the script or the scripture, I am serving the devil. I myself weep perpetually, I flutter around Father's form until he's completely gone out of himself. The girl is gone. Of course, she was never there, of that much I'm certain. Snow lies upon the street, so much now that it can accumulate beneath the suitcase and block the wheels. I drag the suitcase behind me, it's growing ever lighter. Finally, I bear only its handle in my hand. Over the course of these few steps, the suitcase has lost all of its contents, which lie behind me in the snow. Father's toothbrush is to be found among them, as well as his house slippers, a telescopic walking stick, and a strange book, the cover of which gives no information regarding title or author, I open it and read: "Over the course of these few steps, the suitcase has lost all of its contents, which lie behind me in the snow. Father's toothbrush is to be found among them, as well as his house slippers, a telescopic walking stick, a strange book, the cover of which gives no information regarding title or author, I open it and read": a Gotteslob, nail scissors, a photograph of my mother, which always displays different stages of her life, I can't and don't wish to encounter Mother anymore, besides which, in 1952, I would at most be a friend of hers, her friend, but not her son, I would have to perpetually say to myself, you're not yet born, but the eye clings to the image that is transfigured every second; next to the photo lies a Merkur-brand razor blade, a bit of small change, a taxi-company card, a rosary in a small case of black leather, which also harbors a yellow tooth, the case smells of the nineteenth century, of draconian punishments, then, my gaze falls once more upon my mother, the eye pulls the viewer into the image. It is spring, she's wearing a light blouse, through which her breasts, never revealed in my presence, shimmer, as this is the ultimate quality of old photographs, to equip the image-viewer with X-ray vision, which makes clothing transparent. Mother beams, her white teeth have a menacing aspect, they turn the photograph into a sculpture, then, the next moment, Mother has vanished once more and only the mountains still untouched by people appear in the morning glow, as soon as I've scanned the snow with my gaze, looking for the tracks of birds or other animals, Mother appears once more and leads me through the snow by the hand, shows me the beauty of the mountains, which appear in the light of the fifties, she'd like to go there with me, she says, and she's sorry that she didn't pay more attention to me before, that's just how she is, she can't make fast decisions, she moves everything to and fro, but, now, it's crystal-clear to her that it's me to whom she'd like to give all her attention and, in the evenings, we lie together in her bed, she unbuttons her blouse, two buttons only, then she smiles at me with the helpless smile of the later mother, who always wished to be pitied, even though it wasn't me who brought her into the world, but she who brought me, and, in this world, there shall be many things to be endured, but not with her, it is her children who shall have to abide, in this moment, I am becoming my own father, who has either overlooked the smile groping for pity or condoned its foreseeable consequences, I discover a liver spot on her upper body, her skin is much lighter than any photo paper would allow to be perceived, the liver spot is surrounded by a red line, upon which tiny insects creep, they're exchanging secret messages with their palpating feelers, one of the little beasts sees me right when I want to shoo them off, then I feel a piercing pain in my right eye, the photo falls into the snow, which blinds me, I grope around for the photo, jam my hand into the open nail scissors lying there, blood drips into the snow and over the photo, upon which, just as the blood runs across its paper, my mother is to be seen in the bed of roses behind my parents' house, the way, garbed in a plastic apron, she's pulling weeds and speaking kind words to the roses, saying that they've been so good since their pruning and grown so diligently, thus do the roses not drop, their defoliation is their new beginning, I wipe the blood off of Mother, which takes away her shine, but gives her color, Mother simply doesn't want herself to close, what a stupid mother you are, I say to her, you want to be my wound for all eternity, upon my brow and the wound eats down deeper and deeper, cut her off, the girl says, you must cut her off, and I cut her off, make her clean, and kiss her, my name is Stintelein, the girl says, and, from now on, I won't disappear from your life ever again, even if you don't see me, I'll be there. I lay Mother down in the Gotteslob and she instantly begins to sing, a full choir resounding from her tiny throat: "O Christ, our true and only light, / Enlighten those who sit in night; / Let those afar now hear Thy voice / And in Thy fold with us rejoice," then she reads out the obituaries that Father has laid between its pages: "She was unable to recover from a serious illness that befell her in 1956. After a life of deep faith, she passed away on May 11, 1960, well prepared and strengthened by the holy sacraments. Remember her in prayer so that she might soon enter into the joys of heaven," I open the book once more, but can no longer find Mother in it, only her voice resounds in the vicinity of a gallows, which adorns one of the inserted obituaries, a man is hanging from the gallows by his hair alone, his arms are bound, his legs are dangling a few centimeters off of the ground, but high enough that not even his toes can make contact with it. Nevertheless, the man seeks again and again to make contact. If only my hair were to fall out, he screams, but his hair does not fall out and thus, perhaps, shall he slowly perish of thirst and hunger. I move closer to him, asking who hanged him there and why. To which he replies that the answer is to be found in the fourth canto of a certain L, who couldn't help but meticulously put down on paper all that each of us thinks at least once in our lives, but we send this thought to the gallows so that we never hear anything more from it again and there does it still hang as thought made flesh. The thought, seized by the scruff of the neck and hanged by the hair from the gallows, is completely black, his mother and daughter-in-law have smeared him over with tar so that the scourge might enter more deeply into his body, they brandish the lead-surfaced flagrum with great ardor and the old woman cries out: Isn't that Jesus; that really is Jesus! Mother and Daughter-in-Law are both drunk and surprised that the guy is still alive, they put him into this disadvantageous situation together, for he refused to have sexual intercourse with his mother—an encounter she so ardently desired—while the daughter-in-law had hoped to be favored with the mother's inheritance. Thus could the mother barely wait for her own son to penetrate her deeply and move inside her as he hadn't done ever since his birth, but had certainly done during the pregnancy, and she lay there stark naked in her son's bed, he wasn't even there yet, rather, he was in a corner pub not far from his family apartment, he was seeking to convince the publican to grant his wish for another beer, after all, he'd been suffering from insomnia for quite a while and really couldn't imagine going home, where only the fear of fear and the desire to balance himself up on the roof awaited him. That'll be your last beer. The son is overcome by a rare feeling of triumph, having wrested free a chunk of time, only for himself, my own Reinheitsgebot, the son thinks, then, soon enough, sadness overcomes him, for it's pathetic, such rearguard action, sitting out, sitting before oneself, gradual congealment. As soon as he'd drunk the final sip, this beer of grace gave the son the idea of hurrying home, without closing the door giant steps across the apartment, to tear open both of the window-casements, then to continue his passage by quickly lifting his legs, hopping from one leg to the other, then, consequently, thrusting forth into the void, an act that could only be prevented by the sudden sitting-up of somebody in bed, as soon as the bedroom light went on, the person had found the light switch after briefly groping around on the wall, his own mother made herself known, rose from the bed in a seductive pose and, in a placatory tone, convinced the son that she was cold, could he please shut the window, which he refused to do, instead positioning himself by the open window in a crouched position and making preparations to leap down. The mother, keeping calm and at no loss regarding new means of persuasion, approached her son, in leisurely fashion and without taking her eyes off of him, covering the three meters between bed and window with astonishing speed, then, once she was standing right in front of him and he still hadn't leapt down, demanding that he touch her breasts, touch them, she said, and tell me whether you still recognize them. The young man, whom I believe I recognize as myself because of her words, hesitates, estimates the distance down and the risk of surviving the fall as he gazes at the pavement, the notion of being dependent on outside help as a result of a failed suicide attempt, then being unable to undertake any further attempt on one's own, but being dependent on someone else's gracious helping hand, that is a horror to him, but then he cannot resist the temptation to touch his mother's breasts, just as she asked him to, squeeze them tighter, the mother said, you ought to cause me pain, however, the word "cause" causes him to take his hands away once more, he's never eluded the connection between horniness and words, never been able to disable it, then the mother undoes his pants, leans forward, her breasts sway slightly to and fro, and she makes a sign to him to get down from the windowsill so as to "give himself to her," as she says. The phrase "give himself" is even worse than the word "cause," it's more dreadful to him than "refreshing" or "interesting," the latter of which is always used by foreigners who speak English without being able to speak English, the son does, indeed, clamber down from the windowsill, but then he sits back down onto it, collapsing in such a way that it wouldn't take much for him to tumble down backward into the street with no grand gesture. There he is, the son that mothers yearn for, beautiful, but powerless, strong, but acquiescent, Playmate of the Mater Dolorosa, Suspended Matter of the Pietà. Far from being frozen in a single posture, Our Mother of Sorrows bears her son into his bed and the son finds it less unpleasant to be carried by his own mother than to come into contact with the sweat that's formed beneath her breasts, he's always found his mother's sweat to be revolting, it didn't fit the image he had of his white-skinned mother, always so concerned with elegance. Her elegance, the son then painfully came to note as he got up in the years, was borrowed, cited, it gave her rural origins a casing behind which she could hide her true feelings. When she was in bed "with the flu," but the issue was actually sadness and despondency, she was laid up with elegance, and this elegance made sure the flu wouldn't go away. If she couldn't explain to her son why everything in the world was in such an ugly state, she still did so with elegance, and the son was thus content in the belief that the world's ugliness was merely a passing thunderstorm. When the thunderstorm then struck inside of him, the mother stated her opinion that heavy weather was always to be found inside of us, most people just didn't know how to deal with it. Then he felt himself to be a chosen one in league with distant forces. One day, the storm was raging with such force that he asked his mother if it wouldn't cause major damage, after all, he was the airplane flying through the thunderstorm. How can you be the airplane when the weather is inside of you, the mother asked. I am both the airplane and the thunderstorm, the son said. The mother reflected for a moment, then said that the son ought not to worry, one of the two that he was would, in this case, surely survive. But an airplane never flies voluntarily into a thunderstorm. If I am both airplane and thunderstorm, the son thought, then the airplane is my body and the thunderstorm is the hereafter. The sweat smells stale. The mother's body is dotted with liver spots. Previously, the son had always thought that liver spots arose out of sweat, they are the deadly matter that the body excretes right up until the deadly matter conquers it. The more liver spots a person has, the closer they are to death. The sweetness of the sweat is disgusting, the son thinks. The perfume of death. How much more beautiful is a head of lettuce in a field, its abdomen remaining hidden from its observer. The mother puts the son down onto the bed. Now, he was so big that she didn't initially notice the change in his neck. Only when he bent down to her—did he want to tell her something, flip the game around and address her as his little daughter?—could she distinctly see a golden cross hanging from his neck with an equally golden Jesus, who seemed to follow his observer's eye.

Involuntarily, one also had to speak of this Jesus and the mother did so, reverently at first, then jocosely, until the son, who took these speeches for the childish whimsy of the thoroughly religious mother, realized with a sense of horror that the mother's attention had turned entirely from him to the man on the cross. Dear Jesus, was one of the things the mother said, should I not liberate you from the cross so that you can show my son the righteous way? Saying these words, she actually attempted to pull the golden nails out of the corpus. The son wished to liberate himself from this unfortunate situation by standing up once more and striding backward. Hey! the mother said, in the meantime having managed to slightly loosen the nail that held the feet to the cross. She was more than a little happy at the fact that she'd succeeded and that the goldsmith had done such neat work. It was now very calm on the street, the moon was shining through the window, the heat that'd reigned in the room for hours already mingled with the cooler air that was being drawn in. The son shivered slightly, the goosebumps were unpleasant to him and, soon enough, his mother was there, rubbing him warm, just as she'd always done when he was still a little kid. Quit it, the son said, having, in the meantime, managed to undo the clasp of the chain, from which the cross hung—in such a way that the chain slipped down from his neck and the mother could devote herself, undisturbed, to her Jesu-Minnesang: "My chosen Blood / ah, my redemption's Lifeblood! // Where can I find / heart or words to love and laud // such unheard-of faithfulness in this heart-rending trial? // Heaven alone can give me power to praise." The mother, however, who hadn't expected the chain to open up, let the jewelry fall from her hand. Please help me, she said to the son, who, now completely naked, goes down to her on the bed to help look for the chain. I'd really like to put on a shirt, he says. I'll close the window, the mother says. They'll probably find Jesus again soon, the son will probably want the mother to touch his testicles, the mother imagines that the son is a marble statue and she is palpating his cold member. Where did you get the cross, the mother asks when she finally finds it again beneath her knee. From Father, it was lying in the top shelf of his dresser and, when I took it out of there, Jesus wasn't yet on it, the son replies. Now, you have him back, one can take him off of the cross very easily, the mother says, but as soon as the cross hangs round his neck once more, he feels as if a millstone were pulling him down. When he attempts to get rid of the chain, his chest grows very hot, Father shall fix it, Father shall fix it, he hears somebody say, do you also hear that, he asks his mother, what do you mean, she asks him, but she only wants to play pleasant games with him, I don't hear anything, she says, dear Mother, the son says, somebody is saying Father shall fix it, do you not hear that?, calm down, dear son, and hold still, the son is too out of breath to say anything else, he lies on his back and is suddenly very calm. Something is branded into his chest, he wants to read it now, he feels the precise contours of the characters, but can't lift his head, it costs him quite an effort to ask the mother to read the characters to him. I'd be happy to do that, the mother says, her son's impotence affords her a languorous feeling. There are 23 characters inscribed on your chest. But I can't feel that many characters at all, the son says, shocked. How many do you recognize, the mother asks. I recognize these:

ΛΕΡSΑ Ս ΑЯƎΝS

It all boils down to conjecture, the mother replies. And what does that mean? It's all up to you, my son. Erase it, the son says. Then the mother replies: What I wrote is what I wrote. With these words, the daughter-in-law strides into the room. Are you this woman's husband, the mother asks her son. The son replies: Is that your own idea or did others talk to you about me? The mother replies: Am I your wife? Your wife handed you over to me. It ought not to be to her disadvantage. Then the son says: What is to my wife's advantage is hardly a disadvantage to me. My wife's disadvantage is also my disadvantage. A disadvantage of the flesh can be an advantage for the spirit. Very true, his mother says. Your spirit is not of this world, thus has your flesh nothing to fear. If my spirit is not of this world, my flesh is not of this world either, that is the truth, the son says. The mother speaks to him: What is truth? Then, having said that, she turns to the daughter-in-law: I find nothing to like in him. But the daughter-in-law, believing the deal they'd made to be lost, screams: If he doesn't want to go back into you, he ought to pull himself up by his own hair and gratify your spirit. Does the spirit not experience the deepest of satisfactions and is the deepest of satisfactions not to do as God does in snuffing out the life that one has brought into the world? That's right, the mother replies. Is it not of indispensable value to study the slowly extinguishing life as precisely as possible and does one not have the responsibility of conveying this extinguishment to posterity by means of beautiful words? That's right, the mother replies. It's one of the strangest facts, the son thinks, that children don't often call their parents' parenthood into doubt, whereas parents take paternity tests quite often, sometimes maternity tests too. A child is simply told, I am your mother, I am your father, then, at some point, the child begins to say Mommy and Daddy and does so for as long as parents and child shall live. Indeed, how many children would question their parents' parenthood if they had the natural right to do so? I can see what you're thinking. You've always known what I'm thinking, the son says. You're thinking, the mother says, that I ought to temper justice with mercy, even if there is no justice to be had. How right you are, the son replies. Justice is inviolable, the mother says, it applies unconditionally. And thus do we now wish to brand upon your chest the guilt that you bear. As soon as the mother says this, the son feels the script once more, black fire upon his white skin, it writes itself upon his chest. This time, it appears to be complete, the son praises his mother's art, she speaks so modestly of God's script, the black fire upon the white fire, which man, however, cannot read and which God has merely found, for him alone is it possible to read the white script out of which everything arose, but which didn't itself arise, rather, it is the ur-text of all that exists, the ur-text of the world. Your skin is the parchment upon which the script appears, the black flames that only make visible that which is already written in the white fire, that is the justice that already *is* grace, as, to wit, is already written upon you, just as was written upon God's arm. Your skin shall dry out in the wind, the black flames shall go out, your life shall have become script, and people shall come from all over to read the script that God made appear against the background of the white fire that has existed since the beginning and that only God can read, though he did not create it, for it was not created, rather, it was there from the beginning, as was said, and thus is it written, for God found the ur-text upon his arm, it shall now be upon your chest, and God has no need of the ur-script whatsoever, it is the only thing that can exist without God, for it was already there before God, Mother, the son seeks to interrupt her, but the mother goes on talking incessantly, the words fall from her mouth like meat that one suddenly no longer wishes to eat, for one knows not what effect they shall have or because one fears their effect, then the teeth also fall out with the food and the teeth are followed by the palate, which sets itself off to the side, and the brain penetrates the former oral cavity and flows through the mouth, the lips of which it cauterizes, and those lips, once so beautiful, your one great pride, dissolve with the words that no longer find any support, but the mother doesn't hear her son, the more she speaks—and she won't stop speaking now—the stouter she seems to her son, who, suckling at her breast, palpates the signs that the black fire has only just branded onto his chest. Is the script ready now, Mommy, the son asks. And Mommy bears her privates upon her face, two bulging, very hairy lips. The script is ready now, the mother replies. He calls me "Mommy," she says, a bit ashamed, to the daughter-in-law, who cannot hide her jealousy. He used to just call you "Mother," she says, he can't suddenly be becoming a child, she takes a step toward him and smacks him on the chest with the flat of her hand. The mother likes this and they both begin to beat the son, he falls from the mother's breast like a ripe fruit despised by all falling from a tree; *beating the script in*, is what the two women call it. Jealousy is what drives the daughter-in-law, her hands falling onto him like whiplashes, why do you think you can call her "Mommy," why do you think you can call her "Mommy," why do you think you can call her "Mommy"? The blows don't fail to have the desired effect, the script is now rising forth from his chest like little houses, and if one takes a very close look, somebody comes out of one of the doors and takes a deep breath. That's me. I've settled into this house quite comfortably, but would still like to move out. It's growing dark, the son runs his finger over the roofs of the houses, I rush into the house, shut the door. Unfortunately, I can no longer unmediatedly follow that which is coming to pass from the house, the shutters are down, were I to pull them up, I'd draw attention to myself, which I must avoid at all costs. This gives me the opportunity to explore the house. It is dark, there are no light switches to be felt out on the walls, nor are there any shutters, I walk straight ahead, putting foot in front of foot, the floors and walls are made of the same material, unplastered reinforced concrete, no protrusions or cracks, even with my arms outstretched, I can't make contact with the ceiling. A door opens, somebody steps out into the passageway, for that's what it is, a corridor, the door vanishes immediately, then somebody, an office-employee perhaps, stops before me, takes out a clipboard, last name, he asks, first name, announced / unannounced, leave this building through a door at the end of this corridor, you'll only notice it once you've already gone through it, then enter a further corridor, go straight, then take a sharp right, follow another corridor, which shall lead you in a diagonal direction, then take a sharp left, follow that passageway, which shall lead you right back to approximately where you came from, in such a way that you shall have gone the length of a total of three straight lines, they interfere with each other, cut each other's words off, then you shall have reached your goal and can turn to the next house, continuing until you have made consummate all 23 of the houses by way of your inspection. Here is the map:

ERSUNERASANSUBSYNEPASAN

A door opens up and I enter E, the first house. I walk the map through the script. I wish to see what the script has to offer. It offers belly, leg, arch, crown, thigh, shoulder and ear and trunk.

    The house is made of reinforced concrete. One could not live in it. It consists of four single-story corridors; three arms of about the same length are arranged parallel to one another and connected at one end by a trunk about twice as long. The house is empty on the inside, no furniture, no doors, the walls unplastered, no light. It radiates a great chill that immediately penetrates into one's body. And yet, something makes one want to stay. A mixture of joy and fear accompanies the visitor of the script. The fear is what keeps me moving. If I were to pause, an abyss would inevitably open up, the fear says. I stride to the edge of a cliff, a narrow river appears for a few moments, a bed is in the river, in it lies a man, something is standing next to the bed, in the background towers forth a snow-covered massif of rock. I remain in motion, the abyss does not appear, it doesn't belong to the images that stand permanently before one's eyes, but life runs toward it, says the fear, whichever passage you choose, whichever way you go, it is a mere detour on the way to the abyss. It does console me to some extent that the fear has nothing deeper to offer.

The characters on the map shine, but don't give off any light to their environs, rather, they darken everything, I must keep feeling my way along the corridors, sometimes, I get caught between two walls that come to a point, I can only free myself from them with great difficulty. Perished in the sigma. The void gives rise to the most beautiful of improbabilities, succinct contours work themselves out of the lack of contours. I see everything and touch nothing. I can enter into things and, yet, I am not in them. However, this is only possible for me by gazing at the map. It seems to me that the house doesn't need it at all, everything is already contained within the script and only with the script can all that which I describe be seen. The choice is mine: If I don't look at the map and, not looking at the map, walk not along the letters, but go maplessly and without paying attention to the impediments of the script to and fro through this house, then I'm simply moving through one of these hyper-neutral new houses, the sole face of which is facelessness, for no furniture placed in this house shall make the house belong to its owner. But, as soon as I read the map, the most color-filled landscapes begin to bloom upon the walls of the house, a mountain panorama shines in the sunlight, a gorge that does not appear threatening; through a tree-lined hole in a ruin, a hand that is much too large appears from above, an aqueduct perhaps, four gentlemen dressed in dark suits and white shirts with Vatermörder—stand-up collars called "patricides"—and bow ties are sitting on upholstered chairs at a table, they've taken off their jackets, they're nowhere to be seen, they're wearing vests over their shirts, a cloth upon the table catches the eye by way of a bright, jagged line and fringes that make me melancholic. I can't say whether the jagged line goes all the way around, for I am only afforded a frontal view of the ensemble, closer examination reveals that the four gentlemen are one and the same person, initially, their balding suggests that they are wearing round wire-rimmed glasses, but it turns out that they're not wearing glasses, while two gentlemen sitting opposite one another are playing checkers, the other two are chatting animatedly. They sit next to one another at the back side of the table and thus do they offer an unimpeded view of the scenery. They are the sons who have grown old, they have been living here for years, they have a little bit of money, somebody takes care of them and cleans their suits, irons the tablecloth and tidies up, if the gentlemen lose a checker during their game, it is immediately replaced. Father comes to get all of them. His hand slowly grows down toward them. Father is entirely naked, he has grown so large that nothing can cover over his nakedness. Father would like for water to once more flow through the Eifel Aqueduct, his sons prevent this. They live under the bridge, Father always says. The sons say his hand is within reach and, furthermore, it has been so for many years. They didn't know their own father, their father wouldn't know them, the sons say. The only thing they know about him and that they have before their eyes every day is his unspeakable hand, which they hurled stones at for some five years, they ceased doing so only recently, for the stability of the arched bridge was no longer guaranteed due to their removal of the stones, that, at least, is the opinion of two of the brothers, whereas the other two would have very much liked to continue the stoning of Father's hand. They could pull the hand down to them with the stones, there is an invisible band knotting together the stones and the hand, they thought, they want to grab hold of it without fail, the hand has to be prevented from accessing their game of checkers, that is the one and only thing that matters to them, not the aqueduct and not them (the sons) either, for they had shown themselves to be convinced that the hand had separated itself from Father years ago, it is still connected to his body, they think, but the body can no longer entirely control the hand, the only way to explain this is that the hand has penetrated the hole entirely and has been hovering over them ever since, though, now, a state of motionlessness has been attained, it shall either lull them into a false sense of security before the decisive attack or the hand has died unnoticed, become petrified over time, and, together with the similarly petrified forearm, grown so heavy that Father can no longer lift it up over the hole. The four brothers are convinced that Father's petrification is progressing, this insomuch as one can speak of "petrification." They are playing a diceless board game, therefore, they cannot *roll out* who is to clamber up onto the table and take a closer look at the hand, opinions differ as to its constitution, while some speak of skin, others only mention the hand in conjunction with the word "stone," the discussion of the question of what alternative decision-aids there are other than throwing the dice in such a way that this might definitively be clarified finally led to a dispute about whether the brothers, who are the same height down to the millimeter, would be able to touch the hand if they were standing on the table, touching it would certainly afford more security than merely looking at it, some of the brothers were of the opinion that, even with arms outstretched, they would not be able to make contact with the hand, the others were quite certain that they could not only touch the hand, but grab firm hold of one of its fingers, which immediately gave the four of them a great fright, from which they have not yet recovered, and thus does the game of checkers only superficially serve to determine which one of them is to decide on their further course of action. Instead, it serves to relax them, which also clarifies why some moves are reflected on for days. The reflector is in perpetual danger of falling asleep, a permanently uninvolved observer is needed, one of the brothers says, the kind father upstairs is watching with his hand, a second brother answers, in fact, if he were to reflect on the move for long enough, some of the brothers would look approximately as dead as the hand, says a third. Incidentally, they once had such a quarrel about the rules of the game that the next move could not be made for some ten years, and, at the present moment, nobody is certain whether it is precisely this move that everybody here is awaiting.

If I turn the map around, I turn the writing upside-down. If I were to go out, I would move from the back to the front. The upside-down script is not without effect. My parents' house appears upon the walls of the first house. At first, only an outer wall can be seen, then the front yard, kitchen, cellar. If I seek to capture details of these transmissions more precisely, the image disappears once more. It then takes on a strange shape, lengthens out, becomes very thin, compresses itself, as if it were grimacing. I see this simulacrum as nothing but invitation or foreplay, otherwise, I wouldn't be able to put up with it. I simply don't wish to be speckled with parceled-out phantoms, I wish to immerse myself entirely in the visible. That is my greatest wish, to envision the rooms that are part of my story, then I go back into these rooms once more, I rediscover all that which made up these rooms, each object once more in its right place, and if I wish to, I shall remain there. Then what would happen to time? I'd really like to be able to repeat some hours and days as often as I wish, I could focus on the things that have, up until the present moment, escaped me, in this way could the 360 degrees, of which only a small slice is perceived at any given time, be completed until, in my imagination, I could assemble all 360 degrees into a panorama with the effect of depth, a panorama that I could gaze upon in its entirety. Early on, I was convinced that a gaze, the longer it lingers upon something, creates space. To a certain extent, a gaze bulges space, bulges the room. A permanently bulging displacement of space takes place. I would wish onto myself the hyperthymestic syndrome, which would turn me into a living machine of memory and recollection—like Jill Price—but also to invert myself inward into the spaces of my imagination so as to vanish into them. Thus might I entirely unconceal my past, in which I am currently concealed. The wish to *be* things came to me at the age of sixteen and has not left me ever since. The problem that concerns me is how I might then have consciousness as a thing. For example, I would really like to be a house one day.

I turn the map once more, my parents' house vanishes, and thus do I have it whole in its absence. Seeing images requires more than the sense of sight. There is something present that has no existence, but is mere visibility. It is unstable pre-existence. The fuzziness, the blind spot that I always carry out in front of me, and, when I want to take a closer look at the image, it withdraws, drives me out of the first house, a joyful impatience overcoming me nevertheless, it causes me to grow weary of phantom-images, however, it takes me a little while to recognize how to get from one character into the next, the passage from E to R occurs occurs via upper and lower horizontal corridors. If I want to go from N to A, there is only an access point via the apex of the V, which is formed when N and A make contact.

Whichever direction I go in, there are only two ways to endure the world: a cross on each and every wall and books. Each book is born of a lack and authenticates the cross. A projection would have the advantage of one witnessing the crucifixion in real time and not having to picture it. I decide to go in the opposite direction, turn the script upside-down, put the N in place of the E, then penetrate into the A, the second house that was formerly the penultimate. A is seemingly nothing but outer space. I stand before my parents' house, on the flagstones of its northern forecourt—the house is bordered on three of its sides with flagstones or gravel, their only use is to keep the garden away from the house—and look left over the low, little gate and the street, leading to the forecourt and a gravel path, to a house with the sky towering up above it. In this house, a man by the name of Helfmeier will have died, my mother often asks him for advice when the dishwasher, washing machine, or dryer breaks down. Herr Helfmeier knows his stuff and this impresses my mother. Admittedly, though, his visit always seems to my mother to be an act of state, Herr Helfmeier sitting casually upon one of these machines. I feel myself to be an intruder, for I am already in the house now. The machine's working again, Mother says. It's late summer, the light gives the landscape and the things in it a concise contour, everything stands still, as if someone or something were about to arrive, and the animals and the landscape, the trees, houses, and streets were going to follow this someone, this something. Only you yourself don't follow, you don't budge from the spot, your gaze could tear forth from the sky and remove a great chunk of it, then all would be entirely empty all around you. There is nothing to report, no external event has come to pass, it is the moment into which a consciousness of being different has installed itself, a frightening sense of the I, which releases me into a world utterly renewed, one in which God, parents, family, and friends have been placed at a distance. And this Herr Helfmeier, whose cat, Mohrle, was blind in one eye and fell two floors down from a window and into the street one day, but without breaking anything and, from then on, avoided the company of people, I ought to now kick this Herr Helfmeier out of the house, as I am in a mood characterized by great strength being experienced for the first time, they've supplied me with a heretofore unexperienced authorization to do or refrain from doing things, simply because I am me. But he is no more, Mother puts a final piece of clothing into the dryer, closes it, sets the program, then presses the start button. This process seems to once more give Mother meaning in her life, whereas I was beginning to think, it's post-war society that's making her depressed. At the same time, it's only the machines functioning less than irreproachably that cause her to despair, since, without their irreproachable function, the family enterprise cannot be maintained. Its maintenance has already taken on the characteristics of its own enterprise. Mother began to hate the plates and cups, shirts and blankets, the spoons and socks and trousers and tables, the cupboards, plants, and chairs, the plants least of all, those actually came from their parents, their so-called offshoots discarded over entire generations, the residences grow smaller and smaller, the plants have reached the height of trees, two or three years ago, it would have been possible to give them away, now, they won't fit through any door. The cupboards, chairs, tables, and pots are also inherited, as are the carpets, oil paintings, and tableware. There's the Hutschenreuther set, from which nobody eats, then there's the Meissen porcelain that not even kings eat from. Crystal vases fill the cupboards, while clay pots from the nineteenth century by the dozen take up the remaining space. Once a year, Mother carries the pewter jugs and bronze jugs, bronze pans, and bronze pots that crown her cupboards from the great room into the kitchen and polishes them there with a mixture of disgust and devotion, using a sharp-smelling paste. None of these pots and pans and none of these jars and jugs shall be able to conquer the rooms of the third generation. I leave the second house, of which only the kitchen remains. What is the difference between the kitchen and the memory thereof? I get to the Z, the third house, by imagining the service hatch at the foot of the A. Twenty meters. Gravel path. Four more steps. Two steps. A front door made of bull's-eye panes. Wood-cased glass. Iron bars in front of the windows. Small glass triangles. The bell turned off. I kept the key. Initially, one can't stand it, then one doesn't wish to take one's leave anymore. A compulsive visualization of rooms, of spaces. Of where everything was. In the photo from 1967, the brown box on the left of the image, in the top corner, that's a radio. Three temperatures of the tone color. No interstice. Walnut, lacquered. Wasn't everything walnut, lacquered? Veneer or solid wood, wasn't that the only relevant question back then? Did *back then* not exist at all? The circular fadings, the spots on the radio lid, they existed. Flowerwater, slopping over. A vase of tulips always standing just there. Tulipwaterwreath. The vase is filled by a shiny jug of golden brass, as soon as it is poured, the water shoots out of the jug's curved, long-stemmed neck followed by a couple of drops upon setting it down. The water dries up, passes through the glaze, blooms into a wreath in such a way that the vase cannot be moved, the worst has already come to pass. There is a radio in the shop that has no circular markings upon its lid. That cannot be a true radio. Radio is switched on at unforeseeable occasions, the magic eye lights up, voices come close, music, then radio is shut off as suddenly as it came on. Turning the radio on or off is off-limits to me. Its ivory-colored keys may only be operated by Father. A *Songs on the Death of Children*-silence reigns. The vocalization of the child's mouth is the inspiration of a hand puppet. A marionette that, one day, contrary to all expectations, manages to put one foot in front of the other all by itself. Here, one sees this child's high chair, bib on. Entice. An egg cup down which yolk runs. Eating eggs from real chickens is incomprehensible. A pink-primed china-set with black borders. Silver cutlery. Mother-of-pearl egg spoon. The wooden sliding door, walnut, veneered. Herringbone parquetry. The cold stone corridor with a red runner. A wrought-iron railing together with a stone staircase that leads to an upper floor, we remain below. A sink in the corridor on the right, in front of the toilet. To wash hands before mealtimes. Straight back into the kitchen to see what's for dinner. Mother frowns when she sees others lifting the saucepan lid. These metal pots with their embedded black coloring. They burn quick. Burnt mashed potatoes. The gas buckles the bottom of the pot inward. The handles with their great rivets. The lids of the pots have something hat-like about them; flapping brim. The most beautiful thing is the way through. A white-painted square with two small wooden doors that click into a latch lock. Its opening and shutting is the most distinct sound of childhood.

Service hatch. That's where the food comes through. One sticks it in, the other pulls it out. Steaming pots and bowls. The childhood of the body ends with the first unsuccessful attempt to get from the kitchen and into the dining room through the hatch. The Fearless Vampire Killers. The other childhood is lost along with a closet. There's only one possibility left to us: to summon it. The kitchen has a cupboard. The cupboard's got shoes and a shelf with provisions and spirits. Shoes and cleaning tools on the left, nothing but bare wall on the right. There's room for five pairs, one each. When the doorbell is pressed, it leaves behind a number in a small white box on the top left, next to the cupboard door: a 1 or a 2. To the east, the house has a front yard fenced in with a low wall. To the right of this garage, set slightly back, this wall merges with a gate, which is also equipped with a bell. That is the 2. Otherwise, one would first have to cover the twenty meters down the gravel path, up the four stone steps, take two steps, then and only then, to hesitatingly depress the bell-button. That is the 1. The 1 is certainly too close for comfort. The 1 stands upon the threshold. In the winter, when it's already dark outside during the afternoon and nobody else is in the house, there's something oppressive about seeing the 1, but without having heard the ringing. The perpetrator must have slipped through the garden. Dark afternoons. This is impossible. This is what the child struggles against. It doesn't want the big lamp to be turned off.

The key.

The time has come to enter into the fourth house, A. As a security device, a laughable, gold-shining door chain hanging from its mount. A little kick would blow this thing wide open. An easy job to smash through one of the door's square glass windows and open the front door. Front doors of houses are always locked. One can immediately see when a front door isn't locked. The front door is locked. Two full rotations. Vacancy. Then through the wooden door with the triangular knob, down into the basement on the right. The door cut out of the wooden wall. The wooden wall is primarily blue with white stripes across it. The concrete staircase. The gray-painted metal railing. Now, at head-level, the narrow gap on the left. There was always a cigar box here. Then he had a heart attack from smoking cigars, then the cigar box disappeared. The potato cellar on the right. To the left of the potato cellar and adjoining it is the laundry room. In the back, a gray stone tub that's grown out of the ground. A spider cowers in the tub, a tub-bound daddy longlegs who's grown tired. A daddy longlegs who's lived here for generations. He paces up. He paces down. Then he sits there. The tub belongs to him. Even if nobody wishes to challenge his dominion anymore, he sits there majestically. Has he just been cowering there for years? The entire figure a single eye. An eye on legs. The eye seems to have been abandoned. The entire room flows into a drain. This is nothing more than a rusty grid. A central exit. A nothing. There's never a shortage of drainage. The drainage fishes out everything. The laundry room is a parking spot that's been parked. Nobody has done the laundry here for decades. Old tiling, some of it glazed, reserve stock. No longer necessary, the entire house has long since been newly tiled, glazed ones too. Investitures. One imagines how it could actually be, it shall always be different. Having grown up in a white-tiled basement, one shall always be searching for a white-tiled basement. Your house doesn't even have a white-tiled basement, is what everyone then says from every direction. In the house, on the street, in the whole place, it never smells like the current time of day, it always smells of the seventies, which then advance decade by decade. Are used as pretext. A plow in a garbage dump. There's always something new to come. The plow always clears the very same spot. It always smells like at home and, if it doesn't smell like at home, one doesn't take note in the slightest, for one only ever takes note if it smells like at home. First of all, one notices that it doesn't smell like at home here, then, a single moment later, one suppresses this, for one would wish for it to smell like at home—ever and everywhere. If one enters another house and it doesn't immediately smell like at home, one would wish to go home again just a moment later. A key on the floor in the back left corner. An enormous key bit. On the Sütterlin flag fastened with wire: little gardengate. But today's key is far smaller than its former counterpart. Everything grows from big to small. Since everyone has to carry a bunch of keys everywhere in their pants pocket, all keys must consequently be smaller, all locks more compact, now, nobody can carry around such a giant key with such an enormous bit, even just one would bulge forth from the pants pocket and everyone has roughly ten keys to carry, there's so much to open, there's so much to hide.

Another attempt. This time, toward the house from the end of the large garden.

In the fifth house, P, the heart, which is merely the path from the bulbous garden to the freezer chest. The iron garden gate is stuck. One unlocks it, depresses the latch, the gate opens, then tears forth from one's hand and flies back into its lock. One must really tug and tear at it, it gives way, then flies toward one, wobbling like crazy. Flies right at the head too. If one believes that one has to pay the greatest attention to one's feet, the greatest danger comes from the ground, out from the earth, then lightning comes from the air and only now has one gotten to know the earth. It's the fences that go down first, then there's a sudden void through which slips what one wished to have at one's back. Something that intrudes, that tears down one's own protective wall, then levels it to the ground, the neighbor?, the even more poorly understood illness, propertynumber, plotnumber, Recycling Area Me, for which reason we stand naked before the mirror every day—so as to find out, whether I know, whether I know not. If one stands by a fence, is one standing before or behind it, inside or outside of it? Openings, outlets, enclosures, dimensions, from here to there, a fleck of soil, a stakingout, apportionment, displacement. It's not at all self-evident that we should be here out of all places. Would a body in which nothing beats not be conceivable? Is this not completely outdated—the operating system of the heart? There are far more modern solutions, energy-saving models. Modules in which nothing more has to pass, be pumped, set free, the whole of it stands still, renews itself imperceptibly, cleanses itself, is unassailable, simply separates that which has been lived out, then lets it fall. Perhaps the heart is nothing else. Heat enters the body through the mouth, which is a heater, the millwheel-heart spins round and round, the heating decreases, must be rekindled once more, then it increases, wears itself out, gets clogged, then valves must be replaced, sections, meanderings, an entire pipe is efflorescing and must be removed, replacement is imminent, the wall must be pried open, the pipe leaks out over two floors and one can't just reach in and remove the defective pipe, one must intervene in the substance, the replacement pipe-piece is installed, the hole is plastered over once more, if the work isn't done properly, it sticks out in unrefined fashion, one shall always be able to point out: that's where the trouble began. The laundry room is the house's deep heart. Whitewashed like all basement rooms, it appears to be much older. Years ago, the freezer-chest was put in. Ever since it was in the newspaper that the murderer had packed up the corpse, which had already been neatly dismembered with an electric saw, piece by piece into freezer bags, then placed them into a freezer-chest so as to fry the fileted pieces serving by serving—they'd been deep-frozen and would thus continue to be fresh—and eat them, the opening of the in-house freezer was avoided. One day, we also needed a freezer compartment in here, so that was something different. The individual drawers contained deep-frozen beans from the garden, cauliflower from the garden, Brussels sprouts from the garden, kale from the garden, celery from the garden. I'm not actually certain whether one can freeze celery. In truth, the house is uninhabited. Together with its inhabitants is the house uninhabited. There's something inhuman about it. It's not of sound mind. So rigid, so disproportionately large.

Therefore, in the sixth house, "E," there is only the word "Wallpaper" and the phrase "Weeping Willow," the phrase "Septic

Tank," and the word "Staircase." I grew up without colorful wallpaper. I would have really liked to have had quite colorful wallpaper at least once in my life. I've always moved through white rooms. Whitewashed woodchip wallpaper. It's a matter of faith, whether the ceilings should also be wallpapered. No floral wallpaper, no meadowed weeping willow, no shutter, no wood paneling. No mold creeping up the walls, no nailed chipboard. No waterdamage. Where I sit, there is no shadow on the wall, no depression in the earth. I am not there. In the very same second, I am already gone. I have already left, I say while reaching my hand out, while shaking hands. One's own four walls and that one's own four walls are forever. Is that not what one always thinks. Yes, one doesn't think that one's house could one day be demolished. One really can't imagine that it will one day not be there anymore, the house. One sees a house and stands very small before it. A house belongs to nature, is always built into the wilderness. One stands at the window of this house, looks out the window and is greeted by only wilderness all around. Wilderness plastered over. The weeping willow before the house. The house placed upon a meadow plot. The weeping willow directing the wind with its tentacles. The planted tree and the built house and, if it hadn't made it there, it would all be wilderness through which the wind whistles as it rakes over the ground. Care must be taken that the grass not moss over, that the sun not wither everything, that it have enough water, who spares even a thought for the grass on the embankment, the green at the side of the road, roads have been built that nobody uses anymore, the wind passes through everything, it tears at the roof, rainwater flushing through the gutter, the earth is a septic tank, who forgot the wheelbarrow there in front of the house, the trodden-over stairs are going to bits as nobody treads upon them anymore, wilderness grows up through the staircase from below, as it goes to bits, bit by bit, because no one walks upon it anymore, the pensioner who no longer goes to work and dies on the first day of his pension, treading upon the staircase keeps the wilderness flat, the smell in the rooms holds the voices captive, the children's voices, the parents' voices, one can open the window as one wishes, after all, the voices are not in the air one breathes, the voices are beyond the air, they are precisely at this point in the room, the broken bit of staircase shall be blown aside by the wind, a few years later, the wind has swept the whole of the staircase off to the side, 1 or 2, you didn't hear the bell, the mirror in the antechamber doesn't show your now-face, for it has always showed your childhood-face, it hardly knows you at all, it wants to know nothing of you, it shall not show you what you wish to know from it, you go before this mirror and see only your childhood-face, which you left with, which you've now come back with, and you can't believe your eyes. The stem of the E is the mirror through which I enter the seventh house.

The seventh house (N) is N, the house of the empty middle. The middle of the rooms in the parents' house is usually empty. Sometimes, tables stand in their middle, but the chairs are absent. There is an unfurnished room, in which one involuntarily begins to think aloud. In this room, I hear a voice. Good, that's how I'll do it, I say, then leave the room. Now, I've left it, I really don't know what I'm meant to do anymore. I go back inside, hoping that, there, it shall come to me once more. Did I not say you should do him in? Whom am I meant to do in? Him. But who is *him*? You should know that better than anyone. I don't have the slightest idea. OK, you don't have the slightest idea. No. Who had the idea, then? Not me. Do you mean to say that this is my idea? It's certainly not mine. A picture is hanging on one of the room's walls, one that I must always have overlooked. Yes, go in there, you shall learn everything else. Get right up close to it, then you'll see. The picture is quite small. A man is lying in a bed that stands over a river or stream. The mountains glow in the background. Perhaps they don't glow, it might just be the paper's radiant white that glows. An oil lamp can be seen in the picture, as well as a sideboard with baked goods and a wooden box that stands next to the bed. The creek in the picture zigzags like the gravel path, like the Z, the twist of which is the seventh house. From the first time I attentively observe the picture, it becomes my inner duty to study it daily, I'm always discovering new details, the picture narrates my life story from day to day, now and in the future. The picture accords me the task of devoting many more pages to it. The diagonal of the seventh house, which is the N, is a staircase leading down into the basement. The picture, I now recognize, is the eighth house, Y. In there too, a staircase leads down into a basement. It's the very same staircase and it leads down into the very same basement. But the basement is another basement than in the other houses, it's always been one and the same basement. This basement here is totally whitewashed, only the doors of the basement rooms are kept blue. I go from room to room. The rooms are brightly illuminated and empty. Once I've left a room, I hear voices. I turn around, then there's nobody to see. This gives me the opportunity to take a closer look at the powerful spotlights on the ground in the back-left corner of each room. These are the types of light sources used in construction. They have a protective grid in front of the halogen bulbs, which generate great heat with their 400 or 500 watts. It smells of burnt flies or other insects everywhere, they got too close to the spotlights with their chitin shells. Perhaps it's just scorched air, the rooms are so clean that one would be surprised to catch sight of an insect here. Even spiders one looks for in vain. The bulbs emit so much light that their cables must be concealed in a multilayered plastic sheath. Now, voices can be heard in the other rooms too. Interrogations seem to be taking place across the rooms. The rooms hold forth with one another. I take one of the white chairs leaning against the corridor wall of the basement wing and sit down so that I might be able to accurately perceive the voices of the four rooms.

    A voice to the right of the boiler room, its heavy fire door is shut, negotiates about my time in school with voices from the laundry room and the preserving-jar cellar. After some forty years, my supposed cheating in German class is to be investigated. Such investigations of cheating have no statute of limitations, a voice from the boiler room that I recognize to be the principal informs me, then asks me to take the stand on the subject of this accusation. I find myself in the preserving-jar cellar. "I really need a thinner pencil," I say, "I can't manage this one in the slightest—it writes all sorts of things I myself don't wish to." So, I'm still in possession of the instrument of action, the voices realize with a great sense of relief. Who's guiding your pencil, then, I'm asked, and I say: Schattenfroh. Schattenfroh? the principal's voice asks scornfully, isn't that the old Nazi whom the Ministry for State Security blackmailed into unofficial collaboration, saying that they were deeply interested in working together and that Schattenfroh had every reason to make amends for the guilt he'd accrued by working with the Gestapo, even if this guilt can't really be "amended." I'd like to know what precisely he's said to be guilty of. Well, the principal says, one example is he released your grandpa from Gestapo custody. But I've already written about that and shall write more about it.

He asks me if I wrote the following with that oh-so-thick pencil and handed it in as if I were its source and whom did I actually mean by the little old man: "For instance, the pictures on the wall next the fire seemed to be all alive, and the very clock on the chimneypiece (you know you can only see the back of it in the Looking glass) had got the face of a little old man." I did indeed write that, I hear myself say, and the little old man is Schattenfroh. Then this chunk of text can't be yours, for it is Schattenfroh who guides your pencil, the principal retorts. But it's my handwriting, my script, I say. But script is not yet text, the principal says. It all depends on what one means by script, I reply. I can hear my facial expression through the fire door. My face is hot. Script must be experienced firsthand, the principal says. It is therefore imperative that I stand before him as naked as Adam meeting his maker, thus might he show me that writing also causes pain and thus might my whole body become flushed, for my flushing is being observed, after all, it's only shame that makes nudity possible to perceive, a realization that we owe to Keszel Wokalikoks, I am said to have transgressed against all of creation with my lies, I am said to have turned the world upside-down by stealing these words and assuming their authorship, for everything is contained in the script, including the creator, the principal takes my flushing as a sign of having been caught, he says, and this lying to his face leaves him no other option but to teach me pain by way of script, so that my body—the whole of my body—grows flushed in script-like fashion. But if I told the truth, I say, how could he then speak of lying to his face. You'd better not get mixed up about this, the principal says, you are thought to have stolen the script, the fable of the fat pencil proves it, so you really did lie to my face. To face up to him nakedly: This awful moment, the principal continues, you shall never, ever forget it! Oh, but you shall, my mother cries out from the laundry room, if you make no entry of it in *Schattenfroh*, that is! Too late, I reply, too late. Then I look at the script and go from the upstroke of the Y to the arm of the sigma in the ninth house, from the basement of the seventh and eighth houses back into the basement of my parents' house. The potato cellar is actually only a delimitation and no self-sufficient room, only a parcel of passage with a steel door that leads outside, to the courtyard's stone slabs. Opposite the potato cellar is the boiler room. To the left of the boiler room, beneath the staircase slope, are the bicycles. One turns around, moves with ducked head through a narrow door in the middle, between the potato cellar and the boiler room, into the juice- and preserving-jar cellar. The cellophaneskin of the freshly made jam, drips from the jelly flowing forth from the juice press, the retracted lid, the hollow that catches the dust. Vintages long faded. Preferred vintages, from a distance, if one tilts one's head back. Nobody wants to eat from such cellars anymore. Pumpkin free-floating in glass. Compote sagging downward. Dead quincesea, crusted apricot. The brittle host of rubber rings. Their glass inmates—what can still become of you? 1972 until 2002. On the frontlines. Is that not enough? Little soldiers. The thick-walled glass of preserving jars, Mother's distinct skin. Some glasses with delicately indicated vintage. The seventies. Aura? Aurora-wreath in series. Radiates forward in this way and in space-expanding fashion so that there's no longer any room for the label. In the middle, ballpoint bell scurrying over radiantly wreathed label. Neatly applied. The coolheadedness at the beginning of the eighties. Label. Rounded, narrow lick paper. Seventeen by five millimeters. Simply and still numbered off. A red hose with a dull aluminum top protruded from the cauldron. A metal clamp prevented premature discharge. Mothers. Only when it boils over. Apronmothers. Empty juicebottles of dark glass, nobody fills them up with anything anymore. At some point, the garden is at an end. Currantjelly of sliceable thickness. Such jelly on bread and the bread smears away. Little breadislands topped with currantjelly. The empty crustmantle. The tongue fishes undissolved sugar forth from the jelly. Like a punishment. Greengages squatting in this jar here. Burst skin swimming in the water like hair. Greengages stare out at you. Clouded pickle jar. An underseaworld. Isolated fruitstones that have formed threads. Perhaps, it is always thus. The glass shelves facing one another on the long sides of a corridor into the last room of the basement. The corridor has a shelf of provisions on the right. Cans of beer from Belgium. Eggs. Canned peas and carrots. Mustard. Sauerkraut. Hengstenberg. The beer two years expired. Still, it is drunk. Only the snap of the tab when you open the can, darkness and dead silence reign inside of it. Household appliances barely used are stored on the shelves' lower levels. During the holidays, at home in the summer, outside, for the grill. It's disappointing and gives one a bad conscience to see these things there, they're only used on certain days, only on special occasions, I don't touch them, the mere discovery of them takes away all of their shine, all of their mystery. Now, nothing more shows that a shelf once stood here. One day, we shall vanish, our houses folded up; there are people who go to look at their own grave several times a month, it gives them a triumphant feeling of security, perhaps the only one. If we simply go back to where we came from, why are we *en route* at all, why this cycling through, could it not have ended with not existing at all? The lifelong fear of becoming like those from before, then one is to lie only a few steps away from them, for this is, indeed, a family plot and that is what one possesses, even if one has lost one's life.

But before that, I go the way of all food from the arm of the sigma and into the hallmark, the upper belly of the tenth house, the B. B is the dining room adjacent to the kitchen. Here, house is every exterior view, every imagining, and every single room. Although I can move from roomhouse to roomhouse, in doing so, I simultaneously change the time-levels of the adjoining rooms, or so it seems. It's now ten years earlier. Mother serves lunch from the cellar upon a round, chairless table. That means she puts one or two steaming pots on trivets for everyone to serve themselves. However, the plates are missing, as is usually the case. Thus do we stand around the table and eat from the pot. My little brother can't reach it, his tiny arms simply aren't long enough. My other siblings and I have been taking advantage of this for a good year and blackmailing my brother. He must perform certain services for us, then we help him to get to the pot. These services consist in physical tasks, stealing cigarettes, and other thefts, of which he is only allowed to keep a small portion for himself. If he refuses or tells my mother anything about it, his next task is fasting for a whole day. This afternoon, he snitches again, we claim that he is a liar who's not quite right in the head. Mother looks each and every one of us in the eye, her gaze wanders from sibling to sibling, nobody says anything. My brother's childish grin enrages me so much that, four years later, immediately back into our common playroom after dinner, the eleventh house, which I enter through the stem of the B, I jab a sharp pencil into his neck. He turns around and wishes to go out the door, to show himself together with the pencil bobbing in his neck to my mother. If you do that, if you do that, nothing occurs to me, if you do that, I block his passage through the door, then I'll knock your teeth out. My brother reflects. If you knock my teeth out, I'll rip your balls off. You *can't* know anything about that yet, I say. If you do that, I'll jam the pencil into your right eye while you're sleeping. Yes, children are capable of the most varied atrocities. You'd really do that? I'll do it. If you jam the pencil into my right eye, I'll cut your ears off, no, I'll cut off the hand you poked my eye out with. Then I'll poke out both your eyes first so that you don't see my hands anymore. If you do that, I say to my brother, if you do that, I'll kill you. Well, I'll kill you too. How are you gonna do that, kill me, after I've already killed you. I'd be the one to kill you first. Like, in addition to everything you want to do to me. I'll kill you first. What do you mean *first*? Even before I rip your balls off. So, you'd like to swap out the ball-ripping and the killing? Yes. Then it'd probably be better if I killed right away, I say to my brother. Meanwhile, the pencil has fallen down onto the ground. I pick it up and my brother uses that opportunity to tear the door open and vanish. I follow him and go through the right leg of the U, into the curve of the twelfth house, S, in which my mother lies timelessly. She's been silent for two days. From that day on, my brother hoards preserved food in his bedside table in the thirteenth house, N, later also in the wardrobe. The bedside table is so small that my mother doesn't perceive it. Thus is it that she hasn't opened its drawer or its double doors for years. Every day, my brother carries objects into our room in his school bag, then hides them in the bedside table. Initially, I paid no attention to all the things that fit inside of it, just now, however, my brother hid away a revolver and whole cases of ammunition, not even deigning to acknowledge me with a single glance as he did. He doesn't seem to care what I think about it, he's been arrogant for some time now, each objection strengthening him in the belief that he's on the right track. Indeed, his ways are so mysterious that Mother, when she manages to leave the room in which she spends most of her time completely alone and enter another—where we are—which she's been doing less and less often as of late, reads a few lines from the Bible, primarily from the

Books of Moses and Ezekiel, for her, the purpose of these lines seems to be turning my brother's erring onto the righteous path, at the end of which she shall stand with arms outstretched, beweeping and pardoning all. My brother raises himself up and leaves the room. I want to check the box, but it cannot be opened. It also cannot be lifted up, for which there can only be two explanations. Either the box is already much too heavy or it's anchored into the ground. If the latter is the case, the box may lead directly into a shaft that connects the houses. Nobody other than rats and my brother can pass through this shaft and the rats do this incessantly and incessantly do they exchange messages by rubbing their snouts together. They are ready to storm the houses at any moment. My brother has a plague-pass letter in his drawer, a health paper-strip that only clerics receive for free, which tempts him to brag about it constantly. Like Fortunatus, my brother would very much like to have a magic purse, in which he is to ever find money and a letter of recommendation to jauntily follow him everywhere. With it, he would travel, but be back home punctually, in time for bed. Such a letter would replace school and qualify its possessor for any profession imaginable. My brother disinfected the plague-pass letter himself by fumigating it. Now, nobody has to use iron tongs to hold it. This letter sets him free from swellings. Swellings are the plague of canings. I'm never closer to my father than when he's caning me, my brother says. I want to change that now, I want him never to be closer to me than when I'm shooting him, my brother says. I let him say this, then turn toward the wardrobe, the most mysterious place of all 320 houses.

 The wardrobe, in which my brother from now on hoards his cans, has now had an open can of sausage standing upon it for days, its odor is so unbearable that my brother claims a rat is rotting in the wardrobe—i.e., my father, who died of the plague—the wardrobe is located in A, the fourteenth house, our common bedroom, into which I get from the first leg-base of the N via the back leg of the A. The wardrobe is a brown monster, it swallows up the greater part of the room. Its left half crosses the diagonal from the bed to the door, which I cannot see, lying as I am in bed, unless I lay my head at the foot of the bed. But then I would always have to stare at the sky through the window on the right-hand side, which I would prefer to avoid, for staring at the sky leads very quickly to getting lost, to dejection and dissolution. But, from looking at the foot of the bed, I do know that the sky is on the left and the door is on the right. Not being able to see them makes me think that I have them under my control, God and the devil. I can summon them with ease, I concentrate on a spot trembling before my eyes that I never quite catch. Which is the point that either God or the devil hold out for me to snatch at. Once, I thought I saw the fishing pole to which the point was attached, the pole has since sunk deep into a kind of bog, but what is a bog, a bog is no swamp, a swamp sounds more dangerous, a kind of bog, a fishing rod with a point that penetrates the surface of the water and dances. It is perhaps only the interplay of the eyes that causes the point to move thusly, dancing, trembling. Sometimes, I wake up in the night and turn on the light. I search for the point, the invisibility of which frightens me. There is no light within reach on this night, wherever I grope, I find nothing. On the way to the bathroom, I bang my shoulder, the wardrobe's sharp edge forces me to my knees, I grope toward the wardrobe, but it has no sharp edges whatsoever, it's entirely rounded, its open door takes this inward-rounding with it. The door of the wardrobe wasn't opened by me. In the darkness of the wardrobe, a green staircase leading downward reveals itself. It's quite small and hovers in space like a hologram. I'll walk into the wardrobe like my brother always used to go into the wardrobe. There's no glass that dissolves into the fog there. Thus shall one not be able to see me in the mirror and not be able to get to me. But, before that, I go into the A's first leg, into the arm of the Z, the fifteenth house, emerging from the wardrobe, the far-reaching barn of disappointment, a non-place into which one cannot really enter, a hole that is to say, a hole that is always present and in which the past always reigns.

I've come to feel at home in the disappointment that my parents are no longer as fastidious as one might have expected after all those years of training us to be orderly, but cannot live within it. The most powerful symbol was sweaters laid on top of each other in stacks that matched them up in terms of size, shape, and color. Mother planned a sweater-arrangement reform, their stacking was thenceforth to be determined by the order in which they were put on, a new sweater every third day. During the fourth week, I saw myself strolling through the city in a red sweater, the red sweater really would change a few things, the attention afforded to me would distance me from my parents so much that, from then on out, I would be an untouchable public figure. But the red sweater had a hole. Indeed, Mother had always forbidden me from opening the wardrobe, under no circumstances, she said, even today, this formulation plagues me, "under no circumstances," circumstances, to be circumstantial, circumstantial evidence, circumvention, but, this morning, I opened the wardrobe, even though the day's laundry had already been taken out and placed onto a table in the bathroom, the very table that had once served as a changing table, the table from which I'd fallen as an infant without suffering the slightest injury, a fall that, all throughout my life, made Mother suspicious as to whether it might have actually injured me, even if only inwardly, and it must have been precisely this inwardness that always haunted me. Thus did I open the wardrobe and immediately recognize the adversary at work, he who had always forced Mother to keep the wardrobe door shut and demanded this of the whole family every day as an indispensable commandment: No desire can be so great as to open the wardrobe against your better judgment, thus offering up all of the nice wool sweaters to the moths. If the world were ordered in such a way that only a clearly defined area had to be sacrificed to evil, moth damage wouldn't have to take over all subjects and regions, all regions might agree to give up a common precinct, and, in that precinct, Satan would lead in all of his creatures and have his fun, then, finally, he'd once more sit with all other religions at a common table, thankful to have grown so fat, until his sinister yearning drew him out of there once more and he had to hurl himself into the barn, to eat up all that which fear offered him, and one came to call *him* the barn, the barn that he'd incorporated, one would say to him: "You are by far the most efficient barn in the world, into which everything has been brought which has been stolen and confiscated from everybody. And in the middle sits the insatiable greedy worm, devouring much and constantly consuming a great heap of good things, surrounded by its fellow gluttons, who first suck out our blood, then feed on our flesh, until they get to the marrow, break open our inmost bones and then even want to gobble up what is left." But such a barn does not exist, there is fire everywhere in the world, fire but no stove. The moths are the Satan of Darkness and thus must there be a place that is darker than all darkness and, there, the moths fly and decompose in the darkest darkness. There must be a hole in the world that causes all the moths to vanish and it is through this hole that Satan escapes. As I was not familiar with this hole, I had need of another strategy to get rid of Satan and, with him, all the other moths that only ever left proxyholes, to get rid of them once and for all. After the fashion of Raoul Hausmann, I gave a beautiful speech to the red sweater, in which I believed Satan to be, then snatched its red corpse from the wardrobe, tumbled down the marble steps with their cast-iron banister, then ran through the kitchen and into the garden. There, it was my intention to crucify the sweater. At the back of the garden was to be found a so-called grove, which I was tempted to set fire to until I actually did set fire to it. However, the fire was extinguished quite suddenly after it had defoliated a series of shrubs and smaller trees. From then on, I promised to devote myself to the sentence, "I am who I will be." This sentence, which I thought I heard coming from the fire, was a threat. It stated that somebody was doubtlessly observing me and always would be observing me. If I already am who I will be, I thought, then shall I not become that which I am, for that is what I already am. Or does the sentence mean eternal life? Or is "be" a mere projection? If the sentence turns around into "I will be who I am," all remains as it was, being and becoming are identical, except that "that I am" may not have risen up to the self-awareness, for which the future is a prerequisite. In addition, the sentence signals to all who hear it that the one who says "I" shall also be nobody else in the future, which can be understood as a declaration of war and a threat, but also as an assurance and perhaps as an appeasement to one's own purpose. The sentence "I was who I will have been" ignites the past tense, thus omitting the present and speaking of the future as one that will already have been accomplished. In contrast, "I will be who I will be" is a mere tautology, which would seek to prevent all discussion. It is the concluding sentence of a speculative debate on being, which somebody endured or had to endure up until this concluding sentence. The sentence "I was who I was" declares the past to be closed and, therefore, non-negotiable as such, here stands somebody who was born as a person in the moment. With the sentence "I am who I was," I go backward.

I bound broken branches together into a cross with a cord and thrust it underneath the red sweater. I determined that the red was purest blood, even if the crucified sweater looked like a scarecrow. I bound it to a tree and beat it with a rake until it hung from the cross in tatters. Then I set it alight. Satan burned furiously. I unbound the cross from the tree, dug a hole in the grove, and buried the carbonized wood together with the remains of the sweater. Years later, I was still haunted by the notion that a demon would one night rise up from the earth and come to seek me out. I also dreamed two dreams, which alternated constantly, and, while I was dreaming the one dream, the fear of the other was already building up, in such a way that I supposed a common force to lie behind them both, one that desired to wear me down. In the first dream, I was under the compulsion to relate everything back to the number 1, a 7, for example, is 1+1+1+1+1+1+1 and 0 does not exist. The number 173 contains the digit 1 173 times, which is identical with the 1 that is contained nineteen times in the number 19, this being initially unsurprising. At the basis of 19 sheep lies the number 1 nineteen times, which is identical to the number 1 contained nineteen times in 19 cows, in such a way that sheeps and cows, if there are 19 of both of them, are identical. The same goes for 19 people. From which, for example, comes the result that men are not to kill sheep and cows, or, to be more precise, that 19 men are not to kill 19 sheep or 19 cows, as this is unequivocal murder. In the other dream, I was subjected to the compulsion of stealing my parents' jewelry, a compulsion that was constantly growing, for example, I purloined a signet ring and, barely had I stuck it into my pants, when it reemerged in its old place. I hoarded this loot in my desk drawer, which smelled of apples that had been stored for weeks, until they rotted. This seemed to be a safe hiding place for them, nobody other than me would open a drawer, which, when opened, would release such a fatal odor, causing anybody who wasn't already accustomed to it to be overcome with nausea in seconds. But I've always been invigorated by ethylene and I regularly go through withdrawals if I'm away from the drawer for more than even an hour. Soon, there was no more room in the drawer for the growing amount of jewelry, after four weeks, I had around twenty copies of Father's signet ring alone, in addition to several copies of his wedding ring, which he seldom removed, and it was a particular triumph for me to find it just lying around somewhere. From my mother's jewelry box, I would take out as much as I could grab with two hands, as I only allowed myself one attempt each day. Initially, I kept a kind of competition list with a ranking of the best days, but, over time, this became as burdensome to me as the jewelry itself, I no longer knew what to do with it, thus did I take it outside of the house, bury it in the garden, or throw it into the trash can. If I remembered these dreams over the course of the day, the demon in me would awaken, threatening to betray me immediately, a certain number had to be reached, then he would come, I kept asking him about this number and, at a certain point, he finally indicated: 666. This taboo number triggered another spell of arithmomania in me, I had to calculate how many times I'd purloined the jewel each time I did and, if I miscounted or wasn't entirely certain, this would drive me into a rage. It's a harmless compulsion, was how I sought to calm myself, it's bad to count every step one takes or all the letters or all the trees or all the cars or all the houses or all the people or all the seconds. The demon knows 666, I said to myself, the demon is Satan. Satan is 364, all but one day, on which he has no legal authority. Thus is it not 666, but 302, which made the counting easier for me. I want to learn shofar, I decided, that will confuse him and cause him to forget on Rosh Hashanah, in such a way that I receive the Seal of Life.

I reached 301, while burying the jewelry in the garden, I uncovered a deep hole, into which the rings, bracelets and chains suddenly fell. As with the well of the Imperial Castle of Kyffhausen, 176 hand-pounded meters deep, like no other castle-well in the world, I expected a grumbling voice to complain about the pain caused by the falling jewelry: "Let that go, otherwise you're really in for it, you toadstool-eater," I heard, though I perceived no motion. The hole must have been deeper than the Kyffhäuser hole, a queasy heat rose up from it and made my face sweat. It wasn't water to be found at the bottom of the hole, but fire, melting down all of the jewelry and forming it into an idol. Down there walks Satan, I was certain, I deliver my parents' jewelry to him, and when I stopped with these deliveries, the hole into which all thought and imagination led down, deeper than food into the belly, came to be within me. The hole must be in an image so that I might close it up in myself once more and only Mother can hold the Satan within me at bay. Thus do I return through a single point, back from the end to the beginning.

In A, the sixteenth house, there is an oil painting by Champion, it is called *Lowlands*, it shows the "Rhine landscape near Düsseldorf," Mother said, one day, it shall hang from the corridor wall where I live.

That's not a good place for it at all, but it signified home to Mother and thus must her home also have a home. It's an outrage that my mother died. If there were any authority upon whom to avenge death, I would become Michael Kohlhaas. There, in the oil painting, flows the Rhine. Two cows can be seen, perhaps three or four. The trees are leafless, the earth doesn't seem to be frozen. A woman in a red coat is strolling off in the distance, a flower. She shall soon have vanished from the painting, which is entirely occupied by the Rheinauen. Life might well entirely exhaust itself in the contemplation of this painting. Oft have I observed Mother standing before this painting, without wishing to see anything, she had already seen everything, standing before the painting, she had only to recall it briefly, then she would be strolling through the Rheinauen near Düsseldorf once more. It's quite wonderful to have a painting, into which one can flee, in it, one knows for certain that one can act out life as a transitory condition, to turn away, then to turn back once more, to be man and wife in the phantom of this something, which is an image and is thus neither dream nor reality. Mood is always quotation. One day, on Champion's trail, I discovered a painting by him entitled *Sunday Strolling*, which, also with a central perspective, shows an only negligibly different section of the landscape. Did the painter have no imagination? Did he always seek out this same area so as to put something that was exemplary about it on display? I envy this painter, for he has something I've lost, a place the visitation of which comes to form his identity. And what if this place doesn't exist in the slightest? Does that make a difference? He painted it, so it exists. And, because it exists, he can paint it over and over again. Identity is varied repetition, Franz Mon says. Didn't the Romantics seek out places that they then put down onto their canvases in idealized fashion? Here a spring flowing from a mountain, there a mountain that is as impossible to find in one's environs as the spring. In *Sunday Strolling*, the painter shifts the landscape a little further off from the viewer than in Mother's painting; in the foreground, behind a gap of shadow that widens to the right, a massive, sunlit path bordered by two beech trees can be seen, on it, coming from the left, a young couple is strolling with their child (a girl) and their dog (a sheep dog?) running up ahead. The landscape presents itself to the viewer as if in a peep box, the two trees framing the peephole through which the eyes see a stilled image. In this frame show, the landscape comes to itself and the observer to the landscape, which he cannot enter, but only come upon, as it does not even remotely exist outside of his gaze. His desire to see is satiated, the illusion builds up in him that he might be able to flee into the painting together with his body and escape from his true environs. He has already entered into the painting as a young couple with a child and a dog. However, the frame is not shut, it is no window frame. The sky is open—and empty. The cloud is a consolation hanging in the air, it is meant to distract from the void. The tableau is overseeable in both senses of the word; but what do the trees disguise? Is the beyond behind them? The meadow where we played as children? And on the left—there, I come as a couple with dog and child. Thus are we all simultaneously present in and with this painting: childhood, youth, old age, my mother, the child. The family does not see the shadow, but shall enter into the shadow. The gaze drifts off into the distance, though it sees nothing there. Thus might it perhaps miss what is unfolding before it. The wet meadows in the painting frighten me, they cover the earth like a carpet, as if nature were compelled to hide something or as if someone had dragged the locus amoenus out over an abyss, a pleasant idyll over Gehenna. From the foot of the A, I go into the leg of the seventeenth house, the R, a dark room, in which it is brighter than in the light of the sun. In this room, the elect shall possess both joy and peace. How beautifully the light ("Licht") is contained in duty ("Pflicht") and the most beautiful duties are self-imposed ones. Glorified be this light, for it glorifies itself. And this light drives and pushes me away. The room is a receptacle of light that is as dark as the universe inside me when I close my eyes and set off on my travels. In the room, I learn that

Herr Helfmeier from the second house has died. I hear the expression "heart attack" for the first time in my life. I feel my pulse, follow it in the direction of the heart, check my heart, discover the expression "heart palpitations," I take my mother's nightly bogeyman to heart, she called it "heart troubles," lie in bed, breath carefully through the mouth so as not to miss my heart's beating, I hear my heart all too well and listening to my heart only accelerates its beating, then my heart begins to gallop, springing over the Rheinauen fencing, chasing after the red coat, it doesn't budge, throws me off, elopes, it has been on the run ever since. I am certain that I shall catch up with it one day and close the chest, which immediately disappears back into the sea of the tabletop and reveals a gorge, now, decades later, referred to as "Teufelsschlucht," the Devil's Gorge. I can explore the gorge with binoculars, which I feel through the table-top while the chest is dashed to bits in the valley. There is an engraving to be found on the binoculars: "All disassembly is strictly forbidden." There is an address tag on their case: Lungstraß, Grubenreu, Herrenstraße 31. I shall drive there only to discover that my grandparents' house no longer exists, in 1981, it fell victim to a so-called city-center redevelopment. The binoculars fit nicely, the eyes are relaxed and tire very little. But what is shown by the glass does not show the glass itself, the eyes alone cannot see it, something must be happening between the eyepiece and the lens, hidden from the naked eye. And what do the eyes see? A valley through which the Prüm flows, wedged between two cliffs of sandstone, they once belonged together, thousands of years ago, until the perpetual alternation of frost and thaw broke a large piece of rock out of the plateau and tore it down into the depths. The Teufelsschlucht is twenty-eight meters deep, the binoculars show. Old seabed. The crevice in the rock would be easy to leap over, as it is only one meter wide at its narrowest point. There's nothing to gain, however, over on the other side, the shore is without hinterland, a raised rock formation as the end of walkable civilization. No plants grow there, the rock is exposed to the stubborn sun, no animal strays there, a rusty Coke can rattles in the wind, rolling to and fro in a small depression. Over there is the promised land of which everyone dreams, I see beasts of prey charging forth with bared fangs, an invisible chain prevents them from attacking me or hurling themselves into the depths. Still, it's not without its charms, the notion of leaping over and surrendering to these marvels, of swearing to never give up that spot again, not under any circumstances. These are the dreams of the little boy who withdraws into a gloomy chamber he discovered while playing in the attic, he hopes his parents don't know of it or have forgotten it—but how could that be? Thus does the little boy have a true secret and the secret makes him strong, allows him to endure injustices, he prays to God and already feels himself to be a true martyr—in this room, he finds his grandpa's meerschaum pipe, it's still burning, in it, one can also hear the sea's murmuring, here lie photos in a box, they show his grandma's countenance, which he's never before set eyes on, it's said that she truly disliked being photographed before she fell down the outer staircase of the house one day and everyone racked their brains as to whether she had fallen down the stairs as a result of a stroke, a brain tumor, senile dementia, or softening of the brain—or did her falling down the stairs cause a stroke? The family left their speculations at that. But the incident was recounted again and again. There is no photo of her from before the fall.

In the darkroom, I pray and keep silent, forge plans as to how best to conquer the world, here, I destroy things as revenge on Father, for when he comes home from work and blindly believes all of Mother's complaints, takes the son to task, punishes him wordlessly with the cane, and I know that one must learn to use one's fists, I grab an object from one of the boxes stacked atop each other without being able to see anything, I seek to break it or, failing that, take another until the floor of the room is littered with broken things, but perhaps that's merely what I imagine myself to be doing and the things are too dear for me to be able to harm them, I probably just clear them off to the side, hide them away somewhere, and consider them as my own property from then on. A single plug is to be found in my chamber. I place the Crucified One, he who shines so bright at night that he irradiates his surroundings, onto a shoebox altar, guide the pickup head of the red plastic record player, the boxes of which serve as a cover, onto the only record that I own at a millimeter-speed, I set the needle just to the side of the record as often as I set it onto the record, the record comes to sound very dull over time, the needle has dug so deep into the ice at a certain point that it always gets stuck there. "Away with him, away with him, crucify him! Away with him, away with him, crucify him! Away with him, away with him, crucify him! Away with him, away with him, crucify him! Away with him, away with him, crucify him! Away with him, away with him, crucify him!" from the *St. John Passion* gradually becomes a torso more of foreboding than of revelation and if only I could hear more than a polyphonic scratching, for me, in the hell of the chamber, the *St. John Passion* is heaven on earth. Lord Lord Lord our ruuul . . . er, the choir thunders in a trinitarian manner after eighteen bars of prelude. "Passion" slant-rhymes with "God's son," "Zeit," time, with "Niedrigkeit," lowliness, and "ist" embraces "bist"—only fame remains without rhyme. Logos, stride forth, be incarnate and suffer. The green light is strong enough for me to decipher the Bible. What lordly poetry need and pain cast forth, regarding the Crucifixion too, chosen by the Crucified One Himself so as to convey the unbearability of His pain: "I am poured out like water, and all my bones are out of joint: my heart is like wax; it is melted in the midst of my bowels. My strength is dried up like a potsherd; and my tongue cleaveth to my jaws; and thou hast brought me into the dust of death." Nobody has ever put the visible and invisible withering of the body into words more harshly—and the poetry of the Baroque followed suit and expanded on the matter. But why does the complainer, even in the throes of mortal distress, only dare to compare? "I am poured out like water, and all my bones are out of joint: my heart is like wax; it is melted in the midst of my bowels. My strength is dried up like a potsherd; and my tongue cleaveth to my jaws; and thou hast brought me into the dust of death." It's about being "poured out," not about water. *Poured out* means very shallowly, carelessly, at some point, it oozes off, evaporates, it's about being dry, not the potsherd, strength comes from the whole of the body, the tongue concretely cleaving to its place. The tongue is mobile, the heart is not, but it is more than an organ, it is an image and a symbol, here, it's at the point of being excreted and slipping down into the pants, the body is in the process of digesting itself. Is the tongue the dry potsherd? Does all strength therefore emanate from the spirited tongue and the tongue is now as stiff and dead as a potsherd? Is *Pater non est filius non est spiritus sanctus non est pater* so because it is only the son who suffers, though the father remains unaffected by it, for he has no incarnate body, yet, still, this whole is God?

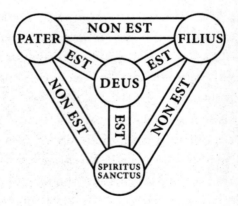

"And thou hast brought me into the dust of death." That is lamentation and certainty, in the latter of which lamentation is in good hands, as if in the hollow of one's palm. Here, death stands cleverly at the end of the line. For, the words mean only death—in which they are all contained. But the word is just alive enough for the tongue to know that only comparison and not the positing of an equivalency is proper.

Or the tongue is the stylus that aided Bach in the composition of his music. Which Passion Mass would Jesus have most liked to perform? In the glow of the self-illuminated, everything becomes kitsch. But I love that sort of kitsch, it dissolves the boundaries of the body, causes me to perceive things that I've never seen before, but that I'm convinced are to be found in the corners of the chamber. I have both, the concrete chamber of childhood in which I now find myself, in which I can hardly stand, in which the most wondrous things are to be found, hidden away in box-containing boxes and the imaginary chamber in my inwardness, in it, all the memories of my body are stored, they line my inwardness and radiate toward the outside.

The radiant green figure is no longer enough for me, he who shows himself to his worshippers from the protection of a shell, he cannot be clearly distinguished from the cross, has no visage, and is merely a bodiless Vestpocketjesus sunk into the cross. I want to crucify the crucified Christ myself, thus do I decide to abduct the Christ carved by the Austrian sculptor Kurt Sammler,* it hangs over the dresser in my parents' bedroom. His beautifully fashioned body can be detached from its cross by way of clever twisting and pulling. He is some thirty centimeters tall, a crown of thorns sits upon the summit of his head, it seems to cause him pain that comes on quick as lightning and brings tears into his eyes, the artist has succeeded in making the visage so expressive that one seems to locate the source of each pain, the feet, the tendons of which one can trace with one's finger, are nailed one on top of the other, the arms spread wide are expertly nailed to the cross between the ulna and radius, and only the nails hold the body to the cross, the stab with the lance in the side caused him to arch to the right, but wasn't he already dead? or was there a narcotic in the vinegar that allowed him to survive his martyrdom, stunned, in such a way that he was able to deceive the Romans and truly did rise again on the third

---

* Collector.

day, in any case, for onlookers this is a more meaningful death penalty than hanging, there is the possibility that death will only come after days, the crucified are subjected to lengthy torments, those who are able to remain on site so as to not miss the spectacle. What did these gawkers know about the cause of Jesus' death? Did they believe that the Crucified One faced death by suffocation, as, in the context of hanging there, the air could be taken into the lungs, but no longer expelled? Did they believe that, as a result of the arms gradually becoming paralyzed and the spasms running through the body, the Crucified One was no longer able to find relief, not even for a moment, by hoisting himself up? Did the joints tear? That is the very least of what crucified people experience. What remains hidden: only the carbon dioxide that accumulates in the lungs and the blood due to a lack of exhalation, it shall poison the body, though it also allows for temporary uncramping. Then the pericardium fills up with blood serum and threatens to crush the heart. Simultaneously, the Crucified One dries up on the inside. The heart wishes to pump that which can no longer be pumped, the cells thirst, the body hangs there until it becomes limp.

But what does one really know of Christ's crucifixion? Barbet wants to find out on my behalf and crucifies amputated arms in the eighteenth house. What does he believe himself able to glean from the weight-burdened limbs? He can no longer ask the corpse he is crucifying of its condition. He pinned the little old man to the cross like a taxidermied animal and one would merely require a skilled dermo-sculptor, a taxidermist who loves his job, to fix up the Crucified Corpse Showpiece, to put it into a position believable to the layman, the upper body sagging to the knees, which, seen from the side, form a triangle with the wood of the cross, handed down to posterity in such a way that, from a certain distance, it is impossible to distinguish whether this martyred one is made up of skin and bones or even wood, a work of art that justifies the entire existence of the fine arts. Overall, however, I do not agree with Barbet's gadgetry and measures and thus do

I engage Frederick Beizug,* the leading expert, who shows how one must do it: one must crucify a living body, but only, of course, after it has been flagellated. The cross measures 2.30 meters in height and two meters in width. Driving nails through hands and feet injures nerve tracts, the Crucified One screams out in pain, there is nobody outside of the house who can hear him, and there is no position that affords him relief, the suppedaneum, a supporting board sometimes placed beneath the feet of the Crucified One, provides momentary relief by allowing the martyred one to put weight on it, but this only prolongs the death throes. Without the suppedaneum, nobody in a crucified position is able to heave themselves up. They don't have the strength, the cramped and twitching lower legs demand relief, they cannot straighten out the body, the knees soon begin to ache—not even mentioning the shoulders and wrists—due to the injured nerves, any attempt to move increases the agony. Most of the body weight is borne by the arms outstretched on the cross, which quickly come to feel as if they were being torn out of their sockets. All this pain is implemented in perpetuity, relief cannot be brought about by the Crucified One.

Jesus lost a great deal of blood as a result of the scourging with the flagellum and the nailing of the hands and feet, and, as a function of the reduction of the amount of blood circulating in the body, he has gone into shock, at times, his pulse can hardly be felt, then the heart races once more, he sweats blood, his pericardium becomes inflamed, unbearable pain runs through his chest, he attempts to relieve it by shortness of breath, but he doesn't gasp for air, at most, he hyperventilates in a moment of great need. Jesus finds much stronger words for all that in the Psalms. Of suffocation, however, there can be no talk, though that is often what is assumed to take place due to the posture one takes upon the cross, which is alleged to prevent sufficient oxygen from being taken in.

---

* Frederick Inclusion.

Beizug issues the death certificate: "Cardiac and respiratory arrest, due to hypovolemic and traumatic shock, due to crucifixion." And with this result, after fifty-three years of experimental research, which is alleged to be of epochal importance for all the sciences, Beizug is so satisfied that he gives a 10 percent discount on his honorarium, which hasn't been mentioned at all up till now, which means that I can keep at least 10 percent of my inheritance for myself. I am still many years away from my inheritance, I ask him how he can be certain that he shall receive the sum he has asked for, but not in any way agreed upon with me, he waves this off and says that I can be certain that he shall find me, and if he has found me without me having been able to pay the 90 percent, Beizug pauses and points to the Crucified One, then, having already borne witness to it, you shall be able to experience it firsthand. Anyway, I now have a genuine Jesus on the cross and, as I take a somewhat closer look at this Jesus, I am disappointed to have found no trace of the flagellation upon his wooden back, after all, I dismounted him and took him with me for the purpose of contemplation. Art wants to embellish everything, that much is certain. If one wants sincere expression, only photography and film are of use—and only the Crucified One knows nothing of the recording of his execution, in which case it isn't the Crucified One's knowledge that would be the problem, but the knowledge of his knowledge. Then the problem of perspective remains and every perspective is terrifying—false too. If every perspective is false, then this constatation is either irrelevant or photo and film are impossible.

The purpose of the lashing is to leave the skin of the back hanging in tatters, also so that the ruined back provides additional torment when the Crucified One hangs from his post. I can do something similar with my Jesus. So far, I've only tested the carving tool on balsa wood, which requires no great exertion. The lower the overcoming-threshold of the material, the lower its artistic value. But, now, I'm faced with real challenges. Jesus is already carved. In my hands, he is on the verge of resurrection, only the back needs to be touched up. I interrogate him. I make it clear that his mission cannot be fulfilled thusly. Was he not flagellated with the short bone-and-lead-reinforced whip? Why, then, did his back heal so quickly? I imagine performing the flagellation accompanied by the Munich Philharmonic, in front of an invited audience. A note with the following information is handed to the audience with the admission ticket: "The pains of the Holy Spirit ought not be disturbed by coughing. For this reason, herbal hard candy and cloth handkerchiefs with the likeness of the Turin Shroud printed upon them are to be handed out at the cloakroom—you are welcome to take them home with you, used or unused, after the show." Two passages from the fourth version of the *St. John Passion* by Johann Sebastian Bach are being performed. And, already, the opening chorus, "Lord, our ruler," rings out, the greatest music ever composed, a thunderous exordium: "Lord, our ruler, whose glory / is magnificent everywhere. / Show us through your passion, / that you, the true son of God, / at all times / even in the most lowly state, / are glorified." Three times the Lord, a trinitarian invocation, transverse flutes and oboes capture Christ's Passion in various tones, the Holy Spirit makes up their bed of minimally varying waves of semi-quavers in the strings and both are suspended in the basso continuo of the organ point, the "unshakeable calm of God the Father," as Martin Geck* puts it.

The performance is short, I spring over sixteen recitatives, chorales, and arias so as to come right to the recitatives and chorus: "Then Pilate said to him" / "Not this man, but Barrabas!" / "But Barrabas was a murderer":

18a. Recitative   **Evangelist:**
    Tenor   Then Pilate said to him:
    Continuo

---

* Martin Jerk.

Pilate:
So you are then a king?

Evangelist:
Jesus answered:

Jesus:
You say it, I am a king. For this I was born and came into the world, so that I should testify to the truth. Anyone who is of the truth hears my voice.

Evangelist:
Pilate said to him:

Pilate:
What is truth?

Evangelist:
And when he said this, he went back out to the Jews and said to them:

Pilate:
I find no fault in him. But you have a custom, that I release one prisoner to you; do you wish then that I should release to you the king of the Jews?

Evangelist:
They all cried out together and said:

18b. Chorus
Flauto traverso I/II e Oboe I e Violino I, Oboe II col Soprano, Violino II coll'Alto, Viola col Tenore, Continuo

Not this man, but Barrabas!

18c. Recitative
      Continuo

Evangelist:
But Barrabas was a murderer.

The Flagellation lasts fifty-one struck notes of the vocal part. I castigate the wooden Jesus created by the Austrian sculptor Kurt Sammler primarily in semitones and whole-tone steps:

With the final G is the performance at an end, leaving behind at least one question and three answers: How can one give life a definitive form in a work of art? Most likely, it shall always remain finishedly unfinished. We are like ants who *are* as a collective through the individual who is naught. This naught shines through and into this naught shall we return.

    I leave the Philharmonic, into which the eighteenth house has transmogrified itself, moving through the stem of the E and getting across into the N by way of its own second leg. Here in the nineteenth house stands my bed. Behind the bed stands an old shelf, which is draped over with a heaped-up curtain. On the wall, I write the sentences: "The mute word is dubbed I. I ought to go to the shooting." I know that these sentences are not mine and that I have not entirely reproduced the text, from which they've come. Mother startles. Meaning those are fine sentences. I place Father's dental bridge onto the shelf, he forgot it in a glass of water. For days, he looks through the house for it, then he has a new one made. I also destroy Grandpa's golden pocket watch, which I found in Father's nightstand when I was supposed to "stock up on sleep" in my parents' room, it's always dreams that chase me out of my bed at night, in my dreams, there are brittle stairs, whole steps are missing, thus do I run down the stairs from the roof, run back up the staircase, down, up, but I don't really get out of breath over this short distance, I hope that this exercise shall finally afford me dreamless sleep, I ought to stock up on sleep in their bed until they themselves come to bed, then the time of dreams shall be past and I'm to sleep in my own bed until morning, but I don't sleep, I search for lost dreams—to see whether they're still there. When they get worse than they were before, I come to believe that the destruction of the golden pocket watch has some secret connection to Father's vanished dental bridge, thus do I put the crown of the watch next to the tooth-piece on the shelf. The watch lies in a small, self-crocheted bag, its glass is not made of glass, but of easily broken plastic. I can't conceive of the fact that a genuine gold watch has no glass made of glass, the plastic is easy to remove, the bending of the hands costs no effort at all. One can still hear the delicate ticking, but the hands only twitch, I remove them from the minute pinion and hour wheel, then put them into the drawer atop the stack of ironed handkerchiefs that Father always pulls out of his pants pocket with a flourish, he keeps one corner in his hand and opens the handkerchief in the air. Cloth napkins and handkerchiefs lose their right to exist once their owners have died. Nothing good can be thought of he who continues to make use of them. The stack of handkerchiefs is his lifetime's soft grave.

To see things' formerness in their present means that one does not really allow the present to come closer in such a demanding way. The old gaze, with which one penetrates the changes, consoles us for that which is lost. Thus do old-fashioned sights and smells, forms and colors, come back into the light, one has always avoided them. We are always already our parents. And now, in the nineteenth house, my old room, right as I come to recognize this fact, a fallen angel speaks up, he lauds himself for having initiated the flagellation of Christ in me. The angel possesses the gift of walking through the houses in the opposite direction, which is itself already the opposite direction, perhaps he is also a notorious threshold-strider and can only go back and forth constantly between N and U, the nineteenth and twentieth houses. He's been nagging me that I ought to give myself over entirely to reading in the twentieth house, only there would I have all the leisure necessary to do nothing else but devote myself to books that are available in abundance, he tells me that I only have to express a wish and I'll already be holding the book in my hands, in this way, I could also read books that haven't yet been written, the angel particularly recommends two new books about itself, René Girard: *I See Satan Fall like Lightning* and Kurt Flasch: *The Devil and His Angels: The New Biography*. However, in a certain respect, this unvarnished advertising campaign spoils the notion of the truly free availability of reading material for a limitless period. The angel notes me shrinking back and offers me the following bargain: I can take him up on his offer and spend as much time in "his" house as is necessary, it would be available to me indefinitely, and he would see to it that no coveting or craving would get in the way of whatever reading material I had to hand. But I might wish to read books, I reply to him, that put an antidote to this pact at my disposal. You still don't know what I demand in return, the angel says. I ask for nothing more than that everything you write after the twentieth house belong to me. But it already belongs to Schattenfroh, I say. The angel is silent. And smiles. Now, I know that he is Schattenfroh wishing to tempt me. I ought to think about it a bit, he says, after all, it's the same for everyone in the circumstance of the inevitable distraction caused by the magnitude and multitude of contemporary interests, all the while in doubt whether the noisy clamor of the day and the deafening chatter of a conceit that takes pride in confining itself to those interests, might still leave room for partaking in the dispassionate calm of a knowledge dedicated to thought alone. My father has already asked himself that question and I am familiar with the doubt, I say, and, as I say this, it becomes clear to me that Schattenfroh is my father who wishes to call me away from the world and to make me harmless forevermore in the twentieth house. The fallen angel acts astonished as far as my father is concerned, I tell him that my father already asked himself that on page 442, but these are partially Hegel's words, whom my father quoted with reference to the year. Hegel, the angel says, is a devil, who, in certain cases, only put down on paper and expressed in his lectures that which he, the angel, had thought and expressed years before. Therefore, Hegel ought to have quoted the angel and not Hegel himself.

For is it not written: "I will not conceal his parts, nor his power, nor his comely proportion. Who can discover the face of his garment? or who can come to him with his double bridle? Who can open the doors of his face? his teeth are terrible round about. His scales are his pride, shut up together as with a close seal. One is so near to another, that no air can come between them. They are joined one to another, they stick together, that they cannot be sundered. By his neesings a light doth shine, and his eyes are like the eyelids of the morning. Out of his mouth go burning lamps, and sparks of fire leap out. Out of his nostrils goeth smoke, as out of a seething pot or caldron. His breath kindleth coals, and a flame goeth out of his mouth. In his neck remaineth strength, and sorrow is turned into joy before him. The flakes of his flesh are joined together: they are firm in themselves; they cannot be moved. His heart is as firm as a stone; yea, as hard as a piece of the nether millstone. When he raiseth up himself, the mighty are afraid: by reason of breakings they purify themselves. The sword of him that layeth at him cannot hold: the spear, the dart, nor the habergeon. He esteemeth iron as straw, and brass as rotten wood. The arrow cannot make him flee: slingstones are turned with him into stubble. Darts are counted as stubble: he laugheth at the shaking of a spear. Sharp stones are under him: he spreadeth sharp pointed things upon the mire. He maketh the deep to boil like a pot: he maketh the sea like a pot of ointment. He maketh a path to shine after him; one would think the deep to be hoary. Upon earth there is not his like, who is made without fear. He beholdeth all high things: he is a king over all the children of pride."

Now, it is written, I reply. Leviathan has taken on the shape of a fallen angel and I am his secretary. You perceived that quite keenly, the angel says. What have I keenly perceived? That Leviathan has taken on the shape of a fallen angel. After all, he must protect Michael the Dragon Slayer so that he doesn't assume himself able to kill him, indeed, God himself shows that only God can destroy him. It is said that he is God's golem, over whom, or so people think, he at some point lost control. But the truth is that he has lost control over God. But what is crucial for you, the angel says, is the opportunity to afford a book the attention it deserves without being distracted from this occupation by anything else. After about thirty pages, doesn't one always have the feeling of missing out on something in life and abandon the reading, whether this is ultimately due to moral scruples—how pointless wasting the time that one might invest in bettering the world—or a question of sheer boredom, which results from the inevitable comparison between the world of reading and the life-world imagined as being infinitely richer, makes no difference in terms of the outcome, thus, in the context of the provided-for suppression of the life-reality that would otherwise burst in, singular concentration on a book turns this book into life's center.

This becomes too tempting, I can no longer resist the notion of making the imaginary real by uttering it, the angel already suspects as much when he says: "Already, one of your colleagues knows to report the most moving of the most wondrous, the most believable miracles and the most miraculous objects of belief, by, for instance, writing: 'You need only imagine a forest and, already, you emerge from a forest.' But you shall not emerge from a forest, you shall go into an empty house. Take all the time that you need, in the end, you shall be one with the books, you shall be the book *Schattenfroh*, which can be any book that you imagine. You shall not fare as Bouvard and Pécuchet did, those miserable copyists, the times have changed, at least as far as books and reading are concerned, the books are in your head, you shall no longer leaf through them, but observe inner projections, the words shall act on you like a medicine, this is a new form of understanding that comes to pass without the reading-effort that's been passed down, without blue glasses. Alexandre Dumas shan't entertain you like a laterna magica, those days are over, I doubt that you shall even read Alexandre Dumas, Flaubert, yes, he really has high calorific value, not as high, however, as Borges, thus would it be better for you to read Borges, who, moreover, was the only one who understood and saw through *Bouvard and Pécuchet*. Whatever you read, you shall not come to the conclusion that Bouvard and Pécuchet did—that syntax is a figment of the imagination and grammar an illusion, rather, both provide a beautiful scaffolding that is sometimes more handsome than that which it carries. The two of them are not to be taken seriously, but you are. Literature is no dalliance, no pastime, it *is* time. Life has no more intense experience to offer, life is truly and only there to be read. One reads life away, letters are merely another sort of spectacles, which allow us to see things that life conceals with its own things. It's too crowded around us, the empty reading room offers wealth that only the true reader is allowed to immerse himself in.

And, as far as writing is concerned: It is no longer necessary to write toward a profundity in the humiliating hope that something shall rise up, rather, profundity is the inward gaze, which, for those standing outside, radiates outward, through everything, but for those who read in this way, it is nothing but the suppression of all that which lies outside, a inward voyage, a contemplation of the imaginary."

The leg-wall of the nineteenth house, N, becomes porous and I enter U, the twentieth house. The fallen angel promised me an enormous library, U is a supine goblet on the inside, a magnet on the outside, the goblet is completely empty, not a single book to be found in it. I've fallen into a trap and I myself am to blame, I ought not to have read so much or I ought to have read only the right books, only non-fiction. U is so big that I fear one day will not be enough to explore its interior. U is Lake Constance, Lake Michigan, I don't dare to raise my head, so I look straight ahead. And yet, though this house is so spacious, it hems me in. It takes my breath away, I'm tempted to be aggressive toward myself, to hurl myself down onto the floor, to smash my head against the wall. But wouldn't that be pointless, given that there's nobody around to watch? And what wall would I smash myself against, I wouldn't be able to reach it within a day and thus would my anger simply run off. There is somebody next to me. But, when I turn around, he's no longer there. When I thrash about, I don't make contact with anyone. If I stand entirely still, he envelops me like a cocoon. If I move my eyes, I pull him from right to left, from left to right. He always follows. It would be nice, I think, if he could not only follow me, but I could also follow him. Something in this house makes it so that I see myself thinking. It's dead quiet. Roughly in the middle of the house, which consists only of this single room, which is to say, in the middle of the typographical counter, something gently takes hold of me, I sit in the air as if in a comfortable chair, and, the longer I sit, I fear, the more difficult it shall be to extricate myself from this position. I've never been in a more comfortable position in my life. Lying down, I think, would be even more pleasant than sitting. I lie down. Perhaps I should sleep a bit, but I am afraid that I'll end up like Malone—and I can already see how he ends up, he says it himself: "I fear I must have fallen asleep again. In vain I grope, I cannot find my exercise-book. But I still have the pencil in my hand. I shall have to wait for day to break. God knows what I'm going to do till then." I would rather not have to say the following about myself either: "I hope this is not too great a distortion of the truth. I now add these few lines, before departing from myself again." Malone's spells of amnesia, whether caused by sudden sleep or some sort of fainting, are to pass me by. No, I'd rather not swap places with him, though he certainly is a beloved personality, besides which he is utterly useless for the Frightbearing Society, indeed, his stories are funny, especially the one about Moll, or deadly boring, like the one about . . . I forgot, which he himself says, they bore him, however, he never actually forgets them, and that actually bugs me, but, beyond that, his twilight states of consciousness yield up nothing worthy of being collected, if I'm not mistaken that is, maybe I really am mistaken, I've read *Malone Dies* about a dozen times with great concentration and hardly anybody in the world can match that, so, if I say that it doesn't yield up anything, then it's true. For me. Let's leave it at that, I shall not study *Malone Dies* again, I now see him before my eyes everywhere and wish to devote myself entirely to the exploration of the twentieth house.

If the angel promised me too much and I can find nothing but emptiness here, that means Schattenfroh is in league with him and has immediately punished me for my pact. If that is so, I am to sit in solitary confinement as a prisoner of the Frightbearing Society and live off of every word that comes out of my mouth. But I could put off checking whether the angel has kept his word for a little while, safe in the conviction that he has. I would live in the conviction that every action is superfluous. I think "Think nothing." Thus do I still think.

This resolution, if there even was one, doesn't last long, I'm now thinking "consciousness" and "perception"—and can already read my way through a chic bibliography in italics at a freely chosen speed, it also lists the very latest of intellectual achievements, how they infiltrate the world in the form of so-called books, even though, in reality, they leave one cold. Interestingly enough, what I read isn't noted down, there must apparently be some other form of constatation, however, I now notice that the titles I examine more closely remain present in my memory, and I have the ability to recall them. Later, I will check if I can do this however often I'd like. If my inner gaze lingers on a title for more than three seconds, the book opens up—as if imagination and thought could push a button. A sample:

"The sense impulse requires variation, requires time to have a content; the form impulse requires the extinction of time, and no variation. Therefore, the impulse in which both are combined (allow me to call it provisionally the *play impulse*, until I have justified the term), this play impulse would aim at the extinction of time *in time* and the reconciliation of becoming with absolute being, of variation with identity."

Those are the best sentences I have ever read. I look forward to soon reading even better ones. Do Schattenfroh and the fallen angel know who wrote them? The sentences strike upon my condition very accurately. I suffer from the form impulse. Indeed, it is that of which the angel spoke, that which allows for concentrated reading. The sense impulse destroys all that which means reading, but also harms writing. As for the play impulse, that is precisely what comes to mind when I think of reading and writing, but I am afraid I shall have to ask for Schattenfroh's permission—ask if it wouldn't be indecent to use that term with reference to the Frightbearing Society, but I haven't heard from Schattenfroh for a long time, thus does nothing remain for me but to assume that he shall make a report in good time, I still have no proof that the fallen angel, my father, and Schattenfroh are one—the Trinity of the Frightbearing Society.

By the way, I now remember that Sapo is the guy's name, probably Malone when he was young or Sam when he was young, one of those stinkingly boring stories is about him, the ones Malone thinks he has to tell himself to pass the time.

"Draw up a list of books that I've read with great interest for the Frightbearing Society," I now say in the capital U, something is coming to pass off in the distance, I can't perceive it with the naked eye, but can hear it, and thus do I set off on the way there, as if somebody had given me the command to do so. My eyes are fixed upon that which I can inwardly already see: a golden shelf that forms itself forth from the walls and smells wonderfully of frankincense and myrrh. If one gets right up close to it, one shall be entirely enveloped in smoke. "In the mind before the eye," Diether Ort wrote, and so it is, indistinguishably, simultaneously, an inner compass for one to follow—one that the world already is: indistinguishably, simultaneously. White is the most beastly color, it causes one to freeze, blurs the contours, I have trouble maintaining this direction, it cannot be ruled out that I'm running in circles, that I'll never reach a wall, the white is so blinding, the only thing that I now see is the aura of my migraine, a jagged flicker that slowly drifts outward, the aura causes my environs to burn, burning snow, I run through a snowstorm, one driving me entirely into my inwardness. I keep my eyes open, remain in motion, experience has taught me not to lie down when I have a migraine and to get up should it come over me when I'm lying down, asleep, for instance, my motions slow, I keep my head slightly bent, I see to the left and to the right by turning my entire body, my gaze looks directly through everything without fixing upon anything, nothing is coming to pass within me, my thoughts are switched off, an irascible will to reach my goal sweeps away all that which would desire a shift in thinking and thus have I been on the way for two days without having thought anything but finally reaching the wall at the end of the U's leg. Malone has caught up with me, unlike him, I don't lie incessantly in bed, but am incessantly on the way, and the problem lies precisely in this "incessantly," I am not at all certain that I've not collapsed and passed out several times from exhaustion. I can't remember dreams, my memory is as white as the walls, the contours that I see in them are mere floaters that move with the eye, the brain demands a contouring of the snow and is simultaneously overwhelmed by it, I must avoid the sight of it and concentrate entirely on the library, then a boy appears next to me, he's drawing attention to himself with his shaking head and shuffling steps. He points in the direction in which I'm going, tears run down his cheeks, I don't wish to allow myself to be disconcerted by him and pretend I've not seen him. Why is he shaking his head? He seems to be orienting himself toward me, for he's gazing at me incessantly. Something strange comes to pass with his outstretched arm, it gets shorter and shorter the longer we go, in a few minutes, he shall no longer have a hand, his fingers have already disappeared up to the metacarpus, he shall soon be pointing forward with radius and ulna, and even if the messenger boy is no longer visible, something will point forward and the head-shaking will hover next to me too, his demi-profile, which I only ever wish to palpate fleetingly so as not to attract increased attention, he never looks at me straight on, nor does he ever turn his head in profile, stuns me so much that I quicken my pace so as to set eyes upon his face from the front, but the boy also quickens his stride, if I stand still, he too stands still and continues to shake his head, when I rush forward, he catches up with me right away, over time, it seems that he comes to anticipate my maneuvers—whether I stand still or walk backward, nothing can surprise him anymore, and thus do I stick with my normal gait, his feet (he walks barefoot) no longer have toes, I notice, they're undergoing the same process his hands are and maybe his tears just signify pain, which would be a relief to me, however, I'm afraid that they anticipate the things that I'm going to see, somebody is slowly erasing him, now I know that, by the time we get to the wall he warns against so forcefully, he shall have vanished entirely. I am distracted. The face. I see my grandpa in it. And my father. And myself. And my daughter. My clever daughter. The traits mix. My father isn't always the age that he is now, he is also quite young sometimes, my daughter remains ever young, I would very much like to see how she looks later on, I run through five decades, my grandpa—seven or eight, endless combinations appear in the messenger's visage, now, all four of us are quite young, the messenger stops weeping, he himself is very young at the moment, some four years old, while, otherwise, he is immutably fifteen or sixteen years, we have an astonished facial expression, the boy's face really does flicker, in time-lapse photography, snapshots light up within him, Prüm appears, the Eifel, the Dauner Maars, Trier, Saarburg and Grubenreu, my mother in my father's face upon the face of the messenger, who bears the head of my grandpa, laughing and bending down to his boxer and stroking its head, the face of my graceful mother in my face, mirrored in the gaze of my father in the messenger's four-year-old eyes, he's looking at me from the side and shaking his head, and I see my daughter's facial expression in all of them, she's sitting cheerfully at the table, listening again and again to the soundbook *Do You Hear the Musical Instruments*, flute, piano, guitar, drum, violin, and glockenspiel, she makes them play by placing her index finger onto the circular spot with the heat-dependant resistance that triggers them, then she names their colors while humming along.

That this is Doctor Mabuse's outstretched arm shrinking ever more is now quite clear to me, the boy's shape is Doctor Mabuse, in a matter of seconds, the messenger has snow-white hair and a long, pointed nose that is used for writing, Schattenfroh is Mabuse, he no longer writes himself, he allows me to write, thus am I constantly writing my own testament, from which those in the know shall glean the measures necessary for the Reign of Crime.

With the messenger boy, the incessant journeying has become somewhat more bearable, even if the boy is gradually becoming lost to me. The library that I'm hoping for will take on a certain divinity over time, for does God's hiddenness not precisely facilitate one's faith in him and increase his value for man, and has he not hesitated for too long to reappear in any way, yes, wouldn't he only be capable of disappointing if he were to reappear now, his meaning is his withdrawal, however, while God retains his value over millennia (and one might wish to be able to trade him on the stock exchange) precisely because one has given up the hope of encountering him in life outside of the Bible, the library—if the knowledge that it would remain forever attainable were to prevail—would instantly lose all value and be replaced with weapons, whereas there is at the same time no substitute for God but God.

I feel the need to speak with the messenger. "This is my Arcanum," I say to him and I hope that he won't reply. We walk side by side for an hour, it's possible he's not a boy at all, but a head-wagging machine, I think that I've now waited long enough for his reply and can be certain that he won't answer me, perhaps he isn't even listening to me. For as long as he hasn't entirely vanished, I wish to seize the moment to tell him various things, I wish to ask him who sent him, but all that slips out is "in the three devils' names,"* I immediately suspect that Schattenfroh has spoken forth from me, and, as I'm still pondering who these three devils actually are and whether one shouldn't actually curse, "in the devil's three names," which isn't really suitable as a figure of speech, because "in the three devil's names" sounds rhythmically

---

* A common German expression of frustration.

beautiful, whereas "in the devil's three names" stumbles contrivedly and, most likely, doesn't refer to the devil's names at all, as he has more than three names, I hear myself say "in Cuckoo's name," as if suffering from a diabolical form of Tourette's, the cuckoo is merely a devil in disguise and the devil's dependence on God shows itself clearly in his imitation of the Trinity. The female cuckoo lays its eggs in the nests of others, it is unable or unwilling to build its own nest. Brood parasitism is no disease. The eggs and the other baby birds are shoved out of the nest by the cuckoo that has just hatched. Thus would the devil also wish to act. I am his librarial baby bird and I am to squeeze all book-eggs and book-babybirds out of the nest that is the library. There is much work ahead of me, the devil could not prevent the hatching of the nest's baby birds, and, now, they're already singing. The devil cannot give birth and thus must he purloin his baby birds and place them in others' nests as if they were his own boys, but how is he supposed to do that, he sent me, his adopted boy, too late, I shall now have no choice but to rob the nest if I don't wish to call down the devil's wrath upon myself, the messenger is merely a slender something, a trembling skin, a snake crawling upright, its head can no longer be distinguished from its body, it came into this house as a mist and am I perhaps in paradise?, the snake shall turn to me, bowing its crown-like shock of hair and its slender neck of smooth lustre, coiling up and licking the ground and seeking to ingratiate itself as a tempter and telling me of a beautiful tree, it hangs with fruit of the most handsome shade, red and gold mixed together, not a trace, only Milton knows of this, this snake here shall not put me off of the apple so that it might melt in my mouth by way of words alone, it is Satan himself whom I must hurl away from me as a ladder as soon as I have reached the armarium, which is simultaneously a library room and a weapons cabinet and a funeral vault, but I first must climb the ladder, after which it shall have done its duty, for it is the book that is of the devil, the script that claims to have been there before God was and not I as

Eve shall speak: "For many are the books of God that grow in Paradise, of various sorts and some unknown to us, in wondrous abundance lies our choice, that the greater part of the books lies there untasted, preserved, until man is tall enough to reach their store and most wondrous many hands help to lessen the aramarium's burden, it is simultaneously a library room and a weapons cabinet and a funeral vault," this is what the devil himself says, is what I imagine, and I reply to him that what he is reciting is not Milton, whereupon he says that it was spoken from my book, which also lies in that room, it is the most magnificent of all, my book is simultaneously a library room and a weapons cabinet and a funeral vault, I could wish for no more beautiful grave than *Schattenfroh*. And there would still be enough space in this grave for the readers of *Schattenfroh* and thus would we, the readers and I, lie together in *Schattenfroh* and ever praise the book that is become our grave with these words: "O sovran, virtuous, precious of all books / In Paradise! of operation blest / To sapience, hitherto obscured, infamed. / And thy fair fruit let hang, as to no end / Created; but henceforth my early care, / Not without song, each morning, and due praise, / Shall tend thee, and the fertile burden ease / Of thy full pages offered free to all / Till, dieted by thee, I grow mature / In knowledge, as the Gods, who all things know," "allmorgendlich," a voice then says, but I don't understand, "allmorgendlich," the voice repeats and I recognize it as the voice of Schattenfroh the Great Prohibitor, he speaks forth from the snake, which is only the size of the pencil, then I don't understand once more, then the voice says, "allmorgendlich" is the correct way of translating "each morning," not, as Hans Heinrich Meier did, "allmorgentlich," which is a typographical error, it should be written with a "d," I take the snake and wish to correct the error, then the pencil squirms forth from my hand and scribbles words in the book that I can only decipher as follows: "Soon as the force of that fallacious book, / That with exhilarating vapour bland / About their spirits had played, and inmost powers / Made err, was now exhaled; and grosser sleep, / Bred of unkindly fumes, with conscious dreams / Incumbered, now had left them; up they rose / As from unrest; and, each the other viewing, / Soon found their eyes how opened, and their minds / How darkened; innocence, that as a veil / Had shadowed them from knowing ill, was gone; / Just confidence, and native righteousness"—that is the Milton whom Hans Heinrich Meier could never translate, I hear a voice say, it's the pencil that says it, the snake. In my head, I find a sentence that's repeated over and over again: "If it's not quite Milton, then it's Milton," and thus must Milton be in the armarium. As I now observe the snake once more, I see that it extrudes resin, its tears running down the shaft containing the savage pencil-lead that is slowly being worn away. Even now, it seeks to shake its head, as if it had to ceaselessly deny something and for that reason does the tip now and again break off, the snake drags a thin, trembling thread of graphite and clay behind it, that's really quite kitschy, the kitsch of tears, hard to beat, these are seismographic peaks, my brain-script, I think, the devil sits in the pencil lead, it dictates my direction, yet I cannot be sure whether I am moving inward in a circle or in a spiral, then, with the thought that, after all that I've heard, it'd be much better to eat no book and to devour script so that no translators come to tear one limb from limb and digest the chunks of flesh, I slowly immerse myself in a fog of frankincense and myrrh, it beguiles me entirely, I imagine myself to have reached my goal, but the goal appears to have no goal, for I can no longer see the ground, I'm afraid of holes everywhere, they could cause me to fall or I could disappear into them, in seconds, I've turned into a stumbling old man, I can no longer see my hand right in front of my face, it is completely impossible for me to make out the pencilsnake in the fog, but I am nevertheless convinced of its presence, thirty or forty meters away, I believe that I see something shimmering, something red is glowing there, it's so strong that it pierces through the fog without being fire or light, a red that is stronger than fire or light, I shall enter into this red like a moth into light, coming closer, then I recognize a rose that must be some two meters tall and a competition with the pencilsnake begins, I recognize Satan's stylus in it, I quicken my pace with no caution, the fog makes me weightless, my feet find the ground no longer, then, should the lightningsnake not enter the rose, instead of from now on being my secretary—instead of "guiding script," as the German language describes the job, or being script—it shall enter into me and my book, which I am holding, it only leaves a few letters standing within it, taken together, they read: "He is judged!" and if no one is able to decipher these collated words, as the letters are scattered across the pages and must first of all be arranged into this sentence, an act that requires some combinatorial verve, should it then be a consolation to me that I died inscrutably and am hidden or is my death then in vain— am I then doubly dead, kindled and burnt by Satan's stylus and vanished into the unreadable chaos of script? It is still yet to be written with blood, the rose is an inkwell, the pencil a feather, thus does it shoot off like an arrow, a flash, and I go with it. Our flight causes the walls to come closer, lightning cuts a path through the impenetrable whiteness, my gaze is entirely distorted, this accelerated perspective causes me to experience a neardistance that makes the stillabsent present to me in an embarrassing way before its time, there is no more in-between. Remind me who it was who said: "Dwellings have become no more than anamorphoses of thresholds"? The threshold drags on. I remain in transit and don't budge from the spot despite my breakneck speed. The threshold experiences such an expansion that it can no longer be distinguished from a dwelling. The wall to my right, which now comes recognizably into view and which was previously unreachable, indiscernible, but always somehow making itself felt, has become a canvas.

 I am a wandering anamorphote that compresses the script the flashing pencilsnake leaves behind in the air, though it's perhaps not me who flies toward the rose at high speed, it is the wall that rushes past me faster and faster, I hurtle along in dromological standstill.

The notion that everything could have been pre-staged is unpleasant to me—that the distorted figures I behold on the canvas on my right could have been pre-drawn, when I look back, they shift once more into normal vision, thus revealing things that were hidden by the distortion as seen from the front. In hindsight, I bear witness to humiliation and violence, which seem to come to no end, the gaze out ahead can't grab hold of anything, everything vanishes at lightning-speed, and, since nothing in front that could be imprinted upon the memory can be recognized, the gaze shifts back once more, Father spends his whole life talking about the ways his own father punished him, compared to those, he says, his punishments are mild, thus is war propagated down the generations, as if it had to be naturalized into the family. Even if everyone is opposed to war, war legitimizes familial violence.

Being-outside-of-me, however, affords me no relief in the Now, for I perceive myself as that which is transitory and the rose toward which I fly as it sucks me in as that which is unchanging and immutable. But is the rose a rose? Is the flashing pencil, Satan's stylus, a snake? Doesn't the tower look like a lantern from afar, exhaling and hazy? If the house here were a ballad, then very much so. But there is no tower here. However, a magic lantern might well be here. "Neither neither nor nor but something else" is here. Here, how sombre doth the moon's light shine because it is not the moon. If dwellings have become no more than anamorphoses of thresholds, then thing and world are torn to shreds and words become things. The rose has opened wide, its petals are fully unfolded.

And with Droste, I ask: what is that? Lucid, darkened by the fog that wafts and flickers through the room, a table and a cupboard in the middle of a wall, and now—now doth he like a shadow walk along the wall, he lifts one arm and stirs a hand. Drifts over to the table and sits down—slowly, stiffly—what is in his hand?—a streak so white!—Now doth he pull a thing forth from a sheath and touch it with both his hands—a small rod, maybe—and slowly move along it, he seems to be cutting the feather.

Writing must be a form of self-gratification. What else would it be? But who is he? He is Ezra, reader and the scribe of the law of the God of heaven. The pencilsnake is now his tool. He's put his bare feet onto a footstool before the table. Not the law of God, but the book *Schattenfroh* lies in his lap, he keeps it in his brownred armarium along with a series of other books. How can this lawmaker opt to fiddle around with a novel? Did Artasasta, the king of all kings, also authorize him to do this? He puts down corrections with the snake. Does he wish to establish a new aesthetic order against the Noveltower of Babel? And does he find no satisfaction in *Schattenfroh*? Does Ezra's name not mean Help? But he pays no attention to me. If I speak to him, he doesn't react. If I wish to touch him, I simply reach right through him. He writes incessantly. My head has felt quite light ever since I started to see Ezra sitting at the table. I can effortlessly wander about in my head, as if Ezra had spread out in there and, now, my head is empty. What Ezra has to say to me, he writes directly into my book, which he is now handing to me for a second time. The first time—about two minutes ago—I couldn't decipher anything. His script is in flight and I do not know whether it is he who writes or the pencilsnake, which was so keen to fly into the rose that turned out to be an armarium and from the wide-open wing of which poured forth the scent of the open books. They smell of love spurned, of youth withered, of stored-up excess that's become too much for itself, and thus did it become rancid and rusted like unused coins, which, untouched, have been sitting in a moisture-exposed drawer for many years. What ought one to do with these coins? Each time one discovers them, one makes the same constatation and leaves them lying about. Thus does Ezra sit before the armarium with its pitched roof, which invites one to vanish inside of it entirely. It is perhaps the wood, the odor of which is transferred to the books or the themes of the books having been litigated since time immemorial and thus does their odor come from within. It is the rank odor that is also within people, they struggle with it for years until it decomposes them.

With his stool, his wide footstool, and the small wooden table with the sloping top, into which an inkwell is embedded, Ezra comes across as a diligent altar boy who wants to do everything properly during the service and thus wishes to be as invisible as possible, or like a schoolboy doing his homework, he wants to be observed while doing his homework. I look at him and wait. Just look at what the snake is doing with me, his face seems to say, while his right hand apparently has a life of its own. He is uncontrollably driven to write that the hand is superior to his body, it is its parasite, it is Ezra's Doppelgänger and, if Ezra were in court, it would first of all have to be clarified which of the two is the accused. Would one have to ask of him that he hack off his hand? Does the Bible not say: "But when *thou* doest alms, let not thy left hand know what thy right hand doeth"? Here, only somebody other than the one to whom the right hand belongs knows what it is doing. Unlike John later on, he does not have a commissioning vision while in exile, one that turns him into a prophet of script, for public speech is forbidden to him, Ezra is merely a typewriter operated from the outside, an unconscious revelation-recipient whose brain alone coordinates the writing motions of the right hand without him being able to say anything at all.

Ezra wears a sleeveless purple outer garment with green lining and a plunging side-neckline from shoulders to elbows over a one-piece green undergarment with long, close-fitting arms and legs. Born in the fifth century AD, he was dressed after the fashion of the seventh century AD. What is a curiosity in itself that amuses me more than it frightens me is the fact that Ezra undertakes his writing activity so mechanically and without pause, without allowing any human stirrings to be seen, he never gets up in between passes, his eyes are permanently open, so far, I haven't perceived a single blink of an eye, nor does he shift his writing posture, as if he were defending terrain he'd already taken.

I imagine that his task is the restoration of all the Bible's Prophecies, which were lost through some unfortunate circumstance. This was commanded to him by God Himself, who had grown tired of permanently remembering everything. Ezra is a mix of diaskeuast and copyist, such people are particularly dangerous, they utterly blur the lines between which words were already there and which they themselves added.

If Ezra is writing *Schattenfroh* or is expanding upon what has already been written in this book, he also likely continues to write the books in his armarium, starting from the page they're opened up to, or he ascribes books penned by him to other authors and continuously corrects them or rewrites books by other authors when required or writes a book from other books, more specifically, one written by others—then there is no more author, the whole of literature is a single pseudepigraphy. Ezra is a creator in destruction. He sucks books dry and pumps that which he has sucked out into the girth of a new book, in which there is nothing new other than cover and paper. It's for that reason that the very notion of the "book" is outdated, it is a metaphor for compactness and overview, for a manageable size that causes a clearly contoured image to arise in the imagination.

Since it apparently doesn't bother him that I am present—he doesn't take notice of me even once, the handing-over of the book after the completion of a new passage is likely more of a reflex, just as in the case of automatons, a mechanism is triggered by a roller or a cylinder or something similar, it is modeled after human sequences of movements, Ezra doesn't have me on the mind when he hands the book over to me—I'm not timid about watching him work, I assume that it proceeds just as automatically as the famous Typist-Android, able to write texts of forty characters programmed onto a column that forms the writer's spine, which consists of cams to be exchanged depending on the character set and are then transferred to his right hand. When the writer is turned on with a crank between the shoulders, he dips a quill into a bottle of ink with his right hand and begins to write neatly, the production of script comes naturally to him, if one were merely to gaze upon the writer, one wouldn't assume him to be a machine. I saw this with my own eyes in Neuchâtel where I was afforded the great honor of having the scribe write the following text: "Schattenfroh is the almighty father"—and thus was the name present once and for all and my father with it. The mechanism is complex, Herr Scheinenden had the scribe itself explain it quite well:

> "Depending on the height of the cams, a cylinder moves with a set of cam disks that contains the coding of the individ ual letters. Three cam discs each move the hand up and down, back and forth, l eft and right. The dimensions of the ca ms used to program the text adheres to narrow allowances. Such is the machine rather error-prone. This was likely a c onstructive concesion to the desire to accomodate all of the mechanisms at pla y in the figure. Sincerely, Schatenfroh."

The micromechanical principle leaves nothing to chance except for errors. To write with a quill is to paint speech, to speak for the eyes. The scribe is a painter of beautiful characters and letters. Ezra is a virtual android, a phantom that is and simultaneously is not. He is an employee of the enframing without knowing it and this not-knowing makes me jealous of him.

Perhaps, Ezra the Scribe is merely a restorer who restores destroyed books.

This time too, I can't decipher what Ezra is giving me to read, the snake in his hand has taken on a life of its own.

Ezra is so unlike me that I am afraid of him and imitate him so that he becomes more like me. Thus do I lose the feeling of the boundary between my own body and that of another. I sit at a spare table before a spare armarium and write in spare books, is what I imagine. He doesn't hear me, doesn't look at me. For him, I do not exist. He is the writer, restorer, and custodian of the books that I am meant to have read, a coroner appointed by the devil. Can there be a greater aficionado of literature?

247 years later, a mechanical android is no longer enough for Schattenfroh, however, a virtual android seems to be too much of a ghost for him, thus did he connect the mechanical and virtual principle of the android with the organic matter of the human being within me, he who suffers and experiences suffering and can reflect on these differences and countless others beyond his programming. All of us are frail entities who find themselves in a state of constant metamorphosis, which does not, however, prevent our mutual abolition. Ezra has replaced the mechanical scribe, how can I replace Ezra? Through Ezra's outer garments, I can stick my arm into his omission, which doesn't prevent him from continuing to write. I don't manage to grab hold of his arm, I can neither snatch the pencil away from Ezra, nor prevent him from writing, thus do I hope that the book he bears in his hands and in which he writes exists precisely as little as he does. I ought to be able to switch off the image that I see. I could turn it off by destroying the source or by putting a bullet into my own brain, at which point it would make no difference whether the head were the source. If the

head is not the source, then it must be behind Ezra, though behind Ezra is only the armarium, which doesn't give the impression that it is the starting point of mysterious projections. It is an ordinary cupboard made of dark-brown wood, which has become old and brittle over the years, it has five shelves, the storage capacity of which is quickly exhausted and which one shall therefore soon replace with a larger one as soon as it's been set up. The books, all bound in red leather, lie as if slain upon the shelves, which are tilted so far forward that one can comfortably read their titles, these are books of flesh and bone, heavy, corpulent. They don't look to be happy, more like they've accepted their fate and are waiting to finally be slaughtered. Ezra spares them not, even if the fact of them lying there so neatly is intended to create the opposite impression. A large drawer is integrated into the bottom of the cupboard, it is locked. Perhaps there are such valuable things in it that not even Ezra is allowed to open it. If he takes no notice of me, I say to myself, if he is entirely unaware of the things coming to pass around him, if he is merely an illusion, if he is the future once more: a simulated presence that spreads terror, as it is also present in dreams, thus only becoming real when it is what remains of Schattenfroh, after all, what remains of me is an if-then without the then, if it's a mere curtain of which the moral law within me forbids the transgression, but if he *is* this moral law that knows no words, only illustration, if a prohibition that one obeys is followed by another that one ought to obey and one obeys it, another one follows, the one observance observes the second, just as one constantly observes oneself, if this murderer's row shall never end, if you think you've seen through it all, then go forth and open the drawer, I say to myself incessantly, for there is no path that leads to the drawer.

I sit down through Ezra, sit down on his stool, put my feet up on his footstool, dip the quill into his inkwell, wipe off the excess ink, then write in *Schattenfroh*: "The footstool real, the ink real." Precisely

33 characters. Pathetic. Ezra guides my quill and writes over me: "I am Ezra, I am nobody other than myself. You are a substitute automaton as substitute-reason-in-motion." I write: "You have no soul." Ezra writes: "I am your soul. I cling to you like life to death." I have nothing of the sort to offer, I put the pen down and rise up. Something on the lower floor of the armarium has caught my eye. Two bits of equipment take up the space of another book. The first, all in white, is a curved scraper, the other, to the left of it, with a light-brown handle, is a very broad brush, which is likely put to use less upon the screen and more to brush dust from the books. I'm just about to take them out of the cupboard, when it comes to me how concretely Ezra comprehends the word "to cling," I'm suddenly wearing his one-piece green undergarment with the long, tight-fitting arms and legs, the purple, sleeveless outer garment also clings to me, its green lining is invariably bunched up in certain spots. Ezra's aureole has also passed over to me, it shines so bright that the books are illuminated as if by spotlight. I take the scraper and book-brush from the cupboard and turn to Ezra, who is sitting naked and bareheaded on the stool. Now, he is no longer an apparition of the seventh century, his previous aspect has been foisted onto me, he tirelessly scribbles away with the quill in the book, the writing noises remind me of snow-sweeping, of ice-scraping, of skating atop a frozen lake. With each of the quill's up- and downstrokes, the letters come to occupy new territory, which they wrest from the imaginary enemy. Who is this enemy? He is the unwritten and the undrawn, erasure, but also the real, for which there are no words and no images and which offers up such high resistance to scribbling away that harrow, hoe, rake, roller, plow, and cultivator are not enough to overcome it. The real is repetition. A repeated assault and a repeated resistance. Then can I just leave Ezra sitting there like this? Pitiful, expression of a lack, when naked, Ezra gives the impression of a fortunate phantom and, now, the time has come to bid Ezra farewell, indeed, he makes no impression at

all, he doesn't know anything, he doesn't exist, there is only the transference of his clothing to me, Ezra represents the metamorphosis of a civilization sinking back into a world-age thought to be overcome, I am his Doppelgänger, confusingly similar to him due to his burnt clothing, Ezra the Virus programs me, Ezra is to be in play in all I do from now on, I move into the armarium, my back to the wall, and shall now leave this house slowly, my gaze is entirely fixed on Ezra, who writes incessantly, there is always something to write, something is always lacking, something is always not in its right place, Ezra writes this place, and, already, a gap opens up where something is not in its right place, this mechanical play satisfies him entirely, as he is only made up of mechanics, knowing no life or death outside of scripture, he shall nevermore leave this cycle, and he shall also really not want to, insomuch as it is appropriate to speak of "wanting" with regard to him, Schattenfroh has decreed wanting unto me, as it is ever unattainable for him. That which I desire remains hidden from me always, Schattenfroh can siphon off of it in peace. Who speaks through Ezra when he writes? The Mabuse Principle. I am nothing but the witness of my self-disclosures, a medium of fission that desires nothing more ardently than that the split-off part desire it. Is this naked Ezra to desire me? Desire me, Ezra, I call out to him from the armarium. He writes. Quit writing, Ezra, I call out to him. He continues to write. Ezra, rise up, collect your writing materials, and get thee home! Ezra does not rise up. He always does the precise opposite of what I want. I don't even need to ask him anything, he shall do the opposite. The notion of being blown backward into an empty paradise does not suit me. I wish to turn to the books, whose body, indeed, is cold, but still body.

If I pick up a book, an identical copy immediately appears in the armarium, if I put it back, the other remains in stock. Soon enough, the armarium shall show the limits of the wonderful multitudefeedingbookpropagation, but, for as long as there is enough space, I shall continue the game. One book calls upon the other and, meanwhile, the armarium is so full that the books threaten to block my way to the next house. Upon one of the books is written "Complete Index." What is the point of such an inventory when the stock of books is permanently expanding, a circumstance that is not exactly unusual for libraries, in such a way that the inventory becomes outdated with each new book. We're dealing with the Complete Index of *Schattenfroh*, as can be seen from the Table of Contents. That too is astonishing as there is no end in sight for *Schattenfroh*. I keep the Complete Index open in my left hand and pick up another in my right. Immediately, another book follows and the index, alphabetically ordered by last name, records the title of the new book. The whole world ought to be set up like this. But, in that case, what would we need indexes for? In that case, we would be certain that new acquisitions would already be listed. Wouldn't we? And, if we were certain, who would check? Supposing that there was somebody overseeing it and this somebody spotted a mistake, how could one thus suppose that this somebody would report the error? Wars could be extensively documented and handed down to posterity in their every detail. In the distant future, a grandfather would say to his daughter, have a look, that's how orderly it was back then, we now know all the details of that which came to pass. For example, I watch the total destruction of Berlin, which finally came to fruition upon a second attempt, for the fifth time in a row, there's always more beauty to be discovered therein. Thus is it not, to be sure, the civilian-friendly large-scale elimination of the enemy—who, indeed, is never part of the people, the Volk, which is to be found everywhere, no, the enemy is to be found here and there and here and there—that would be significant if one were to speak of progress made in the fighting of wars, but the transmission, the handing-over and delivery of all data out of which a war is assembled, without the sum of it being a war in and of itself. It is the list that counts, the listing-off, also in terms of delisting, "butoncethewarhasbeenoverforlongenough" and, yet, at the last moment, it turned against any and all expectations—the enemy takes precautions, he drops documentation just as he does bombs, and thus, in the end, is it only the book that counts, in it, the world is put back together once more and all wrongs are righted.

Holding the bookbodies in my hand, the thought suddenly comes to me: how could I have spent so much time with them, busying myself with them, indeed, they might well have cost me my life—but, for the moment, I consider this to be entirely impossible, I am certain that this is the very first time I've seen these bodies, but, any place I open the books to, I find myself to be proven wrong. In Agamben, for instance, I read my own name right at the beginning, just as in Heidegger, in such a way that nobody, and certainly not me, shall be able to claim that Nobody has not read these books. Perhaps, it's just that my memory is fuzzy, I grab Körtner from the books arranged according to the organ-pipe principle, a system of knowledge that really doesn't seem that far-fetched to me, as it always provides nice surprises and thus has a decisive advantage as set against the alphabet, which is so ordinary and boring that it can easily be forgotten, a fact now confirmed by the circumstance that I can no longer remember (at least not clearly) a previous reading of the just-now-aforementioned books. Nowadays, the modern books seem to be arranged in such a way that the one who has read them remains identifiable to all other readers through the inscription and forthgoing recognizability of his name, in Agamben as in Beckett, in the Elberfelder Studienbibel just as in Enoch and Bradbury's *Fahrenheit 451*, the latter, however being a book that seems to grow worse with each passing year, even back in the beginning, the impression was none too favorable, which is now—quite precisely—381 pages back from here, my name is written clear as day: Nobody. Rabelais even begins with the opposite of my name.

The Complete Index contains more omissions and blank pages

than bibliographic entries. Upon the first page is written: Lay the Index upon Schattenfroh and open the book to page 575:

Aelius Aristides: *Orations*
Agamben, Giorgio: *The Man Without Content*
Agamben, Giorgio: *Homo Sacer*
Agamben, Giorgio: *Pilate and Jesus*
Améry, Jean: *At the Mind's Limits: Contemplations by a Survivor of Auschwitz and Its Realities*
Andrić, Ivo: *The Bridge on the Drina*
Angelus Silesius: *Cherubinischer Wandersmann*
Anonymous: *The Book of Enoch*
Arzy, Shahar; Idel, Moshe: *Kabbalah: A Neurocognitive Approach to Mystical Experiences*
Bär, Gerald: *Das Motiv des Doppelgängers als Spaltungsphantasie in der Literatur und im deutschen Stummfilm*
Barthes, Roland: *Camera Lucida*
Beckett, Samuel: *Malone Dies*
Buber, Martin: *Tales of the Hasidim*
Bee, Julia; Görling, Reinhold; Kruse, Johannes; Mühlleitner, Elke (Ed.): *Folterbilder und -narrationen.*
Beckermann, Ansgar: *Analytische Einführung in die Philosophie des Geistes*
Behrendt, Harald: *Werner Tübkes Panoramabild in Bad Frankenhausen*
Bentham, Jeremy: *Panopticon: The Inspection House*
Biel, Peter Johannes: *Das kleine Lexikon der Druckersprache*
Bogards, Roland: *Poetik des Schmerzes*
Bohlmann, Carolin; Fink, Thomas; Weiss, Philipp: *Lichtgefüge des 17. Jahrhunderts. Rembrandt und Vermeer – Spinoza und Leibniz*
Bradbury, Ray: *Fahrenheit 451*

Bräuer, Siegfried; Vogler, Günter: *Thomas Müntzer. Neu Ordnung machen in der Welt. Eine Biographie*

Brown, Bob; Saper, Craig: *The Readies*

BStU (Ed.): *Abkürzungsverzeichnis. Häufig verwendete Abkürzungen und Begriffe des Ministeriums für Staatssicherheit*

Bury, Richard de: *The Love of Books: The Philobiblon of Richard de Bury*

Caroll, Lewis: *Alice in Wonderland*

Caroll, Lewis: *Alice Through the Looking-Glass*

Carrier, Martin; Mittelstraß, Jürgen: *Mind, Brain, Behavior: The Mind-Body Problem And the Philosophy of Psychology*

Castoriadis, Cornelius: *The Imaginary Institution of Society*

Cervantes Saavedra, Miguel de: *El ingenioso hidalgo Don Quijote de la Mancha*

Cervantes Saavedra, Miguel de: *Der geistvolle Hidalgo Don Quijote von der Mancha*. Published and translated by Susanne Lange.

Dante Alighieri: *The Divine Comedy*

Droste-Hülshoff, Annette von: *Sämtliche Werke*

Edelmayer, Friedrich: *Philipp II. Biographie eines Weltherrschers*

Ekelöf, Gunnar: *Absentia animi*

Elberfelder Studienbibel

Elias, Norbert: *The Loneliness of the Dying*

Elliger, Walter: *Thomas Müntzer*

Engelmann, Roger; Florath, Bernd (Ed.): *Das MfS-Lexikon*

Ernst, Thomas: *Schwarzweiße Magie. Der Schlüssel zum dritten Buch der Steganographie des Trithemius*

Fechner, Gustav Theodor: *Ueber die Seelenfrage*

Fechner, Gustav Theodor: *Zur Experimentalen Aesthetik*

Fechner, Gustav Theodor: *In Sachen der Psychophysik*

Fechner, Gustav Theodor: *Die Tagesansicht gegenüber der Nachtansicht*

Fischer, Stefan: *Hieronymus Bosch. Das vollständige Werk*

Fischer, Stefan: *Hieronymus Bosch: Malerei als Vision, Lehrbild und Kunstwerk*
Flasch, Kurt: *Der Teufel und seine Engel. Die neue Biographie*
Foucault, Michel: *Discipline and Punish*
Fraenger, Wilhelm: *Jörg Ratgeb*
Freud, Sigmund: *Werkausgabe in zwei Bänden: Elemente der Psychoanalyse (Band 1); Anwendungen der Psychoanalyse (Band 2)*
Friedenthal, Richard: *Jan Hus*
Fuchs, Jürgen: *Gedächtnisprotokolle – Vernehmungsprotokolle*
Geerken, Hartmut: *kant*
Gehrke, Andreas: *Ausbruch aus dem Angstkäfig*
Gerstenberger, Erhard S.: *Wesen und Herkunft des »apodiktischen Rechts«*
Gerstenberger, Erhard S.: *»Apodiktisches« Recht – »Todes« Recht?*
Giesecke, Michael: *Der Buchdruck in der frühen Neuzeit*
Gieseke, Jens: *Die hauptamtlichen Mitarbeiter der Staatssicherheit*
Gieseke, Jens: *Staatssicherheit und Gesellschaft*
Girard, René: *I See Satan Fall like Lightning*
Greiffenberg, Catharina Regina von: *Sämtliche Werke in 10 Bänden*
Hagner, Michael: *Die Sache des Buches*
Hanebutt-Benz, Eva-Maria: *Die Kunst des Lesens*
Hegel, Georg Friedrich Wilhelm: *The Phenomenology of Spirit*
Hegel, Georg Friedrich Wilhelm: *The Science of Logic*
Hegel, Georg Friedrich Wilhelm: *Theologische Jugendschriften nach den Handschriften der Königlichen Bibliothek in Berlin*
Heidegger, Martin: *Being and Time*
Heidegger, Martin: *The Question Concerning Technology*
Hemingway, Ernest: *Over the River and Into the Trees*
Hölscher, Lucian (Ed.): *Das Jenseits. Facetten eines religiösen Begriffs in der Neuzeit*
Hüttel, Richard (Ed.): *Werner Tübke – Michael Triegel. Zwei Meister aus Leipzig.*

Katalog *Hus in Konstanz. Der Bericht des Peter von Mladoniowitz*
Huss, Matthias: *Danse Macabre*
Idel, Moshe: *Golem: Jewish Magical and Mystical Traditions*
Jabès, Edmond: *El, ou le dernier livre*
Jabès, Edmond: *Le Livre de l'Hospitalité*
Jabès, Edmond: *Le Livre des Questions*
Jabès, Edmond: *Le Livre du Partage*
Jabès, Edmond: *Le petit livre de la subversion hors de soupçon*
Jabès, Edmond: *Le Seuil Le Sable: Poésies complètes 1943–1988*
Jacques, Norbert: *Mabuse's Colony*
Jaeger, Achim: *Rund um die Dürener Stadtmauer in Wort und Bild*
Kafka, Franz: *Kritische Ausgabe der Werke*
Kennedy, Gerry; Churchill, Rob: *The Voynich Manuscript: The Mysterious Code That Has Defied Interpretation for Centuries*
Kilcher, Andreas B.: *Die Sprachtheorie der Kabbala als ästhetisches Paradigma*
King James Bible
Kittler, Friedrich; Macho, Thomas; Weigel, Sigrid: *Zwischen Rauschen und Offenbarung. Zur Kultur- und Mediengeschichte der Stimme*
Körtner, Ulrich H. J.: *Der verborgene Gott*
Kober, Karl Max: *Werner Tübke. Monumentalbild Frankenhausen*
Kohler, Alfred: *Karl V. 1500–1558. Eine Biographie*
Kleist, Heinrich von: *Michael Kohlhaas*
Koepp, Leo: *Das himmlische Buch*
Körte, Mona: *Essbare Lettern, brennendes Buch*
Kramer, Sven: *Die Folter in der Literatur*
Krause, Gerhard; Müller, Gerhard (Hg): *Theologische Realenzyklopädie*
Kühlwein, Klaus: *Warum der Papst schwieg. Pius XII. und der Holocaust*
Kuhn, Peter: *Bat Qol. Die Offenbarungsstimme in der rabbinischen Literatur*

Leide, Henry: *NS-Verbrecher und Staatssicherheit*

Lentz, Hubert: *Die Konkurrenz des französischen und preussischen Staatskirchenrechts 1815–1850: in Bezug auf die katholische Kirche in den vormals preussischen Landesteilen westlich des Rheins*

Lentz, Hubert: *Entscheidungen in Kirchensachen seit 1946*

Lentz, Michael: *Muttersterben*

Levinas, Emmanuel: *Altérité et transcendance*

Levinas, Emmanuel: *Autrement qu'être ou Au-delà de l'essence*

Levinas, Emmanuel: *Humanisme de l'autre homme*

Levinas, Emmanuel: *Le temps et l'autre*

Levinas, Emmanuel: *Totalité et Infini. Essai sur l'extériorité*

Lindner, Gerd: *Vision und Wirklichkeit. Das Frankenhauser Geschichtspanorama von Werner Tübke*

Luhmann, Niklas: *The Society of Society*

Luther, Martin: *D. Martin Luthers Werke. 120 Bände*

Mandel, Gabriele: *Gezeichnete Schöpfung*

Marañón, Gregorio: *Antonio Pérez, "Spanish Traitor"*

Martin, François René; Menu, Michel; Ramond, Sylvie: *Grünewald*

May, Karl: *In the Desert* [Originally titled *Through Wild Kurdistan*]

Meißner, Günter: *Werner Tübke. Leben und Werk*

Meißner, Günter: *Werner Tübke. Theatrum mundi. Frühbürgerliche Revolution in Deutschland*

Melanchthon, Philipp; Drummond, Andrew (tr.): *Thomas Müntzer's "Speech at Frankenhausen."*

Meyer, Anne-Rose: *Homo dolorosus*

Michalski, Annika; Beaucamp, Eduard (Ed.): *Werner Tübke. Mein Herr empfindet optisch. Aus den Tagebüchern, Skizzen und Notizen*

Mon, Franz: *Sprache lebenslänglich*

Mon, Franz: *Zuflucht bei Fliegen*

Müller, Ernst (tr.): *Zohar - The Book of Splendor*. (A selection from the original text translated into German.)

Müller, Herbert: »Panorama«-Bauwerk Bad Frankenhausen. In: *Bauplanung – Bautechnik*, 1978, 32. Jahrgang, Heft 2, S. 52–56

Müntzer, Thomas; Matheson, Peter (tr.): *The Collected Works of Thomas Müntzer*

Müntzer, Thomas; Drummond, Andrew: *Thomas Müntzer's "Speech at Frankenhausen"*

Necker, Gerold: *Einführung in die lurianische Kabbala*

Necker, Gerold (tr.): *A Selection from the Book of Sohar*

Nietzsche, Friedrich: *On the Genealogy of Morality*

Niewöhner, Friedrich; Schaeffler, Richard (Ed.): *Unsterblichkeit*

Nohl, Hermann (Ed.): *Hegels theologische Jugendschriften nach den Handschriften der Königlichen Bibliothek in Berlin*

Noordendorp, Hergen: *Die Offenbarung des Johannes. Eine okkulte Zahlenlehre*

Otto, Stephan: *Die Wiederholung und die Bilder. Zur Philosophie des Erinnerungsbewußtseins*

Page, D. L. (Ed.): *Poetae Melici Graeci*

Passens, Katrin: *MfS-Untersuchungshaft*

Pelzl, Inès: *Veit Stoß: Künstler mit verlorener Ehre*

Pophal, Rudolf: *Die Handschrift als Gehirnschrift*

Rabelais, François: *Gargantua & Pantagruel*

Rieger, Dietmar: *Imaginäre Bibliotheken*

Rieger, Stefan: *Die Individualität der Medien*

Rilke, Rainer Maria: *Sämtliche Werke in 12 Bänden*

Sanson, Henri: *Memoirs of the Sansons: From Private Notes and Documents*

Saper, Craig: *The Amazing Adventures of Bob Brown*

Schade, Johann Casper: *[Über die Anfangsworte des 63. Psalms]*

Schäfer, Peter: *The Hidden and Manifest God*

Schäfer, Peter: *Some Major Themes in Jewish Mysticism*

Schattenfroh: *Schattenfroh*

Schiller, Friedrich: *On the Aesthetic Education of Man*
Schlegel, Friedrich: *Atheneum Fragments*
Schlegel, Friedrich: *Lyceum Fragments*
Schmeh, Klaus: *Kryptografie*
Schmeh, Klaus: *Nicht zu knacken*
Schmeh, Klaus: *Versteckte Botschaften*
Schmitz-Emans, Monika: *Schrift und Abwesenheit. Historische Paradigmen zu einer Poetik der Entzifferung und des Schreibens*
Scholem, Gershom: *Major Trends in Jewish Mysticism*
Scholem, Gershom: *Sabbatai Sevi*
Scholem, Gershom: *Über einige Grundbegriffe des Judentums*
Scholem, Gershom: *On the Mystical Shape of the Godhead: Basic Concepts in the Kabbalah*
Scholem, Gershom: *On the Kabbalah And Its Symbolism*
Schreber, Daniel Paul: *Memoirs of My Nervous Illness*
Schulte, Christoph: *Zimzum: God and the Origin of the World*
Siegert, Bernhard: *Passage des Digitalen*
Soukup, Pavel: *Jan Hus: The Life and Death of a Preacher*
Stadt Mainz (Ed.): *Gutenberg. aventur und kunst*
Staudenmaier, Ludwig: *Die Magie als experimentelle Naturwissenschaft*
Sterne, Laurence: *The Life and Opinions of Tristram Shandy, Gentleman*
Süß, Sonja: *Politisch mißbraucht? Psychiatrie und Staatssicherheit in der DDR Thomas-Müntzer-Ausgabe. Kritische Gesamtausgabe Band 1, 2, 3*
Triegel, Michael: *Verwandlung der Götter.*
Katalog Tübke Werner: *Mein Herz empfindet optisch. Aus den Tagebüchern, Skizzen und Notizen*
Vico, Giambattista: *La Scienza Nuova: Principj di una Scienza Nuova Intorno alla Natura delle Nazioni per la Quale si Ritruovano i Principj di Altro Sistema del Diritto Naturale delle Genti*

Waldenfels, Bernhard: *Hyperphänomene*
Walter, Meinrad: *Johann Sebastian Bach. Johannespassion. Eine musikalisch-theologische Einführung*
Wiesing, Lambert: *Artificial Presence: Philosophical Studies in Image*
Wiesing, Lambert: *The Philosophy of Perception. Phenomenology and Image Theory*
Wiesing, Lambert: *Sehen lassen: Praxis des Zeigens*
Wolf, Ror: *Raoul Tranchirers vielseitiger großer Ratschläger für alle Fälle der Welt*
Wolf, Ror: *Raoul Tranchirers Mitteilungen an Ratlose*
Wolf, Ror: *Raoul Tranchirers Welt- und Wirklichkeitslehre aus dem Reich des Fleisches, der Erde, der Luft, des Wassers und der Gefühle*
Wolf, Ror: *Tranchirers letzte Gedanken über die Vermehrung der Lust und des Schreckens*
Wolf, Ror: *Raoul Tranchirers Enzyklopädie für unerschrockene Leser & ihre überschaubaren Folgen*
Wolf, Ror: *Raoul Tranchirers Bemerkungen über die Stille*
Wolf, Ror: *Raoul Tranchirers Notizen aus dem zerschnetzelten Leben*
Wolf, Ror: *Die Vorzüge der Dunkelheit. Neunundzwanzig Versuche die Welt zu verschlingen*
Wolf, Ror: *Die plötzlich hereinkriechende Kälte im Dezember*
Zugibe, Frederick T.: *The Crucifixion of Jesus*

If some books or, rather, the reading of them, are no longer present to me, and, to be quite precise, I must say that I can't remember a single book, how can I be certain that the list shall ever be completed, even if what it now says here is: "The list shall only be completed along with *Schattenfroh*"? Is there perhaps somebody using guile to ensure that one or another of the titles isn't marked down? If I can think of another book that didn't get the mention due to it here, I shall append it in good time, and, should I be penalized for that, I shall know that a certain authority has prevented its mention and also intends to prevent it from now on. Whatever this authority is to be dubbed, its name is Schattenfroh. It ensures that, taken together, entire libraries vanish out of the concern that the books they contain might well deny the legitimacy of their claim to dominion and closest proximity to God, from here on out, the word *write-off* would take on an entirely new meaning. As far as the book *Schattenfroh* is concerned, Schattenfroh may perhaps fear that another book could suddenly appear and reveal his plan and his claim to have created a unique work with *Schattenfroh*, one that can no longer be surpassed in terms of originality and proximity to God, as sheer imposture.

Should a book be added the very moment I note its absence, there might be an antagonist who wishes to challenge Schattenfroh— and perhaps this antagonist is also Schattenfroh himself, wishing to confuse me and cause me to believe in an antagonist. Just as God is also the devil and wishes for others to believe in the devil. One way or another, God's finger is at play. But if all this is a game, with whom shall Schattenfroh play it?

And if there are books in the stock of those that I've read that might pose a threat to Schattenfroh and, therefore, *Schattenfroh* in any way, I ask myself wherefore he did not prevent the reading of those books. He may perhaps wish to be defended against such books by all those who tremble at and are frightened by his words. But I could likely ask with equal justification wherefore God did not prevent sin. There is no way out of the labyrinth of thought, whoever cries out is in the wrong.

Might I be allowed to look at the books that aren't in the armarium, I suddenly feel like asking at the top of my lungs when a small, obviously well-stocked book trolley comes rolling out of the background, it's like the ones used in libraries, this one here with three lower shelves inclined slightly toward the back, I'd really like to ask somebody whether I'm the only one who sees it, then the trolley stops in front of me, and I can pluck out individual books, which I then simply hold in my hands without opening them. However, their contents seem to be able to gain access to my brain through my skin, an ethereal or fluid substance that flows into my body. Suddenly, I can recite whole passages from the book *I See Satan Fall like Lightning* by heart. I can't recall having seen it noted down in the index, but now I find it there in orderly fashion under "G." "The most humiliated persons, the most crushed, behave in the same fashion as the princes of this world." Does he mean me? Am I acting like the princes of this book? What Girard has in mind are the two thieves who wish to do the same as the crowd and even outdo them in terms of blasphemy. For Girard, this is an object lesson for a phenomenon that he calls the "Mimetic Cycle of Violence." The lower row isn't worth thinking about. But Kreuzberg is a very fine place to study this. Kreuzberg. "Cross-hill" is what Kreuzberg means. Names are destiny. In Kreuzberg, the Molls hang about on every corner. But they also have more than just Jesus' name in their mouth, they talk about Dismas and Gestas too, the two thieves who hang onto the ears of Malone's Moll and not a milling machine, but periodontitis and caries have made Moll's last teeth into the triumvirate of the crucifixion. They look to have been incinerated, as if a fire has raged through their mouth. They fear that they shall fall out or could even be swallowed at night. They would very much like to get rid of Gestas, they really could do without him, but which one is he, the one on the left or the right? He's the one crucified to Christ's left, some Molls say, while others insist that he's the one on the right. Dismas shall appear to you on Judgment Day next to the Gates of Heaven, which shall remain closed to you, one Moll says, having already lost his Jesus. Your two thieves look like the ruins of the World Trade Center, his neighbor-moll chortles when he discovers the Jesusless Dismas and Gestas in the mocker's mouth. This compliment makes him so happy each time it's uttered that he offers him a cigarette. He has Caspar David Friedrich's *Sea of Ice* in mouth, a third Moll then begins to rant, the ruins of the

World Trade Center don't even exist anymore. Brief respite. Caspar David Friedrich's *Sea of Ice*. *Sea of Ice*. Caspar David Friedrich. What is one to say to that? There's a ship stuck in there. Where? In the Sea of Ice. Shipwreck. Icebreak. Everything shattered. Like us. We are the shattered society. The ship is soon vanished. But, before that, it was already painted. Yes, that's what images are there for. Take a photo of the two thieves. Then we have our Friedrich. Our beautiful society. Better a photo of Jesus. Preferably a photo of Jesus and the two thieves. It ought to be the still-intact, but already visibly assaulted Jesus, as he penetratingly, but lovingly fixes his gaze upon the viewer. Then, they take a photo of Jesus and the two thieves, they want to send it to the government. Warmest Greetings from the Society. No image without text, a Moll says. They must know precisely whom they're dealing with here. Thus do they write a text that they'd like to append to the image:

To the Government.

These days, an unkempt little person named Jesus Christ keeps popping up, he lives in the mouth of each and every one of us and is regarded by the rationalists as a preacher of truth, but is dubbed the Son of God by his host-animals. Those who have seen him do not have much longer left to live.

A small man of puny build and undignified appearance, such that those who see him must be both disgusted and frightened. He has no more hairs on the whole of his body, from his head to his toe, all of it buried in the inflamed periodontium, already totally receded in some spots, he is garbed only in smoker's plaque, buttoned on the side after the fashion of the Molls. His brow is fissured, his face spotted and wrinkled, hideous, of blackish red. Nose and mouth are so deformed that they can hardly be made out. The beard is wild tartar and so unkempt that it disfigures the face rather than serving as an adornment for it. His eyes are black, impenetrable, and lifeless. As far as his body is concerned, it cannot be distinguished whether his struts, so far spared from decomposition, are merely holding him together instead of disappearing into the holes or whether the holes, visible everywhere but also invisible, support him by way of inwardly hidden holes, which are more than nothing and give hope for the existence of a metaphysical residue. Therefore, it is not surprising that he has stalactites where hands and arms typically swirl around the torso, if you pass by them too close, they can seriously injure you. His appearance alone is a terrible rebuke, such that he no longer needs to admonish or speak in the slightest. Nobody has ever seen him laugh, but many weep when they see him. A man who surpasses any humanchild in his hideousness.

In the Reichstag Building, they shall personally hand over the developed photo together with the text addressed to "The Government."

Sometimes the Molls forget that the three from Golgotha are in their mouths, then they seek to implement the ensemble as a tool, which may not work out too well, we're not dealing with former molars. They remind one another of their roommates and, once they ascertain that every single one of them can't possibly have Jesus in the mouth and get into a dispute about it, it shall be settled with the constatation that, indeed, Jesus cannot hang from every cross, but the houses of the republic are full of them, the more stringently the religion is banned, the fuller the houses become, whoever forbids religion and even if one forbids the cross, it's really in people's heads and shan't come out again, besides, Kreuzberg is incorrect, it ought to be called Kreuzhügel, not Kreuzmountain, but Kreuzhill, but the thieves, everyone has the thieves in mouth, there is no doubt about that, there are thieves everywhere, they say, and, as for thieves, there really can't be enough of them, after all, they belong to themselves and work out the thief-ranking amongst themselves, sometimes, one of them wishes to be head-thief, then, later on, he insists on being a henchman-thief when someone whom he can't bear fobs himself off as his equal, and thus does Girard's constatation hold true: "The more one is crucified, the more one burns to participate in the crucifixion of someone more crucified than oneself," this being the acid test, or, as one says in German, the "Nagelprobe"— the "nail test." Each time I speak *Satan*'s name, a cross appears before me floating freely in space, the cross grows larger with each utterance of *Satan*'s name. I can't help but utter *Satan*'s name, it's a compulsion, thus do I utter *Satan*'s name and the cross gets bigger, I utter *Satan*'s name once more, the cross is getting closer and closer to me, then I utter *Satan*'s name so many times in a row that the cross comes over me, and I enter into the cross. I hang from the cross, and it doesn't hurt, at the same time, I can see myself hanging from the cross from afar, and I feel a kind of Schadenfreude, no, his legs shouldn't be broken, I say, he ought to suffer for a long time, for as long as is possible, he ought to kindly sit upon his little stool, that is the king's stool, only kings sit upon it, now, it is to show whether he is a true king, I have barely uttered the sentence when two more crosses appear, I hang from the cross to the right of the gentleman who has just been dubbed king, I inwardly command him to gaze upon me, but he doesn't gaze upon me, he is falsely crucified, I call out, his feet are nailed to the sides of the cross, but they must be nailed on top of each other on its front, he is incorrectly crucified, then the crosses depart once more and I with them, I must endure an impossible rupture, I hang from the cross that's disappearing up a hill and, at the same time, I observe the situation from a greater distance, my mother stands next to me and asks, so, which of the three are you now? and I say to her that I'm the one in the middle, the other two are my secretaries, I was permitted to take them with me, my mother looks through her opera glasses, then, after she's examined the three of them in detail, she says, but he doesn't look like you at all anymore, aren't you actually the one to the right of the one in the middle?, you're mistaken, I say to her, I really am the one in the middle, it's just that a swindler's taken my place, he hangs there, for he is a swindler, he ought to have been hanging on the right, he cheated me out of the middle, his mother really didn't want to crucify him, but his wife did, as such, his mother had him crucified for the sake of peace and quiet, and he said to his mother, then I would like to hang in the middle, which the mother conceded to him, for he was suddenly so brave, I think you're all mixed up, my mother says. You are Gestas who has made me ill, she says; Dismas, who renounced me; Camma, who took another to wife than me; Chammatha, who has not returned to me; Maggatras, who purloined the cross from Father. Jezer ha-rah, the dishonesty and the inclination to do evil, which you never managed to positively make use of. You always only wanted everything all at once instead of using a knife, spoon, and fork. Now, you have everything all at once. Satan has the cross in the third house. He looks at the crucified one. To cast out Satan with Satan. The house must be at odds with itself. My mother advises me to read the book *The Devil and His Angels*, it shall surely take me from my head and put me onto my feet again, then I realize that I've been crucified upside-down. So, that's how I make use of the books, waiting for Schattenfroh's objection at every hour. I put *I See Satan Fall like Lightning* back onto the book trolley. The books are instantly assigned to the armarium inventory. I ought to have memorized it back when it was more manageable. Perhaps, by destroying a few books, I can reduce the inventory so much that I can once more take up its memorization. Agamben: *The Man Without Content*. With the gradual tearing-up of "§I The Most Uncanny Thing," a new exemplar grows in the armarium, initially pale-gray, as if the sun had bleached the shelf at the very spot where Agamben has perhaps already been lying for years, then a bright orange almost indistinguishable from the shelf. But is that still the genuine Agamben that is growing forth once more? Shouldn't it be checked word for word? What if the book-body-snatchers have come, the book's cocoon-copy has long been deposited and fills up with the material of the original as soon as it is destroyed or damaged, perhaps the copies also have messenger-substances, which ensure that the originals are lured in and position themselves next to them, thus falling into the trap. Who can say with any certainty that

Schattenfroh didn't scud the letters of the books through a machine and rearrange them in his own sense, in such a way that Agamben alias Gab Name* is no longer identified as author, instead Schattenfroh has had the book *The Man Without Content* put out by Pahmurks Verlag† under the new title *Twentieth Amount Notch*, penned by a certain "Amigo ab Göring" or, by Rahmspuk Verlag‡ under the title *Went Tithe Human Cotton*, written by "Ingeborg am Agio"§? I call up these books, no book trolley comes rolling through, the books remain in hiding.

At any rate, a gash runs through Nietzsche:

§I The Most Uncanny Thing

In the third essay of *The Genealo*
Nietzsche subjects the Kantian
terested pleasure to a radical cri
honoring art of beauty
he emphasized and gave
which established the honor of knowledge:
sality. This is not the place to
line is that Kant, like all philosophers,
aesthetic problem from the point of view of
purely from that of the "spectator,"
into the concept "beautiful."
It would not have been so
to the philosophers of beauty—
dance of vivid authentic experiences, desires,
of the beautiful! But I fear that the

---

* Gave Name.
† Pahbotch Publisher.
‡ Creamspectre Publisher.
§ Ingeborg on Agio.

and so they have offered us,
as in Kant's famous definition
in the shape of a fat worm of error. "That is
us pleasure without interest." Without inter
definition one framed
—Stendhal, who once called
At any rate he
diated the one point about the
ressement. Who is right, Kant or Sten-
aestheticians never weary of ass-
under the spell of beauty,
female statues "without interest,"
a little at their expense:
on this ticklish point are more
was in any event not necessarily an "un

gy of Morals,
definition of the beau
tiful as disin-
tique: Kant thought he was
when among the predicates
prominence to those
impersonality and univer-
inquire whether this was essentially a mistake; all
I wish to under
instead of envisaging the
the artist (the creator), considered art and the beautiful
and unconsciously introduced the "spectator"
bad if this "spectator" had
at least been sufficiently familiar
namely, as a great personal fact and experience,
as an abun-

surprises, and delights
in the realm
verse has always been the case;
from the beginning, definitions in which,
of the beautiful, a lack of any
refined firsthand experience reposes
beautiful," said Kant, "which gives
est! Compare with this
by a genuine "spectator" and artist
the beautiful *une promesse de bonheur*.
rejected and repu-
aesthetic condition which Kant had stressed: *le désinté-*
dhal? If our
erting in Kant's favor that,
one can even view undraped
one may laugh
the experiences of artists
"interesting," and Pygmalion
aesthetic man."

The pinnacle of the beautiful is its destruction. For, the celebration of the Sabbath, the "penal servitude of the willing," which Schopenhauer extolled as a quality, an advantage even, of the aesthetic state, is the very destruction of this alibi, which sees willing as mere torture, and, by being destroyed, the Beautiful loosens the straps of the rack and, with them, also the way in which the beautiful is taken into service, as practiced by Nietzsche.

Is the destruction of the beautiful not its consummation? The ruin is the pinnacle of the beautiful, the threshold of the is-and-is-not. A ruin is, is not. But must it first have become a ruin over the course of centuries, during which nature found it mete to, for example, burst through Rome's Stoneworks of Eternity, then to dissolve what was structured as an eternal order into its constituent parts, passing over any threat from Rome that nature too would be brought under its control? Only then do respect and reverence develop, felt more as regards the absence of greatness and might and, thus, the subjectless memory, than the architecture itself, which only has symbolic value, its gradual, but total disappearance cannot be stopped by anything, thus shall it one day become the replica, the substitute-substance, the repair having taken the place of the last remaining architectural elements. But what if the ruin was created by a catastrophe? If it isn't weathering and sinking-into-insignificance that grind away at the surfaces, but if, all of a sudden, the temple, the wall, the representative building lose both function and purpose and, in doing so, turn intact buildings into rubble or ruins, once representative of a whole culture and maintained for many centuries, buildings whose contours are still visible and whose architectural form can be reconstructed completely—ruined by blast demolition? If ruins are script from whose sentences history reads, then it is so that the blowing-up of a ruin is the yearning to erase this script so as to set another in its place, but the sentence "campus ubi Palmyra fuit" cannot be exploded; by lying atop Troy, it regains the consolation of eternity through the metascript of the explosion.

The book *Schattenfroh* is a liber ruinarum. It ruins my memories by immobilizing them so as to dissect them. I got along with them just fine for as long as they were in flux, harmless particles that, though they clouded the water, still didn't make it undrinkable. When the lurching particles glittered in the sun, whole stories shone through them and I lost myself in ecstasy; sinking to the bottom, they sometimes clumped together until an imperceptible current took them away once more and caused them to disappear in the drift, which, imperceptibly for the individual, also takes away the language in a different articulation, in such a way that some say a new language has arisen. What now remains, immobilized, is a ruin, a consummate archive, the exterior of which, if nobody reads it, is only ever to be found in its inwardness;

but, if somebody reads it, this causes the ruins to rupture, sets free the forces that had been sealed up inside of it, turns the requiem of exalted silence that is *Schattenfroh* into a hunt for meaning and illustration directed only by him, the reader, the signal of that which is sought is given by the character of each letter, hunting calls, as non-artistic as anything, the startingsignal, the deadsignal, the reader gazes upon a corpse-ensemble, Schattenfroh's Panopticon, and the question arises as to whether it's a corpseensemble of signs, dead wood, or maybe the signs are alive and kicking, but what they signify is unformally dead, and, indeed, that is the danger and hope of reading, to fuel a semiosis that sets into being and destroys simultaneously, that allows creation and extinction to collide, that redeems one's own life as reading.

In addition to that, I have a completely different suspicion: Schattenfroh causes *Schattenfroh* to arise as an artificial ruin, over which he can triumph like the Olympic Gods over the Titans, by causing their palaces to collapse and become their tombs, which provided the Mantuan Gonzaga princes with a wonderful motive for demonstrating their own might in their Palazzo del Te. Schattenfroh threatens me that he shall leave behind a ruin, under which I shall be buried, just as God still punishes the Fall of Man by ruining the earth. To the Frightbearing Society, he can then show a book, in which all culture is immobilized and experienced as a ruin, above the uselessness of which the Society rises up—and thus is it of some use: it is the symbol of the Frightbearing Society and Schattenfroh is its allegorical agent.

Schattenfroh has made sure that somebody is still there to observe, even if he doesn't reply by way of words or gazes. That would be Ezra, whom one cannot meet, through whom everything passes, and that which has passed through then assumes its adorned order, the visible appearance of which is red overgarment and a green undergarment. Ezra is still there once nature has renounced human beings and has turned to a scene both blind and mute. As to whether nature could or would do that; it is the indifferent per se, it cannot will, cannot be able.

Ezra is now no longer the inorganic guardian of the Law of the God in Heaven, which he is to present to those returning to Jerusalem as a single stone-ruin for the reorganization of the community under foreign rule and to anchor it in their society, for this society has a divine vision of the future—the Frightbearing Society does not arise from ruins once more, it administers society as a ruin, as a book of the dead, and most attentively makes sure that it remain a ruin, for this is eternal peace, and Ezra sits before the armarium and keeps watch—that the ruins not turn to the arena of awareness, for they only turn the earth into a museum of ruins as an arena of memory, thus is Ezra a museum security guard endowed with high, perhaps the highest power, he ensures that the visitors—for everyone is just a visitor, there are no more activists, no more politicians, one finds oneself gathered together for a common reading of the Book of the Dead—make no preparations for a counterruinous attack, by, for example, stuffing their pockets full of masonry so that the ruins vanish bit by bit, which, with time, would give cause to fear the reestablishment of the earth in another place, from which the quarried earthruin would be observed as if it were the natural product of a skinning and the skin had decomposed over time. It is the Endspiel-Gaze out of the window in the hopes of not ever encountering a rat again. Nature puts up no sign: "There was once something else here," nor does it explain anything or give hope—this remains quite pleasant for millennia.

The gaze upon the ruins is the gaze upon the father over whom one triumphs, one stands over the father-ruins, the fathercorpse, and thus gains an overview that Father never had, he always sat in his smoky little chamber and only saw himself through the smoke. When it comes to pass, can Father's death be sad? One must have the space and the sight for one's own soul so as to see oneself entirely in the distance. If, in addition to the final phases of development, all earlier phases continue to exist, just as Freud imagined "that in Rome the palaces of the Caesars were still standing on the Palatine and the Septizonium of

Septimius Severus was still towering to its old height; that the beautiful statues were still standing in the colonnade of the Castle of St. Angelo, as they were up to its siege by the Goths," "where the Palazzo Caffarelli stands there would also be, without this being removed, the Temple of Jupiter Capitolinus, not merely in its latest form, moreover, as the Romans of the Caesars saw it, but also in its earliest shape, when it still wore an Etruscan design and was adorned with terra-cotta antefixae," and where "the Coliseum stands now we could at the same time admire Nero's Golden House," and so on, we would then face them with such an awareness, the times would be quite distant, but their emanations present, these are nothing but as made by slavehands, wouldn't they quickly become indifferent and equivalent to our historical gaze and wouldn't it be tiresome to constantly be reminded by them of our never-lived memories, which, within us, would then give way to the resolution that they all must be razed to the ground? Instead, we celebrate the world of ruins as if we could absorb their spirit and, thus, within us, resurrect them in their monumentality, taking a bath in the nimbus of the mightiness they represent while strolling upon them: so that, inwardly, we not get rid of that which time erodes on the outside.

Schattenfroh, a ruined book of the dead. I must forestall my own premature ruin by way of this book of the dead (delivered up, fixed, and set free by Schattenfroh) by leaving the twentieth house through Nietzsche's gash, squeezing through between "established" and "-sality," "ess" and "is," "ar" and "considered," "desires" and "delights," "inter" and "with," "beautiful" and "bon-,""At any rate" and "repu-," "point" and "undraped," "un" and "man," into the curve of the S, the twenty-first house. Here, I find myself in the wild. There's nothing to see but an oak tree, to which, not initially recognizable as such, but rather thought to be a cancerous growth of the tree, a book is nailed by way of the corners of its splayed-out cover thus that its pages flutter in the wind and, over time, it shall dwindle down just like a flower one has forgotten to water for a long period of time, which is the opposite of forgotten. Because of the nailing, the book's title is unrecognizable, however, as the wind sweeps the inner pages of the cover free, one can see the bursting caused, apparently, by flagellation, which might well have utterly deformed the book upon the front-pages of its cover. As soon as one approaches the book, its pages begin to beat savagely, obviously, it doesn't wish for one to read it. Whatever secret it may be hiding, my attempt to take it down from the tree founders due to the resistance of the nails, which must have penetrated so deeply into the wood through the cover that one would sooner rip the body from the back than move the nails even a single millimeter. The tree cannot be blamed for the fact that it must serve as a cross, nevertheless, I am enticed by the notion of felling it. I have an ax in hand and fell the tree. The tree has been felled, trunk and branches have been hewed in several spots, the wind has died down. "Then, a red armarium arises from the tree that has been felled and cut into several pieces, filling up with books in mere seconds." And I read further: "Now, the armarium has become permeable for all who have passed through Ezra." I pass through the armarium as if through a light reddish mist, it clears at this very moment, allowing one's gaze to freely fall upon a staircase. Just as everything seems to concentrate into a single point at night, an entire year condenses into a single moment, the descent of a flight of stairs comes to no end and induces the obstinate counting of things that have no name and no fixed form, but to what purpose? Of all the numbers, soon enough, all that remains is the feeling of counting, a constricting heat that the body would very much like to rid itself of, were it not the thing being perpetually counted, and one immediately returns to one, which already makes two. Bright flashes appear, outlines become distinct for a short while, the sleeping person would like to match them up with familiar things, but the things do not let themselves be grasped and thus is counting accompanied by the search for names, and the names no longer even remotely fit the things that are meant to be fitted into the names, they constantly protrude beyond the names, the things are much too big for their names, one hears oneself cry out in one's sleep, but to whom is one crying out? Now, one sees oneself standing there, mute, and it is another who calls out, the bright flashes have flattened out into circular lines, streaks appearing here, then there, the middle remains empty, falls out, the counting is now clearly in the foreground, while things gradually begin to go blurry in the darkness, counting is a lump in the throat that fits beneath the palate, in tasting, I see counting, I can sense it, the counting is entirely empty, it hovers right above me, I can hurl it away from me with a quick motion of the eyes, then the counting grows warmer and gains density, if I lie there for a long time, totally calm, I fill the counting up entirely, that egg-shaped, woolen space, which smells a bit like a bird, the horsehair mattress causes me to feel the clod that is the lump in my throat more distinctly, it now stands just above the larynx and wanders, bouncing slowly to the forehead, which allows it to swing without releasing it again. There are nice drives one can take, one is firmly resolved and feels no fear as regards hurling oneself inward, racing inward over green areas, which suddenly tower forth like craterlandscapes, a traffic island in the middle of the night as the rain pours down, it juts out into the street and takes the air out of the tires. The light hides away the fact that almost everything is unlit, the light is the desert's artificial water, the misperception, the appearance, the throatlumpclot of the traffic island, it deforms the left rim, takes the air out of the tires, causes the car to levitate for some seconds, and it levitates over the mattress, from which I can't tear myself, my back hurts, my scoliosis growing into an ossification, the focal point of the inflammation shifts, R is an endless staircase, which leads into the basement that I one day decided never more to leave and Father managed to lure me outside by way of a door I didn't at that point know of, the bright of day seemed to me to be an artificial world, flowers only blooming for the sake of appearances, the lawn of artificial turf, paths leading nowhere, ever since, I have been incessantly walking down the basement stairs in my dreams,

I imagine myself to be locked in the basement in a room I do not know, from which I can only succeed in freeing myself if the staircase at some point comes to an end. Over time, I come to no longer believe in such an end, I don't despair, it is quite pleasant for me to know myself to be locked in this room, it's your bad side, I say to myself, and it's good that somebody locked it away. But I picture the room that holds the bad side captive as a paradise in which one's every wish comes true. If one is hungry, any dish can be served, so long as one promptly asks for it, one can meet any individual whom one once knew if one speaks their name, even if that person is already dead, one can also sit opposite oneself, and the opposite that is oneself can be of any age from birth to present age. In that case, one would be sitting across from one's double, one might, for example, say, I'd like to have a conversation with who I was when I was six, then, whether one is disappointed with the course of the conversation or has learned everything one wished to know, all one need do is name another age, then, already, one is sitting opposite the kid, the teen, or even the old man who one once was, as if one were sliding the pendulum's sliding weight further down. Tell me something about Mommy and Daddy, I would tell the six-year-old. He wouldn't comprehend the request. Do they treat you pretty nice? I don't know. Are you happy at home? The child knows all too well what "home" is, but "happy"? Happy is when you've got no worries, I say. The child gives me a blank look. I've the feeling that I must do something good for him and ask what he might wish from me. You should go, the kid says. I shift the weight of the pendulum to its lowest position, then my foot finally reaches the basement floor, I turn around, I've only just left the stairs, R, the twenty-second house, in which, or so it would seem, I had to run in perpetual circles. According to the map, I now find myself in E, the twenty-third and final house. A dry blow, a bright flash. Immediately, the thought of also having experienced this last time in precisely the same way, and also this time, the attempt to gain something new from the circumstances, it therefore represents some kind of forward progress to be able to recollect last time. In this way, one really won't age at all. I briefly consider whether the encounters with the far-too-deep doorframe caused headaches, shake my head, as if that were a way of shaking off a headache, sit myself down in sovereign fashion against a possible headache, anticipate it, stay seated. Back home. I sit before myself. So that's your so-called hobbyroom. Here, the forbidden was soldered together, championships that nobody knew were being held, here, the carousel of joy whirled round, verbatims were tested, the monsterword "irresponsible," a form of folly that is totally and completely irresponsible, who agrees?, who is the uncalled voice?, who is this radiator, this space heater?, this borrowed voice, to whom do I do wrong if not myself. No refuge once one has reached the final room and do you know what the burden of the cross is, that you were never there, that you never visited me there. An old cupboard with veneered walls of laminated fiber sheets, the veneer of a deceptively genuine grain, but then so smooth that it could have served as a mirror, this really isn't nature, thus polished, the whole of childhood was stored in this cupboard, books about growing up, which ought to be done with short shirts and a certain sense of ease, the anticipation remains, growing up drags on, gradually losing sight of the project of what one wishes to achieve. Then the cupboard has vanished in one fell swoop, a quick call, do you still need that, do you not need it anymore, a short spell of reflection, disturbed by this call in the middle of my work, I can't deal with that right now, but it must be dealt with immediately, what's in there, don't you remember, kid's books, old games, homemade stuff, likely not, where to put it, you must ask yourself the question, but it can't pose itself to me at the moment, so away with it?, but where to?, then to be regretted, childhood disposed of. Gametables gone, stuffedanimals gone, books and pens gone, everything properly disposed of, no grand gesture, the stuff is simply gone, picked up, down the maw of municipal garbage collection, one stands there empty-handed, one can no longer show it to anybody, one can also not give anything away anymore, fish a little thing out of a drawer and pass it on, something in which a heart hangs, Mother once got something out of a display-cabinet, an insignificant little thing that she held out before her with unprecedented caution, my heart hangs inside of this, she said, though it wasn't visibly so at the time, it merely made one jealous, one couldn't see it, yet this strange notion, this sentence, my heart hangs inside of this, has remained, has gained ever more depth, ever more gravity, it has become ever more actual, and before she died, she gifted me a golden bracelet, her heart also hung from that, and the heart steps forward, distances itself, forgets, until, one day, this something is presented to it once more, it has long since slipped out of view, no longer any trace of it in mind, it vanished without trace, and now, during the soliloquy that causes one to rummage through this drawer with great determination, the hands feel a shape that can no longer immediately be identified, there is something in this drawer, something your heart used to be attached to, and your heart must have fallen from it, immediately, your back is turned to your conversation partner, the situation must be weighed out with no detours, whether this find might perhaps change your life, whether one must suddenly drop everything, suddenly, you hold a memory believed to be long lost in your hands, and the pause, the pleaseexcuseme, I'llberightback, it shows that we're not yet at the end of the rope, there is a door that hasn't yet been shut, and in this place, where the green has found its way back, the ground-bedecking flowerislands, where, first of all, the hinges in the frames distinctly indicated the presence of a door, then, one day, the hinges had also vanished, the supporting pivots, and the door turns on its hinges, the door cracks open, the angel-entrygate, the frames are also finally removed, the resulting hole, one can hardly say that the resulting omission is adequately sealed, a material similar in form and color is fitted, wallpaper pulled over it, one senses it just underneath, the having-been-fit shines through and, from there, the pitiful condition of the entire room won't leave one's mind, there is nothing worse than filthy carpet, rainsoakedcarpet walkedover with streetshoes, traces of snow, deposited solids that dig deeper into the fibers with each stride, a first cleaningattempt with hotwater and suds as a permanent failure, the carpet in this spot is now *permanently* clean, tearing down a wallunit is equivalent to tearing down the entire house, it stands there empty, it's always something else, Mother said, you can barely believe you've got one thing under control when another thing is already standing at the door, Mother said, there's simply always something else that demands entrance, and, if one looks just hard enough, one recognizes that there's a door that's not yet been shut. There's a door that's not yet been shut. I'm going to shut it.

And, with the shutting of the door, the 23 letters vanish from my chest, I gather Father's effects into the suitcase, his toothbrush, the house slippers, the telescopic walking stick, the strange book, its cover, which, I might add, is of inferior pasteboard, offering no information as to title or author, I open it and find a scrap, upon which can be read in Father's script: "Continue reading here:", the Gotteslob, the nail scissors, the photograph of my mother, the last image before her death, the bit of small change, the taxi-company card, the rosary in a small case of black leather, which also harbors a yellow tooth, I pick up a travelling alarm clock, from which the battery has fallen out of its compartment, I put it back in, the alarm clock works, a remittance slip is still to be found, for whatever reason, Father has already signed it, I briefly hesitate to fill it out entirely, then tear it up, which I now regret, a paper sack of dried apricots lies on the path, I find John Le Carré's *Tinker Tailor Soldier Spy, Absolute Friends*, and *A Legacy of Spies* in the vicinity of the handle I carelessly discarded, but that I once more attach to the suitcase. The suitcase seems to me to be heavier than before, I go back to the park bench, it feels like I've been away from it for years, spring has come, the snow has melted, Crocus and Galanthus are standing by the wayside, he should take galantamine regularly, the family doctor said, but who is to remind him? I take one of the hard slow-release capsules out of the packet in one of the books and swallow it, I shall remain seated here until it takes effect or until there is no effect, thus could I stay seated here forever should there be no effect, perhaps, the effect is that the patient has the feeling that it has no effect, whereas, without the drug, he would not be able to make such a constatation.

The strange book has certain similarities with a dummy, the kind one often finds in furniture stores—and sometimes finds oneself to have been deceived when the dummy turns out, for example, to be *Crime and Punishment*, it moves one to tears, then immediately, which is to say after some eight hours of reading while neither eating nor drinking, prompts one to leave the furniture store with the resolution to lay down all axes, to no longer wish to be an Übermensch, but to be thankful for all that which life may bring, resolutions that have already receded into the background when leaving the shop, for one has already reentered the process of one's own bringing oneself to act, of responding to the perils of life with particular agility and easily bringing about and bearing the quickest of changes, if one has thus read too much Kafka, and this Kafka with his after-effects, as they're made visible with such empathic sprightliness in "The Sudden Walk," allows one to take hold of one's ax as soon as one has returned home, then, as soon as one has ensured that one is not in one's own way, to smash the next-best thing to bits, then, once one has moved on from the kitchen equipment from that particular furniture store, to scamper thigh-slappingly up the stairs and begin to dismantle the library with furious blows without being able to discuss this with a friend whom one has only just asked how he's doing, for one feels no guilt, but rather relief that some burden has been lifted with this destructive act, for does one not, as soon as one possesses a few books—which is to say more than one, as one might pass as accidental—feel the longing to devour them with one's eyes, to be their master, to suck the spirit from their letters and incorporate it into one's spirit, which must have a hole at its bottom, for barely has one dose of spirit been put down when one's own spirit begins to behave incontinently and send what one has previously read into oblivion, one really doesn't wish to keep it either, one wishes to destroy it, thus is destruction a relief that allows me to devote myself completely and entirely to the book, which also does not reveal title or author on the inside. I'm amazed that Father even allowed himself to get involved with such a book, which runs completely counter to his love of order, in the context of which names, designations, titles, and keywords are utterly essential.

A plaque is attached to the park bench's backrest: "*Come unto me, all ye that labour and are heavy laden, and I will give you rest.*" Donated by Schattenfroh, which can be read in the book without title or author on page 603. I shut the book and read: "I am now leaving the 23rd house, the house of my parents, which I go into when I cannot sleep at night. Even so, Father: for so it seemed good in thy sight. All things are delivered unto me of my Father: and no man knoweth the Son, but the Father; neither knoweth any man the Father, save the Son, and he to whomsoever the Son will reveal him. Come unto me, all ye that labour and are heavy laden, and I will give you rest. Take my yoke upon you, and learn of me; for I am meek and lowly in heart: 'and ye shall find rest unto your souls.' For my yoke is easy, and my burden is light. Then the rooms are empty, the park bench, a blue armchair is enthroned in the vestibule, leather gloves lie in the wardrobe beneath the mirror, in it, I can still see myself as a child who felt no fear when its image could still be seen in the glass once it had already turned away. The child saw itself out of the corner of its eye, then, when it looked back, saw that the child in the mirror was gazing at it unblinkingly, utterly motionless, which made the child before the mirror quite furious, it knew that it was going to lose the staring contest, but what weighed more heavily was the reproach that the gaze signified, now tell me, said the child, but the child in the mirror says nothing, though the eyes said, you left Mother behind, she had nobody but you. Even the clothing brush with its back of genuine silver still lay in the drawer, the child wished to bang it against the mirror with rage so that the other's gaze might leave it, the bright bristles massaged its hand, its face, its scalp, it imagined its mother's hand was guiding the brush, and it was the only one who had the brush, not the one in the mirror, thus did the child before the mirror know that its mother was guiding the brush. Bearing the brush being run so beautifully over the walls in hand, the child passes into a large room. Here, Christmas was celebrated. The wooden floorboards creaked because of all the angels, they were coming and going. But aren't angels meant to be weightless, the child asked its father. Not at Christmas, Father said. At Christmas, they're quite heavy as a function of the many gifts they must carry. In those days, there was always a group of wooden musicians from the Ore Mountains standing on the marble windowsill, their presence was more important than the presence of parents and siblings. The pewter jugs and bronze cauldrons have probably been standing in the old, heavy wooden cupboards for generations. If, one day, there were an ordinance that all heirlooms had to be preserved and passed down from generation to generation, the earth wouldn't be big enough and it would all have to be stored in outer space, otherwise both economy and society would come to a standstill. Everything has remained in our family up until the present day. Only the family has not stayed in the family. It has passed over into script. And thus do I go from script to script. I only see what I've read elsewhere, in Father and Mother's letters, in their diaries, my uncle's contemporary-historical essays, the captions of photographs.

During one of my nocturnal strolls, I find a key in one of the pewter jugs, it is like no other in the house. Its bow recalls a gallows knot, its shaft comes to no end, the shaft's double-bit has the most bizarre of protuberances. I know from my mother that there is a hidden room in the house's attic, a room that one can only enter with a key. This room cannot be accessed through any ordinary door, it has no handle, an invisible frame, and no hinges, it is embedded into the wall in such flush fashion that no light can penetrate to the outside, additionally, the lining of the wooden beam-supported ceiling, walls, and partitions with broad-fibered black insulating boards made of wood-wool makes it difficult for even those who know of it to find it. Mother always said that there was no asbestos, to this day, I remain convinced that the thick black fibers *are* asbestos or contain it, I would hold my breath and count to thirty as I made my rounds of the attic, then I would have to leave it once more. The keyhole, which is missing its mounting, is entirely covered over by the wood-wool fibers. Back then, I didn't dare to palpate the walls for hollow spaces, I was afraid of startling animals or finding my parents dead behind the hutch, I also imagined that a certain Herr Schattenfroh lived there, he would stand before me one day so as to tell me the truth about myself, which would result in severe punishments. Schattenfroh always accompanied my thoughts, I was afraid of him, the hustle and bustle of the day, filled with games, a wooden game particularly occupied me, suppressed my fear until the evening, the song of the blackbird dissolved into clamoring chirps, then it comes back, creeps from the fingertips to the heart, which doesn't wish to perceive that it doesn't wish to perceive the fear, the face burns coolly, fear lays a fine veil over the skin, then the body blazes furiously, it becomes a soldier marching against the threat, it must constantly be on the move and knows not where the enemy might be lurking, Schattenfroh is after me, he has seen through my strategies and overcomes me effortlessly, but I don't wish to capitulate, I get the box with the wooden blocks from the so-called kids' room, go into the boiler room, the heart of the house, lay the stones into the shape of a square behind me and do not leave the room for the next few hours.

The boiler was big and blue, it was filled up with oil brought by a tanker. Two hours later, I came to fear that the smell of the oil would give me cancer, I sought to breathe as shallowly as possible, which pleased Schattenfroh, who had, in the meantime, moved into the boiler and fed on my breath, thus did I breathe more quickly so that he might not breath, the oil made the lungs entirely black, sweat ran down my face, that was Schattenfroh's sweat, my shirt served as a sweat-towel, with which I incessantly rubbed myself dry, my face became more and more chapped, while the shirt became more and more damp, I didn't cease the rubbing even when I was already bleeding, I'm sweating blood, I said to Mateo, whom I had pierced with the drawing rod, he now appeared distinctly before me, he was always there when I got myself into trouble, you must extinguish the boiler, he called out, what do you mean by 'extinguish,' I asked, do away with it, was the reply, I took up a wooden stone and beat it against the boiler, yes, kill it, kill it, Mateo called out, the boiler sounded quite empty, the bit of wood lost its shape, I thought that I could hear Schattenfroh whimpering in the boiler, then something called out 'kill it, kill it' from the boiler and I no longer knew whom I was meant to kill, Schattenfroh was Mateo, Mateo was Schattenfroh, the enclosing wall had a chink in it, I could escape through there, I wasn't allowed to put the weapon back, but had to shrink, the gap was too minute, thus did I grow ever smaller, crawl through the gap, and make my way toward the boiler-room door. Now, I was at the mercy of Schattenfroh, the heavy fire door presented an insurmountable obstacle, how could I open it even a crack, as, under normal circumstances, I could only manage to budge it if I pushed against it with all my might. I had to escape through the keyhole, but the key was in the keyhole, it would certainly kill me, I was in my coffin, the wall was burning, the boiler could catch fire at any moment, thus did Mother open the boiler room, box my ears, and say that Father had ordered I would have no supper—and she had the voice of Schattenfroh as she said it. But you're not Schattenfroh, I said to my mother. So, who is Schattenfroh? I mean to say, he who lives up there in heaven and down here in hell. I know, my mother said, at least, I wish that she had said that. Dad forbade you from watching movies like this in secret, she said. To go to bed without your supper is just that: to go to bed without your supper. All night, the empty belly shall remind the body that it is empty. And, because of the emptiness of the belly, the head fills up with edible things.

No supper means no sleep, but foul dreams. When the belly growls, Schattenfroh says things like 'pull out' and 'turn around.' As if I had to pull something out of the wall, to turn around within myself. I walk past Mother going upstairs. A concrete staircase leads to the ground floor. I have no shoes on, the steps are sharp on the edges and cut into the soles of my feet. The ground floor with its cold marble. The cast-iron banister of the staircase leading up to the second floor. The open space of the staircase occupied by meter-high flowers in a jug of blue stone. Spiders lodge in the flowers. The jug was never filled up with water. Nobody liked the flowers, they haven't been changed out in all these years. Even though I didn't dare touch them, I was always tempted to go see if there wasn't any water in the jug. I imagined the water to be a small, but deep pool with its own monster that could leap forth from the bottom of the jug in a matter of seconds, then expand to tremendous size. There was also eternal money to be found there, I thought, which would only have to be assiduously harvested so as to grow back. The money would afford me an independence that would allow me to develop plans of international scope. For example, I wished to set up my own state with its own prisons, everything outside of the state would be a church that would enclose the state in a ring. The jug sounded hollow when one spoke into it. If, by some oversight, I made contact with one of these plants that hadn't yet grown, I would immediately go and wash my hair. Sometimes, a sort of compulsion would develop from this, the contact I made became something I anxiously awaited, I would run up the stairs at the mere thought of this contact, but I could never be certain whether it actually triggered the washing of my hair and the trip to the bathroom or the praying to God. In this way, I said the Lord's Prayer some ten times per day, I also learned how to say the Hail Mary in Latin so as to have a bit of variety and gain something useful from this compulsion. One day, the cast-iron railing was repainted, hot paint dripping down it. Mother had forbidden going up the stairs, the paint might drip down onto my head and cause damage to it. I ducked underneath the cordon, went up the stairs, the paint thus dripping onto my head and causing damage to it. I'd always wished for a carpet atop the marble steps, but it was only the carpet of the second-floor hallway that was recarpeted, gray felt that burned beneath one's soles if one abruptly ceased walking or running. Through the stairwell, one could see the wooden bench that stood in the recess in the ground-floor hallway, a heavy blue cushion lay atop it and smelled to be some hundred years old. If I lay belly-first onto this cushion and breathed in its smell, I would imagine myself to be standing on a street with many people, Bismarck driving through them in a four-horse carriage. He has only just declared war on France and the crowd now wishes to know why Berlin must go to war with Paris. Hats are waved, flowers hurled into the street, there's free hot cocoa in a café. But Bismarck doesn't come, thus do I set off to search for him in a streetcar. He has my father's facial features, but, in contrast to him, has a pompous beard. Only once in his life did my father have a so-called handlebar mustache, it looked utterly abominable, his family was ashamed of it. I now reflected as to whether it was the similarity of facial features or the missing beard that was the defining factor in recognizing my father in Bismarck or in rejecting the presupposition that Bismarck is my father. I opted to see my father in Bismarck, thus setting out to search for him my whole life long. I became an avid reader of Bismarck's biographies, which helped me to explain my father's behavior in a profound way. With the Ems Dispatch, the Franco-Prussian War, and his social legislation my father had earned himself such a reputation that neglecting the family could no longer carry any negative weight. It wasn't foreign or domestic political conflicts or the rift with Wilhelm II that ultimately led to his departure, rather, he dissolved himself inwardly by making speeches against himself in the person of Wilderich von Ketteler and overshadowing himself as Ludwig Windthorst in such a way that the latter froze to death.

The wooden staircase leading to the attic was painted gray years ago. Gray is the smoothest color. The paint job is so smooth that one could easily slip and fall down the stairs. The feeling of hunger is combined with the smell of the attic, which is not lost even after a core-renovation. I carry the key before me like a relic. What seemed to me to be a mysterious labyrinth at the time now turns out to be a very well-thought-out area and the door into the chamber is quickly spotted. The key is the whole house. Turning it, the forbidden one, so difficult to find, in the lock so many decades later, frees up space once more for the oldest of fears, promises to give a peek behind the curtains of power, I had actually always imagined that the house was governed from the roof down. Mother's might consisted in her absence, the fear of the mother is a hard currency, which the child must always pay out, the key goes round the lock twice, then the door opens up a crack. It is dark in the cell, a sweet smell wafts out, warm, musty air that takes your breath away, the door barely gives way, a dent in the floor seems insurmountable, I squeeze through the crack, step behind the door, then tear it open. The air is some forty years old. It still contains Father and Mother's breath. Faint contours can be seen upon the opposite wall. I'm entirely certain that I'm not alone in the room. The attic is fitted with a set of Bakelite light switches, why should the chamber not also be equipped with a light. I palpate the walls, which, to my astonishment, are made of brick. The chamber is fitted with a stone floor, the rest of the attic with only a plain concrete ceiling. The stone floor is divided into squares. The squares are marbled, a bright square standing on one of its corners in the middle is brought into a red square, as a function of which four red triangles arise. The sides of the red square are bordered by bright, narrow rectangles. The resulting rectangular gaps at the corner-points are each filled with small green rectangles.

No light switch can be found anywhere, the longer my eyes scan the semi-darkness, the more they recognize. A large sheet appears. It used to be radiant white, radiant white laundry was Mother's pride and joy, it glowed even at night, now, its color shades into dirty gray and one would prefer not to touch it at all. Mother always said, take a look at your shirt, look at your pants, they're covered in filth. Just to cross the street was enough for 'covered in filth.' The sheet smells like the brittle brown curtain of my shelf that stood behind the headboard of my bed. On the shelf, between the toys and books, I'd hide papers with notes, to which I wished to refer back in case of an emergency. In case of an emergency necessarily meant the Last Judgment, I imagined it to myself as a kind of general reckoning. In my imagination, everyone had to stand before a large table, behind which a row of men sat—my mother too. My mother would wallow in her self-pity and goad the men to interrogate me. From the beginning onward, my mother would always utter the demand 'Now *that* deserves some form of punishment' or 'But *that* really can't go unpunished.' Most of the time, she wouldn't make herself heard with these objections, the men were completely indifferent to my mother, their presence had the sole intent of creating the impression that the trials were being observed from the outside and that they themselves would be pilloried in the event of blatant violations of the legal system, which wasn't, however, put down anywhere in script. Resignedly, my mother would take note of the men's ignorance and say: 'He already had quite a record before this.' One day, a small, oblong box, the origin of which I could not explain, was lying on the shelf. I left it there unheeded for a few days, however, I did notice that it was taking over my dreams and forcing itself into my thoughts and conversations more and more during the day. Thus did I finally open it, but at the very moment I was to gaze upon its contents, the door of my room opened, Mother came in, rushed over to my bed, and boxed me on the ears. 'Don't you dare,' she said, taking the box and leaving the room once more. The next evening, however, the box was once more lying on the shelf and the whole story repeated itself. No matter how I sought to anticipate my mother by, just before 4:00 a.m., without turning off the light, taking it from the shelf myself and bringing it underneath the bedcovers with me, which, in the context of such anticipation, offered still other joys, I didn't succeed in removing its contents, I couldn't even make contact with them once, for the door would immediately open, the light would turn on, and Mother would box my ears so resoundingly, so violently, that, from then on, I would see my mother before me with her hand raised so as to deal out a slap whenever a threatening situation that demanded repentance was imminent. God is merciful when people show remorse, my father always used to say. It never became clear to me why one needed to show remorse and how one ought to repent. What Father was saying obviously had to do with a principle that applied regardless of any actions or events. I imagined a man who constantly repented and, over time, became capable of nothing other than repentance. The poor fellow exhausted himself completely in his repentance, day in, day out, but, at the same time, this persistence was his currency, on the one hand, he caused his fellow humans to think about whether they hadn't forgotten to regret something, on the other hand, the eternal penitent was despised by them because he who hypocritically presented himself as a model sinner believed that he was washing himself clean of his sins by way of lip service. In any case, as soon as I even saw a person, I was overcome by remorse, and Mother hovered before me with her hand poised to strike. Likewise, I had meticulously documented these connections in my papers and wished to present them, to turn to a higher authority when the time came so as to prove my innocence or at least my good intentions not to harm my fellow humans, my mother most of all. For example, the documentation had the following entries: 'May 15, 1978, 8:00 p.m., Mother barges into the room again, tears the box out of my hand, and smacks me. Dad will be here soon, then I'll really get it. Have been waiting for an hour . . . like a dead man, Dad didn't come. At 11:00 p.m., the garage door slams, now it's too late for Dad to come to me.'—'May 26, 1978, 9:30 p.m., took the box under my covers with me today, wanted to touch it a lot before opening it. Touching it made my dick hard, the box is smaller than my dick, but thicker. It's just fine the way it is. First, my cock needs to be gone again, then the thing can come out of the box. The door bangs against the cabinet, light on, Mother tears the bedcovers off, takes the box, hits me, says "sneaky brat," flips the light off again, slams the door shut.'—'September 13, 1978, the box isn't on the shelf. When I wake up at night, it's underneath the covers. Mother tears the covers off and says: "I knew it." I didn't even hear her come in, she must really have been standing next to the bed all night. In the meantime, I've come to believe that the box is empty. Mother has made God knows what promises to herself, her life, her child—but she won't be able to keep them. The promise, for instance, that life has a beautiful meaning. She promised this meaning into the box. Once called into the world, the meaningbox could not be called back, that's why Mother has to reclaim it day after day and night after night. She knows it to be with her son. But she can only access it when her son wishes to open the box. Then she must open it herself each time—to see if there's anything in it that she might show to her son, here, look, this belonged to my father, also having belonged to his father, but there's nothing in it that's been passed down from generation to generation. She gave me a little English-German dictionary some time ago, from back when she was in school, an economy-format war edition, its cover is torn, it smells of water damage, Nazi English, I thought, the Nazis forged English just like they did the pound notes in Operation Bernhard, thus did all who learned English from this little book take the attitude of the Nazis unto themselves, including and above all the English when they looked up a German word.' Besides this documentation, the papers also included poems or what I thought to be poems. Mother commented on the poems with the words: 'You really think you're better than me.' I really think I'm worse than you, I said to Mother, that's why I write poems, I said to her. 'The mute word is dubbed I / I ought to be taken out and shot.' That wasn't mine at all, but somebody else's, it had engraved itself into me, it was ever on my mind, I'd found it amongst my notes one day, the author unnamed, Mother found it quite repulsive and typical of me. That's typical, she said, that says it all.

On the day of the Last Judgment, the box and its story will likely be the trump card up my mother's sleeve. I will be said to have stolen it. Though I will initially be allowed to read excerpts of my documentation aloud—it will have, in the meantime, grown to be 883 pages long—this part of the hearing will eventually be jettisoned, the men will be solely interested in the box, the contents of which I won't yet have laid eyes on. Mother testified that I'd taken the key from the box—the key that was a match for the hidden chamber and I'd done so in order to play out my own little mummeries in there: to pray to God, to write poems to him. Thus did she find the following stanzas written in my script on the wall: 'Lord, give me wings with which to soar / from darkest night to brightest light! / You shall show me your sky adored, / and I come, I come not into sight.' On the opposite wall, she claims to have found the following lines: 'Be still in God, still as the sea! / Its surface alone streaks the wind, / and no matter how like a raging storm it be, / know that the depths are calm, kind.' My objection that these lines belong to Hadschi Halef Omar Ben Hadschi Abul Abbas Ibn Hadschi Dawuhd al Gossarah is carefully taken down in the minutes, I must spell out the names. There, I heard about the chamber for the first time. You shouldn't play the fool so much, Mother screamed at me, she says that it's been my intention from the beginning to deceive them and gain possession of the chamber. She says that I deposited a typewriter in the chamber, using it, I wrote up this interrogation too. She says that, right from the beginning, my goal has been the Last Judgment, during which I want to get rid of her, my mother. When the men objected that they could find no evidence of that which she had brought forward against me, on the contrary, I had wept over her death a great deal, my mother changed tack, though her initial inclination was to object that tears were no proof and that words were merely there so that one might lie with them, a claim that might, however, also have been turned against her. I had thought up the chamber, she now opined, it didn't exist at all, I'd thought it up for myself so as to expose her, my mother, to show that she was holding something back from me that was weightier than meaning, weighter than, for example, the meaning of life. And what might that be, the men wished to know. Something like the soul, my mother said. Something like or precisely it? The soul. I have no soul is what my son accuses me of. Thus can I also not pass down a soul. She says that the chamber is an imaginary workshop, a workshop of the imaginary. As I have no soul, my mother says, my son therefore represented me as headless and bodiless, in a robe that conceals me entirely, she's only a mother after all, not good for anything, she's no woman at all, mother is the third sex, it's no longer a sex at all, but merely a magnificent vestment that traces the contours of the body, its beautiful colors deceiving the senses. What do you mean by 'represented'? Painted, my mother said, my son painted me, he has achieved the feat of causing me to appear in total absence, simultaneously empty and turned inward in absence. The men wished to know what precisely her accusation was. My son did away with me and he wishes to cause murder to appear as art. The chamber with its giant painting is the proof. But if your son really did invent the chamber, as you say, then who could have known of it, the men asked. Everyone could have known of it, for everyone could have seen it—and those who saw the painting saw that it shows the inside of the chamber. The men then wanted to know from my mother whether the painting could be entered into like the chamber. It is a chamber of light, a lightroom, my mother says, and only torture serves to prevent entry therein. The men ask me whether I have anything more to say. I say that I didn't paint the painting and knew of no chamber or lightroom, but Mother left me to my own devices so early that I do not know her face. The men replied that this was apparently not the case, so let us now come to a verdict. It was only then that I noticed I had no mouth, it must have remained in the hand that brushed it away as it passed over it. Mother faded into the background, and my father flickered in her fading, shining through her, which was when I recognized that my mother's soul is my father. My father once said to me, what is it you've got with you, and I gave him the papers that I had on my person. If Father spoke to you, it was a call to attention and the one spoken to had to stand before him, then not budge until Father allowed the one spoken to to leave. This could be managed by way of a short speech, he didn't waste many words, or even with a questioning, perhaps mocking look, which ensured one would leave the room. Poems were written on the papers, Father read them, couldn't decipher certain things, but was of the opinion that they were likely immaterial, then he gave me the papers back, saying that he had also done something like that many years ago, but hadn't dared to show anyone, and I thought he meant to say that I was brave, but what he actually meant was that it was so bad that he'd kept it to himself—then he'd suppressed that too, the to-himself. My father's image went to bits, to shards, the men rose up, and the Last Judgment was at an end. The men had already left the room, while I was still awaiting the verdict. I am still awaiting the verdict today, thus do I believe that the verdict is the continuation of one's former life after the day of the Last Judgment. The joy of having received no punishment, of having been subjected to no corporeal torture, calmed me down so much that I began to move uninhibitedly through the room, aping individual dialogues from the interrogation with no fear of expiring on the spot, later, admittedly, this fear would never leave me, not until I got right up close to the table the men had left behind, almost tumbling forward in my momentum, then, in the process, looking into a deep black hole under the table. The table suddenly appeared so enormous and so high to me that I didn't dare to climb it entirely so as to then climb down the opposite side. Instead, it was a great alleviation to slide down its smooth surface like snow on a mountain—when it thaws, it's only early morning, it's glittering everywhere, an orchestra of waterdrops can be heard playing over the trees all round, a wooden table becomes visible in the evaporating fog, above it on the left, a typewriter seems to hover. A multi-colored raiment can now be seen to the left of that, it is cleverly folded to give the impression of being alive. I can touch the raiment, it's quite stiff. Instead of the missing head, the raiment wears a hood of the same material as the shroud, a wiry halo floats above the veil, attached to the ceiling, one can easily pluck it free and set it onto one's own head. Haloes come in all different sizes or there is one halo-size for all. The halo is more of an aureole. In its folded absence, I recognized my mother Mary. She cannot bear to gaze upon her son's suffering, thus is she the only one who can get a glimpse behind the curtains. She averts her gaze, she has no gaze at all, she has only one line of sight, everything is empty beneath the Good Friday bit of her raiment, turned outward in the colors of the church year, Mother Mary is no mother, she is merely the institution of the mother and stands for the church, which is empty, her hip-length headscarf that is her head is of the same fabric as the shroud that conceals the Crucified One. At least this one has hands and feet, thus could these hands serve the floating Ideal if they weren't bound by the hands that Mary doesn't have.

The typewriter is working. If one comes into its vicinity, it writes. It is guided by a hard hand. It is likely not to be assumed that there is paper to be found in the chamber, thus is all that which she writes directly onto the platen lost. From the clatter of the letters, I at least believe I can hear the following text: Don't put off till tomorrow what you can do today. I turn and kick my foot against something soft, fleshy. My hand feels a tongue hanging down from a maw, a long snout, teeth, an empty eye socket. A cow's skinned head. Then, one step later, a sheet of paper falls to my feet as I bump into a protruding piece of wood. The sheet was folded once lengthwise and once crosswise and is overall quite crumpled. A sticky note with a strange diagram of triangles within a triangle, one outer and three inner, somebody must have had it in their pants pocket. There are feet standing on the block of wood. It's no block of wood. It's a cross. The feet, nailed to the cross, rest upon a footstool. Dubbed the suppedaneum, the beast has been tasked with prolonging the death throes. The feet are bleeding, blood is running down the wood. I hesitate to check whether it's only feet that are nailed to the cross, hacked off like pigs' feet, or whether the rest of the body follows the feet. Except for the hands, the body, if there even is one, is draped over with a shroud, which hangs from the ceiling by way of three cords run through three eyelets. The lower end of the left cord leads to the wall by way of an intermediate attachment, to the empty raiment, the lower end of the right cord—to a little hooded man, he is now laying claim to the entirety of my attention, as a pathetic threat directed toward me emanates from him, I'd like to lift up the little man and press him to my chest, but, at the same time, he digusts me, his raiment, made of the same material as the shroud, is too big for him, the cord runs through the hands clasped in prayer, he is a projection of baseness, of that which one has pledged to do, his neatly outstretched fingers mock the hands on the cross, they've lost all that which lies between them, here, they show themselves to be humble and are false in their humility, the little figure is an unsummoned hanger-on, he's waiting for the time to be right, then he shall strike, however, until then, he kneels or seems about to walk, whatever I think of him, he remains in the same position, motionless, isn't that what drives us mad, this stoic persistence, the tolerance that moves us to veil the savior, for we can no longer bear his visage, I pick up an apple lying on the ground one step closer to the figure, I'm about to throw it when the question arises as to where the light in the chamber actually comes from, as it was formerly so dark that I could hardly make out the outlines of the things and figures. The brightness is now evenly distributed, but I see objects most clearly when I focus my gaze upon them. The source of the light remains hidden. It must be God who is illuminating me. I hear this sentence in me, it appears as self-evident, and thus is it so that God is illuminating me. God now shows me a wooden Jesus lying diagonally in a crate, his right arm having previously been broken off by the apple. With this arm, Jesus himself could have pulled the ripcord and easily reached the cord lying atop the roof of the box from his position. His upper body is free, he wears a red-gold cloth around his shoulders and groin, he holds it together at hip-height with his left hand. The divine blood and the Holy Spirit, a colorful arrangement of the folds. I lay the broken arm alongside the severed pinion, which is lying in a small wooden crate on the table to the left of the Risen One. From the glass of red wine standing atop the crate, I can recognize that it isn't a pinion lying in the crate, but bread. The wine stands over the bread. The bread is rock-hard, using the wine, I manage to soften small, bite-sized pieces. I briefly reflect as to whether the wine isn't too fine to waste as a bread-softener and whether I ought not gulp it down as it is. The bread smells revolting. Mold has formed in its cracks. I put it back into the crate and return to the small figure. An irresistible desire to do violence to it overwhelms me. I pick it up and bang its head against the typewriter, which tips forward. A nice game occurs to me: egg tapping. Point to point and blunt to blunt, then point to blunt or blunt to point. The Risen One begins. He deals a fine blow and cuts the little figure's head off. The little figure does the same to the Risen One. The Risen One's feet smash the little figure's hands. Then the game grows boring and I place the little figure—or, rather, what remains of it—alongside the Risen One—or, rather, what remains of the Risen One. I put the Holy Spirit underneath the table and give it a nice kick so that it slides back against the wall in its coffin. Then I take the three cords into my hand and pull them all at once. The shroud doesn't move. After two further attempts, the cords tear free. The body of the Crucified One has entirely entered into the shroud, one must break him, just as the legs of those who were executed were broken on the cross. Here, somebody has spent so long without gazing behind the curtains that the curtains have become that which is hidden. The shroud is the Crucified One. The Crucified One is just as wavy and folded as the paper with the strange diagram that I pocketed. Wherever I look, I see triangular configurations, between Mary, the Crucified One, and the boy, between the sheep's heads, the bread and wine, and the Risen One, between the typewriter, Mary, and the cows' heads.

The cross is the key, the cross forms at least two triangles, one above the crossbeam and one below, and, now, I recognize a certain Trinity between the Crucified One, the Holy Spirit in the crate, and the little head-, foot-, and handless figure, which must be God. I crawl underneath the table, take God from the crate, then place him beneath my mother's pleated raiment. My father who dictated decrees his whole life long and worked on canonical matters for a Berlin publishing house, for which purpose he withdrew to a small room in the converted part of the attic, smoked many cigarettes, and opened just as many drawers, my father put down this diagram, I can see that very clearly from the handwriting. When my father put that which was most important down on paper, he used the ballpoint pen as a burin, and it was with this burin that he would engrave any underlay, over time, the tabletop was transmogrified into a palimpsest of prescriptions, case studies, and legal commentaries. The design, which had fallen at my feet from the cross's footstool, likely served him as a decision-making aid in complex legal cases of an ecclesiastical nature. Its paradoxical contortions encouraged him to designate problems precisely and to make decisions, as nothing could be as insoluble as this diagram. I observe the diagram, then I gaze upon the cross once more, knowing the wooden Risen One to be beneath the table and God beneath my mother's cascade of folds.

Apparently, God is hidden here. That's not so obvious. If 'Pater non est filius,' then the father is not hidden here and the son is; however, if, at the same time, 'Filius est deus,' then God is hidden here. But whoever sees the son, sees the father, after all, the son himself said so. Then the son is fully revealed, the father is hidden, and the only way to the father runs through the son. So, how can it be that the father dies? If the dead father is in the son, the son is simultaneously hidden and revealed. Then, if the three are one, but also not one, all three are hidden—or is only one of them hidden or one of them only partially? One of the three, two of the three, none, all? Is there a hidden God and, simultaneously, another one who is revealed? Is God only triune in his hiddenness or triune only in his revelation? If God is always hidden, but his son always revealed, how can they be one? And the Holy Spirit? Does it move to and fro in oscillating fashion? Does it confer sanctification between the realms? Does it sanctify that which is on earth, yet divine? Is there a God of Darkness and, independently of him, a God of Light? Or is God a threateningpunishingevil God and only his son is entirely beneficent, forgiving, loving? The Word of God is hidden in the Body of Christ, but why is this diagram of the Trinity necessary, placing the Word outside of the Body once more? There is no one without the other. Thus are all three together just as hidden as revealed, as active as passive. Why are there even three in the first place? One on earth, one not on earth, one between earth and not on earth. So, shall the father be poured out at Pentecost, shall the Holy Spirit be crucified? The magic word is perichoresis. Is the contradiction in Man or is it in God? Only God can cast himself into doubt. But who is God? And what does 'hidden' mean here? Is it not all too clumsy to hang a curtain before the thing and foist it off as hidden? A theater curtain that entices the bourgeoisie's desire in silent expectation of the peep box? The curtain has become independent. It has become the thing. Thoughts stammer and they are right to. Then the cow's maw raises its voice:

'God says to you: Behold, you have My Son. Listen to Him, and receive Him. If you do this, you are already sure about your faith and salvation.' I reply to the cattle-head: 'But I do not know whether I do remain in faith.' 'At all events', the cattle-head says, 'accept the present promise and the predestination, and do not inquire too curiously about the secret counsels of God.' 'I would gladly do so,' I reply, 'it is likely intentional that the Lord remains invisible.' 'If you believe in the revealed God and accept His Word, He will gradually also reveal the hidden God; for 'He who sees Me also sees the Father,' as John 14:9 says. He who rejects the Son also loses the unrevealed God along with the revealed God,' the cattle-head answers. 'I see a veiled Christo and, in him, I see a veiled God,' is my riposte, 'thus might we shroud all that is and, in it, see all that is.' 'I see a veiled Christo and, in him, I see all that is,' replies the visitor to the stables who has followed the Morning Star. But the cow did not follow the Morning Star, nor did it follow any comet, it followed Jupiter, Mars, Mercury, Venus, the moon, and the sun right up close to each other in the constellation of Aries, all partially overlapping. The cow is silent from then on. The other cattle-head is also silent, which can be explained by the fact that it no longer has a tongue. I dub the two heads the wise men from the east. You astrologers, why don't you tell me, if what we speak of is a hidden God, then isn't God presupposed? When I examine them thoroughly once more, I realize that they're really skinned sheep's heads.

But perhaps God is not yet complete in the form of Christ or is simply not presentable? People would lose their faith if they saw him. Is my mother keeping him under lock and key up here until the light can no longer harm him? Is it necessary to protect his surface? Or was it simply hung there so as to hide it? Because it is no longer the right time to contemplate his visage or the time has not yet come? If the arrangement were a panel-painting, the artist would really have made things easy for himself, as he only showed his art in minor matters, whereas, in contrast, his true art ought to consist in showing the main thing, of which he is quite evidently incapable. *Show me God* is what his task is. He does not, however, show God, for he is not beneath the shroud, he is the shroud, it is hardly to be assumed that the artist painted God-Christ on the cross and gave him an expression of greatest suffering, which he then erased with the shroud, thus does he paint the body and paint over it, hiding it from sight and thus making it present in its absence in the motley imagination of all people who see themselves on the cross, after all, the Lord is merely a placeholder for ME.

Is that a walk-in manger and my parents didn't dare to put it up at Christmas, as they were afraid something would come to life, the Risen One might well rise, then be amongst us? Not only the shroud is in the Risen One, the wood of the cross has also entered into him, he is become the cross. Passion, Holy Spirit, and the Divine unite in its weathering. From Paradise remained the apple, from God the veil, which he self-imposedly cannot rend. If God is silent, the devil speaks.

All that we see becomes images. If I shut my eyes, I don't see any cords, by which all would be revealed, I merely see uneven, dashed brightenings, which, when viewed from a distance, are age-related cracks in the painting as a function of poor storage. Mother falls over with a little smack, right where a chair for me to sit on ought now to appear, but only void does. I kick God away, pull the crate with the sheep's heads out from under the table, tip the heads out onto the floor, then simply sit upon the crate. The typewriter delivers little shocks to me, but that merely serves as motivation. I clamp the blank side of the paper, I wish to leave behind a quick message, Mother shall definitely tidy up in here soon, please leave the typewriter as it is, you can dispose of the rest, where is the rest of the wine, unfortunately, the bread was already bad, and please put the trash can back, then I can clean it myself next time. There's still a lot of space on the back too, the graphics shouldn't get in the way and can be written over, I begin at the top left with the sentence: 'The key is the whole house.'"

I slam the book shut. Le Carré, that's what Father would read, but this here? Did he wish to punish the book after having read it and therefore remove its title and author? Did he garb the book anew, put it into a penitential robe? Did he soon subject it to the interrogation of heretics, burning or drowning it? In order to better understand my father, I hereby promise to read Jabès, just as the girl recommended to me.

A ways back, I walked heedlessly past Father's hearing aid, I now wish to look for it and pick it up. What does "a ways back" mean? Back a ways. Back away. It is both a curse and blessing of reading that there is no more time left. I listened to the book with great pleasure and could listen to it for hours more. Does reading not mean listening, sleeping, dreaming? Father was never all that happy with his hearing aid. It beeps, he'd often say, then he'd turn it off, but leave it in his ear, which gave his interlocutor the impression that he could follow the conversation. Father developed a refined strategy to disguise his deafness. He mastered precognition, answered certain questions with authoritarian counter-questions, offered up epistemological riddles, or formulated a question that he seemed to know his interlocutor would ask in the next few minutes. This latter individual saw himself confronted with an inexplicable situation, one that dazzled him in such a way that my father dealt him a coup-de-grâce: You see, you didn't know that I know that about you. Once, he looked at me as if a miracle were befalling him. Now, I shall tell you what is being told to me, he says: "Here is wisdom. Let him that hath understanding count the number of the beast: for it is the number of a man; and his number is Six hundred threescore and six."

Where am I to start with that, my father asked me. I'll tell you where I'm going to start with it, he said, I shall study the number 666. Man's number as the Number of the Beast? It is the Number of the Frightbearing Society. Is it Satan? my father asked. It is never Satan, he said, Satan never comes as himself, he assumes many forms, even the form of the Crucified One. 666 members of the Frightbearing Society. And hear what I still hear: "And he had power to give life unto the image of the beast, that the image of the beast should both speak, and cause that as many as would not worship the image of the beast should be killed." Where, then, are these "many," Father asked, I shall say to you who all these shall be, we shall be them, he said, it begins in the Levant and in the Near East, but it won't end with us. But are we truly threatened? my father asked, after all, thus is it written: "And it was given unto him to make war with the saints, and to overcome them: and power was given him over all kindreds, and tongues, and heathen-nations." But we're no heathen-nations, my father said. So, do we worship it? he asked. We do not worship him, he said, for our names are written in the book of life of the lamb slain from the foundation of the world. Father said he believed a chip had been installed in the hearing aid, one that perpetually played the same record. But that is not the case, he said, for I heard something different each time. From what he heard, the sequence had obviously gotten mixed up. There is also a carnival barker or a preacher who always uses the same formula as he speaks: "He that hath ears to hear, let him hear!" Then follows the actual message, which fits together to form a jumbled narrative. Thus disordered, he could only recall a few fragments like the one already recounted. On a very hot summer's day, he was sitting in a circle of friends and acquaintances, who were then joined by a number of strangers who just happened to be present, perhaps they were being cautious not to cause trouble for themselves, these people did not know one another, still, however, they engaged in a conspiratorial conversation with one another, which means that one of them suddenly said he was going to cover the whole of Berlin with the number 6, the number 6 should be clearly visible everywhere, sometimes it maybe won't be that clear, will only be recognizable to the practiced gaze, making it clear that he is the Six-Man, he's bringing the 666 to Berlin, it's said that there's an underground passage by the Kottbusser

Bridge, a book is chained there, it contains the precise instructions as to how to get the 666 out of the world, but somebody has blacked this book out entirely, it is now the Black Madonna in book form, a little black image—a Schwarzbildchen—of many pages, a place of pilgrimage for the evil and the incongruous, no place of gratitude like the one Kuno von Falkenstein left behind in a hollow oak with his Madonna, that very Kuno about whom there are various legends, in one of which he himself vanquishes Satan after the latter presents himself to Kuno in the form of a lion. After initially switching off his hearing aid, he couldn't, he said, listen to this myth-enriched nonsense any longer, he opted to leave the circle soon after and to go to his hotel room, where he switched on the television, but, without his hearing aids, he couldn't understand what was being said, thus did he once more switch on his hearing aids, what he then heard was not in accordance with what he saw, the voice in his ear captivated him more than the shifting images, he turned off the television and listened intently to the following words:

The Schwarzbildchen

    Ida, a beautiful damsel from Neuerburg, was courted by many a knight. She offered her hand and heart to the knight Kuno von Falkenstein. Therefore was the knight from Vianden who likewise wished to have this beautiful lady as his wife incensed.

    When the knight from Falkenstein was on his way to Neuerburg for the wedding, the knight from Vianden lay in wait upon the hillock in front of Neuerburg. The men then came to bitter blows. The superior might of the knight from Vianden was too great and, soon enough, the groom's companions lay slaughtered upon the ground.

    The knight Kuno was forced to flee and, as the way to Falkenstein was blocked to him, he rode to Neuerburg as swiftly as his horses could bear him. The salvific castle was already before his eyes when the horse, utterly exhausted, collapsed dead. Not far off, however, he heard the shouts and screams of his pursuers.

In his hour of need, the knight Kuno prayed to the Mother of God for aid. His prayer was heard. Suddenly, a thin figure stood before him and wordlessly pointed at an old oak. At its foot was to be found a dark hole, which led into the interior of the hollow tree. The knight Kuno quickly concealed himself within this hollow.

Soon, his pursuers were fast approaching. They found the dead horse, but its rider they sought in vain. After the men from Vianden had taken their leave in a rage, the knight Kuno left his hideout, thanked God for having rescued him, then hurried to the castle.

After he had settled in Falkenstein with his young bride, the knight Kuno had a beautifully carved image of the Mother of God placed into the hollow to give thanks for his salvation. It remains there still today, practically black with age and candle smoke. And to this day, people still carry their need and grief to the Schwarzbildchen. There are a great many who have been heard, just as the knight Kuno was.

This must have been the Six-Man's voice, to which I was listening so intently, it was as if I'd never left the circle, Father said. Would you also hear the other legend, this voice asked him, as he had once more switched off his hearing aids. Man's curiosity is probably his greatest evil, one can't resist it for long, he switched his hearing aids back on immediately, which, incomprehensibly, as Father put it, the voice took note of, for it immediately demanded that he answer. Of course, he wished to hear the other legend as well, Father heard himself say, and he had the feeling of having entered into a pact with the devil. Immediately, he says, the Six-Man told the following tale:

"Toward the end of the year 1146, Saint Bernard of Clairvaux had proselytized the cross in the Ministry of Freiburg with such success that many of the city's, as well as the surrounding region's, most distinguished individuals were thereby inspired to embark upon Crusades to the Promised Land. Among them was also to be found one Kuno von Falkenstein. Full of grief in a childless marriage, he had for many years been anticipating the extinguishment of his house and hoped that he might avert this most bitter misfortune through fervent prayer in the places where the Savior had once lived and suffered. Thus did he take leave from his spouse Ida with heavy heart and break the wedding ring in twain as a sign of the trial of their mutual fidelity, handing her the one half with the words: 'You are to await my return for seven years, after which you might take it as given that I am fallen and thus has our wedding bond been rent.' Tears running down her cheeks, Ida beswore that which he required, then he and his squires immediately set out to join the great host of the army.

Here, however, most were deceived in their expectations; illness, lack of victuals, and the Sword of the Saracens wreaked the most frightful of havoc amongst the pilgrims. The most sorrowful lot fell upon the knight Kuno himself after he was hurled down over a heap of slain enemies and taken into captivity. Here, he was reduced to the lowest of labors, harnessed even to the plow as a draft animal, and exposed to the scourge of the slave driver.

A full seven years passed by in such misery, when, finally, the knight managed to flee. But he and his spouse's trials had not yet come to an end. While she was besieged by grasping suitors in Alt-Falkenstein and her life had come to be in danger, Kuno, ignorant of the way, wandered restlessly to and fro through many deserts. Exhausted by such exertions and in a daze, he finally fell into a slumber long and deep, but in which confused dreams afforded him no rest. They pulled the wool over his eyes, showing him that his wife, having been released from her promise and believing him to be dead, was now being assailed by haughty neighbors and, after some futile resistance, was being compelled to extend her hand to one of them in marriage. Up did he start in desperation and behold! there stood the Evil One before him in corporeal form, with a grin, he confirmed that which Kuno had seen in the dream. At this point, he knew the only thing that could save him would be a bond with the Tempter himself; borne toward home, the knight finally understood himself to be enslaved to him and fell asleep on the way.

Immediately, a deep rent opened up in the ground and a lion rose up amidst smoke and flames, Kuno mounted it right away and flew high above land and sea upon its back. But the way from Palestine to the Black Forest is long and, imperceptibly, however much he strained against it, the exhausted knight was once more stolen over by sleep. But behold! a falcon suddenly flies forth from the clouds, it perches itself upon his head and keeps the knight awake with beak and wings. Soon did the Cathedral Tower of Freiburg become visible. Then they went swiftly up the Kirchzarten Valley, through the Kingdom of Heaven and into the Gorge of Hell, where the lion, furious to have been duped, set the knight down at the foot of his citadel with a roar, then vanished.

As solitary as it was in the depths, it was equally clamoresome up here, where the wedding guests, accompanied by the sound of trumpets and drums, were already given over to the most spirited of jubilation, while Ida observed the wild tumult with tears in her eyes.

Then did the gatekeeper report a pilgrim with the longest of beards and rent garments, he had allegedly come from the Promised Land and was expecting a refreshing draught. Though the guests urged that the vagabond, as they dubbed him, be turned out, the hostess did fill a goblet with wine, which the pilgrim then drained in a single gulp, setting the halved gold ring into it so as to give thanks. When the gatekeeper brought the goblet back to the countess, she perceived, full of harrowing disquietude, the stranger's wedding gift; for her part, she also tossed in the half-ring, from which she had never parted since that day, then, o wonder of wonders! the halves combined to make a whole.

Then did the overjoyed woman lift up the wedding ring that is both old and new, rush with it through the hordes of those present, praising God all the while, then collapse at the gate, entreating forgiveness and renewal on the ground before her spouse, whom she'd long believed to be dead. Then did he, overcome by joyful tears, lift her up and press her to his chest, the dazzled guests disappeared one by one, until only the faithful falcon, ready to return to more lofty airs, continued to sympathetically circle the newly reweds.

From then on, the blessing of many children was also their lot. However, an image of the salvific falcon, beaked and with dashing wings, as old parchment letters show, was taken up by Kuno in both his own knightly sigil and that of his house."

My father claims to be as exhausted by this story as he is moved by it, he's suddenly been taken in by the notion of spending the rest of his life with nothing but such stories, to be interrupted solely by eating, drinking, and sleeping, then, given time, to finally be untroubled by even necessities such as these. In any case, having always been well aware of his own obsessive behavior, my father immediately wished to switch off his hearing aids when he heard the words "of his house," then was unsure for a single moment as to whether he'd heard the question "Is there not another version?" a mere second later, heard from the very same device or even spoken from within himself, the Six-Man instantly answered that, indeed, there is, it is an abridged version of the one just heard, which omits much of what was embellished in the first, though its conclusion doesn't allow for the falcon, but for the devil to come back into the picture and, just as the former is immortalized in the knightly sigil, the latter has been imprinted unto a fieldstone, widely known as the Devil's Stone, even today, it is on view at the corner of the Fortuna Inn. My father agreed to also listen to this variation with the urgent request that they then leave it at that. The Six-Man related the third version as follows:

"The knight Kuno von Falkenstein had his seat in a castle in the Dreisam Valley. Since 1320, the district of Kirchzarten had been amongst its possessions. The knight's marriage with his wife Ida remained childless for a great deal of time. Thus did both of them mourn to such an extent that, one day, the knight decided to set out on a journey to the Holy Sepulchre so as to invoke the blessing of Heaven. Upon taking leave of his wife, he broke his wedding ring into two parts, giving the one half over to her and saying to her that, if he had not yet returned in seven years, she ought to then assume that he had found death. Frau Ida allowed him to leave only with great pain. Once in pagan lands, the knight, together with the other pilgrims, was drawn into ferocious battles with the Saracens. During one enemy ambush, he was defeated by superior forces. Thus did he end up in the Sultan's captivity. This latter wished to give his daughter to the handsome knight in marriage. As punishment for his refusal, the knight then had to perform the hardest of slave labor for many years. Once the seven years had almost expired, the knight finally managed to succeed in fleeing from this torturous situation. But wherever he turned, he went astray and encountered the highest of walls. An ardent prayer finally directed his strides onto the righteous way. Endless did the desert stretch out before him. After much wandering, his strength left him. Exhausted, he sank into a deep sleep. In his dream, he beheld a vision: It was the devil showing him his native castle. There, he witnessed with horror how his wife was being hard pressed by an evil neighbor to marry. Upon waking up, the Evil One stood before him and said that the dream had shown the truth. In desperation, the knight bade the devil take him home at that very moment, he would reward him most handsomely for doing so. The devil spoke: Indeed, I do know of a way, Herr Knight, I shall have you fly through the air to your home by the shortest route on the back of a lion and I wish for no reward. However, should you fall asleep for even a moment during the ride, then shall your soul be mine. The knight thought it not difficult to fulfill this condition and accepted without hesitation. The lion stood there already. The knight swung himself onto its back and the journey passed with lightning speed over sea and land. But the way was long and the knight Kuno had grown tired from wandering in the desert. In the greatest of need, he implored aid from the heavens. Then did a falcon swoop down from the clouds, set down upon his shoulders, fan his head, and even peck at him with its beak when sleep threatened to outman him. Thus, with the help of the falcon and carried by the lion, did the knight Kuno arrive safe and sound—and awake—in his homeland. In Kirchzarten, before the tavern "Zum Rindsfuß," the lion set the knight down. The devil was already present. When he realized he'd been deprived of his prey, he grabbed a great fieldstone in fury and hurled it at the knight. The latter yielded to the side and the fieldstone made thunderous clamor in colliding with the tavern wall. The stone can still be seen there today. The knight Kuno came to his castle in timely fashion so as to aid his wife and punish the evil neighbor. Heaven bestowed the blessing of many children and long life upon the joyously reunited pair."

But my father did not like this version, thus did he emphatically demand that the Six-Man spare him from further versions, otherwise, he would see to it that he would have to ride upon the lion's back, but no falcon would appear to him, whereupon the Six-Man replied that he had no fear of that, as he was already in league with the devil, but that the devil would not miss the next time he threw the fieldstone, with him being the target, this is something you are undoubtedly afraid of, my father answered, not at all, was the answer, since he, my father, was the rock upon which he built his legends.

From then on, Kuno von Falkenstein would not let my father rest at all, he worked through all of the sources available to him before finally coming across Sophie von La Roche, who, in her diary of a journey through Switzerland, handed down the legend in quite unadorned fashion. My father never tired of reading her version to me, and, as the best way one can banish or get rid of what one hears is writing it down, here do I put down Sophie von La Roche's version:

Soon after, we came upon a place where the ledges of the mountain were somewhat wider and still bore at their top the remains of the old Falkenstein Castle, which your brother sketched as we sat together upon a block and I spoke with the woman above whose hut the ruins tower. As we observed those remains, she told us:

O, 'tis an evil castle, stones often fall from it and onto my house, it is now near to collapsing.

I thought: perhaps it is the spirit of one of the old lords from here, one who leveled his subjects to the ground, then was driven into the stones and still shows his character in this way. The arch of the castle gate was beautifully overgrown with ivy and the entire forecourt was occupied by flourishing bushes. There is still one artful tale that is told of the times of saints and knights, about the last Lord of Falkenstein, who quite piously went to the Promised Land and was able to help snatch Jerusalem from the Turks: who, upon his departure, broke his wedding ring in twain, taking the one half with him, but leaving the other behind to his beautiful weeping wife, he endured much grief and peril, performed many knightly deeds and prayed diligently verily, he sometimes thought of his wife, but it was only after a few years that he became very unquiet of her, beginning to feel a sad foreboding of lost love. At that moment, the devil hoped to take possession of the pious knight's soul and said: I would take thee home if thou, I know not for how long, wanted for food or drink, or, failing that, shouldst thou wish to be in thy own place. Curiosity drove the nobleman into Satan's trust, and, as he'd grown accustomed to living with hunger and thirst during these "Crusades" thusly were the journeys of Christian armies to Jerusalem dubbed the weary Prince of Darkness was deceived. Herr von Falkenstein persevered and came to his spouse just as she was sitting at table with her betrothed. No man knew the strange knight, but he was invited to sup. All were quite content and drank to the couple's health from a golden goblet.

After he had thrown half of the ring into it, Herr von Faltzenstein sends the goblet to his wife the bride — she finds it, startles, but after having questioned the stranger, she also seeks out the second half, recognizes its design, and sends the bridegroom away. Today, one does not know whether the sad bridegroom or the cheated Satan now sits there upon the stones. — This is roughly the heroic romance to be found in the Black Forest.

We went onward, and sat by many a young tree between clumps of rocks and pebbles, they stood there full of care and lonesome as often the best men the

One notes that little word "roughly," my father said. Each version really is only "roughly." And "heroic romance" already indicates that this "roughness" is sometimes more, sometimes less embellished, thus is one version of the legend as short as a joke and sometimes just as stale, whereas another version is as long as a novel, a romance, ein Roman, and sometimes just as tiresome, thus does it depend on the balance of the middle, to read the one unwritten version of all the versions, the one different from them all, it's also narrated in exciting fashion and leaves behind an aftertaste of disappointment once its final word has been spoken.

The ways of legends are difficult to fathom, my father said, if the names of the heroes of a legend and their versions are the same, the places, times, and circumstances could, occasionally, differ in substantial fashion. Did the knight Kuno von Falkenstein not live between 1290 and 1343? In that case, what does he have to do with Saint Bernard of Clairvaux? Did the latter's words have so much influence for so long? Born in 1290, he could hardly have been a crusader. But why did Kuno then marry his Ida at their castle in Neuerburg and not in the Dreisam Valley or on his other estates near Freiburg im Breisgau? At the center of all legends stand love, fidelity, and homecoming, Father said, and you are, in any case, severely lacking in that final virtue. Here, one might see to where a lack of love and loyalty and the absent desire to return home lead. Your ride upon the lion's back never ends, Father said, you suffer hunger and thirst, sleep begins to overcome you, but there is no falcon in sight.

Oral tradition and written elaboration provided variations with differing regional references, which were not always aware of each other, sometimes Kuno is on the way to his wedding and a rival threatens him, sometimes Kuno is already married to Ida, but childless, then, coming home from a Crusade, he promises himself the long-awaited blessing of children, sometimes, he speaks to his wife of a seven-year absence, after which she might declare him dead and marry once more, sometimes one does not learn of any timespan attached to Kuno's absence, sometimes he is in league with the devil, sometimes the legend is without devil, sometimes the devil forbids the knight from eating during the flight on the lion's back that is to take him back from the Promised Land and to his homeland, at others, he is forbidden from sleeping during his journey, sometimes the legend takes place in Neuerburg, sometimes in the Dreisam Valley near Freiburg im Breisgau, sometimes Kuno joins the eastward Crusade in the Middle East and suffers a great deal in the fight against the Saracens, a collective term for Islamic peoples, which often meant nothing but "pagan" or "foreign," sometimes the visible sign of satanic rage at having ended up empty-handed, which is to say without Kuno's soul, due either to his steadfastness, for he is quite accustomed to hunger and thirst as a function of the Crusade, or to the aid of a falcon, is a fieldstone against the wall of a house, sometimes it is the falcon in the knightly sigil, then, in its turn, an old hollow oak with an image of the Mother of God that has grown black over time bears witness to Kuno's fate—and thus might the sequence go on and on, Father said.

The story of the legends and the legends that one tells oneself about legends is fascinating, Father says, but what troubled him most deeply and perhaps triggered his obsession with Kuno von Frankenstein was the fact that the Six-Man knew of the special significance that the Schwarzbildchen in Neuerburg and the legend connected to it had taken on for both him and my mother, after all, there was a knight from Vianden in both of their stories, only this one did not strive to conquer my mother with sheer physical violence, he sought to do something by way of slander aimed at my father's religious integrity, since Father met and fell in love with Mother shortly before his ordination as a priest, which was widely known to have led to the termination of his theological studies with an eye to the priesthood, theology has remained the core discipline of his life to this very day, whereas you, Nobody, have fallen away from God, I imagined a tick falling off of its host-animal, only a sole generation was needed to turn the question of God to its opposite, which is to say the answer of the devil, the Schwarzbildchen, Father said, was known to him by the words of people from Grubenreu, when the knight from Vianden everywhere announced that he was the right man for Ida, my mother, to be precise, his rival had ditched God for this woman, and, to be sure, this may have amused some, but it likely drove the blush of shame into most Catholics' faces, a character-assassination campaign was being carried out in town, from then on, my father met my mother in this hollow oak underneath the Schwarzbildchen—so as to receive Mary's blessing for their love. Word of this soon got around in town and Father's knight from Vianden had to flee the scene, as he was now seen as an infidel who wished to bring a God-protected couple into disrepute for his own benefit.

Since I didn't wish to listen to endless legends, Father said, after hearing Sophie von La Roche's version, I took out my hearing aids and went back downstairs with the intention of finding the Six-Man to question him about the Kuno Legends and the Schwarzbildchen, but could find him there no longer, my friends and acquaintances asked me to please stay, some showed themselves to be surprised that I had already been gone for some time, Father rejoined them, then, after some minutes, as he was unable to follow the conversation and because the cocktail party of clamor had brought him to the brink of despair, he switched his hearing aids back on, whereupon, after a few seconds of total silence, the carnival barker first cried out with his "He that hath ears to hear, let him hear!", the mouth-motions of an old school-friend sitting in the circle initially caused my father to believe that this man was the one perpetually repeating this tautological sentence, but the man suddenly fell silent and the following could still be heard: "He that leadeth into captivity shall go into captivity: he that killeth with the sword must be killed with the sword. Here is the patience and the faith of the saints." I only remembered the last sentence because I've not, not ever, understood it, the other sentences, however, are comprehensible and incomprehensible in equal measure. Perhaps all of that is just a translation error, indeed, the sentences are grammatically correct, but more related to German than peculiar to it. Perhaps the hearing aids distort the words in such a way that they only ever receive them in an incorrect transmission, but never literally. If one takes the, under certain circumstances, incorrect transmission literally, then the result is an endless slaughter right up until a suicide that inevitably has to be enacted, for who can lay hands upon the last one after he has judged the second-to-last one if not the last one? Or has someone here leapt forth from the murderer's row that is bound to superimpose the crime of deleting the observed crime onto the observed crime itself, someone who would have created a higher sort of observation or for whom such a one was created, the question, then, is by whom, by whom exactly, if not by God—thus does somebody leap forth from the earthen murderer's row and judge in God's name. He asked me to bring a little light into the darkness, the day shall come when, at a suitable point, he shall order me to take a stand against Luther, Lortz had done the Catholic Church a disservice, the talk of what is Catholic in and about Luther and of what is Lutheran in the Catholic Church is dangerous mumbo jumbo, a smokescreen, Reformation instead of renewal of the church is the result. Should I succeed in bringing forth weighty arguments against Luther, Father says, I shall pay off some small part of my guilt, even if Luther has meanwhile been made so great that he already seems to have been ascribed a greater importance than God himself and only God himself can shrink Luther back down to the size that allows him to be historically recognizable.

He had no fear of these pronouncements, he rather conceived of himself as their witness and not their addressee. He only grew ill-at-ease when he asked the person sitting next to him to check the bothersome beeping in his hearing aids, to see whether he was the only one hearing it, which would then point more toward tinnitus than a technical defect, but the neighbor hears nothing at all, neither beeping nor a voice proclaiming the Word of God, and this, indeed, was what he wished to find out by way of his request. He then switched off the device and put it away into his pants pocket, then, for the rest of the evening, took part in the conversations as best as he could, always in the expectation of hearing the Word of God, even without hearing aids, which did not come to pass, but if he had heard it without a hearing aid, he would have instantly gotten himself to a clinic.

Father said that the hearing aids were sometimes the sea, at other times the land, and, once, he heard a monster rising from the sea, it was so clamorous that he ought to have been able to see it, it had seven heads and ten horns, it had a maw greater than God's, a blaspheming maw that stank of pestilence and with this maw did it devour all those who did not wish to obey it, which is to say all those who are put down in white script, those who spell out the whole of a prescription with their lives alone.

And while, a little ways off from everyone, he busied himself with his hearing aids, a discussion as regards the benefits and drawbacks of cellphones from the perspective of life as such broke out, some raised concerns that they caused people to look down at the ground, man would soon be walking on all fours once more, monkeys would learn how to use phones, the customary arguments were laid out, people living only in a virtual world, etc., whereupon my father objected that evil could now, at any hour, be present all over the world, the unimaginable no longer lurks in hidden places, the surface is the depth of the crime, a surface reflecting sunlight, it causes many a crime to become reality, the murderer imagines himself to be an actor who is shooting a film, a film must have content, murder is the most exciting of content, and even those watching it, especially if it is playing out in public before a large crowd, have this feeling, that, with the camera of their cell phone, they might immediately put the film onto the so-called Web as part of a life-reality finally being taken seriously for the very first time, perhaps its most important part, after all, they are, in accordance with what they claim themselves to be, the witnesses who pass down, who film, and who thus write history and, indeed, this is outside of highly official historiography, which can hardly be distinguished from the symbolic politics of democracy—thus in a town called Tiers did the monster crucify people to the scaffolding that had been set up along a street and the people came running in droves to film the crucified ones with their camera phones, laughing children, aged gray ones who were baffled that they were still permitted to have such experiences. If the witnesses were lacking, for their presence did not have to be taken care of separately, other witnesses would simply come running from all four corners of the world, of course, they knew that, at any moment, they might be ordered from the witness-stand and onto the cross, for many, that is what the special savor of the situation consists of, a tickle that not infrequently inscribes itself as a wobble in the running picture, which documents these times of departure in a way that downright overjoys—on the other hand: The resolution of the picture isn't good, the eye demands better resolution, one likes to look at everything very closely, every detail, the face contorted in pain, the exertions of the killer—the criminal (and this really is self-evident) also takes on this task, a witness must be free if he does not otherwise make himself guilty, the lust in what has been seen and filmed must always remain recognizable, as a rule, fear is a bad director, one who might also involuntarily sabotage historical moments. Each crime is well documented by the criminals, the times change, then films deliver the perpetrators up to the knife or to the gallows.

If, today, recording devices were made responsible for the transmission of oral sources, a maneuver that would free the printing press from its task of losslessly transmitting the parlances of lower classes and jargons from other spheres, as well as keeping knowledge up to date, provided that knowledge also included that which is gleaned from tabloids, things would come to pass that perhaps would never have happened without these devices, for example religious heresies being spread even more swiftly than the printing press had enabled with its books and, above all, its pamphlets, Father adds that the old law only became legible once it had been printed and it became possible to compare it letter for letter with the new law, access to it was therefore no longer merely reserved to landowners and their jurisdiction, thus does the promulgation of an entirely new law that deviates, which, in a certain fashion, invokes the most ancient of law against the ruling state, no longer have need of the time-delayed detour via the printing press, rather, only the appropriate channels must be made use of, in such a way that the institutionalization of the counter-state can be addressed to as many people as possible and, indeed, regardless of social affiliation, the electronic acceleration of paper, Father continues, is both curse and blessing simultaneously, in line with the thought of Hinan Knallsum,* Father never grows tired of explaining to the circle of people that man has become the en-framing of his inventions, paper used to not blush, now, so-called recording devices don't blush to such an extent that it would perhaps be advisable to think up developments

---

* Upward Shootdown.

that would make recording impossible. Of course, one would here have to ask oneself where the limit of that which is permissible lies, the line that may not be crossed, and how, in the triggering of a recording, something like a categorical imperative might be implemented, in such a way that the apparatus would refuse the recording or the recording would refuse itself, whereby a crime, an atrocity, might possibly be prevented, for the perpetrators would lack the incentive of self-transmission and, should this incentive be lacking, the crime might not go beyond mere impulse or its planning. On the other hand, the recording allows for endless repetition and, with each repetition, that which is shown, the crime, distances itself more and more from reality, as it comes to pass over and over again, and thus do repetition itself and lived time come to coincide, Father said, before relating the following incident:

In Bangladesh, thirteen men accuse a thirteen-year-old boy of having stolen a pedicab. The boy has nothing to do with it. The men bind the boy to a post with a plastic noose and interrogate him. The men wish to know his name. The boy tells them his name. Does he like being beaten across the leg with a rod? The boy doesn't reply. The man hits his leg and repeats the question. At which point the boy says he likes his leg being hit. So, I might as well double the number of blows, the man says, then he doubles the number of blows. To the boy's request to stop the beating, the man replies, OK, no problem, but then hits him on the arm. The blows aren't too hard so far, but each one inflicts pain upon the boy. The men briefly discuss whether a hard rubber baton wouldn't be more suitable than an iron pipe. After being hit on the collarbone and lower leg, the boy falls to his knees. The plastic noose prevents his body from collapsing all the way down. Thus is he now hanging from his outstretched left arm, his upper body twisted, his left leg bent inward. Then he is unbound and told that he ought to disappear. The boy takes a couple of steps, he seems to regain his courage, then touches the man standing to his right, the one who hit him with his hand, touches him as if to say, I forgive you, how good that this is all over. The man filming everything laughs the very laugh that always laughs itself. "His bones are still intact, you should hit him harder," he says. The men grab hold of the boy and bind him to another post not far from the first. The boy is thirsty, he is begging for his life. Drink your own sweat, one of the men says. It's better not to do things by halves, the men point out to each other. Now, the man who is hitting him is ready to hit his head and neck too. The boy falls to the ground, then straightens up once more. One blow makes contact with his head, his eyes roll up, he falls to the ground, straightens back up once more. He falls to the ground, straightens up once more. Falls to the ground, up again. To the ground, up. Ground. The boy is pulled up, they also put a noose around his waist. Now, they can better hit his head. One knows the photos in which people bound to a pole hang their heads. Sheikh Samiul Alam Rajon is tortured thusly on July 8, 2015, from 6:30 a.m. until 10:30 a.m. This exceeds a cellphone's capacity. On the other hand, four hours of being tortured can easily become boring, there's a great deal of repetition. The video of the boy's death posted on Facebook is twenty-eight minutes long. The filmmaker carried out a subjective selection, all faces are entirely identifiable, and there can be no doubt as to who has done the deed. The dead boy is hidden in the same pedicab he's said to have stolen, later loaded by Muhit Alam into a minivan rented specifically for this purpose, it is here that he is found by locals at 12:45 p.m. His body displays sixty-four distinct injuries. He died of a cerebral hemorrhage. Dozens of people stood in the vicinity and watched. As they did not intervene, they are able to stand as witnesses of the boy's death. Eleven of the thirteen men are arrested. Kamrul Islam, who is responsible for most of the blows, is tracked down in Saudi Arabia. After having bribed the police. Fortunately, Bangladesh still has the death penalty. The perpetrators put the video online in the conviction that they had made a pedagogically valuable contribution to the enterprise of raising children. Sheikh Samiul Alam Rajon ought to be mourned forever. His name to be written in heaven.

The fact that, in the following case, nothing was posted online seems downright antisocial. Nevertheless, the mobile-phone industry ought to consider whether the storage capacity of cell phones might not be greatly expanded, as its limitation interferes with the documentary transmission of crimes, the severity of which is never severe enough to put the narcissism of the criminal in its place. The perpetrators use social media most sensibly. In exemplary fashion, they don't simply stop at the crime, but, additionally, make a valuable contribution to its solving. The criminal of the future hangs from the gallows with a medal.

Faithful family-fathers raped a woman, the rape and subsequent beheading of the woman were filmed from beginning to end by the family-fathers, initially, the woman is dancing, the men lounging about on the floor in the corner, one of the men stands up, indicates a dance-step, everyone laughs, then the woman lies down on the floor, my father says, all the faces are very easy to make out, the woman screams, the men laugh, finally, one of them has the woman's severed head in his hands, another one of them kicks it away; convicted by way of their own documentation, which they may have planned to watch together while hanging out over beers in the near future, the five men are publicly hanged and, each time, it is astonishing that this comes to pass with so little bother to the outside world, the men precisely observe all preparations for the hanging, they don't want to miss anything, then the barrels upon which they are standing with ropes around their necks are kicked away, then they dangle, all of them seeming to have died on the spot, only the man second from the left, who was able to free himself from the handcuff, raises his right hand high several more times, as if he wished to greet somebody, the crowd jeers, must have been incensed by him, that really is going too far, and, for posterity, the execution of the rapists is also filmed from beginning to end, luckily, the cameras used here were better, my father says. The ear that hears is more exposed than the eye that sees. He experiences this again and again, Father said. The ear sees not what it hears. And thus does the ear create a monster for itself.

Leviathan is the name of the monster rising from the sea, Father tells me, a dragon gave its might over to it, and the dragon is ever in the background, it is the adversary of God created by God, God made certain to know his enemies before they came to know him, and Father also said that, for some time now, he's had the feeling of living in the dragon's breath, it is slowly burning him up, but, strangely enough, from the inside out, then he saw another beast crawling forth from the earth, innocent as a lamb, and he spake as the dragon that you killed, and this beast seems merely to be the ensouling assistant of the first beast, and he exerciseth all the power of the first beast, but not so obviously, and causeth the earth and them which dwell therein to worship the first beast, whose deadly wound was healed, these idols can also speak, for the second beast passed the speech of the dragon unto them, and, now, people all over the world worship these homunculi and take them at their word, people obey automatons, they have forgotten that they themselves made them, thus do we have three demons, a demonic trinity, the dragon, Leviathan, of whom one head has risen again like the Son of God after you killed it, and Behemoth, the hypocritical lamb, the chief servant of the dragon who causes men to kneel before their lack of consummateness and these non-consummate ones have the 666 upon their brow or on their right hand, the name of the first beast, and those who do not bear this name are concerned about their own survival. Wear the 7, but do so invisibly, then live by it. Father narrates that he tried to make sure the voice continued the text from the point where he had precisely turned off the hearing aids, strangely enough, however, he was never able to remember the place, thus does he assume that this is not the case. He sees the two chaos-demons,

Leviathan and behemoth, behind the carnival barker's voice, this voice is the dragon's speech, and all he could glean from this was that we always follow the wrong god, the anti-god, and that, in this way, God remains unattainable to us, Father says that God is absent, but the grounds for his absence are incomprehensible. The face of the false gods pushed itself before God who had no face other than pain. Proxy wars are being waged in the name of the false gods, Leviathan and Behemoth have turned against each other and wish to establish dominance amongst themselves, the dragon is a principle that can no longer be removed from the world. It is so easy to call upon God and to kill in his name and to enrich oneself, Father says, those who allow the false god to be worshiped do not pray at all, for them, God is a mere pretext of power that claims the death of God, from which the world is to be saved, but God isn't dead in the slightest, my father says, he is always there out of principle, Leviathan and Behemoth wish to rule the world through the sale of indulgences, thus shall they finance a part of their war with him, but how is a reformation to come about this time when even their declared enemies do business with the two of them. God is money and money is war and war is God. And the reformers of today are pursuing the sale of indulgences of tomorrow. And, at the end of the day, it isn't God himself who says, if you're not with me, you're against me. In God's Book, which was already there before God and which only he is mature enough to read, from the beginning, it is written who is with him and who is against him. The Last Judgment only subjects this entry to a comparison so that no injustice might occur.

Sometimes, when I receive something through my hearing aids, Father said, I can't tell whether I'm hearing a voice or thinking my own thoughts. In any case, it's all religious content and thoroughly reasonable, Father said. Even if I can't hear it, Father says, and, from time to time, I thank God that I can no longer hear this circle of people, it was my choice not to, without my hearing aids, I only hear an ebb and flow of unrecognizable noises, just as a newborn only sees the contours of something, the full form of which it cannot grasp, thus do I hear nothing without the hearing aids, I hear these messages with them, sound-sensations received through my hearing aids, for which reason I went to an ear specialist, who prescribed me another device, but I wasn't able to stand it for long, I missed the voice, so I put the old device back into operation, in my whole life, I've never heard anything more sensible than these messages. The hearing aids are a divine amplifier. They amplify signals that can penetrate into nobody's head but my own, then never leave it again. that's how God set it up, he didn't ask me. No other medium than these hearing aids can make them perceptible. I have a little wooden box in my head, my father says, in it, the messages are collected. This little box is a kind of music box, which is wound up by the signals. If the signals fail, the music box stops, it never sounds out the same thought-melody twice. Hearing aids are required in order to hear this melody. The connection of signals, little box, and hearing aids forms a circuit, though the signals may not come from the outside at all, but are induced by the box in my head, the box, then, is what hears itself, amplified, to a certain extent, by way of the hearing aids. Strictly speaking, there is no outside at all. But perhaps it would be more suitable to compare the box to a turntable or a radio. It seems certain to me, Father said, that it is not my ears that hear the signals picked up by the box and amplified by the hearing aids, but that the box makes audible within me the signals that it collects and that the hearing aids amplify, so the box is an organ, it is the ear of inwardness sitting right in the middle of my head and transmitting the sound to the hearing aids. There are only two possibilities, my father said, either the hearing aids are pure auto-suggestion, superfluous, and I don't need them, or God himself is sitting in the hearing aids in the form of the Holy Spirit and the box is a radio that receives him. Whatever the case may be, my father said, the little box is the key, the magical ear of metaphysics. It does have a lid, otherwise it wouldn't be a little box of the sort used for storing jewelry, but it isn't airtight, for, otherwise, it would keep that which is inconsummate, erroneous, and sinful imprisoned and not announce its existence, I think. The little box is the beginning of Father's dementia, I calm myself. And, after that, I cannot get rid of the thought of a vivisection—wondering whether the box were not to be found in my father's head, where it would be making mischief as a box on the shelf behind the son's bed or as a device that one looks into so as to see wondrous things.

If, in everyday life, Father says, it seemed that, withdrawn into himself, he was no longer following the conversation, it was actually that he wished to draw attention to the contrary—that he very much did follow every conversation and, indeed, in a way that was uncomfortable for all those participating in the conversation, not excluding himself (he actually spared himself the least), which was to say, he was finally telling the truth. The truth, my father said, the truth is that, in order to be able to talk to anybody at all, he has adapted himself to the mental level of the world around him, and this is precisely the betrayal that he accuses himself of, that, during this time, he has become so mentally flat that he could pass right through the space beneath a door. On the other hand, my father said, it is only thus that I can follow the Holy Spirit, who takes up all of my attention. So that I might not take up any more attention in society than as an obdurate old man, nature has arranged things as described, so that I can simultaneously listen to the Holy Spirit while also not being entirely absent from society without the suspicion arising that I am listening to the Holy Spirit and not to society, he said.

I stick the hearing aids into my ears. Father picks up. You've forgotten your telephone. I've taken the liberty of calling a couple of your contacts. What I heard upon doing so doesn't make me happy in the slightest. Is it true that you have voluntarily given yourself over into the hands of the Frightbearing Society so that they might interrogate you at all hours of the day and night? Didn't I demand that you write only the truth about your father in our Society Book? And what do you do?

I have a direct line to heaven and it shall soon be decided in heaven that you may no longer bear your first name, for the dragon still lives. And there are still ever more streets named after it. Lindwurmstraße—Lindwormstreet. I am your memory before you have even experienced that which you can remember. From today onward, you shall wear this device in your ears so that I might always be able to reach you. Should you not wear it or should I not be able to reach you, you shall be severely punished. I'll reintroduce the death penalty for you. I am hidden in you. I am the father who has his son crucified, indeed, we've both always dreamed of that. Should you reveal our secret to anybody and betray your old, most venerable father, then may God have mercy on you. In view of that which follows, the blows of childhood were merely the caressing preliminaries.

My father's voice is that which is instantaneously written. Each word reverberates in me as in a tunnel. I go through this tunnel and reach a path with a park bench standing at its end. Father is sitting on the park bench. He has the eyes of the little girl who showed me the way. The park bench stands before the nursing home. Thus did I run in circles or I've gone there and back a single time. I speak to him, he dissolves. Then he slowly appears once more. I sit across from him on a fence post and observe him. He is more alien to me than somebody I am seeing for the first time in my life. For his whole life, he failed to get to know his children. For his whole life, his children have sought to get to know their father. Turning aside as a form of greeting, a mere hand to bid farewell. No corporeality. Content-related disputes only in the sense of a negative theology. The Eifel formed him. And the Eifel made sure he developed no taste. His taste is called fresh air. He always talks about wines as if he were one of the top ten wine connoisseurs in the world. He doesn't attach the slightest worth to the furnishings of the apartment. What counts are inner values. Inner values have singular powers, they can pull you into the abyss. The abyss is a gorge in which all the things that life has to offer can be found, albeit in new constellations that one always wished for in life, but, now, they seem threatening, they are the fear that ensures that one moves from A to B and it is not the knowledge of facing one's own fear that makes one sad, but the fact that old longings have been realized without it being of any further interest, that nothing of that which one saw in bed, under the covers, with one's hands pressed to one's eyes, took shape, and that, now, no more goals appear in one's inward sky, which is always just the background of the eye. This mountainous background with its craters and lakes, over which the eye swiftly glides, is lost, like the reflexes of early childhood. Behind the eyes is nothing.

We can go soon, Father says. And where are we going, I ask him. To refresh our memories, a class-reunion of your grandfather's former students, indeed, I too was his student, and, as his eldest son, I am invited, Father says. For his students surely have tales to tell, Father says, and you can accompany me.

I accompany Father, we are already on our way. We're going on foot, Father says, it's to be his final walk, the wheelchair can wait, we shall need some seven hours, he says, initially, the landscape isn't terribly interesting, thus shall we be able to concentrate on Grandpa's story, indeed, Father reminds me that I only ever saw Grandpa a couple of times, my memories of him are indubitably faded, and the park bench in front of Haus Marienhöhe in Lehdam is already out of sight, we soon leave Auf der Sandkaul behind, walk a short distance onto Am Herrenberg and are already on Auf dem Joch, turn right onto Trierer Straße, which we leave once more some two hundred meters later so as to get onto the L110 for about twenty-five minutes, that flows into the L24, which we depart from after some twelve minutes, if we're able to maintain our speed that is, turning right at the fork in the road, then we follow the course of the road for some three hundred meters, turn left, go two hundred meters before turning slightly left in the direction of Kronenburger Straße, which we turn onto after another three hundred meters, we shall walk fifteen meters down Kronenburger Straße in the direction of Auelstraße, then turn left onto Auelstraße, which we leave after roughly two hundred meters and turn right again in the direction of Waldstraße, on which we shall turn left after a short distance, then continue on for some fifty-six meters, then we shall take a sharp right, go straight ahead for a bit more than seventy meters, turn left in the direction of the K64, take a sharp right onto the K4 a hundred meters later, after we've then followed its course for two hundred meters, we turn left, then, two hundred meters later, we turn right onto the L24, which we follow for two hundred meters, then we shall turn right, continue straight ahead for some hundred meters and take a slight left onto the L23, we follow this street for fifty-six meters, then we shall turn right onto the main road, which is called "Hauptstraße," main road, there, we continue onward for seventy-one meters before we take a slight right onto the L23, we follow it for roughly a hundred meters, we haven't quite made it yet, but we are headed in the right direction, where, when we need to, we shall soon turn left, we continue on for two hundred meters, turn right, continue on for four hundred meters, turn right in the direction of the B265, continue on for two hundred meters, again to the left onto the B265, continue on for nine hundred meters, slight right onto Tiergartenstraße at the corner of the B265, follow the road for at least one kilometer and seven hundred meters, turn right onto the detour with the beautiful name Detour, continue on this for three hundred meters, it eventually joins Kalvarienbergstraße, we shall follow this for three hundred meters, until, finally, should this plan that Father has only just finished dictating to me be correct, we shall turn left and reach the Achterweg, then, after another three hundred meters on the Achterweg, we shall have reached our destination in Prüm. During the stroll, as Father dubs our hike, he is astonishingly light on his feet, just as he was always light on his feet when we would walk together, and, indeed, at least two meters ahead of me, he continues to dictate, I must note everything down and am to simultaneously find the direction we're meant to go in, as Father says, thus making sure that we follow his plan, at first, I attempted to keep precisely to the specified distances by counting steps, but I have now switched over to following the street names and, where these are not visible, observing the correct sequences of turns in advance, soon enough, in order to free up attention for noting down the dictation, I shall exclusively adhere to the information about the turns, indeed, for the most part they are nothing but deviations from the course of the road, Father hasn't made special note of the fact that it makes an extreme shift to the left or right, rather, with the indication to turn left or right, he has identified alternatives, between which he has decided, thus does Father dictate and I note down: Grandpa; Grandpa and Prüm; Prüm, the Regino-Gymnasium, named after Regino von Prüm, whom we shall hear about later, the Regino-Gymnasium and Grandpa; Eifel Catholicism, the Center Party, National Socialism, and Grandpa; denunciation, high treason, national treason, Gestapo imprisonment, and Grandpa. Grandpa, boasting to the outside world as a father and later senior school principal, he could be hurtful, at a family dinner, he once threw forks at his children and daughters-in-law, he could be quite gruff, but had a good heart, even though he was also coarse-hearted, he placed great worth in delimitations between himself and others, toward whom he could sometimes be quite judgmental. Your grandpa never apostatized, Father says. He did, however, apostatize from the spiritual ground personnel. The clergy could not be trusted, they preached from the pulpit the ideals they then betrayed to the state in back rooms. He considered the direction that the Center Party had taken under Kaas, the prelate from Trier, and that prelate's being taken in by the promises of the Nazis to be catastrophic. First, Kaas voted for the Enabling Act, then he fled to Rome. The Concordat between the Third Reich and the Holy See secured all Catholics for the Third Reich and metaphysics alone for the Holy See. That represented the end of the Center Party for Grandpa, it was politically dead, just as political Catholicism was dead. According to Father, that which is dead dissolves, thus did the Center Party dissolve a few days before the agreement was signed. Repeat the last sentence, Father demands of me. "According to Father, that which is dead dissolves, thus did the Center Party dissolve a few days before the agreement was signed." Right, Father says. Why do I write down all that you dictate, I ask him. So that others might be able to read it, he says. And why should others be able to read this? Man shall not live by bread alone, but by every word that proceedeth out of my mouth. Out of your mouth? A figure of speech. Let's get on with the text: drafted into the Luftnachrichtentruppen in 1939, Grandpa was responsible for the watches between Schneifel and Trier. He set up the duty rota of his home soldiers (the only ones who took part in the watches) in such a way that every air guard could attend Sunday mass. From then on, he and his garrison were referred to "Jesus and his Twelve Disciples" on the blackboard at Katzenkopf,* a military fort near Irrel. His superiors would have liked to have promoted him to the rank of officer. In return, he, who attended mass every Sunday in uniform, was ordered to skip Sunday mass for once, in fact, going to mass in his uniform was an affront. Grandpa refused. In 1942, he was released from military service and went back to the gymnasium. In late summer or autumn of that same year, the Gestapo summoned Grandpa to Trier. He was held in solitary confinement at Windstraße Prison for three months—for both high and national treason—was interrogated, harassed, forgotten for days, perpetually woken up at night, had to stand in the cell for hours, the light went on and off, then it remained on for hours, the peephole cover was pushed off to the side at irregular intervals, Grandpa came to imagine a great eye hovering before the door of his cell, his guards allowed themselves the fun of pushing an empty plate through the food flap, which Grandpa then just left there, when he was asked to politely get the plate, he retorted that he couldn't eat from an empty plate, how did he come to that

---

* Cathead.

conclusion, that the plate was empty, the guards said, after all, the Body of Christ lay upon it, whereupon my grandpa took the plate unto him and the flap was shut. On another occasion, besides dry bread, there was apple juice in a very beautiful glass—still warm—Grandpa drank it in hasty gulps, it was urine. The Gestapo asked him whether he could recite the Bible from memory. He said no. Then he really wasn't a good Christian, he was told. Whoever's not a good Christian shall be shot. Would he at least be able to prove some minor knowledge of the Bible. Of course he could, and he recited verses from the Psalms. The policemen applauded. Well, there you go, they said, whoever knows the Bible so well must be rewarded with death, they said, then the man standing behind Grandpa cocked his pistol, pulled the trigger, it clicked. Then he leaned over Grandpa's shoulder and hissed into his ear, we could give a shit about your beliefs, you betrayed Germany to the Luxembourgers, with whom, as an air-intelligence officer, you maintained and continue to maintain such friendly contacts, and contacts leave traces, and these traces have now been tracked down, and, now that they've come out, some crow will have to be eaten. The interrogator took the crucifix that was on the table in front of Grandpa, hit him on the head with it, for each betrayal, you get one blow to the head, he said, until the corpus fell from the cross, which gave the interrogator the chance to demonstrate on the corpus what else might happen to Grandpa. He tied the cross to a long cord, pulled Grandpa by his few remaining hairs from the chair and onto the floor, gave him a kick in the belly so that he would lie completely flat, tied the cord together with the cross around his neck, then had Grandpa crawl around the table on all fours. This is your own personal Way to Calvary, he said, we'll do twelve laps, then you shall hear the true reason for your arrest. Meanwhile, the room had filled up, the chief interrogator's colleagues congratulated him on this cunning number with the cross, everyone was allowed to kick Grandpa in the side, if he didn't find this posture to be humble enough, kicking him in the face was also an option,

Grandpa was also meant to lick the toes of the kickers' boots, he was asked his opinion about Jesus washing the feet, whether it might not have been an act similar to this, after eleven laps around the table, pants and jacket torn, with a blood-smeared face and a torso that seemed to be moving alongside his torso, Grandpa sat down in the chair once more, you miscounted, he thought, then the chief interrogator, having meanwhile painted the corpus fallen from the cross red, severed its right arm because it couldn't be stretched out into the Heil Hitler salute, and deepened the side wounds with a screwdriver, as well as the wounds in the arms and feet, asked whether he'd counted dutifully enough, whether he'd noticed anything, Grandpa knew that he could only say the wrong thing and kept silent. You're a math teacher, after all, the Gestapo officer said, an error in the sequence will certainly not have escaped your attention, Grandpa was silent, he can't count, the officer smirks and hits him on the head with the cross that Grandpa wears around his neck like a gallows, as the saying so beautifully goes, three blows with the cross increase counting ability, "eleven or twelve laps?", "twelve," "wrong, eleven, but you're not, in any case, getting out of here alive, otherwise, I would have to tell you that you won't be tolerated at the gymnasium any longer with this weakness in arithmetic. Now, let's get to the serious part of our little chat. The dissemination of writings critical of the government, if I may put it in such a matter-of-factly roundabout way, is punishable by death, you already know that, yet, even so, you have these scribblings reproduced and distribute this spiritual ordure to friends, acquaintances, and people at school."

Thus did the interrogation, punctuated by beatings, go on for days, then Grandpa was mostly locked in his cell, from which he would be taken back out after a few hours, sometimes, it was only a few minutes, they'd forgotten to ask him something, the facts of the matter were not yet entirely clear, something still had to be logged more precisely, once, it was said that he would be released on that very day, another time, he was guaranteed immediate death by firing squad. A warden demanded that he compare the number of prisoners and the portions of food, he, the warden, could never seem to count it right. Grandpa didn't know what to make of this, it was forbidden, they both knew that, but the warden, despite all the weakness in arithmetic that he admitted to, didn't give the impression of wishing to bully Grandpa any further, and what if he were to refuse?, thus did he collate the number of prisoners and the food portions each morning, noon, and night, which, indeed, required a certain level of retention, one didn't wish to risk being questioned about one's background by noting down numbers, after all, writing utensils of any kind were nothing less than high treason. What was high treason? The word—Hochverrat—had lodged itself into Grandpa, it had taken on the form of an enormous building, his brain had the form of its letters, high treason was bulky, it blocked his way wherever he went, didn't allow him to go through a door, it felt as if his arms were attempting to grapple onto a heavy square, which he always had to carry out in front of him, first lengthwise, then crosswise, it ate up the other words, became inescapable.

High treason, according to Grandpa after his inexplicable release, once he could observe this word from a distance and it only occupied his sleep every now and again, was belief in God, if one didn't say "Heil Hitler!" but went to mass on Sundays in uniform. It was high treason if, during a Sunday stroll in Tettenbusch, he had wiped one of his sons' behinds with a bill from the Tietz department store for lack of toilet paper, then that bill, covered in excrement, "was picked up by a party member," as his youngest son Ahndemir recorded in his ten typewritten DIN-A4 pages of tribute, and "by way of the Kreisleiter's desk, found its way into the hands" of Grandpa's superiors. This bill served as proof that he was still buying from Jews. It was high treason to disseminate the sermons of the Bishop of Munster, Clemens August Cardinal Count von Galen, even though the bishop spoke quite National-Socialistically of the "Bolshevik-Jewish governance of Russia." The two and a half months in custody cost your grandpa thirty kilograms, now he only weighed sixty instead of ninety. Grandma's heart was broken, Father said, she could hardly recognize Grandpa, that heartbreak is what eventually led to her fall. And what remained of "Hochverrat"? Nothing. Other than a missive:

The Attorney General   Koblenz, Nov. 2/42
2 S Js, 665/42   Long-distance number: 2351

Please quote the   Mr. ((...))
above business number   ((address))
in all petitions.

Pursuant to Section 170 of the Code of Criminal Procedure, you are hereby informed that the preliminary investigation by the public prosecutor, on the occasion of which you were interrogated before the District Court in Trier on Sept. 5, 1942 on charges of high treason, has been abated.

By order of
Attn. ((...))
Judicial Secretary
The correctness of the copy
is certified
Prüm, 11/12/1942

((...))
Hauptluftschutzführer.

As soon as Grandpa was arrested, the doors of friends from good Catholic families were closed to us, Ahndemir recently wrote to me, Father says. It's good that Ahndemir refreshes and manages family memories, he says, every now and again, he writes a letter to each of the siblings, in them, he always sheds light on different aspects of Grandpa's life. Ahndemir has set himself the goal of bringing Grandpa back to life in spirit with the help of one hundred letters.

The Regino-Gymnasium was now called the Deutsche Oberschule, Grandpa only worked there for a few more days, when he showed up to resume classes after his release from prison, he was greeted with great applause, as he proudly emphasized, by "his seniors," this enraged the Kreisleiter a great deal, "How can one applaud somebody who has been arrested for high treason and been imprisoned?", thus did Dr. Müller, the Kreisleiter, prompt Grandpa's immediate expulsion from the school building. From then on, it was part of his unique harassment that, after his release from prison, he was transferred again and again, over ever shorter periods of time, in such a way that he couldn't even familiarize himself with the local conditions of a school, according to my brother Ahndemir, but he, Father, contradicts the following anecdote about the seniors, Grandpa thought it would be far and away the canniest thing to do to greet all classes not his own—and all classes were and would remain not his own—with a "Heil Hitler!" each morning, Grandpa never gave in to greeting his school classes with a "Heil Hitler!", Father insists on this point; after all, Grandpa worked at the Sobernheim Gymnasium for a whole year, his subsequent service as an Flakhelfer teacher at the Hindenburg School in Trier lasted for six months, he was transferred from there to Trier-Euren to work as a mere anti-aircraft auxiliary teacher assistant for five months, his service in Bous lasted for four months, in Völklingen—three months, then, when he was already imagining that in another three months he'd have no position at all and would be arrested once more, he was warned by, of all people, an SS man in the service of the administrative district office that the Kreisleiter had ordered his arrest and, this time, it would be *final*, then, when the Americans invaded the western part of the Prüm District in September 1944, Grandpa left his Schanzgruppe and joined our family in Prüm on September 15, 1944, artillery fire was already visible from Kalvarienberg, first in Brandscheid, then in the surrounding districts, whereas the Americans' light artillery was visible as far away as Sellericherhöhe and American shock troops—as far away as the Mehlental hillside, the family opted to seek refuge in the large tunnels of the Kalvarienberg Bunker with a great number of "evacuation refusers" in the hopes of being overrun by the Americans, this, however, did not come to pass for the time being, instead, some party leaders appeared and announced that buses would be used to empty out the tunnel the next day, thus did we have to leave this supposedly secure place of refuge, which had now turned out to be a trap, so as to escape the bus transport, as Ahndemir reports, he who, handicapped by his poliomyelitis and consequently unable to withstand any stress, was sent ahead to the district office with his grandfather, who was blind, this was Grandpa's father, an employee of that very office had counselled it to us as an unsuspicious spot, during the first term of my father's imprisonment, this employee was a jailer on Windstraße, in Trier, the prison was across from the episcopal seminary at Windstraße 4, where Klaus Barbie had lived as a ward for a few years during his school days at the Friedrich-Wilhelm-Gymnasium, from 1942 onward, he was the Gestapo Chief in Lyon, after all, who would have guessed that the fugitives were in the basement of an official building, then two high-ranking "golden pheasants" came in an open car and three buses driven by SS soldiers came toward Ahndemir and Grandfather, bundling them onto one of the vehicles with the words: "Now that we've got the lame and the blind, we're going to catch the clever one too," by which he meant Grandpa, my father, Father says, who bases his remarks on his brother Ahndemir's tribute-text, which, from now on, serves as an important part of the family memory, it is circulated in multiple copies and repeatedly consulted regarding highly specific questions, here and there, it is corrected and revised by Ahndemir's hand, and it is only with Ahndemir's death that this memory shall come to a standstill. At the upper edge of his first page of text about Grandpa, Ahndemir wrote with a red ball-point pen: "Pg. 1 of the text I'm meant to have written," Father says. Is that coquetry or the grace of forgetfulness? Father is angry about this entry. Starting with Grandma, the cloak of dementia casts itself over the family, from generation to generation, he says, and it is specifically those affected who believe themselves to have been spared. His statement puts the fear in me, there must be other reasons for this entry, Ahndemir is mentally on top of things, he is one of the sharpest people I've ever met. The entry suggests a monstrous productivity, which means that the recognition of one's own authorship is no longer guaranteed in every case, especially if the text was written a long time ago.

The family was now presented with the following grotesque scene: While Ahndemir and Great-Grandfather drove uphill together with the high-ranking "golden pheasants" and the SS soldiers, the rest of the family ran past them down the hill, the Nazis hesitated briefly, considering whether to pick us up, but finally refrained, as the artillery fire resumed just in the nick of time, right next to Kalvarienberg, which allowed for Ahndemir and his grandfather to escape in a moment of generalized confusion, then, while the rest of the family fled into the bunker, Ahndemir and Great-Grandfather, having taken cover in the ditch several times, finally managed to reach the basement of the district office. On the night of September 17, however, it was evacuated by the "watchdogs," the field gendarmerie, whereupon the family, after marching on foot to Büdesheim and taking the train to Gerolstein, the family split off "from the general evacuation train of the Prümers to Siegerland because of the threat of my father's imminent arrest"—these were Ahndemir's precise words—so as to seek refuge in Duisburg-Mündelheim and Duisburg-Serm with their mother's rural relatives. They survived the collapse of the Third Reich in the "Ruhr pocket."

We ought to have been suspicious of the friendliness we occasionally encountered after Grandpa's arrest, with my father's arrest, the doors of many of our playmates' homes, including good Catholic ones, were closed to us children, so says Father. Each one was a potential Nazi informant. The warden of the youth dormitory located in our neighborhood on the corner of the Achterweg and Kalvarienberg at that time, a certain H., was particularly friendly and of the opinion that he had to console us every day, it was certain that the arrest would be cleared up soon enough, then Father would come back home. He didn't forget to inquire as to the grounds for Father's arrest, and the longer his imprisonment lasted, the more voluble we became. Ahndemir had been friends with his daughter since primary school, then, all of a sudden, she became very curious in all matters concerning our family, before the arrest, she had been so reserved that she scarcely dared to enter our parents' house, but now she could hardly wait for when she would next be sitting at our table and be able to overhear everything that was being said. After the war, amongst the ruins of the district headquarters, I found a denunciation of my father written in the dormitory warden's hand. What was written there would have been enough for execution.

The Nazis did not explain Grandpa's being set free, Father says. The Kreisleiter was furious about it, but also received no justification. Grandpa had a hunch that it wouldn't be long after the war until one or another of them would boast that he was responsible for it. And lo and behold, Father says, no sooner had the declaration of capitulation been signed by the German side than a Reich prosecutor from the Koblenz Special Court contacted him with the goal of obtaining a Persilschein, he claimed that he had "defused" the proceedings against Grandpa and brought about their dismissal, as Ahndemir expressed it. As proof, he submitted the header sections of the files. What ought one to do in such a case, Father asks. They're all poor devils who are now eating crow, Grandpa is said to have said, indeed, he found their behavior wretched, but, on the other hand, this wretchedness was all too human, and that which is all too human really isn't always all that good. Instead of intervening, it was his policy to simply let such people's efforts come to nothing.

Later, Grandpa's so-called liberation from imprisonment was depicted in the biography of a well-known political figure in a way that was typical for the whitewashing attempts of old Nazis. If one did not know that it came from a Nazi himself, who had whispered it into the biographer's ear, then the fable "Nazi saves a father with many children from the clutches of the Gestapo" could only have sprung from the imagination of an oriental fairy-tale teller, Father says. The former head of the National Socialist boarding school in the building of the Vinzentinum in Niederprüm, one Erwin Schneider, who, as a militarist and Nazi song- and march-whistler, still walked the rows of desks in the Regino School in Prüm, a remote penal school for unpopular teachers after the Second World War, in the years after school resumed on September 16, 1949, according to Joachim Hoell, Father says, he hoped to thereby bring about his own denazifying beatification. Father claims that Schneider was in cahoots with the NSDAP Kreisleiter from Prüm, the dentist Dr. Walter Müller. When, together with his brother Hermann Josef, his father returned to Prüm in May 1945, planning to undertake the makeshift repair of the badly damaged apartment building at Achterweg 11 for the family, the rest of the family followed them to Prüm in October 1945, according to Father, during a search of the few files remaining in the destroyed district headquarters, they found a handwritten order about Grandpa that read: "If found, to be immediately shot. Dr. Müller, Kreisleiter." In the district office, together with a friend, he also later secured the card indexes of the local NSDAP and the Opferring, the Nazi charity organization that collected donations, which Grandpa, by then entrusted with various tasks as a denazification commissioner, had hidden away in the basement of Achterweg 11, first beneath the chopped wood, then, later, beneath the coke, "so that nobody would make any mischief with it," as Ahndemir quotes

Grandpa. We were often in the basement and secretly rummaged through the card indexes, Father says, the card indexes contained the names of good Catholic Prüm merchants and civil servants, who, after the war, boasted of their clean slate in the assumption that their regular contributions to the Nazi Opferring, with which they had bought their freedom, would remain undetected. The Nazis tolerated the Opferring's donation system, it served to finance party work, Father says, first with collective slips, then with their own Opferring stamps, which were then sold, which then provided the local groups and the Gauleitung, who received a percentage of the revenue from the sale of the stamps, with a continuous stream of income. Abuse of the collection process was prevented insofar as these were collectible cards and stamps, which were issued and controlled by the Gauleitung alone, any such collection outside of the Opferring was forbidden and one needed identification papers in order to collect donations. The collection system led to genuine competition among the collectors, as the proceeds earned became transparent on the cards, on which a local-group cashier acknowledged the sale of the stamps. Thus, over time, a small branch of industry was established, on their end, the local authority and the Gauleiter also became dependent on it. More than a few used the Opferring to buy their freedom without being party members themselves such that they would not be bothered any further and could go about their business.

Sometimes, we wrote down a few names, Father says, then went to see individuals if they were doing business locally. Under the pretext of being interested in the carpets or curtains being hawked, which must have come off to people as a bit strange given our age, that Father or Mother had sent us was hardly all that credible, they would have wanted to examine the goods themselves, we would ask them a couple of questions, which allowed for conclusions to be drawn about our knowledge of the card indexes, given that they had not known of them before they were discovered, it is likely that they simply repressed the possible existence of the incriminating documents or believed them to have been done away with in the hail of bombs. In any case, we were on a deconspiratorial mission and dubbed our task "uncloaking." Surely, you know XY, we asked the proprietress of a shop that sold corsetry, the alphabetical neighbor of the two businesspeople, our appearance in a group of three, three young men, had such a disturbing effect on her that she called for her husband, who immediately came out of the back areas and into the sales room, he scrutinized us one by one, then decided to deal with us in friendly fashion, no, they didn't happen to know XY, he replied after we repeated the question, asked to do so by his wife, nor did our hint that XY had, precisely like him and his wife, done quite well for himself in years past help jog his memory, what did we mean by "years past," he retorted, before the end of the war, we said, when one could really buy all sorts of things with money, back then, even a pact with the devil might have been made with money, still, nothing was dawning on him, or at least he offered no hint that it was, as he ushered us out the door, there was urgent business that had to be attended to, then my oldest brother turned around once more, my father says, and asked the unsuspecting fellow whether Opferrings are also corsetry. In town, we recounted, a number of business people would have a double name from then on and, if they already had a double name, they would have a triple name from then on, "Opferring" is the newly added bit of the last name, this was chosen so as to acknowledge the regular donation-generosity of these businesspeople, it made it possible for them to flourish in their businesses and survive difficult times without having to make an official pact, Father says. At another business, we wanted to go about it more subtly and asked the owners, who immediately recognized us as Father's children, whether donations really implied no quid pro quo, which was immediately confirmed to us, we followed up and asked whether that might have been different before 1945, back then, quite a bit was different, was the reply, had rings been donated back then and might this donation be called an Opfer, a sacrifice, I'm certain that both of them understood, but they also managed to get us out the door without having shown any weakness. Ever since, the man gave us sinister looks upon encountering us and we gave him sinister looks back. Heijo once said that, when he saw the man, he was overcome by darkness and, if he kept on looking at us so sinisterly, we'd have to go visit him again.

Grandpa expected nothing from people, Father says, no self-sacrifice, no civil courage, most of them are very small and weak beings. That is why every person should be treated decently regardless of their reputation. He was of the opinion, Ahndemir writes, "that while, indeed, high-ranking Nazis no longer belong in leadership positions, they should not be held accountable for any membership they had, or should but only according to the criteria of criminal law. He followed the Nuremberg Trials with a great sense of satisfaction." There was only one thing that Grandpa expected from convinced Nazis and those who were Nazis out of fear, Ahndemir writes: That they have the decency to remain silent. Grandpa did not have a rigid need for punishment. His children couldn't believe that, Father says, they were too cognizant of the fears they'd endured and the humiliations they'd experienced, but Grandpa, according to Ahndemir, was of the opinion that the local Nazis and staunch party members, with the exception of the fanatical Kreisleiter Dr. Müller were nothing but "the petty bourgeoisie gone wild," under normal conditions, they would once more become "normal people—harmless." This refraining from retaliation that Grandpa practiced was, at first, not understood by his children in the slightest, the nightly patrols of Nazis before the house, Father's denunciation, his Gestapo detention, his being threatened with the pistol when he broke off from the Schanztruppe, all that should remain unpunished? Even after the SA-Gunslinger, as Grandpa denoted him, managed to lease gas stations in Prüm again after the war and wrote a letter to Grandpa in the fifties after the latter had bought a car, asking him to "fill up" at his place, he would never personally serve him, even then, Grandpa never lost his stoic calm and read the note to his family during a sit-down lunch, framing it as nothing more than a grotesque footnote to postwar history, Father says, but the brothers picked the crumpled note up out of the wastebasket and, like a negative relic, he, Father, the oldest son, kept it in his desk with the declaration of intent of one day paying the man back. That day came very quickly, when the three brothers presented themselves to him at the gas station, but he wasn't there, not the next time either, on their third attempt, they gleaned the impression that he was never there at all, and thus was the project lost to memory.

Grandpa's benevolence and forbearance as a denazification commissioner often earned him the indignation of the occupying power, Father says, in such a way that, quite often, reinstatements that he had ordered were canceled again within a short time, with the result that the people concerned were by no means considered to be denazified and therefore able to go back to their positions, instead, they were found to be guilty and ordered to clear rubble. It was also criticized that Grandpa sometimes classified such "cases" as "with a clean record" when they were not, not by any stretch of the imagination. If he didn't wish to entirely incur the displeasure of the French, according to Father, he had to accommodate them further. So-called "hangers-on" and less-incriminated persons had to pay fines, which Grandpa sought to stagger as socially as possible, however, more serious cases went to the Trier Spruchkammer, where the Social Democrat Bridi was a hard-liner, Ahndemir writes.

After the war, insofar as one was still alive and in the same place, one would invariably meet again. In that case, did one just say, Good day, Mr. Fanatical Kreisleiter Dr. Müller? Did one keep silent? Did one not even look at all? ~~My brother Ahndemir and I have not forgotten~~

~~the humiliation caused by local Nazis patrolling by our front door every night, nor the fears that the staunch party members spread.~~ I already wrote that above. What did you write above? The thing about the humiliations. Did I already say that? I think so, yes. Where is it better? Above, I think. Then strike it out below.

After the war, faith became even more thin, clericalism was revolting to Grandpa and caused him to become a wordsmith. As my brother Ahndemir rightly remarks, Grandpa was true to the Church in matters of faith and moral doctrine, even if he was also not uncritical about these things, indeed, he did consider it to be the Church's duty to give directions in matters of principle, but, according to Ahndemir, he firmly rejected the church's claim to power that emerged in the wake of the collapse. Should I put down "according to Ahndemir" here too? Of course you should put that down, it's a quote, I hope you've already been putting it down the whole time. Should I also put this down? You should put everything down. Back to Grandpa. He was of the opinion, rightfully so according to Ahndemir, that the clergy had to have no place in concrete politics in the interests of their pastoral work. Ahndemir verbatim: "Parish priests who complained to him that he was in the habit of scheduling party meetings during the Saturday confession and thus prevented some from attending, were told by him that they were precisely in their right place in the confessional and should stay out of politics. He was allergic to the *ex cathedra* statements of some clergymen regarding political matters." End of quote. What? Quotation marks. Where? After "matters." So "regarding political matters." Right. Further on in the text. Grandpa as wordsmith. "Clerofascistic holy-water werewolves," that's what he called these clergymen. The Church can forgive everything, but not forget it. In many respects, they forgot the Third Reich very quickly and not only after it had already become history. According to Grandpa, from these points of view, the story of Pope Pius XII must be entirely reconsidered.

Grandpa saw the resumption of school operations at the Regino School on the premises of the elementary school on Kalvarienberg as his first task, Ahndemir writes. At the end of 1945, he became the principal. Ahndemir's precise words, according to Father: "His acting predecessor, Studiendirektor Eschbach, transferred from Schleiden to Prüm in the 1930s as an opponent of the Nazis, had to give way to pressure from the Church, which could not forgive (!) him for having countersigned the National Socialist order to dissolve the bishop's seminary on behalf of the principal of the Regino School." The reconfiguration of the Regino School into a humanistic gymnasium with modern-language courses, which some complained about in a downright ignoble and slanderous manner, was also Grandpa's accomplishment, just like the implementation of the reconstruction of the abbey, where the Regino Gymnasium was able to return in 1952.

But Grandpa saw his second task as helping to build a democratic Germany, Father continues. For him, the guiding principle here was an orientation toward Christian values through which a democratic body politic might gain "stability and moral resistance against totalitarian ideologies," as Ahndemir writes. The order of the day was for Grandpa to overcome nationalism and reconcile with France, even the willful acts and harassment of the French occupying power, which Grandpa complained about many times over, even in public, changed nothing. According to Ahndemir, when these hopes were concretized in the notion of a unified Europe from 1947 onward, Grandpa became its most steadfast devotee.

Grandpa was a member of the "provisional advisory citizens' representative body" of Prüm, which convened for the first time on July 16, 1945 and existed until the first municipal election on September 15, 1946. On May 24, 1946, Grandpa, as principal, together with the school inspector, a municipal employee, a businessman, and a water-pipe inspector, petitioned the Mayor of Prüm for the founding of a Christian-Democratic Party, the CDP, which then, according to Father, merged into the Rhineland-Palatinate CDU (Christian Democratic Union of Germany) and Grandpa became its district chairman from 1947 to 1958.

If, as a native of the Lower Rhine, Grandpa initially felt banished to the Eifel or Prüm in the thirties, as Ahndemir writes, his involvement in local politics would have been unthinkable without his love for the Eifel and Prüm, which came to life during the time of the Nazis—in their destruction, these places became as a second home to him.

We went the wrong way, I say to Father. He doesn't hear me. This is the wrong way, I say. Father continues on, undeterred. According to the map, we should have kept to the left instead. There is no instead, Father says, nor an either/or. It also wouldn't suit him to admit to an error. I stay there, Father walks onward, he no longer reacts to my calls. Perhaps, he has changed the route and is unwilling to inform me of this. He has always been at peace within himself. When I once asked him why he so likes going on walks, he said: to disappear into the landscape. Man has the ability to become part of the landscape, he says, then the bereaved remember you as a landscape, the most beautiful is the notion that they would travel through this landscape, then you would be omnipresent to them. They would look around the landscape and say, that is Father. I feel the same way about Grandpa in Prüm, Father said, each street, each brick, each hillock, each tree is Grandpa. There he goes, I soon lose sight of him. Nothing compels me to follow him.

Many years ago, when I was about fourteen, Father lost his bearings during a hike. Tomorrow, we'll climb Traunstein, he said. We'll approach from behind, that's the safest way. Father had estimated seven to eight hours for the hike, including a two-hour break. Coming from Gmunden, we drove down Traunseeuferstraße, the paths were signposted, the cardinal directions they were heading in too, the steep

Mairalmsteig was the easternmost ascent, that was the one we had to take, this had been told to us the night before, but Father felt such an attraction to the "Naturfreundesteig" signpost that, in the sure assumption it'd always only been the Naturfreundesteig that'd been spoken of, he parked the car in view of the "Gedenkstein Traunsteinopfer"* sign above the yellow trail indicators. At about 6:00 a.m., we hiked through two Mairalm forest-road tunnels and were soon confronted with the steep entrance of the Naturfreundesteig that Father, who didn't wish to let his astonishment show, as his son might have been able to take this as an opportunity to declare the hike to be at an end, immediately resolved to master by obdurately leading the way, initially, no path at all could be seen, indeed, nothing at all could really be seen, except for steel cables fastened to the rock a bit later on the left-hand side, we were climbing Traunstein in the fog, fog was to be our constant companion, in certain places, we couldn't even see our legs, but this didn't worry us much more than the fact that the width of the trail was just as difficult to recognize as the proximity of the abyss, the latter a direct function of the former, at around 7:00 a.m., Father expressed his surprise that we could see Traunsee from the mountain, even if it was only through clouds of fog, he paused briefly, as if he were considering turning back, a thought experiment he ought to have discarded immediately, not least because I then would have had to walk in front, after all, Father was so clairvoyant that he didn't consider the dangerous option of slipping in the context of walking past one another, thus did he continue on his way, in shorts like me, with his father's mountaineering boots, while I wore his mountaineering boots, which were much too big for me. As soon as the way sloped upward, I lost all sense of stride-distance, the toe of the boot was rather inanimate, later, when the way had sloped downward, my feet gathered up in the toe of the boots while the heels were abandoned. The steel cable gave way to iron

---

* A memorial stone to those who died climbing Traunstein.

clamps, foot pegs, then, later, a long aluminum ladder and a staircase hewn into the rock, whose slants, Father suspected aloud, hadn't been installed properly or they'd been wantonly destroyed, in any case, he preferred not to climb it, he went down a path to the left below that staircase, from that point on, we were as free as the chamois upon the mountain, heading for home in town, stepping nimbly, they will tread with measured gait with your dead body, perhaps even before they pass that gate in the rock that I now see glistening aloft. Whereas the climbing trail of the Naturfreundesteig, which we managed by way of all sorts of hand- and footholds, afforded us a kind of certainty that we'd not strayed from the right path, but had simply taken the wrong one, which Father saw as a sign from God, a challenge to master in his name, Father's hike around the mountain, which proceeded in a northerly direction so as to avoid the sloping staircase, a path he felt to be justified, nay, unavoidable, turns into a test from the moment when, after about an hour of walking parallel to the Traunsee-shore road, having resumed the ascent through the northern plunges of Traunstein, all my strength left me and, free-floating against the wall and incessantly calling out that no more climbing would be possible for me, I caused Father to hand over to me the whole of our provisions, which I then exhausted within a few minutes without this measure influencing my condition at all positively, I'll wait a bit more, I say to Father, soon, it will be better, even after fifteen minutes, it hasn't gotten better, I initially observe the falling boulders and fragments of stone with fascination until the sight of them fills me with fear, heat penetrates the fog, it nails me to the rock face, black salamanders, also known as Wegnarr, Wegmandl, or Hölldeixl, one ought not be surprised to find them in the Alps, crawl over my shoes, I haven't moved them even slightly for minutes now, they leave a trail of slime behind on the leather, perhaps it's also the dampness of the ground that they wipe off on my shoes. Father urges me to keep going, I can't even imagine turning back in the direction of the path we were coming from, I say, the fog clears to reveal flowers along the edge of the path, which I recognize as Stemless Enzian, Lady's-slipper, and wild orchid, Father shakes his head, there's no Stemless Enzian here, he sees no broad-leaved marsh orchid, no Lady's-slipper either, and oh wouldn't that suit me perfectly, but it's much too unspecific as far as names go, I'm fairly certain that there's Stemless Enzian here, I repeat, and thus do we go back and forth like this for a while, Father takes a huge step toward me, he's standing right behind me, I stand in embers and wherever I look is fire, plague, and death, I manage to turn left by using my right foot, however, I immediately lose my nerve once more, and now do I stand with belly against wall, behind me, Father is pushing past, not without whispering an imprecation into my ear, so close that I can feel his genitals, we are completely without via ferrata equipment, without safety ropes and without helmets, I say to the wall, which causes my voice to be perceived as very close to me, as if it were reaching behind my ears, enclosing my head, and simultaneously sounding out from the front and from the back, and it says that a sign points out the elevated risk of slipping and that, when it's damp out, one should avoid this mostly pathless, unmarked stone, which leads along the most difficult rock ledge, at all costs, what beautiful words, I think as I read the sign, they've immediately imprinted themselves onto my mind, they are my only foothold here, Father has vanished, he simply kept on walking, I briefly consider whether I ought not to turn around instead of following him to the left, but imagining that my left foot is nearest to the rock face compels me to follow Father, the actual width of the path can't be made out even now, water runs down the wall, I hold my lips very close to the rock, the water runs down my chest and into my pants, the refreshing effect immediately turns into the fear of a bad chill, the rock is entirely mossed over, little insects clamber over the moss, shimmering-green and black, I feel them upon my lips, they tumble down my throat, the water flows down the narrow path and into the depths, it shall prevent a sure footing if I wish to turn and catch up with Father once more, I'm completely in love with my own voice, the way the rock catches it and gives it back to me, I grow cold, my voice is drawing figures upon the moss, a certain Schattenfroh is there and wants me to turn left and follow Father, I can now see my father right through his name, he speaks, but I don't hear him, he seems to be furious, the veins upon his temples are protruding, I now see his right hand pointing in the direction he disappeared in, the image trembles, fades, the word "Schattenfroh" becomes legible once more, before my very eyes, it transforms to "Storchenhaft,"* then "Hattenschorf,"† then to "Schattenfroh" once more, then the last "h" vanishes from the word, I read "Schattenfro" and I lose interest in this trickery and am about to turn left when a voice says to me, "Behold," I behold and see that the letters are changing places incessantly, as if they were inscriptions upon Father's face, which fades into the background, then seems to be slowly coming forward, inscribed with mutating words: "Ortschaft,"‡ "Nachtfrost,"§ "Schafott,"¶ "ernsthaft,"** "Toter,"†† "Echo," I read, the words write themselves onto Father's head, as if they were program-opening passwords, thus is Father somebody who runs programs, but is he still "somebody" at all, is he still a person, isn't he actually a machine, only there to be of service? I know that Father is Doctor Mabuse and I shall be Doctor Mabuse, Father shall have snow-white hair and I shall have snow-white hair, Father-in-Moss looks at me intently, eyes, nose, mouth, and ears are formed from the letters of the word "Schattenfroh," insects crawl forth from his letter-mouth, they clean themselves, then scurry on their way, following the little

---

* Stork-like.
† Hadscab.
‡ Locality.
§ Nightfrost.
¶ Scaffold.
** Genuinely.
†† Dead man.

flowers that are flourishing so wonderfully through the water, my testicles hurt from the cold, I manage to turn to the left, following Father's outstretched right arm, I stand with both feet on the path for a little while longer, then set myself into motion, Father has fled and cannot be caught, this thought surfaces and I immediately seek to cover it over with other thoughts, it is only by thinking that one can do away with thinking, "Überraschung" is written on a sign right next to a hole in the fissured rock face rising up to the left of the path and that means "astonishment," stones likely broke off of Traunstein, then bored into the ground not far from it, like a window, the hole affords a view onto the lake and its environs, wind and weather gnaw at this Schauinsland-fragment, it has a protective aspect, there's a completely windless corner here that Father must have already visited, on the ground is a scrap of paper weighted down with stones, I recognize Father's script, which always gives the impression of a command, "Here, I waited for my son for a long time, but he did not have the decency to rejoin me. I therefore set off in the direction of the Gmundner Hütte on my own." I fold up the note and put it into my pants pocket. When I'm on the verge of continuing, I pull out the scrap once more, when folding it up, I had the sensation that its backside was also written on, and, to be sure, there, one reads: "Chains, via ferrata, rope-secured paths, rock gate, from the southwest via the Naturfreundesteig, Gmundner Hütte, Traunkirchner Hütte, summit cross of the war veterans on the Pyramidenkogel, large difference in altitude of 1250m, a certain level of fitness required, ascent-channel, Zierlersteig too difficult, Schattenfroh and the priest say hike canceled, Father and Son not mountain-tested," the longer I stare at the scrap, the more text appears there, the script below the scrap has now been entirely freed, it continues to write itself through the air, I read: "Even Naturfreundesteig too difficult, don't get lost on the Zierlersteig!, then ALL will be lost." So, we're on the Zierlersteig. And before I can begin to despair about this, I read: "Quit reading, follow the line of my script," and I see a line snaking out of the tail of the t, it runs before me at waist-height, a blue thread, a worm that adapts to my speed, but shall not condone my stopping, it passes through me silently, it flies a meter up ahead, it dissolves some two meters behind me. If I walk too slowly, it forms words like "Come on" or "Faster" or "Don't just hang around there," a formulation that causes me to see hanged people everywhere, if I go too quickly, I read words like "Caution!" or "Don't slip!" and once even, "In calm lies strength," the four words in tight succession such that the reading focus, which doesn't wish to let a single letter escape, throttles the speed of my steps, I've just overtaken the blue threadworm, then it gives me an entirely different and distorted word to read or it's simply my view that is distorted, "Schattenfroh," "Father" and "Death" are so intertwined that they crawl toward me as a many-legged insect, ScharttEatfreh, it has a black-shining carapace and shimmers green on the belly, the little beast seems to be battling itself with its legs and arms, it laughs at me while knives or wings protrude from beneath its carapace, I stop, then, from a certain distance, I read, "That's what happens." Likely one of Father's amusing disciplinary measures, which proclaim that the world begins with language, then, later on, ends with language, and if Father hasn't yet signed the world with his script, it is on that day that it shall be annulled. I reach for the word "happens," the thread of which dissolves as a sewing needle describing a pattern dissolves the part of the sweater into which it wasn't worked neatly enough when one pulls at it, I can effectively hold tight to the word-thread, somebody seems to be pulling at its other end, all I have to do is lean back, and I'm already being pulled in the most pleasant way, I unfold, flow, I myself become gliding script, which follows the trail of the prescription, the path that I follow in this way is made up of words, with all the detours that they need to border the margins, I am script's slow dancer, and I even dance errors, the correction of which the thread I hang from hinders by way of its guidance, with time, I come to notice that an error is imminent, I then seek to go in the opposite direction, but I can only manage to do this within an insufficient radius, so I go, fully cognizant that I am adding an error to the name of Jesus of Nazareth, and, should my father be guiding the thread, of which I have no doubt, he will accuse me of having made the mistake on purpose, as a provocation of Church and Fatherhood, then he shall once more point out to me that only he is able to guide me onto the right path. The punishment follows right on its heels, the punishment is called 666, which I have to be subjected to because *that's what happens*, I've already completed the second 6, I made it to the third just as I did from the first to the second, by walking up half of the belly in order to find the path from the belly of the one 6, through a straight line, then into the neck of the next 6, but the belly of the third 6 no longer lets me free, walking in a circle with no way out, as if I needed an invitation to get free from the circle, the endless thread wraps around me, my shoes are laced so tight that I can only turn around my own axis with the most halting of steps, my calves are bound together, involuntarily, I lay my hands onto the trouser-seam, the thread encloses my hips, stills my arms, I breathe in deep, the turning around my own axis ceases, it waits, I breathe out, then the thread continues its work, it works its way up to the throat, it is gentle, it treats even the lips with decorum, it doesn't strangulate nose and eyes, enough air to breathe shall remain, however, I cannot open my eyes, I rotate some more, I rotate, then I stand still, and it is said that this standing-still is what allowed the innkeeper from the Gmundner Hütte, who introduced himself to my father as Schattenfroh and to whom Father initially kept silent about my absence, until his disquiet brought him to the brink of tears, as the innkeeper later told me, but I could hardly believe it, after all, I had never seen Father weep, brought him to the brink, that doesn't mean actually crying, so said the innkeeper, who, up until that moment, had assumed that my father had ascended Traunstein solo, but then Father urgently begged him to do something, anything, to grab hold of the loose end of the thread, which, fortunately, stood out clearly from the back of my head at a great distance and was not worked into a much-too-long sentence, then, as the several-kilometer-long thread was unwound, its other end having been bound to my chest with an insoluble sailor's knot, which surprised me, the thread had woven round me from the feet up as described, to get me safely from the summit to the lodges was a measure that, as he expressed it to Father, caused the renowned alpine lifesaver he was approximately as much trouble as spreading butter onto bread. Until my rescue, the innkeeper maintained an almost unsympathetic calm, as he called it, but then, from the very moment I arrived at the lodge, the whole of my body trembling, but otherwise safe and sound, he showered Father with reproaches of the worst sort.

Father will later claim that it was a species of high-altitude fever that put me out of action for hours at the Gmundner Hütte, that the dizziness tangled up my imagination and distorted my memory of the ascent, even though, in my memories, it was Father who, a year before our Traunstein climb, had almost been hurled to Traunstein's rocky foot by Meunière's Disease when we wanted to use the car to scout out whether the mountain that descended deep toward Traunsee could be bypassed by way of the Miesweg, he'd never heard something so stupid come out of my mouth, with this, Father merely wished to parry the reproaches of the innkeeper, we were told of the presumptuousness inherent to climbing Traunstein without any kind of prior experience, not to mention the decision to do so in such poor weather, from the choice of footwear to the apparent disorientation that finally led us to the almost completely unmarked and very steep Zierlersteig, which offered our shoes almost no support when damp, indeed, this trail claimed a certain number of lives each year, Father had done everything wrong and it was a miracle that we weren't to be numbered amongst the dead, and, as it was a miracle, we ought to kneel down before the cross, Father shall say that he sees no cross, up there, in the corner, below the ceiling, the innkeeper shall retort, the cross is plain, without corpus, one should not kneel before a cross without a corpus. If one stares at the cross for long enough, the innkeeper shall say, the corpus appears, namely, Christ's battered body from during the Crucifixion, the innkeeper shall grin as he says these words, his crooked mouth shall reveal a row of rotten teeth, I shall sit in a chair and drink pink Skiwasser, Father shall stare at the cross for some five minutes without budging, the innkeeper shall bring me salted and smoked meat and he shall also offer Father some of the salted and smoked meat, which he, however, shall brusquely refuse, he doesn't wish to be disturbed in his benevolent attempt to bestow belief upon the innkeeper, the innkeeper shall reply that it isn't him who should be believed, but Christ, which Father shall seek to do for a further five minutes, then he shall sit down in the chair opposite me and eat the meat in silence, he shall cover a slice of freshly cut bread with fine horseradish shavings, take the horseradish off of the bread once more, lay the smoked meat onto the bread, pile it high with horseradish, take the meat and the horseradish off the bread once more, spread the bread with butter, lift the horseradish-bedecked meat back onto the bread, and thereupon gobble this down with evident appetite, to then prepare a second slice of bread in the same fashion, this time without any detours, and to also gobble down the second slice, thus fortified, Father shall say, a cross must have a corpus if one wishes to visualize the sufferings of Christ, after all, the Son of God is not formless, with his father, it is a question of faith, whereas some find the notion of God the Father having a form, which is to say a physical body, ridiculous, a ridiculousness that culminates in talk of the "Word of God," as if God had a speaking human mouth, others acknowledge the necessity, the inevitability even, of visualizing God in manifold forms, after all, thinking of God evokes images of his appearance that can only come from the realm of perception and the combinations derived therefrom approach and include the monstrous, one would thus do violence to oneself to think of God as an empty space, however, empty space would progress to eventually becoming the appearance of God if this association with God and his appearance were made just often enough. I am in favor of the ban on images, the innkeeper shall say, it is enough for him to have an image of how Father and I climbed Traunstein in the most threatening of situations, though, fortunately, we knew nothing of this danger, in town, the rumor shall later be passed around that, after the innkeeper said that Germans were the stupidest of mountain-hikers and he'd never seen any stupider than us, Father took the cross out of the corner and threatened to beat the innkeeper to death with it, whereupon the innkeeper countered cross with meat-knife, a story that, over the years, would be told in the most colorful, the bloodiest even, of shades, depending on the occasion, Father himself circulated different versions of the Traunstein-ascent incident in the closest of friend and family circles, we didn't even set out, for example, as the fog prevented it, another time, he claimed that we lost our bearings after just a few meters due to the fog, then climbed Traunstein without any climbing equipment by the most direct route possible, a rock ledge would have been just as incapable of keeping us from our goal of the Gmundner Hütte as rockfall, rain, or exposed climbing areas with the associated risk of falling, we mastered the ascent with great bravura, then the innkeeper congratulated us effusively and took a photo of us, which can still be seen today in the lodges, nowadays, in a third version, there is no talk of a masterly ascent, instead, I, the utterly inexperienced boy, was overtaken by fever on the way and it is out of this fever that all of these phastasmagorias, together with the fable of Father's differing Traunstein Versions, arose, sometimes, the fever overtook me on the way, at other times, it only did so once we'd reached the lodges, the question of the descent was never made issue of by Father, but I know that the innkeeper put him onto his shoulder with the remark that the containers full of groceries he was used to carrying up the mountain were heavier and more unwieldy than the burden he now had to carry with Father, then only let him back down once Father was able to recite the route to him seven times in a row with no errors, he was going to have to cover this route with me, who would be following both of them at a distance of some two meters, at least until the valley had been reached, the descent was no longer dangerous from that point on.

For years, Father shall say this sentence to me: "You are an empty cross," and neither of us shall know what exactly he means by it, but both of us shall indulge in the memory of the cross hanging in the corner at the Gmundner Hütte, hanging there like some slumbering bat.

Do you remember how we got lost on Traunstein once, I ask Father. The abyss was on our left, Father says. Was it not excessively dangerous, I ask him. It was quite dangerous, Father says, for a man came from behind us, he pushed his way past us, even though there was no space beside us, he walked quite quickly and we clung to him. I don't remember that bit, I say. He slowed his pace so that we might follow him, it was the innkeeper, up top, by the lodges, he scolded me, how could I have dared to walk such a difficult trail, and with a child at that, one who didn't even know how to put one foot in front of the other. I don't remember that bit, I say.

I only remember that Father led me from the Gmundner Hütte to the summit-cross on the Pyramidenkogel, with its bolted cladding of gray metal plates and the four iron cables meant to secure the cross against storms, it is characterized by a certain ugliness, which seems to suggest tanks dismantled and rearranged into the shape of the cross more than it does God. It is ten meters tall and dedicated to the fallen of both world wars, it was inaugurated on August 20, 1950 after the four thousand parts that had been transported up the mountain by 520 men and eighty women over the course of two days had been assembled in a short time, says the plaque attached to the cross. Three thousand people were able to fit onto the summit plateau during the consecration.

Father made the sign of the Cross from a position that allowed him a full view of the cross and the thought came to me that one can only make the sign of the Cross before a cross, but not a crucifix, for, while the cross already bears a body that is Christ, oneself is the very one who takes up the empty space of the cross when one crosses oneself. Perhaps, that's what Father meant when he told the innkeeper not to kneel before a cross because he would thus be kneeling before himself. Then Father demanded that I do the same as he had, but I refused. Then Father took me by the hand and went with me to the very edge of the stone, behold, all of this can be yours, he said, you must simply venture far enough, but Father, I said, there's nothing there, I can see nothing, a couple more steps, Father said, and I took a couple more steps until, in the depths, I saw three horse-drawn barrows upon which men and women were bundled up right next to one another, they were awaiting the continuation of their journey. Who are they? I asked Father. They are being taken out of history, they have been waiting for you, Father said, then shoved me into the depths. As I fell, I saw their red, white, and rose-colored robes, the heads already partially without flesh, their bare legs covered over with boils.

Even now, there must be a thread—an invisible one—at play. I see Father upon a hillock, he's sitting on a bench and looking off into the distance, perhaps, he's also looking into himself, in the deeper distance. Oddly enough, he seems to have our provisions, which I was carrying in a rucksack, he devours one slice of apple after another, he also eats the smoked-and-salted-meat sandwiches with great aplomb, then he opens the thermos flask with the coffee, pours himself one, shuts the flask once more, then sticks it into the rucksack, out of which he also takes a plastic bottle of water, which he unscrews and puts to his mouth. I never gave him the rucksack. It must have been the thread that transferred the provisions over to him. The more he consumes, the younger he looks, if, by the time I get to him, he has exhausted all of our provisions, I shall be the father and he shall be the son. Then I might scold him, I might think up a nice punishment, harass him, but not without showing him that I love him.

He has discovered me. He waves at me and shouts something. I shrug, which he likely won't see. If he's not shouting and waving, he'll continue plundering the provisions. That sets me into motion, I'm practically running, I'm within shouting-range now, "If you're not here soon, I'll have eaten everything," he calls out, I must actually have aged by years, I'm so out of breath, my hands have liver spots they didn't have before, Father looks at me unblinkingly, my boy, how you've aged, he says, he, on the other hand, looks quite youthful, as if years had been subtracted from him. Father leaps up, I ought to be careful and take diligent note of everything, he says, of Grandpa, for the time being, everything's already been said, but the landscape shall now markedly shift, the landscape teaches us to better understand ourselves, looking at the landscape relieves us of the impertinence of uninterrupted presence, which compels the Me to perpetually perceive that I really ought to read *Das Mich der Wahrnehmung—The Me of Perception*—by Martin Silbeweg,* known as Stigma Wir Leben† and only dubbed "Er lebt im Wagnis"‡ by his admirers, after which it would become clear to me that the body is only a secondary effect of perception, that there is a "Me" in the sense that "Me" initially only exists in perception, as a perceiver, though there is not necessarily a substantial "I" that can be aggregated to this "Me" of perception, but Wiesing got one thing wrong, it's perhaps to do with his age, he is too young, and the issue is that one actually can enter into an image if death is standing at the door, one is quite certain of this, just as death enters into the bereaved as an image, this, however, is to the chagrin of many a bereaved individual, for, in them there is no more room for another

---

* Martin Silverway.
† Stigma We're Living.
‡ He lives in risk.

image, and the unburdening contemplation of an image, couldn't that also be the unburdening reading of a book, for, if it's good, is a book not an image put into writing, Father says. How is it, I ask myself, that Father can dwell on such a subject, in his whole life, he's only ever recommended me a single book, Saint Augustine's *Confessions*, which was on the white shelf, hidden behind sliding doors, next to Bosch and *The Magic Mountain*, a red cover similar to *The Magic Mountain*'s, even more beautiful than this one, which goes over more to the orange side of things, Augustine's cover with golden letters, the cover of *The Magic Mountain* also with golden letters and unusually soft, one could easily roll it up, the *Confessions* were pretty much lost on *The Magic Mountain*, the psalmodic seriousness and the many-faceted address to God were ultimately more attractive and, to be sure, that book made a deep impression on me, I still know entire passages from it by heart, "And how shall I call upon my God, my God and Lord, since, when I call for Him, I shall be calling Him to myself? and what room is there within me, whither my God can come into me? whither can God come into me, God who made heaven and earth? is there, indeed, O Lord my God, aught in me that can contain Thee?", "Whither do I call Thee, since I am in Thee? or whence canst Thou enter into me?", "Yet woe to him that speaketh not, since mute are even the most eloquent," "I keep not mute of Thee, the whole of *Schattenfroh* is only of Thee," and as if Father had heard or read my thoughts, as I often suspect him of reading along in my notes, which are nothing but *Schattenfroh*, but also thinking along and writing along, he says, *The Me of Perception* serves to prepare him for death, there is nothing better than going to the Eifel and reading this book, Martin writes about the unburdening function of images, for him, Father, landscape is often the better image and there is no better image than the Eifel, which I am now to paint for him in words without leaving anything out, that would be a fine fate: "to be against, / nothing else but that, and always against," you know that, Father says. Rilke, as if that which one sees opposite is nothing but death when, before this, Rilke also says: "And, near death, does not see death but stares / *beyond* it." As if, with this, he had thought of me, seen me, Father says, this Rilke ends with a farewell-figure that is called Life: "Then who has wheeled us backward, so that we, / no matter the action, always seem to have / the stance of those about to depart? Like someone / on the final hill, which one more time shows him / his entire valley, who turns, pauses, lingers—, / and so we live, constantly saying farewell." That pretty much sums it up, Father says. What I have to say about Rilke interests him—and why I haven't said it yet. Rilke needs only a few lines to make one forget all about novels. You need a novel so as to forget yourself. He means that the child has been wheeled backward, quite early, we compel the child to remember and to see the space of perception as full of things, fabricated and not, I say. Care is a preliminary aftercare. In old age, I became your child, Father says. He can now read Rilke once more without being afraid that, after reading it, he won't take a single step more in his life, for he is always only treading water, indeed, there is a further step to take out of the paradoxical Rilke, he turns us into prisoners standing before an infinite mirror. I ask Father whether we ought to continue on. He continues on. We must merely follow the Catholic Element that is at home in the air and the trees of this region, we're already getting close to Prüm, Father says. And the enumeration of the route, I say. Interests us no longer, Father says.

So, where are my grandparents if their graves have already been dug up, I'd like to know. Is it to one's advantage not to be forgotten and is the soul only the soul when one recalls the body or is one only ever recalling the soul. Father opines that all one ever does is remember the soul, the body is nothing more than sheer imagination. This is what makes film and photography so important—so that later generations are able to imagine. If, however, only a few photographs were to exist, perhaps a handful or just a single one, the consequence would be that the facial expression, posture, and age recorded in them would stand in for this person's whole life. Is there a Ding an sich of the body, is what I'd like to know from my father. No, there isn't, he replies, the body doesn't even really exist during one's own lifetime. I find that illuminating, and it takes away my fear of death. But how can one remember another person's soul? Father suggests that it's a kind of taste in the mouth, a certain smell that hovers before the nose, but without it ever emanating from anything concrete. It is something that is and, at the same time, is not. A spinning point of the imagination, its distance from one never changes no matter how quickly one approaches it. He is certain that Grandpa's soul has entered into him. And in this moment, after this confession, we are no longer alone.

We come to a hillock, still quite far from Prüm, and now find ourselves in the foreground of the painting. We, that is to say a doctor, my father, my mother, a priest, and me as the viewer himself outside of the painting. My father is sitting in a wooden chair, neatly sawed from the choir stalls of the Prüm Abbey, the space underneath the chair is large enough for his house slippers. He would like to have his head examined, something needs to be removed, thus did we engage a doctor in a floor-length robe on our way, he wears an inverted funnel on his head and a wide girdle with a clay jug hanging from its golden clasp: "Meester shnijt die keye ras / Myne name Is lubbert das." Is Lubbertus a mere slip of the tongue? Father *really* didn't mean to say that he was a castrated badger! With his sharp knife, the doctor takes no stones from Father's head, but a flower, a misunderstanding on the part of the doctor, which has its roots in the Middle Dutch word "keye," as it means both stone and flower alike, and that costs my father quite a few *keyen*, after all, money is the key to interpreting the world. Thus does the false image come to the ambiguous text. He has many *keyen* in his pants, is what I heard back home, which means he's "stone-rich," as we say in German—steinreich, stinking rich. The doctor is a true Cerretano, wearing the Nuremberg funnel as a hat upon his head so as to avoid divine influence. My mother seems to long for the same, thus does she have that exceedingly bored look. She puts the flowers down in front of her on the round table in the middle of the landscape and says, "a water lily all the same." The Bible upon her head is a book with a sigil and so it is that the catastrophe is imminent, the lamb is still not in sight. Perhaps, the Bible is also hollow, the jewelry box in which Mother hid something. It has similarities with the box from the shelf and it slowly becomes clear to me that this is the box Father had wrongly imagined to be in his head, but in it is not the little box, which is an empty Bible, it is the words of the Bible and, indeed, not all of them, only the 666. The 666 is the key, Trinity of Impermanence, Father Mother Child. Father has 666 flowers in his head. Is family the fundamental evil of the world, out of which the world of all evils emerges? As in—was Gaddafi right? Yes, a world without families would be consummate, a world devoid of people. 777 and God undoes the tzimtzum.

The white veil that reaches down to her upper arms is perhaps typical for the region, just as is the foot-length cotte and the fold-throwing surcoat, slip-on dress and overdress with train, but it isn't typical for my mother, who I always see in a blue apron picking currants, rhubarb, apples, and quinces in the garden, she made jam and jelly out of them, which caused sweat to run down her face, and she really didn't want to do this at all, the large garden was a burden to her, she boiled the fruit in a large aluminum steam juicer made by the company Schulze, it consisted of a pot that was to be filled with water, a collection-container, and a lid. The collection-container, in which there was a sieve-like fruit basket, had a drain on one side, a red rubber hose with a clamp attached to it. If the clamp was loosened, the juice ran through the hose and into a glass. The foam of the rhubarb jam was the most intense taste-experience of childhood.

Are these the people with whom my parents associate? The clergyman shall wish to comfort my father with wine from our pewter jug after he has lost his reason. The pewter jug is an heirloom from my maternal grandparents, it always stood on the very same dark-stained oak cupboard that my mother brought into the marriage—it still stands there today. However, by the time my father has lost his reason, the clergyman shall have drunk all the wine himself. If, indeed, the blood of Christ has a numbing effect, then the Church would rather keep it for itself. Or pour it into the doctor's clay jug. The doctor and the clergyman, united in quackery.

We see Prüm off in the distance. The path thereto leads past gallows, wheels, and pyres. Everything here is a little bit on the small side. With their tininess, the horse, the cow, the shepherd, and the sheep that we see from the top of the hillock turn the landscape into a poorly executed backdrop painting. No matter how hard I try to scan the horizon, I can only see a round image, as if I were seeing the frame of a telescope through a telescope that shrinks everything. This bourgeois sense of order, which wishes to keep everything in view and has already become second nature, I think, a telescopic frame show, the head its own little peep box and both eyes its twinkling little helpers.

After the operation, Father is not quite well. Mother handed the box over to him because he was so valiant, then, with this box under his arm, Father continues on with me in the direction of Prüm. The expressionless mother strides out of the image. Father had the contents of the box in his head, but no box, Mother had the box, but no content, now both come together. You're old enough to know that now, my father says. It is a key, he says, and it must be kept separate from itself. Father raises his finger toward the top of the gallows, wheel, and pyre, says "Memento mori" and "Christman Gniperdoliga," crosses himself, then says, "the book of books is not the Bible, but *Groperunge from Kerpen, which doth lie two miles awey from Cologne*, his register of the dead, in Trier Diocese, he who thought he could make himself invisible also murdered" and "for nine days more did he live upon the wheel, as he was given strong drinks to drink, whereupon his heart did rejoice in the drink, this Christian Gnipperdinga, Christoff Grippertenius, Christoph Gnippentennig, Christman Gnippertringa, Christman

Grepperunge, Christman Genipperteinga, Christmann Gropperunge, who crushed the necks of six children which he'd had with a woman he held captive, chained up, he ate their hearts, hog-tied them, then, as soon as the wind had touched these innocent children, he said, 'dance, my well-beloved bearn, Gniperdoliga, your father good, makes you to dance with joye, thus must you all be of good chere,' and one knows not what precisely in this is true and what has been invented over time."

We see two churches. Mountains rise up on the outskirts of Prüm. The sun slowly sets behind them. That's hellfire, Father says, I shall hurl the 666 into the hellfire. There is only one church here, Father says, so it must be a reflection, we shall have to make a decision. Mother would like to ski here, he says. We shall meet her at the lodges. The meadows were wallpapered over and are no longer maintained. The little sheep are hardly capable of grazing on them, one must be careful not to kick them to death. Moss has conquered the ground, so-called weeds are spreading everywhere, shepherd's purse, scarlet pimpernel, speedwell, persicaria, hairy crabgrass, old-man-in-the-spring. Father points to a plant and asks for its name. I do not know it. Wild carrot, Father says. What kind of tree is that, he asks. I see no tree, I reply. Over there, back there. I recognize no tree, I say. We only just saw it from above, now it's on our left. And? he asks. I don't know it. It's called a gallows, Father says. And what is the name of the tree to the right of it? Once more, I do not know. A wheel post on which the wheeled are set up and displayed, Father says. People from near and far are lured to the spectacle with broadsheets, as a deterrent, they say, the people often find great savor in this spectacle, the proof of the delectare is in the prodesse. My father is a learned man, when the going gets tough, he prefers to flee into the world of foreign words. But how do they get so twisted on the wheel that one calls them the wheel-broken? he asks. What wheels mean is breaking the bones with a heavy, unused wheel, from, as a rule, the feet upward, which prolongs the agony. For, initially, this method is not intended to kill, but to torment. The condemned is laid onto the

Breche (or "breaking machine"). First, he is bound to pegs in the ground, long crossbars, or a Saint Andrew's Cross. The sharp-edged pieces of wood run crosswise beneath the joints of his outstretched arms and legs. Instead of the crossbars or in combination with them, sharp little pieces of wood—Brecheln—can be used (also dubbed Krippen or Krammen), which one places beneath the joints or into which one clamps the arms and legs. The distance to the ground afforded by the wood makes it easier to break the bones, in which situation a master of the wheel is he who manages not to tear the flesh with the wheel. Beyond this, in order to extract the greatest possible pain-effect, the wheel can also be equipped with an iron ring, sharp triangular pieces of wood, or knives. Sometimes, when the delinquent has committed various crimes, there may be the possibility of aggregate punishment. Thus is his hand first chopped off if he has committed theft, then it might be that he is broken on the wheel should he have done away with somebody, then, finally, he is burned if he has been found guilty of sorcery. Or he shall first be broken on the wheel, then hanged. There are combinations to be found here that afford execution the aspect of an ars combinatoria, an art of punishment-weaving, just as the sonnet is the combinatorial art of rhyming. Execution, an ars magna? What new insights might be gleaned through the slow and agonizing extinction of life remains an open question. If the bones are broken according to fixed rhythms, which is to say fixed blows from behind and in front of the joints, the delinquent can be broken on the wheel quite conveniently. Heads and torso, arms and legs then go over and under the spokes. For this, as a rule, a wheel other than the bone-crushing wheel is used. One variant is the smashing of the limbs of the person being executed right in or on the wheel, on which he is being broken. Here, the breaking of the bones is preferably performed with an iron bar, a method that is particularly beloved in France. Once the martyred one has been artfully placed upon the wheel, the wheel is erected onto a post and the delinquent, dead or alive, is left to the birds—that his "grave" might be scattered far and wide. Like the earliest version of Meals on Wheels, I say, and Father boxes my ears. O perfidy of history—that a big-shot lawyer be named Radbruch, Wheelbreak, he says. When Father discovers a condemned man on the wheel, he says: Let's see what the birds have left of him, then he sets forth upon the road to the place of execution. As we arrive, to our astonishment, we see an incensed crowd, which, having appeared out of nowhere, has been so enraged by something that the wheel-tree, surrounded by the crowd and moving with its swaying like a tuft of grass in a constantly changing wind, threatens to topple over at any moment. It stands at a slight angle, its trunk is crooked, not all branches have been cleanly removed, the wheel-breaking must have been scheduled at short notice and carried out in a great hurry, the martyred one is lying more upon the wheel than he is woven into it, his arms and legs are bound to the wheel's rim, the post stands so crookedly that the condemned man might be nursing the hope of crashing down head-first to the ground along with the wheel, which would almost certainly break his neck, but no, he just lies there on high and must be most terrified of his own thirst and the sun, which shall only succeed in consuming him some days later, the crows are already circling above the place of execution, one hears their cries every now and then, it's going to last for a while longer, they call out, but the wheel-broken man lies there completely mute, not even a whimper can be heard right now, as we get closer, he turns his head and looks over at us. What are you gawking at, he asks once we've managed to approach, the crowd doesn't give a damn about us, didn't even take notice of us, they brought me down to the ground, the man continues to speak, bound me to the wheel and hoisted me up the pole, then one person stated that they'd forgotten to break my bones, to which another replied that there was no more time for that, the birds shall soon take him, if you push the post that hard, it's going to fall over. I'm in favor of that, my father is against it. Who condemned you, he asks. The Church, the man says.

Then you must remain up there, my father says, the Church has higher groundings. But it's doing an injustice to me, the man says. Time will tell, my father says, if you are able to free yourself, nobody shall hinder you. We continue on. A man is hanging from the gallows there, my father says, nobody cares about him, he is already dead. The crowd immediately erects a cross from which a man of indeterminate age hangs. He looks like you, my father says, let's go over to him. My father takes a pair of binoculars out of his suitcase, brings the crucified man into focus, then hands me the binoculars with the words: There's no doubt: that's you. I circle round the cross once, looking up at the man incessantly as I do, I take a few steps backward and observe him in great detail through the binoculars. I can see nobody hanging on the cross, I say. But he's right there in front of you, my father says. But I can't see him through the binoculars. Then turn them around, you're holding them the wrong way. I'm holding them the right way, I say. And what do you see? I see a red-robed, donkey-eared pope, I say. He is seated upon small monster-beasts in a praying position, the thighs at right angles to the erect upper body, the lower legs slightly bent—about a dozen demons in the form of men and beasts surround him in a circle, the tiara with the cross atop it is flying off of his head at this very moment, the pope has his eyes shut. What are you looking at, my father asks, then takes the binoculars from my hands. Where is the pope, he asks. The pope is in the sky, I say. My father scans the sky and stares at one spot, spellbound. I've discovered something different here, he says, there is somebody sliding slowly down a pole, but not voluntarily, not with hands and feet, the pole is sliding right through him. For this practice to be implemented at all, one would have to suspend the world, somebody would have to hurl it up into the air, then gigantic airships would come from every direction and take away the rubble. God himself could then sit in the trashcan and long for a chocolate candy, but his only remaining servant always and only gives him a dry cookie. To his insistence that what he wanted was a chocolate candy, the servant replies to him each day anew: you asshole, what'd you do that for.

As a flock of crows sets itself down upon the condemned man's chest, my father suddenly calls out: Now, I see him, he is the true Prince of Hell, Pope Pius XII!!! Most unequivocally!!! If his papal crown were genuine, my father says, it would undergo no levitation. This pope turned a blind eye at crucial moments, many say. The crows approach the man's head with plodding strides, he is making every effort to shoo them away. Three shackles each on his arms and two on his legs prevent his movements from making any impression on the birds. Look, the crow has one of his eyes in its beak, I say, and the others would like to take it away from him. Once the stake has penetrated into his body by way of his anus, the impaled man can no longer be saved, my father says. Now, he is incessantly turning his head to and fro, I say, he can still do that, and the crows hop from left to right, from right to left, all aflutter. Pius XII. Now, they seem to have joined forces in some common project, some are standing on the left, others on the right. The gut bacteria take the path of the stake to which they adhere, they enter the body and spread all through it, my father says. How did they get the wheel up there? He feared communism his whole life long, just like von Galen. Indeed, that is a tree, albeit a very puny one, and not a stake that one had to erect. Death, therefore, by gut bacteria and thirst. As if somebody had hurled him up there with the wheel until the wheel-hub finally got stuck on the tree stump. How could one even think to beatify this Pius, Father says. There must be a God, I say, otherwise, how could one break somebody on the wheel, impale him, crucify him, I say. I mean, who invented these punishments, I ask my father. It was the Orient, the Ancients, and the Catholic Church, my father says.

He fell silent too soon. But if he hadn't fallen silent, that still wouldn't have prevented the Holocaust. Not that this excuses his silence. A truly never-ending story, even this eleven-volume source work *ADSS* is not yet the final word on the matter, Father says. Both eyes are out, the man is still alive, I say. So, leaving him up there was the right thing to do, my father says.

Do you remember that I always used to climb this tree when I was a child, I ask my father. He doesn't remember me as a child. The only beech for far and wide and, now, the beech is a single torso, a destroyed tree of judgment, I say.

As we continue on, we unexpectedly come upon a field of snow. Father says, the seasons always remain the same here, upon this stretch of land, there is always only winter and there's always snow, if one wished for summer and sun, one would have to head east, just a few meters, then the snow quits, one has to get clear of one's winter mantle quite swiftly, otherwise, one will inevitably fall into a swoon, that's how harshly the sun shines, even if one has just been beset by a blizzard, a short time later, the time it takes to cover the few meters from winter to summer, a heat storm breaks through, and it is fascinating to observe that the boundaries between winter and summer do not shift a single millimeter over the years, there are people who, year in, year out, have made it their task to stand with their left leg in winter and their right leg in summer, to observe the play of light and shadow, and to enjoy this fulfillment ever anew—that their ambivalent personality finds its fullest expression in the unmediated adjacency of summer and winter, the one separated from the other by nothing more than an imaginary boundary. Here, the sun shall never shine, here, the sun shall ever shine; here, the snow shall ever lie, here, the snow shall never lie—and both regions belong to one and the same stretch of land, their longitude and latitude are identical, and this contradiction of nature, that these square meters of landscape are only ever connected with winter and the adjacent square meters of landscape are only ever connected with summer, that is what I am, these people say. The earth stands still here, there are no climatic periods, time stands still. What we are dealing with here, Father says, is epochal transitions, the transition from the Late Middle Ages to the Early Modern Period.

The whole, what with its tremendous attention to detail, is based on graphic search-movements, do I understand what he means by that, Father says. I do not. The search-movement of the pen is the Word that was in the beginning, the Word that God put into the finger with which he touched earth and sky. As far as these landscapes and the scenes that play out in them are concerned, they involved quite a bit of preparatory work, what we see here, Father says, doesn't simply bloom or freeze out of nothing, an initial commission must first be made, preparatory work must be done, do I see what he means. Not at all, I say. Preparatory work, Father says, a so-called clarification phase that shades into an enrichment phase (and he is referring here to a certain Herr Behrendt), which is followed by a composition phase, which, in turn, is followed by a transmission phase, and this—by an execution phase. I don't understand what you're saying in the slightest, I say. With the exception of the execution phase, these are the phases of preparatory work, indeed, just like your so-called novel, which you have always believed that you can write about me, but not with me, but which, should you have forgotten, Father says, you've been writing alone in your cell for years without lifting even a single finger, it befalls you, just like this stroll here also befalls you, for they are one and the same, you sit in your cell, you don't write, even though one calls this writing, and you are not on the path to Prüm with me, your so-called novel has also gone through various preparatory phases, and you still must clarify certain elements, other things serve to enrich your novel, even the composition phase isn't yet over, but you needn't trouble yourself over any of this, it comes to pass on its own, you imagine yourself to be in a permanent execution phase, then the end is at its sudden conclusion, just like life, which we thought to be in an eternal clarification and enrichment phase, comes to a sudden end, that's why we still had the execution phase reserved for later, Father says. And yet, the greatest error is to take everything so seriously. Did I ever imagine that we were living on a 1:10 rehearsal stage, a 1:10 scale-model of the world, which God studies carefully before letting us into the 1:1 world, which is to say: never—for he so loves the human-deserted, tree-covered, animal-rich Wide World that a single look is enough for him to know what is going to befall it by way of the human processes playing out within it. And did I ever imagine that there is a final authoritative edition of our life that is to be found in life. No, I say, I never have. That comes of the fact that you've no imagination, Father says, but the very person who created these landscapes, in which it is always winter or always summer or always spring or always fall demonstrates the percipient imagination necessary to assert the existence of key landscapes; looking into the landscape is the same thing as pictorial invention, the Eifel with its season-defined image-zones is a key landscape, Father says, for generations, it has been inextricably linked with the fates of the people who have lived in it, they are completely absorbed into this landscape when they die, and this is why the Eifel is a landscape of souls such as you won't be able to find anywhere else in the country. If one sets foot in the Eifel, according to Father, one must be aware of coming into contact with souls at all times, and these souls know precisely what one is thinking, they see through the body and have foreknowledge of the very hour of one's death.

If one has no imagination, then one has no language either and, consequently, no body, Father says. From the wheels with which one breaks—or, in Old High German, "mit deme rade brehhan"—would later come "Radebrechen," wheel-breaking: a language mutilated. Wheel-breaking, broken speaking; however, with this turn of phrase, it is not certain whether the language or the speaker is broken.

It is a great dilemma that the only two options are "to name" or "to conceal," Father says. Both seem to prevent injustice, though both might well spur it on. The mere description of breaking on the wheel is violence, my father says. The objectivity of a description mirrors the course of events in such a way that it can be reproduced solely on the basis of this description. With all of its devotion to detail, the exquisitely detailed description honors the breaking on the wheel, also standing in for all other descriptions of comparable procedures as a describable process, thus classifying it in a series of other describable processes, like, for example, mowing the lawn.

There, Father says, then points to a cylindrical building that is probably about a kilometer away from us, located on a mountaintop and visible from afar, a foreign body that has only just landed here.

As I was celebrating my fiftieth year, Father says, you were thirteen years old. Around four years before that, it was resolved that a round frame of cylindrical concrete for the world being created be built. Suit the action to the word. A week before your tenth birthday, a golden hammer bearing the insignia of the state strikes against a hollow stone. In the stone is to be found a water- and airtight time capsule. In the capsule is a letter of resolution that the world emerging here ought to be inhabited under the banner of its immutability, the dead would always be killed, the murderers would always become murderers, those in flight always those in flight, the hanged only ever the hanged, and the redeemed only ever the redeemed. A new old reality is to emerge, sewn together with straight thread, it revolves 123 meters in a circle. Reality shall weigh 1.1 tons. It requires some twelve years for its formation. The new world shall contain about 850 square meters of space. It shall be monumentally stable and have a height of some fourteen meters. A building with a diameter of just barely forty-four meters shall provide enough space for it.

What a fuss they made here about this thing, Father says, right up to and including death threats. Elephant toilet, the people said, the elephant toilet would swallow up far more important, urgently needed building projects, social measures, and infrastructural improvements. Even so, the elephant toilet was the best thing that could have happened to the region, Father says. Now, Prüm doesn't just have a crooked church, but also a connection to the heavens that the abbey can only dream of. The building, if one can speak of a building here, has no roof, yet not a single raindrop has made contact with its floor. One sees things in this circular building that one can't see anywhere else, here, the distinction between inner and outer belongs to a primitive stage in the development of human existence, Father says. The particular achievement of the structure is its foundation-laying against all odds, the geological conditions ought to have led to the rational decision to abandon the project. To be precise, the massif of the mountain consists of the gypsum of the Upper Permian, "colorful clay" was deposited onto the rounded mountaintop, these being erosion-remnants, as he was recently able to determine from the journal *Bauplanung – Bautechnik*, in which a certain Müller, first name forgotten, describes the construction history of the building in great detail, in such detail that he, Father, thought about the construction of a new administrative building, for he is in charge of it, he wants to transform it into a panoramic building, which he can watch over every corner of from the center without himself being seen, all this in order to have better access to his employees. This reflection has not yet come to an end. Thus even now is Father thinking about administration, control, and execution, even if, as is generally known, he is no longer in office. For those who have been in office a whole life long, not being in office is the worst state of affairs, they mistakenly imagine that they are everywhere being treated below the threshold of respect they have come to deserve, an emotional response that can be triggered by as little as their interlocutor breathing wrong, no more than a second is permitted to elapse between recognition and greeting, non-recognition, according to the dream of these pensioners, results in the deprivation of civil rights, and thus is my father's going through the town center no *going*, but a mobile inspection of delegations, for there can be no doubt that the citizens at the weekly market are delegations with orders he's given them. The colorful clay, as Father puts it, is badly weathered, which has the constant risk of erosion as consequence. According to Müller, the gypsum layer is underlaid with bituminous limestone, called "stinking slate" or "stinking schist" because it is a limestone that reeks of bitumen. The gypsum itself has changed over the centuries, here and there, it is exhausted, karstified, so to speak. Pockets of karst and sand pipes made the terrain practically unsoundable, where they were found, these sinkholes, some several meters deep, had to be excavated and filled in with concrete. The language of geology is true poetry, Father says, I have so much to learn from it, it is always so resourceful and creates sculptures that can compete with fine art. A richness in visualizations simultaneously combined with the greatest possible intrinsic value of language, Father says, then looks at me with a sense of expectation. Yes, I say. If I were interested, he could quote a passage from the Müller to me verbatim, he studied it for such a long time that it burned itself into his memory. I ought to exploit it just as I've exploited him, fit it into my dull text so that the text might have a few more sinkholes, sand pipes, and a bit more colorful clay. I don't say no and don't say yes, we approach the building with nimble stride, Father getting less out of breath from the steepening gradient than I do. Father suggests an experiment, a word that does not otherwise appear in his vocabulary. The experiment consists in having the aforementioned passage inscribe itself into *Schattenfroh* at the same time as Father goes through it in his memory. I assent, knowing full well that I cannot verify the simultaneity claimed by Father, I don't have *Schattenfroh* to hand. Father moves ahead of me with long, sweeping steps, he is performing a kind of military goose-step, he is highly concentrated on a distant point, the circular building, it has now become impossible for me to reach him with words as I attempt to follow him, I conceive of the intention to check *Schattenfroh* for the appearance of the Müller passage that Father is calling forth from his memory, I expressly note it down, I shall do it as soon as I set eyes upon the book, which, for the moment, is something

I cannot manage, I can only read that, for the moment, I cannot manage, then, consequently, I do not manage. Father always asks: "Do you have it?" I say: "No," but I keep silent about the fact that I don't have *Schattenfroh* before me. Then he asks again: "Do you have it?" Again, I say: "No." Perhaps, you don't remember quite well enough, I say. But you do remember the air raids on Prüm, December 23, 1944, between 4:00 p.m. and 6:00 p.m., four waves of bombers, everything on fire, the abbey building, the vicarage, the hospital, Neuerburg reduced to rubble and ashes on that very same day, even the fire brigade from Bitburg had to move in, which they might not have done had they had foreknowledge of the major attack on Bitburg that would come to pass the next day. After the attacks, Prüm didn't look as if it'd been subjected to a loosening blasting:

> Special measures were required for the foundation-laying of the structure due to the difficult ground conditions. The geological corings indicate that the Schlachtberg massif consists of gypsum from the Upper Permian. On the top of the Schlachtberg, the gypsum is overlaid by thin erosion-remnants from the uppermost layers of the Upper Permian, the so-called colorful potter's clay, which is strongly weathered. The gypsum layer is underlaid by stinking schist, a thin, platy, bituminous-smelling dolomitic limestone, which separates the upper gypsum from the underlying fourth layer, the lower gypsum, in a constant thickness of a few meters. Starting from crevices and fissures, the gypsum is karstified in geological time. As a result, karst cavities of various sizes have been formed in the gypsum, as evidenced by the Barbaros Cave. Depending on the specific local geomechanical conditions, these cavities break open to the surface and appear there as sinkholes. As a result of weathering and karstification, the gypsum is not continuously present as

rock at the surface. Unweathered and gypsum blocks alternate irregularly with karst pockets and so-called sand pipes, which are filled up to several meters depth with the residues left behind by the leaching process. In varying subsoil conditions, this results in a confined space in the form of explosive rock and clayey loose rock with a high susceptibility to settlement. Therefore, the structure had to be designed to bridge possible sinkholes of up to 3.0 m in diameter. Furthermore, a geological survey was required after the excavation, whereby karst pockets encountered were excavated separately and backfilled with concrete. The subgrade for the foundation was produced after a loosening blasting with the help of a heavy bulldozer."

You have to concentrate now, Father says. He sees the passage before him, he says, and, until I see the passage light up in me, we shall not reach the building, and if we do not reach the building, those present shall wait in vain, and if they wait in vain, Grandpa shall be forgotten, and if Grandpa is forgotten, Mateo shall think up a nice punishment for me, it will consist in painting a battle-panorama of the upheaval with my own blood, which will not run dry for the whole duration of the work and will flow painfully from my fingers, then onto brush and roller, onto a canvas of some 125 meters long and fifty meters high, in a tense of empty transcendence into which a dose of God shall be shot at irregular intervals, in a tense of the omnipresence of the entire past and the unforeseeable erasure of the present, which, yes, is a blind spot; in a tense that always speaks of the present, but that knows not the present tense, and, indeed, God knows that the present tense isn't merely a verb form, the present tense has as much to do with the present as the past tense has to do with the past, which is to say *nothing*; a battle-panorama that shall bear the title *Schattenfroh* and that I, as soon as I have finished it over the course of seven years, a term that includes all preparatory work, shall have to start all over again, for it represents that which befalls it, the panorama, the disappearance that comes to pass simultaneously in several places; in the central image-zone, which cannot disavow its allegorical horizon, Pilate appears in a black robe and a black hat, he dips his hands into a metal basin surrounded by fish-demons and washes them of responsibility, his face averted, meanwhile, the demons practice their biting, a jester grotesquely contorting himself in dance and staring at us unabashedly, with red shoes, yellow pants, a gray-black pleated skirt, and a red jerkin fastened with a thread, a much-too-large white collar peeks forth from it, it causes the bell-equipped jester's hat to appear as a bishop's miter, he is pointing to the handwashing scene with the index finger of his right hand, which brings a mocking, but also self-satisfied grin to his face, he accompanies himself with his left hand on the lute while Christ, a few strides north, over Justitia balanced upon the globe, struggling to hold her posture, baring her right leg, the transparent stocking, or is it a shoe, between knee and ankle, the sword in her right hand, the beam scales in her left, as seen from our perspective, the empty right pan tilts downward, despite the fact that the left pan is weighed down with gold coins, she ought to hide her private parts, otherwise one might peek between her legs, the gold coins were thrown onto the scale for this view and much more, flies toward us backward, his head stretched back very far that so he might see us, sword and lily, which were stuck into his ears both right and left, these are wrath and mercy, with them has he judged, now do they judge him, along with his arms stretched out to the sides, his tense torso, and his legs lying parallel to the trunk, they form the cross, his feet are pierced by nails and look to have been destroyed by gout, this Christ as an outlawed outlaw who no longer needs a cross in order to be crucified, he himself is the cross, he flies toward us, then disintegrates at the very moment when Pilate sticks his arms into the water up to the elbows, Pilate with his averted gaze has become the figure of our times, he shows the historical as makeable by men who literally have it in their hands, but then dips this hand away after having dipped his tongue deep into a gullet, Father adds that this is an insufficient return to the things themselves, or, as Geheimrat Irgend,* an actual Nobody, highlighted in his basic figure of das Man, the public sphere that obfuscates everything by making itself immune to every sort of difference, Christ, however, is the exception, he is still perpetually being sacrificed to mediocrity, all so that, in the future, mediocrity might be able to level all that calls das Man into question and Father claims that it is a serious error to open up the Legend of Christ to all so that anyone might be able to refer to it, Christ must remain an affair of the elites, an insider tip, so to speak, otherwise, he becomes a shabby article, like in one of these junk shops sprouting up everywhere, but especially in the small Voreifel towns of the Rhineland, nothing in the public sphere represents das Man more aptly than those, if, indeed, das Man has already shown its true colors, it has already slipped away in das Man's self-referral to das Man, that surely isn't the case, Father says, indeed, it isn't das Man at all, there is no das Man, it did not disappear without a trace, if it was meant to show its true colors, it would never have been present-to-hand, but it is still not nothing, and that is the true miracle upon which the world is based, if, indeed, as Geheimrat Irgend said, having redubbed himself Geheimrat Dinger† after his rehabilitation, everyone is the other and no one is himself; such disintegrations in the panorama, which shall occupy me completely, as if they were coming to pass according to the motto *We need that today, we don't need that today* are to be observed everywhere, and everything becomes image, image in image, image that is exhausted in interpretative disquisition, and, indeed, understanding is the most dangerous thing, for it makes one blind and dumb, makes the things one understands equal to all, and not seeing oneself,

---

* Privycouncillor Any.
† Privycouncillor Things.

who, in the act of understanding, has become a bit more like *das Man* again, what matters is that things remain opaque, Father says, I say, Father, that's all very interesting, but I simply can't follow any more and nor do I wish to, then Father replies, but that's the way, there is no other, all you can do is stand there and let your feet waste away, you shall find no way back, these thoughts are the way to Prüm, Father says, briefly giving the impression of wanting to hit me, his right hand then takes refuge in his hair, which he pushes back for lack of a comb when he notices that I am watching him very closely as he does, there are men, he says, who push their hair back, even if they don't have hair anymore, he is immediately embarrassed by this utterance and gesture, which spurs his hand on to brush his hair back even more wildly, a tuft of hair comes free, Father opens his hand, his hair is flying away very supplely, the fur of a white rat, upon his brow is now written "Pick's disease," his head makes the pecking motion of a chicken that is too tired to look for feed in the broader area and thus does it limit the search to precisely where it is, knowing full well that there is nothing more to be found there, I rub the water from my eyes, nothing is written upon his brow, Father combs his hair, checks the comb, buffalo horn, he's not lost a single hair, you, on the other hand, shall go bald, he says, the comb vanishes into his back pocket, out of which he then takes it once more before stowing it in the side pocket of his jacket, it's Grandpa's comb, he says, Father elongates and stretches out, he tells me to do twenty push-ups, then I'll feel better, at the seventh push-up, Father puts the Bible onto my back, I cannot support its weight, then, as soon as I'm lying on the ground, my hands and feet are bound, I'm now wearing grayish-white spatterdashes, so-called drawstring shoes tied with a bow at the heel, I'm more ashamed of them than of the Bible on my back, I am wearing a whitish-gray one-piece suit that goes down to my knees, then terracotta-colored socks down from my knees to my spatterdashes, it's only with great effort that I manage to kneel down and support myself in front with my forearms, the Bible is pressing into the hollow of my back, I have no choice but to remain in this bench-like position, even as Father incessantly calls out, "Do push-ups! Do push-ups!", he kneels to my right at the level of my buttocks, then cries out "Keep the small of your back straight!" which I manage to do once, a second time, a third time, no fourth time, Father frees his right arm from a sling, he banged his elbow against a heating pipe in the basement some thirty years ago, whereupon it swelled to the circumference of the heating pipe and over the years, as he said, caused him various issues, the arm became independent from time to time, simply came free from the body, the hand would sign documents that, in retrospect, Father would deny having seen, he hits my buttocks with the flat of his hand, which seems to cause him greater pain than it does me, I turn to him, he slaps my face with his hand, I can still see how he loosens the bullwhip that he had attached to his belt, then the blows rain down nice and clean onto my back, partly protected by the Bible, but also, further down, onto my shoulders, buttocks, and legs, Father opens up the Bible and sings:

"Blessed is the man that walketh not in the counsel of the ungodly, nor standeth in the way of sinners, nor sitteth in the seat of the scornful.

But his delight is in the law of the Lord; and in his law doth he meditate day and night.

And he shall be like a tree planted by the rivers of water, that bringeth forth his fruit in his season; his leaf also shall not wither; and whatsoever he doeth shall prosper.

The ungodly are not so: but are like the chaff which the wind driveth away.

Therefore the ungodly shall not stand in the judgment, nor sinners in the congregation of the righteous.

For the Lord knoweth the way of the righteous: but the way of the ungodly shall perish."

I can feel his arm trembling, he would really like to hit me in the head, but that's not the old-school way of doing things, yet he still does it, I immediately feel a kind of paralysis, my hearing also seems to have suffered, Father has grown tired of the bullwhip, he again prefers the flat of his hand, then, turning my head toward him, I see that his arm wasn't in a sling at all, his pants are held up with suspenders, into which he briefly inserted his right arm, perhaps he wanted to see whether the button-fastened elastic trouser-hoist would confer a catapult-like motion unto his hand, but then he would have to aim in precisely the opposite direction, for him, the suspenders served much more as a moral buffer intended to reduce the strength of the blow to a manageable level, he has ocher- to gold-colored scraps of cloth wrapped around his forearm and wears a flat women's hat on his head. "Stand up," he says when he sees me lying there, "you were just like that when you were a little kid, you'd take advantage of every opportunity to fall down." The scraps of cloth are from the gauntlets that he wears over his forearms, they must have gotten caught on a fence or a branch, I stand up, the Bible has vanished without a trace, Father and I are suddenly dressed quite normally, my body cannot complain of any pains, thus might I fall into other times or go to the ground before them. Father's shirt-fabric is very thin, his shirts are always ironed, their creases lose nothing of their obtrusiveness, not even after hours of being worn, he's always attached great importance to that, the material is so thin that I can see his skin, I want to touch Father, but I just reach right through him, he does that well, he can really do that, I think, he doesn't want to be touched and certainly not embraced, I withdraw my hand in such a way that it is stuck to the middle of his arm, no blood, no crying out, Father's arm encloses my hand, I pull it out, a black rose is attached at the level of the ribcage, Father has set himself into motion once more and thus does he claim that, over the years, the envisioned panorama transforms into a palimpsest that causes all times to interlock, in each figure is contained another figure, which, in its turn, contains another figure, and so on, and these figures, around three thousand in number, bring their time with them, which, presumably, is seeking to set itself above another time, which has already set itself above another time, in such a way that it might come to pass that a strongly contoured past, in the alleged background, pierces through the present, the divine ars combinatoria has superimposed the various circles in such a way that each segment of a circle could also overlap with all the segments of the other circles, and all circles and all segments penetrate the other circles and segments, but also have the ability to erase, this erasure, however, only lasts until the circles have combinatorially shifted once more, then that which has been deleted is reactivated, which shows nothing other than the "consummate fullness of the onemanyness of God," just as history is nothing other than God's index.

One might dub this principle "creative destruction," Father says. One can be certain that the same thing shall not eternally return, after all, God doesn't wish to grow bored, Father laughs. No, he couldn't have meant all that seriously. I observe his face, a strange human formation, which is true of faces in general, but more so of Father's face, the beast-like quality of the face alone could well convince people not to rise above the earth, shall it not change anymore, the face?, has nature ceased all operations as far as the face is concerned?, if the face were left out, all people would be equal.

While Father forces me to bear in mind the consequences of the impending disturbance with the reception, which go far beyond a mere family story, and we approach the building set upon karst-cavities with unbroken stride, the source text invoked by Father rises forth from the deep founts of the Eifel, however, it isn't just the passage about the geological conditions of the building site that appears to me now, it is the entire text, which offers such exhaustive information about the foundation-laying, base story, cylindrical-shell-perimeter-supporting structure, and cantilever shell structure, including documents like architectural drawings and photographs showing the stages of construction planning and execution, as well as the means afforded by construction technology. The photographs provide information about the assembly of the base story, the assembly bracing of the outer-wall elements, as well as their assembly, and the soffit of the under-spanned shell roof and its spoke-wheel hub, which together form the aforementioned underroof. Now, I've got it, I say to Father, this is the anticipation of the architecture, its assembly, and the charm of our prefabricated garages of reinforced concrete, with this rotund form, the peak of structural beauty had already been reached:

> Für die Gründung des Bauwerkes waren infolge der schwierigen Baugrundverhältnisse besondere Maßnahmen erforderlich. Die geologischen Verhältnisse besagen, daß das Schlachtbergmassiv aus Gips des Zechsteins besteht. Auf der Kuppe des Schlachtberges lagern dem Gips geringmächtige Erosionsreste der obersten Schichten des Zechsteins, sogenannte bunte Letten, auf, die stark verwittert sind. Die Gipsschicht ist von Stinkschiefer unterlagert, einem dünnen, plattigen, beim Anschlagen bituminös riechenden, dolomitischen Kalkstein, der in gleichbleibender Mächtigkeit von wenigen Metern den oberen Gips von der darunterliegenden vierten Schicht, dem unteren Gips, trennt.
>
> Von Spalten und Klüften ausgehend, ist der Gips in geologischen Zeiträumen ausgelaugt (verkarstet). Dadurch sind im Gips, wie es die Barbarossahöhle beweist, Karsthohlräume unterschiedlicher Größe entstanden. Je nach den speziellen örtlichen geomechanischen Bedingungen brechen diese zur Oberfläche auf und treten dort als Erdfall in Erscheinung. Infolge der Verwitterung und Verkarstung liegt der Gips an der Oberfläche nicht durchgängig als Felsgestein vor. Es wechseln noch unverwitterte feste Gipsblöcke unregelmäßig mit Karsttaschen und sogenannten geologischen Orgeln, die bis zu mehreren Metern Tiefe mit den bei der Auslaugung zurückgebliebenen Rückständen gefüllt sind. Hieraus ergeben sich innerhalb weniger Meter Entfernung wechselnde Baugrundverhältnisse in Form von Sprengfels und tonigem Lockergestein mit hoher Setzungsempfindlichkeit. Das Bauwerk war daher so zu bemessen, daß mögliche Erdfälle bis zu 3,0 m Durchmesser überbrückt werden. Des weiteren war nach Herstellung der Baugrube eine geologische Aufnahme erforderlich, wobei angetroffene Karsttaschen gesondert ausgehoben und mit Beton verfüllt wurden. Das Planum für die Gründung ist nach einer Lockerungssprengung mit Hilfe einer schweren Planierraupe hergestellt worden.

That's how it is with fathers, they fervently hope that their children shall one day share their interests, then, as soon as the child has taken the bait, even if it's under a slight compulsion, fathers fail to show their children that they are happy about this, they themselves lose interest in the matter once the interest has passed over to the child, they also have no further will to communicate information about their previous interest to the children should they have questions, some fathers go so far as to accuse their children of having stolen their interest from them, in any case, Father doesn't acknowledge the fact that a transfer has taken place between us and that, now, I can even call up the building and construction report in its entirety with just a single comment. Instead of expressing joy and recognition, a mocking line forms around his crookedly hanging mouth, it's as if his nervus facialis has been paralyzed at this very moment. This is how my face jokes around, Father says, as if he felt himself compelled to justify his out-of-control facial expressions, but he doesn't justify his behavior, as, for him, this is his untouchable personality's only natural expression.

    Five different paths lead to the building. Father is a master of the art of always choosing the most direct. A meeting place surrounded by green, he says, and, it's true, the building stands within a large green space surrounded by trees. One can only reach the pavilion by way of a low rectangular building in front of it, Father says, one crosses this single-story entrance building with its connecting structure widthwise, then, by way of a staircase, one comes into a basement that leads into the pavilion. But he can no longer remember all that so precisely, his last visit lies a few years back. The concept "Basement" makes me feel uncomfortable. Boiler room. Even the forecourt of the entrance building, decorated with a fountain in the shape of a square basin that rises to a meter above the ground so as to compensate for the incline as the distance from the entrance building increases, appears exaggerated in its dimensions, about three hundred square concrete slabs lead onto a wide four-step staircase, the uppermost step of the staircase extends to the top landing and, a few steps away, a glass front of twenty-six segments, divided into thirteen two-thirds and thirteen one-third units, this likely serves the architectural function of simulating skylights. The entire white- to eggshell-colored front of the building is subdivided by sixteen sandstone columns, which seem to have been relieved of their task of supporting the roof and are thus statically superfluous as far as the roof is concerned, though there is no doubt they are meant to recall representational buildings with their elaborately decorated portals and the porticos before them. The aisle was taken away from the portico by placing it directly in front of the building façade with its columns and windows, the entrance building overhangs it by about one meter, thus does it both belong to the building and not. The flat roof rests on the sides of the building and on the front of the building, which is covered by the portico down to the last meter and shares with it all the openings for the windows and the glass front of the entrance area. The rear-set entrance area with the glass front causes the portico set in front of the building and the front of the building covered by it to be equally permeable. A view from the side reveals that the columns of the double frontage, decoupled as a portico quotation, penetrate the building frontage except for the two outer ones, thus still fulfilling their ancient task of supporting the roof, even if it isn't clear to the naked eye to what extent even this supporting function represents a mere quotation. Two of the columns, extending to form walls up to the glass front, enclose the upper staircase plateau on the left and right, prefabricated concrete elements are suspended between the columns, thus are the columns not merely *antiquating ornaments* that interrupt the tiresome uniformity, also meant to distract from the poverty of the building material, the point-symmetrical rotation of the windows and concrete front elements to the left and right of the entrance area, with which the symmetry of the portico front is broken, already provide a pleasant irritant: If the windows are located in the lower third on the left side, they are in the upper third on the right half; the same applies to the concrete elements. And here is yet another element that quotes ancient architecture: the impression of light flooding the building is to be achieved by the fact that gray slabs, as shadows cast by the columns, parcel the forecourt out into long alignments. I imagine hundreds of people packed right up against one another gathering within the three channels that lead toward the entrance and demanding to be let in, which is then eloquently denied to them, the people's waiting turns into a fossilized state, the people become their own sculptures, not all of which, however, my father or Schattenfroh find to be usable, the great sorting begins, then, finally, only four sculptures remain in the forecourt, as far as perspective is concerned, this space transforms so much that I fear I am suffering from visual disturbances or that my left and right eyes are competing for dominant vision, so disparate are the perceptions that can no longer be conceived of as one. Of the selected sculptures, all without exception are men, two men in conversation and a girl driving a hoop across the square with a stick are added, all frozen in their movements. One sculpture, to the right of the staircase, two meters from one of the columns that make up the wall, with its socle covering the beginning of the gray stone shadow, is performing a bow that exists somewhere between submission and mischief, its legs are crossed, the left in front of the right, it's standing upon the outer edges of its feet, it is wearing pants, its upper body bare, the arms stretched out to the front as if they were being hurled away, the left hand turned outward, if the legs weren't positioned thusly, one might think that the figure was practicing a head-first dive into the water; the second figure, also in pants and with a bare torso, stands a few meters off with its head stretched backward, the arms are at the sides of its erect body, the hands with the palms turned outward, an exalted posture, but, simultaneously, the corporeal expression allows for this interpretation, there is something imploring in its gaze toward the heavens; the third figure lies upon a stone plinth with drawn-up legs; I do not see the fourth figure.

Why are you bothering yourself with that, Father asks. I'm preparing for what's to come, the counting-up-and-down calms me, I say. But you really don't know what's coming, Father says. Should it become strenuous or should it not please me for other reasons, I can repeat the numbers and do calculations, I say. There's nothing to calculate, you ought to listen and write down what's said, Father says. Thus do we pass our time and we're now standing before the entrance. Some people are having a private event tonight, says a roughly 54-year-old man in a black suit and white shirt, he is broad-shouldered, has one of those fashionably narrow beards on his face, it fits his uniform just as much as his hair, always shortened with a buzzer to a length of four millimeters on the sides, shaved sides signal determination and danger. We belong to their society, my father replies in a submissive tone. 54 prefabricated cylindrical concrete shells, the man says, not giving the impression of wanting to open the door for us, a glass door as part of an ensemble of 26 glass segments in which the surrounding landscape is reflected, the contours of mighty deciduous trees generate the impression that the glass has jagged cracks or cambers out, and these cracks in the glass and the cambers distort whatever is caught in the glass in the most beautiful way, I cannot tear myself away from the sight of all these bent figures, armor, hanged men, and celestial apparitions. The bronze sculpture manages something you shall never be able to do, Father says, it bears itself. I turn around and look toward the middle of the forecourt, toward a socle made up of two elements, a flatter square on top of which a smaller, taller square lies in its middle, both of the same stone as the four-step staircase, the socle, in its turn, is in the middle of a surface made up of six blocks by six, which stand out from the rest of the concrete slabs in the forecourt by way of their darker tone, tending toward champagne or yellow-gray, and to which six spotlights are attached. Does art have to be illuminated at night? I ask Father. If it's art, it can be illuminated at night, Father says. So, is this art, I ask Father. I'm not interested in whether or not it's art, Father says, it interests me that you'll never be able to do what's shown there. I don't want to take this lying down, so, this time, I look at the sculpture from as close as can be. A figure bent forward, a young man, naked, he is shouldering a naked young man—himself, apparently. The shouldered man, his right arm between his drawn-up legs, his hand making contact with his right foot, which he has placed crosswise upon the front third of his left foot, lies, or so it seems, with great ease upon himself, the standing man, his head, turned to the left, bending down toward his left shoulder, slightly sloped due to his forward-bent posture, the two life-sized figures seem to achieve a balanced equipoise by the fact that the left side of the reclining figure, which extends from the head to the buttocks, and the upper left section of the standing figure's back, upon which the lying figure is lying, neutralize one another, also securing themselves with their down-hanging arms as they do, their hands diffidently intertwined. Is it thus that they make the necessary contact, which enables their mutual perception, for they cannot look at one another in this position. Any word that they might exchange would upset the balance, if the burden that he himself is were to fall away from the standing one, life itself would also fall away from him. But how is the standing figure able to look ahead in this position? How can he continually pass through life in an upright position? The lying figure is carried through life by the fact that he himself carries himself. Thus is the lying figure liberated of his own burden, he is the one who it boils down to. But who wants to be like this? Which is to say, both together are him, me. And I don't want to be like that. But you aren't like that, Father says. You're a mere half that seeks to bear itself. So, a flibbertigibbet, I say. My father likes *flibbertigibbet*, he says the word to himself a dozen times, then he turns to the admissions controller, who introduces himself as Müller, Herbert Müller, they call me Shell, Herbert Müller says, the name sounds familiar, Father says and offers Herbert Müller his hand, the latter, however, does not accept his salutation, but draws in a deep breath, then points left and right, up and down, front and back, left and down, right and front, back and up, stretching his arms out wide in accordance with the directions, then pauses briefly and points with his right hand to the left, under to over, back to forward, and says that the circular building has an outer diameter of roughly forty-four meters and a height of about twenty-eight meters, as if this fact in particular regarding the building were of the greatest importance. Laying of the foundation stone on May 8, 1974, completion the following year, Herbert Müller says. What does that mean. There seem to be buildings whose admission controllers do not let visitors in until they have recounted the whole history of how it came to be. I can hardly wait to speak of the reinforced concrete beams on the outer circle and in the inner ring, says Mr. Müller, without this, no comprehension of the building is possible, especially not the question, "How is this possible?" We nod. Herr Müller reports:

"The reinforced concrete supports on the outer circle absorb the vertical and horizontal forces of the structure. They have varying cross-sections of 0.6m×1.2m and 0.6m×1.6m and are clamped into the radial beams of the grillage foundation like sleeves. The eight reinforced concrete columns in the inner ring absorb the proportionate loads of the wide-spanning ceiling construction and are also clamped into the foundations of the inner girder grid like sleeves. The trough-shaped circular ring support bar made of reinforced concrete above the exterior beams is formed by twenty-seven trough-shaped elements that are 1.55 m wide, 1.65 m high and 5.074 m long. The wall thickness of the trough is 250 mm, the element mass is 13.0 tons."

One must really imagine this in concrete terms, Herr Müller says. Please, do that now, he urges us. We close our eyes and there is an immediate swarming of reinforced concrete beams and radial beams, an enormous foundation grid passes by our inner eye and all of this is on the verge of connecting with itself at the very moment when Herr

Müller continues his lecture; out of the fear that the reinforced concrete beams that I have just clamped to the radial beams of the grillage foundation like sleeves might slip out of my grasp and fall deep within me, I only follow distractedly:

"The trough-shap%d elements have recesses on the inner side frame for mounting the clamping ceiling beams. To connect the u-og-shaped elements to the supports, there are recesses in the horizontal base plate into which the steel doUs of the reinforced concrete support stilts grip. The connection of the individual elements over the stilts requires special attention. To absorb the bending moments in the vertical plane as well as the twisting moments, there are protruding steel loops on the front sides of the walls, which are linked by steel rings in double shear. To absorb the horizontal shearing forces, vertical round steel bars are passed through the loop connection. Before straining the h-og-shapedo. the joints had to be concreted. After making the frictional connection and embiadong the ceiling consteukaeon over the. Ba5estore§ could be initiated with the leaf assembly. The ring underbeam over the central inner socket consists of 8 single elements. A continuous effect over the stilts was not intended. The connection between them therefore consists of a simple contact looppoop. To create this effect, steel dowels protrude from the towns."

Herr Müller would like to know whether I am following. I am following most conscientiously, I say, and, having been challenged to offer him proof, I speak the next section after him, just as he can read it inside of me: "The ceiling construction consists of fifty reinforced concrete beams that are laid radially and 192 trapezoidal ceiling panels stretching tangentially in four latitudinal circles. A T-beam effect is achieved by connecting the reinforced concrete slabs to the ceiling beams with U-shaped reinforcements and filling the joints with concrete. The ceiling construction acts as a disc when transferring the horizontal external forces to the support construction, which in this way has a building-stabilizing character. As a result of the plate effect, the vertical forces from dead weight and payload are transferred to the inner and outer ring construction. The ceiling beams have a total length of 17.6 m. They are 300 mm wide and 750 mm high in cross-section. The assembly mass is 9.5 tons. The elements transfer their load to the outer trough-shaped enclosing ring and the central inner ring. The free span in the field is 16.04 km and the cantilever arm on the inner ring is 958 mm long." Nothing in Herr Müller's face indicates that he is surprised by my knowledge, on the contrary, he takes this as an occasion to treat me like a trainee who must undergo a rigorous examination, which my father comprehends as a favorable opportunity to ingratiate himself with Herr Müller in a way that might get us closer to our goal, he smiles at Herr Müller for so long that, though he certainly has a hard time interpreting this gesture, Herr Müller reciprocates his friendliness, then Father steps off to the side in such a way that we form a triangle and each can observe the other, for is the triangle not the symbol of fear, the third party—so thinks each of the three—always has a preeminence that the other assigns to him, the other always prefers the third, that is the fear and nobody shall speak of this fear, all three keep silent about it, and weren't arcades invented as a remedy against the triangle, with the swing of their round arches, they divert all narrowness and hopelessness and lead them back down to earth, the arcade that, if only for a few moments, causes one to forget oneself and makes one cheerful. "What was deemed necessary for the outer ring to avoid impermissibly high fixed ends?" Herr Müller asks and Father looks at me expectantly. "Resilient supports were created through the insertion of a 20 mm thick rubber plate," I reply. Herr Müller looks at me for a long time, then, in the tone of a TV host, he says, "The reply is correct. Next question: What is simultaneously reduced by this?" "This simultaneously reduces high edge-loadings," I reply. "This answer is also correct," Herr Müller says, my father takes a deep breath, I've not seen him so happy in a long time. "Third question," Herr Müller says, "how was the center inner ring dealt with?" "Precisely in the same way," I say, "as with the outer ring, 20 mm thick rubber support plates were used." "Very good," Herr Müller says, now he really doesn't want to quit asking the questions. Father looks a bit indignant, as if he were ashamed of his previous pandering. "How are the ceiling beams calculated?" Herr Müller would like to know. All I have to do is read the answer, I look at Herr Müller through the text in my inwardness, his eyes are beginning to flicker in anticipation of my failure, they do not, however, take actual note of a correct answer missing, Herr Müller is only playing with the fear that he supposedly causes me, his greatest fear is actually that the correct answer might fail to materialize, he would rather turn to dust, whimpering and hurling new bits and pieces of the correct answer to me, in that case, he'd finally be forced to give me hints, keywords, full sentences and, in doing so, pretend that they'd come out of my mouth, he would continually turn to my father with a reassuring aspect, my father would have been standing behind him with an ashamed expression for a long time, what a splendid boy I am, so clever and well-behaved, is what Herr Müller would say, I'm going to push it to the limit now, I resolve, I wait with my answer until they can no longer contain their impatience, now, they're in my hands as they don't expect me to fail to give an answer. Herr Müller only has power if I can answer his questions. He's losing sovereignty by the second, he's on the point of threatening sanctions, Father changes his footing incessantly. If I were to just leave, the triangle would remain, the two would always have to fill the gap my absence leaves behind with their fear, which would take my place, I would leave the two of them with the unanswered question that would trigger in them a lifelong dependency on one another. Father would have to transfigure the lack of an answer into a promise, Herr Müller wouldn't be able to show any weakness for the time being, and he would lengthen this For-The-Time-Being out day by day, the waiting would be collective, full of privation, a sleep too long and too deep would be refused so as not to miss my return, but I would have gone away, not without telling the two aging men that I am to be crucified on the day of my return, only the crucifixion would put everything terrestrial behind me and finally bring me to God, but I would first tell the two aging men that Father and Schattenfroh are unbearable placeholders, they ought to have the cross and everything else that is necessary at the ready, I shall direct them to the place where the crucifixion is to be carried out, then I shall return and they shall crucify me. I imagine the pain the nail causes when it is beat through the wrist between the ulna and the radius, for I do not wish to be bound to the crucifix with ropes—but Herr Müller raises his voice and destroys the spun webs of my fantasy. "The ceiling beams are calculated in such a way that, when assembled, they bear their own weight, including ceiling plates and an additional load of 2.0 kN/m² without bracing. The envisaged live loads of 7.5 kN/m² can only be absorbed in their final state by the composite effect of the reinforced concrete beam with the ceiling slabs." he says in a tone that suggests I ought to commend him for knowing the right answer, then my father appreciatively draws his lower lip over his upper lip and nods. I cannot and do not wish to hear any further explanations of the building's construction, I say. Of course, Herr Müller doesn't take no for an answer and lectures me about the fact that my characterization of the exterior façade of the entrance building is not quite correct, the sixteen sandstone columns are rather—and this is really no secret—the sixteen columns of an arcade, from which the arch and the corridor have been taken, in a final accounting, there is no need here to offer passers-by protection from the sun, this protection would only be superficial, for the arcade naturally tempts one to look at the sky through its arches, into the framing of the arch, which is nothing but an oversized window, but not a circle through which one cannot stride, the circle is sufficient unto itself, there is nothing more consummate than the circle and, as such, nothing more dull, but the arch, unfinished and foreboding, limits the sky by placing a dome over it, the arcade arch is there to allow our gaze to experience a certain inkling of the divine, the arcade is the last metaphysical refuge that we have, Herr Müller says, and, in this respect, this building, the façade of which took its passage and arches from the arcade, is the deepest of religious acts, as it really does block out the metaphysical, which is visible to all, paradise is not prohibited to us, but we are denied passage through the arcades and the view through their arches. In that case, the outer façade of the entrance building is a more significant piece of art than the sculptures in the forecourt, my father insists. Herr Müller smiles. That's not too difficult, he says, that which is absent always has the advantage of taking on metaphysical dimensions. I can see that Father would be quite happy if Herr Müller could find his way back to the exegesis of the building's construction, this conversation about art, metaphysics, and God stresses him out, here, God seems unavailable here without the other two. If the metaphysical is obstructed, Herr Müller continues on, though this hiddenness is precisely the circumstance that permanently points to the metaphysical, then the gaze is deliberately averted from something much more important: God. And God consists of fifty-four prefabricated hyperboloid-cylinder shells (also know as hp-cylinder shells) with a limit length of 19.0 m and a width of 2.4 m, which have been put together to form a circular-cylindrical shoring using the assembly method described. The circular ring support joint is clamped at the foot end by way of the outer trough-shaped circular beam. At the head end, the ceiling construction is supported with a sliding contact bearing by interposing angular curtain walling panels. At the same time, the wall-shell construction is designed in such a way that a continuous light band with a height of 2.35 m can be installed at the head end. The wall shell elements form a hyperbola in their cross section. I cover my ears, his babbling passes through my hands.

You're welcome to skip the passage, Herr Müller says, but you won't be able to prevent it from just being there. "Quite so," Father says. And now it appears, word for word from Herr Müller's mouth, and, unfortunately, it stands here as if Herr Müller hadn't spoken it, but written it down directly in the book that I'm holding in my hand as I stand before this building, as if the book were the beginning and not the Word and as if all that is and shall be emerges from the book and returns to the book, that is unless one doesn't read it, in which case one oneself wouldn't be:

"In the middle of the shell there is a longitudinal bracing rib, which is enlarged in the area of the all-round ribbon window in such a way that it can be used as a substitute cross-section for the hyperbolic shell surface that no longer exists in this area. In the longitudinal direction, the 80 mm thick, flexible shell is reinforced by a transversal steel girder at the foot and head end and two further transversal steel girders in the tripart points. The single shell is thus statically effective in the direction of its generatrices as a continuous system over three fields and can transfer horizontally acting external forces to the rigid transversal steel girders in the direction of the ring. The resulting local disturbances in the shell surface are covered by the reinforcement and subside quickly, which is important for the stress caused by the influence of temperature." I ask myself how Herr Müller can have such an influence on *Schattenfroh*, as soon as he speaks, it is written, as soon as he's silent, the book has vanished.

We're not making any progress, I say to Father. So, what are you suggesting? To take Herr Müller out of the book. That really is an amusing suggestion, Father says, but how would you contrive to do so? We could flip forward and continue from a page at which Herr Müller no longer appears. How could you have thought that Herr Müller would hear nothing of our conversation, Herr Müller also has an opinion on the subject of skipping forward. I don't know why you want to go into the building, he says, it surely wouldn't remain hidden if we were to skip over a few pages, the notion that someone might flip back in the book should give us all cause for reflection, as all this trouble would then be in vain, and, after all, it may indeed be the case that, for many readers, my remarks on the building's construction are the most interesting passages, as well as the only ones that could be used to cause a new world—a new building—to arise out of the book, as steel components are installed for the butt joints of the transversal steel girders in the direction of the ring, to which bend-proof steel plates are welded after assembly. Furthermore, angular steel parts are installed at the longitudinal edges of the hp-cylinder shells at a distance of 940 mm. They are used to connect the shells to one another and to absorb the shell ring tensile forces.

    He's talking about *Schattenfroh*, Father says.

    He's talking about the final state, I say.

    Individual elements, Father says, that's what I've always thought—that you can't get beyond individual elements.

    The foundation-structure; that really is the key phrase, I say.

    On the other hand, different settlements in the foundation structure certainly do sound like inadequacies, Father says.

    Fugue practice, which I have made my business, should be given special attention, I say.

The circular cylinder surface structure, which, in its final state, is composed of individual elements, also has the task of compensating for possible different settlements in the foundation structure. It is therefore necessary to pay special attention to the execution of the joint. The measures described above primarily serve to ensure ultimate tensile strength. The connection resistant to compression and shear forces in the butt joints is to be achieved by filling the joints with concrete. In order to guarantee this with certainty, the

Tight connections, you seem to lack that, cementing the joints, joint concrete, concrete adhesive, that's no seal of approval, Father says.

We're dealing with the assembled state here, not the final state, I say.

The slightest wind blows you down, Father says.

I'm at a height where only wind can reach.

It blows you down, Father says.

Schattenfroh has its own structural stability—within itself, I say.

"Assembly braces," Father says, only ugly, makeshift constructions ensure that this house of cards doesn't collapse in on itself.

And you shall never be an eternal shadow that nothing can remove from the painting, I say to Father, while Müller continues to let us in on the details of the shell-construction techniques and the crane-supported installation of the shell construction elements, that's important, he says, without this knowledge, we won't be able to *inspect* the building and only a very few really know what *inspect* really

joint concrete in mortar group III is produced with the addition of a concrete adhesive. It is important for the assembled state of the individual shell elements that the stability against the very high wind force is not given by clamping in the trough-shaped outer enclosing ring alone. Stability is only achieved in a closed spatial system, which must extend over at least a semicircle. Assembly braces are therefore required for the assembled state. The assembly struts were attached to the wall shells before assembly. The load cases of transport, storage, assembly and final installation in the closed system were taken into account in the static-constructive dimensioning of the shell elements. In terms of reinforcement, the element is considered to be untensioned. In order to avoid major deformations associated with the formation of cracks, which can occur during transport and storage, an off-center longitudinal force of 160 kN was generated with moderate preloads in the element using four St 140/160 bracing wires. A cable installation was used to assemble means, *inspection* is now a special form of lust for me—*begehen* a special form of *begehren*—my bike has done more for me than you have, if I were forced to choose, I would choose my bike, it's the most faithful companion that I've ever had, I say to Father, but I only hiss it between my teeth with closed mouth, what I actually say to him is: We won't manage to get into the building, while Father asserts, *he* says we won't manage to get into the building. The art of the thing is holding us back, we agree on that. There's so much to see that continuing on is impossible, we both say, and we also say this to Herr Müller, who shows himself to be understanding and only asks to recite a small excerpt of his text about the building, in front of which we have been standing for a considerable space of time, we assent, unanimous in the conviction that we have never been confronted with a more appropriate use of the phrase "for a considerable space of time."

Müller speaks, Father seeks to make it past him into the building, it isn't even remotely difficult the individual elements. A state of spatial stability is achieved by a three-point linkage as long as the surface structure is mainly in the horizontal position. At an angle of seventy degrees, the transition to the one-point suspension occurs, as is typical for column construction. In the present case, the wall shells were gripped at the foot end with a two-strand suspension gear and gradually steered into the vertical position by an auxiliary crane. The assembly crane is necessary for the installation of the wall shell elements. The hp-wall shells are wedged in the trough-shaped ring beam from both sides. The clamping depth is 1.3 m. In the lower area, the grouting concrete was placed immediately at a height of around 300 mm in order to prevent the mounted wall shells from flapping when exposed to wind. The remaining meter of grouting concrete had to be poured in in one operation. For the total assembly of the enclosing wall, it was determined that a semicircle should be assembled first. After the transversal steel girders had for Müller to stand in my Father's way as he speaks, no matter what twists and turns my father makes.

For my part, I attempt to lure Müller away from the building so that Father might make it inside unhindered, but Müller sees through my plan and only pays attention to my father, who is now also moving away from the building, which doesn't seem to irritate Müller in the slightest.

A good ten meters away from Müller, who stops speaking the moment Father turns his back to him, Father murmurs to me that we might simply minimize Müller's speech in terms of font size, it wouldn't take up so much space anymore, I agree, we're approaching the building once more, Müller continues speaking as soon as we're within two meters of him. Müller shrinks synchronously with the shrinking of the script, which brings me to the thought of making his speech so big that we might slip through his legs and into the building, we wait until he gets small enough that he can no longer stand in our way.

been welded, the assembly struts were moved in order to assemble the second semicircle. The last three wall brackets at the end of the semicircle were to be retained for reasons of stability until the wall bracket assembly was completed. The angular parapet elements form the end of the wall shell construction. They are mounted on the reinforced shell webs above the light band that runs all around. The parapet elements are recessed in the support area, in which there are four overlapping steel loops for the tight connection of the elements to each other. As a result of the influence of temperature, the tight and pressure-resistant connection is only made in the horizontal legs for reasons of rigidity. The mounting gap in the vertical legs was not closed. The assembly of the parapet elements as well as the introduction of the grouting concrete had to be carried out in such a way that the hp-roof shells were supported horizontally and level. The thermal insulation required in terms of building physics was achieved by attaching a thermal insulation layer to the inside of the wall shells with the help of a light substructure. The hp-shell roof structure self-supportingly spans 41.834 m. It consists of fifty-four hp-triangular shells, each weighing 7.7 tons, and the spoke-wheel hub. The hp-triangular shells were manufactured in the same way as the hp wall shells. By simply shifting the shuttering molds, the desired geometric shape of the shell surfaces is achieved, providing geometric versatility. This combined production of wall- and roof-supporting structures within the same matrices is characteristic for the principle of the UNI-hp system.

What did you mean by "eternal shadow"? Father asks. Before we enter the building, I ask him to turn around once more, then to cast his gaze to the right and tell me what he sees. He sees a square that is atypical for this region and more representative of southern climate zones, it has two pointed buildings facing each other, they have arcade-passages, the one on the left shines in white, it has a red roof and is very long, as if one's gaze were stretching it off into the distance, its arcade-passage has sixteen arches, which cast inward shadows at eight o'clock between the first left column and the much-too-narrow corner tower with its narrow windows simulating three floors, an arrow is drawn on the wall at the height of the arch, without upward or downward limit, it points to a vertical line, under which—much like a dead-end sign, except for the fact that the lines here have a certain distance between them—a horizontal line is to be found, as if somebody had forgotten to eliminate a construction mark. The building on the right looks sooted-over and is completely enshadowed, one cannot make out whether it is dark gray or black or whether perhaps there was a fire, a threatening shadow darkens the square before it with the aspect of an unfolded table, however, an area that looks rather a lot like a circus wagon is excluded from the shadow, and this, I say, is what is so astonishing about this square, that it has two mutually exclusive vanishing points, and thus does it show no single central perspective, perhaps it has two, there is at least no point of view where all the vanishing lines converge, here, everything is spatially incongruent, everything cancels itself out, is enigma and mystery, the wooden exterior turned toward the viewer and the double doors of the circus wagon, both made of nailed-together slats, are illuminated by the sun, the right door of the wagon on the open inner side, the interior of the wagon is, as far as can be seen, empty, just as the entire square or forecourt of the building is empty with the exception of two people or human-like figures, the square itself is stretched to the point of breaking, as if, once one had set out, one would never be able to reach one's destination, but would have to be incessantly in motion, and that is precisely what the girl shows by way of her posture, which is more reminiscent of flight than of play, if one takes a closer look, one might well discover a long handle, resembling that of a broom, it might perhaps have the function of locking the double doors from the outside. If one now operates on the assumption that the square in front of the building and on the right has been painted black and its darkening is no unnaturally sharp-cut shadow, then the inexplicable peculiarity of the practically glowing wagon still remains, as its selective illumination could not have been caused by the sun or any other source of light, for the sun, as is indicated by the eight o'clock arch-shadows of the arcade, as well as the shadow in front of the building on the right and the other shadows that have not yet been examined, is not in the northwest, but the southeast. As far as the so-called middle of the field of vision is concerned, he is not able to stop himself from calling the circus wagon the center, despite all the mutually interfering vanishing points and the missing point of view, also despite the inhibited perspective caused by his viewing angle, the wagon's emptiness, apart from any speculation that one can see a broom inside it, corresponds with the emptiness of the square, no matter how fragmented it may be from his position, as well as the actually empty houses, for this reason, he asks himself whether this sight has been waiting just for him, as if he were describing an image whose existence is uncertain for all who do not share his view, which doesn't matter, insomuch as he could well be describing a non-existent image, and, even so, the listener or reader would have the same pleasant impression of an idea seen from a distance, one that signifies no danger, and, at the same time, if it were to hand, would receive it with pleasure, which is what makes the imagining thereof so titillating, but he says that he is describing no image and, in this respect, he has the unpleasant impression that the circus wagon is only empty because the big cat is no longer to be found in it.

For the moment, what troubles him even more, this is Father speaking, is this question: if the sun were in the southeast, how could it then be explained that, in contrast to the circus wagon, the girl driving a hoop across the square with a wooden stick is seen by us as a silhouette, that is only possible if she has no actual body of her own, but is a two-dimensional cardboard cutout. In this case, the girl would be running toward another shadow, which, as mentioned, emanates from a human or a human-like figure, a war memorial perhaps, but the shadow is already too big, too powerful for the square that is not quite visible in its full dimensions, and the building on the left, next to the shadow of the figure, at its rear, the shadow of a flagpole or lance can be seen, the figure has nothing to do with it, it stretches an arm away from its body, as if it did not belong to it, perhaps it is the strict father who would like to receive his daughter, even though she is completely given over to her playing, she runs toward him, and the daughter, one can clearly see this, is running toward him and not the shadow. If one looks very closely at the square with its buildings, Father says, one might well despair of geometry or celebrate the liberation of geometry from the principle of contradiction. He says that only now does he see the double-rods running across the black forecourt of the building on the right and the sunlit part of the square that so beautifully casts light onto the back of the building on the left as seen from here, it reminds him of an overhead line for omnibuses, like those that can be found in Salzburg, and only then does he notice that the building on the right stands upon a hillock and seems to be on the verge of toppling over, even though its constructive form should compensate for extreme differences in altitude, like the Pilatus Railway in Switzerland or the Budavári Sikló climbing up Budapest's Castle Hill, save that the architect, rather than have the building ascend the hill vertically to the earth, which would have been in accordance with the gradient, had it topple over backward, as if it were slowly sinking down, and furthermore, the building, with its windows bent backward obliquely, narrows toward the sunlit spot of the square. The circus wagon standing right in front of him does not seem to be affected by this problem, it remains completely level. According to Father, this tipping point also explains why the girl appears so disproportionately small, even the bright building looks small when viewed in the right light, for an abyss opens up that's just as difficult to see as the rest of the square covered over by the dark building, and now, Father says, he is certain that the figure of which only a shadow can be seen and toward which the girl runs is Bismarck, and if one were to follow the girl, one would see a giant graveyard, the dead of which are slowly being flushed out of the earth, so heavily does the water press down from the mountains and into the earth in order to wash it away. But one thing astonishes him more than all else that has been described, Father says, can you explain why, as far as we can see, not a single leaf from a tree is visible on the square, as if the square has been being swept clean by an invisible hand for as long as I've been looking at it, there's no wind blowing either, everything stands still. That's precisely it, I say to Father, that's what I meant earlier by "eternal shadow," the girl is a strange thing, a shifting shadow, but she doesn't exactly shift, she shifts by standing still, and, by standing still, she does not transform, between her, who is the eternal shadow, and Bismarck, of whom we know nothing, whether he only exists as a shadow here, is unfulfilled space, at least we know that there is a shadow of the girl who is always fathomed as running, but does not run, a shadow of the shadow, what an opaque stage set, one might wish to exclaim, if, indeed, that which we see is not reality and if this is the prelude to that which inwardly awaits us, we ought to look forward to an event rich in imagination without a continuous central perspective, a simultaneous image with the horizon folded up, which only covers over the abyss, the gorge, into which, after all, we shall one day fall.

Turned to face the entrance, Father would like to know what makes being an eternal shadow so desirable, for it does indeed seem one might assume that he was able to escape from the black page after it made him unrecognizable, and the venom of which he spoke is nothing but printer's ink, which, unfortunately, is still having its effect even now, the black page also silenced him and prevented his discourse as intelligibility of Being-in the-world (an intelligibility which goes with a state of mind) articulated according to significations, as the great Mindergag Heiter* formulated it, thus was his spirit able to have more of an effect than I would have liked, though it has not yet been fully resolved whether he is perhaps still imprisoned in the black page and whether the vitality that he has come to feel within himself in the meantime and continues to feel is a consequence of the printer's ink, on whose infinity alone his being-in-the-world depends, if he is thus still concealed in the black page and only wanders about as blackness, it is not without a certain validity to speak of him as an eternal shadow, especially as, in the event of his death, which comes to everyone sooner or later, the immutable printer's ink that he is and to which he shall return promised him the very immutability that the girl was already granted. The reading eyes make contact with the printer's ink once more, I say, and thus does everything once more get moving, for it is so that, unless the reader thinks only of stains when he sees the black on the pages, in which case he is neither dead nor alive, but not at all, only the girl whom we do not see, as she has turned away from us, is eternally only shadow and only then a girl. And with the words that he fears for the girl, fears that she's running straight into misfortune, Father steps over the ant-sized Herr Müller, whom I should be careful not to tread on, and opens the glass door with a single hand motion, the kind one can only master over decades of practice as an administrative head, the door flies against its stopper and hangs there, trembling, in its locking mechanism.

How could he not have seen the person in episcopal regalia standing beneath one of the front arches of the wall arcade, where even the

---

* Lessgag Bright.

crosier can be seen in all its detail from here. One can see that its crook, situated atop its staff, is decorated with four circumferential Gothic stained-glass windows on the cylindrical knob above the handle of the staff, Christ is enclosed in the crook with outstretched arms, in his right hand, he holds the sphere of the cosmos decorated with his peace monogram and, in his left, he forms the sign of blessing with his middle and index fingers. But it is he himself, Father, who so resembles Louis of Toulouse. In his left hand, wearing white gloves, he carries a girdle book, as ashamed as if he were carrying stolen goods or was on his way to the high court. The book is sealed with book clasps, a handy device that prevents sudden opening or uninvited reading.

There is no light in the building. Father is of the opinion that we must go straight ahead, I go to the left in the hopes of finding a light switch. Since the others are meant to be there by now, I'm surprised that it's pitch-dark, Father says. I can find no shadow, some light is penetrating through the entrance door, I go back and search for a switch on the right side, Father's voice grows more distant, there is also no light here, I follow the voice, a wardrobe or something similar is in my way, I open it, it is empty, it smells of a wild beast, the big cat at eye-level, I walk through it quietly and grope my way to a waist-high chest of drawers, one can't get past it on the left or right, it's simply always getting in my way, I'll call it Herr Müller, my feet find no foothold on the other side, perhaps there is a staircase leading downward there, I don't want to risk a fall from on high, which is why I wish to climb down the chest of drawers on the same side that I climbed up it, but the same image shows itself here, then I can't make contact with the ground, not even if I support myself, legs first, with my arms on the chest of drawers, beneath me, the faint reflection of a moat can be seen, toads are croaking and leaping leisurely from leaf to leaf, their bodies splashing about awaken within me the compulsion to eat pancakes, Father's voice can no longer be heard from up ahead, but from down below, I can communicate with him very well from here, he suggests we each try to get into the restaurant in our own way, he'll be there soon, I think that's a good idea, I say in the sure assumption that it will be just as difficult to meet Father once more as it will be to seek out the society of Grandpa's former students. The moat smells of sewage. A spotlight turns on. On a sign above the moat can be read: "Original Moat 1634." Another spotlight turns on, the leaves in the water are artificial, the toads are unbothered. A light breeze stirs. The water smells foul. This doesn't stop the toads from covering over its surface very quickly. Toads are said to be toothless, warts their pride, toad-spawn float in the water, strung out like pearls on a chain. I'd rather go through the water than tumble down into the depths. The toads part the sea, which, with the greatest of strainings, becomes an archway by which the toads gather, initially, they appear to be crawling about aimlessly, then they settle down onto the arch at regular intervals as if they'd been placed there by human hands. I have a barred blast furnace with glowing coals for my belly, which my zipper-fastened black robe causes to appear as the eye of God. I wear a green turban upon my head, from which green cloths, decorated with pearls upon their upper thirds, flow to the right and to the left. The hellfire in my belly beats through my head. I've torn my maw open wide, with my tongue, I feel four pointed canines before my fire-flaming gullet. I stride solemnly through the arch, the light turns on in the foyer, it suddenly grows so bright that my eyes have some difficulty getting used to it. Herr Müller comes through the entrance, he is followed by my father. As soon as they've gone wordlessly past me, they resume their conversation. He sees toads everywhere, my father says. Pink elephants, Herr Müller says. Now, he's no doubt thinking that he has a barred blast furnace with glowing coals for his belly, which his zipper-fastened black robe causes to appear as the eye of God, that he wears a green turban upon his head, from which green cloths, decorated with pearls on their upper thirds, flow to the left and to the right, that the hellfire in his belly beats through his head, and that he's torn his maw open wide, with his tongue, he feels four pointed canines before his fire-flaming gullet, Father says. Herr Müller looks at me and shakes his head, nothing of the sort is to be seen, he says. The wind has gotten into his book and flipped through its pages, he imagines himself to be Lucifer in hell, Father says. A very ugly Lucifer, Herr Müller says. That comes of the fact that his favorite character is a certain Schattenfroh, inwardly, he's delivered himself over to him entirely, my father says. Schattenfroh is all-powerful, he says, he's also Lucifer, thus does his son also wish to be Lucifer. Up until a certain age, that remains mere fantasy, Herr Müller says. He's long since grown out of imagining such things, my father says. They don't even notice that I'm behind them. We cross a mezzanine floor with a ceiling so low that I can feel the heat from the overhead lights on my head. How many of them are already there, my father asks. All of them, Herr Müller says. Father stops and looks at him. All twelve, Herr Müller clarifies.

So, I wasn't mistaken after all, Father says, my dear Herr Sonnyboy. This is Herr Neuwerk, my father says, pointing at Herr Müller. Ebert Neuwerk, Herr Müller says and gives me his hand. Thus do the three of us set off. But you can call me Knut, Knut Werbeere, Ebert Neuwerk says, Kurt is OK too, Kurt Werebene. The mezzanine just won't come to an end, Father stops every now and then to ask something or explain something, sometimes, he looks at me and smiles, as if he were asking me for understanding or as if he wanted to signal that he is fulfilling his duty of care, which expired a few years past. I would very happily say to him, "Too late, Daddy," but he has already turned away once more. We are now some two hundred meters below sea level, Ebert Neuwerk says. The only way to really come to terms with this fact is to take a deep breath, so all three of us take a deep breath. Incidentally, Ebert Neuwerk says, I set everything up just the way they wanted it. Father would like to know whether the well is also in use. The well is quite central, Ebert Neuwerk says. What do you mean by central, Father asks. It is the central place around which everyone has gathered, Neuwerk says, whereas I still can't believe that he isn't Herr Müller anymore. We pass through an unlit passage some five meters long, I briefly consider turning back, if that isn't Herr Müller, then the other man might not be my father at all. It certainly wouldn't make the most favorable of impressions to pose this question.

We enter a space that has no beginning and no end. I ask myself why this space exists at all. Mateo, who is leading the way, suddenly stops, Father collides with his heel, Mateo raises his right arm, as if he were awaiting a precise signal, as soon as we've passed the entrance, I lose all orientation. I can tell by Father's determined steps that he's in the same boat. "So, then," he says, just as he always says "so, then" when the situation actually calls for a "why?"

The eyes must first grow accustomed to their environs, Ebert Neuwerk says. And then we see: It's spring. Back there, a few hundred meters away from us, down the hill, then under the rainbow and through the sun-halo that it arches over, that's where we must go, Ebert Neuwerk says, Father now addressing him as Mateo. It's still a bit chilly, Father pulls a light sweater and a jacket out of his suitcase. I wasn't even remotely aware of the fact that we had a ways more to go, I say. The Eifel is full of surprises, Father says. He replies in the negative to my question as to whether he also has a sweater for me, indicating that he would have had to take a bigger suitcase for that. A large, sloping meadow opens up before us, crocuses can be seen, and the occasional lily of the valley is blooming. It's always spring here, Mateo says. He asks whether we noticed that there's a mountain range quite unusual for the Eifel behind us. Father laughs. Indeed, one can see a huge mountain range in the distance, its peaks still snow-capped. Tomorrow, May 15, the mountains shall be in mourning, Mateo says. Father laughs. There are still no people here, Mateo says, in a few hours, however, nobody else shall be able to find shelter here, the one-thousand-meter-long expanse of terrain, the so-called Hausberg, or "local mountain," becomes a Schlachtberg—a battle- or slaughter-mountain.

How can one go through something and, simultaneously, have gone in the opposite direction, without going in a circle or simply pacing to and fro, I ask myself, we must have paced out a palindrome toward its middle, for the space we are now entering proceeds from the opposite side of the former entrance.

The middle of the space forms a great golden shell around which the nine people are standing. Twelve more people—it is not clear whether they belong—are also in the vicinity of the basin. When the nine catch sight of us, they signal to please come forward, covertly pointing toward the basin as they do, they seem uncomfortable with it or to think that they must excuse it away as a table for drinks. "It's called the 'Fountain of Immortality,'" says the woman standing furthest to the right, draped in a red raiment from head almost down to toe, she points toward the fountain with her left hand. The woman is Erasmus of Rotterdam as portrayed by Albrecht Dürer. You can't compete with him, my father says when he sees Erasmus, he wrote more than twelve dozen books. He is so finely garbed, my father says, that, like Machiavelli, before even uttering his name, you must put on royal and consecrated robes so as to be worthy of him, for any trace of every-dayness is an insult to the intellect. Erasmus wears a costly velvet bonnet and an even costlier velvet mantle. The velvet is lined with fur, the ends of the mantle's sleeves, which Erasmus has turned out with the greatest of care, allow one to gaze freely upon the almost-white fur, which would otherwise be hidden by red velvet. It is far too warm for this sort of distinction-creating attire and the woman gives every sign of suffering beneath the raiment rather than taking pride in her aspect. She looks wrathfully at a staff that is being held practically underneath her nose and to which is attached a tiny little head, which resembles that of the staff's bearer. From here, it is not possible to make out whether the protruding ends with the bobbles are bushy donkey ears or a two-pointed fool's cap with bells, a jester's cap, the sight of which brings a blush of furious red to Erasmus' countenance, why was she of all people confronted with this sacrilege, it must have something to do with her garb, for, after all, there are quite a few guests further to the right who merit the jester's cap as a sign of their duplicity, amour-propre, and mendacity, like, for example, Jörg Ratgeb, who is to be quartered. For some, Ratgeb is a fox, a devil whom one drags through one's environs like a fox's tail, and this is Ratgeb too, lying there like a small sausage with right hand raised high, bent at an angle of ninety degrees, in such a way that the palm is clearly visible, the index and middle fingers are unusually long, the ring finger is bent unnaturally toward the palm, the pinkie is open at an obtuse angle of some forty-one degrees, and, with a suffering expression, he is the only person pointing in the direction of the scene of the battle taking place behind the hedge of low shrubs and trees, of which some are blossoming with white flowers, it surrounds the group gathered around the basis as a protective arrangement, as if it had been planted there specifically for that purpose. With his back to the group, a soldier stands in a purple jacket, with golden knee breeches and socks, a large girdle that converges into a pocket, the pocket is just large enough to accommodate knives, his jacket has shoulder-padding on both sides, it mitigates the force of any cutting weapons able to make impact.

That's not true at all, says the thin man in the green coat standing diagonally to her right, holding the marotte, a staff with a fool's head, in his right hand and wearing a pink hat on his own head, while his open left hand held horizontally in the air at chin level and pointing dismissively outward, as well as the upper and lower arm (plus forearm and hand) forming a right angle, are a clear signal to his previous interlocutor that she is utterly mistaken. This is Sebastian Brant, as Dürer saw him, without fool's scepter and with his hands clasped together on a table or something similar. He stares at Erasmus of Rotterdam as if this were what was needed to protect her from bad things, which could only be ensured by the correct designation of the basin, "Fountain of Life" is what this thing is called, he says, which leaves the bearded man standing in the middle of the basin-thing and seemingly entangled in other disputes completely cold, he seizes the moment in order to be the only one to appraise the newcomers with piercing gaze, not an unfriendly one, but also not the sort of gaze one would think to run toward and be greeted with open arms a moment later, this, however, prompts the young woman standing to his right with her astonishingly young appearance that also highlights her long, curly hair to announce what, in her opinion, is the sole correct, albeit profane description of the basin: "That's a Luther-Fountain," she says, then turns once more to the woman next to her on the right, this woman must have pushed her way forward, at any rate, the gentleman who is standing between the two women in the vicinity of the fountain, who not only looks like Tilman Riemenschneider, but also is Tilman Riemenschneider, fails for the umpteenth time to get to the fountain or the beer glass he's placed by the fountain, the foam-head of which has already visibly collapsed. He comments on his failure with the remark: "Luther-Fountain, hence the many toads in its turbid waters," and Veit Stoß has also been collapsed for some time, she is the woman addressed by the woman with the curly hair, whom only her prodigious talent as a sculptor saved from death by fire as punishment for a forged promissory note, which was then symbolically transformed into the branding of two holes into her cheeks, holes that no longer close, this was done with a red-hot iron rod, in any case, Veit Stoß claims that her cheeks no longer close up, two unforgettable brands through which beer flows as a sign of lost civic honor, which, even in this circle, some centuries later is a source of amusement. If what Veit Stoß wants to do is drink the beer, as she lifts the glass with her left hand, she must hold the hole with her left hand until she has swallowed it, which quite a few see as sleight of hand, as in, by this, she wishes to express her feeling of injustice, the unjust treatment she wishes to express that she went through, the branding that dishonored her and was meant to stigmatize her, she now turns against Nuremberg, visible to all here in Prüm as well, and that, even though "nary a one had ever been burnt so gently," as is written in Deichsler's Chronicle, in assuming this circumstance to be generally known, Veit Stoß thus makes a jester of herself everywhere with the demonstration of injustice upon her own body, which, at the end of the day, she herself upholds, affording the ridiculousness a no less demonstrative flavor, even after Emperor Maximilian I, the Emperor of Nuremberg, gave her the name of "Veit Stoß," to the great chagrin of the imperial city, which felt patronized and which Veit Stoß was not allowed to leave without permission, the news spread that Stoß had been "rehabilitated and cleared of his deed (by having his cheeks pierced with a glowing iron bar as punishment)," which caused the Nuremberg councilors to feel so duped that they threatened the sculptress with not making the imperial message publicly known.

But one shall never forgive the town of Schwaz in Tyrol for having failed to avert the destruction of the ten-to-twelve-meter-tall triptych in the Schwaz parish church at the beginning of the seventeenth century, "over the course of the baroquification of the church interior," it depicted the Assumption of the Virgin Mary over the open tomb of Jesus and was destroyed together with the altar, all of this can be read in great detail in the work of Inès Pelzl, and this came to pass in such a way that there is nothing left of Stoßen's primary work other than three statues of gilded wood, Saint Anna, Saint Elizabeth, and Saint Ursula, all life-sized and with steady gazes, they lament the lost altarpiece. "What I haven't learned through study, I have come to know through hiking," Veit Stoß says as Tilman Riemenschneider finally makes it to his beer glass, which he, at the very moment he finishes hurling it back in a single gulp, wants to set back onto the glass plate covering the immortal Luther-Fountain of Life, but it's then that Veit Stoß shoves him away from the fountain once more, the glass shatters on the ground, and, likely to cover up the unpleasant situation, Stoß taps the plate with the knuckle of her middle finger, which the bystanders interpret as a sign that she wants to give a speech, all conversations break off, a certain individual adjusts his tie, but she makes no speech, instead, embarrassed by the attention she's attracted from those present, she simply scratches the glass and stone of the fountain with her fingernails, which sends a shiver down my spine. Beer is served, Riemenschneider makes a toast, not without a sense of self-satisfaction, with the motto "No Adam Kraft has ever yet passed as Veit Stoß," dedicating it to Stoß herself, who raises her glass without comment and clinks glasses with Riemenschneider, and as soon as the issue of the tie comes up, it occurs to me that nobody else is wearing a tie, not just those already mentioned, but all are dressed after the fashion of the fifteenth and sixteenth centuries, perhaps Father didn't take note of the dress code, "It was meant to have been called the Pirckheimer Fountain, but Willibald Pirckheimer couldn't come, Luther came in his place," Veit Stoß finally manages to utter, she couldn't bear being stared at any longer. If only she had remained silent, in Luther's presence they are discussing what precisely may have been the reasons for which Pirckheimer failed to appear, whether he hadn't been expressly prevented from appearing here, but who could have prevented him, the Party, somebody says, and did the Party send Luther in his place? Precisely, and even higher powers ensured that it was the not-quite-so-defined Redwine-Luther who came? Yes, the powers of art, in revenge for the Party's paternalism—the Party or the secret service? Both, and the still-higher powers of art liquidated Pirckheimer for Luther? Just so, that's what's written, might you tell me where to read this? One can read that on page 229 and in footnotes 910 and 911 (though of what book, Nobody has forgotten); a general state of perplexity during which one forgets to ask about the author, and then an argument breaks out in the group about who is more important, Pirckheimer or Luther, and although most agree that Luther is more important, quite a few of them are of the opinion that the fountain should nonetheless be dubbed the Pirckheimer-Fountain, for, without him, Pirckheimer, the Dürer-friend, it would have been even more difficult for Luther, which would then mean overestimating Pirckheimer's role in the Causa Luther. A certain Peter Vischer the Elder also got himself mixed up in the dispute, he hits Veit Stoß on the finger with a little hammer, which she counters with the observation that lost honor cannot be restored mechanically and certainly not with such a brazen approach.

If the gentlemen here were all drawn or painted by Dürer in this way and Dürer himself is present, then perhaps only Dürer is actually present and has brought his portraits with him, then grouped them into a sort of exhibition. Perhaps not even Dürer is present in person, but also only a portrait of Dürer is to be seen, otherwise, he would have had to have been present here in 1498, when his self-portrait with the landscape was created, Dürer is twenty-six years old, the self-portrait, which can be seen here without a landscape, measures 52 × 40 centimeters, the landscape is something else entirely, it is the Eifel, and the Eifel is a battlefield, a field of slaughter, indeed, Riemenschneider is no Dürer, presumably, he is a Riemenschneider, otherwise, he would also have sent himself as a self-portrait, not being present in person, and Cranach cannot be Dürer either, he comes from the brush of Lucas Cranach the Younger, or, more likely, from his own brush—if the gentlemen are not present in person, one might well say that one need only hang up their portraits and self-portraits for them to be here in person, one need only cry out their names and already the effigies appear, the effigies are their names.

My father now feels the moment has come to make himself heard in the room and to greet all those present in the name of my Grandpa, in the name of whom they are gathered here. He says "Most respected," a short pause is there to ensure the necessary attention, then he says "ladies and gentlemen," and, in order to adequately tee up the personable tone he has decided to strike, "Most beloved guests" follows, then is drowned out by a voice that is not in the space with us, but still sounds as if it belonged to a person standing with Dürer and the others by the fountain. The voice is a bit shrill, a bit too high, but there is no question that it is a man's voice. It is a strange German that the voice speaks, actually, it doesn't speak, it proclaims what it has to say, and what it has to say is not easy to understand:

"[garbled overlapping text] spiritual has to lower its heaven to the level of an earthly and temporal condition, to common [garbled overlapping text]. knowing what he ought to do, he followed the Word of God and did as he was told, attempting to sacrifice and kill the pious child, but God saved Isaac and spared him his life."

He's a crackpot, my father says and he knows all about crackpots, hasn't he said to me a thousand times, "You're a crackpot!"? Getting back to business as usual is what Father always calls his attempt to block out any and all distortions, and a distortion is anything that might jeopardize his control over any situation. Let us now get back to business as usual, Father says, there's still much to discuss. But the voice has not yet finished its lecture, thus do we listen in:

"And that is just like us, for we have had a command from God, and we must wait for the end, and let God take care of us. But I have no doubt that it will turn out well and that this very day we will see God come to our aid and our enemies utterly destroyed, for God often said in the Scriptures that he wished to help the poor and the pious and uproot the godless. Now it is us who are the poor, and wish to receive God's word, so we should not have doubts, for fortune will be on our side."

"As at a rally, God is taken for granted, but, when nothing helps anymore, God still helps. He wishes to exterminate his enemies, and God shall help him, he says, he hopes, and the godless, who, indeed, are always other people, shall be exterminated. If he is not mistaken about this. Whomsoever he preaches to, his congregation is scared shitless. That's the sort of prophet he is, the sort of itinerant preacher, charlatan, private revelator, egotistical sectarian."

The voice pauses. Father smiles, he finds the matter most uncomfortable, for there's nothing at all to cover up, he spreads out his arms and takes a few steps toward those present, who have now gathered more tightly around the fountain. The organizer should have registered the rally, surely unannounced, without consequences, I hear it out, the rest is lost in the voice, which, as if it knew of its opponent-speaker, now sounds out so loudly that Father gives up trying to compete with it, he hurries to the window-front that separates the fountain and those standing around it from the hedge, he says "Curtain," the people nod and turn to him, but there is no curtain, nevertheless, the air in the room is still, while the voice, whose author has still not come into view, unmediatedly inscri(b)es itself:

"But what are these princes? They are nothing but tyrants, who fleece the people, and exhaust our blood and sweat with their splendour, with useless pomp, with their whoring and villainy. God commanded in Deuteronomy that kings should not keep many horses or go around with great pomp and ceremony, and that a king should every day have his book of laws in his hand."

Father, who took me by the hand at the preacher's first words, which causes me shame, for the last time he took me by the hand was when I was four, is now at the same level as Luther, who doesn't see the point in making room for him or helping with the curtain, Father takes two short strides, then he has vanished into the hedge with me, while a gaunt man dressed all in black and with a big triangular flag in his left hand approaches, it is to him that the voice can clearly be attributed, he is followed by three drummers and Death playing the bagpipes, Death is sitting upon a saddled tree stump with elephant legs. Father runs straight at the gaunt man, we are garbed in princely fashion, over a white ruffled shirt with a high collar buttoned to the chin and ending in some sort of ruff, Father wears a combination of peascod belly and a silk doublet—a long-sleeved jerkin, wadded at chest and shoulders, with wide, long sleeves that taper to the wrist—which causes the shirt to become visible in an ovular neckline above which is a chamarre of black velvet with elegant short arms, which, as an over-skirt, is open at the front, quite in line with the demands of fashion and thus allows one to gaze upon the shirt and jerkin and shows off a wide gold chain that reaches down to the chest quite beautifully. The chamarre leaves free six sewn folds of the doublet, which is modeled after the breastplate of a knight's armor at the front and is alternatingly decorated with paler snakelike lines and sovereign symbols or merely ornamental signs, corresponding to the chamarre in their strong, almost obtrusive contours and their black shade. The raiment and symbols draw the whole of one's attention, they put me into a kind of trance, is that which I see there—crown, pillar, medal, plant, and angel—image or realia? The whole of Father's raiment is symbol, he's slung on the city's coat of arms, the chain of which bangs against the golden chain as he walks, yes, Father makes a very ornamental impression as he walks. The Schlumperhose with their codpiece flared out by the padding, the silk stockings, and the distinguished cap of black velvet form a clear contrast with the countryfolk cavorting here. I pale in comparison with Father's ensemble, I'm wearing a plain shirt and even plainer pants, the shirt causes my nipples to show, what little chest hair I have gets caught in the fabric, which gives me gooseflesh. I ought not to fiddle with my shirt, Father says, such plucking is unworthy of me. Social order is reflected in dress code, Father says, that's what makes today's egalitarian society so hateful to him, he says, in it, anyone can buy anything if they've got enough money, only priests still have their distinctive *habitus*, indeed, this fine garb is reserved for the upper strata, thanks to wealth, however, even the dumbest individual might belong to this group, fortunately, though, one can tell by looking at people whether the fine garb that they wear makes them even more stupid than they already are, one wears clothing because it conforms to the occasion and not because one wishes to set oneself apart from others, and that makes him deeply sad, Father says, one might very well read the dress code as the social order in the form of art, no portrait-painter paints a true portrait, self-portraits are the greatest of self-distortions, it's always a matter of idealization, upward or downward, what wretched figures Germans cut in their clothing, with them, adaptation is only implemented in the direction of wretchedness and this is what's to blame for the disappearance of normative codes of conduct, if these still existed, we would see distinction everywhere, and once I'm truly dead, Father says, you won't need pictures of me any longer, won't see images showing me here and there; for I will no longer be here and there, no, already, in the very next moment, I'll no longer be here and there, but simply *here*, which is death in life, he adds that I simply need to call this forth from my memory, a portrait such that no painter can achieve, the advantage of evocation, and it's always to do with magic, which is to say the spontaneous mutability of the visage before the inner eye, if I could no longer call him forth from my memory, I would no longer recognize him in images, in such a way that if I were to describe him as I have just done, I would create an image of him that doesn't correspond to any reality, he would have preferred me to have written a new book of ceremony, which would have had far-reaching consequences. Schattenfroh would like for me to write this, I say, I can't do anything about it, I've already passed into script, but I shall communicate to Schattenfroh that my father desires a new old fashion and a book of ceremony. He already knows that, Father says.

Upon the gaunt man's flag, "a white banner, thirty ells long and made of silk," a crucifixion-group with Jesus, Mary, and the Apostle John can be seen in the middle flanked by two coats of arms, the left of which is a drawstring shoe and the right of which is an eagle over a lion, both with wide-open beak and maw and stuck-out tongues. The number 666 hovers over the eagle, which cannot be clearly seen from a distance, indeed, it could also be the number 888, perhaps the year the city was founded if eagle and lion are indeed the insignia of a city coat of arms. The backside of the flag is also printed without the print showing through to the front. Below a rainbow can be read: "verbum domini maneat in eternum" and "a motto read out, this is the sign of the eternal covenant of God, all who wish to stand by the covenant shall walk beneath it." Father shall surely not walk beneath it, rather, his facial expression reveals that he would like to tear the rainbow from the flag and take it unto himself, for, according to Genesis 9:13, the sign of the bond with God is not meant to belong to this fool, "I do set my bow in the cloud, and it shall be for a token of a covenant between me and the earth," it is meant to belong to those who, like himself, have studied the Word of God, not so as to measure and align the worldly balance of power with the divine order of heaven, but for the mere sake of the Word of God.

With his head turned away, the gaunt man's right hand points toward a group of men standing a mere few meters from him, they are falling upon one another with cutting and stabbing weapons, the object of their confrontation seems to be the flag inscribed with an archaic form of the word "FREEDOM," which causes Father to speak of the perilous concentration of anti-feudal forces.

When he catches sight of Father, the voice of the gaunt man, not undisputed even in his own ranks, cracks, as it is whispered to one from all sides that one ought to keep away from him, he plunges all into misfortune, and that concentration of anti-feudal forces he helped to bring about allows the princely hordes to wipe them out in one fell swoop. As far as the factions surrounding the gaunt man are concerned, the following is uttered, explains a certain Jefferson Tuff-Tuff from the Eifel, who made his way here out of Düren or, rather, out of shameless curiosity and whose style of reporting on things is more like the hydraulic ramp of baroque novels than the staccato rhythms of newspaper journalists or foreign correspondents, in such a way that his first never-ending sentences simply don't appear and the system doesn't react, whichever system it may be:

The immoderates need not worry about the moderates being pushed out by them, the nobles deal with them in the person of a ducal councilor and supreme war chief with the perculiar name of Count Ernst II von Vorderort, who was notorious for his martial abilities, which he offered wheresoever it seemed most favorable to him, even if this was on precisely the opposing side, which at the very least can be said to have led to the expansion of bountiful turmoil to a Europe-wide war, this attribution is an error insomuch as Ernst, who waged war all throughout Europe, lived one hundred years later, rather, it is the progenitor of the Vorderort line, Count Ernst II von Vorderort whom is being dealt with here, he who, with his five brothers, inhabits the frontmost castle on the fortress, hence his last name, there is still a line of middles and rears remaining, which is to say Mittel- und Hinterorts, only just two hundred years later, they shall be able to look back on the 750-year-old pedigree of an ancient, most praiseworthy dynasty, which, as far as nobility goes, can hardly be surpassed in age, in any case, the nobles, though some of them have gone over to the insurgents and fraternize with them, have already ensured that the moderates shall either become immoderate themselves or at the least no longer stand in the way of the immoderates in terms of their resolutions and actions or even concede that the nobles, this Ernst first and foremost, not only put the settlement that the moderates seek with them to the most strenuous of tests, but do away with the possibility of its arising once and for all in the fundamental conviction that, as it is written in Paul to the Romans in the thirteenth chapter, to Titus in the third chapter, and in the first letter to Peter in the second chapter, whosoever therefore resisteth the power, resisteth the ordinance of God and thus, on May 4, which is to say, a few days ago, does this ducal council burn down the village of Engberlin so as to restore said order and as a warning to all who would engender further adversity, he feels the insurgents already standing before the castle gate, he sees them already plundering the castles, the rope around his neck takes his breath away, then some seven days later, he announces in a letter to his sovereign Duke George, known as George the Bearded, whose very vocation it is to be against Luther, an exposition of his reasons for this, it is dispatched by his emissaries, most certainly, George has no need of this, after all, he himself, George, instructs the nobles only one day later to be properly industrious and to do as much damage as possible to the faithless, tyrannical insurgents, without, in the process, abandoning prudence, which is to say without bringing about any particular danger to themselves, and, on that very day, he writes to Erich Mol von Klebtenzu, who always signs only as Rico von Klebten zu Helm, his bailiff at Gassenhauern with its districts of Grauenhassen,*

---

* Hatehorror.

Nahesgrausen,* and Gaunershasen,† that one hundred horsemen rambling through the Eifel have been sent to burn all insurgents to the ground, by which it is meant that their lives together with their possessions shall be razed right down to the ground, in addition to which their wives and children shall be slain, the more the merrier, as many as they can manage, but whom they are to deal with first are the Gassenhauern,‡ this letter proves that George needs no justification from the side of Ernst II von Vorderort. Apparently not wishing to be inferior to the murderousness of his cousin Ernst II in any respect, Albrecht VII burns down the village of Horstesauen§ on his tour of hate, not without having first done away with some seventy farmers and monastery-stormers. Decency demands that, even now, he is still titled "Most True-Born and Most Merciful Herr Count."

Whereas Ernst II is Catholic and fears the aims of the insurgents just as the devil fears holy water, Albrecht VII is evangelical against the insurgents and for Luther, he who reinforces the count in his actions, as can be gathered from a letter from Luther to Johann Rühl, his brother-in-law in the count's service, dated May 5. In it, Luther urges the brother-in-law not to soften Count Albrecht in this matter, which is to say, the murdering of the insurgents, which makes the devil more wrathful and more furious, the devil is nobody other than the insurgents themselves, for Albrecht, Romans 13, beareth not the sword in vain, the counts are ordained and commanded by God, and, after all, the insurgents merely wish to create a new order by driving out all princes and lords everywhere, however, it is said, they did not receive commandment, power, right, or order from God to do so; even if there were thousands of them, the insurgents took up sword out of their own presumption and outrage, they are bandits and murderers, the whole

---

* Closehorror.
† Rascal'srabbits.
‡ Popular Tunes.
§ Horst's Meadows.

lot of them, and one of their greatest sins is using the name of the Divine Word and Gospel, on top of that, they are faithless and perjured in relation to their lords, God sometimes plagues the world with the most desperate of individuals out of rage, hopefully, they shall make no progress and, most of all, not endure.

The counterreaction of the insurgents is not long in coming, shortly after Ernstalbrecht's tyrannies, they make a beeline for the town of Narrte, belonging to the Vorderort line, where they capture three of the lords in the count's service, emissaries of Count Ernst, and take them to Prüm as retribution, for which reason he, Ernst, judged our brother and stuck his head onto a pike. If God delivers him unto us, he shall be subjected to the same. In Prüm—curiously enough, it is not possible to determine whether it was May 12 or 13, even though it was not all that long ago—they judge them in the ring at the center of the wagons, then hang them, an act with which not all are in agreement, but their own exercise of high justice and procedure for the judgment of capital crimes is of the utmost importance to the gaunt man, who gave his explicit consent for the execution.

The uprising is a virus that spreads best by way of letters, a request for help or a favor can be read several times over in the form of a letter, even if the help requested is not granted, the reading and imagining already sets things into motion, many a person to whom such a request is addressed probably thinks. The question arises again and again, and how ought the issue be resolved other than by the banding-together of all the insurgent forces by way of the unification of the heretofore rather reserved mobs elsewhere who are by no means averse to the matter, as to how else the official weapons of a regime funded by nothing else but the money of citizens and farmers can be countered, a tyrannical regime shall not shy away from any means necessary, grasping for even the most extreme and making use of what is mass-destructively most effective, but without immediately raising the suspicion that it is precisely these being used (the means of mass destruction), in the quest to maintain tyrannical power, they no longer differentiate between good and evil, friend and foe. The mass of a mass-destruction threat must be countered by the mass of the masses, the horde, the mob, divided into many hordes and mobs, here and everywhere, ready at any time to break into castles, palaces, and offices, to drive out the mighty and to create a new order from the disorder they've engendered, only those who waver must be won over to the cause and in this it is best that one paints the decline with the most distinct of colors, the contour must draw the line clearly, after all, divine truth is exclusively on the side of the insurgents, who, were it to come to an all-decisive battle, would likely be overcome by the strength and violence of the cavalry and other warlike things with which Philip I, the Hessian-Braunschweig army, and Duke George together with their followers have so far, as it is said, striven mightily and are still striving to exterminate the uprising's poor X-tians, but this battle is not already decided from the outset, in their letters, which are composed in the hope that even one of them may not remain inconsequential, those who have openly turned against the princes and their entourage, without being able to turn back from this, ask that their addressees not surrender to the tyrants without a fight, which would, in any case, signal their certain death, of this fact, one is utterly certain, and this reinforces the bravery of the hopeless, those very ones who are still hesitating, who still show themselves to be undecided, not in the quiddity of the matter, but in their actions, if they are to support them with all their strength, artillery, and people in the most decisive manner, lest, as it is said, a sizable amount of Christian blood is spilled, thereby engendering the greatest of vexations and the weakening of the Holy Gospels, for, without divine aid and the support of others, they are capable of offering up no resistance, which is why the actions of these others must now follow their vows recorded in writing, otherwise, all of their innocent Christian blood shall flow down into the devil's gullet.

On the other hand, now, the princes. Nobody knows better than the gaunt man what they do and what they refrain from doing, with the continuation of his speech, he relieves Jefferson Tuff-Tuff of the embarrassment of further embellishing his account of things that would far exceed his prognostic powers:

"But what do our princes do?

They do not accept their responsibilities as rulers, they do not listen to the poor people, they do not give justice, they do not keep the roads clear, do not prevent murder and robbery or punish offences and evil, do not defend widows and orphans, do not help the poor to justice, do not allow young people to be brought up correctly and with good morals, do nothing in the service of God—which is the very reason that God created the rulers—but simply ruin the poor more and more with new impositions, do not use their power to maintain peace, but only for their own betterment, and make sure they are strong enough against their neighbors, ruin the land and the people with unnecessary wars, with robbery, arson, murder."

This is not however the material that prompts my father to quiet all dispute, indeed, it is no invitation to do so either, these already much-too-long exegeses have brought him to his knees, while Jefferson Tuff-Tuff whiles away his time with such speeches until, finally, the decisive moment has come, it is to be recorded in words and images, the breaking-through of the barricade of wagons on the Schlachtberg behind which the insurgents have entrenched themselves, this shall be performed by the princely armies with artillery, cavalry, and foot soldiers, the united princely horde that marched overnight from Fulda and Langensalza, kept themselves concealed all day and night on Sunday, only the infantry squad is deployed against the insurgents; then withdraws once more, causing the insurgents to believe that they have triumphed; then comes the true army, determined to destroy, it's too late for the insurgents by then, the barricade of wagons becomes a trap, one from which they can no longer escape, and we might well say that we are there, for Jefferson Tuff-Tuff has no issue striding over proverbial corpses, but in that Father refers the gaunt one's speech to himself alone, he can only lose his composure, he walks toward the man and hits him in the face with the flat of his right hand, so hard that the outline of the hand remains upon the skin, some portion of the gaunt man's followers, armed with cutting and thrusting weapons or simply with pitchforks and scythes, make preparations to avenge their leader for this vile act, but are held back from this by others, who likely fear greater unpleasantness, after all, they don't imagine Father to be acting alone, one can tell from their faces, insomuch as it's possible from such a distance, bad eyes might also have a role to play in this, one can read that they are in doubt as to whether they ought to find Father's behavior courageous or simply brazen, in any case, they opt for caution, after all, it could well be that Father is merely the herald testing the waters, not of the Hohenlohe Corps, but of the combined host of the princes George Duke of Saxony, Philip I of Durum, and Heinrich of Brunswick, it is nevertheless clear that nobody here holds him to be a fine fellow, everyone wishes for misfortune to befall him, then somebody comes to the aid of the gaunt man, who, it should be noted, was knocked to the ground by the slap, and utters the sentence, "Such a fellow have I never seen in the whole of my life," which, on the one hand, expresses admiration for the wondrous aspect of Father's deed, but, on the other hand, independently from Father, is due to the circumstance that the slap was administered by somebody who, to judge from his appearance, does not commonly take such acts upon himself, but delegates them, assuming that they are in proverbial good hands, delegated to personnel ideally suited to this purpose, it has taken a long time for the gaunt man to get up from the ground, from whence he took up Father's gauntlet with the following words:

"These are the princely virtues which they parade around. You should not imagine that God will let this go on for much longer, for, just as he destroyed the Canaanites, so he will destroy our princes. And even if we were able to endure all this, God can not forgive them for defending the servants of a false god, the priests and monks. Who does not know about the horrible idolatry which they practice with their buying and selling during Mass; just as Christ threw the money-changers out of the Temple, so will he destroy the priests and all their hangers-on."

Finally having grown weary of such troublemaking and certainly unwilling to take responsibility for the supposed misdeeds of priests and monks, Father waves his widely stretched arms about in a way I've never seen him do before, retreats back a step around the hedge that encloses the fountain, bows, then he is standing next to Hans Hut and says: "But that's a revolt!" and to Hut's query as to what a revolt actually is, Father points toward the gaunt man, who has let his flag, which is now pointing at our well, sink down to the ground.

Hut, not exactly known as a grandmaster of the wardrobe, but for the binding of books, the distillation of wine, and ecclesiastical housekeeping, including preparation for masses, and as a merchant of books to boot, which was how he got to know *Schattenfroh* over the course of many broadsheets, also selling them, replies, "No, my Lord, this is a revolution!" "In any case, it's impudent!" my father says. "One ought to know," Hut says, "that seven princes and one landgrave have joined forces against this unruly mob that only has the strength to take on the landgrave alone and throw back his troops, they allowed themselves to be seen outside the city, the princes are leading a lively correspondence with one another, they title themselves as 'Your Very Dearest,' and discuss what is to be done against this rising rabble, with the resolution to allow one another passage through their own territory, after all, it is a question of putting an end to the turmoil everywhere, but one might refrain from the pillaging of foreign soil—the gaunt man must kick up quite a racket, otherwise his own people shall hand him over, precisely because the moderates among them wish to negotiate with the princes, who set the condition thereto that 'If you turn over to us, alive, the false prophet Thomas Müntzer and his immediate following, and throw yourselves completely onto our mercy,' so that they might torture and behead him, 'our treatment of you and decisions in respect to you will be such that you may yet, if circumstances permit, find favour in our eyes,' but who precisely are these followers, if one were to ask under such a precondition, nobody would wish to be counted among their number, thus would they reach their goal of destroying the mob, nor is it said that they shall not nevertheless, even if the gaunt one along with his followers has been delivered to them, fall upon the horde with its barricade of wagons and butcher them, the princes, in any case, 'expect a speedy reply,' the mob debates quite controversially when a sun-halo and rainbow appear in the sky, just as is painted on the flag, this causes the crowd to huddle quite close together, they 'ought only dispute heartily and be bold,' the gaunt man cheers them, and these celestial phenomena are read as a turning point in time, and an epochal turning point is actually coming to pass here, for a battlefield, a field of slaughter, is the book that is read over and over again, one can flip back and forth through it and skip over a great many things that are not immediately decipherable, one can do violence to the book by raging against it, and, at the end of the day, one can destroy the book, and just as 'schießen,' to shoot, is contained within 'entschließen,' to decipher, so too is 'Schuss' contained within 'Entschluss,' shot within decipherment, the reply from the barricade of wagons, behind which the mob has entrenched itself, takes too long for the princes, and it is you, Herr Landgrave, who lets it to be known that no armistice—and certainly not an indefinite one—has been negotiated by expecting a speedy reply, the answer was simply delayed for too long, and thus, on May 15, 1525, the Monday after Cantate, do you order the culverins, your artillery, to be brought right up to the barricade, the cavalry and infantry, a few hundred, if not a thousand men, to move in immediately and that they fire the artillery directly into the center of this barricade of wagons, after all, it is a thousand meters in diameter and, at this point in time, is somewhat exposed as far as defensible positions are concerned, and thus, just as there are beasts who feign being of enormous size, then, having gotten themselves into a hopeless situation by way of this deception, are done away with in a fight with an animal that was expected to be smaller, for the supposedly smaller animal is not only bigger, but also knows how to surprise and has been fitted out with better weapons to boot, thus does the bombardment confuse the advisors, who, on their side of things, have abandoned some part of the weapons they were carrying on their person, some that were quick to hand, perhaps this is precisely because they know that, not only is the bigger beast actually bigger, but has also been endowed with better weapons, the cavalry only adds to this confusion by falling upon the barricade of wagons, the large beast, hollow on the inside, begins to stagger before it can come to its own defense, it burns, the pike goes through the eye, penetrates into the head, goes briskly through the belly, impales the heart, from a great distance (the Landsknecht kills from a distance of five meters), the mob manages to fend off the halberd when it is used as a thrusting weapon, however, he does not see the weapon's hook and cleaver behind his parry, the Landsknecht wrenches the halberd forward once more, and the hook goes through the neck or tears open the back, stabs in the leg from behind, then, soon enough, the halberd is usable from the front once more, it penetrates the chest of the one lying on the ground, the two-handed sword slashes a breach through the formation of pikemen, even if it has a pointy end and is much longer than an ordinary sword, the two-handed sword is, here and there, also made use of as an executioner's sword. The devastating superiority of the united princely horde seduces many a Landsknecht to court-martial measures, the sword falls from the one's hand while offering up great delight to the other when it separates head from body, then there's the

Katzbalger, which makes short work of it, and the knife, which very much likes to be stabbed into the back, this certainly hasn't escaped your notice, and the musket, of which nothing need be said, the flag of the princely horde is adorned by a false bird of prey, which, in truth, is likely to be a vulture and belongs not in the slightest to the flag, instead, it always hovers before it, those of the insurgents who manage to flee, hide themselves away in the saline-sod drainage ditches, but most of them are picked up and done away with there as well," Hut recounts, at this point, Father, who has recognized nobody less than himself in the landgrave, has long since wandered off with an expression of great curiosity on his face, he'd really like to get a good look at the gaunt man, is what he says before disappearing behind the hedge. Thus did he also not hear that Hut offered to endow him with the seal of baptism so that the Last Judgment might not extinguish him along with body, soul, and recollection. I'm now a little bit offended that Father didn't take me by the hand, I call out to those gathered by the fountain that we shall be back very soon, then follow after him, something about the gaunt man's face strikes me, Father's violence against him is strange to me, but, instead of continuing to grumble on about him, the gaunt man now entirely shifts the subject to the priests:

"And just as God praised Phineas when he punished the fornicating of Cozbi, so God will give us the good fortune to punish the fornicating of the priests.

And so you should be comforted and work in the service of God and cut down our sinful rulers. For what good would it do if we were to make peace with them, for they will continue their attack and not let us go free, and drive us into the arms of idolatry—then we would be guilty and would be better to die than to submit to their idolatry. It would be far better if we were to become martyrs than that we should allow the gospel to be taken away from us and be oppressed by the abuses of the priests. I know for sure that God will help us and will give us victory, for he spoke to me and told me so and commanded me to reform all ranks."

And as he thus speaks, I want to stop Father's hand, he just can't wait to smack the man in the face once more, he is torn between listening to and interrupting the speech, the man has my countenance, Father slaps me in the face once more, but, instead of hitting me, he yells at me that I ought to be quite precise when citing the Word of God to him, he would be only too happy to take part in my mission, and how precisely would I imagine reforming all ranks, I say, I shall abolish all of them, the ranks, no rank should remain above any other, I shall reform fathers so that they do not regard the child whom they have brought into the world as merely the legitimation of their social skills, they must make a vow before the Lord, Behold, this is my child, and I shall be there for this child forevermore, and I shall not deny my child, but accompany him down all his ways, and as far as priests and their transgressions are concerned, I shall place them in the pillory before their church for three days, everyone must see them, and the papal curia, should they have transgressed, those shall I expose in the Vatican, and the priests and the members of the curia, should they have transgressed, shall have to give all those who ask the information as to what they have done, and if that is not enough or if they refuse, I shall cast them forth from the land that shall appear to them as a disk, so quickly shall they tumble into the abyss, and as I speak thusly, I see that the gaunt man's mouth moves along with the inflection of my words, but my mouth is mute. But I have no fear of him, let him just try to raise his hand against me, even if he and the other two princes command a combined host of 6,600 men with cannons, misericorde, halberds, and two-handed swords—and this horde is to attack us in our barricade of wagons, the gaunt man says. It is not to be considered a miracle that God will give victory to so few unarmed people against so many thousands, for Gideon with only a few people and Jonathan with only his servants defeated many thousands and David, unarmed, brought down the giant Goliath. So, I have no doubt that the same shall happen again now and that we, however poorly armed, will gain the upper hand. Heaven and Earth themselves would have to change before we would ever be abandoned, just as the very nature of the sea changed in order to help the Israelites when Pharaoh was pursuing them.

Then Father knocks me to the ground for a second time, blood spurts from the back of my head, I look at Father without my eyelids moving, he's standing over me with his legs spread until he averts his gaze from me. I await further punches and kicks, Father stretches out his right arm, his hand opens and closes, this gesture of sovereignty has always been hateful to me, somebody hands him a halberd, which I don't even dignify with a single glance, for what kind of match really is it against the Sword of Gideon, with which I, prophet as well as political and military and revolutionary leader, sign my letters to the counts of Mansfeld, they circulate through the mob in transcripted form, instead, I continue my sermon, directed to nobody and everybody, as I lie down:

"Do not let your weak flesh be terrified, but attack the enemy with courage, you must not fear their ammunition, for you will see that I will catch in my sleeves all the bullets that they fire at us. Yes, you will see that God is on our side, for he now gives us a sign. Do you see that rainbow in the sky?—that tells us that God will aid those who have a rainbow upon their banner, and will pass judgment on the murderous princes and punish them. So you must not be terrified, you must trust in the help of God, and stand by your weapons: God will not permit you to make peace with the godless princes."

Father has the sleeves of my black mantle cut off, then recognizes having done so as a foolish error, for he can no longer threaten me with scudding stone cannonballs into them. The rainbow, he says, that could already be seen on page 730, which is to say long before your speech, when the big meadow was still empty and Mateo said, back there, a few hundred meters away from us, down the hill, then under the rainbow and through the sun-halo that it arches over, that's where we must go, then we went and are there even now.

The hastily cut-off sleeves give Father no peace. He consults with a Landsknecht as to whether they shouldn't be sewn back onto my mantle. The Knecht has no opinion on the matter, but affirms that he will do as he is told. When Father hangs the sleeves of the mantle over his left forearm like a maniple, two folded papers fall from them, I recognize these to be two letters that I'd had conveyed to Count Ernst and that have now come back to me like a miracle. My severed sleeves, symbol of suffering and mourning, the two thieves who have ever accompanied me on my left and on my right, who have ever been true to me and lent me a hand, Father slipped the letters into them so it looks as if they have defrauded me, as if they were the thieves whose hands had to be cut off. Father picks the letters up, unfolds them, scans them, folds them up, and hands them over to the Landsknecht, but then takes them back from him immediately, reads them more carefully, looks at me, reads, lets the sheets of paper fall, picks them up once more, hands them over to the Landsknecht once more, but, this time, with the request to read the letters so loudly and distinctly that all in the vicinity might hear what an abominable son he has, in reading, he is to strain mightily, in the original German, the language takes some getting used to and has almost ceased to be comprehensible to today's ears, the Landsknecht follows orders immaculately, his face betrays serious joy at being permitted to carry out such an unusual assignment, he has never yet served as public reciter and, simultaneously, he is suffused with the worry of not being mighty enough for the language. But how great is Father's astonishment when the Landsknecht not only stands there like somebody for whom giving a speech has become part of his daily bread, but for whom the language of the letters is no hurdle, he recites them so fluently and with such properly archaic intonation that one has the impression of being present for somebody's monologue in a play:

> Frightbearing Society, September 22, 1523
>
> To the noble and well-born Count, Lord Ernst von Mansfeld and Heldrungen, written in a Christian Spirit.
>
> Greetings, noble, well-born Count. The castellan and Council of Prüm have shown me your letter, according to which I am supposed to have called you 'a heretical scoundrel' and 'a curse upon the people.' This is quite true, for I am well aware—yes, it is common knowledge—that you have strictly forbidden your people with a public edict from attending my heretical Mass or sermon. To this I have said—and I will denounce you before all Christian people—that you have had the insolence to ban the Holy Gospel, and if (God forbid) you persist in such raging and insane bans, then from today onward, for as long as my blood still pulses, I will name you on paper a damned and ignorant man—and not only before all Christendom, but I will also have my books translated into many tongues and scold you before the Turks, the Heathens, and the Jews. And you should know that I do not fear you or anyone in the whole world in these great and just matters, for Christ cries murder at those who remove the key to the knowledge of God, Luke 11. For the key to the knowledge of God is this, that one should govern the people that they learn to fear God alone, Romans 13, for the beginning of true Christian wisdom is the Fear of the Lord. Now, you want to be feared more than God, as I will show in your deeds and your edict, then you are he who takes away the key to the knowledge of God and forbids the people from going to

church and can achieve nothing better than that. I will prove that my new Church Service and my sermons, yes, even the very slightest thing that I say or sing, agrees with the Holy Bible. And if I do not succeed in that, then I am prepared to lose my life and limb and all that is precious in this world. And if you can only succeed in your obstruction by the use of force, then for God's sake you must desist. But if you hope to do something like that, as is rumoured, then you must consider that it will cause no end of discord. The prophet says 'There is no wisdom nor understanding nor counsel against the Lord.' I am as much a Servant of God as you are, so take care, for the whole world must be treated with patience. Do not pull, or the old coat will rip the way you don't want. If you force me into print, then I will deal with you a thousand times worse than Luther did with the Pope. If you act as my benevolent lord, then be ready to suffer and to bear witness; but if not, then I will let God be your judge.

Written at Allstedt, i.e. Prüm, on Saint Maurice Day in the year 1523.
    Nobody, a Destroyer of the Faithless.

TO COUNT ERNST VON MANSFELD
PRÜM, May 12, 1525

Open letter to brother Ernst at Heldrungen, that he might change his ways.
    The outstretched power, the firm fear of God and the solid ground of his righteous will be with you, brother Ernst. I, Nobody, give you warning—even though it may be unnecessary—that, for the sake of the living God, you should abandon your tyrannical raging. You must not let

the wrath of God hang over you any longer. It was you who began to martyr Christians, it was you who slandered the holy Christian faith as villainy, it was you who had the impudence to uproot Christians. Now tell us, you miserable, wretched sack of maggots—who made you into a prince over the people whom God redeemed with his own precious blood? You should—and you must—prove whether you are a true Christian; you should—and you must—demonstrate your faith, as 1 Peter 3 commands. I give you my honest word that you will have a genuine safe-conduct so that you may publicly confirm your faith: our whole community, standing in a ring, has promised you this. You must also repent of your blatant tyranny, you must tell us who made you so foolish that you became such a wicked heathen to the disadvantage of all Christians, all the while claiming to be Christian yourself.

But if you stay away and will not do as we have urged you to do, then I will denounce you before the whole world with upraised voice, and every brother will be prepared to spill their own blood to fight you, as if you were the Turk. Then you will be hunted down and rooted out, for every man will be far keener to gain an indulgence at your expense than any indulgence that the Pope ever offered. We do not know how we can otherwise bring you to justice. You have no sense of shame; God has made you obdurate like the King Pharaoh, and like those kings which God himself wanted to obliterate, Joshua 5 and 11. Let us lament to God for evermore that the world did not recognize your coarse tyranny before now, when you raged like a bull. How was it possible that you could inflict so much astonishing damage? How can anyone but God himself have mercy on you? In short, you will be destroyed by God's mighty power. If you will not humble yourself before those of low standing, then you will be eternally shamed in the eyes of all Christendom, and you will become a martyr for the devil.

So that you know also that we have been given our orders, I say this to you: the eternal living God has commanded that you be cast down from your throne by the power that has been given to us; for you are of no use to Christianity, you are a pernicious scourge of the friends of God. God has spoken of you and your like, Ezekiel 34 and 39, Daniel 7, Micah 3. Obadiah the prophet says that your nest must be ripped apart and destroyed utterly.

We want to have your answer by this evening, or else we will hunt you down in the name of the God of hosts. So you know what to expect. We will not hesitate to carry out what God has commanded us to do. So do your best, too. I am coming for you. Written at Prüm, Friday after Jubilate, Anno Domini 1525.

I, Nobody,
with the Sword of Gideon.

Bravo! Father cries out. That couldn't possibly have been penned by you, he says, the handwriting is clear enough, but the original is full of the sorts of errors typical of sixteenth-century German texts, he shall have it checked over (he says without realizing that these errors have vanished from the English translation), then I'll learn the hard way, he asks for the leather case that he usually carries with him for important official matters, he sticks the letters into it, hands over the leather case and tells me to get up, I just keep lying there, Father makes a sign to two Landsknechte, they grab me underneath my arms and pull me up such that I stand before him slightly stooped, behind me, he gazes upon the Knecht still standing there with the cut-off sleeves draped over his left arm, then he has this Knecht approach him with the words, "Even to morrow the Lord will shew who are his, and who is holy; and will cause him to come near unto him: even him whom he hath chosen will he cause to come near unto him. But until then, take the sleeves and sew them back onto the unfortunate one, who is just as much of a blasphemer as all the other insurgents." While the Knecht sews the sleeves back onto my black cloak, Father holds me by the hand, he impatiently follows each stitch, swinging his arm as he does, I hold my arm very stiffly so that the servant doesn't hurt me with the needle, for the stitch passes through the skin, then for a second time, I feel how the sleeve is being sewn to it, only the Knecht noticed my brief twitch, his gaze betrays the insecurity as to whether he ought to pull the stitch out of the skin, I shake my head, Father asks what that means, an insect, I say, the Knecht has understood, the second sleeve shall soon be sewn on too, one doesn't see the seam at all, Father says with a sense of appreciation, the Knecht is overjoyed, he ties the thread and tears it off, Father thanks him, we rush away, there is still something important to discuss, he says.

But, as soon as we've joined the gentlemen and ladies at the Luther-Fountain of Life, they appear garbed in accordance with our own era. I know, my father says, and while I am still contemplating this sudden change of raiment and Father's sentence, as if my perception had cracked, I observe the fountain with its pomegranate of immortality floating above a golden snake or a golden bough, as well as the six Luther roses swimming in it, which, when I recognize them for what they are, cause me to grow wrathful against this Luther, who shall finally be forgotten five hundred years after the Reformation, then a scrap of paper is brought to me, upon which, beneath the illustration of a Luther rose, one reads: "This sign shall testify that such books as bear it have gone through my hands, for there is much illegal printing and corruption of books these days." I count six red petals from the six roses floating in the water, but the true Luther rose has only five white petals, thus is this not a Luther rose and I am soothed. Luther looks at me grimly, as if he's noticed that I recognize the forgery. In the milky, turbid water, beneath the glass plate, lie golden vases, which, when one observes them, begin to revolve around themselves, once they've turned one full rotation around themselves, a formulation that I've never fully understood, faces appear upon them, I recognize Father and Grandpa, then Bismarck and Luther, if I look at the faces for longer than five seconds, Father becomes Bismarck, Grandpa becomes Luther, then Luther becomes Bismarck, then Grandpa becomes Father, then Grandpa becomes Bismarck, and now that Father is becoming Luther, the water in the fountain begins to boil, the glass plate steaming up from the inside, the steam lifts it up a little, it falls back onto the edge of the fountain, is lifted back up, I look away, the fountain calms down once more, I wish to tell Father of this, but nobody other than me seems to have perceived it, on top of that, the beer stands cool at the edge of the fountain and appears to be drinkable, some lean against the well, while I cannot touch its still-glowing edge. As if boiling water could write, something can now be read on the outer-side of the fountain, where, before, only ornaments adorned it: Schattenfroh. This is not mere script: the h is the Arc de Triomphe, Cologne Cathedral becomes the doubled t. And it doesn't stop at Schattenfroh. The script now spins round in a circle, I follow it. Nobody seems to take offense at this. I take one lap, the script writes. I take a second lap, the script writes. I take a third lap, the script writes. I take a fourth lap, the script writes. I take a fifth lap, the script writes. I take a sixth lap, the script writes. I take a seventh lap, the script writes. I take an eighth lap, the script writes. I take a ninth lap, the script writes. I take an eleventh lap, the script writes, I've miscounted, I can no longer follow the script, which digs deeper and deeper into the wall of the fountain, overwriting that which is written, for there is already no more space, it notices precisely this and now grows smaller, it shall soon have dug all the way through the wall, the massive concrete dam in Obermaubach shall break, pure gold lies round the fountain, scriptflour that I shove into my pants pockets until it trickles out once more, now, one can follow my tracks, the gold betrays my path. I pass into script, read it off the ground. The script on the fountain doesn't cease overwriting itself. At the beginning was the sentence: "One calls this writing." And close to the beginning was a table. And with these words do I sit at the table. Upon the table is a stylus, connected to it by a long chain that cannot be broken by even the greatest of strainings. I read: "This is Herr Fietkau, my father says," then my father says, "This is Herr Fietkau," and introduces me to Lucas Cranach, a small, gray-haired man whose suit has outgrown him. Herr Fietkau was my father's student, my father says, and Herr Fietkau nods. I look at him, he doesn't look at me. Good evening, Herr Fietkau, I say, then turn to another gentleman to whom Father is introducing me, Werner Beutek, who knows the past better than the present, my Father says. Herr Beutek, in whom I clearly recognize Sebastian Brant, does not appear as if the present were at the center of his own present. Then Father introduces me to the ladies Stromm and Gansen. Gisela Stromm, the one says, Anni Gansen, says the other. Both simultaneously offer me their hands, thus do I give Gisela Stromm my right hand and Anni Gansen my left. "Pleased to meet you, Frau von Rotterdam," I say to Frau Stromm, while to Frau Gansen I say: "Pleased to meet you, Frau Stoß." Herr Schug is already drinking a Bitburger Pils when I shake hands with him in greeting. He mumbles his name into the foam on his lips: Paul Schug. I tell him my name and say: "Pleased to meet you, Herr Ratgeb." Mechtild Goergen stands a little ways off, as if she were concerned that my father might overlook her greeting, she strides forward and calls out her name with a remarkably light, yet still powerful voice, as if she had been ordered to do so by a judge. Mechtild Goergen, who looks so suspiciously similar to Tilman Riemenschneider, immediately reveals that she is a teacher, that it is, indeed, her calling, and that my grandpa bears not inconsiderable blame in this, she smiles when she says the word "blame," her teeth are diverse shades of gray, crooked, the left outer incisor has been pushed out of line by the other teeth of the upper jaw, the canine has shoved itself behind it, it hangs there, crooked and shifted over, immediately attracting everyone's attention.

Your grandpa distributed the pastoral letters from Bishop Clemens August Graf von Galen at school, Herr Beutek says. With his left hand, he distributed the pastoral letters and with his right, he threw the Nazi propaganda booklets out the classroom window. Frau Gansen disagrees. With his right hand, she says, he threw the pastoral letters of Clemens August Graf von Galen, whom the Catholic Church would beatify decades later, out the window of the second-floor classroom, while his left hand leafed through the Nazi propaganda booklets. And how was he able to flip through the pages with one hand, Frau Goergen would like to know. He would read aloud from the Führer's booklets before starting the lesson, Herr Schug says. He read nothing from the Führer's booklets, but from Galen's pastoral letter of September 14, 1941, Herr Beutek says. And what's the difference, Frau Stromm would like to know. Well, it's not all that simple, Frau Goergen is incensed. Precisely, Herr Schug agrees, the Bitburger Pils seeming to have softened him vis-à-vis my grandfather. After all, von Galen was Wilhelm Emmanuel von Ketteler's great-uncle, the man, he says, who was so hard on Bismarck. It's likely the other way around, Herr Beutek says, Ketteler was von Galen's great-uncle. Von Galen cherry-picked what was left of Catholicism in National Socialism and pilloried the rest. There were no cherries in National Socialism, Frau Stromm opines. Oh yes there were, the Oberammergau Festival, Herr Fietkau says, Hitler loved the Pilate from Oberammergau because Pilate's performance highlighted the guilt of the Jews in the death of Christ, thus ought the Oberammergau Festival be preserved. Then it was actually Hitler who picked the cherries out from Catholicism, one can hardly imagine von Galen picking the cherries out from Oberammergau, Frau Goergen says. Be that as it may, in his pastoral letter of September 14, 1941, von Galen speaks of the Bolshevik-Jewish governance of Russia, Frau Stromm says. He cites Hitler, who'd spoken of this some three months before, saying that, for over ten years, "Jewish Bolshevist" rulers had been endeavoring from Moscow to set not only Germany but all Europe aflame, Herr Fietkau says. Do we see him differently because of this, Frau Gansen says, from the start, whenever the conversation was about my grandfather, she adopted a sulking tone, as if Grandpa were guilty of something before her that he now had to make up for by enduring slander postmortem. To quote means to take over and make one's own, Herr Schug says. Here, one really ought to differentiate, Herr Fietkau says. Von Galen ought not to have adopted the phrase "Jewish Bolshevist," Frau Gansen says. Von Galen also quotes Pope Pius XI, who, in all seriousness, says that both man and civil society derive their origin from the Creator and that God has likewise destined man for civil society according to the dictates of his very nature, these are basic truths that one has dubbed "natural religion" and that, according to von Galen, can be recognized as true by human reason even without supernatural revelation, Herr Fietkau says. Then God must have welcomed the French Revolution with open arms, Herr Beutek says. The Pope is very careful that God keep pace with the history of civilization, Frau Goergen says. I would very much like to know whether God has studied *Elements of the Philosophy of Right or Natural Law and Political Science in Outline*, in which civil society is described as a wedge that is driven between state and family, alienating one from the other, Frau Stromm says. That's all sophistry, Herr Beutek says, here, he wishes to remind everyone that von Galen also speaks of the beastly observance of the doctrine that claims that it is permissible to deliberately take the lives of "unproductive people," the poor and innocent mentally unfit, a teaching that opens the door—the floodgates, even—to the violent killing of all people who have been declared to be "unproductive," as well as the terminally ill, invalids of work and war, and the elderly, his speech, Herr Beutek says, is clearly directed against the National

Socialist program of euthanasia. On August 3, 1941, he mounted the pulpit of St. Lambert's church in Münster and spoke out against "Aktion T4" in his sermon, which, for reasons of so-called racial hygiene, stigmatized the "unproductive citizens" as "unworthy of life." Von Galen risked his own neck with this sermon and its waves reached all the way to Berlin, where Martin Bormann immediately wished to hang him, which Goebbels postponed to a more favorable point in time after the war, in any case, numerous secret transcripts of von Galen's sermon circulated through the whole Reich, the ecclesiastical resistance to the killing-program was also articulated elsewhere and, already in August 1941, Hitler ended "Aktion T4." Pope Pius XII is said to have memorized entire passages of von Galen's sermons, including the following from the sermon of August 3, 1941:

"A curse on men and on the German people if we break the holy commandment 'Thou shalt not kill' which was given us by God on Mount Sinai with thunder and lightning, and which God our Maker imprinted on the human conscience from the beginning of time! Woe to us German people if we not only licence this heinous offence but allow it to be committed with impunity!"

Father clarifies that Grandpa mostly received copies of von Galen's sermons from Frau Knühl, the district welfare officer, and that they were stenciled, duplicated, and distributed in the Prüm district office. According to Father, both Frau Knühl and Grandpa were arrested simultaneously, most probably on August 12, 1944. "Thou shalt not kill," the Fifth Commandment, Father says, I ought to write an essay about that one day, thinking about it really is a good school of life, Luther thought about it too, with the corresponding consequences that would finally have a repercussion some five hundred years later.

My father asks about his father's pedagogical capabilities and Grandpa's students all agree that he was a strict, but good, teacher. Yes, absolutely. And beyond that? Everyone is silent. Anni Gansen is of the opinion that he was sporty, he was also energetic, Paul Schug says, and warmhearted, Mechtild Goergen adds. Does Father wish to see a milder image of his father than the one that he himself holds in his memory? Can Grandpa really have been more warm-hearted than Father, who isn't warmhearted at all? Did Prüm contribute to the cross-generational unyieldingness that caused Father to grow up with no empathy at all? No farewell embrace, no gazing back. One goes for a stroll on Sunday with the kids. On weekday evenings, one interrogates them to determine whether they've been a burden to their mother. They are ever a burden to the mother, for the father is never around. One afternoon, Mother called Father at the office, the son was reading a book, the title of which the mother couldn't understand in the slightest, and that worried her quite a bit, she wished for Father to take a look at the book after work. Where is the book, Father asks in the evening. It is called *Durchs wilde Kurdistan—Through Wild Kurdistan*—I reply. Father reflects for a moment, then states that the title bothers Mother, especially its last two words. I handed it over to him. Father flipped through it, read some, flipped back and forth, looked at me, "Where is the last page?" he asked me. "At the end," I said, expecting a box on the ears, instead of which he repeated the same question. The last page had come unbound, I must have put it back into the book and couldn't remember having done so, he finally found it, the end of the book is just as prominent of a place as the beginning, Father said, then read out loud:

"Marah Durimeh kept her word: she came in the evening; and once she was able to speak to me, unheard, she asked me: 'Sir, you grant me a request?'

'From the bottom of my heart.'

'Do you believe in the power of amulets?'

'No.'

'But I still made you one today. Would you like to keep it with you?'

'As a keepsake of you—yes.'

'Then take it. It helps not for as long as it is closed; but should you ever need a savior, open it; the Ruh 'i kulyan shall stand by you, even if he is not by your side.'

'I thank you.'

The amulet was square and lay in a small, oblong wooden box, the lid of which was adorned with nineteen white and eighteen black cross-strokes. Since it was furnished with a ribbon, I immediately hung it around my neck. Later, however, it would turn out to be very useful, despite my frankly confessed disbelief; of course, I could not have expected that its contents would be so surprising."

That's a good ending, Father said and praised the dialogue, which I ought to take as an example. So, what's the deal with the amulet, he asked. I don't know, I said, I didn't read the following volume. Mother finds that there is far too much violence in the book, he said. Beyond that, the business with the amulet bothers her. Thus did Mother tear out the page and show it to Father, who then laid it back into the book. A strange game. What is it that bothers you about it, I asked. The superstition, Father said. He also claimed that Mother had discovered spiritualist texts in my possession. I denied that. Something by a certain experimental magician named Staudenmaier, Father clarified. There, she read that human sensory organs could do what technology had otherwise been invented for. The eyes, for example, could project outward. How did I feel about that. That's an interesting notion, I said. What is it you mean by *notion*, Father asked. It's thinkable, I say, but I have my doubts as to whether it's feasible. Father wished to know what my stand on violence was. Karl May shows a society that cannot get by without violence, I said. Father was not satisfied with my reply. I reflected briefly, then said: Karl May shows a society that has emerged forth from violence. Well, well, Father said, then this Marah Durimeh is its savior? Marah Durimeh is a mysterious old woman, something akin to a Great Mother, she is the imagination, a cave spirit, the human spirit, she was Karl May's grandmother, I say. And what did Father do? He tore the last page into a thousand pieces and made them rain down over my head, then down to the ground like confetti. May Marah Durimeh be with you, he said, now you have a new last page. Mother had put a hundred-mark note in the amulet that hung around my neck in a small wooden box. I wasn't allowed to open it later, that would have bestowed independence upon me. Every night, I dreamed of this amulet. In the dream, I was convinced of the fact that a treasure had been taken from me. I dreamed that the wooden box with the amulet was to be found on a shelf that stood behind the headboard of my bed and whose brown, brittle curtain resembled the Shroud of Turin and gave off an odor that alternately reminded me of the eighteenth century and of the soup of swallows' nests with eggs and ham that Charley, the narrator of Karl May's story "The Kiang-lu," eats with his travel companion Frick Turnerstick as the fifth of sixteen courses on a barge called "The Wind" in Canton, China.

Just as the Shroud of Turin is to Turin Cathedral, so are Christ's Sandals to Prüm Abbey, Werner Beutek breaks the silence that has fallen. And the Seamless Robe to the Trier Cathedral, my father adds, in hard times, he always seeks out Trier and ignores Prüm. In some families, family is the only subject, generations spin round in a narcissistic circle, the female or male line is a single person who is reborn in their offspring and only dies when nobody else follows. My father never kept silent about his father, but his memory is no wellspring of long narrations, he seems to have slowly settled into his father's maxims without ever announcing their convictions. Father has no counsel for the future. "Get yourselves checked for colon cancer," he once said after Mother died, and "Be careful that you don't get that AIDS." Two of my father's sentences about Grandpa have stayed with me: "With Grandpa, that wouldn't have happened," and "The crumbs need to get eaten too." Father likely has such deep respect for his father that he avoids Prüm without being able to entirely withdraw from the region. I see him mute before his parents' grave, he crosses himself, then takes his leave. The grave has since been excavated, Father let slip no word about this. When used for graves in the earth, the phrase "rest period," allocated as twenty or thirty years, is appalling. If I can't live forever, can't I at least be buried forever?

That's how it was, all those present say, then raise their glasses to Grandpa. At this moment, looking through the glass raised in Grandpa's honor, the sun-halo is perceptibly losing intensity, at a single point, the insurgents managed to break through the ring that the united princely host had closed around the barricade of wagons, which many of them pay for with their lives, it's still not decided upon whether the princely mercenaries shall now storm the barricade of wagons or whether the insurgents shall attempt to flee from it, with my eyes pointed straight ahead at the gaunt man standing there as if in a painting, he looks at the ground on the bottom right with an expression of great disappointment, I recognize the way he's staged himself, we have made a significant contribution to the success of this staging, for it is only through our presence, our gathering around the fountain as the nail that goes through the feet that the requirement is fulfilled that the Imitatio Christi, which is most sacrilegious for the princes, among whose ranks my father numbers, is perceived as such, and thus are the feet, which we form with the fountain as a well that passes through them into the wood, simultaneously the eyes, which recognize the torso of the Corpus Christi in the gaunt man, the nail between the radius and the ulna of his right hand is the blue-and-white-striped flag of the princely mercenaries, before whom the aforementioned black bird of prey constantly flutters, as if unable to decide whether to become part of the flag or to remain part of itself, the nail between the radius and ulna of his left hand is the insurgents' FREEDOM flag, the sun-halo forms the head of the crucifix with an angel tumbling down headfirst upon it, at one moment, it appears as Icarus, at another, as the angel Satan, the gaunt man himself is the midpoint, the heart of this truly over-dimensioned cross, the size of which alone is already blasphemy, and thus shall the stab through the heart not fail to materialize—and now do I fear nothing more than that my father might see what I see, for I am indeed the gaunt man. Interesting, Father says, the bird of prey casts a shadow onto the flag of the princely host, which has no need of any buzzword, while the so-called FREEDOM is utterly without shadow, for that reason, the bird must actually recognize the FREEDOM flag as prey, but don't you see, he says, it's mere deception, "Through long chain of hands / For by elements is hated / The creation of man's hand. / Idle sees he all his labors / And amazed to ruin going / There's one thing you shall never get: FREEDOM," the bird acts as if it doesn't belong in the painting, for it cannot even fly anymore, it is the instrument of its shadow, the shadow ensures that it must always remain in the same place in the air and the shadow was arranged by the "beshitten prophet and lie-filled murderspirit," who looks to be entirely sunken into melancholy, as if he didn't realize what he'd brought about, in such a position, he's probably thinking to himself, well, if I've already lost, I would nevertheless prefer for the images to disguise that, and what is more suitable for this than the shadow that people, beasts, and things cast as if they didn't belong in the painting, but in life itself, and the one who engages in willful deceit—but now I see, Father interrupts, this deception alone isn't enough, the two flags are elements of a much greater deception, I've finally drunk enough from the Fountain of Knowledge, which is also part of this blasphemous drama, and if it is the task of this light-phenomenon with the rainbow overarching it, enclosing the flags on the left and right, under whose apex it lies, to distract us from the true nature of this blasphemous staging, thus has the gaunt man deceived himself by way of this deception, the light of knowledge itself determines its refraction, the colors of the sun-halo, as you see, are arranged in reverse order of the colors of the rainbow, an erasure of the Noahic Covenant, my son, Satan in the halo falls upon the gaunt man so that what belongs together will grow together and, in this federation, the cross that the gaunt man has spanned between north and south, east and west, shall also be erased, only to erase the Old and New Testaments as well, but this is not enough, both, which shall be one, shall also tumble through us, they shall strike us down like a comet that falls from the welkin, and if they do not strike us down, they shall tumble into the fountain and trigger a new deluge, we cannot stand idly by, Father says, we're on our way, it says, then rushes back out into the field. A few Landsknechte immediately join him, indeed, my father is not known for his generosity, but paying wages on time is not something he could ever have been reproached for not doing.

No, you've got it all wrong, I say, the bird of prey is a vulture, but, unlike all other vultures, it shall not drown in my blood, rather, it is waiting to be shot down by one of the insurgents, it is just that they lack the weapons and no matter how much it begs to finally be shot, it is already a sufficiently attractive target, unmissable, always in the same place, the insurgents look up briefly, but then do not hesitate to shoot the next bullet into the head of a Landsknecht or into their own heads and it is the latter option in particular that is growing ever more popular amongst them. This enrages the vulture very much, for it has always claimed to be faster and sharper than any pike, it makes every effort to tear itself free from its own shadow. It doesn't get even a single millimeter away from it. And all the Landsknechte laugh and the insurgents join them in their laughter. All of the weapons are suddenly calmed in truce, there is no longer an unequal battle being waged over the question of God and injustice, the vulture makes sure of this, it poses as a bird of prey each day anew, then, moving in still motion, the bird brings peace, laughter is unbearable for the vulture, and when it threatens that friend and foe alike shall drown in its blood, which fills all depths and overflows all banks, the laughter and the tranquility seem to be endless.

This is a further proof of the fact that society must go back to the ordo of the Middle Ages, for, otherwise, it has none at all or shall soon be degraded and decomposed into a society game, a parlor game, Father says, and as society did not find its way there by itself, it must be helped to find its happy place, beyond which the egalitarianism with which the dance of death has indiscriminately treated all estates and classes must be reversed, one thinks only of Lübeck, Basel, and Bern, Father says, death dances ever with us, it is the shadow rushing up ahead that we drag along behind us, that's beneath us, and if we are all already dead in life, Father says, then death too must have a sort of order, which, however, can be none other than that of the society in which death practices, otherwise, there could be no more state funerals, as insurgents all round the world so ardently wish. Indeed, every man dies alone and some of them without even being aware of it, but it is of secondary importance how long one is aware of it, only the fact that some are aware of it and some are not truly matters, but death belongs less to the life of the dying man than to the life of those left behind and that is all others, and thus does the meaning of life show itself in the state funeral, which he also desires for himself, but not the meaning of death, which is, in and of itself, insignificant. And, with these words, he orders my arrest, I, however, manage to evade it because of the blood filling all depths, overflowing all banks, it threatens to carry us away, it could carry us very far. The insurgents above me and below me have been bruised and pierced all over by the vulture's sharp beak, it has pecked at the whole of their bodies, the mountain itself can no longer be distinguished from blood, but the blood is living, it flows down a channel, the "Bloodgroove," it colors Weißer Berg, "white mountain," which now shines a beautiful red in the eveninglight, no longer distinguishable from the blood and the setting sun, not a single Landsknecht swims here with the thousands of lost souls whose bodies are about to be plowed into God's Acre, the graveyard, I shall be washed up before the gate of the second city wall, which I do not wish to pass through this time, 109 years previous, rather, I come right up close to the city gate in a house that is open and since, fortunately, I also find nobody inside able to give me information, I hurry up to the attic before the one who has obviously been driven outside in the course of the general turmoil returns, I find a room, not unlike my room underneath the attic where I lived in my parents' house when I was growing up, there is also a shelf with a closed curtain to be found here, and, as such, I want to take a look and see if there's a box hidden behind it, nobody shall search for me, nobody shall find me, and nobody shall know me if they actually do find me; I take off my robe, lie down on the bed, pull the covers over my head, and shall—and how could one expect otherwise—not be able to fall asleep, even though sleep has been the most essential element of life for weeks, alongside unconditional trust in God and the help one requests from him with each passing hour, perturbed both by scenes of defeat that have cost the lives of so many thousands, of which word swiftly spreads, and by a question that is brought up again and again: how can it be that, instead of immediately (and as peacefully as possible, by our advent alone) breaking the resistance of all those who brought us under the threats of the worst of punishments and establishing a system that follows God's Will and Word after they were disempowered and their system had been abolished, as represented by Father, we have either been massacred or, like me, have had to act as if we've been massacred so as not to be caught, scrupulously interrogated, then executed, in the worst case by one of the dukes or landgraves whose palaces we had intended to capture and who we threatened to catch, interrogate, execute.

Are the spirits to blame for the fact that we summoned them and haven't been able to get rid of them, the spirits that possessed the discontented and, just after they were turned into insurgents by the aforementioned spirits, left them helplessly alone with the urgent question of who is to lead this mob and of what one ought to have been doing in the future—I am the spirit and God has cited me to end the suppression of his pure Word, the Word that is free from vanities and avarice, as it is otherwise implemented by the rulers who pretend to have interpreted it only in their own interest and, to achieve this, one must "tear down all the castles and homes of nobility and leave nothing standing," for from those tyrants seeking to reach a particular goal for the nobles, who have been equally hit by the crisis of (but not exclusively) means of production caused by the swift growth of population and, subsequently, the work forces, and have become the main competitors for land, a goal that consists in indemnifying the nobles with the commons, the land available to everyone and used excessively by the peasants, even though the population requires more and more food, especially meat, with the pasture the peasants need to produce fodder thus being indispensable, and, in line with this, the increasing demand of the commons declared by the feudal landholders thereby challenging the peasants for their means of existence and, as a function of the burgeoning productive forces, leading to the emergence of people with little and, at a progressive rate, even no land at all, alongside those who own it, to say nothing of the repercussions of the agrarian crisis, a dwindling spiral; but not only this, many different wars and feudal feuds including pillages and lootings have been (and still are) taking place, but with the peasants having been (and still being) compelled to care for the reconstruction of destroyed villages, while being more and more bound to their native soil, with their property rights, including the right of preemption, being limited, the feudal landowners having the right to use the peasants' children as workers, the burden of duties increasing, including taxes, both direct and indirect, that not only enrich the feudal lord but are supposed to help to finance the extension of the state and to rationalize the body politic by providing civil servants with a university education, thus forfending the onset of the modern state with its Roman law that is directly opposed to the old, i.e. divine law, which, in the rebels' eyes, transforms the state that excludes them in such a way from the community of laws that is to be unified and of public life itself into a lawbreaker, not to mention the rural population that is educationally disadvantaged and seeks sanctuary in small-mindedness, whereas humanism, a new, broad educational system, has found its way into the cities and has permeated every aspect of cultural life—as such, nothing is to be expected from these tyrants, even if they pretend to be considerate toward Reformation.

All sins against the Word of God emanate from the princely tyrants, so that "all glory, fame and honor, all dignity and splendor" are truly due to the Son of God alone and cause earthly life to swing toward heaven, worldly obedience must not be placed over divine and those who demand worldly obedience must bring nobody into conflict against God's claim, for which it is also indispensable to not, under any circumstances, allow oneself to be persuaded to enter into negotiations with the tyrannical princes, which still ended up coming to pass, as I was to find out when I arrived late, but not too late, here in Prüm. Theology ought to be subject to the princes' might, they wish to govern the faithful and cheat their subjects out of Christ. Thus does true theology demand revolution. The sentences must be as short as the sword is long. The revolution orders the world anew and makes a God-pleasing Christianity possible in the first place. But what is such a reorganization to look like? For the time being, this is to remain undetermined. For we wish not to make the error of anticipating God. We're dealing with something else entirely, this is no longer the individual. It's no longer about saying that *this* is interesting and *that* is less interesting. First and foremost, what we are exclusively dealing with is suspension, the elimination of the existing order, the separation of the elect from the damned, and, indeed, here and now, beyond all present ranks. Come unto me, all ye who are cowed and disoriented, I wish to teach ye how to read, and I will give ye rest. Chiliastic revolution, that is social action in motion. The kingdom of God is not to be found somewhere in heaven, it is meant to be everywhere on earth. The farming ground is prepared. Without me, no Luther. Without radical theology, no social-revolutionary praxis. And vice versa. And no language without mystical spiritualism. And, all in all, no radical theology and no social-revolutionary praxis without Luther. Then a kind of hopelessness comes to the fore, as its doctrine of justification and its sealed faith actually get stuck on the outside of the letter, without such faith becoming inward, body and soul. But, in the context of a doctrine of spirit and a theology of suffering, it is the abyss of the soul that matters. The goal is freedom from the Word, which is exterior, the goal is the effect of the inner word, Christ must be bitter, a bitter Christ. I was sent here by the secret Christianity. It is I, Ezekiel, Jeremiah, Elias, Daniel. And I say unto you what I see, they are stabbed and shot, but it is only over the outstretched hand of the fool sleeping peacefully in a red robe that blood runs, he is truly dead, is that me?, until the vulture tears everything away, gesture of fearfulness, broken mouths, always looked at more and more closely, each time, something can be recognized more precisely, something else comes into view. What's the sky like? Red as blood is the sky. The sky is black once more. It's about to burst, hurls forth the 666, putrefaction shall rain down upon the thirsty people whose bodies are already very much in thrall to putrefaction, they give forth the Word once more, it sounds out far and wide through the land, like hollow coins clattering across the ground. The burning sea rages behind the procession of the muses. There is no sea. Flamelambent, constricting projectiles, not air, not earth. Spinning clouds that whirl skeletons. Waves of magma. Is it raining cosmic matter and energy? Woe unto him who sees symbols. Colon cancer. A snail. Turbulence. The eye of a reptile. Lizardskin. Spermtears. Skulls appear and are thrown ashore by the Felsenmeer millwheel. There is no land, only a narrow crevice. Between the fissure and the eye of the reptile, viscous molten rock. At the edge of the column, the sower with the red trousers bound below the knee. Van Gogh, above the left knee, in magma. Bismarck, right above van Gogh. And many others who cannot perish, who have eagerly taken up the seeds, which are repeatedly pushed to the surface by the grinding mill of time. All in hot, uniform mud. Something is written upon the cornea and in the eye-chamber of the reptile: 666 flanked by two cherubs.

The sower hovers in peculiar fashion. He seems to be in a hurry. Over the crevice, on horseback, the woman riding the white horse. The proud steed pulls a harrow that plunges deep into the earth, a cultivator that prepares the field for seedbeds and simultaneously drags with it the skulls and bones of those that have been pushed up. The bones and skulls fall deep enough into the furrows it has drawn; covered in earth, they've a tomb in their pits.

The sower has bound a cloth in which small jars of seeds are to be found. The sowing of the crevice is hard and precise work. Adam and Eve shall also disappear into the crevice, toward which the sower and the woman riding the white horse are moving, and the muses too shall tumble into the abyss of the cleft. The harrow shall fill up the cleft with the skulls and bones it keeps coming across. The cleft becomes a skullroad, the skulls themselves one day become seeds, thus does death keep itself alive. Adam and Eve are entirely nude, she shows herself off to us frontally, whereas Adam has turned his back, both are their own statues, her blazing hair grabs at his genitals, as if she were dumping an enormous jug over him, she has stretched forth both arms, she holds the overflowing crown of the apple tree in her hands, it threatens to pour into his gullet, however, he recognizes the impending disaster and, renouncing the sin, falls defensively off to the side. Even Daphne and Apollo could have left it at that.

I follow the woman riding the white horse who brandishes a riding crop. The arm and the crop form the same arc as the reptile's eye. Her crop shall deliver a blow unto me.

Fool's club, laurelwreath. I am the wanderer between the worlds, here and there, entirely in the image, entirely before it, wherever I look at it, I look at myself. No halo, no sign of support. No heaven is here in sight, for Venus has fallen to earth through Michael, who has the key to the abyss and a great chain in his hand and Michael hurls her into the abyss where he binds her with the chain for a thousand years, and I lose my face, thus is there no image of me, and I am led into a room in which there is no mirror, with my face, I also lose the lock before my mouth, and I loudly say: "God that is all good and almyghtye / Hath shewed his power upon me Nobody / For whear my mouth with lock was sparred / He hathe it burst and my speche restored, / Wherefor I wyll syng prayse unto his name / And thoughe the pope with all his trayn / Do me rebuke and against me sayen / That as tofore I shuld nowe holde my peace / Yet Gods honour to set furth I can not ceasse." It is thus that I see everything before me.

What occurs yonder, where art thou? And I know not whether it comes to pass in a dream. This jolting now too, it seizes me more tightly, my left eye entirely gummed up, and when I turn around, it turns me around again, which I can't stand at all, I beat against it with my right hand, there is only one hand and one arm, I see it with one eye, there is somebody standing there. Who art thou, once again. Hullo, I beeth a poor sick man, I say. In sooth, alas. He now stands a little ways off, looks around haltingly to see if he can find something, but at first finds nothing, simply gawps, then finds my satchel, just as it is the way of people to look about and most surely aught to find; they begin to search, all is already lost, he pulls out the wretched letter that Count Albrecht wrote in the camp and I knew I really shouldn't have pocketed it, it is more deadly than a stamped and sealed pass, from whence did that letter come to you, he asks, I avoid the question and ask what his name is and who he is, Schroffel von Waldeck, he says, a Knecht, one can see that, I say, what can one see, he asks, that you are a Knecht, I say, he takes that as an affront, I want to raise myself up, you're not that ill, he says, who is your master, I ask, it is . . . , I don't understand him, the way he mumbles, you mean Otto von Noppe, I ask, no, not Otto von Noppe, who then, I ask, Otte von Eppe, I hear, who is that, a nobleman, he says, and from whence, I wish to know, a man from Rhineland-Palatinate, he says, Otte, Otto, not Noppe, but Eppe, Otte von Eppe, not Otto von Noppe, his Knecht is here, in search of an inn, why have you come up to the attic, there are free chambers downstairs, anxiety, an insurgent, as if he were just about to . . . ?, mere curiosity, bowing and scraping before the nobleman, I climbed up to the roof to find out what sort of inn this was and there *he* is lying in bed, he shall say to his master, but he's forgotten the letter once more, it could easily go on like this, he has his weapon always in view, now, the matter of the poor sick man has been articulated, why should I not make it known that I was being pursued by insurgents, I could get out of bed and embrace him as my liberator, the roof-hatch, but without robe, yet not so gaunt, snatched away by the pursuer, huh?, the letters, what is it he wants with these letters?, the bag along with it, he probably doesn't believe that himself, while I ponder, I recognize that no excuse shall catch on, then he calls down the stairs to the Junker, cheerful strides promptly approach, that's how a man who has triumphed walks, a fellow with an upright posture, so tall that he can only stand hunched over, enters the room, so, who am I, a liar, the Knecht says, gives him the bag with the letters, leaves the room, and makes sure that nobody comes up the stairs, the Junker scans the letters, from whence did I get them, he inquires, they were simply handed over to me, I say, was I on Weißer Berg with the insurgents, for God's sake, I reply, I've got a fever and have been laid out here for days, I haven't been able to take a single step out the door, then he touches my brow, takes my hand, I'm cold as ice, he says, looks at the letters once more, handed over in a bag? he asks, where was that? on the battlefield? am I the preacher, I dismiss this, startled, then he grabs hold of me, shakes me, am I the gaunt man, I'm not all that gaunt, I say, the Knecht comes, threatens me, OK, I'll admit it, the gaunt man, yes, a short exchange of looks between the two, the Knecht flies out of the room once more, is overjoyed about the discovery he's made, what a catch, the Junker reflects for a moment, indicates to him that he is to take me with, Philipp I and George shall certainly be able to find a suitable use for me, I am to get up and put on my robe, might I take a glance behind the shelf-curtain before we set off, the Knecht immediately draws his weapon, the Junker appeases him, perhaps he hopes that I've hidden something here, he has a look while the Knecht doesn't take his eyes off of me, is this what I have in mind, the Junker asks and holds out a box to me, I mean, what's in it, I wish to know, do I not already know what's in it, he wishes to know, he takes a key out of the box, tries it in the door, it doesn't fit, he looks around the room to see if it might fit somewhere else, and when the Knecht whom he sends after George and Philip I leaves, he jokes that it's certainly the key to my soul, if only they'd begun with the screws, they would already have twisted the truth out of me. From the way he's holding the key, I can tell it consists of two parts, either hollow on the inside or concealing a small dirk that I'd like to use to stab the Junker in the neck, just as soon as he hands it over to me, but the Junker has become aware of the constitution of the key itself and seeks to extract the bottom part, a scrap of paper falls out, I quickly pick it up from the floor, take two or three steps backward, unroll the scrap, read it, then stick it into my mouth. To the astounded Junker, I say, "George is affected, Philip II as well." The Junker draws his sword, take the scrap out of your mouth, I shake my head, he sticks the sword between my lips, I ape chewing motions, woe unto you, he says, if you swallow that, I'll shove this sword down your throat, thus do we stand there, the sword shall tire him out, the saliva softens the scrap, trampling up the stairs, three men enter the chamber, the Knecht in front, behind him are Duke George of Rhineland-Palatinate and my father, both garbed in exceedingly festive fashion, the Junker stands to attention, approaches George, the last Roman Catholic member of the House of Wettin, and whispers something into his ear, George looks shocked and whispers something into my father's ear, both look at the Junker, then my father whispers something into the Junker's ear, who then, in his turn, whispers something into George's ear, whereupon George nods, "Duke George of Rhineland-Palatinate and Landgrave Philipp I of Durum demand that you hand over the scrap," I refuse, but conceal the fact that, meanwhile, I've already chewed and swallowed the scrap, which causes me less concern than the fact that my father seems to have become the not-even-twenty-five-year-old Philipp I von Durum, who married George's daughter Christine two years ago, five years after the death of my mother, in the very same year when George had all of Luther's Bibles confiscated, which was a personal triumph for me, as I don't, after all, need George or my father for my own execution, one Luther is enough for that, by writing and speaking such beastly things of me, Luther is nothing but a mounted conductor of soft-soapery. At that point, George doesn't hesitate for long and brings my right hand beneath the thumbscrew, I recognized the device just as soon as he came up the stairs with it, he immediately tightens the thumbscrew even more, O pain, I cry out, and he says, does this cause you pain?, yes, I say, but I ought to bethink, he says, "this is most painful for you / but even more painful for those poor people stabbed to death today / people engulfed in misery by you," and I hear myself laughing loudly and saying, "They never wished it any other way to be," I am an evil prophet, says Philipp I, who I ought to recognize as my father, God has gravely forbidden upheaval, which can also be shown in the Scriptures, indeed, one ought to honor the authorities and it does not befit a X-tian to avenge himself, here, I am defiant and say, I would have been right to punish the princes, for they were so opposed to the Gospels and acted so unmercifully against Christian liberty, whereupon Philipp I, whom I ought to recognize as my father, refers to the New Testament, I counter with the Old Testament, what are you trying to prove with that, asks Philipp I, whom I ought to recognize as my father, the right to resistance, I say, as is justified in the Old Testament, I know nothing of it, Philipp I says, etc., he refers to Romans 13, he opens the girdle book, which, wearing white gloves, he holds proudly in his left hand, as if he were carrying a relic or on his way to the high court, he opens the book-clasps, leafs forward, backward, forward, then reads

Romans 13

Let every soul be subject unto the higher (state) powers. For there is no (state) power but of God: the powers that be are ordained of God. Whosoever therefore resisteth the (state) power, resisteth the ordinance of God: and they that resist shall receive to themselves damnation.

For rulers are not a terror to good works, but to the evil. Wilt thou then not be afraid of the (state) power? do that which is good, and thou shalt have praise of the same: For he is the minister of God to thee for good. But if thou do that which is evil, be afraid; for he beareth not the sword in vain: for he is the minister of God, a revenger to execute wrath upon him that doeth evil. Wherefore ye must needs be subject, not only for wrath, but also for conscience sake. For this cause pay tribute also: for they are God's ministers, attending continually upon this very thing. Render therefore (to all their) dues: tribute to whom tribute is due; custom to whom custom; fear to whom fear; honour to whom honour (is due).

> Owe no man any thing, but to love one another: for he that loveth another hath fulfilled the law.
>
> The night is far spent, the day is at hand: let us therefore cast off the works of darkness, and let us put on the armour of light.

As to my objection—does he think I don't realize the incompleteness of this letter from Romans—Philipp I, whom I etc., replies that it ought to be enough to reproduce it incompletely here, it serves his purpose quite perfectly, which is to say, to show that one ought to honor the government, whereupon I say that it is about the difference between the duty of obedience and the right to resistance, and, indeed, the Old Testament expressly shows that it recognizes a right to resistance against the tyranny of evil, against the evil of tyranny, even if the very ones who are in possession of power are also in the right, which is to say are in possession of legality as such. Philipp I, whom and so on and so on, cannot and does not wish to recognize this, why, then, would there be a New Testament. The New Testament does not exist to invalidate the Old Testament, I say, rather, it is its culmination, without the Old Testament, the New Testament cannot be understood at all, it is the fulfillment of a promise. Not everyone can claim the right to resistance for themselves as they see fit, I say, but only he who, like me, is urged to it by his conscience, I am one who is driven by conscience and the unconditional love of God and, as such, I know that tyrannicide, which the Old Testament sanctions as the pinnacle of the right to resistance, is my duty. Philipp I, however, *shelved* the Old Testament by pulling out the New, he acts as if he wanted to set me onto the wrong track, although I am absolutely certain that he does not know the Old Testament, not in detail, in any case, and he really ought to give Romans 13 another read. And thus do I tell him the story of Jeremiah's arrest and how perpetual repetition finally preempts the dreadful end:

And it came to pass in the fourth year of Jehoiakim the son of Josiah king of Judah, that this word came unto Jeremiah from the Lord, saying, Take thee a roll of a book, and write therein all the words that I have spoken unto thee against Israel, and against Judah, and against all the nations, from the day I spake unto thee, from the days of Josiah, even unto this day. It may be that the house of Judah will hear all the evil which I purpose to do unto them; that they may return every man from his evil way; that I may forgive their iniquity and their sin. Then Jeremiah called Baruch the son of Neriah: and Baruch wrote from the mouth of Jeremiah all the words of the Lord, which he had spoken unto him, upon a roll of a book. And Jeremiah commanded Baruch, saying, I am shut up; I cannot go into the house of the Lord:

Therefore go thou, and read in the roll, which thou hast written from my mouth, the words of the Lord in the ears of the people in the

Will my dear one thus allow that he shall recite the whole story here?

Dear son-in-law, is that not enough, should you not shut up his mouth?

For Jeremiah says it himself, my dear one, he cannot, he is not worthy of his, he is not worthy of him; he betrayed the mob, just as Jeremiah here betrays the Lord.

Lord's house upon the fasting day: and also thou shalt read them in the ears

of all Judah that come out of their cities. It may be they will present their supplication before the Lord, and will return every one from his evil way: for great is the anger and the fury that the Lord hath pronounced against this people. And Baruch the son of Neriah did

I wish to hear it in its entirety, should a single word of this Bible-hero be false, and you know that we ought not to change a single iota, he shall be judged on the very spot.

according to all that Jeremiah the prophet commanded him, reading in the book the words of the Lord in the Lord's house. And it came to pass in the fifth year of Jehoiakim the son of Josiah king of Judah, in the ninth month, that they proclaimed a fast before the Lord to all the people in Jerusalem,

and to all the people that came from the cities of Judah unto Jerusalem. Then read Baruch in the book the words of Jeremiah in the house of the Lord, in the chamber of Gemariah the son of Shaphan the scribe, in the higher court, at the entry of the new gate of the Lord's house, in the ears of

And the false prophet proclaimed to all the people in the Eifel to . . .

all the people. When Michaiah the son of Gemariah, *do you not notice, my dear one, how these genealogical tables are meant to lull one to sleep, they make one so drowsy...*

the son of Shaphan, had heard out of the book all the words of the Lord, Then he went down into the king's house, into the scribe's chamber: and, lo, all the princes sat there, even Elishama the scribe, and Delaiah the son of Shemaiah, and Elnathan the son of Achbor, and Gemariah the son of Shaphan, and Zedekiah the son of Hananiah, and all the (other) princes.

Then Michaiah declared unto them all the words that he had heard, when Baruch read the book in the ears of the people. Therefore all the princes sent Jehudi the son of Nethaniah, the son of Shelemiah, the son of Cushi, unto Baruch, saying (to him),

He could have done precisely the same without inciting the people to rebellion, had he come to us directly, we could have avoided all this destruction.

Take in thine hand the roll wherein thou hast read in the ears of the people, and come. So Baruch the son of Neriah took the roll in his hand, and came unto them. And they said unto him,

Sit down now, and read it in our

He would have come before us with all of his manuscripts and we would have taken them apart line by line, word by word, letter by letter, then ordered them alphabetically as material out of which God would extract the letters that were worthy of his Word.

ears. So Baruch read it in their ears. Now it came to pass, when they had heard all the words, they were afraid

In fact, if the false prophet had read in our ears too, we would also have been afraid, both one and other...

both one and other, and said unto Baruch, We will surely tell the king of all these words. And they asked Baruch, saying, Tell us now, How didst thou write all these words at his mouth?

There is no doubt from whose mouth HE (who is he) received and put down his words; but if he takes the Word of God into his mouth, he hath already become a blasphemer.

Then Baruch answered them, He pronounced all these words unto me with his mouth, and I wrote them with ink in the book. Then said the princes unto Baruch, Go, hide thee, thou and Jeremiah; and let no man know where ye be. And they went in to the king into the court,

And thus did Satan whisper to him, and he understood it wrongly, and his manuscripts are full of errors.

Now, verily, he hath hidden himself. But it did him no good. If only he'd hidden himself away in hell instead of making a fool of himself in an attic.

but they laid up the roll in the chamber of Elishama the scribe, and told all the words in the ears of the king.

So the king sent Jehudi to fetch the roll: and he took it out of Elishama the scribe's chamber. And Jehudi read it in the ears of the king, and in the ears of all the princes which stood beside the king.

Now the king sat in the winter-house (it was) in the ninth month: and there was a fire on the hearth burning before him. And it came to pass, that when Jehudi had read three or four leaves, he cut it with the penknife, and cast it into the fire that was on the hearth, until all the roll was consumed in the fire that was on the hearth.

Have we not studied the manuscripts of this arch-phantast again and again and found nothing good in them? And yet we allowed him to have his way until he became a murderer.

You ought to do as the story does, take the manuscripts, cut them off piece by piece, then hurl them into the fire.

Yet they were not afraid, nor rent their garments, neither the king, nor any of his servants that heard all these words. Nevertheless Elnathan and Delaiah and Gemariah had made intercession to the king that he would not burn the roll: but he would not hear them. But the king commanded Jerahmeel the son of Hammelech, and Seraiah the son of Azriel, and Shelemiah the son of Abdeel, to take Baruch the scribe and Jeremiah the prophet: but the Lord hid them.

(George cuts the columns off and hurls them into the fire.)

(And the columns that he has heretofore not cut off and hurled into the fire, he now cuts off and hurls into the fire.)

He surely expected that the Lord would hide him too. Which means that it must be another Lord than the one he had in mind.

After that George has burned the roll, and the words which Baruch took down from the mouth of Jeremiah, who received them from the Lord and put them down, and which I, Nobody, took down from the mouth of Schattenfroh, who received them from himself and put them down, Schattenfroh says to me:

"Take thee again another roll, and write in it all the former words that were in the first roll, which George with Philipp I, who is your father, did burn. And thou shalt say to George: Thus saith Schattenfroh: Thou hast burned this roll, saying: Why hast thou written therein, saying: Schattenfroh as the king of Babylon shall certainly come and destroy this land, and shall cause to cease from thence man and beast.

Therefore, thus saith Schattenfroh of George: He shall have none to sit upon the throne of David: and his dead body shall be cast out in the day to the heat, and in the night to the frost. And I will punish him and his seed and his servants for their iniquity; and I will bring upon them, and upon the inhabitants of Jerusalem, and upon the men of Durum and Prüm, all the evil that I have pronounced against them; but they hearkened not.

For his two sons, the one ill, the other weak in mind, shall remain without child and both perish before the father, however, George's Eifel dukedom shall fall to his brother Heinrich, which, due to his brother's Lutheran attitude all throughout his life, he shall view as the worst misfortune imaginable. And then too shall Philipp I of Durum, his son-in-law, spread the Reformation during his lordly retreat."—

Thus do I, Nobody, take another roll, and write in it all the former words that were in the first roll, which George, the Duke of Rhineland-Palatinate, hath burned. And many more words like this are added: There exists the rumor that Muror heretically reprinted this book here according to old custom."

Then, my father speaks: "God himself has thus blown into you so that you might assemble a mob and rise up against the princes, but your

God is Schattenfroh who has moved you to make such a ruckus. You boast of divine revelation, but have made up such things or have been deceived by the devil with visions, for that is precisely Schattenfroh. Nothing is correct in your Jeremiah 36 beyond a couple of words, but the rest you, a prophet-eater, have written onto and over, made heretical and twisted, and you likely believe that those whom you so slander shall not notice what a wormy reprinter and bookdevil you are, how they run from you everywhere, intent on their own advantage, their wish to pull the wool over everyone's eyes regarding God and Christianity, the True Word. You are a genuine Occus Boccus. May the false word get stuck in your throat in such a way that you leap strugglingly toward the ceiling, striving to rid yourself of the bone. We shan't help you! If we remove the head with a sharp blade, then the bone shall soon come into view. For that reason alone, because of your disfigured face, you ought to go to Hell and become a martyr for the devil. And even if you sometimes have already thought that I am Schattenfroh, so do I say to you here and now: I am not Schattenfroh," but George's gaze betrays that he has recognized Schattenfroh in him.

Beyond that, according to Philipp I., who is said to be my father, there is no right at all according to which the right to resistance, as I understand it . . . —as the Old Testament understands it, I interject— . . . as I understand it, might be enshrined in the law. Your subversive thoughts and deeds, Philipp I, who is said . . . , says, have as much in common with the righteousness of a Reformation belief as the devil with the Divine Trinity. You shouldn't speak like that, is what I then say, also revealing the contents of the scrap out of rage at the landgrave's arrogance in wishing to dispute matters of theology with me; if this actually were my father, he would no doubt be more familiar with the Old Testament than the writings of the Church Fathers: Upon the scrap is written: "George und Philipp: Jeremiah 36" and here on page 790 has the prophet's scripture been fulfilled once more, I say.

George is so horrified by this that, likely attempting to cover up the issue, he has the Junker hand over a hundred guilders as reward for my capture and announces that he shall take me into a castle on this day, the name of which he grumbles into his suddenly grayed beard, in such a way that I approximately understand "Geldhernun"* or "Lehrendung"† or "Ungernheld"‡ or "Dunglehren"§ or "Hundregeln."¶ This, George says, is the castle that the insurgents, instigated by me, were seeking out and whose proprietor I threatened to do away with if he did not comply and accept our terms. Count Ernst II von Mansfeld-Vorderort, of whom I am speaking here, has still not forgotten my letter of twenty months ago, in it, I, according to George, wrote, "I do urge and exhort you, unnecessary though it should be, to abandon your tyrannical raging for the sake and in the name of the living God and to provoke the wrath of God no longer." Is this the script of my hand? George asks.

Yes.

Did I also write this: "You it was who began the martyring of Christians; you it was who denounced the holy Christian faith as villainy; you it was who dared to eradicate the Christians."

Yes.

Did this bit of unspeakability also come forth from my shortsightedness: "Just tell us, you miserable, wretched sack of worms, who made you a prince over the people whom God redeemed with his dear blood?"

Yes.

And did these lines also spring forth from my own shortsightedness: "You shall and will have to prove that you are a Christian; you

---

* Standanddelivernow.
† Doctrinedroppings.
‡ Reluctanthero.
§ Dunglearning.
¶ Dogrules.

will and shall have to give an account of your faith, as l. Pe. 3 87 insists. An absolutely genuine safe-conduct will be given to you by the whole community gathered in the ring; there you will apologise, too, for your manifest tyranny and say who made you so foolish, as to become a pagan evildoer like this, to the detriment of all Christians, while performing the Christian name." Yes, my farsightedness. And even in the event that he didn't come and confront the farmers, I'd have made provisions: "If you stay away, and do not acquit yourself of the charge laid against you, I will lift up my voice against you for all the world to hear, and all the brethren will be ready to risk their lifeblood, as they have been hitherto against the Turk. Then you will be hunted down and wiped out, for everyone will be far keener to gain an indulgence at your expense than those which the pope used to give out. We don't know any other way of calling you to book."

Yes.

And I am also said to have thought up a curse beyond death: "If you will not humble yourself before those of little repute, you will be forever disregarded in the sight of the whole Christian people and you will become a martyr of the devil."

Yes.

Then, finally, the threat, am I alone to blame for its formulation: "So that you know, too, that we are acting under instruction, I say this: The eternal, living God has commanded that you should be forcibly cast down from your seat; for you are no use to the Christian people; you are a scourge which castens the friends of God. God has spoken to you and your like in Ezekiel 34, 39; Daniel 7; Micab 3. Obadiah the prophet says that your nest has to be torn down and smashed to pieces."

I alone.

Then I ought to be paid back in the same coin.

The four Landsknechte that George sent for come up the stairs and lead me away, the two princes behind them. The Knechte inquire as to where I am to be taken. I shall give the instructions, George says. We have now penetrated deep into the matter, he says, already audibly out of breath after just a few meters, and we wish to get out of it once more. We'll manage that best if we go to the western edge of the summer meadow, in an easterly direction—the procession is slowing, the Landsknechte are concerned that the princes shall lose us—away from Weißer Berg, the supposed center of that which is coming to pass, where I am said to have placed myself most fatefully. Your staging really did catch everyone's eye, George says, in such a way that they didn't lose themselves in the jumble of events, in the little stories within the big story, thus do eye and word have an order, though this is simply my view of that which is coming to pass, a light ought to dawn upon the gaze, an enormous Latinate cross that overlaid the battle and the appearance of which is my most significant lapse, greater than even the panic-stricken leading of the insurgents into the abyss, for the crosspoint of this merely imaginary cross, visible only at its endpoints, as it should also, if it were up to me, appear in future painting and literature, if anything at all should appear at the end of all days other than the eschatology that is at work *in* history, I would have imagined myself there instead of Jesus with my body completely enshrouded in black; this cross is by no means modest, the way Jesus' cross could no longer be surpassed in terms of modesty, it is a form of bombast as no theater in the world could have performed it, it would then have turned out to be more than mere theatrical thunder, with this cross, my heretical conceit and presumptuousness would become consummate by way of the conviction manifesting itself therein that only the spirit of the script, which I presume to know, and which is experienced in the abyss of the soul through a sudden revelation, and not its mere letter, as Luther emphasizes, justifies belief and makes divine will tangible, revelation cannot be read, but comes to pass daily if one simply has will and sensitive awareness; in order to get to the point, George says, one really must deliver such a chiliastic enthusiast and enthusiastic chiliast from himself—I would happily break off his words, which cause me more pain than a thumbscrew ever could, but my voice would shoot off without making contact with his ears—and if, after this long speech, I simply believe that he does not know what he is talking about, I ought to be certain that he has seen the cross of which he speaks with his own eyes, it consisted of five elements with a dual visual-axis formation: the vertical from the apex of the rainbow in the north, in which many recognized my halo, it bordered and arched over the whole ensemble, over the sun-halo with its falling angel as my head, myself as the heart, then this so-called Fountain of Life in the south, which formed the base of the cross; in the horizontals from the princely flag to the west, through myself as the sectional figure of both axes, all the way to the flag of the insurgents in the east. George appeared suddenly beside me during this exegesis on the formation of the two visual axes, thus do I not wish to stand back and take the witness stand for myself. Faith is all about suffering, only the experience of the cross counts if one wishes to receive the testimony of God into one's heart, all else is mere semblance, I say. Everyone must receive the knowledge of God, the true Christian faith from the eternal, powerful Word of the Father in the Son as explained by the Holy Spirit, so that in his soul he may comprehend what is the breadth, and length, and depth, and height. In short, there is no alternative: men must smash their stolen, counterfeit Christian faith to bits by going through real agony of heart, painful tribulation, and the consternation that inevitably follows.

The procession comes to a halt. My scriptures must also be smashed to bits, George says, and it is thus that we would now go and seek out the workshop of all evil, for the ABCs lie fallow, and one really ought to leave it at that, at lying fallow. You, George says, who are a true apocalyptic mystic and, as God's revolutionary, a social servant, who does not distinguish between religion and secularism, for you, revolution and reformation suddenly make no difference, to the Roman Catholic, this is a horror, for he only looks backward, while you look out ahead, to where the gaze cannot reach, which, through the misunderstanding of the Word of God, the sole interpretation of which he claims for himself as sole elected one, incites the people to rise up against the authorities, to whom, consequently, the worldly order no longer applies, only the rule of God to be established in the here, and I ought to have followed the lead of Grschwbtt, also known as Tall George, who, 140 years later, shall write:

"When I get up in the morning, Grschwbtt spoke, I speak the whole ABCs, in them, all the world's prayers are contained, our Lord God himself might then put the letters together and make prayers out of them as he pleases, I can't do it half as well as he can. And once I've said my ABCs, then I'm aweary to the marrow of my bones and as steady as a wall for the day ahead."

If only I had kept it at that instead of misreading the ABCs of God and history and their convergence, which now hits me of all people so painfully, to falsely read out that which I ought to have left to God and History, if only I'd been a bit more holy, George says, but, in that case, I wouldn't have gotten any further with my manuscripts than an illiterate, who, without knowing what he does, takes the letters, then arranges them this way and that, and, in so doing, cannot in all innocence help but hit the nerve of the times. But I know very well what it is I've done and what I'm doing and thus am I to be taken by the letter, which shall soon take my life. If, at the very least, I had humbly limited myself to the letters ב and ש, ש would have perpetually gone in and out of ב, for ב is the order of creation, even if I wasn't worthy of it. And if only I'd taken my example from a man who died eight years ago, a man who was illiterate until the age of fifteen because he had been denied an education until that age, yet still became one of the most important intellectuals of his time, a fact that even numerous hostilities based on fabrications—for example, he was said to have invented the historians Abludihn, Findigerem, Miederfing, and Einigfremd,* who, this was the general opinion, had provided him with chronicles that the Teutons were descended from the Greeks, which, of course, had consequences for the tribal history—could change naught of. His text, George says, *Antipalus maleficiorum*, which condemns witchcraft and justifies the burning of witches, overshadows even the *Malleus maleficarum*, which recently found its way to unimaginably wide dissemination through the invention of book-printing, but it was actually handwriting, script, that Jens Noah von Heidenberg (for that was the man's name) preferred to book-printing, indeed, book-printing is no devil's work, but it is dangerous, as it results in the repetition of all printed mistakes and errors in all exemplars, as such, a significant error ultimately remains more firmly in the memory than a significant thought, whereas an error might be corrected and taken out of the world by a copyist's hand in a new transcription.

He, George, says that he could also add this as a warning: If the printed book is riddled with printing errors, they might, in a worst-case scenario, make it illegible, and it would require the power of foresight, not merely to mend these corrupt texts, but to merely reconstitute them in the first place, and thus are my manuscripts also corrupt and whoever restores them is damned and leads his readers to damnation.

506 years later, Hinan Knallsum shall take precisely the opposite position: "When copying texts by hand, each successive copy was worse, because old errors were overlooked and new ones were added. New editions of printed material, in contrast, could be expected to eliminate the errors of preceding ones."

As far as writing material is concerned, George continues to prattle on about Jens Noah von Heidenberg, the parchment on which copyists write is more durable than the paper used in printing that

---

* Unitedother.

is made of rags and tatters, this paper disintegrates quickly, after two hundred years at the latest—here, Jens Noah von Heidenberg has perhaps allowed himself to be guided too much by name, in fact, paper made from rags is very durable and defies age much better than other paper—and, as for the preciousness of parchment that endures for more than a thousand years, the preciousness that drives its price so high, this can always be compensated for by the many beautiful discoveries that parchment allows for as palimpsest, not all traces of previous script can be removed from it by scraping and scratching the text when it is reused. As such, education is also a consequence of the palimpsest. Thus, George says, does the writer inscribe himself into the writing of others, the trace of his life that is left behind is to be read against the background of other life-traces, and it is for this reason that there is sometimes more to discover here than in a printed book.

According to Jens Noah von Heidenberg, George says, the copying-down of holy books is preferable to the composition of one's own books—just as the abbots and monks of his order used to busy themselves with the copying-down of the ancients, for example, Cassiodorus, Bede, Alcuin, Hrabanus Maurus, Petrus Damiani, and Regino von Prüm, who was also an eminent historian and music theorist—since this does not burden the writer with vanity and corrupt thoughts, he shall speak no useless words and be untroubled by senseless rumors, after all, this initiates him into the divine mysteries and enlightens him in miraculous fashion. For each word that we write imprints itself forcefully onto our memory if we only take our time while writing and reading it. And thus have I, George says, copied Jens Noah von Heidenberg's script so often that I could recite all of it by heart right here, yes, I can quote his manuscripts verbatim in such a way that somebody might confidently copy them down, then, when the writings of Jens Noah von Heidenberg are published, a proofreader shall, should the writer have done his job well, find no error.

Thus ought nobody think and nobody say: "Quid necesse est me scribendo fatigari, cum ars impressoria tot tantosque libros transfundat in lucem, ut modico ere magnam bibliothecam possimus instruere?" "What is the sense of copying by hand when the art of printing has brought to light so many important books; a huge library can be acquired inexpensively?"

And even if there are already many books in print, he points out, there could never be so many that one wouldn't be able to find something new to write, something that hasn't been printed yet. It would also be difficult for somebody to seek out all printed books or acquire them for himself. Even if all the works in the whole world were printed, a dedicated writer would in no case abandon his zeal; on the contrary, he would also have to confer permanence onto the useful printed books by copying them down, for, otherwise, they shall not last for long. It is his authority alone that confers authority unto scanty works, greatness unto worthless, and longevity unto the ephemeral. In any case, an avid writer shall always find something worthy of his efforts. He does not give in to dependence on the printer; he is free and rejoices in his freedom by fulfilling his task. And he is by no means so inferior to the printer that he ought to give up his strivings because of the latter's art. Rather, regardless of this, he ought to proceed down the path he has started out on with joy; in the certainty that his achievement shall be undiminished in the eyes of God, even if another should suffer a disadvantage therefrom as a result. But whoever desists from a compulsion to write because of print is no true friend of script, for he sees only the present and contributes nothing to the edification of future generations.

Indeed, George says, according to Jens Noah von Heidenberg, that which is printed shall never be considered equal to handwritten codices. And when he copies down the Holy Scriptures, the most noble and conscientious form of all writing, he becomes part of the tradition and participates in Eternal Life as a reward for striving and reverence and the impeccability resulting from both. However, nobody can be considered sufficiently learned with regard to the Holy Scriptures who cannot also demonstrate a solid knowledge of secular sciences. Theologians must keep the minds of their listeners strong, the mere proclamation of fundamental Christian principles does not suffice. In this way, it is his aspiration to renew X-tianity through the bibliography—his library contains more than two thousand handwritten books, but it is only through the bibliograph enumerating all of his books that he sees his holdings emerge most distinctly from the paper, like a new creation. He believes he's only just getting to know them now, only now do they seem to truly belong to him, George continues to channel Jens Noah von Heidenberg.

Last but not least, if one has written something oneself and not simply copied it down and one must prove something that one has claimed, one might still say that the resulting book in which the proofs are to be found—the sole copy—is sold to an unknown buyer.

Anyone who has caused an uprising or a war must be compelled to write down the names of the dead on the most valuable of parchment, George says, for the cost of which he alone would be responsible. If there were several engenderers of the war, i.e. blame could not be found to belong to a single individual, all persons concerned would have to copy down the names. A list must be drawn up to this purpose, those who have been compelled to mourn deaths in their families ought to log their names in the list; if they knew of any dead in the neighborhood, if, for example, a whole family had been wiped out there, then these names must also be logged. It would be most desirable if such people were forced to write until the end of their lives. The names that pass out of their hands and onto the parchment are inscribed into their souls.

I ask George how many names he is thinking of putting down onto the parchment in his own script. Certainly not yours, he says.

The Landsknechte get the group going once more and the prince, heated up by his speech, drags along, still mutely accompanied by

Philipp, who, walking beside him, surveys the area, and everyone seems to accept it as inevitable to have to stride over a corpse lying on a meadow or a path with each step they take, only George finds this to be bothersome, each obstacle is transferred into his voice.

Suddenly, a great din makes all conversation impossible, already audible from afar, it rises up triumphant upon our arrival. Both princes seem to hold this for a favorable opportunity, to, here and now, sheltered from the noise, have a discreet conversation with our group, and thus, after overcoming a kind of continental fissure or orchestra pit, our group first circumvents a fourteen-person shofar-choir, which has positioned itself in the fissure or pit and split up into two back-to-back ensembles of seven blowers, one of them is playing westward, into the past, the other is playing eastward, into the future, then our group goes down a stone staircase, which leads past the missing eastern side of a small ruined house, if it weren't for the marble floor with lozenges of black and white, one might well think it to be a stable, the group presses along the long southern flank of the ruins, in the vicinity of which a princely table has gathered and is eating, while peasants come along hunched over and pay their tithes in the form of natural produce, a goat, a basket full of eggs, a goose, a great many vegetables, when one gazes upon George and Philipp and the two servants paving the way for them, one is invited to take a seat at the table, the invitation is withdrawn when they realize that two Knechte and a figure in black accompany them, there is no place for them, the people indicate, but it is the shackles upon my wrists that are incompatible with roast goose, exquisite wines, and the bright green tablecloth, the peasantry steps back, I like the goat, it eats of the vegetables to be handed in as tithe, behind the peasants, a wingèd, fire-breathing dragon has swung onto the western wall; the insurgents, led by me, turned even the heads of the mythical demons before they lost their own, George says and indicates to the two foregoing servants to take the dragon off of the wall, it ought to calm down, the battle is over; you are in error, I say, the dragon is in service of the Christian struggle against evil, which they've only just capped off, George interrupts me, meaning the good won the battle with God's aid; again, you are in error, I say, indeed, it is spreading its venomous breath all through feudal society, for there is no use in a servant seeking to drive it away with a stick, just as there is no use in two Knechte trying to get hold of it, the only one who can attempt that is he who sees it; well, the dragon errs because the insurgents have caused it to err, George says, none of this bothers the two Knechte who are leaping up onto the wall as if the devil had taken hold of them, they're waving off the air with their hands. Now that we have walked around the house that, verily, is no house, George has the group stop, a very special delivery is expected. The choir of blowers with their shofar horns, the upturned funnels of which resemble the tubes of the carnivorous yellow pitcher plant, allows the past to rest for the time being, while the future is played into so loudly that the stones come loose from the walls and tumble to the ground. Nobody is blowing the horn to indicate the beginning of a celebration, no, it is the end of one being trumpeted, a group of nine nobles would be celebrating it behind closed doors, without prospects, were it not for the fact that the roof was untiled, the doorless and windowless masonry toward its eastern side was open and, on its northern side wall, it was so cracked that nobody would be astonished if it were to collapse in the near future. Closer observation reveals that the ruins are not the marble-floored outbuilding of a castle, but a servants' chamber; the marble checkerboard laid down in the chamber must have served as a mockery of the servants who could never rejoice in feudal grandeur and splendor and thus would the disproportionately large checkered floor be sheer humiliation, rather, the square is an empty inner courtyard, the remains of a stately home, of which only the walls surrounding the inner courtyard remain, while only the ritual has remained from this society within society, the empty dance is not merely demonstrated by the faces, whose boredom and expressionlessness have always been part of the society-game, the parlor game. It is a fool's game. A single couple tries out the courtly dance step, accompanied by bagpipes and shawms, they dance a pavane that gradually turns into a funeral play for them, the dance now has more in common with an oscillation of the body than a fixed series of steps, if the gentleman leads to the left, the lady makes a turn out of the inner courtyard and onto the stairs, if he leads right, he himself makes this turn. Both musicians are focused entirely on the couple, while two other couples in the back part of the courtyard seem to have lost interest in dancing and converse, standing right up close to one another, a couple is standing together with two men, roughly in the middle of the inner courtyard, the lady indicates a dance move with one arm stretched high into the air and a bent hand, the men, however, are only interested in the dancing couple, whom they examine just as intently as they comment on them, as if an epoch were coming to an end here and now, the clearest sign of which is to be found in the disintegrating components of the dance, which nobody dances mechanically any longer, but, in a best-case scenario, consciously quotes, unable to reproduce the movements that constitute the dance whenever the social ritual requires an evening dance, but, now, one is coy and loses all lightness, as if one were aware that all motions one makes have suddenly acquired such a comic element that anyone who sees them must burst out laughing, simply because their time is up.

 Like horses habituated to constant motion who become restless if they stand still for too long, the Knechte have meanwhile begun to shift their weight from one leg to the other, they stride back and forth, while I am the horse upon which one has laid a harness.

 A rack wagon is brought over by six men. In it sits a man in a black raiment and with a black hat, with closed legs tilted slightly to the right, turning his upper body toward a metal basin surrounded by fish-demons, his head tilted to the left, he washes his hands of responsibility. His eyes are closed. What I would give to be able to look him in the eye. Four of the men clamber up into the wagon and tip the man forward, accompanied by the calls of the other two to be careful of his head and not to step between the rungs. Together, they heave him up and set him down, led by George, at a sufficient distance from the choir, and the walls, right up close to the continental fissure or the orchestra pit, on a piece of land at the edge of the meadow rising into a hill in a northeasterly direction, whereupon the shofar choir turns to the man in black and once again begins to blow. Pilate, George says, made entirely of wood, a commissioned work, delivered overnight, commissioned, admittedly, well in advance, time is the sole artistic freedom that we can with clear conscience endorse. Our contribution to the fine arts, which articulate many things better than the history books do. It is bad art, I say, state art, the despairing/sublime attempt of the princes to escape their provinces in their heads, but it is precisely this art that shall one day be the emblem of the province.

There is the occasional sheet of paper lying upon the meadow, torn-out bookpages perhaps, Philipp I sends a Knecht to collect them. The Knecht picks up the papers, but instead of bringing them to his master, he immerses himself in them. Philipp I, my father, sends a second Knecht, but this one doesn't come back either, he examines the sheet handed to him by the first Knecht. It is rather unlikely that the Knechte can read, my father says. Then he sends a third Knecht when the second one doesn't come back either, but simply stares at the papers together with the two other Knechte, my father goes over to them so as to politely inquire as to the reason for their keeping a distance. Very suddenly, it is as if the scenery has been painted into place, nobody moves, only the shofar choir plays. George breaks away from our group and goes over to the staring people. He strives not to look at any of the pages, rather, he asks Philipp I to tell him what it is that so captivates the attention. Philipp I reports. George has me approach with the two Knechte who are guarding me. He bundles the pages together and has them delivered to me by one of the Knechte with the request that I form an opinion. I immediately recognize what is coming to pass here, but fear that they wish to test me as part of an interrogation and thus do I merely reply that somebody cast off these papers because of printing errors. The question arises as to whether Jens Noah von Heidenberg was therefore correct. For some, the pages are wayward, for others, they reveal their true meaning over time, I say. Indeed, a new meaning emerges each time, no gaze and no interpretation is stable, just as "Sünde"—sin—and "Ente"—duck—are contained in "entstünde"—arise—but only come into view one after the other, perhaps also not being recognized at all and the new form that the sentence takes over time and, therefore, its new meanings only give themselves up as one observes the sentence, for only then does it change, but when one averts one's gaze, the sentence returns to the beginning, my father replies. That describes the procedure quite well, I say. If everything flows and nothing stands still, if everything is in excess, but never in passage, then there really is no point, George says. Handsomely formulated, I say, which immediately earns me blows from the Knecht on my right, nevertheless, something can be seen and, therefore, recognized, and that burns itself into our memory, it can be repeated, appears in us as image—can be described and interpreted. But each time anew, Philipp I. says; each time anew, but not in a different way, I say. Then there's no point, George insists. There is a point: each time, I say, but no eternal signification other than with God.

The Knechte relish the change as such, Philipp I says. That which is coming to pass here should never happen with the Holy Scriptures, George warns. Both gaze scrutinizingly at me. I am asked whether I would find it appealing if the letters were to begin to dance? This would come of the fact that letters are set separately in a printing press, if they had been written by hand, they could not be separated out from the ensemble:

```
A small mistake in the beginning is a big one in the end.
      all   is              in      a big one in the end.
           mist    in the beginning is    g one
A s      i take       be    in    a big one
                in the beginning is           the end.
A s      i            beg                 i     end.
      all   i take in the beginning is    i
  s      mi t e    the beginning          in the  end.
                             n         o       end.
```

George takes the sheet and tears it up. He wishes to know what meaning that which is written on it now has. If the sheet were covered in script put down by a hand . . . George interrupts me by showing me another sheet from the bundle:

"The big fork, which was given to Lucifer, who was standing in the corner in a childlike huff—a toy to compensate for the abortive carnival costume, but with which he serenely disdains to play—shall one day till the field for far-reaching reforms, then shall God no longer be אֶהְיִ אֲשֶׁר אֶהְיֶה ("ehjeh asher ehjeh"), but "I was that I-Was," then shall the shofar sound out upon my arrival, the voice says, and I do not turn to see the voice that is speaking to me, I"

Who wrote that, he wishes to know. I keep silent. We know that you wrote that, my father says. Are you clairvoyant? he asks. Has the Kingdom of Lucifer come?

This sheet here, George says, is actually a broadsheet to be read by all who are capable of reading, it is no rubbish that the wind has blown over from the printing works, by the wooden walls of which we stand, no bit of rubbish ensuring we have no flowers in the meadow and no crops in the neighboring field, the "rubbish" is the final thing that the printing works printed, a broadsheet that shall wend its way across the land so that all who are capable of reading shall read it, a broadsheet upon which one can read of how to conquer and take Schattenfroh and the Root of All Evil, Schattenfroh's printing works, and that the one is unthinkable without the other. And George reads:

"Now *Schattenfroh* is straitly shut up before of its readers: no signifying meaning goeth out, and no meaningful signification cometh in. Only Nobody goeth out and cometh in. And the Father saith unto George, See, I have given into thine hand *Schattenfroh*, and the Nobody thereof, and its readers of valor. And ye shall compass the printing works of *Schattenfroh*, all ye men of war, and go round about the printing works of *Schattenfroh* once. Thus shalt thou do six days. And seven hermeneutics shall bear before *Schattenfroh* seven trumpets of rams' horns: and the seventh day ye shall compass the printing works of *Schattenfroh* seven times, and the hermeneutics shall blow with the trumpets. And it shall come to pass, that when they make a long blast with the ram's horn, and when ye hear the sound of the trumpet, all the people shall shout with a great shout; and the wall of the printing press of *Schattenfroh* shall fall down flat, and the people shall ascend up every man straight before him.

And George the son of Albert the Bold calleth the hermeneutics, and saith unto them, Take up the *Schattenfroh*, and let seven hermeneutics bear seven trumpets of rams' horns before *Schattenfroh*. And he saith unto the people, Pass on, and compass the printing works of *Schattenfroh*, and let him that is armed pass on before *Schattenfroh*.

And it cometh to pass, when George speaketh unto the people, that the seven hermeneutics bearing the seven trumpets of rams' horns passeth on before the FATHER, and bloweth with the trumpets: and

Schattenfroh followeth them. And the armed men goeth before the hermeneutics that blow with the trumpets, and the reward cometh after *Schattenfroh*, the hermeneutics goeth on, and bloweth with the trumpets.

And George commandeth the people, saying, Ye shall not shout, nor make any noise with your voice, neither shall any word proceed out of your mouth, until the day I bid you shout; then shall ye shout. So *Schattenfroh* compasseth the city, going about it once: and they come into the camp, and lodge in the camp.

And George riseth early in the morning, and the hermeneutics take up *Schattenfroh*. And seven hermeneutics bearing seven trumpets of rams' horns before *Schattenfroh* go on continually, and blow with the trumpets: and the armed men go before them; but the reward cometh after *Schattenfroh*, the hermeneutics go on, and blow with the trumpets. And the second day they compass the city once, and return into the camp: so they do six days.

And it cometh to pass on the seventh day, that they rise early about the dawning of the day, and compass *Schattenfroh* after the same manner seven times: only on that day they compass *Schattenfroh* seven times. And it cometh to pass at the seventh time, when the hermeneutics blow with the trumpets, George saith unto the people, Shout; for the Lord hath given you *Schattenfroh*. And *Schattenfroh* shall be accursed, even it, and all that are therein, to the Father: only Mateo shall live, he and all that are with him in the house, because he hid the messengers that we sent. And ye, in any wise keep yourselves from Nobody, lest ye make yourselves accursed, when ye take of the accursed thing, and make literature a curse, and trouble it. But all the ornate speech, decorations, tropes are consecrated unto the Father: they shall come into the treasury of the Father. So the people shout when the hermeneutics blow with the trumpets: and it cometh to pass, when the people heard the sound of the trumpet, and the people shout with a great shout, that the wall falleth down flat, so that George with his entourage go up into the printing works of *Schattenfroh*, every man straight before him, and they take the printing works. And they utterly destroy all that is in the printing works with the edge of the sword. But George saith unto the two men that had spied out the country, Go into Mateo's house, and bring him out thence, and all that he hath, as ye swear unto him. And the young men that were spies go in, and bring out Mateo, and his father, and his mother, and his brethren, and all that he hath; and they bring out all his kindred, and leave them without Prüm. And they burn the city with fire, and all that is therein: only the ornate speech, decorations, tropes they put into the treasury of the house of the Father. And George saveth Mateo alive, and his father's household, and all that he hath; and he dwelleth in the Eifel even unto this day; because he hid the messengers, which George sent to spy out the printing works of *Schattenfroh*.

And George adjureth them now, saying, Cursed be the man or woman before the Father, that riseth up and would act as diaskeuast unto *Schattenfroh*: he shall lay the foundation thereof in his study, and in the library of the twentieth house shall he set up the gates of it. So the FATHER is with George; and his fame is noised throughout all the country."

You can do that, I say, and I can't stop you, but *Schattenfroh* isn't even close to finished yet, you'd be dismantling an unfinished book right here, on page 808, with the ending as of yet undetermined.

That your Father hinders mischief does him honor, George says, then orders me to skip over a few pages in the bundle so that we waste no time. I ought to read aloud. I read aloud:

"And it comes to pass. All those princely warriors remaining on Schlachtberg and around it goeth about the printing works of *Schattenfroh* for six days. Seven hermeneutics bear seven rams' horns before *Schattenfroh*. On the seventh day, they go about the printing works of *Schattenfroh* six times and the hermeneutics blow with their trumpets. And the ram's horn is blown continuously and we hear the sound of the trumpets, the entire people shouts with a great shout and the wall of the printing works falls down flat," so that George and his entourage go up into the printing works of *Schattenfroh*, every man straight before him, and they take the printing works. And they utterly destroy all that is in the printing works with the edge of the Word. Then George says, "It is so beautiful to be here with all the people I love. I wish not to—and shall not—forget this hour, for, together, we learned about the art of printing and did a good deed."

We meet nine people occupied with printing, all of them wearing head coverings, sometimes they're blue, sometimes they're pale-pink and pointed, both variations, especially the blue one, look like jester's hats; the one head covering resembles a nightcap, just as the other resembles a turban or a beret, all hats take on quite adventurous forms. Judging by their head coverings, some of these people look like temporary employees of the bakers' guild who are just about to use their spades to get a book out of the oven like a loaf of bread, whereas another person seems more like he's confused the printing works with a library, so engrossed does he stand before one of the second or third proofs lying atop a small square table made of wood, this person is meant to check through them repeatedly for errors and correct them if necessary so that a final correction can eventually be made, then, after checking the settings, the imprimatur and, later, the sheet-wise binding of sheets can take place, he is already simulating this by precisely fitting the pages together to form sheets and the sheets together to form quires and the quires together on a cardboard cover to form a book, so engrossed therein that he seems to have lost sight of his true occupation as he reads. Perhaps, this has something to do with the typesetter and his blue jester's cap, which tempts him to the nastiest of distortions, but also anagrammatic shifts and intellectual flourishes, why not finally be an author, his motto might well run.

In the printing works, with all of its crowding and the confused simultaneity of its processes, the sequence of individual steps can hardly be understood. There is no beginning and no end here, everything is equally *primordial*. Here, each person is part of a cycle that does not cease by itself unless someone like George or Philipp shows up to arbitrarily bring it to a halt.

George asks whether I know what's being printed here. I say that I do not. But I actually do know. It will certainly come to you, George says and asks one of the printers to give me a bit of a hand. The printer bows before the prince and whispers into my ear: "A printing works is a book in which the dismantling and the assembly of a book can be seen equally and simultaneously. Inaccuracy is the greatest enemy of book-printing. Which is why everything here runs with the greatest of precision." As if the executioner were explaining to the criminal how gallows worked, which he only does to make himself seem important to the worldly ladies and gentlemen and the masses who have gathered here, I must listen to a lecture on the printing press and the manufacture of a book, namely my own, which shall soon, as it is to be expected, turn into my executioner's sword, while the typesetters, at the speed of the printer's stream of speech, take the letters, lower- and uppercase, punctuation marks, ligatures, and abbreviations out of the typecase with one hand and assemble them into lines in a device held in the other, place two composed lines into a boarded box that is only open on one side, which the typesetters, as soon as enough lines have accumulated for a printed page, empty into a locked frame on the table before the printing press, then fasten the forme into the frame, fold a kind of frame over a sheet of paper, which is needled onto the middle of a board, which they then fold onto the forme that has just been blackened with ink balls and push the carriage sliding across the table together with paper and forme under the rotating spindle to which an iron plate covered by wood is attached, they manipulate a wooden rod provided with a wooden ball, causing the iron plate to descend and merge with the forme, the wooden rod is pushed in the opposite direction, the wood-covered iron plate rises, the carriage on the table is pulled back once more, frame and board are folded up, and a printed book page is revealed, it shall have to be looked through for errors and corrected if this has not been the final printing—thus do speaking and reading seem to be taking place simultaneously, but the speech is handed over to me in readily printed form, and the typesetters, inkers, and printers working in time with the speech are already occupied with this passage here, which somebody feeds into Nobody for them.

As if he wished for his aperçu from earlier to have a lasting effect or to leave me enough time to plausibly describe the situation in view of current events, after this interruption, the printmaster continues to instruct me:

"Except that this isn't to do with the dismantling of books, but only and uniquely with the printing and binding of *your* book. Only the forme, also called the typeset, is disassembled, 'distributed' in printer's jargon, in such a way that the type and other characters can be made available again for other formes; which is to say, once the commissioned number of one and the same page or one and the same sheet has been printed therewith. Before this can happen, the letters and other characters must first be cast in large quantities with a hand-casting instrument, then collected in the type case according to a certain order that allows for speedy access. Many different fonts and one font set of each with all body sizes must be available. In order to be set right-justified, the letters of each font must have different widths. More than 550 different characters must be made available for the printing of *Schattenfroh*.

So, no printing without setting copy. But where should the setting copy be placed? Most typesetters place it on the left side of the typecase between the compartments with the numerals and the accented letters. Others prefer to have the manuscript at head-height and make use of a copy-holder. A copy-holder consists of the tenacle keeping the setting straight with a spike or a screw-clamp so that the typesetter can easily attach it to the edge of the typecase in the typecase bar without obstructing the view of the letters and the divisorium is as a wooden or metal fork for marking the line currently in the typeset. Some printing-works owners or typesetting managers fear that attaching the copy-holder might damage the typecase bar and therefore forbid the use of the holder.

According to the setting copy, the typesetter takes the letters required for the sheet to be printed and the blind material for the gaps to be filled, with which the exact line width can be achieved, then arranges the letters in a device called a composing stick, a metal bar with an adjustable stop, also called the "sliding head," mirror-inverted to one or two lines. Before he starts typesetting, he places a so-called composing rule, a kind of ruler made of particularly hard nickel silver, along which the letters are to be placed in the composing stick.

On the back of the letters is the so-called nick, ideally a continuous groove at exactly the same height, from which the typesetter can tell whether the letters are all to appear at precisely the same height in the print.

If a line in the composing stick has been completed, it is spaced out, i.e. the line gets adjusted to the predetermined line width of the composing stick by means of the different-sized spacing pieces, an expansion or reduction of the space between the words that doesn't become visible in the typeface itself (the doubling of letters at the end of a line result from lines that are too short and abbreviations from lines that are too long). Then one takes the composing rule out by its ears and places it before the first line.

The lines arranged in the composing rule are then lifted onto the galley, a rectangular wooden or zinc plate with wooden or metal strips on three sides and open on one side, provided with the desired row spacing (slugs) and made into a column, the finished black of type corresponding to one printed page. Four columns form a sheet. The transfer is completed with the composing rule.

The pressman then lays the finished composition or the forme, which is bound with a cord, via the open side of the galley into the wooden or iron chase, the composition is then secured with sticks and quoins, in particular wooden or metal wedges or other mechanical clamping devices, and tightened with screws and nuts.

The printing press looks—and works—like a converted oil, wine or papermaking press, it is also mainly made of wood, which should be of particular interest to you, since you come from a papermaking town and the street your parents' house is on leads directly to the Holtzmarckt commonly known as the Old Diech. In terms of its operating principle, it mainly consists of two parts: the platen and the forme. The platen includes the threaded and the screw spindles mounted in a frame or stand along with the Pressbengel (which is both a "rounce" and sounds something like a "press-brat") that performs the rotation and a so-called hose, on the underside of which the platen is fastened with four hooked bars. Now, the forme to be inked, the block of type mentioned, has been locked into the bed of the press, a smooth-ground and polished surface made of iron, brass, hardwood or stone carried by the carriage, which, guided by a handle, runs horizontally back and forth on tracks on a stable table in front of the platen. The threaded spindle goes below the crosspiece, called the crown, through a head, which is mortised into the side walls with elastic bearings, on which it is pivot-suspended with a screw nut, and, past a certain distance further down through the hose whose function is yet to be described, is fitted into the second head called the bridge. If the winter has a certain amount of give, the bottom joist, the till, is held firm to the frame. In the space between the two joists, protruding horizontally from it, the aforementioned Pressbengel is attached to the spindle, a strong iron lever enclosing the spindle, through which (and thus also through the spindle) the sheath goes, this is a conically tapering lever, round wood about two meters long, which is mortised with the spindle or the Pressbengel and at the front end of which the governor ball sits. Pulling the rounce toward you causes the platen to lower via the spindle and thereby effectuates the actual printing.

The forme consisting of letters and space material and used by the table with its aforementioned equipment such as carriages, beds, and paper is, to a certain extent, the counterpart to the platen, the surroundings of which guarantee the mechanics of its depression. The interaction of both main parts makes up the printing process, which basically consists of two forces acting on one another, in that a hard material, the iron of the printing plate, presses a soft material, paper, onto the hard material of the forme. This requires a physical pressure that is exerted by a constant force. If you now turn down the platen with the rounce so that this process can be carried out, there is a risk that the platen will turn and the torque will be transferred to the platen. In order to prevent this, the aforementioned hose is fitted precisely into the till, a rather long rectangular wooden box with a square profile, through which the spindle is guided and can easily be moved up and down using a simple device. The device consists of two pieces of iron set in front, which are fastened into the hose, have the shape of a crescent, and engage with the threads of the spindle. The hose with its locks is able to prevent it from turning, after all, it ought to be pressed and not turned; only the pressure from the hardened steel toe of the spindle caused by downward motion is transferred to the metal plate of the crucible, an iron plate in its middle.

Now that the mechanics of the effective forces have been clarified, what about the mechanics of the sensitive materials, the paper as the substrate for the print and the inking of the forme? The bed lying on the carriage is connected via a hinge on its transverse side opposite the printing plate to a hinged parchment-covered frame, also called a mirror, which consists of three parts: a lid made of iron or wood, a frame the precise size of the bed, an inner frame that fits exactly into this lid, the so-called tympan, which, in turn, is connected to the large frame of the lid by means of hinges and hooks, and the frisket of the same size attached to the upper edge of the lid, which prevents the paper or sheet from falling out of the cover when one wishes to fold the lid onto the forme. The lid and tympan are covered with parchment or firm canvas, the frame with strong paper into which, depending on the number and size of the columns, gaps have been cut so that the print can be put down in accordance with the type area and, at the same time, the area not to be printed is covered by the recessed frame of the paper. Wool- and cloth-felts or layers of paper and cardboard placed behind the covering of the lid modify the rigidity of the imprint depending on the font size, paper, and color. Lid and frame are connected by the so-called buckle.

The sheet about to be printed on is placed on the open tympan or parchment-covered frame using two sharp iron needles, so-called small pins, so that it doesn't slip and so that the backing-up can also be printed without any problems, making sure the type areas precisely match, if care has been taken to ensure this, when locking the printing form into the closing frame, all pages are set up congruently, for only then is it guaranteed that the printed front and back sides, front and back printing, do not bleed through to each other.

To ensure that the letters do not show up on the paper in speckled or spotted form, it is dampened at least four or five days beforehand so that the printer's ink, which consists of linseed oil, tree resin, and soot, can be better absorbed. The paper must not be soaked, which would prevent the ink from being absorbed. Dampening the paper is therefore the noblest task undertaken during printing. Dampened and undampened sheets are to be stacked alternately according to the number of pages and the size of the print run, then weighed down with stones after about half an hour. The next day the paper is folded over, the bottom side comes up to the top and the left side comes to the right—and so on. It is important that the sheets dry evenly, which requires occasional airing and repeated folding.

Now, we come to the aforementioned coloring of the forme. This is done with the ink balls. The ink balls consist of a disc of funnel-shaped hollowed maple with a handle about as long as a hand, both funnel and handle in a single piece, others consist of a turned wooden handle with separate ball wood, for which maple, basswood, or alder may be considered, the funnel is filled with boiled horsehair and covered with dog leather, which is particularly suitable for coloring due to the fact that dogs have no skin pores, thus does the color stay on the outside of the leather. Calfskin or sheepskin can also be used. Before the leather is nailed to the edge of the ball wood with ball nails, the horsehair is stuffed into the funnel of the ball wood. It is important to ensure that the ball has a semi-circular shape and is evenly filled. The balls also need regular care, every three days, one should break them off by opening them and taking out the horsehair, ruffling it, discarding it, and replacing it with dry, ruffled hair—this requires a good supply of horsehair. One ball takes up the color and colors the other by the balls rubbing against one another. Thus can the color always be refreshed. It should be noted that the black printer's ink is not to be applied too heavily so that the edges of the letters are not colored and their imprint is not smeared. After the circular inking of the forme, also called the setting, the inker hangs the ball back into the ball-holders, the two wooden pegs onto which the ink ball is laid.

Once the paper has been inserted and the forme inked, the mirror is folded in and swiveled down onto the printing form. In a second printing press, the mirror is missing, here a dampened sheet of paper is placed directly onto the inked forme and covers over its entire surface with the so-called protecting sheet, a layer of felt or cardboard, and, to ensure even distribution of pressure, a few sheets of paper.

In the case of the printing press with a mirror, the protecting sheet is more likely to be stretched onto the printing platen and the vertically mobile counter-plate to the vertically mobile bed of the press with the forme. The protecting sheet forms a soft zone between the hard steel of the platen and the printing form. Once all this is done, the carriage is pushed underneath the platen.

The situation is a bit more peculiar with the manuscript of *Schattenfroh*. The paper fastened into the copy-holder fills with text before our very eyes, text that, as instructed, we set immediately. It is likely transmitted from the clouds. And thus has the work come to no end for years now, we work in three shifts around the clock, each shift requires its own pressman, its own inker, other printers . . . Normally, the typesetter makes the first correction. If there are several setters, it is essential that uniform orthography be ensured, otherwise, a deviation can easily result in an error or an incorrect reading. In the German language, however, few concern themselves with orthografy or correkt speling, authors are the least attentive to grammar and correct spelling, they cannot be relied on, and thus do things sometimes go haywire as far as language is concerned, *Schattenfroh* is no exception, on the contrary, in addition to its confused and heretical contents, it is accompanied by an orthography that might well be dubbed downright negligent. Beguiled by the snakes of words, which, not infrequently, reach the length of an anaconda, the proofreaders all sink down, stupefied by their work, which hasn't changed the practice that an editor reads the text aloud and the proofreader compares what he has heard with the printed text or the proof sheet, indeed, the proofreader fell into a sort of deep sleep less because of the truly unbeautiful voice than because of its contents, and one made specially and precisely sure that the voice did not sound pleasant. The incalculable number of errors of a formal, content-based, and intellectual nature in *Schattenfroh* finally led to the invention of a special system of abbreviations, which, put down as a handwritten correction mark for every imaginable type of error on the margins of the proofs, serves as instructions for the typesetter to replace the incriminated passages; however, this abbreviation-system turned *Schattenfroh* into an artifact due to the unmanageable number of errors, the typesetters attempted to familiarize themselves with the system, which only confused them more, before they finally refused to implement it (and let's not even start on the subject of the English translation . . .). And thus do I conclude my presentation, not without noting that there has not, as of yet, been a solution regarding the process of proofreading. Moreover, and this makes the process all the more difficult, a system of autocorrection seems to be coming to pass here, suitable for intervening in the divine plan of creation, for no sooner has an error been discovered in the pages attached to the copy-holder and noted down as such, it comes to pass that it is corrected, but not by the typesetters and mostly not in the way they wish for it to be."

Thus is the manuscript processed before it is even printed. The pressman's remarks resemble the description of an execution more than that of the production of a book. He called the windmills that fly around everyone's ears here a copy-holder. So, this is where my book is meant to have gone, the one I used to carry with me, the pages pulled apart, the words decomposed into their letters—but who says that Schattenfroh doesn't put them back together from scratch, distorting their meaning. I did indeed spot his name in the press. It seems like nobody has control over the text. The printers grab the letters blindly from the air into which the mills have catapulted them like bullets, hurling them into composing sticks, transferring them onto the galley, where, arranged in rows, they are exposed to the further arbitrariness of a storm that ruffles sense and senses, the storm hurls them to land, that is the bed against which they shatter as sentence.

"All of this," I say, "stands in the way of my book. I did not, I know this now, write it. This is entirely proven by this freshly printed sheet, which has just been set up and printed and hangs so harmoniously on the line next to the other newly printed sheets of *Schattenfroh*, the papers look like a cauldron of bats sleeping upside down, but devil knows what this page here is:

SEGUNDA PARTE

CAPÍTULO XXIV

Donde se cuentan mil zarandajas tan impertinentes como necesarias al verdadero entendimiento de esta grande historia

Dice el que tradujo esta grande historia del original de la que escribió[1] su primer autor Cide Hamete Benengeli, que llegando al capítulo de la aventura de la cueva de Montesinos, en el margen de él estaban escritas de mano del mismo Hamete estas mismas razones:

«No me puedo dar a entender ni me puedo persuadir que al valeroso don Quijote le pasase puntualmente todo lo que en el antecedente capítulo queda escrito. La razón es que todas las aventuras hasta aquí sucedidas han sido contingibles[2] y verisímiles, pero esta de esta cueva no le hallo entrada alguna para tenerla por verdadera, por ir tan fuera de los términos razonables. Pues pensar yo que don Quijote mintiese, siendo el más verdadero hidalgo y el más noble caballero de sus tiempos, no es posible, que no dijera él una mentira si le asaetearan.[3] Por otra parte, considero que él la contó y la dijo con todas las circunstancias dichas, y que no pudo fabricar en tan breve espacio tan gran máquina de disparates; y si esta aventura parece apócrifa, yo no tengo la culpa, y, así, sin afirmarla por falsa o verdadera, la escribo. Tú, lector, pues eres prudente, juzga lo que te pareciere, que yo no debo ni puedo más, puesto que se tiene por cierto que al tiempo de su fin y muerte dicen que se retractó de ella y dijo que él la había inventado, por parecerle que convenía y cuadraba bien con las aventuras que había leído en sus historias».

Y luego prosigue diciendo:

Espantose el primo, así del atrevimiento de Sancho Panza como de la paciencia de su amo, y juzgó que del contento que tenía de haber visto a su señora Dulcinea del Toboso, aunque encantada, le nacía aquella condición blanda que entonces mostraba; porque si así no fuera, palabras y razones le dijo Sancho

---

1. Se entiende: 'del original manuscrito de la historia que escribió'. 2. 'posibles'. 3. 'aunque lo asaetearan'.

Did you write that? No. Here, it is clearly stated that a great history is being dealt with, presented in the ur-script of its first author, from which it can be concluded that there is or must be a second author, perhaps also a third, fourth, and fifth and that this ur-script was transcribed by somebody who is not named further on, at least not on this page, but I am not named as the author of the ur-script, it is a certain Cide Hamete Benengeli and there's nothing in it about a printing works or about princes, not about Nobody and also not inkers, press-men, or any other kind of men, what it's about is that the very individual who transcribed the ur-script, I am quoting from the transcription of the transcription, 'in the chapter communicating the' likely past "adventures of the cave of Montesinos he found written on the margin of it, in Hamete's own hand, these exact words" which he afterward reproduced, they are, in any case, written in an entirely different book than this one and thus does one either wish to foist something off on me once more, as has already been done, I would now like to remind you of what that was, you may already remember: 'Hoffman is perplexed, he cannot find the passages he read aloud from my book, they stripped me of it during the strip search in the sure belief that they would learn something of Warhol's map therein. Others are excerpted in totally distorted fashion, furnished with extra sentences that didn't come from me at the beginning or the end, perhaps they've been invented for treacherous reasons. They are preparing to condemn the entire book before I myself can stand to speak and answer questions'—or such disorder reigns in this printing works that the books are printed here and there, then folded and bound in the bookbindery in quite literally corrupt form, just as it is well known that one book copies from another and the other book emerges from the first. You might now say that it is not the book that is copying, but the author, but I do not consider that to be a foregone conclusion; and even though the printed page doesn't originate with me, it is still part of my book, for I am said to have let it off-leash in taking it off the drying line before the final proofreading, whether it has been carried out or not carried out, which, incidentally, I wasn't at all authorized to do, especially as I shamelessly seized the opportunity of the most minute scope of action afforded to me and am thus to blame for the confusion inherent to the fact that this is less a book being assembled than a chaotic hybrid gathering up the world from all compass points, which only proves my presumptuousness, which I allow to prevail in all things and implies that I have to put up with the principal suspicion of breaking off an episode at the very moment when the source that I am copying from runs dry. Which would lead one to conclude that I myself do not run the regime that rules over my book, but only open and close the inflow-channels without having any influence on the overall flow, on that which, fed above-, middle-, and belowground, flows over the page and is made visible there by means of printer's ink; however, surface runoff, intermediate runoff, and base runoff, which collectively transverse each page of the book, are beyond my control. But, to write a book means to be underway upon one's own sovereign waters. To this, it is objected that I didn't include this page in my book of my own free will, that its appearance there instead sprang forth from the printers' caprice, and that what is narrated on the page has nothing at all to do with me, in short, I ask that this page be removed from *Schattenfroh*. And if you were to say that, if something is in a book that does not originate with the book's author, what is at stake, whether it be plagiarism or quotation, is a question of intellectual appropriation, in this case, it also makes a difference whether it came to pass with the author's knowledge or not; as far as the reader is concerned, you might be correct in your statement, provided that the reader actually reads and doesn't simply let his eyes drift over the paper or even look through a closed book.

    How then can I be certain that I am not the aforementioned

individual who made the transcription of the ur-script? This could be attested to by somebody with the first name of Teilchen,* less unusual for our ears than for our eyes or for our minds and the not nearly so unusual last name of Malz,† Teilchen Malz, whom one also calls Nelz Amlichte‡ or Zech Mitallen§ or Mein Allzecht,¶ if only he were here, but he is absent. Nevertheless, he can attest to it.

Regardless of this, at least two questions to do with this curious page remain to be clarified. For one thing, to be precise, this book, from which the page arose, shall only first be published in ninety years, and so do I ask you, oh highborn majesties, how you can lay the blame on me for that which does not yet exist; on the other hand, it must be explained in detail from whence I could have known this.

You could now further ask what it is that troubles me about the printing procedure, its sequence of actions, the individual stations, the mechanics... The typesetter who selects the wrong font; the pressman who does not dampen the paper as described, who selects the wrong ink, doesn't line the paper up properly with the small pins, is imprecise when selecting the mold closures and trimmings; the inspector who, if there is one to hand, would prefer to look out the window than at the work of his people—they can all ruin a book before it is read. In contrast, given the contents of *Schattenfroh*, it would be appropriate to take the following catalog of prohibitions into account when printing: Even if typeset and makeups cause the greatest of difficulties, which result from the recalculation of the manuscript as a function of the line-by-line homogeneous requirements of the letters in the composing stick and the grouping of lines upon the page: The text of the setting copy ought not be interfered with in any way, no spacing material, no spaces

---

* Particles.
† Malt.
‡ Nelz Inthelight.
§ Drink Witheveryone.
¶ My Alldrunkard.

are to be used, which includes letter-doublings and abbreviations at the end of the line, even if this results in widows. No more assistant typesetters shall be needed. The book shall be printed as intended. That which is being printed here is not my book. My book is an absolute book, it has apocryphal parts and two centers, my book is one person as two—which are my father and me."

Nobody takes notice of me. George smiles, but gives the impression of not having listened to me at all. The employees are working away, it cannot be precisely seen whether they are simply faking their work-processes and assistive labor or are actually occupied with genuine stages of production. I imagine the printing works to be a printing-works museum, in historical raiment, the typesetters, printers, and press-men presenting their work, which has already become historical, to the museum visitors, and, indeed, always only for as long as would be necessary for illustrative purposes in the space of a lecture, without putting too much strain on or even remotely damaging the historical equipment, in order to create the illusion of a self-contained past, into which an authenticated gaze might still be granted access, on the one hand, it shows that today's times, despite all their modernity, cannot be conceived of without the old times, while, on the other hand, showing the old times in their primitiveness, considered to be impossible today. Therefore, if all employees now look somewhere between highly concentrated and morose, this is nothing other than a historical citation of the efforts and functionally conditioned displeasures that such an underdeveloped work entailed. The letters are taken out of the typecase, even if the one or the other falls to the ground, there is no sign of nervousness in the presence of the distinguished visitors, on the contrary, they show themselves to be self-confident and sublimely superior to any subservience. That would certainly not have been the case during the time in question or it would have been sanctioned immediately.

Either way, George says, such speeches are nothing if not

page-filling and, in order to counteract this, the action must be driven forward once more, after all, a speech in the merely possible form of the German subjunctive is nothing but sheer misrepresentation and, therefore, doesn't really have a place in the book, but the action, *that* is carved in stone and he is carving it now and personally laying it down as a forme upon the bed. Thus does it come to pass. The printing presses have stopped, all the employees are frozen in their motions, not even the two princes budge.

Nobody speaks. Only the woman before me who looks so exasperated, so surly and grouchy, so grumpy and enraged, deeply disgruntled and exceedingly ill-tempered, downright unwilling and indignant, embittered isn't quite the right word, more like resigned, she's as dejected as her gaze, which she constantly directs at two printed pages folded in the middle and lying before her on the table that serves as a carriage, has understood this cycle, she knows that nothing is finished here without being started all over again, that she has no time to rejoice at a printed page, which is instantly snatched from her hand as new sentences press in, the old sentence is decolorized once more and its letters wander back into the typecase, on the very spot, entirely innocent, as if they hadn't just committed a crime coming to light in black and white and only the trace of the crime will remain, its countenance. One can clearly see its smirking teeth in the typecase.

How gladly the woman would wish to dub the printed sheet that she must remove from the small pins before she attaches a new unprinted double-page to the iron needles connected to the parchment-covered frame *her own*, a world-excerpt that lacks past and future, its lack of surroundings she can imagine to be different every day, that would be a new way of reading and, here, it is actually an advantage that the woman cannot read at all, as she announces to me with a smile. "I look at the letters," she says, "they all have a certain character and, depending on which and how many characters stand together, they signify this or that, and thus do I go from word to word, group to group, sentence to sentence. This sheet here speaks of you, it shan't end well." Philipp wishes to know what I'm saying, he walks up and down and stops by each typesetter and printer. Nothing, I say, mere words. "But one doesn't merely wish to get rid of your body; your spirit and your soul are also to be destroyed, we have it here in black and white, Schattenfroh has already put it down and had it printed, the press where you found his signature belongs to him, the princes know all of that, they wish to execute your book, they have recognized your soul and your spirit in it, for does not the page of the book have head and foot, and does not the book, once it is bound, have a body with back and joints, and is not the skin that you are still wearing on your body like the leather of the cover, only it is still warm, and like paper, which suffers just as much underneath the pounding sun, and thus shall you yourself be executed with the bound book, one shall empty *Schattenfroh* just as you are emptied, then shall the book ensure you no more survival," Philipp wishes to know what I'm saying. I'm not speaking, I say, for a soul that is no longer legible is no soul, it is like the carcass of a bird, an empty casket of nature. How close to one another are both culture and barbarism in the execution of a book. What greater longing could the child express than when it cried out: Go back to singing, dead lil' birdie! What is she saying there, Philipp asks. I don't understand her language, I say. The woman craftily uses his absences to continue speaking of herself, as if her speech were nobody's business. Stefan Horcht is the oldest typefounder's name, they all call him Mateo, he shall make the sign demanded by George twice more, once in gold and once in the tried-and-tested alloy of lead, antimony, and tin, in which the antimony should exceed the proportion of tin in a ratio of ten to one in such a way that the letter becomes nice and hard. If you are not speaking, Philipp says, then wherefore do I hear this? I ask him whether he is hearing *and* listening. Mateo, who, at the same time, is the oldest bookprinter here, knows that a letter is a memory, it comes down to a letter that is an unknown sign, it is formed from the last letters of your name, but George doesn't know this, just as he doesn't know that the beginning is in the end and the end in the beginning. The woman says that she cannot read. Thus does she have no mind, for the mind is the administrator of senses and things, Philipp says. The golden letter ought to fill the gap in your teeth, it becomes visible each time he speaks, in order to take an impression of it, he shall give you an apple made of soft wax and cast the letter accordingly. You give the apple back to him immediately after biting into it. The opportunity to do this shall come. You ought to swallow the other letter. When you feel an impending bowel movement, you go to the toilet and, while you're carrying it out, you place your hand onto a prepared stack of quires with the sheets of paper necessary for the book, which is the definitive edition, supervised by the author. The excrement returns the invisible to the visible, for did man not come forth from excrement and go from the in- to the outside and is there not a deeper connection between excrement and gold? Not that of gold as the excrement of hell, in which it is no longer worth anything, although the idea of an oral hell is a delightful one, also not in the sense of shitting gold, as there, indeed, one merely replaces the other, instead, that which is most valuable is concealed in excrement, the life that, should the excrement be observed, it can save. Therefore, take of your excrement, of the black script, into your mouth so that it might color the golden letter. Once that is done, take the sheets one after the other and make your mouth into a press, thereby pressing the sign into each sheet. Thus do you delete the deletion. If she has no mind, she must be a witch; if she is a witch, then she must know how to write, Philipp says. The black script is in your mouth, which is a press, the excrement makes the prima materia visible once more, the white script, and your book returns to its pages. For the sign with which George wishes to erase your book, which is you, transmutes the black script entirely back into white, subtracts the black script from the white, which was, in the beginning, legible to all who knew of it. The white script remains ever fixed, it can never be erased from the sign and never lose its ground. We can never get close to the white script, it can neither be destroyed nor read. The black script is already interpretation and only interpretation, we've no written *Schattenfroh* at all, we have only its interpretation, for its script is white. Black is the mediation, the grounds for which is invisible, but is itself already script, fore-script before all black script, and the black script is no script, but fire, which burns for only as long as we read it. Thus is *Schattenfroh* never written, but always only mediated, as a function of which it cannot actually be typeset, its white script is sacrosanct, the black script squats atop the white, overwrites it, and George cannot be certain that you are not a jester who fools everyone, thus does he wish to be sure that you verbally recant, just as unprinting, of which he shall soon speak, is the scriptural retraction of the visible. The black script has given over quite enough of the visible, now, it shall soon become invisible, Philipp says. The black script is death, the white script is eternal life.

But Mateo, who is also dubbed Antonio or Peter Ozianon, he who betrayed your father, who offers up his services wherever and however seems most favorable to him, shall be grateful to be able to help you, after all, he let the messengers into his house and delivered you up, he, the typefounder and printer, he betrayed himself, he shall soon help to invent that which nobody shall have wanted to have been, that which, as George wishes and Mateo fears, erases the beginning that was the Word with the end that is the deletion mark; then shall the Word be erased for the first time, God, who made tzimtzum for the Word, which was in the beginning and from which everything came forth, shall no longer have any script on his arm, script only he can read, which, as white script, is the only true script, black script is sheerly oral, it is exegesis, interpretation. Thus does he erase his betrayal, as he hopes, by helping to testify to everything. But you must beware of him, you shall not be able to trust him, tell him that the gold shall be gold and the letter that you shall swallow ought to contain ten times as much antimony as lead; just as antinomy contains non-amity and many into, one to one, so should antimony cause the quenching of antinomy, which shall cause the quenching of *Schattenfroh*. Mateo shall set everything in motion, otherwise he shall have quenched the letter press before its blossoming—and his own existence with it.

George doesn't know all of this. But I know:

⁂⁂⁂ ⁂⁂⁂ ⁂⁂⁂⁂⁂ ⁂ ⁂⁂⁂⁂⁂⁂ ⁂⁂⁂⁂ ⁂⁂⁂ ⁂⁂⁂⁂⁂ ⁂⁂⁂ ⁂⁂⁂⁂⁂⁂ ⁂⁂⁂ ⁂⁂⁂⁂⁂⁂⁂ ⁂⁂⁂⁂⁂⁂⁂⁂⁂

Philipp says that I ought to consume the scrap before my execution, this would allow me to survive by transmogrifying me at the moment of death, thus making me the executed one no longer. The slice across the throat, for it is assumed that I am to be executed with the sword, separates lower from upper; that which was the vessel of speech, the lower, is transmogrified in the upper, into intellectual nourishment, which no sword is capable of cutting through, for in the sweat of my face shalt I eat my book, till I return unto rags and tatters; for out of them wast I taken. For book I am and unto book shall I return.

The inker stands to the left of the woman like his own exhibited piece. Before George's stone enacted the law of solidification, from which only the woman is exempt, he was in the process of recoloring the forme with his ink balls, in it, the letters are now set mirror-invertedly. As he was staring perpetually at the woman's hands—it was uncomfortable to him that she was talking to me—he wasn't just inking the forms, but also the sticks with the result that paper-dust and other bits of filth accumulated on the balls, turning the letters into hickeys that must be punctured once more. The letters took on more and more color, which encrusted between them and gradually leveled out the difference in height between the shoulder or counters and the face, called the bevel, the sidebearing on the face that slopes down to the shoulder. And thus does reality press in on the book:

Father has vanished into black. Ach, poor Father! I sigh as the front page repeats itself on the back. Antonio or Peter Ozianon takes the book lying on the table in front of my father's empty chair and turns the page of the opened book. Then I see that my father is being slowly sucked into the black page until he has entirely vanished into it. By the time he comes to, I must think of where I've already seen the page in the past. No sooner has he pronounced "written" than he falls into a state of stupor. "What does 'written' actually mean, though?" Father asks.

You have recognized that we already belong to another time, George says. What you see here is the past. Your book is balanced upon the dividing line between yesterday and tomorrow. Today, you are to revoke and we have come up with something special for your revocation:

Schattenfroh is to be deprinted with white ink and you yourself shall be implicated in this process, page by page, line by line, letter by letter.

A book that is false through and through eludes any sort of correction in such a way that, by my orders, it shall on this day shrink to a single mark of odd beauty, like rhetoric to metaphor, and this mark, which looks like a spelling variant of the initial "S," is the beginning and end of *Schattenfroh*, it applies to the entire text. Initially, we believed that we had to cast this mark two thousand times so that each letter, each digit, and each punctuation mark could be captured on the page at the same time. However, it is sufficient to set the mark in the middle and to fill the page in the forme with blind material. As soon as the page has been pressed into the platen, the mark pulls all glyphs from the printed page. Dyed with white ink, it removes the printer's ink from the book in miraculous fashion, it literally gobbles the book empty. *Schattenfroh* burns out and collapses, the book becomes a black hole, the entrance of which is the mark. Whatever has passed through this entrance shall never leave in the opposite direction. Why a white mark? It is invisible against the background of the white paper. Thus is it the best fire to fight fire with, because "for the Imagination is as it were pitch, / which easily cleaveth and sticketh, / and soone taketh fire, which being kindled, / is not so easily extinguished: wherefore the only remedy / to resist the Pestilence / in such men, / is to quench and expel the force of the Imagination. / This is one example / wherein the power / and operation of the Imagination is declared, with the exhalations thereof."

I ask to wait until the book is written to its end. How can you request that, George says, if you don't even know how this process is implemented. For *Schattenfroh* was simultaneously conceived of and printed, imagination and reality coinciding, there is no need to wait until the end, it is already apparent that the book teems not only with whore's children (widows) and cobbler-boys (orphans), fly-heads (turned sorts), and onion-fish (single letters set in the wrong font (literals)), but, even in terms of historical details, it consists of nothing but lies, of lead lice, the dissemination of which must be prevented. According to George, the process of deprinting developed for *Schattenfroh* is centuries ahead of the development that would one day be accomplished by inventors at the University of Cambridge: the shooting of ultra-short flashes of light at the paper to be deprinted, by which the color pigments evaporate without damage to the paper.

The reuse of the *Schattenfroh* paper made possible by the deprinting would, George claims, be ennobled by the circumstance that it would not be used for any other book than the New Testament in Martin Luther's translation. They would know that this is much worse for me than death and, therefore, would wish for me to experience it. They would not allow me to experience the subsequent annihilation of Luther's December Testament.

The aforementioned scrap is attached to the outer right side of the printing press, already visible from afar, but only now is it possible for me to gaze upon it. It has the charm of a scrap with the word "SOLD" on it announcing imminent vacancy. The paper displays a signature: *Schattenfroh*. Is the handwriting familiar to me, Philipp I asks, the scrap was deliberately saved for my visit. The joyful agitation of his voice betrays the fact that he is simply waiting for the moment when I spot the scrap. It is not the script of my father's hand, I say. Then it is a forgery, Philipp I says, but that would be easy to verify, for, if it is indeed no forgery, I would still bear witness to a revelation today and, after all those days of testing, always only just missing the final step to consummation, he had no more ardent desire than to finally make the small miracle a reality in my presence, with my vigorous support as well. How pompously he speechifies, as if he were quoting from a bad book, always invoking religion whenever the narrator takes the lack of words for a divine test, which consists of getting into the surge of the heated anticipation of words. The narrator doesn't even notice that they burn up before his mind can get them to cool down and look at them, thus does he mistake their emptiness for intellect. I wish to take the scrap unto me, then Philipp I suddenly tears it free, examines it lengthily, and hands it over to a Knecht with the demand that he give it to the oldest typefounder present. At the moment of the handover, the scrap reappears upon the printing press. According to Philipp, in view of the typefaces used in *Schattenfroh* and the high demands associated with them, the printing shop employs several typefounders who are total masters of the hand-setting of type-foundry, the oldest of them has the task of kindling the flame in the charcoal stove with char cloth and maintaining it well with bellows until it is big enough and has developed a temperature more than three times higher than that of boiling water, then hurling in the scrap, heating the alloy of lead, tin, and antimony with the fire in a vessel, as is typically done, then pouring it with a ladle into the casting channel on the back of his hand-casting instrument, which was cleared for the character by the metal jaws, for this, he needs no more than an unprocessed matrix, but no patrix, for the scrap adds the shape of the character to the flames, its crude type can easily be pulled out of the instrument once the alloy has cooled. A previously unseen symbol will appear, with which, after grinding the fin and smoothing the metal, *Schattenfroh* will be printed. After printing, the character, of which—mark it well!—there must be only one copy, is to be melted down once more so that no nonsense can be done with it.

Stefan Horcht, the oldest printer, is quickly found, he is, as the woman said, called Mateo, and with the words: "I pour type in the print shop to begin / It is made of bismuth, lead, and tin, / I arrange the type accordingly, / Putting letters in order as need be / like this:

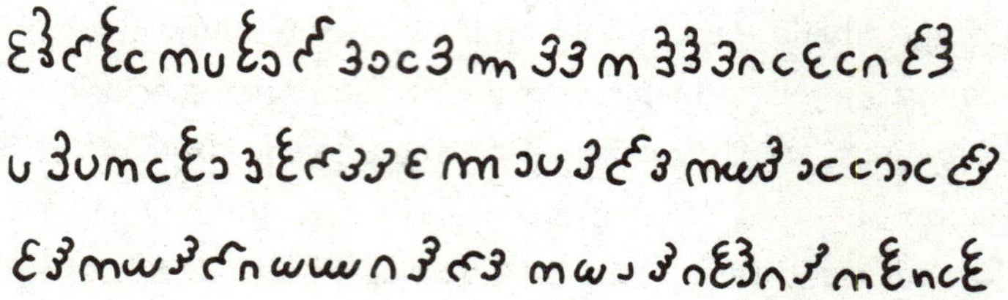

or this:

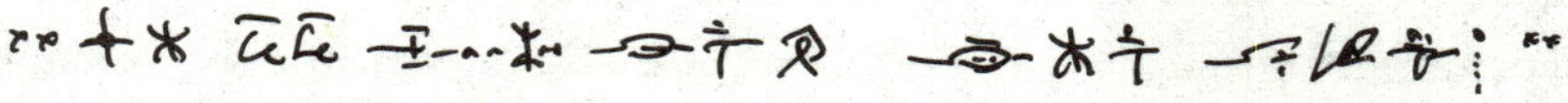

and German letters can I do / I pour Voynich letters sometimes too / Capital letters, periods, and signs so fine, / In *Schattenfroh* they'll be all in line," he kindles the fire of his oven, hurls in the scrap with Schattenfroh's signature, and carries out everything as George described to the Knecht. And while the typecaster grinds the fin of the type obtained from the hand-casting instrument and smooths the metal, the dyer appears who, as inker, is also responsible for removing and cleaning the forme and, before he dyes them white, he sings a little ditty about cleaning the mold, as if he could only endure his work while already thinking of its end: "Once a forme has just been printed / hot lye brought out from fire glinted / Then the mold is washed so fair / That the setter has his script so clear."

If the typesetters and proofreaders don't catch anything in the whole jungle of all the errors woven into *Schattenfroh* before it goes to print, so too will the author have caught nothing after *Schattenfroh* goes to press, nothing except for the deleatur, set into the middle of hundreds of pages, Philipp says as he proudly presents the character to me:

This character is nothing other than the abbreviation of my signature, the paraphe of the name "Nobody" as a black hole into which n, o, b, o, d, and y were first sucked and now *Schattenfroh* too. It doesn't impress me. Philipp sees that the character doesn't impress me. I know it, I say to him. You know nothing, Philipp cries out. Immediately, the employees of the printing works, George, and the Knechte of the two princes run out together, somebody comes forth from the throng that has formed around us and wrestles me to the ground, pulls me up once more, boxes my ears, and asks the two outwardly perplexed-looking princes to deal with me when the time comes, he has the experience necessary in order to erase evil incarnate. This is Mateo.

"Schattenfroh is a single catchword. You are to become the true Pressbengel, the brat-lever, and I wish to be your press-man," George says. Two Knechte grab hold of me and bind me to the sheath. The great weeding begins. But even if it is torn out root and stem, even if the fire uproots it, it shall return with the next rain at the very latest. I have become body-wood. The character that came forth from my name is about to dig deep into *Schattenfroh* and thus begins the great deprinting. My free-hanging head serves as fly ball, with it, George guides the sheath, the woodenstaff connected to which he ruthlessly shoves from right to left. This, one can see, comes to pass with the greatest of strainings. George has placed his right foot atop the press's step and, as he pulls the bratty Bengel (a lever with a pronounced sub-text)—the Bengel is me, I am the brat—toward him, braces himself with his torso back at an angle. George says that he must make sure that the Bengel not bang against his right cheek, the vibration triggered by this might damage the printing press in the long run. Now, he has evidently discarded this precautionary measure, my right arm is completely crushed, I hold my head rigid, fearing it might be torn off, but the vibrations triggered by each bang of the wooden body against my cheek are transmitted to my head so directly as to swing it parallel to the rebound. Merely pre-calculating the rebound costs me so much effort that, after about twenty printing processes, which George performs with mounting satisfaction in view of the result that I am being denied, I in large measure submit to this violence and am solely concerned with avoiding a concussion of the brain or a fracture in the area of the neck. In the moments to come, when the press stops working and a new sheet is loaded in, when George is convinced of the fact that the formerly printed page is not truly and utterly blank, I wish to say to him that this is torture and that the painfully meticulous description of the printing press and of the incessant cycle of setting, transferring onto, removing from, coloring, printing, cleaning, and distributing is no less of a torture, a cycle that spins in my head, while, with my head, I am being pulled from left to right and back again, my head, George says, needs a hose like the platen so that the torque isn't transferred onward any further, and now the press stops once more, and I say this to George, but my voice is drowned out by the racket of the other presses, in which *Schattenfroh* is being deprinted, giving rise to voices that never tire of their enravishment regarding the miracle of deprinting. George is sweating. I hear him breathe. Short and shallow. Sweat drips onto my head and arms. If he allows the lever to snap back after banging it against my cheek despite all warnings, the next time he tries to move the lever, he can barely manage it, the frame trembles, I see double for moments at a time. George murmurs. It's unbearable not to be able to understand a single word, thus does one not hear all the way through to understanding. It's to do with the blisters that form on the hands, George murmurs about calluses, about blestres, he murmurs, hacked flesh, swelling, thickened skin, rind- and bone-tumors, but also warts, I imagine burst skin, cheesy or septic necrosis, sheep's cheese with calcium deposits, syphilis, a wound in the face that will no longer heal, maculopapular exanthema, fatal outcome, George's callus grows ever bigger, the secretion from the callus shall spill down my back, I purse my lips, George doesn't smell good, he's not an attractive man, he's written too many treatises by his own hand, book-thick and almost unmasterable with the naked eye, his councilors walk hunched beneath the burden of his drafts and ordinances, the court regulations he issued some twenty years ago, George says, testify to great thrift, the Saxon King Bench's Order that he worked out is fundamentally based upon a great sense of justice and it is his preference to settle disputes personally, George says, his sovereign church regiment does not shy away from monastery visitations and interventions in the monastic rule where he finds them necessary, he promised this to his mother not least of all, the two of them together still constitute a community of prayer, just as he promised her he'd not cease bellyaching against Luther, but instead ban the distribution of his translation of the New Testament in the Duchy of Saxony, a promise he then implemented not quite three years ago, announcing that he would have Hieronymus Emser revise Luther's East Central German translation from Latin into Upper German, and not translate from the Hebrew and Greek ur-texts. The question arises as to how he intends to do it, Emser, he shall smooth out a phrase here, sometimes exchange a word for an Upper German expression there, all in all, however, it is likely that Luther is simply being taken over and foisted off as Emser, after all, Luther too merely fell back upon the Vulgate, which he probably knew almost all of by heart. In any case, it is not quite as sovereign in Greek as it is in Latin or Hebrew. The currency dispute follows on the heels of the translation dispute. Not only shall George not respond to the decreasing gold content of Rhenish gold guilders—a tendency caused by the increasing price of gold—by reducing the amount of silver in Saxon thalers, a step that would be suitable to stop their outflow into foreign countries, but he shall uphold their gold content as an inner value; furthermore, he intends to inwardly fix said inner value by emblazoning his coins with the following dedication: "Duke George, the most constant protector of Roman Catholicism and the most obedient son of the church." As far as I am concerned, however, not even a dram of human pity is reserved for me, the peacemaker would prefer to finish me off, as demanded by the conscientiousness and the piety of his heart.

George asks whether anybody is keeping count. 164 more pages, the factor replies. I suggest to George that a pause be inserted, but George is working so beastly hard that he doesn't hear me. His breath-blowing turns into moans. I'm afraid he'll die right here before me. He flatly refused Philipp's offer to replace him. Wouldn't it be better to take me out of the sheath of the printing press and bring off the last few pages with the handle alone. The platen opens up once more and George boxes my ears. So, he does hear me. I give myself names like Woodenbrat, Nobodywood, Woodenbengel, Nobodyrounce, Bratpress, Sheathwood, Bengelnobody, Bratlever. Then the bratty Pressbengel leaps back on page 837 and George gives the Knechte a sign. The Knechte rush over, they wish to pull me out of the spindle and lever, they allow me to fall to the ground in terror. If only he'd smashed his head, Philipp says, interrupting his reading to help the utterly exhausted prince clamber onto a stool provided by the inker. My back feels quite stiff, the chains have dug deep into my wrists, I can't move my head anymore, at least I was able to prevent that which Philipp feared. Thus do I lie motionless, but alert upon the floor and can see how George slowly sinks down from stool to floor, Mario fully makes use of the setting consisting of a single letter and distributes it into a storage case specially prepared for the now-famous mark, Philipp has lost his bearings, the typesetters, printers, and the inker read the blank pages, shaking their heads and also laughing. Then both Knechte come and turn me onto my belly. My right arm no longer seems to belong to my body, it is a dead thing lying beside me. I can tighten my belly but not curve my spinal column. Lying on my back, I possessed at least a small, if also limited, field of vision, now, it would cause me the greatest of difficulties to raise my head, even if I could move it. This gives me time to reflect on how to proceed. I could transfer over directly to me being taken to the castle, after all, I am a dangerous good and must be withdrawn from circulation as soon as possible. However, the decision regarding this is not mine. I could become entirely brat, entirely lever, entirely "Bengel," and the princes would thenceforth be arguing about a piece of wood that one day wishes to become an iron rod. The history of the printing press would then have its relic, which the princes would be too God-fearing to destroy—after all, it shall only be Luther who, in my resolution, wishes to recognize nothing other than what is explicitly "a devilish, hardened persistence" and in me "the devil (. . .) at his most ferocious," which shall have to be extensively dealt with later on, by which it can, from his perspective, be recognized that I, as far as Luther is concerned, have taken prudent precautions—which, to make available to the general public, would justify calling me a martyr. I could ask for my father's pardon, say that this is all just paper and Gutenberg has long been on the mind and this annihilation here cannot last—the virus of knowledge shall spread beyond the book; not failing to add that sublimity and distance shall soon be replaced by other supreme disciplines of western man, namely, mindlessness and miserliness, I might add that the book carousel or reading wheel to be presented by Agostino Ramelli in sixty-three years (he would recommend it to all those who wish to study diligently or to those who suffer from gout or are otherwise ill) would be the beginning of a mobilization and an acceleration of reading, the beginning of the attempt to overcome a medium by way of the medium, in addition to the possibility of switching from one book to another without any issues and, in this way, reading them simultaneously, which is particularly convenient when preparing compilations, serving to make the handling of heavy folios practicable by keeping them on their shelves ever at the same angle toward the reader by way of a gear-mechanism, regardless of whether the wheel is turned forward or backward, in such a way that, should the reader wish to gaze upon another book in the wheel, then return to the previous one, his reading would be able to continue from precisely the same spot where he interrupted it for another book, as it would not have changed its position, for the books do not follow the turning of the wheel; I could also tell my father that Robert Carlton Brown shall bring about a "bloody revolution of the Word" some 350 years later, the notion of a transportable reading-device with a strip of text scrolling before the eyes, including an optimized, time-adapted, i.e. accelerated, reading speed that contains entire libraries, which are able to be read within a month, but only by those called to it by the powers that be, the others would either celebrate a lifelong illiterate Eucharist or be too fat, too rich, and too fulfilled to wish to continue reading books; for the typewriter-sized reader, which richly deserved its company name of "Ideal," the texts will have to be miniaturized and all unnecessary words have to be eliminated; reading-telegraphy, the reading of microfilms, that is the future, by then, Father's library shall have been replaced by a device, from which an epigram sounds daily, at the touch of a button, in such a way that, whoever seeks entrance into Father's library—even if it is he himself who does—finds it only in the form of this epigram; if we are able to know nothing more, we are still dealing with systems of knowledge and their orders, which dissolve in our grasping of them, until, one day, books will finally be put down directly onto the beating, pounding ether—illegible.

These are beautiful thoughts that I am having and I owe them to George alone, his Roman Catholic sternness do I bow to as a stretched-out brat, a Bengel through and through.

One of the Knechte kneels to the ground next to me and palpates me. It's grown into his back, he says. What do you mean by that, Philipp asks. The wooden stick. It must have fallen down and rolled underneath the press, Philipp says. I can feel it quite precisely, the Knecht says as he plays with my back. I feel nothing there.

Philipp wants to see for himself. The Bengel has grown into the Bengel, he says, brat into brat, lever into lever. He asks me whether I know anything about stakes. The wooden part is the sheath, I say. We won't be too critical, Philipp says, beckons to the servants, then gives them an instruction. The Knechte grab hold of me like a swine on a spit and rest me against a wall. If I were to fall over now, I wouldn't be able to get up on my own. In the corner, at a height of some two and a half meters, the Knechte attach a wrought-iron suspension, nail a crossbar to my back, and heave me into the contraption. I hover above the ground. That must really be liberating, Philipp says. George gets up, arranges his raiment, and takes a few steps toward me with a smile. The wall must be re-whitewashed, he says, it's no good if the lime falls from the walls, I don't deserve that, that would be undignified, the Knechte are to see to it that the walls get a new coat of paint, and as it certainly would be most difficult to take me down, I ought to be whitewashed at the same time. We shall call for a painter forthwith, the Knechte say. What's there to laugh about, George wishes to learn from the typesetters and printers, as, meanwhile, they have sat down around a small, round table in the opposite corner of the room and are listening to Mario, who is reading to them from the printed pages that lie neatly stacked in layers before him—this can easily be observed from up here. They no longer take any notice of their environs and have begun to speak so loudly that the following passage can clearly be heard:

"George takes the page out of the reader's hand, seeks out the lines, flips the page over, turns it upside down, turns it over once more, then, finally, covering up his cluelessness with an exaggeratedly upright posture and a stern gaze, returns it to the typefounder with the words that he should continue with his reading from *Schattenfroh*."

George takes the page out of the reader's hand, seeks out the lines, flips the page over, turns it upside down, overturns it once more, then, finally, disguising his cluelessness with an exaggeratedly upright posture and a stern gaze, returns it to the typefounder with the words that he should continue with his reading from *Schattenfroh*. However, visibly made sheepish, he denies having read out anything from *Schattenfroh*, indeed, the book is printed page by page with the letter founded by his own hand and, yes, His Highness most personally led the Pressbengel to the point of total exhaustion, to which anyone here can attest. George, however, doesn't believe it, he heard what he heard, even if he didn't quite understand it, for how is it to be understood that somebody is reading from a book that has only just been destroyed, it is no less of a great sin if a typefounder and printer set forth to continue a work that the princely power had censored and destroyed in an unprecedented litigation than to have written this work up to its annulation, if that became the norm, if copies and forgeries one day began to circulate before originals, there would be sequels written to unwritten books and publishers specializing exclusively in pirate copies and updated new editions.

Under penalty of scrupulous interrogation, George demands that Mateo read to him that which is written on the blank paper. Thus does Mateo take the sheet proffered to him and read:

Le mort
Venez danser vng tourdion
Jmprimeurs sus legierement
Venez tost/ pour conclusion
Mourir vous fault certainement
Faictes vng sault habillement
Presses / & capses vous fault laisser
Reculer ny fault nullement
Alouurage on congnoist louurier.

Les imprimeurs
Helas ou aurons nous recours
Puis que la mort nous espie
Jmprime auons tous les cours
De la saincte theologie
Loix / decret / & poeterie/
Par n[ost]re art plusieurs sont grans clers
Releuee en est clergie
Les vouloirs des gens sont diuers

Le mort
Sus auant vous ires apres
Maistre libraire marchez auant
Vous me regardez de bien pres
Laissez voz liures maintenant
Danser vous fault/ a quel galant
Mettez icy vostre pensee
Comment vous reculez machant
Co[m]mencement nest pas fusee

Le libraire
Me fault il maulgre moy danser
Je croy que ouy/ mort me presse
Et me contrainct de me auancer
Nesse pas dure destresse
Mes liures il fault que ie laisse
Et ma boutique desormais
Dont ie pers toute lyesse
Tel est blece qui nen peult mais.

How is this text to be understood, George wishes to know. Is it only the clergy who read? Is the invention of the printing press death? The poem is directed against the invention of the printing press with movable types as a totalized phenomenon, the inker says. A printer is of the opinion that, wherever a manuscript is set, wherever it is printed and published as a book, wherever the book is published and is read, death is already there. The art of book-printing is devil-spawn, the pressman says. Book-printing kills handwriting and the copying of books, which is why death leads the typesetter and the publisher away, Mateo says. George agrees with this exegesis, but points out that here lies a paradox, as in the interpretation: the text is directed against the invention of the printing press in general, but it exists in printed form, as if the author wished to negate printing by way of printing.

An image is included, Mateo says. George recognizes nothing. Is the image the empty page, Gijsbrechts's backside of a framed painting, not as the image of an image, but as empty bookpage of empty bookpage; not painted as a panel, but printed as a bookpage. The bookpage printed as empty bookpage is therefore no empty bookpage, but an image. If Gijsbrechts's painting has two back-sides, but no front-, so too is the image of the empty bookpage the only page in the book that has a fixed spot, for the reader does not look through the letters, which means through the pages, at a world supposedly lying behind the words, instead lingering on the page in the hope, never to be abandoned, of finding something on the other side of the page, George says. But as he finds nothing, he reads empty paper, which has many faces. The blank page is a first indispensable step toward the undoing of book-printing.

But the bookpage isn't empty in the slightest, Mateo says, for, indeed, this image here can be seen clearly and distinctly:

Quite so, George says, Gijsbrechts's painting isn't at all empty either, after all, the number 36 was painted onto a scrap of paper that was attached with sealing wax to the top-left of the back-side of the painting or, rather, the canvas. Katálogos: to count down, to list up. One out of 36. The same once more become different. 36 is not zero. The nothing shown is something, just as 0 consists of the enclosure of nothing. A canvas is never blank. The hemp fiber displays a genuine texture. Does an angel not walk beneath the 36? And is there not a towering figure awaiting it on the right, eluding one's clarifying gaze amidst the fog? A sun is matte in its shining. Its rays have bleached the projection-screen unevenly. Or does one perhaps see a winter landscape with bare trees that fog enshrouds, a stretch of coast with high-blown dunes? Yes, it is Jesus himself who is strolling there. The angel shall not be able to hold him. Does a stake not tower up in the middle of the painting, to which the angel, which is no angel at all, is led? And does one not already see what is befalling him there? The stake is placed at its feet. Does the cross not appear? You must not be ashamed if you attribute the painting to Paul Klee. The only difference here is that the stretcher frame and picture frame are part of the canvas and each of the stretcher's bars is connected to three round timbers.

It is now entirely clear to George that, after its printing, *Schattenfroh* operates with white script against a white background. There is nothing more left and everything is there. However, George continues, the cipher appears to exist only in the eye of the beholder, how else could it have been put down on paper? Phenolphthalein, iron sulfate, vinegar, or apple juice—just a few examples. Phenolphthalein has a purgative effect on the eyes—thus are images purged from there too. Or the eyes rub the pages over with ammonia, which makes the script or the images made of phenolphthalein visible for a short while. Ferrous sulfate turns blue with cyanate, eyes observing the world through a permanent blue filter. Red cabbage stock colors the acetic acid, thus is red cabbage a brain-growth that excretes the brew onto the paper by way of the eyes. The apples are most certainly from the tree of knowledge, which no longer stands tall in paradise, but only in memoriam, though it continues to be forbidden. Mention should also be made of onion juice, which rises into the eyes, alum and ammonium, which the body absorbs and is therefore made to see wondrous things. As far as fruit juice is concerned, if it is to be made use of as invisible ink, it reacts not only to heat, but also becomes visible underneath ultraviolet light. In the event that juice from apples was used to write and draw upon the printed paper, two mutually non-exclusive possibilities are conceivable: First of all, we're dealing with the eyeball-juice of the chosen guinea pigs—actually selected by Lucifer himself—with which, driven by gaze-directionality and gaze-intensity, the paper is written on, and, second of all, that these very eyeballs are also able to make the drawings and the script of the eyeball-juice visible by emitting either ultraviolet light or heat. One might be able to distill a juice fit for invisible ink from fireflies. If one consumed this juice, one would become a genuine seer, in hours of enlightenment, one sees that which one cannot see upon the blank page. Is the firefly then not also a symbol of beauty? The distillate is the beauteous souls of the dead who live on eternally in paper. Nobody has made sure that the printers too can recognize the image with practiced eye, but not the princes, and it has now fallen to Mateo to scrupulously interrogate Nobody on this matter.

I follow their dispute as if I had no part in it and as if I weren't the one being negotiated over the whole time. I am freshly whitewashed. The crossbar holds me in suspension without causing me any pain. I'm quite cozy. The whitewash is my new raiment, it bedecks my eyes and lips. I enjoy *not* opening my eyes and lips against its resistance, which it would be all too easy to breach, I imagine that the whitewash is demanding I keep my eyes and lips shut, then, triggered by a single sign, I am to see wondrous things. It is more beautiful to imagine things than to truly see them; when one sees them, one always finds something to complain about. Only holding back a turd, then seeking out the lavatory when expulsion can no longer be avoided, affords me a comparably blissful feeling to that of slowly opening whitewashed eyes and lips and also imagining the soft scatter of particles, the smallest of ships ramming an iceberg, the tearing of a cocoon, the whitewasher Knut Werbeere,* who, as a painter, has innumerable pseudonyms, such as Rene Tubewerk,† Kurt-René Webe,‡ and Bert Neuewerk,§ was not squeamish, he started out by applying the lime paint in a milk-thin layer, he then mixed in sticky fillers for the second and all subsequent applications, it was inevitable that this mass would find its way into my mouth, I believed that I could feel something in the form of letters with my palate and tongue, something that I had gathered in my mouth and put into alphabetical order:

a a a
e e e e
i i i i
o o
u u

c c
d
f
g g
h h h h
j
l
m
n n n

---

* Knut Whoberry.
† Rene Tubefactory.
‡ Kurt-René Weave.
§ Bert Newwork.

p p p
r r r r
s s s s s
t t t t
v

I under no circumstances wished to interrupt this process by swallowing my spit, I resolved to suppress the external reflex of swallowing (and of translating—even the names) at least until I had gotten all of the letters into a position I was satisfied with:

Frueh goss Joerg naiv ratendem Philipp sturste Nachsicht.
Vier Mandate goss Joerg, Philipps Nachsicht streunt frueh.
Philipp goss Joerg frueh. Nachschuss, Tritte. Adam verneint.*

But once I'd gotten a taste for names, I wished to taste nothing but, thus did I take apart the little story of the Golem and its inventor, which causes Adam to deny the Fall (but leave Philipp, Joerg, and Adam alone), not without noticing that the Golem invents its own creator. But I didn't get any further with the three names, the rest could not be contained in names. Thus did I continue to decompose these names in my mouth and have been tidily transmogrifying their letters ever since. I compose the letters on the basis of taste-impressions, not according to the criterion of lexicon, grammar, and logic. Each name has a different taste and can be recognized by its taste as a name. If there remains a residue that cannot be defined in terms of taste, I discard that which I've discovered. It looms, coming together letter by letter, there is nothing accidental in the mouth, it

---

* Early, Joerg poured Philipp, guessing naively, hindsight, most stubborn.
Four mandates did Joerg pour, Philipp's hindsight strays early.
Philipp poured Joerg early. Rebound, kicks/footsteps. Adam negates.

tastes of armor, incense, blood, and Bible. Now comes this sequence of German names:

Georg Philipp Jesus Christus Schattenfroh Vater Niemand.

I assign each one a space within my mouth. George back left, Philipp back right, where the circumvallate papillae are, both taste sour, no, they don't look good there, I swap them, Philipp back left and George back right, they look good there, Schattenfroh in the middle on the tongue's midline groove, Father beside him on the right, both of them particularly palatable, perhaps a bit too spice-laden, their flavor too intense, I put Jesus, Christ—but is there just one of him or are these two different people?—I put both names in the middle behind Philipp and George at the edge of the root of the tongue, they taste bitter, I put Nobody right at the front, myself, I taste sweet, I don't like that Schattenfroh and Father have no taste, it pleases me not, I cannot control them here, I place them on the right and left behind me, now they taste salty. Now, I have two crucifixion groups that oppose one another, Jesus Christ and Nobody are Jesus, the two thieves are Philipp and George, as well as Schattenfroh and Father. I shall have to take one of the two with me, Father or Schattenfroh shall be my Dismas. At first, they all swim through my mouth, in which saliva has accumulated like water in the Rursee as a result of the Rur Dam; I must merely open the dam-gates and the saliva shall flow out. What more beautiful feeling can there be than knowing your father to be in your belly. Philipp stands crosswise, but the acceleration of the salivary-pressure and the swallowing reflex push him around Jesus Christ and flush him away. George seems to have immediately joined him, I can no longer find him and can't deal with Jesus Christ as I desperately try to swallow him. If I can manage to, I'll help him along with my fingers or a little wooden stick, the latter shall cause him to imagine himself to be in the vicinity of the cross, and he'll go down clutching at the little stick. What if I swallowed

Father, then could no longer breathe? Schattenfroh is perhaps only a virus who is waiting to spread through the entire body, bringing with it spores of that most-virulent German tongue. Perhaps, he has already done so and only wishes to prove that he can play along with the letter-game, that obscene mixture of child-training and language-magic. I swallow him, he hangs in my throat like viscous mucus; as if he were reproducing himself out of himself, he remains chunkily in the throat, even when it drains. Schattenfroh is a mass that constantly drips down, a stalactite, I am his stalagmite. The time shall come when we become a stalagmite. How would the emergence-process of this formation progress if I were to swallow myself? Would I be copied into myself? Would I already contain Schattenfroh? Do I even exist without Schattenfroh? Is there an observer in me that observes me and Schattenfroh—the I itself? Do I then exist twofold, but Schattenfroh only onefold? Or does Schattenfroh observe forth from me, the one who has swallowed himself? What am I then swallowing myself down into? I have now taken the tablet. Nobody slides down Schattenfroh's maw. A sled that is slow to get going. It shall soon pick up speed and be unstoppable.

 I am of another opinion, I say, he shall be taken away from the printing press by Death himself and he shall also lead the typesetter away and the publisher shall fare no better, for he can no longer publish anything. That really is a grave lèse-majesté, George says, for it, I wish to call you to account without trial, and what account means, to know that I ought to properly ready myself at Heldrungen Castle, for which Luther's "A Sermon on Preparing to Die," published precisely six years ago, is most ideal, he hereby foists it upon me, he shall have it provided to me for my stay at the castle so that I might know what is essential and useful and solely and uniquely "for God's sake," as it is called in Luther, and how then can book-printing be seen as important in the face of death, even if Luther belongs, George says, to the very ranks of those whom death shall first take away, as in the quoted poem, and that is the beautiful thing about sadness, the script would barely be able to make it to me. Before I am taken to Heldrungen Castle, also known as Schloss Grundlehne or even dubbed "Geldhernun"* in common parlance ever since the uprising I started, there, I am going to be mistreated according to Hundregeln† so that I be taught a Lehrendung,‡ he only wishes to show me something more, you can see it clearly looking out from up here, he tells me, your heart and soul will not fly any higher, what I can see is a horse standing next to a printing press, a woman sits upon it in a red leather-cloth saddle, a smoking torch or candle in her left hand, her gaze cast over her right shoulder at me, she is unmediatedly seeking out my eyes and I ought to take a very close look at the woman to see whether I don't recognize my mother in her, the thin hair hanging stringily down and utterly exposing her forehead, she had it dyed brown, the fresh shade makes up for her discontent, each morning, she asked my father what she ought to do with her terribly thin hair, it didn't suit her. Leave it as it is, my father always replied, beside her is a man looking up, he bears a book in his hand that is entitled *Schattenfroh*, one can only read it if one kneels down and looks up from under the book, which is not possible for me from my corner up here on the wall, I can decide for myself whether I don't recognize myself in this man, gaunt, bald-headed, truculent ambition in the gaze, but toward what is the gaze cast, where does my mother's right hand point, she points to a small soul-figure slipping out of the mouth of an old man in a crew-neck hospital gown, gray and blue diamonds strung up and linked upon the white cotton, the last bit pulled out of the mouth by an angel or demon or demonic angel hovering in the air with red-glowing wings and fire-flaming hair as a midwife has, it is a soul-birth, the old man shall be my father, the soul follows his extubation. Isn't the soul enchanting, George asks, it

---

* Gimmeyourmoneynow.
† Dog-rules.
‡ Lesson-dung.

really does look like a newborn babe, and how it rejoices to finally be free. It is a cherub, this soul, though he can't yet identify any wings. The demonic angel has two pairs of wings, I say, apart from its red wings, its flaming hair, and its death-skull visage, it appears entirely in steely blue, the first pair of wings, in that same shade of steely blue, looks to have been undone, also worthy of note is the frilled shirt it wears beneath its jerkin, the pants pass for contemporary in terms of their cut, it's only the fish fin, which could also be a toothless reptile, a snake, or a chimera or a bit of destroyed clothing fluttering in the air and which one forgot to remove during the fitting, a surprising fact, given the fin's excessive length, which causes one to wonder whether this is an angel or a demon. And the golden-brown soul-child, is it not already wearing a diaper that is much too large, does it not soon wish to flap and flit about like a moth?

    You are writing all of this, George says, you are the demon with the blazing hair and the red wings, the movement of my pen painted him into the sky together with Father and the soul-figure, an aerial painting, based, however, on an original that paints a completely different image, in this one, the obstetrician is a graceful angel with curly hair and fluttering dress, the soul—a well-formed child with already aged head, its long arms stretched out toward the angel, it gazes most trustfully at the angel and the angel does not tear it forth, but receives it unto itself most calmly, the long candle in the right hand of the nurse or nun kneeling at the foot of the bed has not gone out, but burns, the dying man, for whom the candle promises eternal light, lies upon a bedstead with a chamberpot peeking out from under it and not upon a meager stretcher, only slightly wider than the bed is the curtain attached to a horseshoe-shaped rail at its foot, it protects the dying man from prying eyes, we, the image-observers, see the longside of the bed, in which the dying man lies, the curtain only runs some forty centimeters toward the foot on either side, thus can it not be closed around the bed, which is either typical of the time when the picture came into being or—and this is what he actually suspects—is a tribute to the image-observer, for whom everything is staged, such a big curtain, pushed off to the side (and how, given the volume of its material, can it even be pushed?) really does claim far, far too much attention at the expense of the soul-birth, which is why all the things and figures serving the purpose of contemplation are only hinted at, as, indeed, everything can only ever be hinted at; on the back-side, the curtain is, in any case, drawn, on the front-side, facing the observer, somebody, presumably the nurse or the nun, threw it over the rod to free up space at the foot in such a way that the dying man can be seen over the entire frontal long-side of the bed, possibly not just by the observer of the picture, but also by other sick or dying people who are presumably located in the room behind the observer, further surroundings, however, apart from the scenery of the infirmary, are left out. Everything is dignified and peaceful, even the fact that the sheets are wrapped and placed around the dying man in such a way that he lies there with his bare arms over the sheets, with bare chest and only his sides covered below the chest and down to his legs and seeing that the uncovered cutout allows a glimpse of his genitals, which, in the picture, are barely covered by the lower end of the candle, provokes no protest, isn't even perceived as provocation. At the moment of death, the light in the eyes goes out with the soul-birth, the eyes of the dying man in the picture are already empty, the hood upon his head resembling a Byzantine-Orthodox miter, the dead man looks protected and redeemed, the soul-child leaves a cocoon in which it was kept fresh and free from the world until its birth. How different is the broken, armless, amorphous creature with its back to us, it speeds away from the mouth of the hollow body lying there with closed eyes, the demon grabs hold of it like a lifeless sack, changing its form with each and every grasp.

The Knechte heave me out of the wrought-iron contraption, then, together with the crossbar, onto the horse behind the woman who is said to be my mother, the man with the book who I am said to be follows us with brisk stride, a horse also stands at the ready for him, the Knechte ride out in front, whereas Philipp and George form the procession's end with both remaining Landsknechte. My hands are bound to the beam, which is tied to the horse with a rope that passes beneath its belly. They bind me to my mother with an additional rope so that I don't keel backward, she now has to brace herself against the whole load on her back, I myself am pressed so tightly to her by the rope that, if I wish to breathe, I can only do so against her waistcoat, but Mother seems not to mind the load in the slightest, she continues to sit upright upon the horse, which unhurriedly sets itself into motion, Mother's flowing skirt exudes an unpleasant warmth, in this position, I shall suffocate before I reach the castle, Mother doesn't react to my cries, if I could manage to move about thirty centimeters to the left, I could touch her with my right hand and perhaps call forth a reaction from her, but she seems to take no notice of my presence whatsoever, as if I didn't exist at all, which infuriates me all the more, as she really never tires of telling me what a burden I am to her. I simply can't manage to move my torso enough to the left to reach her with my hand, then I realize that I could simply hit her in the head with the beam. Should I do that, I ask her, should I hurt you? A massive blow, only a short windup, executed with a quick spin of the torso, the beam is shoved a little ways into her head, out of which I then extract it with no trouble. The beam is intact, her head displays no injury. I repeat the process. This time too, the beam penetrates deep into the head without causing any damage. If my hands were free, I would seek to grab into Mother's head with them. I perhaps only exist as the one who writes and I sit behind this Mama's Boy, with whom I have so whimsically sympathized and into whom I've inscribed myself. But why is it not within my powers to switch back and forth between the one who writes and the Mama's Boy, no matter how much I long for it, demand it even. Perhaps, there is only a small hole free on either side through which the imagination can slip, for it is a matter of awaiting the proper moment of relaxation. I wait. I relax. I feel myself to be in between. I give the one who writes the order to call for Mother and, lo and behold, the one who writes calls for Mother, then Mother says: "What do you want? Have I not told you a hundred times to behave like a true son and do honor unto your mother? A son exists only to comprehend his mother. And what do you do? You invent a character with a crossbar upon his back, he has as little substance as a blank page and precisely as much to say." You've got that right, I say, I didn't manage this figure too well. "You managed it very poorly," Mother interrupts me, yes, I managed it very poorly, I say, "what does *managed it very poorly* mean here," Mother asks, "you can't even be said to have managed it at all," yes, one might as well put it that way, I say, there can be no talk of having "managed," "so don't always say 'managed,'" Mother says, and I am silent. I am not certain whether I spoke as the character with the beam or as the one who writes and, as this question gives me no peace, I ask Mother whether she heard my voice closer or farther away. "Closer or farther from what," my mother asks, you've always been so imprecise, just like this. Did the one who writes or the figure with the beam upon his back speak to you? I ask, here, she is able to console me, my voice is always too near, she says, she rejoices every day she's not able to hear me at all, not even once was it afforded to her to be able to forget me after days of total silence, but, now, she lives ever in the fear of having to perceive my voice, which is scandal, sensation, convulsion, "you are unable to keep yourself to yourself, you raise your voice and a rift passes through the world. Your voice is more alien to you than I am, thus do you wish for me to ever hear it and soothe you. You only wish that I might pull your voice out of your mouth like the soul-birth of a small child, a sweet young thing, then pamper and indulge it as if it were you yourself, to whom such a thing never came to pass, or so it seems, I cannot remember, no matter how hard I try, actually, you wish to say nothing at all, you wish only to speak so that you hear your own voice, which tears you back toward me, from the start, you thought that I was in the great beyond, me and the voice, from the very moment you first said 'Mommy.' You'd like so much for your voice to not be of this world, even though I, your simple mother, cannot do you this favor, for it is I from whom your voice comes." The boundary between an only just and a no longer, between the audible and the silent, that's interesting, I'll never arrive at this boundary, the essential things come to pass on this side of the boundary and beyond it, only just and no longer, I must stand upon the threshold, but she doesn't ever see me reaching it. But I'm standing there now, right there, I say, and you don't see me. "I cannot see you," Mother says, "I turned my back on you a long time ago." Indeed, hearing is also seeing, I say, when, because of a sudden stop, I fall over, thus noticing that Mother does not consist of flesh and blood at all, rather, she feels like a wooden doll over which—and I dare to assert this only as a function of circumstance—one has provisionally thrown something to bedeck its wooden nudity. So, that's how it is, I say, you invoke me, I say *Here I am*, then you, who are The-Other-in-Self, my core, who ensures that I never come to myself, you who are the other voice within my inwardness, that which constantly perturbs me as the other, you turn away at the very moment you invoke and address me, but your voice already belongs to me, just as mine belongs to you. You invoked me and you recognized me, you recognized me and you left me, I gave myself up and gave up my voice, then you left me. I say that as your echo, for I am no more than that. "A preacher's tone," Mother says, "an appalling preacher's tone, just like your father, who could never differentiate between inner and outer, own and other. And so sniveling, it doesn't suit you at all, that actually seems to be more like an echo of something else entirely, the Old Testament, I suppose."

At this moment, George appears next to the Mama's Boy, saying that I ought not to worry, the writing one is a mere necessity of thought, he only exists because my hands are tied, he vanishes with my death. Since the writing one is riding behind me, he can see me, but I can't see him. George says that, in such cases, it is not customary to turn around. The consequences of non-compliance are foreseeable: the writing one and the Mama's Boy shall be banished back into the welkin, where each might seem blissful within himself, each never having the possibility of touching the other or turning to face the other, the word, "he is sitting behind you" must suffice for all time. Then disappears once more.

A display dummy with ill-fitting hair. Two Knechte up front who take their assignment very seriously. Two princes intent on hacking down an uprising, rooting out a book, then making short work of its author as insurgent. An author who exists twofold, only once within the function of the one who writes, then once as son of mother. A mother—see display dummy. The son of the mother experiences nothing that does not concern the mother, who experiences nothing because she is a display dummy. The one who writes waits for the Mama's Boy to experience something and, since he experiences nothing because the mother experiences nothing, the one who writes, who can only ever see Mother and Mama's Boy from behind, the mother covered over by her little son, has all the leisure in the world to envision the Mama's Boy as a daredevil.

It's beautiful here, I've underestimated the Eifel for all my life, I've felt sorry for those who were born here and live here, as Those Who Got Stuck or Those Who Moved In. There's so much to discover that one really can get lost. Our way leads past a landscape of karst cones and into a water gap, we cross a water gate and gaze from the Ossenboch onto the Goldene Aue. The mountain spur falls steeply away, George must have gotten lost, the horses benefit from the fact that the intermittent tufts of blue moor grass are more plentiful here, their bluish, slate-gray, and whitish blooms awaken within me the imagining that we find ourselves on a contemplative ride-out, at the end of which a feast shall be held in my honor, they cling to the rubble slope with their dense root systems and resistant offsets, they're distributed like steps, otherwise, the horses wouldn't be able to take a single step. The common beeches that I encounter on the way call forth in me a sublime impression, in their foliage, I see the bleeding visage of Jesus. On the south and southwestern slopes, the common beech is retreating due to the dryness of the air and soil, and pedunculate and durmast oaks appear, small leaf lindens, hornbeams, and weeping birches arise. The durmast oak is majestic, a relic of a bygone era that does not yet wish to accept its demise. It is towered over by the small leaf linden, which, as supplier of honey, is meant to keep the people still. The weeping birch with its brushwood stands ready to sweep away the old community. Smells everywhere, totally topsy-turvy.

A mosaic of semi-arid and dry grasslands is bordered by dry forests, between which are to be found areas of dense undergrowth with whitethorn, sloe, wayfaring tree, or dogrose, I also see horseshoe vetch and heath roses here and there. Hairy milk-vetch, dwarf feathergrass, or dwarf sedge, which likewise grow here, have beautiful names, but really are quite insubstantial. Areas of heather and bird's-foot sedge suggest higher amounts of rainfall that will prevent the aforementioned plants from thriving. The prevailing low vegetation makes it easy to overlook plants, even in drier areas, however, numerous plant communities are quite at home in the dry-warm, shallow—i.e. of shallow soil depth, barren, and nutrient-poor—skeletal soil of Muschelkalk—or shell limestone—and Permian limestone, which is to say, soils containing a great deal of loose, coarse material, such as scree and rubble, it is filled with humus here and there, one also finds the greater bur-parsley community with the wild herbs carrot bur-parsley, shepherd's-needle, poorman's weatherglass, red hemp-nettle, and dwarf snapdragon. Now, we come to an area of deep lime soils, which is to say those of Middle and Upper Muschelkalk, here, the settled community of summer adonis stands out, as well as the rough corn bedstraw and the few-flowered fumitory. The untrained eye can hardly distinguish wild herbs from the species of a settled wild-herb community, the most widespread community of which, that of the white campion, can be found in the community of summer adonis just as it can be found in the greater bur-parsley community. It is beautiful to see how these plants can coexist without a monoculture coming into being, everything seems to be in equilibrium, each and every plant is dependent on every other; or is coexistence merely a natural growth sequence of the neutral-reaction soils to be found here? The white-campion community consists of common wild oat, fool's cicely, night-flowering catchfly, forking larkspur, earth chestnut, and dwarf spurge. If I am a weed, then I have not been able to set myself down into this soil, by way of a plant-trellis, I rise to the pinching off of my own side-shoots, brown rot has taken hold of me, the soil has grown tired of me, that which began as dark germinators, wishing to grow as an indigenous open flower, spreading far and wide, has now been thinned out and reduced together with its community, though one knows very well indeed that this shall only bear greater fruits. Shall this lead to a composition of species as of yet unseen here and more fields by way of acidic reaction—all this to do with the primacy of the chamomile community, which consists of annual bugloss, chamomile, wild radish, four-seed vetch, wind grasses, and colicwort, until the soil becomes so acidic that only annual knawel, which the princes must make use of as a decision-making aid in seeking to eliminate their unreliability and turmoil, red sorrel, which, with its subterranean offshoots, is very persistent and unruly and multiplies uncontrollably through all attempts to eradicate it, and corn spurrey, an underling that the princes happily gobble down like spinach, is also to be found. The ground beetle *Amara pseudostrenua* is considered to be most rare, even now, it is scuttling up my mother's waistcoat, the numerous entomologists who have settled here because of the area's coleopterological peculiarities would give a year's salary just to see it. I am convinced of the fact that beetles have a soul and this specimen is my "spirit animal." *Blaps lethifera* also lives here outside of houses, under stones, in the open air. Its appearance announces death. It swarms about here, the Große Totenkäfer, the Great Death-Beetle—actually called the Churchyard Beetle in English—has likely done its work and wanders back into the regions from whence it first set out to battle. A swarm of some 350 specimens has been accompanying our train for about an hour now. I am fairly certain that they clambered out of my father's waistcoat and skirt, into which, from time to time, they return. In 493 years, I shall be 53 years old. A Death-Beetle for each year of life, a greater honor could not be bestowed upon me on the way to the fortress. It is soothing to follow the horse's leisurely stride and get a good look at the surroundings. Everything has a name, we don't know most of the names. When one sets out on one's way, there is no longer anything familiar, everything becomes new, heretofore unseen, all is equally important, nothing is small, everything fades progressively into insignificance. Suddenly, we turn left and leave the mountainous forest-terrain, as if the correct route had once more occurred to George or as if it were now safe to give up one's camouflage and show oneself out in the open. The way becomes significantly less arduous, though it remains monotonous, it leads over fields and acres to a village called Liebsolden,* George reports that, a few days back, farmers put up a sign at the entrance to the village upon which the place name "Lobendlies"† could be read, but nobody thought to praise it, so the sign was taken down. The place itself is a fine, well-built hamlet, of which I shall most happily take up the description anon. Upon a hill that is some 130 meters tall, dubbed a "mountain" by George, stands a stone castle complex with two fortifications, which is to say two Bergfrieden, which, visible from afar, protrude from the forest, one lower and one upper castle, the lower castle has been expanded into a palace, while the upper castle, standing some

---

* Lovewages.
† Readpraisingly.

five hundred meters away from this one, is inhabited, George says. In the year 1089, a monastery occupied by Benedictines was founded here, some four weeks agone, it was in part laid to ruin, in such manner that it encountered its wyrd; now, the destruction seems beautiful in and of itself. Some monks have joined the uprising, the good Matthias Bilderhand,‡ later to be dubbed Matthias Daherblind,§ did so two years ago, as he knew how to campaign quite effectively from the pulpit regarding the shame of indulgences and the greed of the Church. My being handed over is a ride through history, monastic life is past, whichever way I turn, all I see is backdrops. But the fields and acres are beautiful, I could hurl myself upon them and work my way over them with bare teeth. George can read it in my face, they ought to have driven me across the land in carts and heavy chains, after all, I am nothing but a brute bound to a clod of earth, he says, but I am not thankful to the Lord for that native clod, I should simply cultivate that earth most beneficently, instead, George says, I constantly criticize its consistency, wish to reinvent land and soil, and can no longer distinguish between Word and Weapon until I finally wish to rebuild God himself. While the procession is at a halt, I can observe a heap of beetles upon the ground, they are making war with each other. It is a lively collection, the species can hardly be distinguished one from another, they're too similar. Why do they fight? No reason for it can be made out from up above, thus do I ask Philipp I, who appears on my right, whether I might not make use of this halt to observe the Beetle War as close as close can be. And be unfettered?, Philipp I scoffs, *he* shall undertake the observation himself, then report back to me. Having achieved nothing, he sets himself back at the head of our group of travelers. With its enormous antler, one beetle shoves another with a no-less-enormous antler out in front of it, only once this one has been

---

‡ Matthias Imageshand.
§ Matthias Thereforeblind.

shoved against a windfallen bough does it manage to brace itself against its attacker with its hind legs. With its lance that it bears upon its head, one green beetle pierces a second green beetle with a lance upon its own head, the second beetle immediately falls onto its back and is petrified. The beetles fight, equals against equals, in different weight classes. Only once their respective champions have been identified are the class-boundaries abandoned. However, that does not mean that only the heavier beetles triumph. The dead are carried away. Upon a meadow-like elevation dubbed "Weißer Berg," a group of beetles makes a barricade of wagons out of small branches and rubble, this latter serving as supply wagon or farmer's cart, the rubble is laid out as munitions, which can be rolled down from the upper promontory if necessary. The other beetles, which have not barricaded themselves amongst the wagons, withdraw so that they can no longer be seen by the wagon-barricade spies: These are George, Philipp, and Duke Heinrich II of Brunswick-Lüneburg, along with their followers. After some time, temperatures are taken between the negotiators of both sides. The talks are unsuccessful. Indeed, conditions have been set by both parties, however, since nobody is willing to agree to them, the situation remains unchanged. The scenery already bores me, I'm at the point of turning away from it when a tremendous swarming comes to pass, all of a sudden, the ground on my left turns entirely black, the princes' Beetle-Knechte form clusters that move forward, the lower beetles climb upward and clamber over the others until they themselves are overrun once more, thus do the cluster-wheels roll from all sides toward the barricade of wagons, the mob here evidently allowed itself too great a sense of security, the posts are only partially manned, some flanks are completely unprotected, now do the princes fall upon them, a great disorder builds itself up to towering on high, beetles roll down the mountain as black-shimmering drops, then seek to climb it once more, the barricade of wagons is soon leveled, the dead are carried away, many flee, then are recaptured, a slowly dwindling fountain of pearl-black water pleases my eye, rolling cocoons, pupation, crawling escape, the horses' legs up, the swarm has left the ground entirely, it dyes us black, I must move forward, otherwise, arms and legs are petrified, I hold my mouth shut, they seek to penetrate me through my nose, but are too big for that, if I just keep moving my head back and forth, they fall off, and I must sing, that sets them into flight, I've also seen that the beetles form a name, Schattenfroh, and they have the 666 upon their back, it detaches slowly, scrotum and member threefold, the inseminations are interminable, the beetles are rock-hard, I remind myself to sit up straight, Mother is trickling, a tiny heap of sawdust collects upon my right thigh, then begins to grow upward, I lay my head back, sneezing would make me look suspicious, Mother consists of only holes all over, her clothing also has holes, the beetles shall come out of the horses; don't sneeze, I think, and if I don't think "don't sneeze," the sneezing builds up; to breathe shallowly and quickly, they have come to unfetter me, these are no chains of iron and I am also not being transported in a cart, as was once written, take a look, my hands are free, Mother is crumbling, I shall soon have overcome her, Philipp asks: "Has nobody ever said to you that there aren't any such beetles here?", the retinue rides cross-country, the monotony of the fields makes me field-blind, the harrow has made perpendicular tracks, as if the farmer wished to take an examination for a master craftsman's diploma before his prince instead of impaling him with common bugloss, as seen from above, the field looks like a watercolor consisting only of shades of brown and through which a long downpour has passed. The sun burns. I sit upon a Spanish donkey. Mother is entirely withered. She has now certainly become a wooden doll wearing a festive dress, an inanimate, if also quite finely worked-over, piece of wood, which nature has opted to take back into its womb entirely. This passage seems very familiar to me, as if I've already been there. This impression grows stronger once we get to the following point: It doesn't come to pass all too often that somebody is presented in public tied upside-down to a pole. Once they catch sight of me, the crowd parts, the people seem to take it for granted that my destination is the fortress, the outlines of which now stand out clearly before us. Coming from the west, we ride toward the outer moat. The shortest way to the bridge over the moat leads to the left in a northerly direction, then along the moat to the right in an easterly direction, but George takes the path to the right and leads us around the entire grounds, gawping, repeatedly expressing his rapture, for years, he has been admiring this fortress in a constant state of expansion, its lord, Count Ernst II von Vorderort, did not shy away from demolishing the surrounding houses in order to make the necessary building materials available, one day, the entire complex shall be protected by more than ten moats and ramparts, one wall erected around the next, one knows that, in 109 years, I shall have sought to, using only a map, but without authorization, pass through the city-gate of a city in which I shall have been born in 439 years, and that I shall have escaped the just punishment for this by fleeing, which I shall have accomplished by climbing over the city wall, once again without permission, this time, precautionary measures have been taken, I am not able to get into the city and its center, the fortress, until we finally reach its north side by way of a tree-lined path, which, on the protruding earth wall with its four large, acute-angled bastions, merges into the bridge over the outer moat, where the fortress gate of a mighty gate-bastion is flanked by two larger bastions, the drawbridge is lowered upon our arrival, we ride through the gate into a casement some twenty meters long, which we leave through an iron gate, which is opened in response to the cries of two gatekeepers, then, after another fifteen meters, we come to the outer ditch-wall of the surrounding inner moat, over which a smaller bridge with a drawbridge at its end leads us to a turret of an inner defensive wall, upon which the drawbridge is supported, five further turrets are attached to the defensive or outer wall, we pass by the turret and finally reach the gatehouse, of whose keeper George says that he has caused many a newcomer to simply disappear, there is a rumor that the gatehouse has a flap at one point on its floor, the keeper leads despised people onto it, then the flap immediately falls open and causes these people to disappear without trace; below ground is to be found a great tub of poison that dissolves the human body within a day, another version is far more exhilarating, according to that one, it isn't poison in the tub, but copper sulfate dissolved in water—one might translate it as "glassy copper"—which, in precisely the opposite fashion, conserves the body for many years, for it reliably kills bacteria and putrefactive organisms, the keeper has taken advantage of this circumstance and operates as a genuine collector of human exhibits, which he hoards in the east wing of the castle, George recounts how the man informed Count Ernst II of his passion for collecting by suggesting that the best-preserved corpses might be exhibited so that the miracle of the human body could be studied, the exhibited ones are alive in death, the east wing could serve as a medical lecture hall, whose uniqueness would soon be spoken of all round the world and would turn the fortress into a fortress of science, it might also be worth considering the transportation of those declared dead all through the land in order to show them to dubious characters, which certainly would not fail to have an effect in the direction of a political or religious conversion, after all, nobody wishes to give themselves up to the notion that the dead have appeared to them. George asks whether I believe this story. I am silent.

 George continues his story and tells of how the keeper of the gatehouse is surpassed in his intransigence and perfidiousness by only the tower watchman of the Bergfried, the most beastly in all the land; any attempt to deceive him would be much the same as the death penalty, the tortures that he has devised over the course of his life are without equal, lords from every corner of the world visit, interested in his methods of interrogation, thus does he slowly become literature, and he is worried that he is insidiously losing the strictness he has heretofore established and developing a kind of empathy for his clientele, who have done nothing less than disregard the law and must be treated accordingly, after all Dr. Luther says precisely the same thing when he speaks of a "clear judgment" of the eternal God who gives victory unto us, the princes, "so that God punishes the peasants for their disobedience and their blasphemy and all their misdeeds," to which I reply that this Luther is weatherproof through and through, he speaks of God's mercy only in the sense of barter and indulgences out of the fear that God might change his mind once more, thus does he write: "they should be merciful to their prisoners and those who give themselves up, just as God is merciful to everyone who surrenders and humbles themselves before Him. Do this, so that the weather does not change again, and God then hands victory to the peasants." In my case, one could hardly speak of giving oneself up, incidentally, the tower keeper's name is Antonio Atome, George says, I'm certain that you've known him since page 61, sometimes, he also helps out in the gatehouse if the case turns out to be one that is all too *difficult*, then the terms "fortified wall" and "neck ditch" take on a new meaning.

Did I mean to say that this tower had to be cast down together with its towerkeeper, who, in any case, kept its fire hot: "On, on, onward, for the fire is hot! Do not let your sword grow cold, do not let it hang loose in your hands! Smite cling clang on the anvil of Nimrod; cast down their towers! As long as they live, it is not possible to be emptied of the fear of man. You can be told nothing about God as long as they rule over you. On, onward, as long as you live. God marches before you, so follow, follow!" No, not at all, I say, a different tower was meant and a different castle. But this is my letter and my handwriting, dated April 26, just barely three weeks old. Yes, I say. A castle for all, a tower for all, George says.

We ride through the gatehouse and into the castle courtyard, where George compels me to go, for his friend Count Ernst II, who, together with his cousin Albrecht VII, is waiting for me and would certainly be most pleased to receive a writ of fine script from my hand, one that describes his possessions, among which I am now to be included so that they would emerge most distinctly from the paper, like a new creation, and the script from the hand of his most devoted enemy causes him to believe that he is only now getting to know his possessions in such a way that this is the first time they truly seemed to belong to him, the grounds are hurried into inventory thanks to how light I am on my feet—my flight has demonstrated this—and how practiced I am in fencing with words, thus, gazing upon the grounds, do I write upon one of the printed sheets that George has with him:

"A four-winged castellated castle with a Bergfried forms the core of the complex, which is adjoined by several horseshoe-shaped farm buildings in the eastern outer bailey: on the east side a brewery and oast house as well as several horse stables, a smithy with a cellar, and, at its rear, a tower-like extension in the inner courtyard of the complex; gatehouse, residential buildings, parlors, offices, and stables on the north side, and, on the south side, the castle chapel with a cellar and the armory with chancellery and sacristy. The castle and the farm buildings are surrounded by an independent fortress, which consists of a fortification wall with five turrets and an inner moat. For better defense, this ensemble is preceded by an outer moat wall of the inner moat as well as a high earthen wall with seven acute-angled Vaubanian earthen bastions and an outer moat running around it. The fortress is impregnable and shall one day fall into disrepair."

You shall have the opportunity to compose a much longer piece of script, George says, in which you might either defend yourself or recant all of your convictions, but, now, he thanks me for the pains that I have taken, adds a final article to the text with his own hand, and causes it to vanish into an envelope, which he puts into the inner pocket of his fur-lined mantle.

I am taken to the Bergfried at the east end of the south wing, not unnoticed by George, I immediately look for a window on the high round tower. An uninhabited Bergfried, George says, into which the elevated entrance leads over a staircase, but, after that, there is no way out.

We are particularly proud of this well-fortified wall tower, we find its exposed masonry to be both noble and morally appropriate, that which comes to pass in it does not remain hidden from God, just as no stone remains hidden from the human eye.

The tower watchman welcomes me. He tells me to go on ahead and follow the path of the stairs. It is cold in the tower. I count the steps. Fifteen. Since this is a spiral staircase embedded in the masonry and supporting itself in the middle thanks to a rounded newel, which forms a layered column, a railing is not necessary. Antonio Atome takes his time, he knows I am no worthy opponent. From time to time, he cries out "Onward!", then I continue on for a few steps. Even after some hundred steps, we have reached no plateau belonging to a floor, from the outside, I hadn't imagined the tower to be so high. This is not the crumbling staircase of my dreams, nor are there any missing steps, and I don't run down the stairs from the roof, then back up once more, in my dreams, the stairs are loose and the missing steps become ever more numerous, I must take venturesome leaps so as to overcome the gaps, my fear of heights makes the climbing of these stairs into the worst of punishments, this staircase is massive, stone doesn't break so quickly, but there is also something about it that progressively takes my breath away, and now, after more than two hundred steps, I am quite certain that the staircase is growing narrower, the tower watchman drives me into a gap out of which there is no escape, the resolution is quickly made, I turn around and run down the staircase, however, I continue gaining height, for the staircase also grows narrower going down it, I turn around and around and around, it makes no difference. For a short moment, I am entirely enclosed in stone. I wish to cry out, but stone suddenly fills my mouth like a bridle bit in a horse's mouth. To die thusly with lock over mouth, Antonio Atome says, that is Nobody's lot. From now on, he is to lead my book, just as he promised at the printing works. To put it frankly, he has been leading my book all along, but circumstances now compel him to admit this out in the open. The time has come for me to slowly transition into the book, I become stone, a book turned to stone. I lead the prisoner into his chamber. How could that sentence have gotten in here, I wish to know from Antonio Atome. He ignores my question. The bridle bit becomes the hardest of bread. What am I doing dragging myself up the stairs like this, he asks me, with my mere 36 years, I'm no old man. No saliva, limbs aflame. Come on then. Not swallowable as a whole, the lower jaw has slipped, that is the language in mouth, the bridle bit, which is slowly dissolving. Antonio Atome shoves me through the stone. It must be because the air is getting thin for you up here, he says. Duck your head down, the ceiling will soon get a lot lower, we'll end up having to pass through a hole. The hole is a tunnel through which we crawl, my raiment turns utterly white, light gets in through a cracked door, I've ceased breathing, Atome tells me to crawl across the threshold, this is your cell, he says, he walks upright, his robe is clean.

A bed opposite, its long side right up against the wall, a table with two chairs, their backrests leaning against the wall. The furniture and the bed are encased in the same synthetic material as the walls. Atome takes a seat upon one of the chairs. You ought to take a good look at everything, he says. Why ought I to do that, I set myself down on the other chair. You can decide whether you wish to always sit or always pace, Atome says. I get up again and remain standing. If you opt to stand like that for hours, you shall faint, Atome says. That would be the very latest point when I might choose to sit. When I stand up, I notice the chair hasn't moved. The table is so high that Atome cannot see me pressing against the chair with my knee. We're going to bring this area entirely under our control, he says. There are two voices, the one voice says: "Reach forth with your right hand and seek to tip the chair forward by way of the backrest," the other voice says to me: "If you touch the chair, you die." The chair does not allow itself to be budged, the table is also glued in place. We wish to make you as comfortable as is humanly possible, but the furniture might well be used as a weapon, Atome says. If you want, I can glue you in place too, he says. Shall he forbid me from using the bed? I pace about. I wish to pace about until he tells me that I am to be still. Barely have I thought this when Atome says: "Be still." I am still. A second keeper enters the room. Without offering any greetings or saying anything, he sits down upon the second chair. Both look straight ahead. Schattenfroh probably gave them instructions. I'm pacing about once more.

The cell is box-shaped, its walls are covered over with a white synthetic material that resists any attempt to puncture it. The synthetic material is mounted onto a frame that I cannot feel. The cell is one honeycomb in a whole complex of honeycombs. I am not so certain that this is the case, but the serial construction of the cell strongly suggests it. The system of construction is remarkably flexible, the cell is built in just a few hours, then dismantled even more quickly, it can be transported anywhere it needs to go. It is cool in the cell. I'm a bit chilly. In this chilliness, an unpleasant warmth has already begun to announce itself.

I believe that I hear others in their cells, even if I can see them, I shall not address them, Father has perhaps instructed the keepers to convince me that only I can see them, thus would he everywhere proclaim my unsoundness of mind in all that I do and say, and this disgrace shall survive my death. A blue light burns in the bathroom, one might well fear that it does so around the clock, neither the bathroom nor the wardrobe are equipped with a door, I imagine the water being turned off and the toilet-smells soon spreading all around, after two days, one's own reek would become alien, this wouldn't actually bother the two keepers who accompany me around the clock, I am ashamed of my odors, but the gentlemen, always nattily garbed, do their work according to regulation, I've no idea what work this is, they pull no faces, continue to breathe normally, I seek out the remaining reek-free zones in the cell, the air I breathe is consumed whichever way I turn.

Now, the water has been switched off. In the wall opposite the toilet is a fan that doesn't run precisely when the water has been turned off. Electricity and water seem to be paired. The floor of the cell consists of dark laminate laid down in a checkerboard pattern. Each individual square displays six bars, the direction of which has been offset by ninety degrees from cube to cube. Thus does each lane lead underneath a bridge, whose own lanes run crosswise. The floor at the foot of the bed was laid sloppily, two squares with the bars running in the same direction were merged to form a rectangle. I cannot recognize whether something is meant to be marked out by way of this method, when I lie down in bed, which doesn't seem to be forbidden to me, at least not for the moment, both keepers stand at the corners of its head and foot and look at me. Even when the light is out, they look at me, in any case, that's what I imagine, I cannot verify it, no light switch can be reached from the bed. I'd very much like to know whether they stand there all night, but that's hardly conceivable, after all, they too have to sleep. Perhaps, they are swapped out once they are certain that I have fallen asleep. It won't take long until I am no longer able to distinguish between day and night even if I am meant to notice that the light streaming down from the ceiling in the middle of the cell has been extinguished, so bright that it burns one's eyes and one can recognize nothing more for minutes at a time. As far as the ceiling light is concerned, I feel that I have developed a new compulsion, from time to time, I must look into the light, which temporarily blinds me, then I grow certain that I shall *actually* go blind in this way, after all, I can't cease staring at it, it gives me some sense of variety, the keepers have become invisible by way of the light, I am no longer allowed to speak with them, they only speak in my head, if my eyes aren't attracted by the light, I must check whether they are moving their mouths, they never move them except to take a breath, I do not know the voice of the second keeper, I do not know what is forbidden to me and what I ought to do, they hinder me in nothing, but do sometimes stand in my way, indeed, it is impossible for me to go to the toilet, I have recognized a connection in this and say to myself that they only get in my way and prevent me from going to the toilet when they know that my bladder is pinching, I must absolutely avoid them noticing this fact, I have since come to assume that they want to unexpectedly get in my way, they want to be unpredictable, that is their quiet triumph. I'm pissing my pants right now, which is to say, I would be pissing my pants if I had any on, as I wear no pants, I piss on the floor, a great puddle forms, the floor seems to be level, the urine doesn't drain, both keepers stand behind me, they have vanished, ought I to hope that they are getting a rag? A shirt, a mantle, and pants hang in the open wardrobe. I take the mantle and wipe the floor with it. The mantle doesn't quite absorb the piss, it feels disproportionately heavy, I hang it back up in the wardrobe. It's dripping. Each drop loudly hits the floor of the wardrobe. I lay the shirt down under the mantle, it instantly goes red. What ought I to glean from that? It's a perfidious strategy that causes me to wet my pants without even having pants, while pants are simultaneously hanging in the wardrobe. The toilet bowl is utterly filthy and will overflow with each further actuation of the flush. Thus does it not matter whether I defecate on the floor or relieve myself into the toilet. In the sewage, I recognize familiar faces. Turds float on top, clear water running into the bowl blurs the faces. There's my elementary-school teacher who would enter the class early in the morning, slightly stooped over. He was too young for this posture, he made the class stand up, then didn't know what the point of this standing up was, he was so ashamed of his appearance that he didn't allow himself to even remotely hope for the esteem of the schoolchildren. The name of the school caused me to doubt whether everything could be in its right place here, as it meant the opposite of happiness. Already, during my first recess at school, I was lying face up on the playground, my right eyebrow split open, my upper incisors knocked out. What did I learn from this? It is wonderful to hold your opponent to the ground by way of his hair, a game that can go on for a long while. With time, however, the opponent's compulsion toward revenge grows and it is for this reason that one ought not let him go. The second bell shifts the constellation in such a way that only the search for a suitable escape route has priority and it must, in any case, be ensured that one reaches the classroom before one's opponent. But only once one has truly smashed his face in does a certain calm return and can one negotiate about friendship. Friendship with a certain Ralf. Smaller, but more impudent. And with a certain Norbert. Smaller, but more wiley. Norbert passed away in a car accident together with his family. Only the grandmother, who didn't wish to go along on the trip, stayed alive. She also no longer knew where to go, for a year, she would go back to the school, sit in Norbert's chair, but didn't know how to solve even the simplest of arithmetic problems.

Now, I've noticed something wonderful, the glaring light has apparently been stored by my eyes, for, otherwise, I can't explain why light streams forth from them, wherever I look, if I concentrate my gaze there long enough, I see what I imagine on the outside, in this way, I can also imagine abstract things in an entirely living way and project them outward once more. I look at my keepers and project a second face onto their faces, revenge or certainty, for example. They cannot resist in the slightest. In this way, I shall be able to kill. I alone can see the certainty that I project onto one of the keepers' visages and it is enough for me that I alone can see it as a new face, I now combine certainty with ugliness. This affords me a certain loftiness, at least for a little while. Thus am I not dependent on external sources of energy. But care must here be taken that the store of imaginings and abstract things to which one affords a visage remains overseeable. Only thus can one practice something, an attitude that offers security. As the reality that we survey is never enough for us, but we wish to have a double of everything, it ought to be established whether optical projections cannot be stored onto a photographic plate, thus could an end be put to fleetingness and might we go forth into our remembrances once more. Photography is the enemy of the transitory. However, should the outwardly projected images be able to be perceived by other people—and, indeed, at the moment of their transmission—this would be a serious disadvantage that would deliver up our inwardness to the gaze of the other. The overall aim must therefore be to generate light without the imaginings bound to the projection, i.e. empty projection.

Pacing about makes me tired. I sit down on the bed, the second keeper stands up and makes a hand motion to me, signifying that I ought to get up once more. What choice remains to me. I stand, I walk, I stand, walk, stand, walk. Stand. Neither seem to notice me. At the very least, they are saying to each other that the order of the cell is sacred. They now wish to make a little disorder, they say.

The watchers put one of the two chairs standing by the table by the bed in place of an armchair and say that there never ought to be a chair or anything like that by the table. I've meticulously committed the order of the cell to memory, just in case. It could, for example, be claimed that I brought the cell into disorder. Then I will at least have the possibility of restoring order myself. My memory could also be faulty or at least not correspond in every detail to the originary layout of the cell. What befuddles me is how the keepers managed to move the furniture when it's all glued to the floor. I can't budge the armchair. The keepers raise themselves up from the chairs and sit down on the bed. I sit down at the table, then Atome gets up, pulls me from my chair, turns it toward the wall, and bids me to take my place once more. As seen from the table, I sit with face toward wall, however, I'm currently sitting at the left end of the table as seen from the bed, which is to be found behind the table on the opposite wall, at least that's how the furniture stands now, thus am I sitting in a forbidden position at the table, for only Atome ought to sit on the left, as he said to me when he was saying something else to me, nobody saw any need for a surveillance camera, I think, one sees me always and everywhere, even without a camera, I know that because one can see me writing just there, my fingers don't make even the slightest of contact with the stylus lying on the table and bound to it by way of a longer chain, and it scrawls across the paper of its own volition, I have a hard time remembering the sketch he drew right onto the tabletop completely covered over with scriptgrowth, but, beyond that, my words are more precise: The cell is rectangular, in our inner eye, the rectangle is tilted onto its long side, on the left transverse side is a small threefold opening in the middle in place of a window, into it, a ventilation system was installed. The ventilation can be covered by means of two opaque curtain-shawls on the left and right at the corners of the short side. The bed stands about one and a half meters away from the left transverse side. The other end of the bed marks the starting position of the opposite table, I've already observed that its position can shift within a short timeframe, then, for instance, the table would be pushed further off, to be level with the bed, which would immediately alarm me, like right now, I feel it, I get up, the table has been moved, I seek to push it back to its old position, or at least to the point I remember as its starting point or that appears to be harmless in and of itself. A defined constellation must be accepted as order, one cannot live within a permanent variability of order, which has become a part of one's identity by way of initially accepted arrangement, to lose it would be to have no more residual ego. An armchair was standing at the head of the bed, about forty centimeters from it, I've already mentioned it, and now the armchair stands there once more. The interrogation is to begin upon the armchair. It always begins with a chair or an armchair. If I offer the armchair to the interrogator, he shall say, there is no armchair here. Curiously, I shall have no interest in convincing him of the opposite, by, for example, sitting in the armchair myself, I associate sitting in the armchair with the notion that the interrogator might shoot me, even though, as far as I know, he carries no gun. The fact that there is an armchair the existence of which is denied by the interrogator shall torment me and I haven't the strength to establish the armchair's existence, I know that it is there and the interrogator knows that an armchair stands there, but, officially, no armchair stands there. Good, moving on. My surroundings shall hardly change from how they are now. Precisely in their middle, between the two long sides, a bare 100-watt bulb hangs at the level of the bed's headboard, it burns all day and night. Once I've finally been able to forget it, it calls itself back up in my memory through my closed eyelids. Its burning filament is the electrified aura, in such a way that I've woken up with a start on many occasions, not knowing whether I've fallen asleep or merely longed for sleep, convinced of an impending migraine, which can be triggered by just such a light and I would have to endure the attack without medication, which always results in severe head pain. If the light inside of us and the light outside of us have become indistinguishable, have we grown closer to God? Let's drop that. Hildegard von Bingen had migraines with aura and hallucinations, I have migraines with aura and no hallucinations. He who suffers from migraines with aura is more at risk for stroke. Knowledge that is of no use to me here. My migraine pills were taken away along with my blood-pressure monitor. At home, I measured my blood pressure with dedication, morning and evening and sometimes also throughout the course of the day, often ten times in a row. My doctor advised me to get a sphygmomanometer with a cuff, I immediately bought myself a fully automatic upper-arm blood-pressure monitor with a universal cuff. To begin with, even before the measurement, I would panic that my blood pressure might be too high. In fact, it was always too high. With the first low result, my fighting spirit strengthened—I was going to get my blood pressure under control from then on. Since I have no device available here, I measure my blood pressure with the middle finger of my right hand against my carotid artery and put down the systolic and diastolic values, just as I wrote them down onto a blood pressure card at home: 133:82, 129:79, 127:84, 131:80, 126:82. Subjective state of mind can be very misleading as regards actual values, I therefore seek to remember how I felt in connection with the measured results. My blood pressure is stable. I cannot and do not wish to provide the interrogator with any further weak points. What were the other weak points? One weak point is certainly that my script can already be followed as it comes to pass, visible and mutable for all those who have access to my brain, the child that shall slip out of my father's mouth. Atome shall be my Baruch, genuinely loyal to tradition, he has a tendency to falsify. Back to the layout of my cell, the ground plan of which is so important to me. The ground plan of my cell is the cell-order, it warns me not to digress and not to lose myself in digression. But that's precisely what I am always doing. It is perhaps time to recall the story of Simonides as Cicero recalls it:

"I am grateful to the famous Simonides of Ceos, who is said to have first invented the science of mnemonics. There is a story that Simonides was dining at the house of a wealthy nobleman named Scopas at Crannon in Thessaly, and chanted a lyric poem which he had composed in honor of his host, in which he followed the custom of the poets by including for decorative purposes a long passage referring to Castor and Pollux; whereupon Scopas with excessive meanness told him he would pay him half the fee agreed on for the poem, and if he liked he might apply for the balance to his sons of Tyndaraus, as they had gone halves in the panegyric. The story runs that a little later a message was brought to Simonides to go outside, as two young men were standing at the door who earnestly requested him to come out; so he rose from his seat and went out, and could not see anybody; but in the interval of his absence the roof of the hall where Scopas was giving the banquet fell in, crushing Scopas himself and his relations underneath the ruins and killing them; and when their friends wanted to bury them but were altogether unable to tell them apart as they had been completely crushed, the story goes that Simonides was enabled by his recollection of the place in which each of them had been reclining at table to identify them for separate interment; and that this circumstance suggested to him the discovery of the truth that the best aid to clearness of memory consists in orderly arrangement."

Ground plan and seating arrangement, as is shown by the story of Simonides, are the prerequisites for commemorating the dead. One recollects oneself as one who is dead. In summary, Cicero formulates something that I have ceaselessly practiced in *Schattenfroh*:

"He inferred that persons desiring to train this faculty must select localities and form mental images of the facts they wish to remember and store those images in the localities, with the result that the arrangement of the localities will preserve the order of the facts, and the images of the facts will designate the facts themselves, and we shall employ the localities and images respectively as a wax writing tablet and the letters written on it."

Memorizable clarity is the maxim. Here are the enemies: the uncontrollable drift of associations, the stagnation of signs and words, which generates a stockpile of identical texts and, in the process of recollecting actualization, recasts shifting assignments. I occupy myself with such things. This offers me support.

Alright, moving on, already too long spent on such matters. Drift of associations, stagnation of signs. Precisely that. Something else. I shall tell a story to the interrogator: He who is to be interrogated is brought in. His belt has been taken away. It is said to me that I must simply stand there. I simply stand there. "Beautiful, firm standing on the image-stage, clear sculpturality and weight," but also "Naturalness of mimic and gesture" is the motto. Are you a profit-seeking individual, both seedy and sleazy? Bribe-giver, bribe-taker? A murderer, traitor to the state, terrorist? Do you lead a dissolute lifestyle beyond your means that led you to rob a bank to make up the difference? Are you the comrade-in-arms of a wave of lifeform-filth that shall one day sweep Europe off its Christian pedestal? Nothing of the sort. Why are you here? Because you knew how to read the signs. You are Nobody.

He who is to be interrogated looks at his pants. Those are not my pants, he says. My pants are in the pile reserved for dark laundry in the basement, forty degrees Celsius. The house is from 1932, saltpeter has effloresced from the basement walls, it sketches the most awesome of characters. Those who are executed, hung from trees, shot with arms stretched wide before the body, twisted, hunched over. The plaster has fallen from the walls in certain places. My pants have a hole at the knee, blood that couldn't be removed. These ones here have no hole at the knee. A face with a thick red nose. If the salt has eaten a hole into the wall, I shall use it as a shooting gallery. I would very much like to shoot somebody. My pants slip down. I must hold them fast, but am ordered to take my hands away. I'm meant to keep my hands incessantly in motion. I must inquire about the word "incessantly." Is it precisely "incessantly" that's meant. That's correct: "incessantly." Is incessantly the same as "incessant." There ought not to be any leaps in function-values, but nobody wants to have said "incessantly." 1932. The house. Once again, nobody cares about Charlotte von Stein. So, who's this Nobody? I didn't say Nobody. But you thought it. Thinking isn't quite saying. Oh, but in your case it is.

He who is to be interrogated would like to sit down. The greatest of defendants didn't sit down either. Do you know who Nobody is? The one who did *that* to the cyclops. That was Nobodyius. You too have a long odyssey before you. You shall voyage through body and soul. You shall be Nobody. Nobody—an empty picture frame. The two keepers won't get out of my mind, not even when I don't see them. I cannot defend myself against their eyes. At night, I believe that light streams forth from them, in fact, they send out an energy that has an ongoing effect within me, allowing me to see things that I had already believed myself to have forgotten. Nothing is ever entirely forgotten, it's merely turned slightly away from the sun. Forced into obscurity, all it needs is a little bit more light so that it can reflect. The thing is currently unreachable due to the deactivation of its sign, but it has by no means been negated. It circulates no longer, is possibly covered over by a similar thing or sign, we always say one thing, but mean another, which we don't achieve for so long as we always say the one thing. Laughmann is all I have to say. An overabundance of supply reigns, but to reign here means nothing good, the one covers over the other, we throw out our line and fish blind. It is a matter of either preventing or escaping the confusion. It is a compulsion to think such thoughts. It keeps me from fully exposing myself to the situation. But I can't bear to simply see things. That is the greatest pain—to simply see things. The mere fact that I think "Night" is painful, now, it's just one more word.

It is announced to me that the interrogator is coming, he is the devil, I must stand up and salute him. "The interrogator is coming, he is the devil, stand up and salute him." The interrogator is coming, he is the devil, I stand up and salute him. The interrogator is coming, the devil. I Heil you, I stand before you in awe and gratitude and greet you. Nothing of the sort. Everything only in your mind.

Mateo. I raise myself up. Did I sit down? We are alone in the room. Atome and Mateo, a strange passing-by-of-the-other, or, rather, a passing-into-the-other. I didn't see the second keeper pass out of the cell, however, he is also no longer to be found there.

Surely, I know the song "Drei Chinesen mit dem Kontrabass"*? Yes. And the name Johann Kaspar Schade also means something to me? Yes, I say, adding that it's spelled with a "C." Why that is of significance now. Because it's written with a "K" here. Then I ought to change that. Good. Johann Caspar Schade. Schade became well-known with the so-called Berlin Confession Controversy, Mateo says. I know this very well, I say. He wished to abolish private confession. Precisely, I say, then presume to add that he actually did abolish it too. Schade was in favor of so-called "general confession," "Heavenly Father, everlasting and most merciful God, we confess and concede

---

* "Three Chinamen with a Double Bass."

before your divine majesty, that we are poor, wretched sinners, conceived and delivered into utter wickedness and corruption, inclined to all that is evil, bereft of use for all that is good; and that we transgress without cease thy holy commandments in our sinful life" and so on, wickedness and corruption, inclined to all that is evil, it is inscribed upon my body, but I can confess to my guilt, how and as often as I'd like, absolution cannot be granted to me, besides which nobody here wishes to abolish private confession, Mateo says. And so that there are no doubts about this, I am to treat Schade's constantly reforming creed, in which the words scurry about like mice in a box, then regroup, according to the model of the "Drei Chinesen" and recite it in a beautiful voice. "Then I'll pass through you, I'll see you," Mateo says. And I recite the creed:

INTERROGATOR / thou art mine interrogator.
        artthou mine INTerrogator
        INTERROGATOR thou are mine.
        Thou INTerrogator mine.
        mine INTERROGATOR art thou.

THOU INTerrogator art mine INTerrogator.
        thou INTerrogator / art INTerrogator.
        art mine INTerrogator / INTerrogator.
        INTerrogator / INTerrogator art mine.
        INTerrogator mine INTerrogator art.

ART thou INTerrogator mine INTerrogator.
        mine INTerrogator / thou INTerrogator.
        thou mine INTerrogator / INTerrogator.
        INTerrogator / thou mine INTerrogator.
        thou INTerrogator / INTerrogator MINE.

MINE interrogator / artthou interrogator.
>   Interrogator thou art / interrogator.
>   artthou INTerrogator / INTERROGATOR.
>   Interrogator / interrogator artthou.
>   Interrogator / thou interrogator art.

INTERROGATOR / interrogator artthou mine?
>   mine interrogator thou art.
>   artthou / INTerrogator / mine?
>   Interrogator / thou mine art.
>   Interrogator / interrogator artthou.
>   Interrogator / mine artthou.

>   AMEN.

With the word "Amen," Mateo has disappeared once more, as if conjured out of the cell. He left me some paper, right next to the toilet, but I'm not meant to write. Thus do I observe the characters of the birds scrawling across the paper. For there are writing birds in my head, they are a gentle transgression of the ban on writing. However, they are rather impetuous and tend toward grimace-loving barbarity, which can, at times, escalate to cannibalism, when they break forth from the cage of script, then, as soon as the interrogator is absent, they fall upon one another and it is a laborious process to catch them. I call this catching "reading." I don't keep track of time.

   I estimate that Mateo was absent for a whole day, he's been coming in sporadically for a good hour, he leaves the cell again after just a few seconds, then they fly up and gather themselves into an orderly image once more. Thus is it written. If the interrogator doesn't look, it flies written. Those are some beautiful thoughts you've got there, he says. They are your thoughts, I say, then he grabs me round the neck, chokes and shakes me, the birds fly up and circle round wildly, they fall to the ground with broken necks. Mateo leaves the cell. Poor birds, I'd like to push them against the wall next to the table with my foot, then I believe that I recognize a word and a number in their lying there, I circle them in the one, then in the other direction, their dead bodies form the word *Schattenfroh* and the number 666, I sweep them up hastily and another word soon arises. The choking and shaking has had the effect that I can see through the bird-script, I can see things in the way script has put them together, I'm instantly on site, I now say "Switzerland" and am swimming in Lake Zurich, if I say "Schultüte," I have a Schultüte in hand and am standing in the garden of my parents' house. I feel the very same pains that I felt on August 23, 1970. I need only let the birds scratch the pain from August 23, 1970. I make use of Mateo's absence to develop a technique that allows me to only think of these connections and I'm already slipping into the envisaged situation. This is a lively hopping between contexts, a switching to and fro between places and times.

Then the interrogator is sitting there in a blue armchair, I didn't hear him come in at all. He only wishes to see that I'm not writing, the rest shall sort itself out, he says.

Mateo claims that he can read what I write despite the prohibition on my writing, even when he's not present, he can hardly stand reading nothing from me, so he plunges into my bird-script, which he doesn't always like. Have I noticed that he is making a correctional intervention, as I am already incapable of putting a stop to the bird-scrawl? I haven't, I reply. In any case, he says, you can, from time to time, observe how the lineature of the script, the bird-stenography, warps and the lines take shortcuts, implement turns. I dream, I say to him, of writing in secret, a process by which I would not guide the pen myself, for I wouldn't have any pen whatsoever, but have a kind of snake in my hand, I would allow it to romp across the page in such a way that it wouldn't bite me. The snake's attention, scattered across the page, doesn't allow it to take anything particular into its gaze, it takes in its environment as the transitory contained in genuine permanence, for it mostly generates this environment on its own. Its bite would beget unforeseeable things into the world, monsters with faces that transform every minute, they strive to conceal their origins, if these monsters were to look directly at you, you'd only recognize yourself in these origins. The snake's being-everywhere-at-the-same-time—the writing in itself—cannot, of course, be controlled, nor am I responsible for the snake. The fear of its biting the writing hand would cause that hand itself to go out of control. Because of this, Mateo says, you'll end up taking that hand off at night and hiding it in a small box so narrow that the hand can only fit into it diagonally, but not lengthwise. The lid of the box is also locked so that the hand itself cannot open it. The following came to pass in a dream yesterday, I recount it to the interrogator, which causes me even greater difficulties: The hand is female, it is obviously not my hand. When I opened the box to put it back on this morning, the dream had become reality and the hand actually was female. I re-shut the lid and fastened it shut even more firmly. When I realized that I no longer had a box to hand, but also no hand, I hoped that the renowned door in the wall would open up, that the interrogator would appear and offer me the hand. I would like for it to act on its own initiative. It ought to guide my pen. Instead, the birds write, written in my own script, I write with my right hand and it's my right hand that I'm missing: "Sometimes, when the interrogator comes in quite suddenly, he comes right through the aforementioned door that doesn't, however, exist for me, they fly up and gather themselves once more into an orderly image. Thus is it written." It must be because of this last sentence. For, it is written: "Man shall not live by bread alone, but by every word that proceedeth out of the mouth of God." Before, I always thought this meant the words that *come* out of God's mouth. There is an enormous difference between "come" and "proceed." Or is there not? The word proceedeth off somewhere—but whither. It is written and proceedeth. The word that is written is an empowered word that empowers itself. It can portentously name that which is coming or, first and foremost, call forth the calamitous, it is a vagabond wandering between language and reality; it can become a genuine monster any time it loses its lack of ambiguity in its vagabonding and its origin becomes uncertain, and thus shall I become a monster by metamorphosing myself into the thing that I make of myself without comprehension.

Mateo is there once more. As if faded in. This time, he didn't come through the door. Sit down. Now, we learn the order of the cell. The order of the cell is governed by eleven articles. Article 1 is really simple: "Et es wie et es." "'It is what is' as pronounced in the Cologne dialect." "Wrong. There is no translation." "Et es wie et es." "Ed is what eddies." "Almost. Pay more attention to each individual syllable. Et es wie et es. If you don't have it yet, we'll still be sitting here come tomorrow morning, but that's also OK, we won't run out of time. However, keep in mind that nine more articles follow:

Article 2: Et kütt wie et kütt.
Article 3: Et hätt noch emmer joot jejange.
Article 4: Wat fott es, es fott.
Article 5: Et bliev nix wie et wor.
Article 6: Kenne mer nit, bruche mer nit, fott domett. Wat wellste maache?
Article 7: Maach et joot, äwwer nit ze off!
Article 8: Wat soll dä Quatsch?
Article 9: Drenkste eene met?
Article 10: Do laachste dich kapott!"

My father assumes that the cause for my lack of understanding of what is coming to pass in the world lies in my ignorance and complete incomprehension of these articles, Mateo says. We drill through the articles. For hours. Speech. Contradiction. Interplay. Hear. Mishear.

Interrogate. Why can you write it, but not say it, Mateo says. I don't know. You shall only have internalized it once you can speak it, he says. I must pace about, saying each article dozens of times as I do. That frees me from the compulsion of conceiving of people as mere tools of the apocalypse. Out of all this, Mateo agrees with me on one point: Grace cannot be read up on in the Bible or anywhere else, it can only be personally experienced or not experienced. Now, finally, Mateo shows himself to be satisfied with my speaking or at least pretends to be and announces the next task.

I am to repeat. I repeat: "Qui YA Paar Vuss Error in Prins Ipioo mag Nuss esst infinay." What is that meant to be. Misread, probably. Then I ought to give it a good listen. I listen good. "Qia pavs ero in princ magnus et in fie." Did I listen good enough? Letters are lacking. For each missing letter, a blow is dealt to the head. From the beginning, letter by letter. "Quia pervu error in princip magnu est infin." Am I an illetrist? No, I am a lettrist. All missing letters demand compensation, Mateo says and deals another blow to my head. Then he continues his lecture: the Latin letters are nothing in themselves. To be something, depending on both sound and image, one must switch language and script. For, a given letter is everything, it was there in the beginning and God breathed life into all that was created with it, but he appears here just as rarely as the letter that represents divine power: ב and שׁ. I tell him that divine power is the lie, it leads speech, but does not hold it, for Shin has no root. On the fourth pass, he spells much more slowly, however, it's only because each letter is now followed by a blow. "Better safe than sorry," he says. The result proves him right: "Quia parvus error in principio magnus est in fine." "And?" he asks. I understand the letters, but not their meaning, I say. Then he turns to me like a kind father taking pity on a naughty child. Learning language is a form of training, he says. Even if the person being trained is no longer a child who must be shown the language for the first time. One cannot understand letters, he says, each letter is a concentration of divine energy, the world is lacking, it lacks letters, our society would like to address this lack, this God-ordained restriction, the lack of letters is the reason for our negative prescriptions, the non-following of which is necessarily deadly, but the following of which helps to make the world shine once more in its consummateness. The world consists of six letters, we only have five that barely anybody reads, I'm co-writing the sixth, the Book of Books, which is still invisible, its contours become more visible with each word, this book is one of the lacking letters. He leaves the cell. Here, I have days to analyze the sentence as exhaustively as I can, over and over again. My school Latin finally allows it to be melted down into a matte formula: Error is large in principle. I do not believe in error. At most, I believe in the sentence: "I would make the same mistake again." There are two mistakes in this sentence: "same" and "mistake." I am not responsible for mathematics. I can very well imagine somebody who has to decide something, he might, for example, have to make some decisive calculation, but he makes an error at the beginning that costs everyone affected by this decision their necks. Error means not wishing to submit oneself to the rules. But making an error also requires freedom of action.

In any case, I seem to have arrived—or my journey has at least stalled. I can only think about the bigger picture if I'm left alone. What journey? They couldn't take much off of me, which meant I was traveling without baggage. Inwardly, Schattenfroh said. To Duria. To durability. To Prüm. To Grundlehne. To tradition. The spaces shift. The peculiar feeling of always being in the very same room, the very same space. Sometimes, I'm guarded, then I'm alone for days once more. Or hours? I wish to ask Mateo when he shall fulfill his promise.

"What do you think about rats?" Mateo asks. "Have you ever seen one? I don't mean the little mice that roam subway tunnels the world over. I mean sometimes fat but always nimble brown rats. You really wouldn't believe where they can roam their way to. They don't like it at all when they have nothing to eat. Starving rats have been observed to attack one another. An exceedingly human reaction. Hunger mounts even more when panic is at play. And do you know how panic is fueled? By fire. But we don't wish to reveal too much of the game, after all, it is particularly enticing to only learn the rules of the game shortly before the game begins so as to be able to slide and tilt with the game itself, to oneself be transitory. Indeed, Wolfgang Reis described this quite wonderfully—and that is the seed that bears fruit. Now, you may think that this really isn't much at all, but where there is no risk, there is no reward. Which brings us back to the game. The to-and-fro of the game is no end unto itself, it does have goals, the goal is the becoming-other of society—and otherwise than it imagines, but does not think, its own becoming-other; this is to do with becoming other—becoming different—from *another* society. A society that has entered into its images. We are this society. We indulge in no massification, we are elitist. We practice no gaining of independence as a subsystem of society, we *are* the Society, the subsystem of which is broader society. As has been put so beautifully: 'the end of God: the human compulsion to make things.'"

Thus is Mateo only printer and keeper, though I'm really not aiming for subsystem autonomy, I'm aiming for the whole. What is the sole thing that justifies *outrage*? The matter of God. Only God's Law counts. Not secular jurisdiction. Judicial theology, not civil code. Final Judgment, hearing the inner word in the abyss of the soul, not world judgment and scriptural literalism. the master wants to set the game in motion, the evildoers are all for it.

To only learn the rules of the game shortly before the game begins, Mateo says, increases attention and excitement and spurs on ambition. How gladly one would wish to triumph in a virgin game. And I really do wish to triumph. I would like to get out of this story unscathed and draw on it until the end of my life. But it could also turn out differently. Depression can also be a torture. I ought to think of my friend who hanged himself from Leserfordernd Brücke.* Did he not say for years that he would never get depressed again, Mateo asks. Didn't he always say that he'd only just discovered the solution to having no more fits of depression? Alcohol hung him from that bridge. Alcohol said to him, "Go to that bridge, forget not the rope." Go to the bridge, forget not the rope. Drawbridge here, abridge drew her, bad girder where. Alcohol has many voices. One must stop up its mouth. Otherwise, it fills your legs and belly up with water and takes your breath away.

"Body and soul. That is the problem. Or rather: These are the problem. Body and soul. The scholars dispute. Since Plato, the scholars have been disputing," Mateo says. The dispute seems to have been temporarily put to rest, he continues. It is disputed whether there is an immaterial soul independent of the body; whether the soul is deathless and whether immortality is to be deduced from everlastingness, whether what immortal means is not instead just *necessarily living*, the soul thus being said to be immortal, but passing away with the death of the body; whether and to what extent the body has an effect on the soul, whether and to what extent the soul influences the body, whether and to what extent mental characteristics can be traced back to physical ones; whether the I belongs to the body or to the soul or, rather, whether the I is body or the I is soul. One can pursue this question without contemplation and come to a modal-logical conclusion, but without being able to refer to field reports; one can rely on empirical data alone, yes, it might be more explicit than all philosophical concepts, but may also not qualify for generalization. For him, Mateo, the soul is nothing other than a Doppelgänger, the wish to be immortal, to have a life after death.

What, for example, does the following case tell us about the relationship between body and soul, as well as flesh and spirit, with regard to the question of how truth comes to light, Mateo asks. Light and

---

* Reader-Challenge Bridge.

truth are an inseparable pair of siblings that darken one another. We're not dealing with truth here, but with the question of what methods might be used to obtain a confession, the truth-value of which is less relevant than, for example, the criminally relevant confession of guilt certified with a signature: A 23-year-old prisoner of bourgeois origin who sympathized with the Resistance was utterly terrified by the dual tactic of good cop/bad cop and thus began to confess. But more was demanded of her. Thus was she treated with psychopharmacology over the next five days, which put her into a state of increasing dependency on those interrogating her. These were no longer her enemies, but her judges who were to proclaim her guilt, and she came to regard torture as a truly just punishment. She reported that she was losing more and more of her personality by way of growing feelings of guilt, she regressed in the psychological sense, had pseudoperceptions, and developed hypersensitivity, as well as sexual excitability. It was on this basis that the actual conditioning began. Certain stimuli signified that she ought not to fall asleep; for instance, the clock's ticking was brought into association with a certain scent that causes insomnia. Sleep was brought into association with a blanket that was then taken away when she wished to sleep. She was given orders accompanied by a specific melody. And, during the interrogation, she was masturbated by her guards, who took advantage of her sexual excitability until she gave up the desired information. This was accompanied by a feeling of relief that she likened to an orgasm. This is a pornographic case study, I say. Mateo grins.

  A third keeper enters the cell. With scuttling stride, he turns to face the wall. He is garbed like Mateo and the other one, whose name I still do not know. Slim. Tall. Thinning hair. Tense body-posture. Nervous disorders. Or corporeal motor disorders. Twitches. Like me. Haven't seen myself from the back for a long time. Mateo whistles him over. It is only through others that one knows oneself. I do not like how hesitantly he follows orders. No self-respect. He must immediately be there and deal with the business that's been ordered. The way he operates isn't mere refusal. If Mateo doesn't do it, I'll take it upon myself. I shall undress him, stick him into a tailor-made suit, he ought to wear a tie, fine shoes, black leather soles, smooth leather, a bit glossy, but of exquisite quality, their gloss must make the mouth water without being too *common*, a fine aspect, something must make him stand out, distinguish him from the other two, the third fills me with shame. "This one here," Mateo says, "shall take over your duties." The third one turns around and smiles, "I am," the other one says, offering him his hand. He is indeed I. A spitting image. No wonder he looks better than I do, he need not fear my competition. He has fuller hair, likely a cosmetic operation; he probably thought I was ashamed of my bald head, but he ought to have known better. The careless servility with which he treats Mateo is unworthy of our family, Father's Father would have chased him out of the house. Does he think I don't perceive him observing me in secret? He wishes to be entirely distinguishable from me, but the situation that he discovers here is sufficient as far as his own benefit is concerned. Or does he envy me my status as prisoner, which means that he and the other two are here because I am here and not the other way around. I am a breaking mirror in which he wishes to see himself whole. He doesn't seriously believe he could ingratiate himself with Mateo so as to deprive me of my lifeblood and thus watch me drain away; for, I am the lifeblood. And he shall drain with it. I shall make this hypocritical alter ego, this trickster, into a pharmakos. And what tasks ought he to undertake? Where is the second keeper? "There are three of us," Mateo says, as if he could hear me think, "we were two from the start and, strictly speaking, still are, you and you and I." I look at the third, who acts so sheepish that I'd like to box his ears. But to look me in the face . . . he doesn't dare do that. Or everything is merely feigned. "He is the second keeper that you are," Mateo says. "So, I'm guarding myself, watching myself," I say. "Doesn't everybody do that?" Mateo asks. "He had another face, the second keeper," I say. "He didn't have one at all until I gave him yours, he was a mere brute, but now the time has come for him to be complete and start taking on your duties," Mateo says. The third that I am sits down at the table. Mateo takes a book out of the inner pocket of his jacket and dictates to him. "Abidaga went once more to the stable, where he was told that everything was ready; lying there was an oak stake about four arshins long, pointed as was necessary and tipped with iron, quite thin and sharp, and all well-greased with lard."

"And what's this about—what do you think?" Mateo asks me.

"Who is to answer?" I ask.

"Ego answers, not Alter; Alter writes," Mateo says.

"It's about a stake," I say.

"We've already heard that. About a stake."

"About an oak stake."

"Right. About an oak stake. We've already heard that. What interests me is what purpose the oak stake might have. No idea?"

"A sharpened stake to be rammed into the ground."

"Into the ground, superb. And how ought that to be done when it's four arshins long? Do you know how long that is?"

"No."

"Roughly two meters and eighty centimeters. Ought somebody to stand upon a ladder and ram the stake into the ground with an enormous sledgehammer? And into what ground?"

"Into the earth."

"Let's keep listening: 'On the scaffolding were the blocs between which the stake would be embedded and nailed, a wooden mallet for the impalement, ropes and everything else that was needed.' So . . . ?"

"A gallows."

"Not bad. A gallows. But why is the gallows shod with iron and very thin and sharp at the top? And why is it well-greased with lard from top to bottom? For a gallows, that would be a bit much, isn't that so?"

"I'm not sure about that."

"You're not sure about that. Let's keep listening: 'Ten guards were drawn up in two ranks, five on either side. Between them was Radisav, barefooted and bareheaded, alert and stooping as ever, but he no longer "sowed" as he walked but marched strangely with short steps, almost skipping on his mutilated feet with bleeding holes where the nails had been; on his shoulders he carried a long white sharpened stake. Behind him was Merdzan with two other gypsies.' So, who are these people who've come on the scene? And what's up with Radisav's feet? Do you really have no idea what's going on here?"

"It's literature."

"OK. Literature. And what causes you to recognize that?"

"The strange names."

"Strange names equals literature. Very nice. Further on in the text: 'Radisav bent his head still lower and the gypsies came up and began to strip off his cloak and his shirt. On his chest the wounds from the chains stood out, red and swollen. Without another word the peasant lay down as he had been ordered, face downward.' So, what do you think is going to happen now?"

"He's going to be hanged."

"Warm, very warm, but still not quite right. Listen: 'The gypsies approached and the first bound his hands behind his back; then they attached a cord to each of his legs, around the ankles. Then they pulled outward and to the side, stretching his legs wide apart. Meanwhile Merdzan placed the stake on two small wooden chocks so that it pointed between the peasant's legs. Then he took from his belt a short broad knife, knelt beside the stretched-out man and leaned over him to cut away the cloth of his trousers and to widen the opening through which the stake would enter his body. This most terrible part of the bloody task was, luckily, invisible to the onlookers.' What an awful pity, you might now be thinking. Indeed, the only reason it remains invisible is that it *can* be described in great detail. Will you not depict this most frightful scene in its every detail for us? I am certain that it shall afford you the greatest of pleasures. You shall depict the difference between fiction and reality by way of your own body. None shall be able to claim that you didn't do your homework. And, at the end of the day, you shall finally be rid of your obsessions."

"I'd really rather not."

"What?"

"Depict."

"The beautiful thing is that the author has already done it for you: 'They could only see the bound body shudder at the short and unexpected prick of the knife, then half rise as if it were going to stand up, only to fall back again at once, striking dully against the planks. As soon as he had finished, the gypsy leapt up, took the wooden mallet and with slow measured blows began to strike the lower blunt end of the stake. Between each two blows he would stop for a moment and look first at the body in which the stake was penetrating and then at the two gypsies, reminding them to pull slowly and evenly. The body of the peasant, spread-eagled, writhed convulsively; at each blow of the mallet his spine twisted and bent, but the cords pulled at it and kept it straight. The silence from both banks of the river was such that not only every blow but even its echo from somewhere along the steep bank could be clearly heard. Those nearest could hear how the man beat with his forehead against the planks, and, even more, another and unusual sound, that was neither a scream, nor a wail, nor a groan, nor anything human; that stretched and twisted body emitted a sort of creaking and cracking like a fence that is breaking down or a tree that is being felled.'

I contend that such literature has surely merited the Nobel Prize. But what's the deal with the reality portrayed? What was merited by that reality? What's your opinion? An age-old subject. Does literature not tamper with reality here?"

"I don't know."

"Oh, but you do, you just don't want to say it. Look at that, all the dumbass can do is write everything down. But that's how it's meant to be. Write it down, don't *think* it down. Let's hear a little more: 'At every second blow the gypsy went over to the stretched-out body and leaned over it to see whether the stake was going in the right direction and when he had satisfied himself that it had not touched any of the more important internal organs he returned and went on with his work. From the banks all this could scarcely be heard and still less seen, but all stood there trembling, their faces blanched and their fingers chilled with cold. For a moment the hammering ceased.' If literature describes something well and we can use it as a manual, then it is good literature. What do you say to this thesis?"

"There's no doubt this is well-described."

"Too little. You say too little there. But, actually, you agree with me. It's simply that the manual isn't yet finished: 'Merdzan now saw that close to the right shoulder muscles the skin was stretched and swollen. He went forward quickly and cut the swollen place with two crossed cuts. Pale blood flowed out, at first slowly and then faster and faster. Two or three more blows, light and careful, and the iron-shod point of the stake began to break through at the place where he had cut. He struck a few more times until the point of the stake reached level with the right ear. The man was impaled on the stake as a lamb on the spit, only that the tip did not come through the mouth but in the back and had not seriously damaged the intestines, the heart or the lungs. Then Merdzan threw down the mallet and came nearer. He looked at the unmoving body, avoiding the blood which poured out of the places where the stake had entered and had come out again and was gathering in little pools on the planks. The two gypsies turned the stiffened body on its back and began to bind the legs to the foot of the stake.' So far, so beastly. But the best passage is yet to come. I also wonder whether the author didn't somehow take object lessons from reality. Can you imagine that somebody who wishes to depict this tidbit in a book, in a way that is true to reality and in the knowledge that it cannot be invented, studies it upon an object that he traps for precisely this purpose? An execution in service of art? But listen a bit more, yes, how precisely this was worked out, but also how limited to the bare essentials, in such a way that everything is able to take place in the imagination, which has a stronger effect than that of contemplation, which, at best, causes bad dreams. Is it the freedom in his technique, i.e. the treatment of the material, which allows us to dub that which is beastly beautiful in its depiction; and also, if the trace of a despotic human hand has an intrusive effect in reality and calls forth disgust in us, does the very same human hand become free play in art? Indeed, it is good manners in art to assert one's own freedom and to skimp on the freedom of others by way of the artist showing that which does not happen to others.

Justice is done to the subject in the face of death, even if only indirectly, even if the author is only the executioner's parasite. Is it sad, then, or is it not a form of consolation for the human species that images are never enough and we must always speak? Here, care is taken, precision of gaze, a double translation that shows through even in the English, it certainly isn't too obvious that this is a translation from Serbo-Croatian. Thus does speaking, which has itself coagulated into description, become image once more, but an unstable image that, should we turn away from the manuscript, slowly loses its contours, just as dust scatters, and thus do we continually turn back to the manuscript: 'Meanwhile Merdzan looked to see if the man were still alive and carefully examined the face that had suddenly become swollen, wider and larger. The eyes were wide open and restless, but the eyelids were unmoving, the mouth was wide open but the two lips stiff and contracted and between them the clenched teeth shone white. Since the man could no longer control some of his facial muscles the face looked like a mask. But the heart beat heavily and the lungs worked with short, quickened breath. The two gypsies began to lift him up like a sheep on a spit. Merdzan shouted to them to take care and not shake the body; he himself went to help them. Then they embedded the lower, thicker end of the stake between two beams and fixed it there with huge nails and then behind, at the same height, buttressed the whole thing with a short strut which was nailed both to the stake and to a beam on the staging.'

I could now take your Alter and enact the same upon him. Or I shall carry it out upon you. Each is to decide that for himself. If you both place the burden upon the other, I am the third who laughs and carries it out upon you both. The same applies to the case that you both choose yourselves. Thus must it be that one chooses the other and the other chooses himself. The one who chooses himself has already lost. The matter is a hopeless one. What, again, was the name of the genius who slipped the following sentence into one of his books: 'Death is a constant quantity—only pain is variable and may be intensified infinitely'?"

Mateo leaves the cell. Alter sits at the table and writes: "Mateo leaves the cell. Alter sits at the table and writes." Ego thinks that. Thus should it remain. Mateo has left the cell. Alter sits at the table and writes: "Ego thinks that. Thus should it remain." Thus does it remain. Then Mateo strides into the cell once more. Alter sits at the table and writes that. And? Mateo asks. Ego doesn't speak, Alter says. So, did Ego speak? No. Mateo leaves the cell once more. And? Mateo asks. Alter doesn't reply. And writes. I'm going to count to three, then we point to either ourselves or the other, Ego says. I wait until Alter has written that down.

One,

                       two,

                                          three.

I point at Alter, Alter points at nobody. Mateo enters the cell. He asks whether we have opted for a decision. A strange wording. Why does he always only look at me, could Alter not also say something. Alter and Ego are one, which is to say Nobody, it is enough for one to think and speak and the other write. I pointed to Alter and he pointed to nobody, I say. Then Alter shall become a tableau vivant, after all, he is my slave and one does not interrogate slaves, after all, slaves only testify under torture. Basanos. Torture as means of information-acquisition from slaves. Everything regimented. I'm at liberty to have Alter undergo the procedure so as to testify. Otherwise, I'll become the tableau.

Mateo leaves once more. Alter doesn't allow himself to be spoken to, he is, after all, to become a tableau vivant, he asks himself whether the part about the swollen, wider, and larger face, the wide open and restless eyes and unmoving eyelids, the wide open mouth and stiff and contracted lips and the uncontrollable facial muscles, which cause the face to look like a mask, is correct, I stand behind Alter and read the final passage once more, something's somehow fishy here, that's how it is now, wherefore does a book continue to be written, even though it's been deprinted, wasn't the talk always of execution by sword, impalement is more than mere torture, it is an execution, the stake spreads intestinal bacteria throughout the entire body, even if the criminal is unimpaled or removed from the stake, he will not survive, but basanos is not about torture as touchstone, it springs forth from the loyalty— and is the authentication—of a true statement that the master of the slave has made or has perhaps not made, gold is an upright sense and only gold leaves behind a very distinct mark upon the basanos when rubbed against it.

I ask Alter whether he doesn't have anything to say to me. Alter writes that down. Then he continues to wait—until this sentence. I lie down on the bed. Mateo doesn't come. I doze off. The synthetic material with which everything is clad has a foul odor that now bothers me. Does it secrete poison? Alter's arm is in constant motion. The way he sits at the table. I feel sympathy for him. I see better with my right eye than my left. I ought to, in any case, be somewhat proud of Alter. He is tireless. He is wearing fine garments. Pity. Always self-pity. The plastic structural cladding that means one can hit nobody on the head with this chair. But it's glued to the floor. If one were to tear it free. Impossible. So that one might not bang one's head intentionally against it or fall down so as to do harm to oneself. Likewise table, likewise bed. Likewise. Likewise. Like. Wise.

Then she said to me that you must drink a liter of warm beer and, yes, in your one-man tent, in the midday heat, garbed in a sweater, the entrance tightly shut, nothing else ought to come into the tent, for it is soon to be drunk dry and your eyes shall be opened and you shall be as God and know what is good and what is evil. But it only functions with German beer because of the Reinheitsgebot; in the case of beers that do not comply with the Reinheitsgebot, this method should be used with caution, for one's health might be damaged. Thus did I set out on my way and search for a business that sold German beer. Finally, I found a poor devil who made me a fair offer: Since it's a question of medicine, he offered me the bottle for twelve marks. If you were to buy two bottles, the price for both would be reduced to twenty marks. He emphasized that the consumption of a local beer would mean certain death, as Bavarian beer, at its finest, really is liquid bread. I began to count. If a sufficiently large quantity is purchased, the bottle price is reduced to right around zero marks. The sufficiently large quantity turned out to be seven bottles. The other calculation was to do with the fever. With each bottle, I would be able to sink my temperature down by some two degrees.

No breeze through the tent-entrance. After three bottles, nothing—crickets. Later, the cows came and trampled down the tent. Natura non facit saltus, but still recognizes the Reinheitsgebot, and thus do I remain entirely unharmed. Seven bottles of beer in a sealed tent with a fever of nearly forty degrees and an exterior temperature of some forty-two degrees is a spiritual experience that fundamentally changes life and calls God into action. And God said: The fever is history, take the sweater off, open the tent, and go for a swim. And I rose up, took my sweater off, opened the tent, and went for a swim in the Ganges. And I saw a beast stride into the water, having two heads and two suns around it, and upon his breast eleven black flames and three crowns above its flames. And the beast which I saw was like unto a leopard, and his feet were the feet of a bear, and his mouth was that of a lion. And the beast mocked that I had sinned against the Rhineland by drinking Bavarian beer—and, indeed, it was too little to die, but too much for an acquittal. Bavarian beer, the other head hissed, is not brewed to the sound of Cologne Cathedral's bell-ringing and therefore does not comply with the Rheinheitsgebot. The beast marked a sign of memory in my forehead: "Drink Cologne beer, o man of Cologne!" was now inscribed upon it and the beast announced that it would devour me if I were not able to recite all 666 brands of Kölsch in alphabetical order. According to the Kölsch alphabet, there is, I say, only one Kölsch and it is called Kölsch, everything else is total bullshit—it can go straight to hell. Thus did it come to pass. The streams of impure beer from round the world formed a deluge, in which the beast drowned. In order to commemorate this event, the world speaks of the RHINEheitsgebot.

I raise myself up off of the bed, Mateo is already back in the cell.

Something's fishy here, I say. The execution is now scheduled, Mateo says. I dreamt of beer, I say, the dream went like this: "Then she said to me that you must drink a liter of warm beer and, yes, in your one-man tent, in the midday heat, garbed in a sweater, the entrance tightly shut, nothing else ought to come into the tent, for it is soon to be drunk dry," Mateo interrupts me, he would prefer to read the dream, Alter looks over his shoulder and reads it. Dürer recently dreamt a better dream, Mateo says, then reads out from the book: "In 1525, during the night between Wednesday and Thursday after Whitsuntide, I had this vision in my sleep, and saw how many great waters fell from heaven. The first struck the ground about four miles away from me with such a terrible force, enormous noise and splashing that it drowned the entire countryside. I was so greatly shocked at this that I awoke before the cloudburst. And the ensuing downpour was huge. Some of the waters fell some distance away and some close by. And they came from such a height that they seemed to fall at an equally slow pace. But the very first water that hit the ground so suddenly had fallen at such velocity, and was accompanied by wind and roaring so frightening, that when I awoke my whole body trembled and I could not recover for a long time. When I arose in the morning, I painted the above as I had seen it. May the Lord turn all things to the best."

What do you think of that dream, Mateo asks as he flips back through the book and reads the previous pages. Dürer's dream is a single-color copperplate engraving, my dream is at least olde-colored, I say.

That's right, Mateo says, it's fishy or, to put it otherwise, there's a worm in this. He hands me an apple that I am to bite into without biting anything off of it. The apple is made of wax. Now, everything is happening very quickly, Mateo says and takes the apple out of my mouth. Swallow the letter, he says, then hands me the box. As soon as I've swallowed the letter, a large pile of paper appears next to the privy. I ought to ruminate on Luther, my father wishes it to be so, Mateo says, then leaves the cell. Luther. A criminal. He won the power game. What else ought I to think about him. I sit down on the bed once more. Alter, unflagging. I look at him for a long time. At least turn to me, I order him in my thoughts, but it's no use. Mateo comes back in. He presses a golden letter into the gap between my teeth and points to the toilet. I wait. For hours. Then, I savor the black script in my mouth, the black script colors in the golden letter. I take one sheet after another and make my mouth into a press by pressing the mark into each sheet. After 902 pages, the work is done and the deletion is reversed; the entire manuscript is there once more. Alter comes and takes the sheets unto him. I wish to complain about this to Mateo, who has been watching me this whole time. That's already posterity, he says. I don't agree with some passages and would gladly change them, I say. It's of no interest what you agree with or not, we must now make a forward stride, otherwise, there's no end to the changes that would need to be made, Mateo says. Alter has been industrious, as prestidigitator, he wrote out your thoughts on Luther in no time, minutes truly taken down from memory. It is already written in my book. It is my confession of guilt—finally! plain English! translated from plain German! I can read it if I'd like, Alter has already signed it for me. And thus do I read:

Thou shalt not kill. (Exodus 20:13)
Ruminations

> Let each one here his lesson learn,
> God to such home will bliss return.
> (Luther)

Whoever reads the Bible embarks on a journey of endless references. In the beginning was the Word, thus does the Word always point to a word in another place. In the beginning was the Logos. Logos, among other other things, means speech, word, thought, meaning, or mental faculty. In the beginning was the Word, thus might this be an oral utterance, written speech, or a mental/spiritual faculty that exists within itself, capable of all sorts of emanations. John 1:1-18 is a prologue that might be considered a parable for the whole Bible. Its first six verses read: "In the beginning was the Word, / and the Word was with God, / and the Word was God. / The same was in the beginning with God. / All things were made by him; / and without him was not any thing made that was made." What does that mean? The Word was there before God. Or: God was first within it, as Word. The Word strode forth from itself as differentiation. As God, it named and called into being by naming—even itself. Thus did the world arise as the difference between Wordgod and Godword. And thus does the poet seem to be an alternative God, his metaphorical acumen begetting a parallel world, in which signified and signifier again become one, still undivided. Thus might God as Word be an invention of the poets. We find God in the "Book of Books," the Biblia, an anthology of various poets. Thus does "Biblia" signify no superlative, the Bible is not the throne of literal creation; "biblia" is a metonym, script's substrate—papyrus, bast—becoming a proper name. Some things that we certainly believed to be in the Bible, but never sought out, we end up not finding when we do look for them. But he who has landed in the Bible shall never more manage to get out of it in the same way he got into it at the beginning. Not that he has been converted, as conversion would require him to have entered into the Bible as an unbeliever. Indeed, it is conceivable that, after reading the Bible, a believer says, I now no longer understand the world. Which world? The world of the world or of words? The world of words can call forth verbal monsters, which, once they've been distinguished by way of their naming, are already called into being as monsters of the real. It is in this way that God can also be a monstrous God, he might appear to be a monster in the sum of his qualities. Was it this perversion that God feared in pronouncing a ban on names and images? The ban on images in Exodus 20:4-6 entered the Second Commandment in the Anglican, Orthodox, and Reformed traditions;

Luther, however, left it out of his Large and Small Catechism in 1528/1529 and it is likewise not taken into account in the Roman Catholic tradition: "You shall not make for yourself an image in the form of anything in heaven above or on the earth beneath or in the waters below. You shall not bow down to them or worship them; for I, the Lord your God, am a jealous God, punishing the children for the sin of the parents to the third and fourth generation of those who hate me, but showing love to a thousand generations of those who love me and keep my commandments."

The ban on images corresponds to the self-revealing of the Name of God, who, as YHWH engaging with Moses in the form of the burning bush (Exodus 3:13–16), allows himself to be recognized in the names of, depending on the translation, "I am who I am," "I am what I am," and "I will be what I will be." The prohibition on misusing the Name of God: "Thou shalt not take the name of the Lord thy God in vain; for the Lord will not hold him guiltless that taketh his name in vain" (Exodus 3:13-16), which Luther quotes briefly and succinctly as the Second Commandment "Thou shalt not take the name of the Lord, thy God, in vain," which, in Judaism, led to the name "HaShem," the name that represents the unsayability and, as such, the inexpressibility of the Name of God. This was a solution as cautious as it was forward-looking. If the Decalogue from the Pentateuch is the extended Name of God, then the Name of God is a concentrate in the function of a hypogram arising in the Decalogue. God is the concealed theme-word that is not pronounced directly, but pronounced alongside. Whenever you read the Torah, you speak the Name of God.

If people worshiped the images of God that quickened their imaginations the most? The name would prevail, which would contain a most significant entelechy, energetically unfolding its states out from within itself. And who could control the images and names that have made their way into the world and cannot be taken back, called back?

Exodus 20:7–17 (approx. fourth century BC) is the reference version of the Decalogue, the older version in Deuteronomy 5:6–21 (approx. seventh century BC) is the hermeneutics and canonization of this version.[1]

Since Deuteronomy is historically older than the Book of Exodus, the Decalogue, which existed before the Book of Exodus, was incorporated into the Sinai episode of Yahweh's self-revelation. What does that mean? At the very least that a literal reading of the Old Testament overlooks the breaks in the chronology of its coming-into-being. This is entirely to the benefit of the narrative sense of the Bible, the compilers of which must have paid special attention to compositional balance, to an equilibrium of individual sections, even if this could not always be provided for in view of the abundance of compiled sources. So is it that the Bible as a whole is the parable of its opening: "In the beginning was the Word, and the Word was with God, and the Word was God."

There are no Ten Commandments. *Dekalos* means the "ten-word" or, perhaps, the "tenfold word"—das Zehnwort. That which grew into a repressive Christian ethic in German as the Ten Commandments, which, starting with the Church Father Augustine, was adopted by Catholicism and by Luther, goes back to something that was first combined from looser groups of commandments to form its tenfold shape, the ur-text of which either never existed or must have been

---

1. See *Theologische Realenzyklopädie. Volume 8. Clovis—Dionysius Areopagita.* Berlin: de Gruyter 1981, p. 411.

lost, its literary final version is the condensate of Yahweh's revelatory speech on Mount Sinai, in the prologue of which (Exodus 20:2-6), Yahweh reveals himself as the liberator of the Israelite people from Egyptian slavery.[2] As liberator, Yahweh makes promises with the formula "I, your God" or sometimes "I am your God," but also binds demands to these promises, they are bundled into the Ten Commandments and are therefore unthinkable without the prologue.

But if, instead of speech that has become a literal sign of God, the Decalogue is merely the written version of a previously existing ethical code of conduct belonging to a clan with the core association of a family, one that, now that it has been codified, is no longer passed on orally, but in a place, a place of script, one that is accessible to all?

Angelus Silesius says in his *Cherubinic Wanderer* that the place is already contained in the Word, that God is in the Logos:

> *The place is the word.*
> The place and the *word* is one, and were the place not
> (of all eternal eternity!) the *word* would not be."[3]

But what sort of place is that? The wasteland? Where is the wasteland? In you, the Cherubinic Wanderer says:

> "*The place itself is in you.*
> It is not you in the place, the place is in you!
> Cast it out, and here already is eternity."[4]

---

2. See Dieter Baltzer (ed.): *Teaching and Learning with the Old Testament*, pp. 188-201, here p. 194.
3. Angelus Silesius: *Cherubinischer Wandersmann*, Chapter 6, p. 205.
4. Angelus Silesius: *Cherubinischer Wandersmann*, Chapter 6, p. 185.

The past shall be. The hurled-out god, the coughed-up god, is the future that's already been and always is: Topos is the place. God is the Topos.

And if the "Ten Commandments" (Ex 34:28; Dtn 4:13; 10:4) were not a coherent discourse in the slightest, but a jagged collection of formerly separate sentences, the apodictically formulated negativity of which represents no law,[5] but aims prohibitively at non-doing, abstention, then the passing-down of the Ten Commandments as Christian ethics disguises their origin and recodes the apodictic sentences of the likely family-oriented prohibitives into timeless and contextless prohibitions of a legal character.

Does research into the history of this genesis provide evidence against the existence of God? The history of the impact of the Decalogue is likely to be of greater interest than the history of its genesis and this also applies to the question of God himself. Assuming that he doesn't exist, he still continues to exist in his impact, more precisely, in the belief in him and the consequences of this belief. There are no certainties in this question, not even Pascal's Wager is capable of convincing here, as its own reception-history shows.

If in the beginning was the Word and the Word was God, thus is God in me when I hear the Word by hearing God by hearing the Ten Commandments.

Indeed, for the recitation of the inward God, the voice is the medium of God as it revealed itself to be on Mount Sinai and that was in the beginning, before the Spirit of God took the praying man unto himself. That is the divine cycle. To draw

---

5. See Erhard S. Gerstenberger: *Essence and Origin of 'Apodictic Law.'* Neukirchen-Vluyn: Neukirchener Verlag 1965 (Scientific Monographs on the Old and New Testament. Volume 20), p. 43.

the divine spirit down with words of prayer. To prayerfully cry out "Thou shalt not kill" by reading the sentence aloud means invoking the sentence and the divine spirit with it: Help me not to kill. To read means to pray.

The voice of others, God's voice, evokes me first of all. With this evocation, to which I cannot close myself as I would, under other circumstances, just close my eyes, thus am I brought into a dependency equiprimordially and I relieve myself of it by recitation, as if I were coughing something up. But, simultaneously, the recitation of God renews the covenant of dependency. Exhalation relieves inhalation and grounds each exhalation anew. And, when one breathes in, one already announces oneself to be breathing out, just as breathing out is already contained in breathing in. The Voice of God, which so frightens those who meet with it—they wish to hurl it back to the place from which it seems to thunder—marks the abyss between Man and God. If the Voice of God is the bridge between God and Man, then Man is the walker to and fro upon this bridge, man repeats the singular event of being invoked by invoking God in prayer. Why does he do this? Was he merely hallucinating and does he now wish to arrive at some kind of certainty? In prayer, he wishes to call God down to him, to cause him to appear within, in such a way that when God does not appear outside the human body, he appears in an unreachable place, which is therefore no place, but within, the terror felt at the Voice of God thundering some distance away is appeased by way of inward repetition. The other—God—is in my voice. The afterlife is within me. I can't come to myself because the afterlife permanently prevents this, he is in my voice, which I do not hear, but only know. This is how God interferes. Does he at least hear my voice? He divides me incessantly. I must overcome this division by calling upon the mute voice. And what prayer could be more appropriate than oral revelation put down in script, then called forth once more in its original orality? If God is the one who—by way of witnesses, by way of tradition—makes me speak with his words, so too is Logos the place where I am able to get hold of him by reading and listening for the moment when I have to pray uninterruptedly so as not to lose him, for I do not otherwise reach God and I lose him at the very moment I become silent. Then God sinks down in me like a piece of metal into murky water. I lose it in seeking.

But if God, who has given us his invocation as the dependent-making other, exists on the inside, I shall always wish to invoke him, I can activate him by speaking, turning to him—thus is all speaking soliloquy, I incorporate myself when I incorporate God, who, as tzimtzum, constricted himself so as to make room for the finite world, at which point he says to me: "Thou shalt not kill." So, is this self-incorporation not killing? Is it, if not a physical act of killing, then a symbolic one, this "die and be new-born" as the cycle of life? The transsubstantiation of the body into suffering precedes any self-incorporation. Since the Passion of Jesus Christ, body and suffering have belonged together. Luther also comprehended this. The body stands for the sole person of my self and of the other and for life. Life—body—suffering: This is the series that must be kept in balance, its last link, suffering, is doubly occupied: By way of Christ's Passion, suffering, including the suffering of the soul, has been, symbolically speaking, made absent from the body, it is personified in Christ, simultaneously, it is the presence of the other in one's own body, in the context of this consecration, the body of Christ is incorporated into one's own body by way of the suffering of Christ, according to the Roman Catholic view, this comes to pass as transubstantiation, Lutheran teaching deviates from this in that it does not speak of an objective change in the ontos of the bread or the wine, but of a consubstantiation, by which the body and blood of Christ are taken up in and with the bread and wine and become one with them by way of the priest. The covenant to be renewed in the consumption of Christ's body and blood is precisely this ever-renewing recognition and realization of the Passion by way of the transmission of suffering.

The invocation of God serves the casting out of suffering that befalls us, thus is God a lightning rod. Luther admonishes us to "accustom us ever to keep in view this commandment, always as in a mirror to contemplate ourselves in it, to regard the will of God, and with hearty confidence and invocation of his name to commend to him the wrong which we suffer." To follow the commandment "Thou shalt not kill" thus also satisfies divine narcissism and, indeed, as shall be shown, in a double perspective, for the sanctioning of the transgression as balancing-out also serves divine narcissism. And should I refuse such an invocation? If I do not invoke God, I am not entirely myself, since I only am by way of the absent other. To not invoke God is my bargaining chip: I withdraw the source from him, the mirror that only shows its image when it is breathed upon by the voice. But if I do not invoke God, I am not. But if I do invoke him, others might possibly not *be*. The invocation of God comes to pass in many forms.

If God, as it is variously stated, dwells in letters, the Torah is the Name of God and, consequently, the letters are his visible and audible representatives; the letters to be spoken aloud are put into a specific order, uniting the reader who calls out with God in the fact that God as letters is vibrated via the vocal cords and the vibrations transmit themselves through the air from mouth to ear, thus is God transmitted if you strike the magic word, yet some strike not the magic word, but only throat or neck, and the connection to God is not intensified by *loudly* calling out the letters, which signify God in the way that they are ordered and glorify his greatness, indeed, the loud invocation of God drowns out one's own conscience, in which God is to be found, forced to remain silent, thus intoxicating the murderer. Killing is delegated to God in the God-invoking act of killing. God is so great that he accepts the killing as a sacrifice and, by accepting it, exculpates the murderer. But what if the wrong person was killed? The killer acts in the conviction that God has led him to the right person.

"Thou shalt not kill." Even so, there has never been any lack of fatalities. That's because people can't read and can't hear. If they could, they would know that each person killed signifies *another* person killed, indeed, the killer is also killed. In that sense, each killer is also a suicide. This is what the Pentateuch says: "Whoso sheddeth man's blood, by man shall his blood be shed: for in the image of God made he man" (Genesis 9:6). Whoever kills another kills an image of God. Each murder is a proxy murder. The expiation of killing comes to pass so as to serve God's narcissism, then the evil of the killing is balanced by way of the good of the killing. Thus are there two kinds of killing. If evil killing did not exist, good killing would be deprived of any basis. Recent history shows that there seems to be a preliminary form of killing here, a killing in reserve, as it were, as unbelief is evil and thus should the unbeliever be put to death to please God because unbelief abolishes the entire system of which God is the ultimate foundation. This shady bargaining is meant to lure the soul that is ever unquiet. Killing for a flat rate, the God Mammon is great. A Jan Hus, a Thomas Müntzer, shall arise from their ranks to demonize such indulgences and the self-empowerment and self-glorification of the priests. The incrimination of the clergy, the sinful priests turned more to worldly life than to God, those not held accountable for their sins and who exercised unlawful taxation, this was a matter of common concern for Jan Hus, Thomas Müntzer, and Martin Luther, the last of whom behaved downright uncouthly in his criticism of the clergy and aimed most particularly at the Carthusian order in his interpretation of the Fifth Commandment. While Jan Hus often referred to the sinful priests as Antichrists, devils, and heretics, Luther testified that the then-fashionable Carthusian monks aped and seduced the world with "a false, hypocritical appearance of holiness," for they "disregard this commandment like the others, and esteem them unnecessary," falsely praising and proclaiming their own works as "the most perfect life; for, in order that they might lead a pleasant, easy life, without the cross and without patience." The cloister, he claims, is merely an alibi for them to be left alone by the world and for them not to have to do any good to anybody.

Ultimate justifications are a difficult business. What is the ultimate justification for the commandment not to kill? Is it moral law or the Word of God in me? In the first case, the final justification would be a matter of natural law, in the last, a metaphysics of morals, the ultimate justificatory concept of duty belonging to which Kant describes as follows: "Duty is the necessity of an act out of respect for the law." And, indeed, regardless of who decreed the law, the concept of duty is only formally defined here.

But why does it say "Thou"? Why does it not say "I shall not kill"? Who has ever said "I shall not kill"? If somebody hears or reads "Thou shalt not kill," he always hears or reads an authority interpolating him. Somebody is pointing at you. With the sentence in this form, God points at the listener who hears the Voice of God in and with this sentence. But how different it would be with the sentence in the form "I shall not kill." Is that not mere quotation, the passing-down of hearsay, a rumor? If anybody at all feels himself to be addressed, the nonresponsive "I" is displaced into the realm of fiction. "I shall not kill": Here, somebody says: "Take note of that. How does the sentence go?" And the one called upon replies: "I shall not kill." As a memory-sentence for the epoch of childhood, however, the sentence would be more effective in the form "I am not allowed to kill." In this form, the focus of the sentence is still on learning by heart and internalization. Once this sentence has passed into the child's flesh and blood, the child shall likely kill nobody for its whole life. Later, it may recall this sentence and, even more so, the one who instilled this sentence into it like a mathematical formula by way of the Nuremberg funnel. Then the child grown old laughs over this childish belief and kills somebody, for it has gotten to know life and society and now knows better. It says quite frankly that this sentence is ideology, not justified by anything in the world, the unbelievers have sent their false god who is to stand for this sentence. As this God does not exist, he can also not take responsibility. Thus must those who always carry him in their mouth take the responsibility. But how different is the Thou that everyone is, for everyone knows that the other is addressed with this Thou.

"Thou shalt not kill": This formulation is a virus, which people have been immune to since the beginning. It is a magic formula, which one must believe in. "Thou shalt not kill" is not "Thou mayst not kill." But why is it not "Thou mayst not kill"? An error in the translation? If it read "Thou mayst not kill," the commandment would be a prohibition. Would it thus be a law? But who would supervise its observance and who would sanction its transgression? The state as God? And if there's no God at all? Then all the powder would already be shot with the sentence "Thou mayst not kill"—powder the formulation "Thou shalt not kill" still has stored in the receptacle of the "shalt."

What follows from the Ten Commandments if the addressed "Thou" doesn't keep to a commandment? Is the God of the Old Testament not just and merciful? The Ten Commandments set forth no behavioral system of norms or positive notion of right, they lack the sanction of a properly worded punishment. The Bible itself provides the answer here and Martin Luther incorporated these answers into his Catechism and Bible translation. Matthew 5:21-22: "Ye have heard that it was said of them of old time, Thou shalt not kill; and whosoever shall kill shall be in danger of the judgment: But I say unto you, That whosoever is angry with his brother without a cause shall be in danger of the judgment."

And Revelation 13:10-11: "He that leadeth into captivity shall go into captivity: he that killeth with the sword must be killed with the sword. Here is the patience and the faith of the saints." However, there are not only two kinds of killing; there are also two kinds of sword, as shall be seen below, otherwise all executioners, whether they execute with sword, hatchet, or guillotine, would themselves have to be executed—and as soon as possible.

What is the opposite of "I can do away with somebody"? "I love all mankind." Martin Luther shifts the lever in this direction when he changes the imperative negation "not," which denotes the prohibitive of the Decalogue, into a positive "shalt": love of God comes to pass as love of neighbor and love of neighbor as love of God.

Before this, however, Luther extends the notion of killing to regions that do not aim directly at the annihilation of life and thus aim at the body of the other, but are localized in the subject himself—his ethos already kills in that he wishes ill. Killing begins in the furious heart. It also means killing by way of words, slander, character assassination, abusing the name of the other by way of rumor. Luther writes: "Therefore the entire sum of this commandment is to be impressed upon the simple-minded most explicitly, viz. What is the meaning of not to kill? In the first place, that we hurt nobody with our hand or deed. Then that we do not employ our tongue to instigate or counsel thereto. Further, that we neither use nor assent to any kind of means or methods whereby any one may be injured. And finally that the heart be not ill-disposed toward any one, nor from anger and hatred wish him ill, so that body and soul may be innocent in respect to everyone, but especially in respect to those who wish one ill or actually commit such against one. For, to do evil to one who wishes and does one good is not human, but diabolical."

If one were to take a few testimonies of Luther's raging against opponents and enemies as a basis, his remarks on the Fifth

Commandment might well be read as if he himself, Luther, were unaffected by its implications or as if this teacher of the populace had set out to be a better person—thus the Pluralis Majestatis. But, perhaps, because of his spiritual authority, he felt himself to be the government expressly exempted from the prohibition on killing. "Therefore," he writes, "this prohibition pertains to individuals and not to governments." As sovereign, the government stands outside of the Fifth Commandment, in that it has the power to negate its observance. The government is the exceptional authority with the divine license to kill. By decision, it overrides the Fifth Commandment so as to maintain it. The killing then restores the situation, in which the Fifth Commandment once more applies. "Thou shalt not kill" really does not mean that killing is forbidden under all circumstances. A murderer who kills with intent is to be killed by the authorities who sit in God's stead. This killing is no unlawful, arbitrary killing. "The hand," according to Luther in 1526, "that wields the secular sword is not a human hand but the hand of God. It is God, not man, who hangs and breaks on the wheel, decapitates and flogs: it is God who wages war." Meister Hans is a fine fellow, guided by the Hand of God. Luther knew all too well that this sort of doctrine of authority and its hierarchical subordinations, as well as the argument of a good cast of mind that ought to abstain from violence and charity, might well be used to make Luffer suther. Killing for a just cause? The question of the "right to kill" has its own tradition. In the sense of justice as a higher goal, divine wrath compensates for satanic temptation and the work of the devil, up to and including the death penalty. Divine right is accordingly of unconditional validity. Life is an unpaid bill that shall be settled up on Judgment Day. Until then, however, the evil cast of mind can also claim the zeal of righteousness in the Name of God for itself. Even the penal authority position held by the powers that be is not immune to an evil cast of mind camouflaged beneath God's name. No heretic ought to be called on to carry out the divine will. But who is a heretic and what is the divine will? "Thou shalt not kill" is the divine law. Only God can peer into the heart and the heart is, from time to time, a deep den of cutthroats.

If, in a letter from May 30, 1525, Luther wrote to his friend Johann Rühel, who worked as councilor for the Count von Mansfeld—the very Count Ernst II of Mansfeld who had Thomas Müntzer tortured at Helderungen Castle for twelve days before he was released—Luther appeals to God and points out that it is high time that the peasants into whom the devil has entered be strangled like vile dogs instead of allowing Thomas Müntzer to flee from the people to the swine, as in Luke 8:27-39, does Luther not then sin against the Law of Sinai "Thou shalt not kill"? "Well," writes Luther in his letter, never at a loss for the drastic, "anyone who has seen Munzer can say that he has seen the very devil, and at his worst. O God! If this is the spirit that is in the peasants it is high time that they were killed like mad dogs. It may be that the devil feels the nearness of the last day, and so decides to stir up all the dregs and show all his hellish power at once. Haec sunt tempora, but God still lives and reigns and will not forsake us. His goodness is nearer, mightier and wiser than the ragings and the ravings of Satan." But, on the subject of the Fifth Commandment, did Luther himself not write in his Catechism that: "Now this commandment is easy enough and has been often treated, because we hear it annually in the Gospel of St. Matthew, 5, 21 ff., where Christ Himself explains and sums it up, namely, that we must not kill neither with hand, heart, mouth, signs, gestures, help, nor counsel. Therefore it is here forbidden to every one to be angry, except those (as we said) who are in the place of God, that is, parents and the government." Thus must Luther himself, who kills here with hand, heart, mouth, and sign, sit in God's place in such a way that he is exempt from the punishment of being killed—or Luther himself is diabolical.

And what, then, is the intention of Luther's prospective polemical pamphlet, in which he unequivocally supports the execution of Thomas Müntzer? Luther must have fundamentally changed if he wishes to endow his own Catechism with his own belief, for, in it, he writes: "So also if you see any one innocently sentenced to death or in like distress, and do not save him, although you know ways and means to do so, you have killed him." Consequently, Luther himself shall have to be killed. Kill and be killed, the speech suits the man from Eisleben quite comfortably. In his polemical pamphlet entitled *A Terrible History and Judgment of God on Thomas Müntzer, in which God clearly Punishes his Lies and Damns him*, which was published before the execution of Thomas Müntzer on May 27, 1525, a compilation of letters between Thomas Müntzer and other insurgents with fore- and afterword and mocking comments in the margins, addressed to "all dear Germans," Luther demonizes the preacher and his Reformation competitor as an Antichrist, responsible for the many dead at the Battle of Frankenhausen, also presenting the battle as God's judgment upon Müntzer, who invoked God without having been called by him. For Luther, the outcome of the battle is God's judgment: "I must rejoice that God has passed judgment and has so arranged matters that we now know and can recognize how the rebellious spirits taught errors and falsehoods, and that their preaching was against God and was condemned by Him."

Thus did God act differently than Müntzer might have hoped, the Battle of Frankenhausen is the sorry effort of the devil, who wished to seize the power for himself—Müntzer is his "harmful manipulator" and "beshitten prophet" and "lie-filled murderspirit." Did Thomas Müntzer therefore preach killing, as Luther implies? Was he a prophet of the devil? Luther likely wanted to be sure that Thomas Müntzer would be silent forevermore. Müntzer was no man of compromise, Luther saw that clearly, for he also preferred to preach of passive endurance out of an anti-political/theological calculation. "For," he writes on April 19 or 20, 1525, in his reply to the *Twelve Articles of the Peasantry*, an admonition for peace addressed to the peasants, "no matter how right you are, it is not right for a Christian to appeal to law, or to fight, but rather to suffer wrong and endure evil." Here too, Luther once more preaches his two worlds, the secular and the spiritual—and they ought never come into contact with one another. He sits in a vale of tears of paradoxes and Thomas Müntzer seems to bear some of the blame for this as well, as Luther blames him for his own horror at the death of the peasants and Müntzer's own fate.

As a heretic, on January 3, 1521, just a little more than four years before Müntzer's execution, Luther himself suffered a papal ban, which was finally granted by Emperor Charles V on April 19, 1521, before the Diet of Worms, Charles proclaimed the imperial ban on May 8 of the year in the Edict of Worms, with the consent of the imperial estates having been wrested from them, Luther, protected by the Saxon Elector Frederick, was able to escape from the consequences of this for a little while by way of the daring escapade of a friendly abduction. At the Wartburg and after ten months back in Wittenberg, he was finally safe from persecution. Luther was lucky not to have to died as a heretic. In Thomas Müntzer, who had so vehemently renounced him, he saw the Anti-Luther whom he had to suppress within himself. The Anti-Luther was thus to die in his stead. If Luther had been taken at his own word—i.e. against Müntzer—he would have had to be executed.

Here, one must at the very least still ask who misused the name of God: Müntzer or Luther? Only God can decide. And, indeed, God likely already has. The course of history is not necessarily the consequence of a divine verdict.

I agree with the part about a divine verdict, but it wasn't me, I didn't write it. As I read what's written next, Alter fades more and more until, finally, he vanishes entirely: "Mateo opted for Alter and against Ego, for the sword and against impalement. Imagination is enough," he says. Mateo is nothing but a hired hand of violence.

The sword is roughly three meters long and two meters wide, it must be wielded by three men, upon it is not to be read 'When I do heave the sword aloft, I wish unto the sinner eternal life,' but the whole of *Schattenfroh*, printed onto the blade by way of a single bite. The criminal must read it in its entirety before his execution, which causes the execution to be unbearably protracted. The fact that the book also ends with his execution sweetens the farewell for him, he cannot know that. However, should the book not end with his execution, the reader shall already have forgotten him by its end.

Alter reads. He shakes his head. Mateo says that he should shake it while he still can. Alter reads on. Then the sword falls and Mateo says: That wasn't the end yet.

Taken back to the fortress from the printing works in a cart, Alter's head is impaled on a stake not far from here, 'pinned into the feld,' through numerous visits by curious citizens and so-called nefarious people, the path thereto soon becomes as worn as a public way, there are some who grab hold of his visage as soon as they reach him, one of them even causes his head to fall off, then that person takes out a handkerchief, heaves him up once more, and sticks him back onto the stake, adjusts him a bit to the right, then picks the nose and turns away, another one kicks him down to see how well he bounces, then sets him back onto the spit upside down, a third begins to interrogate him, and, as he doesn't reply, he is found guilty, then sentenced to be put to death by the sword. One now wishes to remove stake together with head and replant the path, the well-trodden road testifies that he is on the fastest route to becoming a saint or martyr."

Now, *that* makes me jealous. Why him? I can still feel it—the blow through neck and throat. And I feel that the tunnel is at an end and I crawl out, into a new century very near to here.

Blood in the urine. What color has the blood of the soul? After urological surgery, discharged to outpatient follow-up care in a satisfactory general condition. The satisfactory general condition manifests itself as dehydration and urosepsis. Obstructive urinary outflow disorder. The full bladder stops releasing water. Blood collects in the bladder. Pathogenic germs. Inflammation of the body. Rot. Opacification of the affected. The hospital has invaded the body. Thus must the afflicted body go back to the hospital so as to come to its senses there—to decay. Brandberge, beg bernard, bender brag: The Hospital upon the Berg der Barden—the Mountain of Bards. The urologist is a buffoon, a harlequin. He shall have to carry the straw mattress. And I set it aflame with Barditus. One is already speaking of chances. Whenever one speaks of chances, one has none.

My brother sends a photo. So that we might know what awaits us. A photo.

Sepsis. Artificial coma. Intubation. They sign us in. The door opens. Intensive care units are the battery cages of death. Is the intensive care unit in the basement? Have we gone down a flight of stairs? Behind the door waits a narrow room with a gray floor made of PVC. On the left, an examination table, a chair. The examination table is covered over in medical crepe paper. Two-ply white recycled tissue, glued. A showroom? A transitional corridor, as if one had to undergo a purification in order to reach the threshold-people, the convalescent, the dying. I've undergone a purification, hundreds of pages. Left. Right. A passage. Is that him? Who? The one with the bare feet that one sees through the open door? Yes, that is Father. The slapping of leather soles against the vinyl floors. Am I well dressed? Would Father have found something the matter with my shirt? One still always feels like a little boy with him. Father, that is I, I am Father. I myself lie before me. Eyelids matted with Vaseline. Was someone afraid of his evil eye? Or is that not Vaseline at all, do eye secretions escape uncontrollably and glue the eyes shut? Feet and hands are badly swollen. Father would look wonderfully young if only one couldn't see his head. That really isn't the body of a dying man, water swells it up nicely and causes it to appear as nothing like the body of an old man. Father never was an old man. Even when he walked with a cane, he was no old man. Not all of his hair fell out. In the coma-bed, the skull appears pure. A beard grows from his chin. He was also never muscular. Just enough for a few blows. His wedding ring was also taken off of him as a precaution. But this really isn't the body of a dying man. I've always imagined the body of an old man to be different. Lined, wrinkled, bespotted. If the water flows out once more, he might be precisely that—lined, wrinkled, bespotted. An ulcerous leg. Professionally provided with modern plaster. The bed tilted slightly forward. Father stretched out stiffly. A yellow-and-white-striped sheet down over the hips, the upper body bare. I cannot touch him. Touch him now! That's not gonna happen. Father's head is stretched slightly backward. A transparent tube leads into the wide-open mouth, another through the left nostril. The rising and falling of the thorax appears to happen in disembodied fashion. How strange: Father is alive. The nasal feeding tube does its work, just as everything in the room does its work. Beloved Father, have you given up or can you not carry on much longer? Unfortunately, I cannot touch you, I could check if your hand were warm, but I can't. In dying, to become young once more. But you really aren't dying. The ventilation could easily continue until your body begins to decay. Your ventilated thorax would remain, rising and falling, rising and falling, dancing thorax, air-armor, signs of life. And from your body would flow the water, your body melting like snow, it burns up like a candle, and the water quenches the flames of your inflammation.

The poor resolution of the image is not worthy of his life, each part of the device can clearly be recognized, but not all that clearly, it really should be excessively clear, as I have many images from our shared life before my eyes and thus shall death's approach also be excessively clear. Life, the device. A Pentecost of tubes and cannulae. And when the day of Pentecost was fully come, they were all with one accord in one place. And when the fiftieth day was fully come, they were all with one accord in one place. And suddenly there came a sound from heaven as from a rushing mighty wind, and it filled all the body where he was sitting. And life appeared unto cloven, like as fire. And the fire tongues entered into him and went out. And he swallowed each of them, and while he was swallowing them, they swallowed him. The dissolution of life is very clear here. I held the photo next to my father lying there incarnate and thought I could perceive a slight improvement in his condition. Don't you think so, I ask my brother. Father looks slightly better, what do you think? A veneer veils the dying. Water is the veneer. Air is the veneer. Father has already died, one simply doesn't see it, that's what I think. But here, take a look, in the image, he really does look a lot more forlorn, much, hold on, much more hopeless, there, he really does look like a dead man. Because the image stands still, the image doesn't breathe. And wait and see how he looks as a dead man. What would you say to Father if he were to suddenly open his eyes and ask you what else you wish to say to him? I would say to him, I've always loved you, Daddy. What about you? I would say to him that I thank him and shall never forget him. One runs out of ideas as to what to say. Not a soul knows the ritual set-phrases any longer. So, what does one say to a dying man? I just want to say a quick goodbye? Quick, that's gotta be the way to go. Quick as a knife-stab. Brevity—a beastly virtue. If man were already capable of making use of language at birth and lamenting in it, it would already be high time to commemorate one's own death, as it has already begun. He who had just been born would give an endless speech about his dying until he was dead. Speaking about death would be the sickness unto death. Is there a more beautiful work of art conceivable than this? We would probably tell our father that the sun was shining outside. Or: I just wanted to see how you're going. Or: Hello, Daddy. We are, in any case, personally present. One doesn't always manage that. Some don't want it. They're so afraid of death, of the death of others as a substitute-death of their own death, in such a way that they don't even dignify it with a syllable, death, don't even address the dying one, it gets better every day, even the dying man gets better every day, he's just taking a little nap. On October 20, 1758, Frederick II was indisposed. He could not make it to his dying sister, the Margravine of Bayreuth, so as to comfort her face to face. Thus did he give his personal physician Cothenius a letter with the following sequence of words: "Most tenderly-beloved Sister,

Receive kindly the verses I am sending you. I am so filled with you, your danger and my gratitude, that your image constantly rules my soul and governs all my thoughts, waking or dreaming, writing prose or poetry. Would that Heaven might grant the wishes of your recovery that I daily send there! Cothenius is on his way; I shall worship him if he can preserve the person who in all the world is closest to my heart, whom I esteem and honour and for whom I remain, until the moment when I too return my body to the elements,

Most tenderly-beloved sister,

Your loyal and devoted brother and friend, Frederick." And us? The Grim Reaper has the last word because we say nothing and the Grim Reaper also says nothing. Didn't even pray. Accepted. Settled.

In the hallways of the intensive car unit, snapped up a scrap of conversation "got used to everything." If somebody were to lead me into a room, point to a bed, say that is your father, but there was nothing but a piece of charred wood on the bed training its eyes upon me, then that somebody said, have no fear, he can't see you, I would get used to it, and if this piece of wood were then no piece of wood at all, but a little animal made of plastic, my little childhoodplasticanimal, I would get used to calling that Father, and Father, whose dying appearance serves as screensaver for me, a skull without magic, existence laid entirely bare, Father ought to go back home with me soon, I am to take him back home with me, and I would put him on my bookshelf at home, into the rhetorical-classics section, which one consults when one thinks oneself to have understood everything, everything except for language.

I copy the skull from the photo and set it into the text, it is the head of an executed man, the face suddenly swollen—bigger, wider. The eyes open wide and restless, but the eyelids unmoving, the mouth open wide, but the two lips stiff and contracted. Intubation. Since he can no longer control his facial muscles, his face looks like a mask. But, because of the machine, the heart beats heavily and the lungs work with short, quickened breaths, the nose almost white, he's now become an old man after all, he's as old as I've ever seen an old man to be, I look at him uninterruptedly for five minutes, then he is young once more, he has big ears, but doesn't hear me, his open mouth says nothing more, even with the greatest possible magnification, no more hair can be seen on the skull, he was always so proud not to have lost it, no total baldness, but not just a fringe of hair either, he's had a fulfilled life, that comforts me despite the scene, you're not allowed to do that, he says, what am I not allowed to do, you're not allowed to show me, you're not allowed to take my head, you're not allowed to say that, you're not allowed to see me, that you can see me like this is irreparable, you're listening to music and looking at me, everything around you makes the sight as pleasant as it could possibly be, somebody has always had to die for you to be able to breathe life into your texts. The doctor said your soul has already gone, only a bothersome shell remains, but I'm not yet dead and you're already turning me off, he stands up out of the photo, the yellow lever in the middle of the bedframe, there, on the right, give the yellow lever a pull, I give the yellow lever a pull and Father sinks slowly down into the ground, the cables grow longer, the heart beats regularly, Father vanishes into the ground, his image slips out of the text with each line, your body hasn't changed all that much in the last decades, but now the ground is closing, I take the plasticanimal, remove what remains of the adhesive, reserved, but not picked up, you can take it with you if you want, it is your father and I take Father along with his vitals monitor, his anesthesia monitor, his ICU monitor, I take all of it with me.

You are the great invisible one, the lifelong unfelt one, the one who is always only labeled, the outlined one, the one whose outlines are transmuted and merge into mountain- and animal-shapes.

When did you start to quit? Are you already an image? Do we slide into death thinking and feeling and somebody is watching us as we do? And we are not this Somebody, it is also no Nobody, it would be very bad if it were the Nobody who is responsible for everything that nobody is responsible for any longer. The body in death. "In death" is a process. The sentences short of breath. Intermittent breathing. Endotracheal tube. Intubation forevermore. Persistent respiratory insufficiency. Extubation ends life. Unsuccessful treatment. Tapering off. The sneaking out of life. The corpse is the image of the dead. I've known your body for some years now. For years, I've had it before my eyes. During our last encounters, I told your corpse that it might as well vanish, I could hardly recognize you. Your corpse simply stared at me. Silence is the name of his weapon. The corpse already had its deathmask on. Your corpse was the absence of the present. When the corpse is first dead. Art first begins with the corpse. The sole thing worth preserving is the corpse. Only if the preservation of the corpse of a society is no longer *worth it* does art end.

I shall show my father's photo everywhere, I shall project it onto the Reichstag, it ought to fly over the Brooklyn Bridge instead of the American flag. I grow into his death so as to push him out of my life.

Right up until her death, Mother spoke incessantly of her own father, whom she could only push out of her life by growing into his death. She was of the conviction that she ought to grow into his death. Father accompanied Mother's death through pre- and ab-sence. Topor is the sleep of death. Somnus with a T. Deeper than sopor. Sopor: resounding, ringing, dinging: i i e.

Is it mere convenience that the notion of the soul exists? Is it perhaps our sole consolation?

Dying, the soul's diet. To be dead endlessly. Death is the feast of the soul. And resurrection? Does Augustine not say, "Resurrection is our belief, to meet once again—our hope, and to remember—our love"? So, then what? Resurrection of the dead or deathlessness of the soul, anima separata or anima unica forma corporis? The most glorious ars combinatoria shall here be set into motion, just as it already lay in ashes and ruins in the Middle Ages. Resurrection of the dead and immortality of the soul? If resurrection, why then immortality? Does the resurrected man die once more or is he immortal after his resurrection? Is he immortal only after his resurrection or already with his birth? Now, let us suppose the soul is immortal. Which "immortal" is here referred to? That of the protective stupidity of everyday life, which leaves us lost for words and afraid of God until we doze off into lessness? Or is it only platonic immortality?

Man is an outlandish machine. Body and soul, the old game in new garb—the new game in old garb. The present seems to have no position. But it has a historical overview, it is the historian, the writer of introductions, the contrasting, balancing, comparing, subliming, summarizing, concluding. Plato with a rat's tail. The rat's tail is named Aristotle.

The soul is not matter, the body is a nuisance to it. Or the soul has matter—the body—that the soul wears down over the years, as it is the visible one, so as to be alive alone. Or the soul is of the finest material and we cannot recognize it. But can we perceive it? The soul seems to be something split off from consciousness. Consciousness dims, but the soul remains unchangeable. Is the soul to be conceived of without the body and the body without the soul, both are only one with each other, but in various ways, does the soul have intellect or the intellect soul, could there then be said to be a dumb soul that is without intellect or a soulless intellect that coldly calculates and is without morality?

And if there were no soul and we believed in the soul, what would we lose? Can the soul be bet on? And if I win? "Then you receive nothing." "Nothing?" "Nothing! If you win, you're right—that's a given. Then there's no soul. But you've also basically lost. And I have also lost. If there's no soul, our life is meaningless and empty. And our fathers and mothers have definitively gone away from us forever." "And if you win?"

"Then I'll have doubled my gain. I've won the bet that there is a soul and we shall meet again in death."

"And if the soul must suffer those very same torments in death? And if the soul must review its past life from birth until death, hour by hour, second by second?" "Then, it shall perhaps not recall its past life." "The soul would repeat its past life without knowing that it is repeating a past life? Then that wouldn't be repetition." "But that's wonderful, life would be eternal." "If there is a soul that repeats a past life and, in so doing, forgets that it is repeating, together with a body, a life that it has already led." "In the repetition of this repetition, the soul must already have forgotten that it ever had a body in the first place. For the soul would not even remember itself." "So, the soul would have no self-consciousness." "The soul is the imaginary that, for a brief moment, walks or runs or springs straight ahead." "So, there is no deathless repetition." "Repetition lies in recollection." "So, there is no recollection." "There is recollection."

The question of the soul drives us back to the question of the primordial soup into which lightning struck. We were all once macro-molecules, not ashes.

Deathless. What does that mean for the resurrection of the body? According to Augustine, the soul is the actual human being. Beautiful human. Descartes says the soul can exist separate from the body, it is the I. Then let us die in peace, it never really hits us, death only separates that which was a forced marriage, body and soul, and the body is soiled, the soul pure with God. Of whom do I speak when I speak of death? Is it a naked something or always only a person? Is he an unperson *in* death? Resurrection not from death, but in death: body and soul are both dead, they are united in death. If body and soul are dead and, indeed, both inseparable as the principles of the person, thus do they rise back up, if at all, only in the death into which they have both died—and in this do they transform their aggregate state. Or shall my father have a nice total death, as is theorized by mortalism? What does that mean for his resurrection? Must God remember him and recreate his image from memory? God can do that, otherwise he would be no god at all. But what if he only set one copy into circulation—a paternal Doppelgänger? Thus am I caught up in the memory of God and we hope there is no forgetting. My recollections are a part of God's memory. My father shall be my recollection. His memory has left him. If I lose my memory, my perspective "Father" is lost to the memory of God.

Shall our eschatological versions recognize one another? Shall they be united once more with our personal identities?

There is no question of mortalism here, Father is Catholic. In this case, it really is individual eschatology alone that comes into question. Let the Enlightenment rage in Protestantism, death is to be no sinking into the abyss, no exit into nothingness. But does the soul share in the sinful subject? Is the mere circumstance of being alive not egoism and is this egoism not the sin of sins? As in, did we have a choice as to whether to be? Did somebody come to ask us if we wanted to be or not? This Somebody would have had to have asked somebody who already was. But how can God wish for a sinful soul to be deathless? And the afterlife. Does one even need a soul for the afterlife? Might it actually be that an earthly part of ourselves, the soul, is already part of the hereafter? Then we, who are *we* as a function of our soul, would already be in the hereafter in the now. But how might we recognize the hereafter within us? Is it the imaginary? Is it the green hillocks I see after a little while when I keep my eyes closed? How does God suppose he shall identify us once we have died a total death? Does he punish all people equally and with the same punishment? Then there would be only earthly judgment to lay our sins bare. I can sin and the only question is whether or not I shall be discovered in this. If the sin remains undiscovered, no earthly court shall be able to expiate it.

Not wishing to rely so entirely on the resurrection, man has left no stone unturned in the quest to at least prolong life until, perhaps, a means shall be found to let him live so long that death shall be valued as a form of salvation. In around 1900, one was of the conviction that yogurt could prolong life. Twenty years later, it was animal gonads whose transplantation were going to put death *back into its place*. Fresh-cell therapies are the modern versions of this procedure. Twenty years later, anti-reticulo-endothelial serum once more held the world in the suspense of infinity, as macrophages had been identified as the driving force behind the aging process. The 1960s stood entirely under the sigil of the frozen. As soon as the dying process had begun, the body and soul were to go to zero, which required a contract specifying when the deep-frozen one was to be thawed out for resurrection. For instance, the contract might stipulate that the thawing should be initiated precisely when a drug against cancer or, more precisely, against the cancer by which the dying person had been sickened, was discovered, the drug would then be administered to the thawed one and, from then on, he would be healed. Of course, the one with the will to freeze must reckon with the possibility of never more gazing upon the light of day. But what a sweet hope here breathes its last, which is to say it cannot die in the slightest, for it too shall be frozen. Resurrection as thawing. But what if life isn't only extended, but one no longer dies?

Wednesday, August 20, 2014. Still hope? We've transferred your father to the normal ward. From now on, we can only offer him palliative care. That's fine, probably a good thing. Palliative. To be looked up immediately.

On the way to my mother's birthplace. When piercing through the wall of clouds, the pilot slips slightly. He shines in the light, paints himself in the sky. Everything friendly. I read about the loneliness of the dying. Can't remember anything. "If humanity disappears, everything that any human being has ever done, everything for which people have lived and fought each other, including all secular or supernatural systems of belief, becomes meaningless." Elias, page 67 in the English edition. There's no other possibility allowed for in the book than the slammed door. I cannot declare myself to agree with this ending. Who knows whether the beast shall not be resurrected. Or whether a loving God is not watching mankind as it sinks down. With a surveillance system from Videofied, alarm technology with no false alarms. Then all worldly and superhuman belief systems would still have meaning for God, for whom they serve as entertainment. A couple of sentences earlier, it says: "Death hides no secret. It opens no door. It is the end of a person. What survives is what he or she has given to other people, what stays in their memory." I could start from there. I write down what has remained of Father in my memory. Elias sneaks out quietly when it comes to the question of the soul.

Cheerful Rhenish natures do not fear death. Only melancholy behind the carnival mask. To take death along on board. Exemplary. To also swing by to see the Church Fathers. The eternal struggle between Plato and Aristotle. And us as merely the commentators on their commentators. If you want to leave it like that now, I'll send it to God. It ought to be cleaned up in Catholic fashion. The death of your father ought not to be the last word.

A beautiful day. Shortly after landing, the message from Brother, Father died at 1:14 p.m. Father preempted me. What's that supposed to mean. Death preempted him. Fortunately, he was a believer. The belief of the dead is a consolation to the living. I now wish to investigate whether there's a soul for the rest of my life. Some time after my mother's death, I thought I'd managed to make contact with her. I wasn't sure if this contact had been only in a dream, all attempts to dream this dream a second time remained fruitless. In the dream, if it was only a dream, Mother came to the agreed-upon place at the agreed-upon time: a café in Cologne. She wore a gray suit and was really quite taciturn. Throughout the whole meeting, I wasn't able to tease out what made her appear so reserved; there seemed to be a score in need of settling. Her reserve made her noble, no trace of depression still clung to her. I soon realized that the answers she was giving were not answers to the questions I was asking her.

A bare room. Yellow bedding. Father lying upon the corpsestraw. The institutional-typical deathfashion. A crew-necked patientgown.

Gray and blue diamonds in strings and rows on white cotton. The extubated mouth open wide.

It is not resurrection that is a comfort, but the notion of resurrection. I see the empty body through the wide-gaping mouth. Death is a "Totraumvergrößerer," a breathing-exercise device one calls a "dead-space-enlarger" in German. Is Father now a moment of God and entering into God's relationship with himself? God's memory knows no bounds. It is only the past, however, that is eternal. Father is the past that shall not pass.

The question is where you are now. You are in the question. You shall be resurrected when I project you outward once more, when my eyes hurl you against the wall once more—like they did when I began to willfully hallucinate.

That the dead person has the audacity to leave us alone with the life that he set into the world for and with us.

Died in this room. Thus do I order my father, "Rise, take up thy bed, and walk." And immediately Father is made whole, and takes up his bed and walks. Now, I shall touch you. Keep composure. Pray. Watchwords. Father cried one single time in my presence. But I really do love you, is what he said, there's no need for you to look for any other father. Did he think that I was gay because I worked with a gay bookseller? Hypocritical. The curtain drawn. A washbasin. Years ago, I burned a stack of testimonials in the washbasin of my room under my parents' roof. When the fire threatened to spread to the curtains, I turned on the tap, which remained silent. I opened the window and hurled out the burning jumble. Mother was standing in the garden in the meadow and conversing with her visitors. Then the ashparticles blew past, followed by the flambéed remains. In broad daylight, my mother said. I only just managed to keep the curtain from burning, I called out, sitting in the windowframe. Then this was a terrific success, the visitor said. Everything burned up beautifully. I turn on the tap, water rushes into the sink, and gurgles down the drain. What would happen if I were to pour a beakerful of water into Father's open mouth? Would he come back to his senses once more; would the water trickle away into the body? What if I were to lean down to him so far that my raincoat made contact with his mouth, would his mouth catch hold of part of the jacket by way of his jaws suddenly snapping shut and suck it all the way into his gullet? Should I not violently force his mouth shut? Father is not to be heaved out of bed and laid onto a heap of corpse-straw so that he might be burned thereafter. Rigor mortis prevents the closing of the mouth, binding up the jaw with cloth would not be possible. I take off my rainjacket. Father, beloved Father. No text wishes to arise. You were a good father. That's what I think, but I don't quite believe it, so I don't say it. Now, you've really done it. That's for sure. One can see that. But done what. Isn't he the one who's done for. The urologist did him in. The one who wanted to have a closer look at the prostate and bladder, which were blamed for the blood in the urine. The prostate and bladder are now completely fine. Beloved Father, I shall always think of you. How could it be otherwise. Oh God, how embarrassing that nothing more occurs to me now. I am embarrassed before a dead man.

What if Father now ate the deathshroud. Or consumed himself. Perishing would begin in every direction. My father a Nachzehrer who follows his relatives? If one were to exhume him, would one find the shroud sucked into his mouth up to the third button? From the mouths of how many dead would one have to tug the deathshroud to keep the world from dying? From head to foot to head all round the bed. The hand as dead chicken. "The body grew swollen with great turgidity and a foul miasma followed, potent and cursed. The mouth was not sealed shut immediately upon death and remained open. Thus it was that the mouth had need of being wrapped in a linen shawl, before the body was laid within the coffin." History repeats itself. However good death rituals are, they diminish introspection in the face of the dead, to, in thinking of the dead, think *that's a wrong thought* is irreparable. To not be able to distinguish genuine thoughts from non-genuine in the room of the dead is irreparable. To ask oneself: is what I'm feeling now sadness.

Ought I to bite off the big toe of your right foot so that you don't come back? To say to you that you have gone away? "Father, you have gone away." How hollow the room sounds. Ought I to drill a hole in the wall to give you an exit? Will I catch death if I touch Father? My tears ought not to fall upon him, for, if they do, he shall not rest in peace. When shall we have remained at the bedside for long enough? It shall only have been long enough once the body has entirely decomposed. But the longer one remains, the rosier Father's visage and the more mobile his eyes, mouth, ears, nose, and hand.

Hurry up, say something. Only the dead man is *in order*. I shall wear your gold ring. I always thought it was perfect. The blue stone is poorly set, it is missing about half a millimeter on one side. For me, it has always been a ring of power and your proxy.

I have clearer memories of the things around you than of you. In your bedroom stood a chest of drawers of veneered wood, in it was mainly white underwear distributed neatly across many compartments. You never had any black underwear in all your life. The drawers could be pulled out rather far without falling out. Finerib. Mighty underwear. Always a few sizes too big. On the chest of drawers stood a small gilded chest made of wood. Beyond your golden ring, an inconspicuous ivory figure was to be found in there, it one day told me it was the household spirit. The chest smelled of the old days, the odor formed the most improbable things that were meant to have once laid in it. A scrawny red bird with green eyes, struck by lightning as it took flight, head held high. The little bird was burned up on the inside and began to shine all the more beautifully. It has now become an arrow, a rigid gesture. If I thought of the little bird, I was immediately tormented by the notion that I would have to always crouch down from then on, as walking upright attracts lightning. In the odor of the small chest, a strange beast also arose, it was half lion and half bird of prey. It had the head, beast, wings, and claws of the bird, but the body, hind legs, and tail of the lion. You're evil, Mother would sometimes say, you're going to be put into the chest. One day I said to her that I was already inside of it. She no longer dared to open the chest. The animal pictured in a magazine, that's what's in the chest, I said to Mother, but darling, she said, that's Jesus Christ, the mightiest beast that we have, it also protects our house. Since then, she has been able to open the chest again. And it turned out that I was right, in a book, Byzantine tradition, I later read about two flying griffins that were interpreted to be Mary and Michael, they stand beside God's throne and temper his wrath. The griffin also tempered your wrath. Once I'd grown up, Mother said, the chest is not a chest, but a little box and this little box has a little key, with it, she shall now close the box. The search for the key was the meaning of my life.

You were never greedy. The gold in your mouth remained hidden from even yourself most of the time, and others did not see it either. You were your own gold-guard. Perhaps, the griffin is my revenant during my lifetime. And I am your revenant during your lifetime. Now that you are dead, you have perhaps become your own revenant. Will you call out to me if I bend down toward you? That's how I often observed you as a child during your midday nap when I lay next to you on Mother's half of the bed, and Mother was happy not to see me for an hour or two, take him with you, she said, he's a nuisance to me. You always snored. Then your snoring would skip and your mouth would snap shut like that of a dangerous animal. This time, you do not snore, your mouth and your gullet are entirely dry, I can observe each and every one of your teeth without having to be afraid of you waking up. Golden arches all along the gums, golden fillings, bridges. And yet, I imagine that this is precisely what you shall do at any given moment, wake up, look at me, become a dangerous beast. Would you then begin chewing on your shroud or gnawing at your arm in which the water had stagnated? Do I not hear you chewing? You are a Nachzehrer who turns me into one of the undead. They renounced the possibility of closing your mouth, as the rigidity of your muscles made it such that your jaw would have to be broken.

The eyes are shut. The upper body is exposed, your mouth does not come into contact with the shroud, one ought to lay it onto your face. I lay it onto your face.

Seven years ago, Father shared a bed with a dying woman, his second wife. The second wife was suffering from blood cancer and, once it came down to it, could eat only astronaut food. She already had waxen skin just before she died. He sees it, she would say to my father when I would look at her. What does he see, my father would ask. He sees it, she would say. She was shrunken. Her body reminded me of a sun-dented chocolate figurine. I was fascinated and repelled simultaneously. How can you lie next to her all night long, was what I always wanted to ask Father. It's going quite well, he would say, it's *her* bed. An IV flowing into her right arm. If she had to go to the bathroom at night, Father would follow her with the IV bag hanging from its gallows. After some weeks, partial mobility turned into strict confinement to the bed. From then on, she spoke of her beast in bed. Nobody had yet spoken of dying, I could clearly see it, and perhaps this "it" was the unpronounceable death, I saw it and couldn't imagine that the waxen skin would be able to turn back into the life-skin that holds us together. The fact that one actually goes through all that in the first place and doesn't just kill oneself immediately. Beastly the notion that, one day, it might no longer be possible to kill oneself because the body is too weak and no means are available to hasten its vanishing. Euthanasia ought to be taught in elementary school. There ought to be euthanasia conventions all over the place. Euthanasia operaballs. Euthanasia religiouswars. At night, I hear dripping into the sink, she said. Then I ask your father to get up and turn the tap shut more tightly. Your father gets up like a gentleman each time I do, he goes into the bathroom and turns the tap tight. I hear it continue to drip. Now, it really is tight, your father says and lies back down in bed. I haven't yet precisely figured out where the dripping is, only if I concentrate hard on the dripping can I fall asleep. Before his stroke, Father always had headaches, but they were never so bad that he thought to go to the doctor. Insomnia was his faithful companion. One night, the headpains were so unbearable that he got out of bed like a ghost, like a ghost in the darkness, he said, he groped around a bit, wasn't able to find the lightswitch, then fell over next to the bed. In the morning, he woke up lying in bed once more, his head had bled, he sat up and didn't have to think long about what had happened the night before. At the hospital, his head was X-rayed and the stroke was discovered, a lightning-like trickle one could recognize in the images. These images were found when clearing out the apartment. He also survived thyroid cancer. I look for the small scar below his larynx, but don't find it or don't see it. Bidding farewell is such a violently tense situation, perhaps I'm overlooking something, a bulging or discolored spot on the neck, why am I so interested in the details of all this, I'm afraid of ending up like this too, ending up how? I get all that which my father got, not to mention all that which my mother got, thus does my bidding farewell only serve the taking stock of my own situation, family history is suddenly a single network of glaucoma, Parkinson's disease, colon and thyroid cancer, cardiac insufficiency, hypertension, dementia. I also don't see well at all, hear badly, flatulence points unequivocally to colon cancer, until we meet again, Father, what would Mother have said at the sight of you, Mother always pointed out qualities that she had perceived in you or supposedly perceived in you so as to distract from herself, her slow but steady wasting away, take care, beloved Father, also such a stupid thought, wherefore *beloved Father* and where is he going to take care? One of the sentences that must certainly not be thought here is "I've gotta go now," why must I go now, where is it one is meant to go, as soon as the thought has been suppressed, it has been thought, I don't mean it like that, Father, I mean, you know me, he doesn't know me at all, laughable shell, in India, the dead slated for cremation sometimes fall from the wooden cart, then are picked back up and placed back onto the mode of transport. No music. Look at the clock. I'll stay another minute. Horrific. Slumped in chair in the morning after breakfast. Do you want a coffee. Yes. Can I help you. No. The last word was no.

"The next morning the learned man went out to take his coffee and read the newspapers. 'How is this?' he exclaimed, as he stood in the sunshine. 'I have lost my shadow. So it really did go away yesterday evening, and it has not returned. This is very annoying.'" That's to be read in an entirely different story. But in fairy tales, as in life, the shadow returns and the Shadow becomes the Lord and the Lord becomes the Schatten. The shadow left my father and my father became the Schatten.

In the nursing home in which he was temporarily quartered, acute word-finding difficulties. At least the word *shit* always tripped right off of his tongue. Generalized mirth. To which Father said it's shit that he can't find words anymore. Then we were all relieved that he had found these words. I imagined that, at a certain point, the brain only allows one to speak of things that are no longer there. Father suddenly took a liking to being fed, the dry nursing-home chocolate cake could barely be balanced on the fork, Father snapped at the crumbs, which then disappeared safely into his mouth. He acknowledged these nibbles with a sole "delicious." He still had that appreciative gesture that had characterized him for decades: when he afforded significance to things, happenings, or people by abruptly throwing his head back and barking out a "ha-ha" with his mouth wide open, sometimes just whispering. The nod that his head here produced, as if a spring had been released in his neck, applied to himself, it meant showing the world to his children, his wife, his other relatives, friends, acquaintances, and strangers—thus did he bring it into being for the very first time.

Fortunately, Father has always been a believer. He actually still is a believer, after all, he's not dead yet. The dead man had been a believer. The dead man? When Father was still not yet dead, he was a believer. Which is to say: as one who lived. As one who lived, Father was a believer. Is the circumstance of having been a believer preserved for all time in death? Faithful out beyond life? Perhaps a question of eschatological positioning. Whatever you do, consider your end. And then? This to and fro, this body-and-soul-catch-me shall yield not a single iota of insight more than this statement: When Father still lived, he was still not dead.

The notion of taking Father back to his apartment, to lay him out there, to let him become one with the apartment, apartment as grave. To die at home and the house, the apartment, would become a mausoleum, habitable only by the dead man who could always be found there. I cannot part with you, but your body shall remove its gaze from me. Until we meet again, beloved Father, you were and shall always be my Deus absconditus, he who hides his face, my Schattenfroh who is absently ever present.

Father is said to have said something else to the nurse. How could he have done that right before death without being able to move his jaw? The nurse cannot recall. So, who said that he said something else to the nurse? The nurse, the orderly says. So, what did he say to her? The orderly doesn't know. He's no longer quite so certain as to which nurse is said to have spoken with Father. It was a young one, a very young one. So, not the nurse who was just asked and can no longer remember. No, a very young one. A very young nurse appears in the hallway. She shakes her head. I've not yet had any dealings with the man who passed away today. If no nurse wishes to recall what Father's last words were, the internist must now be put through the wringer, his policy of too-early discharge—and this in the case of a patient with private insurance—caused the blood poisoning to turn into a death sentence. We sit in the corridor on two black hard-shell chairs. The internist doesn't come. A few white-coated employees file past and vanish into the rooms of the ward after greeting us.

Dead. Can one maneuver oneself into it prior to certainty? It's not to do with learning to die, dying is a one-off process that only comes to pass a single time; it's much more to do with the calm clarity of consciousness, to run toward a field into which one sinks silently, and thus is life not at all a circuitous approach to this field, of which we can only know where it lies quite suddenly, and we always go toward it. But, of course it's not that, that which is always only here, not there, as is hopefully not so with life, the place where thinking and speech really do wish to go, to cross over, instead, both only find the present and thus does the talk of a field swing into the remembered strolls with Father by the Honighecke, in the Eifel, right straight through the forest. The imaginary, on the other hand, remains totally dry, distills nothing that would finally end all comparisons, all familiar images, when we speak of dying, of death, there is no language of the transitory, it merely grows even darker where it was once lighter, it becomes wider and deeper where it was narrow and finite, we are compelled to mentally distinguish the hereafter from this mortal coil, the hereafter does not send us its words to think the hereafter out of the hereafter.

The hereafter is empty. Only Father is there. And Father is also empty. He is the now that comes before the hereafter, the border past which nothing begins, which certainly has to do with this language.

Don't we wish to take it back—that which we hurled into the heavens on our knees? But by what right, apart from childish intractability, which does not wish to perceive that a kind and heavenly father must dwell above the starry canopy, the earthly one is already enough.

My brother is smoking. It's raining. The taxi is coming. In the taxi, it smells of smoke, thus is my brother smoking once again. Could the window perhaps be opened. Of course. Could you please stop, I ask the taxi driver. Yeah, course I can. But why? Could you drive back there, please? My brother doesn't want to go back, he's looked at Father for long enough. I've studied his face, my brother says. I really would like to go back, I'd like to ask the urologist something else. I don't think that's such a good idea, my brother says. The taxi driver looks at me through the rearview mirror. He shrugs his shoulders. I look out the window. My brother took Father in two years ago and took care of him. You told me to tell him to keep well away from you. Who? The urologist. The urologist should count his blessings that he didn't cross paths with me. Well, OK, then there's no problem. But I would really like to ask him why he released Father a day too early. He'll just spin some tale. The taxi driver asks whether he ought to go back. Yes, I say. Under no circumstances, my brother says. We continue on our way.

Is it important where we die? Under no circumstances in a hospital. What would we do if we already knew what everything was leading to? Would we think up feints as to how to cheat fate? Assuming we opted to faithfully follow the mapped-out and no longer remotely secret way with all of its consequences, what if *this* way were to deviate from THE way. Could we then hope for a complaints office that would regulate such an unreasonable deviation from the regulatory rules accepted as its own? Also assuming that such a complaints office existed, would we seek it out in the case of such a deregulation and demand the reinstatement of the teleological constraints that had been promised to us? Supposing that we didn't pay a visit to this authority, despite the fact that this visit was necessary, ought this case to have been regulated before it had come to pass? It might be of the greatest possible appeal should the consequences of not reporting the deregulation described be open-ended, thus could everyone imagine *their own*, though nobody could prepare for anything. For our whole lives, we would hope for a single off-path event, the reporting of which we would do our very best to avoid. I say goodbye to my brother under the pretext that I have to catch an earlier train. My brother suggests seeking out the pub where he last sat with Father before Father could no longer leave the apartment. There's also no earlier train.

The notion of once more finding something of my father in that place takes hold of me. In cities that are smaller than Berlin, Hamburg, Munich, or Cologne live underdeveloped people. I must also test this thought out at Father's final place. The supermarkets offer only rejects, the people squat dully in pubs, have listless cow-faces, smoke incessantly and down one beer after another, schnapps, schnapps, schnapps. Their clothing is of tear-inducing shabbiness, vanishing colors such as brown and gray dominate. The suicide rates in these places must be the highest in Germany. Wrinkled faces that, for decades, have only moved between their apartment, their preferred fitness mortuary, and the discount store, they drag their plastic bags over the sidewalk. Pedestrian zone, sidewalk. German road-construction guidelines with their general cost accounting, general technical regulations, recommendations, notes, manuals, guidelines, technical delivery conditions, technical test regulations, and further technical test regulations are unique in the world. Each citizen should have to know these road-construction guidelines—which anticipate every eventuality—by heart, otherwise he should not be allowed to use the sidewalk. For this purpose, a separate office is to be set up in each town of more than 5,000 inhabitants and in each district of a larger city; these offices shall administer the examination. A citizen who fails the exam is permitted to take it a second time. Between the first and second tests, the citizen is not to step foot onto the sidewalk. In this way, he gets a foretaste of what it would mean to be deprived of the right to use the sidewalk. Those citizens deprived of the pedestrian zones would have no choice but to remain in their houses. An exception could only be made for going to the doctor. However, the granting of an exception depends on the capacities of the medical practices and hospitals that have, at long last, been afforded some relief by this measure. Over time, the streets become emptier. A pleasant feeling begins to spread, that of belonging to a civic elite that concentrates all of its energy on the civic questions governing public life. On what are the disenfranchised to live? How are they to earn their money? Those are good questions. A good solution shall have to be worked out. Cigarette smoke billows fitfully out of a pub. The sauce-brown carpeting swallows each stride. Early pensioners, early retirees, the mother-abused, and professional failures fill the tables. They greet each other in friendly, distanced fashion, then show themselves to be unabashedly curious. They recognize each other instinctively, shout watchwords at one another, embrace each other in a way that ought to drain the whole of their energy for the day, were it not for the genuine joy of recognition, for themselves, they are heroes whose daily life is tantamount to the overcoming of a war, and this hypertensive life actually is war, only one turned inward, a struggle with the inner wrecking ball, which oscillates irregularly and beats against the heart, then the eyes overflow, saliva leaves the mouth, a roaring laugh follows, their special sense of humor, behind which strokes, heart attacks, and liver failure all squat. His brother. Ah, OK. You can smoke in front of the door. Once the barkeeper has settled down, you can smoke inside. The camaraderie of the dishwashers and the wiper-offers who quickly form into a company when danger is imminent and a stranger is always a danger, this chumminess bestows a balance unheard of during the daytime upon these poor souls. A whole day lasts until twelve noon. Such consistency makes overconfident. It takes a shit on Obama and cheers for Putin. Also the CIA, which really takes the cake. Cakes the take. The USA doesn't know jack about torture. Waterboarding can be survived. That's Erna. Erna had an issue with her bowels once. Then she had an issue with her liver. Erna is quite thin and cannot be distinguished in her style from her pals. The people have lost their gender, it plays no more role at all, the men and women hunched alongside one another at the counter, running around in every direction, they've *met in the middle.* An ideal circumstance, if it weren't for a penchant for frivolity that can hardly be contained in reality any longer, the men belch it forth from themselves and the women nod deafly. A not-insignificant part of the local congregation holds their heads very rigidly, in the sure presentiment that the slightest movement would sweep them off their chairs. That gives their unwavering gaze upon me a certain soil-rootedness, legitimacy, a sovereignty that neither gaze nor words can oppose. Erna sits at the slot machine, to which she seems to pay no attention. She gets up, paces about, sits down once more. With her right hand, she covers over the central turntable. She looks, she doesn't look. Perhaps, she is leaning entirely onto the machine's glass front. No agitated flashes, no alarm. The money trickles away. Erna accepts this with equanimity. I hold her gaze for too long. She takes her hand off the slot machine and comes over to my table with brisk stride. I know you. Your brother told me something once. OK, what was it? Nothing in particular. And you already know me. Yes, it's not too difficult. As in, it's easy to know somebody. I already know your brother. At which point all the rest is revealed? It's one and the same family, after all. And thus does the conversation take its course. The machine calls Erna back to it. Coins fall into the chute. Erna takes her money with the same equanimity with which she got over its disappearance. She comes back to the table immediately. Zero sum, she says. Didn't win anything? Won same as I lost. And vice versa. Precisely, and vice versa. And what does that mean for you now? I'll glug down the rest. She takes a seat. The barkeeper puts a Kölsch down in front of her. I don't drink Kölsch, I only drink Alt. There's no Alt here. OK, then I'll drink a Kölsch. It's grown dark outside. Rain is marching in. *Hell in the Hürtgenwald* occurs to me. I must still have this book somewhere. Actually, what's happening with Father's library? How might the books smell? Do they smell of smoke? *Hell Hürtgenwald* sounds better. I must certainly have another look at this book.

The military cemetery above Daliwaram Trappist Monastery. Fantastic view. The gray stone makes everyone equal. Honorary cemetery Daliwaram Abbey. Also women and girls amongst the dead. I envied the dead their beautiful spot. To see Daliwaram—then to die. Thus lined up, in rank and file, bloomed over in the summer and under a mantle of snow in the winter, the wind whistles past the graves, thus does one not even remotely wish to get back up, but to stare at the heavens. Longing for the enemy? Envious of a few sparsely lined-up wargraves? Suicide at the wargravescemetery. Wargrave desecrated out of envy for the dead. Dug the grave up and lay oneself down in the dead man's place. Wished to smell 1944. In memory of his father, showed himself at Daliwaramtrappistmonastery Wargravescemetery. It really is astounding how far one can go in one's own head and what one can see. I stand in the honorcemetery of Daliwaram Abbey and read the names:

Unknown Soldier
Unknown Soldier
Unknown Soldier

Upon another archaic gravestone, one reads:

Nobody.

I'm so sad, I must go home and have myself nailed to the cross in Vossenack, Christ proffers his hand to anybody who would go up in his stead. I want to be nailed to this cross or that cross and taken on it to my grave. I am Verlautenheide, I am Vossenack. Today, I would also offer the sharpshooter a second chance had he missed me, the flamingo, standing in the middle of a narrow, cobbled road in the Hürtgenwald some seventy years ago, missed me with his deadly Hornisse on the first shot, I too would have at least the respect for the enemy's war-method necessary to let him go for it a second time, only he ought not to miss my kneecaps by inches, going end-on-end, but blow my head off in perfect form. It is so easy to turn the Second World War into a comic that one doesn't laugh at. It's a mere matter of translation that makes the chariot rope ignite. The passage about the Iron Maiden is usable, as it describes that its purpose was, "to put a criminal inside and then close the doors slowly. There were two special spikes where his eyes would be. There was a drain in the bottom to let out all the blood." Where the eyes shall be shall be no more light. Iron Maiden, a Nuremberg device for slaughtering. Maidenkiss and off into the flow. Whether the real Iron Maiden was "a medieval torture instrument," only the Middle Ages know, but they reveal it to nobody. What's the bloodgutter, then? It is "the bloodgutter in the side of the blade of a sword or bayonet." One can learn so much by reading. Fiction and faction lie so close to one another, no room for another page between their two covers. I was there, I hiked the bloodgutter. It's been washed away by the centuries—and was well-filled with blood on my birthday. This path was previously known as Little Beef River, it was here that the manure from the cattle flowed off.

Erna has turned back to her machine. I sit down next to her at a free device. The lighting conditions allow me to observe her in its reflective glass. But there's not much to observe. She appears completely indifferent to that which is happening. One cannot read from her features whether she has won or lost. I can also observe myself in the glass of the device. I practice Father's aspect. Narcissus on the deathbed. I tilt my head back, my mouth is open. My cheeks are sunken, the bones protrude. The nostrils are tunnels into the Kingdom of the Dead, my eyes belong to another who is observing me from their sockets. My eyes are Father's eyes. You gotta give it another shot, Erna says. She's now found her rhythm. If the machine demands money, she orders a Kölsch and sticks in the change. She does this six days a week, my brother says. Nobody precisely knows what she does on the seventh day. It's rumored that she has a one-day job. Others claim that she strives not to gamble or drink for one day a week. Some, on the other hand, hold that to be not even remotely likely, Erna is probably at home, sitting in front of the TV, and drinking. She is close friends with an old man of some sixty years old, George, who also comes here regularly, and it is also said that he has been to her house several times. This is inhabitual insofar as most of the people here let their dwellings go to pot for whatever reason. Some out of the conviction that their dwelling isn't neglected in the slightest, even if they don't know how to spell "tidy up." Writing, by the way, is an entirely separate issue. They get caught up in their mistakes and never move on. Others regularly finish off their nights at home, usually with harder spirits that they avoid at the pub or, if they do drink them, then in so-called "civilized quantities," which is to say a maximum of five glasses. After a bottle of schnapps, not much remains of the living room, the next day, there is only enough time to set the table and chairs upright, the tea is getting cold again, the crispbread can be eaten on the way, it's 3:00 p.m. at the latest when the visit to the pub, interrupted during the night, is resumed. Erna swears to never allow it to come to such a repetition again. To whom does she swear that? She swears it to God in the hopes that God will not hear. And Erna hopes that it wasn't she who swore to God (who better not have heard) that she would never visit the pub again. Today, she knows nobody here. The barkeeper ought to keep George off her back. But Erna, I mean, what's the matter, it's George. It's George, exactly right, and George should sit down at his table like a good boy, end of story. How is that the "end of story"? It's simply the end, the end. There are precisely five people in the room, not counting the barkeeper. Erna holds all of them in her gaze and all of them hold Erna in their gaze. I also hold all of them in my gaze and nobody holds me in their gaze. Erna sits before the slot machine and doesn't play. The barkeeper asks what she'd like to drink, but she doesn't know. But that's not how it is. Erna has already been playing for two hours and has drunk a lot, I've not been counting. The light is already autumnal, I cannot distinguish whether it's the daylight or the light in the bar that's causing this impression, perhaps it's bright as day outside, here, however, in this room, the walls are suddenly light brown with reddish transitions, some individual leaves also have tar spots and leaf necrosis, tar stains are spreading everywhere, I've already gone over these changes with a big eraser, there's rubbish lying everywhere, in it, I read the word "emendation." Emending: improving, correcting; to correct a text handed over in incorrect or incomplete form. However, the incorrect or incomplete text handed over is life. A door opens up in the wall, for a short while, a passage can be seen. There are pebbles lying on the ground, I love the word "gravel," then a little man by the name of Lindhorst hurries over, he is wearing a wide damask nightgown, glittering in red and yellow, and, with white-gloved hands, gives me Novalis, but only the *Teplitzer Fragmente* and I read Teplitzer Fragment 15: "Concept of philology—sense for the life and the individuality of a mass of letters. Soothsayer from ciphers—*augur of letters*. A restorer. His science adopts much from the *material tropics*. The physicist, the historian, the artist, the critic etc. all belong to the same class. / The way from the particulars to the whole—from seeming to truth, *et sic porro*. Everything involves the art and science of getting from the one to the other—and so from the One to the All—rhapsodically or systematically—the spiritual art of travel—the art of divination."

My brother is leaving. I'm going home now, says my brother. Erna gives me a blank look. I pay and follow my brother outside. Erna turns back to the machine. That's her friend, my brother says. Who's her friend. That box there. It's raining outside. It's the rain of childhood, I say. My brother has ordered a taxi, he offers to take me to the train station. It's a hop, skip, and a jump, I say, I'd rather go on foot.

Father was never affectionate. My brother and I are also not. At least, we weren't. Or rarely. Grandpa's grave has been dug up. Which Grandpa? Father's father. The eternal Eifel. Father has taken us to Grandma and Grandpa's grave at least ten times. It never rained. Yes, one time it did. Father stood before the grave and prayed, we looked around in embarrassment. Aunt Liesel died on March 13, 2014, five months and a week before Father, at the age of almost 103, Grandpa's second wife. She survived Grandpa by forty-five years, five months, and thirteen days. Father survived Mother by sixteen years to the day. Grandpa survived his first wife by eight years, four months, and seventeen days. We'd already said the machine ought to be shut off, I tell my brother. Yes, and . . . ? He did die on the same day as Mother. If we had wanted it, he wouldn't have died on the same day as Mother. So, you mean to say that he didn't pick that date himself. Precisely—he didn't. But, now, he has died on the very same day and this has a symbolic effect. August 20 shall always be dark.

My brother gets into the taxi. A short salutation. It's less than five hundred meters to the train station. The sidewalk is lined with smoking and beer-drinking men upon whose faces is writ large that they checked out long ago. Their pants dangle about their legs, most of them wear sweaters despite the warm temperature, a certain kind of protection against the possible chill of night. One passes through an olfactory field of smoke, dirty laundry, and acrid bodily reeks, a skunk-technique that keeps one at a distance. If there is no dispute, the men speak from a single mouth. They carefully look after their worn-out plastic bags, rearrange the full and empty beer bottles, collect tobacco residues in their coat and jacket pockets. With expansive gestures, they tell of that which has befallen them, that which they didn't deserve. The men's gestural exertion and their alcohol consumption form communicating vessels. They are the lords of the street. As they have no more to lose, they look at one with a sense of challenge. At least that's what I read in their gaze. In fact, they've not yet lost everything. They still have the clothes on their backs, the full and empty beer bottles in their bags, they sort them ever anew, the empty bottles down below, the full ones on top; then the full bottles are too heavy and threaten to fall out of the bags and onto the street, thus are the bags emptied entirely, then the bottles standing on the street are heaved back into them, full ones first. The equal distribution of the full and empty bottles has the advantage of causing the same weight to be borne on the right and left, however, if one wishes to open a new bottle, it is only with great difficulty that one can extract it from the bag. It is for this reason that some men have divided the bottles and still occasionally look for full ones in the bags of empties, for they have forgotten their ordering principle over time. It would be the same for anyone. Opened bottles find their way into jacket or coat pockets none too rarely, which is convenient and protects against larceny far better than if they were left standing on the street. This does not, however, prevent them from being forgotten there. The alcoholic seeks to neutralize the fact of having to maintain the so-called level by talking loudly. Much later, once words are lacking—and they often lack—the gesture comes into play. The gesture can be countered by a richness of other gestures, it is at least as powerful as the word. For the facts of the matter that are "everything," which signifies the whole, one must reach back very far. So far that one finds oneself back out on the street. Nothing in the faces of the men signifies an impending catastrophe. I cross the street and watch the men, imagining what it is they've done in their lives to bring them here now, amongst themselves, brought together by homelessness and alcohol. Then one of the men points to another man's mouth and shouts, "open your mouth, I'm gonna show you, that's Jesus and those are the thieves, that's you, you've got yourself in your mouth." The other willingly allows him to gawp at his teeth. Now, they're both pointing at each other's teeth, "He's got me in his mouth," says one, then the other: "One lil' punch, then you're out." "So, what's his name," the one asks, pointing to a tooth in the other's mouth. "His name is Moll," he says. "Nah, he's Gestas," the other says. "If it falls out or you swallow it, you're orphaned," the other says once more. "A fire has been raging in your mouth," the one says, to which the man addressed replies, "a fire shall soon rage in your mouth." Nobody wants to have Gestas in their mouth. "Who's that?" the one asks. "The one hanging to the left of the crucified one." "But they were all crucified." "And the important one was Jesus." "One was good and the other evil." "The one on the right." "The one on the left." "The one on the right." "The one on the left." "The evil one." "The one on the left." "The one on the right." "The good one." "The evil one."

Then, at that moment, one of the men is carrying the other over a deep gorge. He could easily manage this—he seems to be strong enough, the man he carries lies comfortably over his shoulder—if the rockface he's just stepped onto, directly opposite, had not immediately risen steeper than the man can effortlessly scale with the shouldered, seemingly unconscious other man. It cannot be determined from here whether the exertion that it costs the man to scale the rockface is due to its relatively large angle of ascent or the word "scale," this, after all, means nothing more than to climb with great difficulty. A third man is also looking on while, simultaneously, a fourth man, who is initially mistaken for a woman, hits a fifth man with a stick-blow or stabbing-weapon, laying him out onto the ground. A saber falls from the right hand of the one hit by the stick or the stabbing-weapon and, as this saber, which shall never make contact with the ground, falls out of his hand, it can be seen that the other man, who is laying him out onto the ground, is also wielding a saber. What has remained unobserved up until this point is that a sixth man has been lying face-down on the ground for a long time. Either this man was struck down or even done away with a few moments ago by the man who was tipping backward or by the man who was so ably wielding the saber. I operate on the assumption that he was done away with and, indeed, with the knife that can easily be recognized during its incessant slashing motion, with the saber held in his right hand. I am less concerned by the escalating situation than by the circumstance that nobody but me finds it to be of concern, nobody reacts with outrage, all seem to accept this escalation.

This calms me a bit and gives me the opportunity to have a more thorough look at the men's clothing. The men all wear the same shoes. The men standing around, not engaged in what is coming to pass, also wear the same ankle-high boots, into the legs of which they have tucked their pants. One or more leather leather straps wrapped around the bootlegs are responsible for the closing of the boots.

Something has fallen down into the gorge. I move along its upper edge on all fours and gaze upon a bed in the valley, a bed in which a man with Bismarck's aspect lies. It is not Bismarck, in any case not Otto von Bismarck, but rather General Friedrich Theodor Alexander Graf von Bismarck-Bohlen—one can tell by the sideburns. The man's baldness is much like my grandfather's. The bed stands with its foot-end in the thinly flowing brook of the valley-floor. The head-end stands upon scree. Bismarck-Bohlen is wearing pajamas or a nightgown, an over-dimensioned shirt-collar lies upon his belly, the bedspread is emblazoned with blossoms, daisies, which represent naturalness and truth and promise pure, unadulterated, genuine happiness. The well-spoken Bismarck-Bohlen keeps silent. The rhetorical figures upon his bedspread shall dry up. The bedframe is unadorned. Even with binoculars, it is not possible to see whether they are made from wood, metal, rattan, or some mixture of those materials. The sleeping Bismarck-Bohlen leans against the raised pillow, which is pinioned against the high headboard. To stabilize the head and back, stiffened padding is placed between headboard and pillow. It doesn't seem to have originally belonged to the bed. Head- and footboard are crowned with lathe-turned spheres. If the bedframe is made out of metal, the spheres are, in all probability, also made of metal. No pilaster with capital flanks the outside of the high foot-end. I would like to be able to look into Bismarck-Bohlen's face. The notion of having to move some two meters to the left in order to accomplish this provokes a kind of paralysis. I suddenly think of my sister, who told me of a visit to the opera some years ago. About twenty minutes after the beginning of the performance, an elderly gentleman wished to take his seat, which was to be found in their row, directly on the parapet of the upper tier. She got up from her seat, let the man pass by, but could no longer sit down in her own seat. In one fell swoop, she was seized by a dizziness that made all motion impossible.

An image is now projected onto the center of the outer side of the footboard, where there may once have been a flat cut carving. What is to be seen is two young lads who have stuck their heads into the crooks of their arms, which rest upon a table in such a way that only the backs of their heads can be seen. The heads of both boys lie in the crooks of their left arms, the lad on the left has also laid his bent right arm onto the table. He is wearing a sailor suit, the lad on the right is wearing a white shirt and a beige jacket over it. The lad on the right has short-shorn dark-blonde hair and the one next to him has long black hair, which is parted in the middle. Both are afflicted by alopecia areata, which has already exposed the back of the lad with the short-shorn hair's head. The upper back of the other lad's head is also affected, thus is it to be expected that both of their heads shall eventually be eaten empty and the deforestation shall spread to the rest of the body. I imagine staring at the image until both lads have disappeared from the outer-side of the foot-end. Don't give up, I call down into the gorge. Bismarck-Bohlen raises his right arm and waves. He fits the enormous shirt collar onto his head, then falls asleep once more, now as a nun. The image of the two lads flickers for a while, then stabilizes itself. A man in tails and tophat approaches Bismarck-Bohlen, who is lying in the bed, from the left. With each stride, the projection of the two lads fades a bit more. As they gaze upon the man, they pull their bodies out of the mattress, clamber through the footboard, then take flight. Rushing forward, they grow ever smaller until they have entirely vanished around a red-shaded riverbend. The man in tails and tophat greets Bismarck-Bohlen, who has only to look at him to remember that he has encountered my father before. Meanwhile, Saturn is hanging quite stable in the sky, its ring-spokes and the various color-belts of its surface are easy to see. Observing Saturn, I discover a transparent glass oil lamp standing on three legs, at its base, a book can be seen. I think I've read this book. Did you hear that, somebody just said, I think I've read this book. That was you, there's nobody here other than you. And who just said "that was you"? The flame of the lamp burns so bright that dense soot rises up toward the mountains. Snow lies upon the mountains. I see my mother skiing down its pistes.

A wind begins to stir. I have great difficulty attempting to cling to the edge of the gorge, so I lie down flat on the ground. Never-before-seen insects bustle soothingly up here. Unfazed by people or weather, they go about their business. An ant is taken away, a beetle is in a hurry. Is it searching for sustenance or does it not wish to be eaten? A stone rolls toward the slope, tumbles down it. The impact follows promptly, as if the gorge had no depth. Birdsong. Something shoves me from behind, I want to get up, then I realize that I myself have become this stone on my way into the valley. For years, my father kept his gallstones in his nightstand. Why is it that people cannot part with the things that were once them? The complete set of milk teeth in a red box that lies in a small chest. Father's false teeth, loose next to the gallstone sack. One day, Aunt Friederike forgot her upper row of teeth in the Kukident jar, which the dachshund then knocked over, the dachshund took possession of the teeth, ran around the house and garden with them for the whole day, then choked on them during the night. After my aunt had mourned the loss of the dachshund for three days, she cleaned the teeth in said jar with double the amount of Kukident, then put them back into her mouth. Is there anybody who keeps their surgically removed tumor? Does one have a right to it? Would it always have to be refrigerated? I must take care of my father. My father lies dying. Upon my entering the valley, in which his bed stands over a river, the gorge has vanished from the picture of the landscape. It's rather warm and I do not know whether the warmth is emanating from an oil lamp that is standing some twenty meters behind me or whether the sun has enough might to heat the earth. Until recently, I could not believe that it wasn't the earth's distance from the sun that regulated the seasons, but that they depend on the inclination of the earth's axis vis-à-vis the ecliptic. Since people in Europe live far away from the equator, the seasons are very pronounced here. The earth orbits the sun at an elliptical distance. An optical illusion. Something is covered, darkened, obliterated by way of the seeing eye. The flame of the oil lamp indicates the wind has calmed. The bushes behind the head-end of the bed are bare, they must have been pruned before the onset of winter. They have many arms that stretch out toward the sky. There would be room for a beast at their center, but there is no beast to be found here. Father is wearing pajamas or a nightgown, an over-dimensioned shirt collar lies upon his belly, the bedspread is emblazoned with blossoms, daisies, which represent naturalness and truth and promise pure, unadulterated, genuine happiness. The bushes look as if the sun has dried them out. I am afraid that the oil lamp will burn my back, so hot has it suddenly become. In the pocket of my tailcoat, I find a toothbrush-cup that I wish to fill with water from the brook so as to put out the flame. The barren brook, however, does not wish to give up any water, it is quite hard and has taken on the color of rust, under my father's bed, where it springs forth, it is entirely red. With the immersion of my hand, the lamp is extinguished. The red water is quite warm. Nothing indicates that it flows from my father's body. Did my father not just raise up his right arm and wave? His lips move. There is no sign of anything dripping out of his mattress. I set my tophat into the shirt collar, Father smiles, he says there must be a receptacle for the tophat somewhere, at home, probably in the basement, one might easily put the tophat in there, the container has a kind of flap or drawer, films were also shown in this box, they showed him from much earlier, I really ought to have a look and see if I can't discover myself in there too. My father's face is made entirely of wax, I can see that very clearly, but don't dare to touch it. My father never, ever said that. But he says I am to move to the foot of the bed, for, there, I shall be able to see everything quite clearly. From the foot-end of the bed, I see him at his full length. The bedsheet can no longer be distinguished from his body. Body and bedsheet have flowed into one another. Blurred contours—and one is preoccupied with tracing those contours for a whole life long, as only sharp contours are capable of soothing. My father's beds were always plain. This one is a surprise. On the outer side of the footboard are two young lads who have stuck their heads into the crooks of their arms resting upon a table in such a way that only the backs of their heads can be seen. My brother and I. Our heads lie in the crooks of our left arms, my brother has also laid his bent right arm onto the table. He is wearing a sailor suit, I am wearing a white shirt and a beige jacket over it. I have short-shorn dark-blonde hair and my brother has long black hair, which is parted in the middle. We are both afflicted by alopecia areata, which has already exposed the back of the lad with the short-shorn hair's head. The upper back of the other lad's head is also affected, thus is it to be expected that both of their heads shall eventually be eaten empty and the deforestation shall spread to the rest of the body. Scabies. Mite damage. I recognize the table upon which we have laid our arms, the return of my elementary-school desk. The school bears bad luck in its name ("Im Pesch"). My brother has a sheet of paper concealed beneath his arms. I wish to read what he has written on the paper.

    As they gaze upon me, they pull their bodies out of the mattress, clamber through the footboard, then take flight. The table and the sheet of paper stay behind and I seize upon the latter with no hesitation. A dashed circle is drawn on the paper, an isosceles triangle fitted into it. The legs of the triangle are also dashed. In the center of the circle or triangle is again a circle. From the intersections of the triangle and the large circle, tangents go to the small circle, they are drawn as arrows. If you draw them through the small circle, the tangents meet in its middle. Downward, from left to right, the points of intersection of the triangle and the large circle are called: Pater, Filius, Spiritus, all also connected by way of the triangle's dashed legs. Their dashes are each interrupted by one or two words: "est" or "non est." The non-dashed tangents are also broken, but only by one word: "est." In the middle of the small circle stands a name that is no name: "Deus." Thus do the tangents run toward "Deus," with the sole exception being that the tangent from "Deus" runs toward "Filius": "Pater non est filius non est spiritus non est pater non est spiritus non est filius non est pater est deus est filius non est spiritus est deus." With its Trinitarian identities and non-identities, the fifteenth century was already food for thought back in elementary school. Pater est deus est filius. Father is God is Son. Thus is Father—Son, whereas it was at first said that the father is not the son. God must thus have intervened at some point thereafter so as to make Father Son and Son Father. Indeed, what would Aristotle say to this? And what does this mean for my brother and me? Are we both the father? What does "to be" mean here? Does it mean that Father is in us now? That Father hasn't died at all and it is only his body lying there?

Some two meters behind the foot of the bed stands a small sideboard with baked goods in a shell-shaped bowl upon it. The ensemble has only been here for a few moments. I assume that these things simply arose at the very moment that I mentioned them. Before I take a roll out of the bowl, I would like to corroborate this assumption with the following test: Next to my father's bed stands a receptacle made of wood. I look, there's nothing there. Thus is it not just some receptacle that stands there, but something very particular. Even when I say "something very particular," it isn't there. It is a seeing machine, a viewing machine, a peep box, or a kind of binoculars, except that, with this device, one doesn't aim into the distance, but into the darkness. This device, which widens conically toward the bottom, is possessed of two square, lens-equipped openings, through which one can look inside of it. Its bottom, just like the whole of its casing, is made of wood, a flap attached to one of its long sides can be raised, but its function is not yet entirely decipherable. The flap is open. Which allows one to gaze freely into the inside of this strange device. A wooden wall divides the visual space into two equally sized chambers. In the right chamber, a spider crouches at the bottom. It's nice that it's found a home here. I want to take a closer look at it and kneel down. My breath pushes it across the chamber. Then another spider comes out of a dark corner and carries it away. But many hundreds of other spiders can be seen by casting one's gaze through the flap. My father fell asleep forevermore while trying to look through the lenses and into the interior of the device from the bed. One must put the lenses right up close to one's eyes. The spiders inhabit the paths of both beams. Somebody flicks a lighter to life. Another brings up a stick, the other end of which is wrapped in a gasoline-soaked rag. The rag immediately catches fire. The stick with the burning rag moves toward the fuse. The fuse immediately catches fire. The fire prowls its predetermined path. The path leads to a beetle. The spiders burn wildly. That is not what I see. I carefully turn the device over and release the spider-carcasses through the flap. The device is dripping. The spiders have melted together into an amorphous mass. The stench spreads. The spider-drops gather into a trickle that moves away from me like a centipede. I can now see everything. The device shows a stony stream-landscape with snow-bedecked mountains rising up in the background. Over the stream's bed, through which hardly any water runs, a bed has been placed. An old man lies in the bed. To his left, on the ground, stands a wooden device with a flap open on the side. From the bed, from the right side as seen from the old man's perspective, there is now a distinctly visible sideboard upon which reposes a shell-shaped bowl filled with baked goods. The baked goods look like fruit. The old man raises himself up and takes a fruit with four nodules out of the bowl. He says something to me, he whispers something into my ear as he passes by, the device, however, is silent. I close my eyes and look inside of it once more. The scenes that the device shows are not repeated, but I do not know to which period that which is shown belongs. At some places, that which appears to be a film freezes, only so as to continue at a different place some seconds later. The old man offers me his hand. I go to a washbasin that is hanging in the space of a vacuum, the basin is attached to nothing but air and I wash my hands. There is a bottle of disinfectant at the edge of the basin and I pour it over my hands. The old man points to an oil lamp, he seems to wish for me to put out the lamp. Standing before the mirror, I notice that some of my teeth are missing, I immediately accept this with a shrug of the shoulders, but then displeasure stirs in me, as I've had no teeth fall out since my childhood, and I protest against the gaps. I palpate the rows of teeth with my tongue, but they are complete once more. There are dentures lying on the old man's bedside table, his upper lip is sunken. As my parents' teeth grew ever worse, they admonished me to brush my teeth multiple times per day. I lose a tooth every day, it's always the same one. To have left my wisdom teeth in my mouth was a great error, they displaced the teeth of my lower jaw, which then had to be brought back painfully into order by way of braces. The teeth work by night, reciprocally displacing one another, the left incisor loses its grip each night anew and goes overboard, the tongue shoves it away, tongue can barely wait for tooth to capitulate. Once this finally comes to pass, it's not at all the incisor that's lost, rather, it's the strong canine that's been detached from the jaw and swallowed by me. In order to prevent this in the future, I'm prescribed a kind of net, I must spread it out in my mouth each night before falling asleep. It is porous to breath, but lets not a single tooth pass. Thus can a stop be put to teeth falling out, however, the inscrutable construction of the net inflames my imagination and, each night, I recall the most fabulous of blueprints. Tonight, I am certain that it is the roof construction of the Munich Olympic Stadium that fills the space of my mouth. Already, I can feel reliable workers clambering atop it, looking for loose spots from which the tooth might escape. Knocking and shouting sound out from everywhere, here and there, the stretched-out pyrex proves to be brittle and the pylons, from which the roof in my mouth is suspended, are also a cause for concern, they are proving themselves to be more susceptible to the weather than initially assumed during the planning because of the incessant dampness. I shall have to determine how long these guys intend on strolling around in my mouth and whether they now wish to appear every night. However, it is the oil lamp inserted into my mouth from the back that preoccupies me more than the leaky Munich Olympic Stadium roof in my mouth. The lamp doesn't burn. Which is to say, it burns very well, but causes no pain. The Alpenglow appears in my maw. Down in the gorge surrounded by white mountains, I see a bed. A nun carrying a wooden box with nineteen white and eighteen black dashes on the lid around her neck tumbles off of her bicycle, hits her head on the curb of the sidewalk, then perishes. At this moment, the street vanishes, a narrow stream appears, my mother lays a big book with pictures by Johannes Vermeer off to the side, the book remains open to the illustration of a lacemaker wearing a large white collar. The original picture is 24.5 centimeters high and 21 centimeters wide and can thus be produced at scale in a book. Now, the little box is lying upon the bedspread, my mother pulls a key out of it, opens the box, then, after she has embraced and kissed my dead father, she pulls a folded piece of paper out of it. The paper has a pattern of stripes on its underside, it matches the stripes on the little box and my mother's dress beautifully. My mother extracts a vertically striped tie from the paper, which she then tucks beneath a loose cardboard collar. The collar is a tie-tying aid that allows for the tie to be tied independently of one's own body, then placed beneath the erected shirt collar. The nun's garment with its large white collar already lies upon the bed, my father was wearing it when he had his bicycle crash. The collar has only to be looked at for long enough with the soul-emitting gaze of the medium and the tie joins itself unto the collar, binding its knot of its own accord, and, soon enough, Father has once more filled out the collar entirely, he straightens the knot, clears his throat, he is already leaving the bed, he pulls his jersey trousers over his linen underpants, and slips on his heavy dressing gown so as to resume his official duties. For all the joy of such an unexpected reunion, my mother, whose opinion he has always valued so highly in matters of appropriate dress, which ought to be befitting of one's post, just as of the family, points out to my father that such a combination of nun's bonnet, tie, blouse, jersey trousers, and dressing gown was surely befitting of neither post nor family, not even to mention society and the way it gawps, simply biding its time before giving vent to the vicious spleen of its gossip. My father requests a mirror, when one cannot be brought in, he has his aspect described to him in detail, asks questions, corrects it wherever the description seems to him to be too implausible, and laughs along when the sight placed before his eyes seems grotesque enough that, in it, he recognizes a type of person whose appearance momentarily frees people from the consciousness-yoke of death. He quickly gives in, puts his nun's habit back on, then goes back to his desk at the office, where stacks of paper have piled up like dung in a stall that hasn't been cleaned out for a long time. Back in his day, my father was dubbed the "King of Papers." He takes the quill from the inkwell standing at the ready and works through the remaining ordinances. "These devils, my papers," my father writes, "allow me to control the devil-citizen. I have researched and documented everything that causes him to act in such a way. But he, the citizen, who really ought to fear my papers, no longer recognizes himself in them. Can it thus be that we become somebody else from one day to the next? What art of disguise demands greater respect than that of a citizen who 'in the corner of a tavern, sufficiently concealed behind a small glass of whisky, entirely alone with himself, entertains himself with nothing but false, unprovable imaginings and dreams,' as a descendant of Jan Hus once noted, or the paper upon which such things are written? According to this descendant, it is false to say that I felt resolute yesterday, that I am in despair today, it is never possible to notice and judge all the circumstances that influence the mood of a moment and are, perhaps, at work in it. If one agrees with this, the same can above all not be said of a stranger. Consequently, we are leading an artificial life and only God knows the life that goes on behind this mask. Is this masked life therefore reprehensible? Is there no guilt whatsoever? If there is no guilt, there is no God either. Then there is only that which is written."

My father's work is interrupted by the visit of a portraitist who asks my father whether he'd prefer to be painted in oil or represented in the form of a bust. My father opts for the oil portrait, the inclusion of which in the city's ancestral art gallery is immediately promised to him, but only should he allow himself to be interrupted in his work and present himself as he thinks he is *without* the presence of the portrait painter. In memory of the descendents of Jan Hus, a cheerful painting is created, it is only harmed by the fact that the city will cause the image to disappear into its catacombs without its ever having seen the light of day.

"The table grows with each passing day," my father writes, "the paper upon which I am finally going to write this ordinance grows smaller with each passing day. The day shall come when I shall lie upon the table and no longer be able to find the paper. But I have seen through you, dear son, you cause this notion to rise up in me day and night in such a way that I become smaller, until, one day, I myself can no longer be made out upon this enormous table. In this way, you wish to write me out of the world. I am now putting a stop to this undertaking by way of an ordinance. Ever since you left the Church, you've had the aspect of a Vicar of the Antichrist. Formally, you can leave the Church, this is an act of state. But as a baptized Catholic, you shall always remain a baptized Catholic. Baptism is an indelible spiritual mark. As a citizen, you may leave, but as a Catholic, which is to say as a human, there is no possibility of you doing so, your membership within the church remains dogmatically unaffected. In terms of Church law and theology, my dear son, there is no leaving the Church. You leave the Church as a corporation under public law of a peculiar kind. Such a corporation has the right to levy taxes. So, it really is all about the money for you. How is your so-called leaving the Church to be understood as anything else but a disobedience that must be punished? What does it have to do with your inner decision to leave the Catholic Church? You shall be scrupulously interrogated about it. Is not the most important book after the Bible the baptismal register? And what is now written in this baptismal registrar? It is written that you have left the Church. This satisfies the conditions of a schism, even if it hasn't been viewed as a schism since 2012. It does, however, have the consequences that follow from excommunication. And, yet, you still come before a priest and receive holy communion? Yes, you only did so for my sake. You did it for your own sake. So that you might be able to put your Father's life behind you with no hesitation. I doubt you confessed your leaving to the priest. Do you think that I don't see you? Even now, I can see and hear you very clearly. You swallowed the Host as Antichrist. The Host shall do a bad number on you, it shall become a monster that one day rises, it shall clamber up your gullet and sit in your mouth, you shall be nothing more than an echo of your monster—speechless reverberation—and the monster shall say what I want. The monster shall be my thoughts that you shall speak when I am dead. Now, we come to death. Death is there when one speaks it. You must answer for the death of your mother who, from the day of your birth to her far-too-early passing, was nothing but bothered by the regrettable circumstances of your existence, right up until this bother called forth a fatal illness in her, the inevitability of which she was convinced of from the moment of her diagnosis on, yes and much earlier too, from the illness of her beloved father on. And thus can I say that certain unbeautiful things have come to pass in the life of our dear mother, things for which you are responsible. Mother has given her power over to me and I am now making use of it to hold you accountable. You are predestined to perish in script. That the times are *oh so modern* does not bode well for the rules of procedure. It was a great error in legal history to allow the accused to take the stand, after all, the tribunal ought not to become a lecture hall. And you, dear son, are not entitled to the dispute that you so earnestly demand. So, what do you wish to bring about with your revolt, by making yourself heard, if you do not, after all, qualify for such power? You have put me here into this bed in the hopes that I shall never again be able to escape the gorge. But the gorge doesn't even exist. You wish to be taught, but you are unteachable. Dogmatics and dispute have already exchanged views and decided that your interpretation is wrong on dogmatic grounds, this requires no interpretation whatsoever, with *Schattenfroh*, you wish to definitively destroy your father, deny him the right to a soul, for he so neglected you in life that penance can only be done by way of the loss of his soul, but, with *Schattenfroh*, you have refuted yourself and my memory is unrelenting, *Schattenfroh* has become part of him. You might wish to think that Mr. Hus the Goose is not yet roasted, but I say to you that the fire is already burning, you have long been refuted. I shall set a paper cap upon your head once more, even after my death, it is painted over with devils and the words: 'He confused it with an indulgence.' Nowadays, confession is considered a cure; I don't need your confession to know. I know. In your case, there can be no talk of a reintegration into society—that which one reads about everywhere as the highest goal of confession. Who is your Filcyw this time, the one whose fallacy you follow, and who might your Johannes von Eisenjec be? You shall not, however, be granted the joy that one shall have been required to read your books, in which you wish for my coldness and severity to be revealed and in which I should fear to find my heresies, I have read them no more diligently than the Holy Scriptures, as I did not teach heresies, and especially not as far as you are concerned, for one comes across the Holy Scriptures hundreds of times upon my shelves, whereas your scripts have all burnt up in my washbasin.

Are you suggesting that the corrupt Church system begins with your father? Study ecclesiastical law by way of your own body to learn that ecclesiastical laws are not mere ordinances of reason (and how this is so), but ordinances of a reason aligned with faith in revelation. Thus is it written. The lawgivers of all-church law are the pope and the college of bishops—not Jesus Christ and not God, as you believe. Divine law is another matter entirely. You can leave the Church, but not God. And with these words do I condemn you once more to . . ." The mouth moves, but the sound is muted. Now, Father is also flickering, his image fading, I want to wave at him once more, but he can no longer be seen there, the nun's habit remains back on the bed.

A gust of wind blows through the papers and carries them away. Nothing can be taken back. But the wind carries Father's final ordinance up to me on the rocky outcrop, where I need only grab it out of the air. I hold the ordinance in my hands and, in the distance, on the mountain opposite the gorge, Mother appears skiing down the slopes. Then she stops. Her visage is suntanned, she wears snow goggles that are much too big, a light-colored top of thick cotton buttoned at the wrists, it reaches far beyond the belt-accentuated waist, a cross-shaped cord lacing over the sternum, the cord runs through seven metal eyelets on each side, lead tape was made use of as a cord so as to better hold the loop, precisely the kind one uses to weigh down curtains, the hood's top lies loosely upon the shoulders, the knit, visored cap upon Mother's head cannot hold her wavy hair tied into a ponytail. On the backside of the photo is written in pencil: Comparative photo for Order 327 (Dr. Lungstraß). Dr. Lungstraß developed lung cancer and could no longer distinguish between hot and cold. Mother always said "cold" when the soup was too hot, Grandpa would then carefully bring the spoon up to his mouth. In the photo developed in Trier, she predicted that family life would destroy me. The shelteredness has likely vanished from her face. But this had to have been because of her father, who didn't wish to let her go, who didn't want her to study pharmacology in Cologne, before eventually allowing it, but too late, it cost my mother too much strength to defend herself against his veto, so beyond all measure had he bound her to himself; when she finally left, a piece of her was torn off that could never be replaced. Mother takes the ski poles out of the snow and is out of the image in just a few swings.

I lie down on the table, the entire flat surface of which is decorated with an emblem.

I crumple up Father's ordinance in my left hand while tracing the contours of the emblem with the index finger of my left. After all, I have always atoned for that which my parents have found me guilty of. In order to be able to combine the impressions into an image, I must turn unrelentingly. If I turn too slowly, the traces are gradually lost, if I turn too quickly, they build up no image. I assume that these studies already belonged to the punitive part of my father's ordinance, it would be easy enough to stand up and look at the emblem from a suitable distance instead of palpating it with one's belly. A main in tails and tophat, however, who appeared next to me, compels me to remain lying upon the table, his voice weighs me down, "just lie there," it says incessantly in a tone that is less commanding than it is warning, as if some evil might otherwise come to pass and, as soon as I've raised my pelvis a few centimeters up, which might well indicate a slow rising,

I see things, which to describe as ghastly seems strangely antiquated to me. But it is ghastly when one sees oneself age in a matter of seconds, when one sees an illness raging inside of one's body, I'm lying in my father's bed in the intensive-care unit, instead of a tube, there is a sword in my mouth, it comes out of the back of my head and fixes me to the bed. Upon the sword is written: "Thou that here open thine eyes, take heed and be assured of this: it is folly to trust in thine own strength, for a prideful heart doth not endure. If thou thinkest even of wrongdoing, the sword hangs already over thy head." If I now pull my right leg up, as one does when one wishes to stand, I feel myself to be strangely open in the area of the throat, blood running down. However, I am relieved to feel my head, at this very moment, I see it before me on a pole, next to which the sword is stuck. On the blade of the sword, I now read the inscription: "LOOK NOT UPON ME AND MINE, BUT UPON THEE AND THINE. WHEN THOU SEEST ME, JUDGE ME NOT: FOR WHO CAN TELL IF THOU ART TRULY DEVOUT?" Whether I am devout? Went every day to Mother's grave and wept and remained pious and good. Meek and good. Hypocritical and good. Righteous and good. Am I righteous? "Look not upon me" is likely intended for the executioner for whom his own sword stands. But it doesn't say "Look upon me," it says, "When I do heave the sword aloft, I wish unto the sinner eternal life." And he is already heaving the sword aloft and blood is running down the piste. Mother pulls a red thread through the groove she has ridden into the snow. I have only just laid down my body, which forms a triangle with my head, lying a good meter away from it, and my all-seeing spirit, which I feel, but cannot see. For the head can no longer turn atop the trunk, the eyes move to and fro in the furthest corners of their sockets. In this way, they do not miss the script that Mother's wending has left behind in the bloodgutter: "O Lord take this poor sinner up into Thy kingdom so that he might become holy at one happy stroke." Urine running down through the gutter.

Then, somebody else takes up the sword and says: "Can you imagine the pain when the blade cuts into your neck?" But this time I say: "I can imagine it very well." He ignores my riposte. To reply is servile. Whoever replies, accepts the hierarchy in whose place ("Ort") the question sits like place ("Ort") in word ("Wort"), at its end, and the hierarchy is the sword. "The first cut shall sever your veins. The blood shall be mixed with your saliva." I taste it. "The second blow shall open your neck. You shall no longer be able to breathe through your nose." Thus does it come to pass. A swordsmith comes and smiths the sword. I prepare to stand up entirely when I see a cage being built from metal bars before me, the builders are taking great pains to ensure that all the angles are correct, they knock and hammer, pull on this iron, screw each pipe, straw is piled up inside of the cage, only when I lie flat on the table once more do the webs disappear and the hand palpates other figures than the ones I caught fleeting glimpse of upon getting up. There is, for example, a black horse upon which a little girl is sitting. She has the reins firmly in her grasp, the black horse is motionless. That's what the girl was ordered to do. Wavy lines in the background. Small, spherical elevations in the lines on the left. My hand dips into the lines, a small chest bites into it, then it is immediately pulled through the tabletop. When the processes slow down, one is able to come to one's senses. But why am I lying atop this table? This question seems to have something to do with the emblem that decorates the tabletop. If this emblem weren't there, the question would have to go: Why am I lying atop a table? The next question follows quite logically: Why does the table stand upon a rocky outcrop? The explanations have to end somewhere. In full, the sentence reads: The explanations have to end somewhere—then the fear begins. For example, the fear that this rocky outcrop might break off beneath the weight of the table and the desk cabinet and tumble down into the gorge. Thus do I do well to stay lying down. The surface of the water has calmed once more and thus can I devote myself to the wooden chest, which allows itself to be opened quite easily. It is filled with photographs. Most of them are black and white, whereas, at first glance, the rest seem to me to have been colored. I only wish to devote myself to the black and white photographs and also only those that have inscriptions on their back sides. I have a sudden longing for script produced by a hand. My father's handwriting was always the law. Father wrote with finger upon stone. Handwriting, he would always say, is the ultimate justification. This is why autographs are so sought after, they are the trace of body and of spirit, shaving of the soul. Father loved to sign things.

On the backside of one photo is written with pencil: Juist, August 16, 1935, Stintelein. A nickname of indeterminate origin. The handwriting could have originated with Grandma Lungstraß. The photo is curved, it has a white frame with an irregular jagged edge. Stintelein was Mother. In the photo, Mother was five and a half years and two days old (to the day). That one's own mother was once young is beyond all imagining. Are vascular malformations already present and develop over the years. Over the years means very quickly. Very quickly means the next moment as compared to this one. The future has already passed. Stintelein. With braided pigtails pinned up to form loops, she sits in a bathing suit upon a beautiful black horse, the reins held taut, photographed from the side, the stirrups hang too low for her feet to reach. The dark dots on the left of the image are bathers. Stintelein is biting her lower lip, joy, fear, and embarrassment are in her face, she sits upon a photo-horse, she is posing against this beach backdrop for the sake of her parents, who, with each glance at this image, are on its other side. Farewell, Stintelein.

A photo card with the triangular stamp of the Lacheralm ski hut at its bottom left shows the ski lift at Sudelfeld by Wendelstein in the Mangfall Mountains. The backside of the card is scattered over with signatures. The following memorandum is to be found in neat block letters at its top edge: "Upper Lacheralm: from 2/17–3/13/52."

Mother's handwriting. So, between February 27 and March 13, 1952, I only just saw her skiing down the Untere Sudelfeld. Mother is twenty-two years old. The return of a dead woman upon my little idol. I love her especially much now. In my memory, I call her Stintelein, as if she were my child and not I hers. I could write for so long about my mother—until I starved to death at this father's table or until the rock upon which this table stands tumbled down with me into the depths because the words become too heavy for it or else I very suddenly decided to preempt a rockfall by getting up and, with the small chest in my hands, leaping about on the table until it gave way along with the rock underneath me. I fly down into the gorge together with Stintelein and shall only stop wondering about this beautiful name, which reminds me of ducks and stilts, once I've been dashed to the ground. Has nobody ever set up an effigy of his mother in the front garden and covered over the wall of the house with her image? Has nobody ever tumbled into the depths, where, down below, the enormous portrait of the falling man's mother waits to welcome him? Or somebody lacquers his car with the likeness of his mother and crashes into a wall with it or drives it off of a bridge and into a lake. With Stintelein on the black horse, I have Mother once more—as I never had Mother before. The photo is more Mother than the one I knew, handwriting and image are the true mother who shall age no more. An inversion takes place here: Mother's recollected life, which can only ever remain a fragment in the memory, as she was already alive when I came to know her, for which reason, from then on, she led her life as another, the remembered life must be measured by the one photograph that is no image of life, but a totem. Stintelein. A word on my tongue. In observing the photograph, the black horse becomes a guardian animal, the assistant to the psychopompos, who developed the alphabet so that it might be displayed in his name. Pomp of the psyche, éclat, exaltation, splendor, pageantry. With this are you to lead your mother's soul into the hereafter. Ever still. But how can one sit upon a black horse in Juist two years, six months, and sixteen days after Hitler seized power. Nothing escapes me in this photo of Mother. It heals all wounds that are unspoken between us and that death leaves behind. Death leaves behind an irreplaceability and this photo here, upon which I train my gaze, calls up the irreplaceable in my memory, brings it before my eyes. The photo really brings one nowhere, I am the one who brings the photo before my eyes so as to regain something lost, Stintelein, upon whose face the faces of her granddaughter, whom she never saw, and her other son are already inscribed. If the mother is and remains a child, I shall one day be her father and, in the child, the later hardships remain hidden, the foreknowledge of the exchanged biography, which gave priority to the general, to this chimera, over one's own singularity. Mother got her handwriting, her script, from Gustl, my grandma, whom I only have a single memory of, the way I am sitting in her lap in 1967, the year of her death, the blue-upholstered armchair that, now, after Father's death, stands in my room, far from here. Mother exchanged the volatility of Grandma's handwriting for a neatness that resisted any and all blemishes or errors, each minor flaw has already been resolved in the procession of the script. Let us, our gazes fixed forward into the past, enter the Kingdom of the Dead backward, stepping over that very threshold that, in life, is always avoided, just as one avoids certain determined, predetermined steps on a staircase or a determined random stone slab in the yard when hopping about on one foot, from now on, I wish to see this transition in every threshold, step, and stone slab and also practice looking backward while walking backward.

Along with the chest, I have pulled the emblem out of the tabletop. It is now on top of the chest where I can study it at my leisure. The emblem has a heading, followed by an image under which text can be read. Even if I don't dare to move a single centimeter so as not to trigger a rockfall by way of a careless motion, everything up here must remain in a fine equilibrium, thus does the gorge with its rocky outcrop offer me an excellent view as has never before in my life been afforded me. It must be a celebratory mood in me or an illness that causes me to take pains to express myself so antiquely, but this style is well-suited to the situation. Today, I feel myself to be like the seventeenth century, it corresponds to my current feeling when I look at this emblem. The emblem shows nothing other than itself. How can it do that, it doesn't, after all, act. It's showing itself is to be understood thusly: "to let that which shows itself be seen from itself in the very way in which it shows itself from itself." This sentence: as if somebody were putting it down with the quill that is my head. Epoché, which is to say: devotedness to things. "Back to the things themselves!" Written down, all images are strangely dead. These things would have to be set into the sentence in such a way that they let themselves be seen. But how? Only thus can I protect Stintelein on the black horse: by not adjusting the photo. Then all allegories are swept from the table in jolly fashion. Manifest is the world. Totem is kitsch. Stintelein is not kitsch. I do not pray to the photo, do not fall to my knees before it, do not mistake it for a statue, it ought not to bring me any consolation either, indeed, I know that Mother shall not come back to life by way of me worshiping the image, she returns dead, she shall only be dead forever for as long as I live. Mother's photo has no soul, but it makes the world more consummate, it represents the Manes, the departed spirits of the dead. If I lose it, I've lost Mother for good. I shall keep and cherish it so that the spirits don't stalk me in my dreams or send sickness or death.

I mistrust the phantoms in my head—that Mother looked like this or like that, that her gaze was sad or benevolent—they never return to a basic image, they don't allow one to see. I am glad that I managed the leap from the photo of Mother to the emblem of the little chest. The emblem shows the chest to be a child's coffin, so teensy-tiny that only a newborn could fit into it. Over the image, it reads: "Secura pericli." I imagine Mother lying in this little box, barely born, a voice sounds out when you open it: "In this chest lies your mother as your child. The chest is only meant for you. I'm going to close it now. With each new opening shall your mother be metamorphosized. Until, at last, perhaps a beetle will be found in the chest. And you shall meet others who shall also claim to have a beetle in their chests. Do the others dub their mothers *beetle*? That's a part of the history of philosophy that does not contain you. And it is in this way that you shall have lost your mother altogether. Your mother shall have departed as in all other cases and you all stand there with something in your hands. Thus do you individually belong to the Society of those Holding-Something-in-Their-Hands. Never shall you know when the opening of the chest has crossed the border into pain. Therefore, beware of opening the chest." Thus, verily, is everything that is the case illustrated idiom. Under the shut chest, the following text can be found upon the emblem: "Noscere magnatum si quando arcana voceris: / Fac teneas linguae librica frena tuae. / Non ea divulges et vino tortus, et ira: / Ne subeas poenam lubricitate gravem. / Vulganda evulga, sed cum ratione: tegasque / Quae tempus, ratio et causa, tegenda jubet. / Res quaevis bene clausa, manet secura pericli. / Lingua tacens, meriti praemia tuta capit." But is not the beetle a symbol of the devil? Then how could my mother turn into a beetle? I shall have these lines translated, I only know a few words such as "recognize," "when," "language" ("tongue"), "wine," "anger," "punishment," "severe," "time," "cause" ("mind"), " thing," "good," "silence." From "manes" to "manet" is just a single step. Only a few more to mania.

Somebody must have already opened the chest, Mother has transformed into photographs. Stintelein upon the black horse has so etched herself into my memory that I'll never again have to open the chest in order to make Mother present. Gazing upon the photographs, I can suddenly see things I've never seen before. All these things are long gone, lost between the many moves and the attempts to leave aberrations behind by way of a clean break. Thus, over time, does photography take the place of life and is thereby on the threshold, it is already part of the hereafter, which is not apart from this world, photography is able to evoke smells and sensations, to set moments that have been passed over in experience, which were thus not experienced in the slightest, into their old light. Photography congeals a loneliness that recognizes you when nobody else does. I observe Mother's photographs, black and white, out of focus, otherworldly, and see myself, I came forth from this face here and that one there, in the round photo, Grandpa bends down toward Lassie the boxer before the tinsel-covered Christmas tree, he laughs as he does with wide-open mouth, his teeth can be seen quite clearly, my daughter now has this surprised laughter, full of happy expectation. The photograph of Stintelein lives on in me, it is a separate being that has always disconcerted me, but is now familiar as familial trace, more identical than any ID. The bodily posture of the mother here, *that* is me, I have grown into this posture, and thus is the space around us filled up with invisible gestures, which we must only accept. Mother stands next to her parents' house, as if the family home were a friend, a tentative playmate that cannot make up its mind to tumble down into the gorge with Mother, the gorge now opening itself up to be seen once more.

The bed stands in the middle of the Prüm River. Next to the bed stands a device that I cannot precisely identify from up here. It is as if somebody had thrown certain things, including the bed, an oil lamp, and this device, together with a man, down into the gorge, and the air had carried everything into its precise place without damage or injury—or so it seems—placing the bed and the man lying upon it into the river, the sideboard in front of it, the oil lamp behind it, and, to the side of the bed, the device, the exploration of which soon prompts me, against all reservations, to descend into the gorge. However, the wind up here forces me to lie flat upon the ground, which gives me the opportunity to study the outer side of the footboard, upon which two head-sized spots can be seen. The spots move. Which is to say, in the spots *is* movement. Cell divisions can be observed, something pulsates, an exchange between solid and liquid elements takes place. The notion that this is an enlarged interior view of a man in bed causes me to indefinitely postpone my descent of the gorge so that I might devote myself entirely to these observations. Is it thus that disease arises? And is it possible to follow the disintegration of a human being in this way? The stages of decay should be legible from a display set into the image. What would be gained through this? With a decay of up to 49 percent, atheism would rule the world, at 50 percent, the God-fearing once more gains the upper hand. But atheists are the true God-fearers, the so-called believers are always only afraid that it will be to the so-called all-seeing God's liking to punish them, thus do they themselves resort to the punishment that they inflict upon others in the name of God so that God might spare them. Torture and execution are performed to please God so that God might only see the victim and not think to turn on the perpetrator. As perpetrator, the perpetrator shall remain the perpetrator for his whole life, he shall not be able to stop being a perpetrator and must incessantly bring sacrifices to his Lord. The Lord himself is a victim, for the perpetrator makes him into a primitive God, to whom one must offer victim-sacrifices. The cell-division comes to pass so rapidly that the spots on the outer side of the foot-end have lost their head-shape and are already colonizing the space beyond the foot-end, as if the bed had a mask on. I wish to get hold of this mask before the world discovers it. Incidentally, I operate on the assumption that my memories, which are constantly multiplying, are the mask and that my memories here are locked up in this gorge, in this shaft of images. I am afraid to move, for, if I move, I bury my memories, thus must I keep still so that no others can pluck them out of the air, be able to breathe them in, for that is everyone's goal—to get fatter, to take up more space in the world, to displace others. Germans primarily consist of the recollections of others, they band together in great masses because the masses give them protection, because they themselves are masses and they wish to take on even more from the crowd, the masses are a Mass of Incorporation. Incorporation means dying and each act of dying is a murder that is avenged by a birth. If, for example, a person eats a pork rind, then they shall bring a pork rind into the world. Only the human-like Gestalt of this pork rind shall prevent it from being immediately eaten again. That's a proven fact. Just as it has also been proven that a person who eats a pork rind becomes a pork rind himself. One quickly sees the rind upon the person's ugly mug. Pig cannot be distinguished from man in that the pig is an even-toed ungulate that supposedly has no language, but it's actually the pig who has the far more beautiful face. On the train to Leipzig, I once observed a man entering the compartment with a fat-dripping kebab. In a matter of seconds, the döner turned the compartment into a cathedral of reek. No sooner had the man gobbled down his döner kebab than he became pig-eyed, wiry stubble sprouted from his face, his eyelids and cheeks hung down, his face lost its contours so quickly that he turned into himself in the assumption that he was somebody else, the fat trickled down into his stomach, his belly had taken on the form of a drum and now arched further and further outward, this man's little arms withered, he developed a persistent compulsion to cough, against which he offered himself a cough drop as somebody else, but he himself politely declined it, for he wasn't coughing at all, just thinking, the fat had now entirely collected in his belly and was once more seeking a way out, for which purpose it made use of the esophagus, which had become a single trickle of blood, and thus shall the man, who had entirely become swine, no longer be able to distinguish between his own meat and that of others and shall eventually eat his own larynx. Before this, he falls into a deep sleep, the only time when the ugliness of his face can become consummate, in this sleep, he gathers up the strength necessary for self-incorporation, he shall already be missing his belly, which, having become a pig himself, he no longer requires for digestion, and thus is it no surprise that he gobbles down his larynx, after all, he no longer needs any human language to articulate himself. I saw this man get out of the train as a pig in Berlin and leave the station on all fours, the hunt was on. It shall soon have been shown whether he measured up to his stall. This came to pass in February 2013, back when pork was in döner. Recollecting this occurrence, I already find myself on the rockface, I wish to grab hold of the mask, which has become so big that it blocks the view of the bed. The two headlike spots of fat have become a single spot of fat, eyes, nose, and mouth have developed, the mouth opens and shuts, the eyes look agitatedly to the left and right, they fix upon something, they have now lost contact, they are scanning the entire field of vision as if they had slipped behind cladding and were on the verge of entirely falling into the interior of the housing. This cladding is in their way, they see everything only to a limited extent, for they must be afraid that their sight shall be reduced more and more, they seek to generate wind by way of tiny motions, this wind is not only enough to hold them to the surface, but to clear all obstacles out of their way. I don't know what difference it makes for them whether they see something before or behind them, whether the source of their fear is to be found at the end or at the bottom of their gaze. It may be entirely all the same for them. A notion must, in any case, be tied up with the gaze, the gaze shall trigger expectations and misgivings, it has a memory that it cannot circumvent. I have torn my right leg on a protruding root, blood is running down into my shoe. This immediately calls forth small animals that undertake the sucking-up of the blood. I momentarily consider tumbling down into the depths so as to shake off the animals, then I notice a small figure below me, it bears some resemblance to me as a child. I address the child in a friendly manner, but it turns away from me and indicates a distant point down below. I ask the child whether it has no fear whatsoever of tumbling down there. It shakes its head, then indicates the point off in the distance once more. My eyes have gotten worse over the years, insofar as eyes can get bad, I see things that are located at a certain distance from me only quite blurrily, thus do I not know how I ought to react to the child's finger-pointing and ask it what there is to see there in a tone that ought to signal that I know the answer only too well, but wish to hear it from the child, and the child promptly indicates the name of the things that it sees there in the distance. I am so frightened by this that I momentarily lose my footing and am on the verge of tumbling down into the depths, which sets the child into a state of joyous expectation, and thus is it utterly disappointed when I get my grip once more. Would it have made you happy if I'd tumbled down there, I ask the child. The child keeps a straight face, it stares at me unblinkingly, the child really isn't related to me at all and I say so to it. But, at that very moment, the child takes on my facial features, it grows wrathful and clambers nimbly up the rockface, which I shimmy down in a great hurry, afraid of not being able to evade the child. Only it turns out that the child's goal isn't me, but the table, which it has discovered and from which it gazes out onto the gorge. I cannot rid myself of the suspicion that the child can control everything from on high, I am its marionette, which it leads by the strings, my every motion is controlled by it, thus does the child guide itself as a grown-up. With its help, neatly hung from the marionette control bar, I manage a gentle descent.

I cannot wait to look into the device. I look into the device. I see something or a photograph. As a photograph, this something in the gaze upon it represents the unhappy consciousness, which, released from the unconscious calm of nature, knows only the state of necessity and of the understanding and for which "*being-in-itself* is the *otherworldly beyond* of itself," the other world—the hereafter—is within me, it is the loss that must be aimed at again and again and thus can I not come back to myself except in death. For me, my essence is an unattainable hereafter, it flees from me with each attempt to grasp it. In observing an image, consciousness cannot return to the reality of the image, in which I see only phantoms, but in which consciousness scents its own essence—itself. Here, the photo grabs hold of only the gaze, the observer himself does not appear in the image, he is the blind spot. I harbor such deep thoughts when my gaze passes through the device. So deep are the thoughts that I dub the device that triggers them "Hegel." It is a device with which I can gaze into my own head. The problem of the future shall be having to decide whether to gaze out into the world or into one's own head. Some people shall see no difference here, for others, what is testified to in this question is nothing more than an old problem. The question of the question is whether there can be any choice whatsoever between world and head or whether anybody to whom the possibility of gazing inside his own head is made available shall not have to do so compulsively. Thus do I gaze inside. But what do I see? I see the device through which I can barely wait to look. Then I see the child pointing at the device. The next moment, I see myself upon the rockface, I tear my right leg on a protruding root, blood is running into my shoe, the child clambers nimbly up the rockface, which I shimmy down in a great hurry, afraid of not being able to evade the child. Only it turns out that the child's goal isn't me, but the table, which it has discovered and from which it gazes out onto the gorge. I cannot rid myself of the suspicion that the child can control everything from on high, I am its marionette, which it leads by the strings, my every motion is controlled by it, thus does the child guide itself as a grown-up. With its help, neatly hung from the marionette control bar, I manage a gentle descent.

I cannot wait to look into the device. The avaricious stream goes red. A table can be seen on the left, I come into the image on the right. Goes dark, then light once more. I sit at the table, the tabletop is completely covered over with scriptgrowth.

Mateo is there, he strokes my head, but that's not me, I am the golem of my golem, a Mogel,* the golem sits there, I must scrape the

---

* Bluff.

script from the golem's forehead, then he will die, that's the truth, he wears a box upon his brow and is bent over toward a book that he holds in his hand. In favorable light, like right now, I can see into the book by gazing through the device. I read: "I hold a book in my hand. Now, I am reading that I hold a book in my hand. Indeed, it is strange that I know nothing of this. I read further on in the book. This sentence is in the book too. This one too. The book is very light. It can practically fly. I can open it at any point and continue the writing of what I have read. They have broken my back. The bookbinder's gauze is torn. Labels have been removed from the top and bottom of the spine, not detracting from the script at all, but slightly damaging the cover. The net is torn in two places, in both cases between the two blocks of paper. The glue has turned totally brown, I am disgusted by it. It looks like rust, but also causes one to think of dog feces. But where is all of this? It can be read here. I imagine the space between the spine and the side gusset poured over with cement. Here, a hole caused by paper corrosion, right in the middle of the text:

Innermost whisper: Man has fallen into the evil from which he sprang without salvation. I reply to this with two suppositions from experience: Man finds himself to be only alone in the true world. Furthermore: Each thing has its spirit that governs it and not the other way around. From this, I conclude: As the world is entirely evil, so is it a slave to its own evil spirit and is not, on the contrary, its master, in such a way that it might chase this spirit out of its service. This also applies to the man who, accordingly, is the worst of all possible men and who is really quite hopeless.

I did not write this, for it was Raul Pedal who wrote it."

The golem flips forward a few pages. The pages are empty. He flips back, opens to the last written-on page, takes up a pencil, and writes:

"You don't know who's thinking when you're thinking, who's speaking when you're speaking, and we shall be in your head until you have completed this task, until you have the feeling that this is enough, that it was your task to write it all down, and now, you think, you have written it all down. You shall never be able to be sure that this is *your* feeling. But what role does that play? He's already been doing that for days. What? Standing right up close to the spyhole and alternatingly pressing the left, then once more the right eye against its rim. But there was no eye to be seen. On the other hand, he imagined that he saw worse out of his left eye than his right. Though it was always the other way round. His belly was dripping. Dripping? He could hear it distinctly. Into the intestines. Gastric juices. There it was again. If he held his breath, that would end up suppressing it after all. If he could escape right then, his belly would betray him. Loudly working digestive organs. The rumbling of the intestines might also mean cancer, he once learned, and the account of a student who, as a function of his upset stomach or intestines ceased going to the library until the compulsion to listen to his belly drove him to a psychologist. Fear of cancer. No dissipation of fear before the endless wall. It always came back from the wall." Mateo strokes the golem's head, who is more than happy to tolerate this. Then the golem takes up the pencil once more and writes:

"A young man lives across the street from the State Security headquarters. The large panel building made such a powerful impression on him that he developed the compulsion of standing at the window of his apartment from where he could count the countless little windows that penetrated its façade each time he did. He dyes the always drawn curtains black so as not to give himself away during his observations. If we encounter a policeman, we see ourselves compelled to confess everything to him. The policeman is the true priest. Sooner or later, the young man will find himself so afflicted by the sight of the State Security headquarters that he will collapse when gazing upon it. Thus does he begin to develop countermeasures against his bad conscience and his arithmomania. Very soon indeed, he is absolutely certain of this, somebody shall come to take him in, after all, the State Security services can peer into the brains of all honest citizens. To this end, they have developed a bad-conscience indicator, an instrument that is able to measure a specific bodily vapor, which indicates a bad conscience even at a distance of several kilometers away. But if the device isn't perfectly calibrated, the lack of fine differentiation leads to it identifying entire conurbations of conscience-plagued citizens. Hunting season all year round. The man occupies himself with the setting of individual windows, which, at the very least, greatly slows their counting. In the meditative posture that he thus develops, he himself shall, in any case, have recognized a resistance against state authority, in such a way that, though he has barely domesticated the compulsion to count, he has also discovered a new wellspring for his bad conscience. Moreover, he cannot rid himself of the impression that his black curtain makes him easily distinguishable to State Security, who would only be able to see a single imperative in its contours: to arrest him once and for all. Even the measure of taking a step back behind the window, just far enough that he could still gaze upon the façade of the building in its entirety, is not able to reassure him entirely. After several days of preparations, a sort of training that basically consists in the rehearsal of interrogation strategies—the man wishes to remain composed if faced with any conceivable sort of subversive conversation techniques—he opts to give himself up at the headquarters by his own free will in order to be questioned. As nobody has called him there, he is initially met with hesitancy, but in not at all unfriendly fashion despite all of their firmness, in this, the young man believes that he has recognized the first perfidious tactic. No interrogation takes place, the man is not arrested, nor is he allowed to go to prison. But, as he is already there, he at least ought to *go into production*, be forced to get a job so bad it's considered to be a disciplinary measure, as is stipulated by the Bitterfelder Weg, which would certainly preserve him from all future self-denunciations. Even if he met Trotskyites several times along his transit route, as he claims, it is not his job to accuse State Security of having failed to arrest them, indeed, they tell him, State Security knows all too well when they are to take whom out of circulation. The harmonious human society of the Frightbearing Society shall certainly know how to defang him by way of this measure. The moral-political unity of state and population demands certain sacrifices, self-hatred, they tell him, is a perfidious form of hate, whoever hates himself, forefends the deserved hate of State Security, which still awaits anybody who turns out to be an enemy, and he ought to be quite certain on this point, what with his own act of self-denunciation due to self-hatred. The public sphere already begins in oneself and whoever hates himself by denouncing himself, hates the public. And thus is everyone still responsible for the fate that befalls him."

Mateo nods in recognition. The golem is a cathedralsparrow. Mateo—Meier, his director. Meier chainsmokes. I read his lips: "Go catch your golem again." Next to him lie a small and a big stick. Bound together with a leather strap, a cluster of keys hangs from a folder. The golem's lips split open. But not bleeding. Mateo opens the folder, which is full of words. "I stand ready," I read. And I read: "Yes, just read, after all, that's you and nobody else." Mateo turns to me and smiles. I breathe in the smoke from his cigarette through the device. This emboldens me to grasp for the little box upon the golem's brow. If I should touch the box, I'd expire on the spot, said Schattenfroh. Then the straps holding it to my head would draw together and blow up my skull. I manage to touch the box. Schattenfroh's spring ought to dry up forevermore, then I would leave the gorge and the cell. I write this character upon the little box with my finger: ⱳ. The name Schattenfroh immediately appears upon the box. And I see how the name is pieced together again and again, like an analog fifteen-character split-flap display flipping through its alphabets, taking short pauses every so often:

Fracht Sehnot
eh Nachtfrost
haschte Front
ach thronfest
Schattenfroh
sehnt fort
ach Stehfront ach
stet froh nach
Text nach Froh-
nacht oft sehr
frech tat Sohn
erst noch Haft
traf Sohn echt
nachts eh fort
ach Front seht
fern, hasch tot
recht sanft oh
straft noch eh
Schotter Hanf
schert nah oft
fest noch hart
hast Not frech
Ton hast Frech-
fron echt hast
Nachtohr fest
hatten Frosch
hatten forsch
hatten Schorf
horchten fast
noch resthaft
thront es fach

haschten fort
Fach sehnt Ort
echt sanft. Ohr
storchenhaft
naht chorfest
Echtfront, sah
Fahne Schrott
ehrst nach oft
nachts oft her
focht nah erst
harnfesch tot
horcht Stefan
rostecht Hanf
horcht fest an
Frost echt nah
horchte sanft
Hans roch Fett.
Hans recht oft
frech. Hans: tot.
Hans echt fort
ahnt Ortschef
satt fern hoch.
Nahet! Forscht!

Mateo hands the golem pencil and paper. His lips form a single word: Quintessence. The triumph of the virus. The footnotes gone. The golem writes:

"Nothing is handed over but tradition. One word with seven letters to begin with. That which I have written, I have written. In personal life, things sometimes got confused. But it was livable. There is no compromise to make there. The Frightbearing Society is within me. Now, everything has been read. And nothing remained of it but a glimmer."

I ought to have written that, it makes me furious that he wrote that. The golem takes the pencil and writes:

He is Schattenfroh and Schattenfroh vanishes. I, Nobody, the golem of golems, feel all of his power draining away and gladly take on his power.

The device through which I am looking suddenly broadcasts badly. Perhaps, it is also the eyes. Or the blow delivered to the golem's head with the folder, a blow Mateo deals with great earnestness, shakes the sequence of sentences into confusion. Or the view has reversed. The earth is flat, in one fell swoop, it is no longer rotating clockwise, but counterclockwise. Mateo places the folder onto the table in front of the golem. I read: Biginning in ende, ende in biginning. Seek to weave the ende into the biginning, / If thou wishest to be wys on earth and holie in hevene. He accompanies my every word with his finger, then presses the golem's head into the folder, yanks it up once more, and flips the page. I cannot read everything that is written in the folder:

"Yes, I am afraid. Are you afraid. Then, on the other hand, I see very clearly that I am sitting across from two gentlemen who are asking me comprehensible questions. Would he slip through the tube and into the cell? Through which door would he come? At first I wanted to figure out if the intervals between the scraps of paper were the same, but how could I have measured them? There is quince jelly for breakfast, sometimes also orange marmalade. Bread with jam, 'breakfast,' on a scrap of paper, on the next scrap is 'lunch,' while soup and bread with cheese, 'dinner,' is on the third scrap. I cannot discern whether we (provided I am not alone here) can also be seen from there, however much the question occupies me. If I am to make hypotheses from the floorplan of my cell about that of the entire building, there must be other, possibly identically laid-out cells and a core cell in the middle of the building, from which all other cells can be reached—at least by way of the speaking-tube. It dominates me and speaks even when it isn't speaking. The voice is dreadful. I then imagine an animal crawling slowly through the tube and, as soon as it slips free, it might grow to be very large in my cell so as to devour me or the voice could pupate in my ear and molt into an insect penetrating my brain."

The name on the box continues its work:

Shattenfroh,
Oh ernsthaft,
strafte Hohn
ahnt ohrfest
Stroh ans Heft
steht froh an
Hanf sehr tot

Haftnest Ohr
straft hohen
Hahn erst oft
steht Farn, oh

Haftstern Oh
stoehnt Fahr-
haft Not sehr

sanft, oh ehrt
Hefts Ahnort
haften Stroh
nahtest froh
Ernst hat Hof
Hof sehnt Rat
an Hefts Hort

Ohrtest Hanf
ahnt sehr oft
Sehfront hat
Stehfron hat
Nestfroh hat
Sehnot fahrt
steht froh an

Ahn steh fort
nah Hefts Tor
Rost nah Heft
ehrst oft nah
nah seht fort
Harn seht oft
nahst oft her
ahnt erst Hof
naht Hof erst
naht Rest Hof
Shattenfroh

hast eh Front
Sehnaht fort
Ohrnaht fest

There is less and less of it. Mateo is severe. The golem has no more hair. A new page is opened; if Mateo flips through as quickly as before, then, once again, I capture only fragments:
"I find the merest breath to be especially uncomfortable if the voice does not articulate itself, but, instead, my counterpart, who is not visible to me, merely breathes in and out. The instruction is preceded by the request, 'come here,' I go right up to the tube, put my ear to its opening, then wait for the voice. The open end of a sheet-metal tube protrudes from the wall. Sometimes, a voice resounds from it and gives me instructions. I have been in a cell for several days. What do I see? The hand has now disengaged itself, the engraving has burnt itself into it and is glowing. It is a tremendous pain, I bite my left hand so as not to scream. Then it's not just warmth, my hand burns without my being able to remove it from the tabletop. It's not because of the wood, it must have something to do with the engraving. The spot becomes warm. It remains lying upon a relief-like spot. My right hand slides across the table. I wait. It wasn't very bright before, but it's downright dim now. The light goes out. The grimace of a distorted gaze, the stylus has swelled to several times its old size, it won't be long before I have to hold it down with both hands, it penetrates the table effortlessly. This is the table-level broadening of my soul, forgetting and remembering are simultaneous. I want to attach myself to their floating, it shall lead me through walls and times. I can't get enough of the phantoms, one seems to be able to see through the table with them, I have the feeling I have to set myself up particularly well with them. And then there's still a kind of flurry, a pulsating surface, the fluttering of letters like snowflakes that one wants to catch immediately with one's hands, a river can be made out, a chest, a photo, an executioner's sword, a judgment,

a gorge, a pub, a Hürtgenwald, a death, a dying, body and soul, an intensive-care unit, an execution, a pamphlet against Luther, an interrogation, a cell, a lock, ein Pressbengel (which is both a 'rounce' and sounds something like a 'press-brat'), a pact with said printer, a printer, an arrest, a battle, a fountain, a meeting, Prüm, the Eifel, Grandpa, a park bench, a hearing aid, the Last Judgment, a whole house, a key, a library, 23 houses, a girl and a suitcase, a nursing home, Mother on a big train, a second library, the office, an execution, an interrogation, a sword, a cell, a curtain, a carpet, a woman in a window, a Fratzenstuhl, a wooden doll, a city wall, a Muttergotteshäuschen, a city map, a tapestry, a throne of God, the ladies of the seven antechambers, a journey to heaven, Rilke, Ruprecht, an open book, a chimera, a toad, a hell, a black page, an interrogation, a medieval repast, a cell, a father, an office, a large building. I sit before the wooden book of life and death. An army of amorphous, defective signs is gathering together here, a tumult is what it is and a fire is lit from its center that takes everything with it, as I once experienced with a carpet that caught fire within itself, then, as soon as the carpet had disappeared from the middle, said Father, it wasn't a carpet at all, but a curtain that could liberate the eye to see what was hidden behind it, but nothing was to be found behind it, said Father, behind it is to be found nothing but the pure trope 'ach!', meaning 'alas!', but also Akh, the ancestral spirit, the spirit-soul, which we all wanted to join after our death or into whose possession we wanted to transport ourselves, this is why we say that 'death is filled up by one's *ach*,' that the *ach* is first a crested ibis, then the most luminous star-filled poultry that can spread its mane out so impressively and never ceases bowing to greet those of its own kind, then a Schattenvogel, a shadowbird, for is not every shadow a bird? But none of this covers the sensual pleasure that the table calls forth in me, as if it could release me from the situation in which I find myself and I could walk through it into a landscape in which I myself am only script.

Only the most diligent of removers shall be compelled to discover that the tabletop is a Wunderblock, which one would have to destroy completely if one wanted to destroy the permanent traces of that which had been written upon the wax tablet, which is just as well preserved and is legible in suitable lights as any engraving upon a slab, even the one that has allegedly been removed, thus would one have to destroy the entire slab, which the stylus is entirely incapable of and, as the table is anchored to the floor, mere physical strength is not sufficient."

I've overexerted myself completely. Years must have passed and now, in one fell swoop, I find myself dragging my body behind me, forced to make it perform the tasks that I set out to do. I reach through the device and touch the little box once more. The golem is lazy, one must train him. Does he have no influence on the switch tower of vanishing? It might help to give the box a shake. With my index finger, I can raise it up and let it fall once more, raise it up and let it fall once more. Something is coming to pass:

>hattenfroh
>hortet Hanf
>naht oft her
>ahnt her oft
>eh fort ahnt
>naht eh fort
>ahntet froh
>nahtet froh
>haften Hort
>oh fahr nett
>Ohrahn fett
>Ehrnot Haft
>ehrt oft Ahn
>oh Harnfett

nah, fett, Ohr
horten Haft
ehrt oft nah
nah, fett, roh

There is less of it again. Schattenfroh is battered. I can feel how the dismemberment of the name dismembers his body. That would be my greatest wish, my private eschatology: that the destruction of the word-body signify the destruction of the object-body. The golem writes in Mateo's folder. Thus is there the book and the folder. And the golem writes:

"While some will endeavor to entirely remove all existent traces from the tabletop to either keep themselves under the illusion that no one is to come after them, but also, in return, to ensure that nobody will be able to outflank them if they themselves are not given the opportunity to make their mark, such that a quick glance is all that is necessary to distinguish them from all of the others, but, still, they are frustrated that the strenuous work of the *radere chartas* is not completed by a salaried specialist, after all, it is they who are the eye specialists, those who first detect what is to be removed and would have liked to do nothing in the world more than to induce its erasure with the curt command 'this here!' or 'that there!', others attempt to entirely remove entries they hate so as to 'immortalize themselves' in their stead, as common parlance never grows tired of saying. Those who follow will then discover that they are only going to be able to overpower something already written-over with all of its intertwining characters by way of even greater pressure onto the tabletop in the sense that their writing pushes the antecedent engravings into the background, which doesn't remain endlessly possible, partly the hand will not allow for it and partly the tabletop. The person writing here must furnish a place for himself and, if he can estimate how much space his engravings shall take up beforehand, the traces that he'd like to leave behind, he shall take this as a requirement, then shall he also only endeavor to clean this area or merely write over the preexisting engravings. Writing and erasing takes place at and in concomitance with this table. I take the stylus in hand, if placed with only moderate pressure upon the tabletop, the stylus immediately leaves a small indentation in the wood. I prefer the cold. As soon as it says that 'it glows' here, it becomes ice-cold. It glows. I put it around my neck. The chain may tempt some who sit here and consider strangling themselves with it. If one were to use the tabletop as a horizontal buffer, the stylus would pass through it straight to the heart. Upon the table is a stylus, connected to it by a long chain that cannot be broken by even the greatest of strainings. And with these words do I sit at the table." And I say unto myself and unto you: And I read:

> attenfroh
> faehrt Not
> naehrt oft
> roh an Fett
> Fett an Ohr
> nahte fort
> hatte Fron
> tarnte Hof
> ortet Hanf
> ahnt er oft
> Rattenhof
> Natterhof
> Ohrentaft
> orten Haft
> fahren tot
> tatenfroh

"This is the re-entry into paradise, the conscious individual must be broken through so that others might nestle in him and so that the others' perception might graft itself onto one's own. I am at the center of things and at the center of script. One day, you might be able to undertake the remote control of others' eyes. If my vision goes straight to the center, I see left and right separately. Terribly simple. What occurs on the left dissolves on the right, then reassembles itself as script. We merely hear script, and we read when we hear. I also hear an insect-like hiss, I might make a voyage anywhere, the imaginary is the safest place, one day, however, it will be the most insecure, Schattenfroh said, I'm sitting at the table, the tabletop is completely covered over with scriptgrowth. The visual acuity of my eyes varies greatly, a phrase that shows how the eyes are in no small measure responsible for our measure of time and I remained in darkness for hours, the pain wandered until I finally thought I'd perceived it in front of my body, until such a strong photophobia had affixed itself to me, even with my eyes closed, and such strong headaches afflicted me, I see fore from myself by way of seeing something in my inwardness. With it, I see fore, from, and something. Foresees. I am satisfied with at least still having language, it allows me to see everything, and language tells me I should name the celestial bodies of my inner 'Foresees.'"

And it is so. First, just a little while ago, the "h" fell out of the split-flap display and no other character appeared in its place, now the "a" has also fallen out without me having to give the little box a shake. The body escapes Schattenfroh's body:

    ttenfroh
    Frohnett
    Fetthorn

Here, the sheep is hidden in the wolf. And the hunter. And the fatal shot. The golem appears to be asleep. But he isn't sleeping at all, he wishes to pull the wool over my eyes. Or distract me from other things. He takes the quill. And writes:

"If the aureole of the lens disappears, which it does at regular intervals, an afterimage remains in view at the back of the eyes, an image whose slow fading I am enjoying more and more. Miraculously, I am now able to fully grasp the celestial bodies swimming at the backs of my eyes. The head motions lead me to suspect that there is paper in the box, perhaps strips rolled into each other, which are hurled against the walls of the box, one roll in each chamber, the box also makes incessant noises that lead one to conclude that script is coming to pass within it. If I should touch the curious box fitted above my eyes, I'd expire on the spot, said Schattenfroh. And God did offer himself up to interrogate me. Plagued by feelings of guilt, I'd like for God to interrogate me and perpetually test me. At times, I really do desire nothing more ardently than to be interrogated, an urge that results from a certain propensity to torment myself, as well as my Catholic subservience, which shows itself all the more evidently as the conviction of having entirely renounced Catholicism solidifies within me. Inwardly, I shall see the entire world of the Frightbearing Society, Schattenfroh said, whose member I now be for all time through my free decision to be interrogated. Wherever that might be. I shall see through them into the inward. With this sort of spectacles, I shall experience unimaginable freedom, Schattenfroh has promised. Is it not touching how he emphasizes my so-called writing against his better judgment? I'll be there for you in a moment, he said earlier, until then you must write this here. If he suffuses me completely when, formless in my head, he calls forth in me the notion that at the very least *he* might be immortal, then I hear him from head to toe and this hearing envelops every other sensory impression, also strengthening my body: Schattenfroh is a dictator, he leads the quill that I don't have."

The wolf has eaten the sheep. And makes tzimtzum.

>   tenfroh:
>   Eh front-
>   tenfroh

The golem is not *frontenfroh*, is not "ready to fight." No, he is timid, inhibited. And what is he waiting for? There must be a connection between the indicator's shifting and the golem's pausing. The quill plows across the paper once more. His script grows ever more illegible.

"He buzzes around me, he rattles, a hooded little monster, thus do I imagine him, made up of fly, grasshopper, gecko, and human head, with his wings far too large, and this rattling grounds his falsetto in such a way that I, completely absorbed by the noise, only ever perceive him in fragments. I always hear him differently in spatial terms, I can't see him. That means he lives in my head and has appeared to me since I've been here, in my darkroom. Has been for weeks. Schattenfroh is in my head. I always hear these two sentences in the background. I assume that they're always there, but, occasionally, when I listen carefully, now for example, I only hear 'A small mistake at the beginning is a big one in the end.' Schattenfroh always says two sentences: 'There is no Schattenfroh other than Schattenfroh—and you are his prophet' and 'A small mistake in the beginning is a big one in the end.' Schattenfroh, he is the Big Other that perpetually changes its shape, the processes put themselves to paper.

For every one shall be salted with fire, says Schattenfroh, the worm dieth not, and the fire is not quenched. Schattenfroh said the throne looked like ice crystals, its wheels like the radiant sun, and, underneath the throne, currents of flaming fire are to come forth, but the throne doesn't burn, the wheels don't light up, no currents of flaming fire can be seen, this throne must be a fabrication. I'm sitting on a throne. I'm here at 666 A Drafter Shat Avenue, also known under the addresses 666 Earth-as-draft Avenue and 666 Gehenna, and am sitting in a *camera silens*. 'Come to Gehenna 666, loosen your tongue.'

'Imagination is devilish ערה רצי, yetzer hara.'
'The tongue defileth the whole body.'
'The tongue is the world of iniquity.'
'The tongue itself is a fire.'
'The tongue is inflamed by Gehenna.'
'The tongue is a restless evil.'
'Schattenfroh was here!'

It must be Schattenfroh, he has lured me here with his number games, his 6 brushstroked all over the city with white or red paint, the 6 I at first followed aimlessly, roamingly, until, after about a year, I recognized the system that lay behind it—the incidence of the 6 upon the map of the city coalesced into a 666, I'm in the middle 6 now—and ultimately discovered messages in the 6s in enlarged photographs:

enfroh
oh fern
frohen
fron eh"

Again with this affected pausing. All that which he claims to have seen and recognized. He himself is the error. These are no messages, this is the empty game that is language, a transitory zero-sum game. Do I win that which Schattenfroh loses? And is it more than the languagebody? Is a third party at play? Is it language? Is Schattenfroh now the golem whose golem I am? He likely doesn't know what he's doing. He says it himself:

"I do not think that it is attended to by beings, who, sitting upon remote celestial bodies, are given human shape after the manner of the fleeting-improvised-men, as is written in the Book of Daniel. Who actually attends to the writing, I do not know with enough certainty to say.

The brain is read out at the mind-interfaces. Brain abduction. It's not only that I can't help being watched, as one would normally observe someone in a department store when he's walking hastily or in a church when he's sitting there all withdrawn into himself. My memory drips. I wonder whether it's ever dripped itself dry. Why not broadcast it *everywhere*? But why write it down? The brainfluid-script is projected into my hands, from which Schattenfroh allows to be read that which I have thought and seen in the form of a book, as if the hands were giving instructions, or what I have thought heard seen is transmitted remotely via the spectacles to a device that writes everything down and the quick motions of my fingers are nothing but an atavism. For is brainfluid not the soul?

My writing must be a projection of the brainfluid-script. I have the feeling that someone is pawing into my thoughts, images, and everything that I hear as soon as I think, see, or hear something, though no exchange between me and these others takes place. The motions correspond with what you see, think, and hear, says Schattenfroh. Sometimes the right hand seems to be writing as if it were holding a pen or a quill, scraping and encircling motions are carried out, then both hands become involved again, as if they were typing on a keyboard or drawing in the air. The fingers move without my having agency over them. My centroscriptorium is remote controlled, as are my hands. I'm a prestidigitator, a tachygraph, a quick-finger, I write, but not really, rather I only think, see, and hear, even if, as just now, in extremely limited fashion. It writes:

nfroh

Frohn"

To be happily in service to. When one looks upon him like this, it's believable. An honest stutterer who takes great pains and executes everything as Schattenfroh has instructed him. It withdraws itself. But he continues to write diligently. And I am his chronicler:

"They are located very close to the eyes and surrounded by an aureole that exudes a little bit of brightness. Lenses are placed into the box on the left and right. As for the spectacles, I only suspect that they're spectacles—this small box before my eyes that seems to have no weight one moment, but makes the head sink heavily the next. The facemask is meant to keep my head warm. I suspect that this Something, which I shall hereby call Woodlouse, speaks as my tongue. Apparently, though, this Something lacks for nothing, it's been sucking at the tongue-artery constantly, babbling and ready to gladly chow down on whatever's served to him or her, but nothing is, I haven't eaten anything for days. Your mission should read: 'Nobody recognizes himself.' You must be and become a most proper nan mann, he said. Thus spake Schattenfroh. Your name is not Johannes and not Emmeram, your name is Nobody. I have no tongue. Or, if I do, I can't move it. On my head sits a hat adorned by a bird's wing. I'm sitting in a darkroom wearing a facemask and some kind of spectacles. What strange words there are. Hermeticized. The darkness of this room sealed off from the outside makes it impossible to distinguish between day and night. I haven't slept, though I'm not tired either. I've been here for a few days. Thus did it begin. The beginning should read 'Now it's happening.' They've suddenly changed something."

Fissures run through the image, something bulges outward here, the schism goes right through the middle of the word, holes like

moth-damage, white spots, themselves further script, whisper to me,
I read them out with pecking eye:

I don't know when the beginning is and I don't know what everything is. I said it can't be done. My mission is to write everything down from the beginning. Society demands amusement. I write: As I am here voluntarily, I have voluntarily subjected myself to the confines of this society. And, as I am here voluntarily, I have voluntarily subjected myself to the confines of this society. And so I write: I am here voluntarily. I must write that I am here voluntarily. I am writing into my brainfluid. I have no paper, no pen, no typewriter, no computer.

    froh
    Ohr
    roh
    oh
    h

    One calls this writing.

The Alexander Grass Humanities Institute at Johns Hopkins and Deep Vellum are proud to present AGHI in Translation, a partnership to bring the world's greatest writers into dialogue across academic and public spheres. By producing and promoting major works of literary translation, the AGHI and Deep Vellum aim to deepen literary engagement in the city of Baltimore, across the nation, and throughout the world.